Praise for
Bob Dylan: Outlaw Blues

'Few music biographers have the wit and wisdom necessary to catch the many nuances and details of Bob Dylan's amazing life. Spencer Leigh certainly does, which makes *Outlaw Blues* such a tasty prospect. Bob Dylan's story is well-documented by Spencer Leigh, finding new directions in the incredible maze of Dylan's life.'

Colin Hall, Beatles biographer and custodian of *Mendips*

'Bob Dylan is the most influential songwriter of the last half century and I know of no more perceptive pundit than Spencer Leigh.'

Gary Osborne, Songwriter, 'Forever Autumn', 'Amoreuse'

'Spencer's work is meticulously researched and this tribute to the great Bob Dylan is no exception. His writing is imbued with an obvious respect for his subject and their work. Spencer is excellent!"

Charlie Landsborough

'As a lyricist myself, I am interested in Spencer's take on Bob Dylan's songs. Writing a book is a massive task. Well done, mate.'

Barry Mason, Songwriter 'The Last Waltz', 'Delilah'

'I always know when I read a Spencer Leigh book I will get fresh insight into the music and lives of his subjects. I am tremendously excited how his acute research and profound musical knowledge challenges the many diamond facets of Bob Dylan.'

Barb Jungr, who has recorded three albums of Dylan songs

'There simply aren't enough books about Bob Dylan. So complex is he as a human being, a songwriter, a poet, a guitarist, a pianist, a vocalist (never a mere singer), enough words can never be written about him. Dylan is to this day – inscrutable and unfathomable.

Thank you, Spencer, for this, I feel some corners have been brightened, yet still you've left us plenty to ponder for ourselves, such is any great writer's wish.'

Ian McNabb, Singer-songwriter and musician

'Spencer Leigh has almost interviewed everybody, and always knows the right questions to ask. His enthusiasm for music history glows out of every sentence he writes.'

Peter Doggett, Former editor *Record Collector* for 17 years and noted biographer

'Spencer for me is an absolute icon. His passion for music is inspirational. I love the way he can convey it with his writing and his broadcasting. Long may he reign!'

Janice Long, BBC Radio 2

'Spencer is a fine researcher and writer. I always look forward to reading the connections he makes, and especially in this, between Bob and the Beatles. I think there's quite of lot of them!'

Hunter Davies, Official Beatles biographer

Praise for
Spencer Leigh

'Having read Spencer Leigh's engaging Buddy Holly biography, I am eagerly anticipating the author's new book on Bob Dylan. The detail embedded in the Holly book (and throughout Leigh's previous work) ensures that the Dylan book will prove to be fascinating and essential.'

Simon Wells, Biographer of The Who and the Rolling Stones

'One can guarantee that Spencer Leigh's books are not only entertaining and informative, but also thoroughly researched and cross-referenced. I have continued to use them as 'go to' texts for my own research for they are full of primary source materials one seldom finds elsewhere.'

Mike Brocken, University lecturer on popular music

'I can absolutely recommend any of Spencer Leigh's books.'

Ian Kennedy, BBC Radio Merseyside

'Spencer Leigh knows so much about popular music. He is a mine of information and we are so pleased to have him as one of our contributors.'

Dr Alex May, *Oxford Dictionary of National Biography*

BOB DYLAN
Outlaw Blues

Spencer Leigh

Published by McNidder & Grace
21 Bridge Street
Carmarthen
SA31 3JS
Wales, UK

www.mcnidderandgrace.com

First published in 2020
©Spencer Leigh
www.spencerleigh.co.uk

All rights reserved. No part of this work may be reproduced or transmitted in any form or by any means, electronic or mechanical, including photocopy, recording, or any information storage or retrieval system, without permission in writing from the publisher.

Spencer Leigh has asserted his right to be identified as the author of this work in accordance with the Copyright, Designs and Patents Act 1988.

Every effort has been made to obtain necessary permission with reference to copyright material. The publisher apologises if, inadvertently, any sources remain unacknowledged and will be glad to make the necessary arrangements at the earliest opportunity.

A catalogue record for this work is available from the British Library.

ISBN: 9780857162052
Ebook: 9780857162069

Designed by JS Typesetting Ltd, Wales
Cover design: Lara Peralta
Cover picture: Bob Dylan at Sheffield in 1965 by Harry Goodwin.

Printed and bound in the United Kingdom by Short Run Press Ltd

About the author

The journalist, acclaimed author and BBC broadcaster Spencer Leigh is an authority on popular music, especially the Beatles. He has written many music biographies including, most recently, Simon & Garfunkel, Elvis Presley, Frank Sinatra and Buddy Holly.

Spencer Leigh has been broadcasting his weekly show, *On the Beat*, on BBC Radio Merseyside for over 30 years and he has interviewed thousands of musicians. He has written over twenty-five books, hundreds of album sleeve notes and he writes obituaries of musicians for the Guardian, the Independent and the Oxford Dictionary of National Biography.

Spencer is an Honoured Friend at Sir Paul McCartney's Liverpool Institute of Performing Arts (LIPA) and has a Gold Badge of Merit from the British Academy of Composers and Songwriters

'I kinda figure my life speaks for itself.'
Bob Dylan, 1986

'No way.'
Spencer Leigh, 2020

Foreword
from Ian McNabb

There simply aren't enough books about Bob Dylan. So complex is he as a human being, a songwriter, a poet, a guitarist, a pianist, a vocalist (never a mere singer), hell, even a welder for all I know (I was delighted when I heard he loved to make wrought-iron gates – imagine his store *Gates of Freedom*), enough words can never be written about him. Dylan is, to this day inscrutable and unfathomable.

In the 2019 *Rolling Thunder Revue* documentary he even decided to add some more shaky and plainly false myths to his legend. Most artists of his dotage and breadth of work we have been able to summarise and analyse and contextualise and booglarise and file away, but Zimmo? Nope.

His songs straddle many styles on record and when you see him perform live you never know if 'Blowin' in the Wind' / 'Shelter from the Storm' / 'Lovesick' / 'Lonesome Day Blues' etc. will be a dustbowl lament or a four-on-the-floor boogie. I have seen him do both, as hopefully have you dear reader. I have seen ballads turned into rockers and 40s-style jump'n'jivers turned into funeral marches. No artist has played with their own music so thrillingly and so often carelessly.

His work has been with us for so long now that it feels so familiar yet still so... unsolved...which is the only word I can think of. Another book of analysis is only more than welcome to this particular long-time fan. Thank you, Spencer, for doing this. I feel some corners have been brightened, yet still you've left us plenty to ponder for ourselves, such is any great writer's wish. Whatever the artist gives of themselves, they always want us to find ourselves in their work. Thank you, Bob, thank you, Spencer and most importantly thank you, Quinn the Eskimo, whoever the fuck you are.

Always carry a lightbulb.

Contents

Foreword from Ian McNabb v

Introduction: A Complete Unknown? ix

Chapter 1. Talkin' Minnesotan Blues 1
    I. I Pity The Poor Immigrant 1
    II. So Much Older Then: 1941–1958 5
    III. Play: *Girl from the North Country* 15

Chapter 2. On the Road 17
    I. Blues and Beats 17
    II. So Much Older Then: 1959–1960 30

Chapter 3. Talkin' New York 42
    I. Hey, Hey Woody Guthrie 42
    II. So Much Older Then: 1961–1962 55
    III. Film: *Inside Llewyn Davis* 83

Chapter 4. 'It's Something I Learned over in England' 85
    I. Come Writers and Critics 85
    II. So Much Older Then: December 1962–January 1963 94

Chapter 5. A Lone Guitar and a Point of View 103
    I. The Cruel War 103
    II. So Much Older Then: 1963–1964 113
    III. I Can't Help If I'm Lucky 142
    IV. There but for Fortune: Phil Ochs 142
    V. Hawk-eyed: Ronnie Hawkins and the Hawks 144

Chapter 6. Electricity + Eccentricity / No Limit 150
    I. Big Bang Factors 150
    II. So Much Older Then: 1965–July 1966 162
    III. Reviews: *World's Fair* 216

Chapter 7. Life in the Country 218
    I. Illegal Smile 218
    II. So Much Older Then: August 1966–August 1969 222

Chapter 8. Help Bob Dylan Sink the Isle of Wight 249
    I. Festival Life 249
    II. So Much Older Then: August 1969–1971 256

Chapter 9. Framed 266
    I. Musicians Making Movies 266
    II. So Much Older Then: 1972–1973 269

Chapter 10. And the New Bob Dylan is… 278
    I. With Bob on Our Side 278
    II. So Much Older Then: 1974–September 1975 290

Chapter 11. The Thunder Rolls 301
    I. Pulled into Nazareth 301
    II. So Much Older Then: October 1975–1978 314

Chapter 12. The Missionary Times 330
    I. Religion and Rock 330
    II. So Much Older Then: 1979–1984 333

Chapter 13. What Was It You Wanted? 351
    I. Saving the World 351
    II. So Much Older Then: 1985–1989 356

Chapter 14. Gruff and Ready 378
    I. Tombstone Blues 378
    II. So Much Older Now: 1990–1999 388

Chapter 15. 'Me, I'm Still on the Road' 414
    I. Don't Start Me Talkin' 414
    II. So Much Older Now: 2000–2012 417

Chapter 16. Oh Mama, Can This Really be the End? 439
    I. Nobel-minded 439
    II. So Much Older Now: 2013–2020 445
    III. Drawing Blanks? 447

Acknowledgements 452

The Wicked Messenger – A Bob Dylan Bibliography 462

Appendix 1. Bob Dylan – US and UK discography 465

Appendix 2. The Band – US and UK discography 481

Appendix 3. Take What You Need: Covering Bob Dylan 484

Appendix 4. Odds and Ends: Bob Dylan Lists 497

Index 501

Please note:

The film title, *Dont Look Back*, does not have an apostrophe. It looks wrong, I know, but it's right. The director D.A. Pennebaker thought it had more urgency that way: to each his own.

The song variously known as 'Stuck Inside of Mobile with the Memphis Blues Again', 'Stuck Inside of Mobile with the' (on the first UK copy of *Blonde on Blonde*) and 'Memphis Blues Again' is referred to as 'Memphis Blues Again' throughout the text.

Introduction: A Complete Unknown?

Mystery Train

Once upon a time…a fairy tale beginning.

Once upon a time…the opening words of Bob Dylan's most famous song, 'Like a Rolling Stone', released in 1965 and a regular contender for the best single of all time.

Once upon a time…but this book is not fiction. This is a true story that happens to read like fiction.

Most performers create their work for public approval, but at the centre of this book is a mercurial man who doesn't trust his audience. If he feels he is getting too much acclaim, he veers in another direction. Inevitably, he has slowed down because of age, vocal restrictions and the ability to play a guitar, but he doesn't want to be a nostalgia act and so he is very different from Paul McCartney, Rod Stewart or the Rolling Stones. He rarely encourages an audience to sing along and even today he may act strangely on stage, practically obliterating the melodies of his famous compositions. Sometimes this is accidental, sometimes deliberate, but this restlessness has given him the most volatile career of anyone in popular music.

Accept that from the start that almost everything about Bob Dylan is unusual or different. True, there is the familiar trajectory of someone starting in small clubs, building up a following, having hit records and becoming a superstar – it applies to Bob Dylan but in a supremely unique way.

In 'Like a Rolling Stone', Dylan asks his adversary how it feels to be 'a complete unknown', and maybe that appeals to him. He wrote crazy, idiosyncratic songs, very different from anything else around, and he was regularly featured in magazines and newspapers, and yet the public knew little about him. He created his own back history – a fairy tale, if you like: lies, if you must – as though his true story of getting to Greenwich Village in the early 60s wasn't worth telling. When he scorned his followers in the thinly-veiled 'Positively 4th Street', it was self-evident that the real story was as enthralling as anything he could invent.

In Dylan's view, his creativity was what mattered and his private life was nobody's business but his own. Look at the documentary film of his 1965 UK tour, *Dont Look Back*, and see how journalists walked on eggshells. He didn't suffer fools gladly and he didn't like daft, impertinent or probing questions. On another occasion, he said, 'You wouldn't ask these questions of a carpenter, would you?' Fair enough, but you can't expect public acclaim without attracting media attention.

Bob Dylan: Outlaw Blues attempts to get as close as we can to the real Bob Dylan. Some say he is enigmatic but that word is an admission of failure: it simply means the writer doesn't know. When I researched biographies of Elvis Presley and Frank Sinatra, I felt that the more that I learnt about them, the more accurate the assessment would be. With Bob Dylan there are false trails and locked doors: he has something in common with illusionists as he knows how to misdirect the public, journalists and biographers. Even if somebody got to 95% of Dylan, there will still be that 5% that nobody knows about, which could change the whole picture. As the director of the documentary *Dont Look Back*, D.A. Pennebaker said to Andy Gill in 2007, 'Bob Dylan and David Bowie live in a part of the brain that we know nothing about.'

As a result, it is difficult to predict Dylan's reactions. Time and again, I have determined what would a reasonable person do in such circumstances but as he told his official biographer, Robert Shelton, 'I hate to do the predictable.'

In 2006, Bob Dylan ended the Halloween edition of his *Theme Time Radio Hour* programme by saying goodbye, pausing, and then going 'Boo!' His career has been like that. The singer / songwriter Gillian Welch gave Emmylou Harris a talisman WWDD (What Would Dylan Do?) as a guide for songwriters.

So, this is the story of Bob Dylan, who is quirky as hell and wholly unpredictable. The story is, for the most part, told chronologically and please read it as though you don't know what happens next. As Joan Baez laughed, 'You can't second guess with Bob Dylan. I never know what he is going to do next. Maybe I'm just bright enough to know that I'll never know with him.'

Dylan knows that elusiveness attracts – of course he does. In 2001, he told Robert Hilburn, 'A lot of my songs are misinterpreted by people who don't know any better.' Fair enough but he could easily resolve this with a couple of radio programmes explaining just where his critics had gone wrong. But Dylan will never provide footnotes for his songs. He likes mysteries. Given the choice between being coherent or being secretive, Dylan would take the latter.

The mysteriousness suits him fine. Dylan may be sceptical about his songs being scrutinised in universities but by saying no more than a few cryptic comments about them, he has created a growth industry. Some of his songs remain as impenetrable as Ingmar Bergman's films. 'Desolation Row' opens with the line, 'They're selling postcards of the hanging': what on earth is that about? Actually, I do believe I have solved that one.

It's a good ploy. Fred Dellar, a noted *New Musical Express* journalist, says, 'Dylan obviously thinks it is good to be mysterious. He writes lyrics which can be interpreted in so many different ways and many authors have tried to decipher them. Dylan caters to this. If he did suddenly explain something properly, people would say, "No, no, it doesn't mean that", and disagree with him. The fact that he has made himself a man of mystery has elongated his career. It makes him much more interesting as people want to know more.'

A former editor of *Melody Maker*, Ray Coleman, knew Bob Dylan. 'Dylan's a shrewd and cunning manipulator. He thinks that the longer we can be kept guessing, the longer the interest in his work will remain. 'Subterranean Homesick Blues' is a great track, full of innuendo, but no one knows what it's about. Maybe it's about nothing at all but it would be nice if Dylan did a song-by-song breakdown the way that John Lennon did.'

Dylan sometimes says that his songs mean exactly what you want them to mean: it's a glib explanation and not what we want. We want to know what the songs mean to Bob Dylan. And he will never tell us. I suspect that he has a sly smile when he reads of writers and academics searching for his sources, his intentions and his meanings. John Lennon joked that the Beatles' 'I Am the Walrus' would confuse the academics, and Dylan has done this time and again.

As much as I like Bob Dylan, this book is not hagiography and I am prepared to revise my opinions along the way. Indeed, Bob Dylan has been a moveable feast for me as I have gone back and forth about the qualities of some albums for years. There is a possibility that he is a fraud, a con man, an emperor wearing new clothes. Indeed, one of the thrills of writing this book is coming to grips with what has obsessed me, off and on, for 56 years. There is something wonderful about being alive at the same time as Bob Dylan.

In keeping with Bob Dylan's personality, the structure of *Bob Dylan: Outlaw Blues* is unusual, but I think it tells a better story this way. The general format is to split the chapters into two parts: the first describes the background to something significant in Bob Dylan's life and the second continues Bob's story on a day-to-day basis. If you just want Bob's story, then you can read the second sections on their own. If that is how you want to read the book, fine: I'm flattered that you want to read the book at all, but the overall picture is important and tells a much broader story.

The first parts of the chapters take up various themes and events in Dylan's life and put them into context. What were the attractions of Woody Guthrie, the old-time blues singers and country music? How did Bob Dylan fit into the Civil Rights movement? What is the history of protest songwriting? What other performers have deliberately alienated audiences in the way that Bob Dylan did in 1965/6? What was the relationship between Bob Dylan and The Band and, indeed, Bob Dylan and the Beatles? What are Bob Dylan's personal beliefs and how have they changed with the years? Why is Bob Dylan below par at major events, notably *Live Aid*? How does Dylan measure up to other Nobel prize winners?

Over the years I have spoken to hundreds of musicians about Bob Dylan and you will find a lot of contrasting views in this book. To me, that is one of the best things about him. If I collected all my quotes about the Beatles together, most people would be speaking as one about their music, but with Bob Dylan the assessments are all over the place.

I think you will enjoy the range of opinions and when combined with the many details of Bob Dylan's life, I am sure you are going to find a lot of things that you haven't read before. I have had an enormously enjoyable time putting this book together and I hope I can share this feeling with you.

And, considering all he has gone through, Bob Dylan's greatest achievement could be in reaching his 80th birthday. Salute him when his birthday comes.

CHAPTER 1
Talkin' Minnesotan Blues

'Get born.'
Bob Dylan holds up a placard for his first video, 'Subterranean Homesick Blues', 1965

'You always know who you are. I just don't know who I'm gonna become.'
Bob Dylan to Sam Shepard, Esquire magazine, 1987

I. I Pity the Poor Immigrant

The opening verse of Bob Dylan's 'With God on Our Side' contains the line, 'The country I come from is called the Midwest.' The nation Bob Dylan comes from is called the United States of America, and, according to the Census Bureau, the Midwest refers to the central states in the north, two of which, North Dakota and Minnesota, share a border with Canada.

The Voyageurs National Park is along the border between Minnesota and Canada. Its name comes from French-Canadian trappers who transported their pelts to Montreal by canoe, which took months. It was, and largely still is, a wilderness, populated by eagles, moose, bears and now tourists. There are some boarding houses and many visitors travel by kayak. The camping tips say: boil drinking water, check mercury levels before eating fish, look out for mosquitoes the size of small birds, and watch out for bears, obviously of any size.

Bob Dylan comes from Minnesota. During the ice age, the glaciers flattened most of the area and created thousands of lakes, while rivers ran along the eastern and western borders. In the winter, all those lakes could be frozen.

The name Minnesota is a Sioux word meaning 'land of sky-tinted water' while the name of the city Minneapolis is a mixture of Sioux and Greek and meaning 'water city' and it does have numerous lakes and parks. The lover Minnehaha in Longfellow's poem, *The Song of Hiawatha* (1855) means 'laughing water' – so now you know how Minne translates. My favourite name belongs to the small town of Pipestone, Minnesota. It was named because the Native Americans used its soft red clay to make peace pipes.

As a child in the 1870s, Laura Ingalls Wilder travelled with her family to these new frontiers. Part of her journey was in Minnesota and she put her experience into a series of books generically known as *Little House on the Prairie*. In the 1970s it became a long-running TV series with over 200 episodes.

Rochester, a city in southern Minnesota, was created by migrants from Rochester, New York. It was devastated by a tornado in 1883 and as a result, Dr. William Mayo and his sons established the Mayo Clinic, the first group practice in the world. Today the city is regarded as one of most highly educated cities in the world.

The immigrants had originally come from Europe: British, French, German and Scandinavian, and with the callous cruelty of the day, they eased out the American Indian tribes. They made their living as farmers, fur traders and lumberjacks. Minneapolis was founded on money from the flour and saw mills.

A town called Pig's Eye developed in the 1840s and became the state capital, St. Paul. Like Rome, it was built on seven hills and there are preservation orders to maintain the old buildings. One of the tourist attractions, Fort Snelling, dates from 1819. Nowadays, half of the state's population lives around the twin cities of Minneapolis and St. Paul with friendly rivalry between them. St. Paul favours its old stone buildings while Minneapolis welcomes modern architecture. Minneapolis was the setting for *The Mary Tyler Moore Show*.

It is very cold around the twin cities with the temperature regularly around –6°C in winter. It is ideal for skiing and it's chilly in autumn and spring. In July and August, it is hot and clammy. Minnesotans joke that they have two seasons – winter and road repair. Dylan has remarked, 'I'm used to four seasons, California's got but one.'

Dave Rave is a Canadian Elvis Costello. He wrote and recorded an album, *Ashtray Makeup*, with a Minnesotan group, the Governors in 2012. The opening track is 'St. Paul' and another song is 'Duluth'. 'I go to Minnesota a few times a year and it is a fun place to be, especially in Minneapolis,' says Dave, a man who welcomes a challenge, 'I purposefully go at the coldest time of the year – that is in January. It is great for rock music, and the Replacements and Soul Asylum are from the area. It is pop music with an edge and that is what I like. There was a big flood in Duluth and we wrote a song about it. St. Paul is right next to Minneapolis and is a great city. I am writing about what is in front of me. We are going to make it there, as the song says, because they need some entertainment.'

Perhaps because so much of the year is viciously cold, the crime rates are low as the locals are engrossed in keeping warm. As Bob Dylan remarked, 'You couldn't be a rebel – it's so cold, you couldn't be bad.' There is however plenty of violent crime in the film and TV series of *Fargo*, also set in the north of America, albeit fictional. As the crime writer Mark Billingham told me, 'You can't beat blood on snow. That's one reason why Scandi Noir is so popular.'

The hitmaker Bobby Vee (1943–2016) hailed from Fargo, North Dakota with a Finnish and Norwegian lineage. He appreciated Bob Dylan's imagery. 'I have sung 'On a Night like This' and 'Forever Young'. He comes from northern Minnesota which is a fabulous place. It is cold but it is beautiful all the year around. He often writes about cabins and the frost on the windows, so those are the images of his youth. I can visualise being back home as soon as I hear some of his descriptions.'

The most famous entertainers to come from Minneapolis are the Andrews Sisters, who are associated with the war years and performing with Bing Crosby. F. Scott Fitzgerald was born in St. Paul in 1896 and his first novel, *This Side of Paradise* (1915), was partially set in Minnesota. The filmmakers Joel and Ethan Coen are from there, St. Louis Park to be precise. Joel's wife, Frances McDormand plays a police chief from Minnesota in their film, *Fargo* (1996).

The fictional characters don't need local accents. There isn't one but the all-purpose Scandinavian phrase, 'uff da', is in the language which means 'oops!' Other popular phrases are 'alrightee', 'doncha know', 'you betcha' and 'okey dokey'. To avoid an argument, a resident may say, 'That's different'.

There are now 2.5m people living in the twin cities, which has been described as a cultural Eden on the prairie. I'm not so certain of that as just outside the cities is the Mall of

America, a monument to consumerism with over 500 stores, opening in 1992. Its owners will have to be astute to avoid the downsizing in retail stores in the western world.

The famed engineering company, Honeywell, was founded in Minneapolis and it retained its links with the area after moving its headquarters to New Jersey. There are 3,500 Honeywell workers in Minnesota. The 3M Company (the Minnesota Mining and Manufacturing Company) is another mammoth concern, still based in the area.

The American Indians realised that there was something unusual about the land and they talked of a great spirit being there. They were right – the earth was filled with iron ore and powerfully magnetic. The so-called Iron Range was discovered in the 1850s and more than a quarter of the USA's iron ore was to come from there. The deposits played a crucial part in armaments for the two world wars.

Born in 1856, Franz Dietrich Von Ahlen left Hannover when 18. He moved to America, became Frank Hibbing and farmed in Wisconsin. After losing three fingers in an accident, he studied law and operated from Duluth as a land broker. When iron ore was discovered on the Mesabi Range in 1890, he led an expedition of 30 men and tapped a large vein, thus creating a vast mine. He established Hibbing in 1893.

The first residents in Hibbing were the lumberjacks who were building the houses for the miners. At first, it was cheap buildings in muddy streets and the tough workers would get into saloon brawls. Typhoid was a killer but the town prospered and Von Ahlen became rich before he died in 1897 at the age of 40. Not even wealth could save you from appendicitis, it would seem.

The Mesabi Iron Range, just north of Hibbing, which itself was 200 miles north of the twin cities, was the main mining area. Underground mines were built at first but the ore was often only lightly buried so this marked the start of open cast mining which has annihilated so many areas.

The deposits became so valuable and so important that the mine-owners wanted to move the entire town of Hibbing so that they could strip the area – and they did. The academic and Dylan scholar, C.P. Lee went on a Bob Dylan tour that included Hibbing: 'Hibbing is like nothing you can imagine. I was with a busload of academics and we went through this flat wasteland, and we thought, "How could Dylan have come out of here?" When we left, we thought, "Why aren't there more Dylans in Hibbing?" It is unique: they have created the world's largest hole by extracting iron ore. In the 1920s, the mayor made a deal with the mine-owners. They wanted to use the area where the town was and they said that they would cut the houses off at ground level and move the entire town two miles west and so in 1925 they did just that. The mayor gave them a list of demands and the residents still get a percentage of the iron ore. The high school has marble halls, gold-plated door knobs and crystal chandeliers and the auditorium is based on the New York Opera House. The Americans with us had seldom seen this opulence in universities. Every child in Hibbing gets free medical and dental care. All their text books are paid for and yet Hibbing has but one main street.'

The stage at Hibbing High School is so palatial that everything else must have been an anti-climax to Bob Dylan. It's a shame that the Pope John Paul II didn't invite him to play the Sistine Chapel in 1997, but we'll get to that later.

The Second World War brought even more prosperity to the region but the deposits in some mines were exhausted. Now there is the Hull-Rust Pit outside Hibbing that is three miles long, one mile wide and 500 feet deep and is advertised as a tourist attraction. Strip-mining has created the biggest slagheap in the world.

When Bob Dylan recorded his album, *The Times They Are A-Changin'*, in 1963, one song that showed the times were a-changin' was the bleak 'North Country Blues'. It is a desolate song in which Dylan plays a miner's daughter who becomes another miner's wife. Illness, serious injuries and fatal accidents are never far away and when the ore can be obtained cheaper in South America ('where the miners work almost for nothing'), her husband moves away, leaving her with three children. She is in a dying town, knowing her children will have to leave if they want to work.

In 1966 when Bob Dylan's biographer Robert Shelton told him that he had been to Hibbing, Dylan said, 'You see that great ugly hole in the ground where that open pit mine was? They think up there that it's beautiful. They are doing that now to the whole country.' A poignant song on the subject, sharper even than Dylan's, is 'Paradise' by John Prine, which describes how strip mining affects the townsfolk of Muhlenberg County, Kentucky.

In 1914, an enterprising Swede, Carl Eric Wickman started a small bus service to take workers from Hibbing to the mine in Alice at 15 cents a ride. He teamed up with another bus service that was going 60 miles to Duluth and this grew into the Greyhound Bus Company. It became increasingly important as airlines generally went to big cities and trains were axed on certain routes. The Greyhound became the only public transport system in some areas, a modern stagecoach if you like. There is a museum to celebrate Greyhound buses in Hibbing.

Ironically, times have changed and you can't travel to the museum by Greyhound as they have stopped services to Hibbing. Even more ironically, Hibbing has a tourist exhibition for Greyhound buses but does not have one for its most famous son, Bob Dylan. There is a small collection of memorabilia on display in the public library but the privately-owned, themed restaurant, Zimmy's, closed in 2014.

Are there any other candidates for Hibbing's most famous or even most infamous inhabitant? Not really. Vincent Bugliosi who prosecuted Charles Manson came from Hibbing and so did Jeno Paulucci, who founded Jeno's Pizza, and the baseball star Roger Maris. I'm clutching at straws here, or billiard balls. The pool player Rudolf Wanderone was known as Minnesota Fats but he didn't come from the area. He adopted Jackie Gleason's moniker in *The Hustler* (1961) and claimed that the film was about him.

The hit recorder of 'Young Girl', a highly dubious song in today's climate, Gary Puckett was born in Hibbing in 1942 but raised in Union Gap, Washington. He didn't attend the same school as Bob Dylan which is a pity as he would have only been a year behind.

Just 35 miles away is Grand Rapids where Frances Gumm was born in 1922. She became Judy Garland and there is a Judy Garland Museum in Grand Rapids. You can read Yip Harburg's lyric for 'Over the Rainbow' as a song about wanting to escape and incidentally, David Bowie wrote 'Starman' after playing around with that song.

Judy Garland was a chameleon-like movie star who often created new looks for herself. You can see that too with Bob Dylan even if you only glance at the jackets of his different albums.

Seventy-six miles from Hibbing and 150 miles from the twin cities is Duluth. It was named in the seventeenth century after a French officer, Daniel Du Luth, who brokered a peace agreement with the Ojibwa and Sioux tribes which led to an agreement with the French to develop a fur trade. Minnesota is alongside Superior, Wisconsin and there are 30 miles of waterfront, making it the largest inland harbour in the US. Duluth exported timber and iron ore to Chicago and Pittsburgh and was known as the 'air-conditioned city' because of relatively mild winters and cool summers, but it's usually windy.

Duluth does have some dark history. In 1918, a right-wing group, the Knights of Liberty tarred and feathered an anti-war Finnish immigrant. His death was ruled a suicide, though how you can tar and feather yourself is a mystery.

Duluth to St. Paul is now on Interstate 35, but Highway 61 is still functional and goes through forgotten towns. As the Dylan scholar, Michael Gray wrote, 'These people feel proud that they can endure this climate. Its heartland ruggedness, they like to think, puts iron in their souls.'

In June 1920, six black workers with a travelling circus were arrested and accused of raping a 19-year-old white girl. Three of the men were taken from the cells and hanged from lamp posts. The crowd posed with the bodies and the lynching featured on postcards with the greeting, 'Wish you were here?', presumably to deter others from settling in Duluth. In 2002 Duluth erected a memorial to the murdered men. One of Dylan's most mysterious lines is the opening of 'Desolation Row': 'They're selling postcards of the hanging.' Could that lynch mob also explain 'the haunted, frightened trees' in 'Mr. Tambourine Man'? It seems credible that Dylan knew of the murders and it's even possible that a relative or two was in the crowd. We'll get to 'Desolation Row' later, but maybe it is imbued with the spirit of Billie Holiday's 'Strange Fruit'.

In 1937 Bessie Smith died on Highway 61 near Clarksdale, Mississippi. Elvis grew up on Highway 61 and it went past the Lorraine Motel where Martin Luther King was shot. In 1964, David 'Honeyboy' Edwards cut 'Highway 61', which almost certainly prompted Bob Dylan's 'Highway 61 Revisited'.

Over a thousand miles long, Highway 61 is as familiar as Route 66, which is largely down to Bob Dylan, but there is little mythic about it today. The little towns are even smaller, often uninhabited and there are gigantic billboards along the way.

Going north from Duluth, you can travel through the wilderness, waterfalls and state parks to reach the Canadian border. Along the way is the International Wolf Centre – so take your pick if you are a Dylan tourist – the call of the wild or the call of the weird. Duluth Public Library is now the Bob Dylan Historical Library, but what's in a name?

We will be seeing how Dylan's early life influenced his songs and his poetry. He writes directly about Hibbing on the liner notes for *The Times They Are A-Changin'* and also in his sardonic poem, 'My Life in a Stolen Moment'. The main character in his book, *Tarantula*, talks about making a Faustian pact to escape. Even when you hate somewhere, something or someone, it can have a bearing on what you write – and Bob Dylan is living proof of that.

And so too is Sinclair Lewis. This Minnesotan from Sauk Centre won a Nobel Prize before Bob Dylan. His portrayal of small-town life in *Main Street* (1920) was a bestseller but the citizens of Sauk Centre were not amused, thinking that they had been portrayed as bigots and simpletons. Lewis stuck with this rather depressing theme in his work but nonetheless, he won the Nobel Prize in Literature in 1930, the first American to do so. His childhood home is now a museum in Sauk Centre. (The town is named after the Sauk tribe but fascinatingly, centre is spelt the British way.)

II. So Much Older Then: 1941–1958

In 1978, Bob Dylan said, 'I don't know how Jewish I am. These blue eyes are Russian.'

Dylan's family name of Zimmerman is German, not Russian. Many Germans immigrated to Russia around the time of Catherine the Great in the late eighteenth century. A century later, the Russian ruler Nicholas II blamed the Jews for his problems and permitted violence against them. In November 1905 the anti-Semitic hysteria was so rampant in Odessa that over 1,000 Jews were killed in one day.

Dylan's grandfather, the fantastically-named Zigman Zimmerman was born in Odessa in 1875 and owned a shoe factory in the Ukraine. The name means 'carpenter' so who knows what Tim Hardin was thinking when he wrote 'If I Were a Carpenter'? Not to mention Ziggy Stardust. Zigman had no idea how long his factory or indeed his family would survive in Odessa. He fled the country in 1907 and sailed to America.

Zigman found the small but bustling port of Duluth, Minnesota entirely suitable. It already had a Jewish community and Zigman was used to its climate. Zigman sent for his wife Anna and family in 1910. There were Maurice, Minnie and Paul, and another three children – Jake, Abram and Max – were born in the US. It is possible that Jake was born in Odessa and that Zigman used the opportunity to register his birth in the US, and who could blame him.

At first, Zigman was selling clothes off a horse and cart to workmen and their wives. Once he had mastered English, he was selling shoes in the Fair Department store in Duluth. He established his own business, the Zimmerman Furniture and Appliance Company, selling furniture and kitchenware. Anna worked from home as a dressmaker.

Bob Dylan's father, Abram (Abe) Zimmerman was born in Duluth on 19 October 1911. He attended Central High School in Duluth where the pupils were of immigrant stock, mostly Scandinavian. It was an impressively large building with a clock tower, although the writer Michael Gray remarked of its colour, 'Looks like it's been built out of dogshit.' Abe was doing part-time work, delivering newspapers and shining shoes from the age of seven. There was no media entertainment and even baseball was played on stony ground.

The Zimmermans lived on Lake Avenue, across the road from the high school, and so they were not on the hill like most of the Jewish community. One of Abe's brothers started a taxi service in Duluth in the early 1920s and apparently, the Zimmermans were the first in the area with a telephone, although if they were the first, who were they going to call? By 1920 Zigman opened his own shoe store and was a persuasive salesman. In 1925 the Zimmermans moved to a larger property.

Abe was humorous, quiet and good-looking, speaking Yiddish to his family but otherwise English. In 1929 he started as a messenger with Standard Oil. He saved enough money to allow his mother to visit her sister in New York. Although he was laid off after two weeks, he was reinstated a fortnight later and was able to pay for the journey. He became a clerical worker earning $60 a month for a six-day week and he clung to this job as the nature of his work saved him from conscription.

Abe met his future wife, Beatty in 1931, when she visited Duluth. She lived in Hibbing and was part of an immigrant family of entrepreneurs. B'chezer Edelstein was a blacksmith from Lithuania and in 1902, he came to Halifax, Nova Scotia with his wife Lybba and four children. Now calling himself Benjamin Harold Edelstein, he and his family moved to Superior, Wisconsin and then Hibbing, Minnesota. He had his own forge and he manufactured cast-iron stoves. They had 10 children and in the 1920s, he and his brother Julius were showing films in Hibbing, first in tent shows and then in their own movie theatre, the Gopher, which opened in 1925. It was exciting to visit a cinema back then, even more so when sound came along.

When Lybba died in 1942, the brothers dedicated a new cinema to her. By all accounts,

Ben was a tough and stubborn businessman. He was Bob Dylan's great-grandfather and Bob would have known him as he survived until 1961 when he was in his nineties.

Ben and Lybba's oldest child, Florence Sara, was born in 1892, and in 1911, she married Ben Stone in Hibbing. Ben Stone is a very American name but don't be fooled. Ben was Benjamin David Solemovitz, born in 1883, and he came from an immigrant family of Lithuanian Jews. His sister Ida had been murdered in 1906 by a Scotsman who had planned to marry her.

Ben sold clothing to miners and he could wash them in his Sample Shop in Stevenson, which had been named after a successful miner and was 12 miles from Hibbing. When the mine's resources had been exhausted, he moved into Hibbing and opened Stone's Clothing in a former bank building, keeping his stock in a vault. He did well and could afford a four-door Essex car, which they needed as they had a growing family – Vernon, Beatrice, Lewis and Irene. Bob Dylan's mother, Beatrice, known as Beatty, was born on 16 June 1915 and had an independent spirit, being able to drive from the age of 14, simply from watching her father, a trait picked up by her son. She was to say, 'Bobby is very much like I am. You either do it or you don't.' Beatty was warm-hearted and fun but she spoke fast, leaving little room for answers.

On New Year's Eve 1931, Abe met the blue-eyed blonde Beatty at a party. The Depression had taken hold and Abe later said, 'She didn't know anyone else who had a job.' As Abe lived in Duluth and Beatty in Hibbing, the winter storms kept them apart.

The inhabitants of Hibbing were 90% Catholic and rather than get married in Duluth with its choice of four synagogues, they waited for a visiting rabbi to marry them in Hibbing. They were married in Hibbing on 10 June 1934 when Abe was 22 and Beatty almost 19 but they settled in Lake Avenue, Duluth. They had a honeymoon in Chicago and moved in with Abe's mother on East Fifth Street. Zigman and Anna were separated and there were five people in the house – Anna, Abe and Beatty, and Abe's brothers, Paul and Maurice. This was constraining and so Abe and Beatty moved to 519 Third Avenue East. Zigman still lived in Duluth but he died in July 1936, following a heart attack during a heatwave.

Abe was earning $100 a month as a stock clerk at Standard Oil and Beatty sold clothes at a department store, Mangol's. They both wanted a family. The collage in the first volume of *The Bootleg Series* (which despite the title was an official release in 1991) reproduces an old driving licence. It gives Bob's date of birth as 11 May 1941, which is mystifying as he was born 13 days later. It also gives his adult height as 5 foot 11 inches when he is three inches shorter. Welcome to the crazy world of Bob Dylan.

It was a difficult birth as Beatty had a crooked bone at the end of her spine. The doctor operated and after a forced labour, Robert Allen Zimmerman was born at 9.05pm on 24 May 1941 at St. Mary's Hospital, Duluth. He weighed 8 pounds 13 ounces and had blond hair and blue eyes and was lucky to be alive. He was also given a Jewish name, Shabtai Zisel ben Avraham, but Robert Allen was how he was known.

Bob Dylan was a Gemini – who are said to blow hot and cold. Robert Shelton tried to make something of this in his biography, but as I think the signs of the zodiac have no bearing on a personality, I am ignoring this and similar sentiments.

Similarly the folk singer Julie Felix says, 'Bob is a Gemini and they were two heavenly twins; one fell to earth, and the one in heaven was always trying to reach the one on earth, and vice versa. There is never a feeling of contentment in a Gemini. They are always striving to find that other half within themselves. That drives Dylan a lot, I feel, and the majority of his songs are a search or a complaint about injustices, both on a personal level and a collective level. The earlier songs were on a collective level but the older he got, the more he has internalised this.'

By 1941, America had not joined the war, but the reports were grim and over 70,000 Jews had been killed in Odessa. When President Clinton was elected in 1993, Bob Dylan said on stage, 'I was born in 1941, the year they bombed Pearl Harbour and I've been in darkness ever since.' It was a great line, suggesting more than it meant. The bombing of Pearl Harbour by the Japanese brought America into the war. On the other hand, it could be a reference to the wars and conflicts in which the US has been involved since 1945. There was a gap up to the Korean war but since then, there has been considerable military action. Often they have been comparatively small conflicts for the Americans, if not for their enemies.

Beatty put ribbons in Bob's hair, thinking he was pretty enough to be a girl. The photograph of him at 18 months shows his chubby cheeks. He was talking early and fond of saying, 'I will be two in May.' At first, he didn't like going to Nettleton School and he had to be dragged there, kicking and screaming. School never got any better for him. He had however, a love of poetry and he could memorise poems he liked.

Right from the start, Bob was singing, his first recordings being on his father's office Dictaphone. Their second son, David Benjamin Zimmerman, was born in February 1946. Perhaps to ensure that David wasn't getting all the attention, Bob sang 'Some Sunday Morning', a current success for Helen Forrest and Dick Haymes, at a Mother's Day event he attended with his grandma. When asked to repeat the song at his aunt's wedding reception at a social club in Duluth, he said, 'If it's quiet, I will sing.' He reprised his song, again a perfect choice as it was a wedding song. An uncle raised a collection for him but he gave it back, saying he sang for free. I wonder if a young Chuck Berry did the same?

Showing a professionalism beyond his years, he had an encore to hand, 'Ac-cent-tchu-ate the Positive', a million seller for Bing Crosby with those girls from Minneapolis, the Andrews Sisters. Both songs are from films but Bob would have picked them up from the radio or possibly a record as his parents did have some 78s.

In 1998 Dylan said while playing Duluth, 'I was born on the hill over there. Glad to see it's still there. My first girlfriend came from here. She was conceited and I used to call her Mimi.' I suspect this was a feeble joke on 'me, me' but you never know with Dylan.

Dylan rarely mentions his childhood. The family gatherings at which he sang suggest that there were more, but we know nothing of them. Was he a lonely child? What were his fears, his emotions, did he cry much, how did he feel about being Jewish, did he accept authority? Bob has never said, but we know the answer to the last one.

The war ended in 1945 but Abe had his own problems at Standard Oil. He had tried to keep out the infamous Teamsters Union but the work force disagreed and signed up.

In 1946 Abe contracted polio but the hospital in Duluth didn't have the right equipment. He discharged himself after a week, making his own way home and crawling up the steps to the front door. He was off work for six months and it left him with a limp so he couldn't play ball games effectively with his children. Despite his efforts on the company's behalf, Standard Oil's management was not sympathetic and laid him off.

With no reason to stay in Duluth, Abe and Beatty moved in with Beatty's parents, Ben and Florence, at 2323 Third Avenue East in Hibbing. Bob had only been in Duluth for the first five years and when asked for his memories, he could only recall the sound of the foghorns.

That new address was handy for Bob as the Alice School was next door, but Abe and Beatty wanted their own home. Their offer on another house was accepted and they kindly gave the current owners, the Madden family, time to move out. Mr. Madden had died and the Zimmermans appreciated it was a stressful time.

Their new address was 2425 7th Avenue East, a detached house in a good residential area. It is now Bob Dylan Drive, but the home is not a museum nor is it open to visitors. It is a beige stucco house unlike anything else around. Bob has visited it twice: once in the 1970s with his wife Sara and then with a black Labrador in 1984.

Hibbing had prospered during the war and Abe was soon selling furniture and electrical goods at Micka Electric with his brothers, Paul and Maurice. He and his brothers were a good team: Abe could do the books, Paul the selling and Maurice, being an electrician, the fitting. One of their slogans was 'A kitchen range for the Iron Range.'

Beatty worked at Feldman's Department Store so she was out during the day. Until their grandmother, Florence Stone, moved in, the children would return from school to an empty house.

Bob was quiet and well-behaved but he avoided things he didn't like. He joined the boy scouts and wore the uniform but he left within a month. He liked the comic book series, *Classics Illustrated*, which reworked out-of-copyright adventure novels. Abe enjoyed solving the *New York Times* crosswords and Bob developed a love for the English language and the choice of words.

The Zimmermans had a piano but Bob didn't want lessons: that was too much like hard work. When he was 11, a relative, Harriet Rutstein, a music teacher who had graduated from the University of Minnesota, attempted to teach him. Bob said, 'I'm going to play the piano the way I want to.' That is still his approach, experimenting until he hits something he likes. Bob started playing the harmonica and when he was 12, he got his first guitar. David was a better student and became a competent classical pianist.

The school's music teacher tried to interest Bob in the school band, but he showed no flair for the trumpet or the saxophone. He bought a Spanish guitar tutor, which cost him $1, but he was largely on his own unpredictable path. Soon, he was playing some kind of music, sketching and writing stories and poems, but he had little interest in conventional school work. He told his grandmother that he wanted to be an architect but that involved a great deal of learning.

In 1951 Bob wrote each of his parents a poem, one for Mother's Day, one for Father's Day. Writing about his dad, he wrote, 'Though it's hard for him to believe, I try each day to please him in every little way.'

Because Bob's family owned the Lybba cinema, he could get in free. He liked westerns but even if he saw *The Gunfighter* (1950) with Gregory Peck, it is doubtful whether a young boy, even Dylan, would have picked up its complexities. He wrote about his love of Gregory Peck and that film in 'Brownsville Girl'.

According to his memoir, *Chronicles, Volume One* (2004), Dylan found life in Hibbing idyllic and he enjoyed the circus coming to town, which is referred to in 'Desolation Row'. He listened to baseball commentaries on the radio.

Bob would visit his grandfather Ben Stone after school and Ben picked up on his intelligence, realising that once something took his interest there was no stopping him. Ben died in 1952 and his wife, Florence went to live with Abe and Beatty. When Bob visited the house in the 1970s, he said, 'This was grandma's room.'

The war was over and everyone wanted to get on with their lives. Conformity and complacency ruled the day and when *Life* magazine in 1950 asked the youth for their heroes, they chose President Roosevelt, General MacArthur, the wholesome cowboy actor Roy Rogers and the clean-cut Doris Day. Nothing to shake the system there but soon the younger generation would be saying, 'Let's go bonkers!'

Because of the demand for iron and steel, Hibbing's economy had prospered in the war years and although it would benefit from the Korean War, business was not so good in peacetime. Abe had to repossess goods from non-payers and occasionally Abe would take Bob to his clients, something that deeply disturbed the young child. He would come to think that business was corrupt and people should not be humiliated.

Abe had many friends and was a part of the Hibbing Rotary and in 1952, the family had the first TV sets in Hibbing – well, they did sell them, after all. Bob favoured variety shows and westerns. He liked *Wyatt Earp* and *Gunsmoke* (*Gunlaw* in the UK), which featured James Arness as Matt Dillon, both starting in 1955. Episodes seem hammy and wholly predictable today but they were very popular at the time.

Bob loved to pretend he was an outlaw but later turned on childish games. He said of toy guns, 'They are as much to be held responsible for the death and destruction of the planet as any important arms manufacturer. They're just doing it for little people. They're the ones who start the assembly lines of death.'

When Bob started collecting 78s, his first obsession was with the country singer Hank Williams as he hadn't yet picked up on black R&B. We now know that Hank wrote several hit songs about his tortured relationship with his wife, Audrey. How soon Bob realised their authenticity, we don't know but he must have sensed it. In 1991 he told an interviewer, 'Hank Williams' songs are not love songs. You're degrading them by calling them love songs. They are songs from the tree of life.'

Bob mourned Hank's death on New Year's Day in 1953 and his admiration for Hank has grown with the years. He said, 'In time I came to know that Hank's recorded songs were the archetypal rules of poetic songwriting.' Listen to the imagery in 'I'm So Lonesome I Could Cry' and you can see what he means. He added that Hank didn't have a pretty voice but it was full of conviction, something he took on board for himself.

Another early influence was Johnnie Ray, albeit a middle-of-the-road singer in his day. On the face of it, he was a smart-suited nightclub entertainer, usually wearing a tux, but he was a real emotional guy who got so overwrought that he became known as the Prince of Wails. His signature song was 'Cry' and audiences would wait for him to break down on stage. Johnnie Ray was gay and his career was ruined in 1959 when he was arrested for soliciting in a toilet in Detroit. He'd been set up by the police and he said he would never play Detroit again. Like Hank Williams, Bob Dylan picked up on the genuine emotion in his voice. Johnnie Ray is a footnote in popular music but he can be seen as John the Baptist to Elvis Presley's Jesus, the man who suggested what would be coming.

Bob had to study Hebrew for his bar mitzvah when he was 13: that is when you are deemed old enough to understand the Commandments and agree to follow them. Rabbi Reuben Maier was impressed with his grasp of Hebrew when he chanted the Commandments, little knowing that Bob would soon be living by his own directives. Bob was dressed in white, looking like a younger version of himself at the Isle of Wight Festival.

There were still no synagogues in Hibbing so the visiting rabbi had taught Bob his lines upstairs from 'a rock'n'roll café' (Bob's words). Bob was hearing black American R&B

for the first time, albeit fleetingly, but he found the stations on the radio and assimilated the fast-talking jive of disc jockeys from Chicago. He learnt songs quickly as he never knew when he would hear them again.

'The Drunkard's Son', a lyric in Bob Dylan's handwriting, has been discovered and is dated from 1954. This was considered an important find by some Dylan scholars, but Bob was transcribing a Hank Snow lyric with a few mistakes or amendments, possibly as he was writing it down from the radio. Everyone did it: you would scribble down lyrics as you heard them and then copy them out decently, filling in gaps as best you could. Indeed, there was a lyric, 'Everybody But Me', in Stu Sutcliffe's handwriting which was considered an early Beatles' song but in reality, came from a Ricky Nelson album.

Starting in 1954, Bob Dylan went to a Jewish summer camp, this one the Theodor Herzl Camp outside of Webster, Wisconsin. The idea of Bob, even a young Bob, socialising and joining in approved activities, seems unlikely but he got on okay and made friends – Louis Kemp, for example, became an administrator for his *Rolling Thunder* revue in the 1970s. There is a photograph of Bob as a bullfighter using a towel for a cape.

Bob had concerns about summer camp as he was on medication for asthma: he grew out of it but some say Bob always had a blocked nose. Bob met his first girlfriend, Judy Rubin, at summer camp. Short pants, romance.

Bob befriended Larry Kegan from St. Paul. In August 1954 he was a step ahead of Bob Dylan as he sang in a doo-wop group with three black boys. Bob was impressed.

Over in Canada, Dylan's future organist Garth Hudson found himself loving doo-wop records but for a different reason: 'The tenor sax solos were so short. When the doo-wop era came in, there would be only 12 bars for a tenor sax solo and some of them were masterpieces.'

In 1955 Bob was affected by reading John Steinbeck's novel, *The Grapes of Wrath*, which is about farmers losing their living in the Oklahoma dustbowl and he wrote a 15-page essay about it. This was paving the way towards Woody Guthrie.

Bob saw some JD movies (Juvenile Delinquent movies now have their own genre). *The Blackboard Jungle*, set in the Bronx starred Glenn Ford as the harassed teacher and Sidney Poitier as the oldest pupil in the American school system – he was getting on for 30. Adolescents would dance in the aisles when they heard 'Rock Around the Clock' by Bill Haley and his Comets on the soundtrack. This kick-started the teenage revolution, although Haley himself looked like a variety entertainer.

Bob associated himself with two American actors: Marlon Brando, and James Dean who starred in *East of Eden* and *Rebel Without a Cause*. He died while racing illegally on a highway in September 1955 and his final film, *Giant*, was released posthumously in 1956. Through his uncle, Bob saw *Rebel without a Cause* several times. He had Dean's pictures on his bedroom wall and dressed like him in a red-zipper jacket and tight jeans. Abe, fed up with his obsession, tore the photos from the wall, which could have itself been a scene from *Rebel without a Cause*.

At the time, James Dean's acting style was very convincing and many artists have sung about him including the Eagles and Phil Ochs. A character from Andy Warhol's Factory in Lou Reed's 'Walk on the Wild Side' believes she is James Dean. When Bob Dylan appeared at the Newport Folk Festival, he sent his parents a review that was headed, *Rebel with a Cause*. Just how Bob saw himself at the time.

Marlon Brando was another naturalistic actor, mumbling away and pretending to be a JD, although he was older than Sidney Poitier. His biker film, *The Wild One* (1954), contains an exchange where Brando is asked what he is rebelling against. His marvellous response is 'What'd you got?' Bob wanted a leather jacket like that and is often seen in them to this day. In 1997 Dylan said that Brando was 'brave, fearless and undaunted', which is another way of saying he was an awkward bugger.

Bob's closest schoolfriend was John Bucklen, whose family did not have much money as his father had been injured in a railway accident. John's sister was seven years older than he was and he and Bob would visit her. They cut songs on a reel-to-reel tape recorder. In 1993 snatches were used in a BBC TV *Arena* documentary about Highway 61 and we also learnt that the young Bob Dylan thought Johnny Cash was boring. The songs include a Bob Dylan original 'Hey Little Richard', 'Jenny Jenny', 'Buzz Buzz Buzz' and probably from hearing Elvis, the standard 'Blue Moon'. Dylan may have had John and his sister in mind when he wrote 'Bob Dylan's Dream'.

In 1955 John Bucklen found a radio station, KTHS from Little Rock, was playing rock'n'roll and told Bob, and they heard the *No-Name Jive Show*, presented by Gatemouth Page from Shreveport, 'Gatemouth' being an endearing nickname for someone who talks too much. They learnt that *Groovy's Boogie* was presented by the owner of Stan's Record Shop in Shreveport, which did mail order. If Bob was listening at home, he could play along on piano to most of the tracks. After seeing Little Richard on film, he played the piano standing up.

Talking of 'Tutti Frutti' and 'Blue Suede Shoes', Bob said that they were 'great catch-phrases and driving pulse rhythms and you could get high on the energy but they didn't reflect life in a serious way.'

Los Angeles singer / songwriter Andrew Gold commented, 'You could have a whole discussion about meaningful lyrics versus vapid, silly lyrics. It is not so much what you say as the overall effect. When Little Richard goes 'Awopbopaloobop', it doesn't mean anything other than 'I'm having fun' but it shows you how it feels. Some songs go 'I love you' and don't have any emotion, so 'Tutti Frutti' is a more meaningful lyric than something written in English.' Spot on, mate.

Although Bob's cousin Lewis Stone was the station manager at WMFG in Hibbing, he had no intention of programming the new music and Bob criticised its square schedules.

Bob realised that some independent labels like Chess and Sun put out a succession of great singles. He and John loved Gene Vincent, who was the first white rocker who seemed like a hood. He and John bought blue caps at Feldman's and would mime to the records. Abe caught them and thought they were acting silly.

Bob still liked the more mainstream rock personalities, saying in 1987, 'When I first heard Elvis' voice, I just knew that I wasn't going to work for anybody and nobody was gonna be my boss. Hearing Elvis for the first time was like busting out of jail.'

The legal age for driving in Minnesota was 15, so in 1956, Abe let Bob drive his car. Abe and Beatty bought Bob a customised 1950 pink Ford convertible for his sixteenth birthday. Bob always got what he wanted. His relationship with his parents was okay, certainly nothing out of the ordinary.

On an early trip, Bob and John Bucklen went looking for the DJ Jim Dandy (real name, Jim Reese) with WHLB in Virginia, Minnesota. They found him and were surprised that he was black as he had sounded white. Bob was entranced by his record collection and wanted to know more about the black roots to the new music.

As well as music, he and John Bucklen were hung up on motorcycles and Bob got a Harley Davidson 45 in 1956. It was a good bike but not their big model and Brando had a Triumph Thunderbird in *The Wild One*.

A few members from the Hibbing High marching band jammed with Bob and called themselves the Shadow Blasters. They auditioned for *College Capers*, an annual talent show at Hibbing Community College, which was short on performers. Not for the last time, Bob said 'Play loud' and they did. They performed Little Richard's 'Jenny Jenny' and were not allowed on the show itself, one teacher describing his vocal as 'African shrieking'. Dylan considered this an endorsement.

By now Dylan had an electric guitar. His first guitar was from a Sears-Roebuck catalogue, but he replaced it with a solid-body Surpo with gold sunburst, which cost $60. He met two musicians, LeRoy Hoikkala and Monte Edwardson, at the Erickson Music Centre in Hibbing. In October 1956, they became the Golden Chords, so-called because of LeRoy's gold-coloured drum kit.

On Christmas Eve 1956, Dylan and two other boys, Howard Rutman and Larry Kegan pooled their resources and made a record in St. Paul, Minnesota. Dylan pounded the piano as they performed truncated versions of current successes: 'Ready Teddy', 'Boppin' the Blues', 'Lawdy Miss Clawdy', 'In the Still of The Night', 'Let the Good Times Roll' and 'Earth Angel'. 'Confidential', a US Top 20 hit for Sonny Knight in 1956, stayed with Dylan and he subsequently recorded it with The Band. Kegan kept the aluminium disc and relatives tried to sell it after his death in 2001. The asking price was $150,000 but there were no takers. Bob did perform with Kegan and his friends in the Jokers. They had cardigans with 'Jokers' on the front and possibly appeared on a TV show in the twin cities. Bob sang with them on and off, mostly off, for two years.

On 5 April 1957 the Golden Chords played at a Hibbing High School show called *Jacket Jamboree* in that glorious auditorium. Bob played the Steinway, singing and playing 'Jenny Jenny' and 'True Fine Mama' as loudly as he could. When he broke a pedal, everyone laughed, but some teenagers wanted to hear more. It was at least the second time Dylan had faced controversy – and it didn't bother him. He'd enjoyed it: again, another character trait. If we could go back in time and see the Golden Chords, we would hear them play rock'n'roll badly.

The Golden Chords could only play in venues with pianos and they found a home in Van Feldt's snack bar and another in a barbecue joint, Collier's on Sunday afternoons. Bob bought an Ozark Supro for $60 and he was keen to play his electric guitar in public. Monte Edwardson showed him a few chords. The Golden Chords were the first to perform a Bob Dylan composition, a blues song called 'Big Black Train'.

When Bob was out with LeRoy Hiokkala on their bikes they had to wait for a big black train. Bob got impatient and when it reached the end, Bob roared, 'Let's go' and drove off, oblivious of a train in the other direction. He couldn't stop in time but the bike skidded and went out of control, throwing him clear – a very lucky escape.

Around the same time, Bob swerved to avoid a three-year-old who had run out into the road, but not sufficiently well and the child had to be taken to hospital. The child was okay but Bob was badly shaken. Abe settled out of court for $4,000.

In October 1957 Bob was dating a Finnish girl, Marvel Echo Star Helstrom, who lived three miles outside Hibbing at Maple Hill. She lived in a shack with no hot water. Her father Matt was an odd job man who poached beavers and didn't think much of Robert

Allen Zimmerman. Bob and Echo would meet after school and go to a café and Bob rarely had money on him. This was unreasonable as Echo had so little of her own.

In keeping with her unique name, Echo was a stunning blonde who wanted to be a movie star and Bob was hell-bent on being a musician. After he had been away for a few days, he told her he had made a record – 'Do You Want to Dance' by Bobby Freeman. This was patently ridiculous but he must have thought that his voice was sufficiently strong to pull off the deceit. Echo and Bob were together for a year and broke up after Bob had dated her best friend, DeeDee Lockhart. Was Echo the girl from the north country? Possibly: she believes so but we will come to another candidate.

Bob was dating others at the same time including a farmer's daughter, Betty Anderson. This didn't get far as Bob was very wary of the farmer, but he also felt that way about Echo's father, living on the edge of a wood and partly making his living as a hunter, even killing bears.

On Valentine's Day 1958, the Golden Chords played the Winter Frolic Talent Contest, a Chamber of Commerce event in the Memorial Building, Hibbing. The teenagers in the audience liked them and they must have been a welcome relief from a mime artist, a tap dancer and an acrobat. They hoped to win but the adult judges placed them second. Giving them the trophy would have been endorsing rock 'n' roll. A couple more weeks and a couple more gigs and the Golden Chords split up.

In March 1958 Larry Kegan had an accident: he missed a wave and dived into shallow water at Miami Beach. He became a paraplegic and then a car accident ten years later made it worse. He was a quadriplegic and Bob saw him several times before his death in 2001.

On 6 April 1958 Bob took part in another *Jacket Jamboree* at Hibbing High, this time in a new group with John Bucklen and Bill Marinac with three girls doing backup. The songs included 'As Time Goes By' as well as Danny and the Juniors' current hit, 'Rock and Roll Is Here to Stay' and a live performance of one of his own songs. Not that it was any great shakes – he had simply adapted Little Richard and was singing, 'I got a girl and her name is Echo'. I don't know how he rhymed the name but there are intriguing possibilities.

Bob Dylan remarked, 'I read somewhere that 'That'll be the Day' was a line Buddy Holly had heard in a movie, and I started realising that you can take things from everyday life. You can go anywhere and have your ears open and hear something. If it has resonance you can use it in a song.'

In the summer of 1958 Dylan was going to the twin cities, not to prepare for university but to further his musical career. Dylan's parents were hoping that he would work the music out of his system, settle down to university life and become a lawyer. His mother told him that he had the ability to win the Nobel Prize if only he did something constructive.

No chance of that. He had an idea for a new band, Elston Gunnn and the Rock Boppers. He would be the three n'd Mr. Gunnn, the full name combining Elvis with the TV detective, Peter Gunn as well as being close to Judy Garland's family name of Gumm.

In August 1958 the Satin Tones were booked to play the St. Louis County Fair in Hibbing and Dylan was recruited on a recommendation. The group consisted of Marshall Shamblott (piano), Dennis Nylen (upright bass) and Bob's cousin, Bill Cohen (drums). It went okay as they played Hibbing Armory and may have appeared on regional TV.

Bob had already heard a number of beautiful folk songs from the Everly Brothers and their seminal album, *Songs Our Daddy Taught Us,* released in December 1958 and including

'Rovin' Gambler', 'Barbara Allen' and 'Who's Gonna Shoe Your Pretty Little Feet'. Both Dylan and Paul Simon have shown a strong affection for this album in interviews and performance. We will see in the next chapter how Bob enjoyed the archive collections of Harry Smith but the Everlys came first.

Whoa-oh! One of the big singles in the Christmas market for 1958 was 'Gotta Travel On'. It was written, or at least adapted from a 19th century British folk song, by Paul Clayton, whom Bob would meet in 1959. Clayton recorded it himself but the hit version was by Billy Grammer, which had a goodtime, singalong feel and acted as a template for Trini Lopez. For our purposes, the most thought-provoking version comes from the Weavers who included Pete Seeger: this folk quartet sang to their own acoustic accompaniment but sometimes with an orchestra. On this occasion and several years before the Bob Dylan controversy. Pete Seeger had gone electric. Nobody noticed.

In 1959 Bob Dylan went to the University of Minnesota, but he didn't study and as you will find out, he turned it into the gap year to end all gap years. Soon Hibbing would be one too many mornings and a thousand miles behind.

III. Play: *Girl from the North Country*

For many years there had been talk of putting Bob Dylan's songs into a stage musical and many approaches had been turned down by his management. A jukebox musical format worked for Buddy Holly, Roy Orbison, the Four Seasons, Abba, Rod Stewart and Queen, amongst many others, but it didn't seem right for Bob Dylan. The standard jukebox musical ends with the audience on their feet clapping along mindlessly to up-tempo hits, which was hardly Dylan's métier.

Any play or film featuring Bob Dylan as a named character was unlikely to win his support and pseudonyms are used in the films *Factory Girl* and *I'm Not There*. However, he did permit *Comme une pierre qui* in Paris in 2015 which was based on Greil Marcus' book about the making of *Like a Rolling Stone*.

Diehard Dylan fans have not been keen to push for Dylan productions in the theatre and indeed, a jukebox musical would be a new way to annoy them. However, occasionally his songs have appeared on stage. In London in 2017, a production of *Hamlet* at the Almeida used 'Spirit on the Water', 'Not Dark Yet' and 'One More Cup of Coffee', while *Roman Tragedies* at the Barbican employed 'The Times They Are A-Changin'' and 'Not Dark Yet'.

David Bowie's persona is often seen as artifice when he portrays a character such as Ziggy Stardust, while Dylan is regarded as someone who is defiantly himself, sometime to his own detriment. I don't think this is true: Dylan is as much into play-acting as Bowie. Indeed, if any play about Dylan's life were to succeed, I would choose the Woodstock idyll with The Band and the making of the *Basement Tapes,* simply because Dylan is out of the public eye.

A very adroit approach was taken in 2017 for the Old Vic production, *Girl from the North Country.* The play was written and directed by Conor McPherson, who had had a West End success with *The Weir.* He had been given the full run of Dylan's catalogue and I liked his choices. It was by no means a greatest hits production as 'Mr. Tambourine Man', 'The Times They Are A-Changin'' and 'Blowin' in the Wind' were missing and there was relatively little from the 60s. Both 'Make You Feel My Love' (known through Adele) and

'Forever Young' were included. I liked the choices immensely and I liked the way that McPherson merged songs together.

Conor McPherson had been to Minnesota and seen how cold it was and he decided to set the play in a cheap boarding house in Duluth in 1934, that is, before Bob was born. He was a musician himself which surely helped with the arrangements. The instruments had to fit the period and most of the time we have an *O Brother, Where Art Thou* set up, albeit with deeper songs. The arrangement for 'I Want You' transformed it into a close cousin of Paul Simon's 'Homeward Bound'. The play itself was good but there were too many characters for what is really a one-hour play with an hour of music. Ron Cook excelled as the doctor, almost mimicking Robert Mitchum.

Setting the play before Dylan was born meant he could never be a part of it, but did his songs contain a DNA that relates to Minnesota? I think that is what Conor McPherson was revealing. McPherson saw how the songs could bring out the characters and their emotions and in so doing, he cast new light on the old songs. In short, it was a very cold area with warm-hearted people.

CHAPTER 2

On the Road

I. Blues and Beats

Forgive me if I'm stating the bleeding obvious but no performer works in a vacuum and what they do is profoundly linked to the artists who have influenced them. By and large, a young performer copies a favourite artist and learns his songs, gradually finding his own voice. It is surely significant that the major players from the last 60 years have had many pivotal influences – Elvis Presley (who fused country, blues and R&B), John Lennon and Paul McCartney (early rock'n'roll, American R&B, Brill Building pop), David Bowie (Mod era, show tunes, Weimar cabaret), Bob Dylan (early blues, country, rock'n'roll, Woody Guthrie) and Bruce Springsteen (early rock'n'roll, Bob Dylan). At the MTV awards in 1989, Elizabeth Taylor called Michael Jackson the King of Pop, Rock and Soul, which was shortened to the King of Pop, but the Hollywood star had observed Jackson's crossover potential, which came from combining genres.

Religious upbringing acts as a trigger too. Would Paul McCartney have written 'Let It Be' if he didn't know the English hymnal? Didn't Leonard Cohen modify minor key laments that he heard in the synagogue? Cole Porter envied Irving Berlin for knowing so many Jewish tunes as he knew they inspired him.

Bob Dylan was not specifically influenced by Jewish melodies but right from the start, his lyrics contained biblical references, a constant theme in his work. This is significant when discussing Dylan, but maybe less so with other songwriters. Consider this: if you're a musician working on the road, you stay in hotel rooms. You're writing a song and you're looking for images and what is always to hand – a Gideon's Bible. The Bible is full of memorable phrases and poetic images – look at the Book of Revelation: you could get ideas for *Blonde on Blonde* from that and maybe Bob Dylan did.

Bob Dylan has the widest range of influences of any major artist. If he is asked about his influences, he rarely says the same thing twice but his inspirations include Woody Guthrie, Hank Williams, Jimmie Rodgers, Smokey Robinson, Elvis Presley, Buddy Holly, Roy Orbison, Charlie Rich and Curtis Mayfield. His 100 *Theme Time Radio Hour* shows are packed with recommendations. As we will see, Bob Dylan travelled around between 1960 and 1962, often spending nights with fellow musicians or promoters. I don't think he missed an opportunity of seeing what was in their record collections.

In the previous chapter, we saw how Bob Dylan's creative spirit was being nurtured in Hibbing by what he heard on the radio: Hank Williams and Elvis Presley – and what he saw in the cinema: Marlon Brando and James Dean. He was a sponge and very soon he was soaking up the early blues guys and the American Beat writers, who included Jack Kerouac and Allen Ginsberg. We will look at the bluesmen and the Beats in the first part of this chapter and in the next chapter, we will turn to Dylan's most significant and obvious influence, Woody Guthrie.

Quite simply, you can't expect any songwriter to start from nothing: it's how they learn to write and it is what they do with those influences that counts.

Tom Russell offers this songwriting advice: 'Find out who you are; find out where you came from; and listen to the roots of the music. Bob Dylan and Johnny Cash can sing thousands of folk songs that go right back. A lot of modern songwriters can't do that and they don't understand that if you can sing Woody Guthrie, Hank Williams and these old folk songs you have a base for understanding where you want to go.'

The origins of the blues is a long, fascinating but convoluted story. The Chess blues singer and songwriter Willie Dixon liked to say the first blues were sung in the Garden of Eden but the blues as we know it starts with the slaves who were transported from Africa to America. They sang chants and hollers in the fields in the hope of making their gruelling labour bearable. They sang about what was happening around them, their only instruments being harmonicas and acoustic guitars with rudimentary percussion. There would be spirituals praising the Lord, although they had little to thank Him for, even when emancipated, and there would be blues, which told it like it was.

Even when emancipated, the repetitive routine for the black sharecroppers was working hard during the week, going to a juke joint on Saturday and seeking forgiveness for Saturday's sins on Sunday. The word 'juke' (originally 'jook') came from an African word for depravity, and the bars offered a heady mix of dancing, drinking and prostitution.

The lyrics and themes of those blues songs reveal how black people were feeling in America. The blues lyrics of the 1920s were far stranger and far more explicit than you might think.

Bob Dylan wrote on the sleeve for *The Freewheelin' Bob Dylan*: 'What made the real blues singers so great is that they were able to state all the problems they had, but at the same time they were standing outside of them and could look at them. And in that way they had them beat.'

The American singer and activist, Odetta, commented, 'I knew that the blues is generally as projected to the mainstream is "I found you, you left me" and the songs are about women as sex objects or whatever. Certainly that is a part of the blues but there are also many other areas of their lives that are reflected in those songs: you know, we got up, we got dressed and we had to go to work.'

From the early 1920s, the best of the blues performers were making 78rpm records invariably aimed at the black market, although some artists did cross over, notably Mamie Smith (her 'Crazy Blues' from 1923 was the first big blues hit, albeit made with jazz musicians), Bessie Smith and Ma Rainey, but these days Robert Johnson is better known.

Robert Johnson was born in 1911 in Hazlehurst, Mississippi and his best-known songs are 'Milkcow Calf's Boogie', shortened to 'Milkcow Blues' and recorded by Elvis Presley, Eddie Cochran and Ricky Nelson, and 'Sweet Home Chicago', which became famous through the Blues Brothers on stage and film. He wrote 'Rambling on My Mind', 'Cross Road Blues', 'Hellhound on My Trail' and 'Love In Vain'. The melody of Buddy Holly's 'Midnight Special' was based around Robert Johnson's '32-20 Blues': Johnson's song, incidentally, is misogyny at its worst (he's going to shoot his woman with a Winchester), but these were different times. Johnson made a Faustian pact with the Devil at the crossroads where Highway 49 crossed with Highway 61. Even if this was somebody in a Halloween suit having the devil of a time, Johnson believed it was true and it played on his mind: 'I got to keep movin', There's a hellhound on my trail.' The Devil certainly wasn't responsible for his death as that was down to very human attributes. His luck ran out in 1938 as he was poisoned by the jealous boyfriend of his current lover. Much is made of rock artists dying at 27 (Jimi Hendrix, Janis Joplin, Jim Morrison, Amy Winehouse) but Robert and his misbehaving johnson were there first.

In that same year, the record producer John Hammond was planning a celebratory concert, *From Spirituals to Swing*, at Carnegie Hall and wanted to feature Robert Johnson. When Johnson died, he replaced him with another gifted blues singer, Big Bill Broonzy.

Robert Johnson's singles had only ever sold in their thousands but in 1990, Columbia compiled *The Complete Recordings*, a 2CD set of everything they had. With astute marketing, it sold a million copies. Dylan commented, 'It's hard to imagine sharecroppers or plantation field hands at hop joints relating to songs like these. You have to wonder if Johnson was playing for an audience only he could see, one far off in the future.' Sometimes Johnson wasn't so sure about the audiences who were there: he might perform with his back to them so that no one could see how he played and hence, no rival could steal his chords.

Johnson's recordings have influenced Eric Clapton, Led Zeppelin, the Rolling Stones and Peter Green, who has recorded his entire songbook. In June 2000 a court determined that his royalties belonged to a retired truck driver, Claud Johnson, whose mother had a brief romance with the musician in 1931. Someone had seen them having sex! A few weeks later it was determined that the Rolling Stones had 'improperly borrowed' two of his songs, 'Love In Vain' and 'Stop Breakin' Down', so Claud became a rich man in his retirement. The folk singer Happy Traum comments, 'Some of the blues guys were very influential but they only made money if they had reputable publishers who cared about them. The royalties could be enormous. Skip James who wrote and performed 'I'm So Glad' in 1931 was working on the margins but these young hot kids like Cream were coming along and selling millions of records of their songs.'

Charley Patton was another blues singer with a short life: he was born in 1891 on a plantation in Bolton, Mississippi and he spent many years on the huge Dockery Farms plantation. He sang both blues and spirituals and he was excellent at telling dramatic stories ('Frankie and Albert'). He had a hoarse, hollering vocal style and he played a driving, rhythmic guitar with excellent timing. He sang about his women, good sex ('Shake it and Break it') and the plight of the black man. He wrote about the droughts ('Dry Well Blues', 'High Water Everywhere') and he even sang pop hits (Sophie Tucker's 'Some of These Days'). Don't be put off by surface noise: these are fine performances. Charley Patton died from a heart attack in 1934 and his style was a strong influence on Big Joe Williams and Howlin' Wolf.

Victoria Spivey, who was born in Houston in 1906, began her musical career playing the piano to accompany silent films, but she moved to New Orleans and had a hit record with 'Black Snake Blues' in 1926. Her songs were often personal and she sang about her father's death in 'When I Was Seven'. Victoria was a versatile singer, working with both jazz groups and swing bands, and she became infamous for the dirty blues, 'My Handy Man' and 'Organ Grinder Blues'. She settled in Greenwich Village and, starting in 1962, recorded both herself and other artists on her own Spivey label. She died in New York in 1976.

Many blues performers were disabled and were even promoted on this basis – Peg Leg Howell, Peg Leg Sam, Blind Lemon Jefferson and Blind Willie McTell, for example. They could not work in the fields and so they learnt to play guitars and some realised that they could make a living from it. They often developed powerful voices because they were singing in the streets or in crowded bar-rooms.

A good, or rather exceptional, example is Blind Lemon Jefferson who was born in 1893 and raised in Wortham, Texas, which is close to Dallas where he mostly worked. Jefferson was blind from birth and in his twenties, he was singing in cafés, bars and even brothels. He felt safer carrying a gun and he was arrested for firing it from time to time. Not wanting to be confined to a 12-bar format, he developed his own form of blues, He recorded nearly 100 tracks for Paramount, some of them selling 100,000 copies. His best-known recording is 'Match Box Blues', recorded in 1927, which was adapted by Carl Perkins and turned into a rock'n'roll standard. As an example as to how lines flit from song to song, I've just been playing Sam Cooke's 'Somebody Have Mercy' from 1962. One of its lines, 'I'm standing here wonderin' if a matchbox will hold my clothes'.

Blind Lemon Jefferson was not a star like Louis Armstrong but he was able to afford a car with a chauffeur. In 1929 he was abandoned by his driver in a snow storm and froze to death on the streets of Chicago. His body was returned to Wortham for burial but his grave wasn't given an official marker until 1967.

Ironically, one of his best-known titles is 'See that My Grave Is Kept Clean', also known as 'One Kind Favour'. Bob Dylan was to record that song but the white blues singer, Geoff Muldaur, born in 1943, was to take it literally. 'I moved to New Orleans when I was 18. I'd heard some great musicians and I got the idea at 7am to grab some other people and get some brooms together and hitch-hike to Texas to sweep the grave of Blind Lemon Jefferson. It was an ill-fated journey and I found myself in jail in Lafayette, Louisiana. The idea stayed with me and so a few years later, I flew to Fort Worth and got into a car with some friends to find the grave. By then they had moved it and the Texas Blues Society had put a little marker there and his mother and sister were buried in another part of this little graveyard, a lovely place with a little slit-rail fence and scissor-tailed flycatchers.'

In one song, Bob Dylan wrote, 'Nobody can sing the blues like Blind Willie McTell.' The hottest blues guitarist today, Joe Bonamassa says, 'I love Bob Dylan and I love "No one Can Sing the Blues like Blind Willie McTell" – that's a fair statement!' Maybe, but did Dylan mean that Blind Willie McTell was the best blues singer in the world or that he sang the blues differently from anybody else? Dylan biographer Michael Gray comments, 'I'd say the latter. The difficulty is that the pre-war blues is an era in which the blues is communal, it is a shared thing. It is not for the artist to convey his own individual artistry, angst and genius. The job of the blues singer is to express the community, the feelings and emotions and ideas of the community, which is why you get the same blues stanza moving about from song to song and from singer to singer, often creating a non-sequitur as it goes. The blues lyrics are one great shifting ocean of a poem so to start picking out specific people is against the spirit of how the music was created. On the other hand, there are people who stand out and Blind Willie McTell, like Robert Johnson or Howlin' Wolf, is one of them.'

Ralph McTell: 'I took my name from Blind Willie McTell and I agree with Bob Dylan. He had the most beautiful voice and he had a lovely sense of no borders and no boundaries. He would sing pop songs, blues and spirituals and he was a master of the 12-string blues guitar. He is often more interested in playing the guitar than in playing the songs but Willie had a clear high tenor voice and there is no one like him, hence 'No one can sing the blues like Blind Willie McTell'. Most of the blues singers are growly and gruff. He wrote the classic 'Statesboro Blues' and having heard that, I had to have a 12-string guitar. When I was quite young, I became that bloke who plays that Blind Willie McTell number. When it was time to shed one identity and put on another, it was nice to call myself Ralph McTell, and it's not done too badly for me. When I tried to change the name back some time later, the record label said, "Ralph May? No, no McTell is so much better." (Laughs)' (He was named Ralph because his dad liked the classical composer, Ralph Vaughan Williams.)

Blind Willie McTell was born in Thompson, Georgia around 1903 and spent much of his life performing around Atlanta. He was attracted to the 12-string guitar which he had heard played by Blind Lemon Jefferson and he recorded for a variety of labels in the 30s: nobody bothered much about contracts back then. McTell sang for Columbia, Decca and Victor, but for most of the time he was out on the street as making records didn't change his life. He would play at fish fries, picnics, dances and anywhere he could get an audience, both black and white. He was a busker really, although that seems a derogatory term for someone so exceptional.

His full name was Willie Samuel McTell and he sometimes used the pseudonym, Georgia Sam, which was picked up by Dylan in 'Highway 61 Revisited'. He recorded a duet 'Rough Alley Blues' with his wife Kate in 1931 and this inspired 'Lay Lady Lay'. One of its lines is 'Lay across my big brass bed'. Willie is as good as ever, but Kate is unlistenable.

In 1940 Blind Willie made a series of famous recordings interspersed with conversation for the Library of Congress and their researcher, John Lomax. His post-war blues include 'Broke Down Engine Blues' (Atlantic, 1949), which has been recorded by Dylan, but his most famous recording was 'Statesboro Blues', given a stadium workout at Fillmore East by the Allman Brothers in 1971. The most intriguing record of his career came near the end: in 1956, a friend Ed Rhodes, who owned a record store, had him play for a few friends and taped the results. It's not very bluesy but it does show that he was a great entertainer. He died in 1959.

In that year Sam Charters wrote about him in *The Country Blues* and the accompanying album included 'Statesboro Blues'. The book led to New York promoters wanting to book these veteran performers and when people went looking for Blind Willie McTell, they discovered that he had died alone and unknown a few months earlier.

As the guitarist Bob Brozman said, 'These guys didn't play the blues to get the blues. They played the blues to get rid of them.'

Known affectionately as Leadbelly, Huddie Ledbetter was born in 1888 in Mooringsport, which is close to Shreveport, Louisiana and he, more than anyone, became a walking repository of song, any sort of songs. He learnt anything that appealed to him, and furthermore, he was a prolific songwriter. Now, getting on for a century later, it is difficult to state definitively what he wrote, what he collected and what he rewrote. Over the years, he often recorded new versions of songs he had recorded previously so his songs were works in progress. He worked with many other musicians and recorded with Josh White, Sonny Terry and Woody Guthrie.

Leadbelly knew Blind Lemon Jefferson in Texas and learnt from him. He wrote a song, 'My Friend Blind Lemon'. Leadbelly could play several instruments but like several blues performers, he favoured the 12-string guitar.

Eric Bibb, who recorded the tribute album, *Leadbelly's Gold* (2016), says, 'Leadbelly was a human jukebox – he could hear a song once and if he liked it, he would retain it – he had a huge repertoire and it spanned many, many styles and genres. He knew cowboy songs, he knew blues, he knew Cajun songs, he knew children's songs, he knew ragtime, he knew spirituals and he knew songs that were really old. A lot of his songs formed the cornerstone of the folk revival.' The songs associated with him include 'Rock Island Line', 'Diggin' My Potatoes', 'Bring a Little Water, Sylvie', 'Midnight Special', 'Cottonfields' and 'Goodnight Irene', so Lonnie Donegan and the Beach Boys have reasons to be cheerful.

Burl Ives recalled, 'Huddie Ledbetter was a very gentle man. He loved to sing and play the 12-string guitar and that's what got him into trouble. He was a great artist who thrilled the ladies. The girls would flock around him and the men didn't like that. They'd get jealous. They'd start a ruckus and, well, Leadbelly was good at defending himself.'

Oscar Brand: 'We did a show together in a club in Boston and some southerner was heckling him, "Hey, boy!" When you say "boy" to a black man that is as insulting as you can get, you're half a man, in other words. "Hey, boy, sing us something about the cotton fields down home." This went on for a little while and Leadbelly sang a song I had never heard sing before and I suspect it was because he was making it up, (sings) "When I was a little bitty baby". That became one of his great songs and I'm convinced that he made it up there and then.' Strangely, his publishers Essex Music didn't copyright this song until it was a US hit for the Highwaymen in 1961, and the original label said that the composer was Dave Fisher, one of the Highwaymen.

In the early years, Leadbelly was an imposing figure – a well-built, tough man living in the red-light district of Shreveport and enjoying a fight. He was found guilty of both murder and attempted murder and was incarcerated. The folk song collectors, John and Alan Lomax, met him on a field trip and recorded him for the Library of Congress, eventually being able to secure a pardon from the Governor of Texas. Leadbelly worked as a chauffeur for the Lomaxes as they collected their songs. They presented him in concert and he became, in a complete turnaround, the darling of New York Society.

Eric Bibb: 'My father saw Leadbelly at the Village Vanguard in the late 40s, 1948 probably, and he was flamboyant with a double-breasted suit, colourful bowtie, a big pinkie ring and a red sash like a cummerbund. Howlin' Wolf was bigger physically but Leadbelly was a dapper dresser and very conscious of his style. He always had shined shoes and a clean white shirt.'

There is no doubt that the sophisticated audiences were entranced to see somebody with such a notorious past. 'Bourgeois Blues' gives an idea of Leadbelly's true feelings.

Oscar Brand: 'Leadbelly didn't like anybody looking down their noses at him, thinking he was a lower-class minstrel or a fool. He got on very well with Woody Guthrie and Woody got on well with him, far more comfortably than he did with most people. Leadbelly had been through dark places and Woody had been through some other dark places and so they had something in common.'

When Leadbelly played in Paris, he put a tea towel over his left hand so that fellow guitarists could not see his fingering: shades of Robert Johnson there. 'That may be true,' says Geoff Muldaur, 'but this guy was a genius. You can't learn to play like that, just as nobody can play like Django Reinhardt. No other player had his ferocity or his strength: you can only find some other way to do them.'

Leadbelly died in December 1949 in New York City and he is now viewed as an important crossover artist. There is an amusing critique of Leadbelly in the film, *Eat the Document*, when Bob Dylan is talking to a fan about him. He says, 'He wasn't too articulate, can't make out too much of what he has to say.' That could be a critique of Dylan himself. However, it is unfair: much of Leadbelly's speech was captured on primitive machinery and it was not stored well by the Library of Congress, leading to a deterioration in audibility.

Many of the blues performers were too old, too drunk or too dead to benefit from the interest in vintage blues performers which came out of the Greenwich Village folk revival of the late 1950s. It was great that it happened but it was a bit too late for them.

Big Bill Broonzy was born in Lake Dick, Arkansas in 1893 and he developed a powerful voice as he ploughed the fields with his mule. He did army service in the Great War and settled in Chicago. He was recording from the 1920s and often worked as a session guitarist. He played at the *From Spirituals to Swing* concert at Carnegie Hall in 1938 where he was introduced as the 'Mississippi Plough-hand'.

His repertoire included 'Trouble in Mind' and the heart-breaking 'When Do I Get to Be Called a Man'. When he worked as a janitor at Iowa State University in 1950, the students taught him how to read and write. He came to the UK and worked with Chris Barber's Jazz Band before dying of cancer of the throat in 1958.

Big Bill was among George Harrison's favourite musicians although he didn't see him at the Cavern in 1957. Broonzy arrived at Lime Street Station but fell off the train, causing him to be introduced as 'Big Bill Bruised Knees'. Broonzy was given a bottle of whisky which he finished in the half-hour before going on stage. He went into a transport café and asked if everything was with chips. On being told it was, he said, 'In that case I'll have a double Scotch with chips.'

The blues duo Sonny Terry and Brownie McGhee had started as individual performers. Sonny Terry had been born in Greensboro, North Carolina in 1911 and he lost his sight in two childhood accidents. He found he could play the harmonica to increase the efficiency of horses ploughing the fields, and then he started playing with Blind Boy Fuller. In 1938 Sonny Terry, along with Big Bill Broonzy, played the *From Spirituals to Swing* concert at Carnegie Hall for John Hammond. He was recorded by the Lomaxes for the Library of Congress. Sonny Terry was evicted by one of New York's most notorious landlords, Fred C. Trump, Donald's father. In 1950 Woody Guthrie wrote the highly critical 'Old Man Trump' and Woody himself had a lease on one of his Beach Haven apartments in Brooklyn.

After Blind Boy Fuller's death in 1941, Sonny formed a full-time partnership with Brownie McGhee. McGhee had been born in Knoxville, Tennessee in 1915 and had recorded blues that sounded so like Blind Boy Fuller that the record company put Blind Boy Fuller Number 2 on the label. His brother, Sticks McGhee, had a hit with 'Drinkin' Wine, Spo-dee-o-dee' in 1946.

Sonny Terry and Brownie McGhee became a popular touring duo, playing in Europe and working with Chris Barber's Jazz Band. Keen to oblige his fans, Sonny Terry would come to the stage door with a rubber stamp and pad and would offer his autograph in that way.

Bonnie Dobson: 'On 6 May 1960 I went to the States for my first tour with Sonny Terry and Brownie McGhee. They were playing at the Exodus in Denver for three weeks – there were two shows a night, three at weekends and they were like a bickering, ill-matched couple.'

When the duo did some dates with the Clancy Brothers, they watched Brownie down a whole bottle of cough medicine before a show. 'Need it for the throat, man,' said Brownie.

Paddy Clancy retorted, 'Jesus, Brownie, this stuff is mostly codeine. This stuff is as addictive as hell.'

Brownie McGhee: 'Not true, man. I've been taking it for 40 years and I ain't addicted yet.'

Happy Traum learnt 'Careless Love' from Brownie McGhee. 'That is a very old song and people would sing it around the campfire. Blues artists like Lonnie Johnson have done it. I learnt it from Brownie McGhee who was my guitar teacher back in the late 50s and early 60s. Brownie had a wonderful version of the song which turned it from a hardcore folk song into a blues song. I recorded it with John Sebastian playing harmonica, and so it was a Brownie McGhee and Sonny Terry moment for me.'

In 1986 Sonny Terry recorded a version of Robert Johnson's 'Crossroad Blues' for the film, *Crossroads*. He died in New York just before the film was released. Happy Traum wrote a songbook, *Guitar Styles of Brownie McGhee* (1971) in which McGhee reminisced about his life. Brownie died in Oakland, California in 1996.

Rev. Gary Davis was born in Laurens, California in 1896 and was blinded as a child. He learnt the guitar and was performing from the age of 15. He married in 1943 and came to New York. He was sometimes billed as 'Blind Gary Davis, the Singing Reverend'.

Happy Traum: 'Gary Davis was a street preacher and musician but he did have a church in the Bronx for a while and then one in Queens. He played on the streets for years but when people found out his brilliance, he was brought into the concert halls and night clubs. He mostly played gospel songs but if he got enough booze inside him, he would play the blues. Peter, Paul and Mary recorded 'If I Had My Way (Samson and Delilah)' which was a big hit and he suddenly saw a bit of money and he ended up okay. On the strength of mostly white performers, funnily enough, these guys made some money.'

Chris Smither: 'Whether you got religion or the blues from Gary depended on whether his wife was with him or not, and usually she was. He was usually drunk and he would be very drunk when he played the blues. It didn't really matter what he was singing about– what was important were his guitar stylings and his vocals. Skip James would sing about the Devil in one way and Rev. Gary Davis would sing about the Devil in another. It depended on whether or not you approved of the Devil that determined whether you did gospel music or the blues. (Laughs)'

In the 60s, Maddy Prior from Steeleye Span drove him around on a UK tour: 'He was the most amazing bloke, an old man who loved booze and he always found people who'd buy him drinks. Sometimes he'd be about to go on stage and he'd say, 'Miss Maddy, I done drunk too much.' I tried to stop people buying him drinks but then he'd get mad about it so in the end, I let him get on with it. He did some wonderful talking during the performances about his life in New York.' Indeed, the audiences at his UK gigs were often as drunk as he was.

Rev. Gary Davis never made much money from his ministry – he was to benefit from the blues revival and he died in 1972.

John Lee Hooker was born in Clarksdale, Mississippi in 1917 and his stepfather taught him to play guitar so that they could play dances. As an adult, he moved to Cincinnati and sang with gospel groups and then in 1943, he lived in Detroit and developed a very distinctive vocal and guitar style. His 'Boogie Chillen' established him in 1948. He was often best as a solo act as his erratic timing made it difficult for others. He recorded for numerous labels sometimes using pseudonyms, and he had his lasting success with Vee-Jay from 1955, in particular with 'Dimples' and 'Boom Boom', which became mainstays of the British Invasion.

John Lee Hooker would not stick to the 12-bar format and might go to 11 and 14. He would make mischief as he would tell audiences, 'These white guys can't play the blues.' The Groundhogs found this interesting and enjoyed their time with him. Tony (T.S.) McPhee: 'John Lee Hooker was illiterate and could hardly write his name. If he was asked for an autograph, he would be struggling. We would help him out by saying "Bad pen, John" and things like that. Once he got the hang of it, his signature got longer and longer and the n's were always backwards. He is to be congratulated for working out how to do it, not like Big Joe Williams who just wrote XXX. John liked the girls over here and he would be fondling them in the band room. He was a fabulous guy but you would have to watch him on stage as he could make changes in the middle of a bar.'

In his apocalyptic 'Man of Peace', Bob Dylan refers to John Lee Hooker's 'Crawlin' Kingsnake' and to Howlin' Wolf in the same line. Howlin' Wolf – who was born Chester Burnett in West Point, Mississippi 1910 – was an immensely powerful man and an equally powerful singer. He was strongly influenced by Charley Patton but the howlin' was very definitely his own (or the wolf's). He recorded for Chess and many of his songs were taken up by 60s beat groups – 'Smokestack Lightnin'', 'The Red Rooster', which as 'Little Red Rooster' for the Rolling Stones became the first blues song to become a UK Number 1. Wolf's warlike singing was a major influence on Captain Beefheart. Through the beat groups, Wolf found a new audience, even making an album in London, and he died in 1976. Maybe it's as well that Mississippi John Hurt had that appellation or he might have been confused with a British actor. He was born in 1893 and he developed a relaxed form of blues singing. His best-known song is 'Candy Man', which is not to be muddled with the Fred Neil song. The blues-based singer / songwriter Chris Smither says, 'I first heard Mississippi John Hurt on an album of the blues at Newport in 1963, which is an amazing record even to this day. I had never really heard anyone playing like that. Mississippi John Hurt is not strictly speaking a blues man. People lump him in that category because of where he's from and his age as by the time they rediscovered him, he was an old black man. He didn't sound like Robert Johnson or Skip James, but instead he was a songster with a very nice, syncopated picking style.' Both Tom Paxton and Happy Traum were to write songs about Mississippi John Hurt and although he enjoyed his revival, he died in 1966.

Like the blues musicians, the Beat writers travelled around but with them, it was more a lifestyle choice than an economic necessity. They liked to hit the road, Jack (Kerouac).

Speaking generally, life was fairly conventional after the Second World War, which is perfectly understandable. Countries had been devastated; cities had to be rebuilt; and individuals, usually without psychiatric help, were returning to residential life and restoring their finances. It was feared that the next big threat would come from the Soviet Union and this led to the Communist witch-hunt led by the Republican politician, Senator Joe McCarthy.

On the whole, there was a clamping down of individuals who wanted to behave, well, like individuals, and this turned them into outsiders. You could see it on the Left Bank in Paris (Jean-Paul Sartre, Juliette Greco), the Angry Young Men in Britain (John Osborne, Kingsley Amis, Alan Sillitoe) and the Beat Generation in New York and San Francisco (William Burroughs, Jack Kerouac, Allen Ginsberg). The excessively off-beat and highly eccentric trio of Burroughs, Kerouac and Ginsberg had met at Columbia University in New York in the 1940s and relocated to San Francisco.

The first attempt by Jack Kerouac at writing about their crazy lifestyle was submitted to *The New Yorker* and although they rejected it, they spotted his talent and wrote to his agent: 'We read with a great deal of interest *Go, Go, Go*, and it makes us hope that he will have other short stories to send us. We hope that Mr. Kerouac will try something for us that is not about this particular group of wild kids.'

The phrase, 'the Beat Generation', was coined by Jack Kerouac in 1948 and became common usage in 1952 following a feature in the *New York Times*. Kerouac explained that 'Beat' to him meant 'beatitude' and not 'beat up', and he was sincere as he saw the holy in everyday exchanges. But they took drugs and drank heavily: they were beat up all right. 'Beat' also refers to the rhythms of jazz music, usually modern jazz, and their favourites were Charlie Parker and Dizzy Gillespie. Allowing for the cost of their habits, they had little money for anything else and their lives lurched from one crisis to another.

The novelist Charles Bukowski, who had a daytime job at the post office, is often classed with the Beats but he didn't care for their egotism and gregariousness. In his view, the Beats believed that being in the limelight was more significant than doing the actual work. Bukowski's advice to would-be writers couldn't be faulted; 'Do some living and get yourself a typewriter.'

Michael McClure was at the first meeting of the Beat poets in San Francisco in 1955. He wanted to get away from academic views of poetry and he was to say to Bob Dylan, 'How do you write a hit song and become a millionaire?' Dylan gave him one of his harmonicas and told him to sing his poems. He didn't quite take that advice but he did work with the Doors. He is best known for his play, *The Beard* (1965), which is based on a fictitious meeting between Jean Harlow and Billy the Kid – well, it would have to be fictitious, wouldn't it?

What goes around comes around and the Beat Generation can be contrasted with the Lost Generation of the 1920s, which established Ernest Hemingway, F. Scott Fitzgerald and Gertrude Stein. Similarly, you can see how the Beat Generation influenced the 60s, Hunter S. Thompson being a prime example.

In 1951 while William Burroughs and his wife Joan were in Mexico, they were shooting heroin and Bill, finding his libido had returned, was seeking male prostitutes. His wife was taunting him publicly and he got out a gun and said, 'It's time for our William Tell act', although they had never done this before. She put her glass of gin on her head but Burroughs missed it and killed her. Burroughs was granted bail and his attorney founded two locals who would testify that the gun had gone off accidentally, an early example of 'better call Saul'. When Burroughs' lawyer fled the country because of his own misdemeanours, Burroughs did the same and he was given a two-year suspended sentence in his absence but obviously he didn't return to Mexico.

I met William Burroughs once, around 1985. He was the coldest, most cadaverous person I've ever met, totally expressionless and next to him, Andy Warhol, a close consort of the Beats, seemed animated.

Jack Kerouac took to the road with his buddies and his journeys from 1947 to 1951 were turned into one continuous journey which became the novel, *On the Road*. It was several journeys melded into one, but it was written on one huge scroll of teletype paper. He glued one roll to another, loaded it into his typewriter and off he went: he did nothing else for three weeks. I say 'novel' because the publishers didn't like the use of real names and told him to disguise them. It was partly fact and partly fiction because he had exaggerated their adventures to make a better story.

One of Viking Books' reasons for changing the names was because they felt it was unacceptable to call Allen Ginsburg a homosexual and there was a danger that he might sue, although he was comfortable with his sexuality and it was an open secret.

A biographer of the Beats, Mike Evans, says, 'It wasn't as romantic as it sounds. Kerouac's first trip from New York to the West Coast got him as far as the city limits and he turned back because it was raining. He got a bus back and was very dispirited. Then a couple of days later, he gritted his teeth and tried again. It was a mixture of modes of transport and on his first trip he got a Greyhound bus to Illinois and then did some hitchhiking and got to Denver, Colorado and took a train from there. The book gives the impression of it being one marathon journey but there are several journeys, both on his own and with Neal Cassady and other characters he met along the way. Sometimes they would deliver a hire car back to its destination. You could drive one back for free. Neal Cassady had a free pass on the trains because he had been a guard for ten years. They could not afford to take planes. Cassady was a wild man who wanted to be a writer while Kerouac was rather conservative and a very good writer who wanted to be a wild man.'

Kerouac was writing about extraordinary people who were experimenting with their lives as well as their art. In 1956 Allen Ginsberg published his marathon poem on the state of America, *Howl*, which celebrated the Beat Generation. It broke the rules of conventional poetry and, more significantly, was prosecuted for obscenity.

The howlin' Ginsberg told the *Wall Street Journal* in 1966, 'Every American wants more and more of the world and why not, you only live once. But the mistake made in America is persons accumulate more and more dead matter, machinery and possessions at the expense of what really counts: feelings.'

By time of *Howl*, Kerouac, although a published journalist, had six unpublished novels. *On the Road* was published after many changes in 1957. The *New York Times* called it 'breathtaking' and its cult status was soon assured. The book became a landmark of bohemian life and the text of the original scroll was finally published in 2009. The scroll itself with all its amendments and crossings-out was displayed at the British Library.

The incidents in *On the Road* happened several years before publication and rather like John Osborne's *Look back in Anger* (1956), the main characters are moved by jazz and not rock'n'roll. Moriarty (Neal Cassady) modelled himself on Slim Gaillard with his creative and humorous jive talking, a precursor to rap. Kerouac likened his book to jazz by referring to its 'spontaneous prose', which is akin to jazzmen improvising. He typed and typed onto that gigantic scroll, improvising scenes and conversations as he went along. I suppose if you can't be bothered to put another piece of paper in the typewriter as it would break the flow, you don't bother with paragraph marks and other niceties of punctuation.

In 2014 Mike Scott of the Waterboys wrote about going on a Kerouac-styled journey in the ten-minute 'Long Strange Golden Road' on *Modern Blues*: 'Jack Kerouac was a big inspiration on me. I loved *On the Road* when I first read it. I must have been about 20 years old. I've read it four or five times since. It is one of those great lifetime books. I read the original scroll just before I wrote the songs for this album. That is the main reason that I included that quote from Kerouac just before 'Long Strange Golden Road'. I found the first verse of that song in one of my old journals. I had forgotten I had written it. I wasn't even convinced that I had written it because I couldn't remember writing it. So I googled the phrases to check if it had been written by someone else. I established it was mine and then wrote the rest of the song.'

Paris was particularly influential because it was a haven for American jazz musicians, particularly black ones, after the War. It attracted the Beats and they settled in a hotel that became known as the Beat Hotel. It was at 9 Rue Gît-le-Coeur just off Place Saint-Germain and several of them lived there for a year or so and there was a crossover relationship between French and American bohemians.

Several songwriters have written about the Beat generation and indeed the Beat Hotel including Donovan, Tom Russell, Eric Andersen, Allan Taylor and Mike Scott from the Waterboys. Allan Taylor says, 'The Beat Hotel was a hotel in Paris that was frequented by the Beats from 1956 to 1963. It was full of poets and anarchic artists. William Burroughs, Allen Ginsberg and Gregory Corso were residents and Jack Kerouac dropped by on his way up from Italy. I was fascinated by this place and eventually went to see it. It is now a four-star hotel! It was a fascinating period of artistic anarchy which appealed to me as a young man. You don't want to do anything normal as a young man. I read Jack Kerouac's *On the Road* when I was 16 or 17, and it was the best and most influential book I have ever read insofar as to how I wanted to live my life and what I wanted to do with it.'

The equivalent to the Beat Hotel in Paris was the Chelsea Hotel in New York and the Beats stayed there off and on when they had the money. When the Chelsea Hotel was built in 1884, it was the tallest building in New York. It was a dark, broody place, certainly not a luxury hotel, but its very weirdness added to its attraction. It became a home for artists, musicians and writers including O. Henry, Thomas Wolfe, Aaron Copland, Willem de Kooning and Arthur C. Clarke. The Beats would sleep on each other's floors to save money. Bob Dylan was to write 'Sad-Eyed Lady of the Lowlands' there and Leonard Cohen wrote about a fling with Janis Joplin in 'Chelsea Hotel, Number 2'. Sid Vicious' girlfriend, Nancy Spungen died of a stab wound at the Chelsea Hotel, possibly administered by Vicious who was arrested. When he was released on bail, he took an overdose and died.

Donovan is fascinated by these artists who had dropped out of American life, and is keen to highlight his own involvement in the 1960s. 'In the 1950s life was just trying to get itself together after the Second World War. There was this extraordinary closing down of free expression and so William Burroughs, Allen Ginsberg and Jack Kerouac started writing about this alternative society that would soon want to express itself. At first it was only happening in bohemian cafés, art schools, poetry circles and folk clubs, but soon this explosion would launch itself on the world and I was at the forefront with many of these artists to present this new consciousness. The 60s was a renaissance. What was the Renaissance in Florence? It was a rediscovery of pagan beliefs, Greek sculpture, philosophy, art and music and a freedom that was unheard of before the fifteenth century. From the 1950s in the western world, all manners of freedoms and new ways of looking at the world came about.'

While Ginsberg and Kerouac were writing their epic works, William Burroughs was working on *The Naked Lunch*. When Kerouac went to visit Burroughs in Tangier, he ended up typing some of it while Burroughs enjoyed the company of $3 whores. Shortly before its publication in 1959, Burroughs with Ginsberg, the poet Gregory Corso and the playwright Alan Ansen shuffled the sections in the book so that it was no longer sequential. Its reputation is partly based on the order of the text being accidental but it wasn't. They were trying to find a new order for the story. As published, *The Naked Lunch* is readable if disjointed: if they were really creating a collage, surely a lot of it would be impenetrable.

Mike Evans: 'William Burroughs evolved a technique when he was in Paris after he had written *The Naked Lunch* where he used to cut up pieces from newspapers and shuffle them about and see how they fell. You would get an instant poem. He started doing it with his own work. He would write a paragraph and then another paragraph and he would jumble it up. It was implying that each paragraph stood in its own right and it didn't have to be part of a logical sequence.'

There is a hanging scene in *The Naked Lunch* which Burroughs with Alan Ansen recreated in a notorious photograph: who in their right minds would play such games with Burroughs? The scene in the book is one reason why the book was banned. Mike Evans: '*The Naked Lunch* was controversial because of the profanities and the four-letter words. It was hard to read and so it was controversial in the same way that *Ulysses* was hard to read but what got it banned is that people were afraid that others would read it. That's the irony. The powers-that-be banned books that were hard to read on the grounds that everybody would read them and get corrupted. I got a copy of *The Naked Lunch* in a brown paper parcel from a connection in Paris as it was only published there, and it was in English. It was a rite of passage really.'

Kerouac, Ginsberg and Burroughs wrote many other works, but these three books – *On the Road*, *Howl*, *The Naked Lunch* – cemented their reputations. Perhaps they never would have been published, at least not in such unconventional forms, if they had not encouraged each other.

Robert Lowell has said that the Beats were like an unscored libretto, but Bob Dylan has been more generous. Dylan has had a fascination with the Beats and he loved the concept of collage and cut-ups. He liked their freedom and their experiments in writing. Indeed, his own poems often ignore capital letters and conventional syntax, just like Ginsberg's. He wrote a foreword to an anthology of Ginsberg's work. He has praised the poet Lawrence Ferlinghetti, notably for *I Am Waiting* and *Coney Island of My Mind*.

Bob Dylan has singled out *Mexico City Blues*, a mammoth poem by Jack Kerouac, which was published in 1959. In it, Kerouac discusses his spontaneous prose, his conversion to Buddhism and the fact that he didn't publish a novel between *The Town and the City* (1950) and *On the Road* (1957).

Donovan: 'In the bohemian crowd that I was running with, we all passed around books and Jack Kerouac introduced me to the word Zen. I became fascinated by it and with the lack of any meaningful Christian meditation, I was seeking how to meditate. I wanted to know what Buddhism was all about. How do you enter the spiritual world? I started to study Buddhism.'

'*On The Road* was a big influence on all of us, not just Bob Dylan', says Roger McGuinn. 'We all jumped into the Beat Generation with that. I can remember when we went to Jack Kerouac's grave in Lowell, Massachusetts on the *Rolling Thunder* tour and paid our homage to him.'

Maybe the mistake of subsequent generations is that they have been reading fantasy novels and comic books, but that all started with *Lord of the Rings*, actually published in 1954. It became hip in the psychedelic 60s.

Allen Ginsberg was prolific but he never topped the candour of *Howl*. Ginsberg saw himself as an international ambassador for poetry and a modern-day prophet. When Ginsberg came to Liverpool in 1965, he claimed the city was at the centre of the creative universe, a quote Liverpool has used to good effect ever since. The fact that he had said it about Prague a few weeks earlier is overlooked, except possibly in Prague.

Jack Kerouac died, aged 47, in his mother's house in Florida as *The Galloping Gourmet* was on TV. His mother, who had been paralysed by a stroke, survived him. Mike Evans: 'Jack Kerouac was the most conservative of the Beat writers and he got more conservative as he got older: he hated the hippies which the Beat movement had produced, and he became a flag-waving patriot and he died in 1969. Burroughs hated the system but he lived with conspiracy theories that the whole system was corrupt and it was all down to the individual. He was a true anarchist. Ginsberg thought that you could change things if enough people thought the same way so he became politically involved in legalising marijuana and banning the bomb and women's rights and gay rights.'

Because of their free-spirited nature and spiritual vision, the Beats should continue to come across fresh to new generations as their image – their brand, if you like – is so strong. William Burroughs was a major influence on U2 – so it's his fault then.

Allen Ginsberg said, 'The purpose of art is to provide relief from your own paranoia and the paranoia of others. You write to relieve the pain of others.' This can be twinned with Jack Kerouac appearing on *The Steve Allen Show* in 1959 and being asked to define 'Beat' by its host. Jack answered with one word, 'Sympathetic'.

IV. So Much Older Then: 1959–1960

On 9 January 1959 there was another *Jacket Jamboree* at Hibbing High and Bob was making his third appearance, this time leading Elston Gunnn and the Rock Boppers. Starting as he meant to go on, Bob said, 'No rehearsals. Let's go on stage and see what happens.'

Few of the rock'n'roll touring packages came to the Midwest during the winter as the sheer logistics of getting from gig to gig in treacherous conditions made them a nightmare. Because Buddy Holly had split with his manager Norman Petty and moved to New York, he wanted some ready cash as he would have to fight for what Petty owed him. He agreed to top the *Winter Dance Party* with Dion and the Belmonts, 17-year-old Ritchie Valens and the singing DJ, the Big Bopper. On paper, this was a brilliant show but the reality was somewhat different. They travelled in old school buses, ill-equipped for bad weather and when one broke down, it was replaced by another. The heating rarely worked and the musicians were ill, Holly's drummer being hospitalised with frostbite. The upside was playing to teenage audiences who were highly appreciative that they had made the effort to visit them.

Bob Dylan saw the tour at the Duluth Armoury on 31 January 1959. He loved the whole show – the doo-wop of Dion and the Belmonts, the Latin rock of Ritchie Valens and the humour of the Big Bopper but he was especially taken with Buddy Holly.

Buddy Holly knew exactly what he was doing. He had his own ideas and worked out his own arrangements and even by the standards of the day, he had an unusual, even strange voice. He used simple, straightforward language to write endearing songs that are still heard today. It's easy to see how Bob Dylan was drawn to him and his songs. Even Holly's phrasing in 'Midnight Shift' is very close to Bob Dylan in 1966 and we will come across several other links as the book progresses.

Tall and lanky, Holly was a friendly boy next door figure with a Fender Stratocaster. Bob liked the way he could make a powerful statement in simple language and he sat up front so that he could see how Holly played guitar.

Bob was on a high after Buddy played Duluth. The next day the tour played the Riverside Ballroom in Green Bay, Wisconsin and then on February 2, the Surf Ballroom in Clear Lake, Iowa. The coach was so dilapidated and the roads so treacherous that Buddy,

Ritchie and the Big Bopper hired a plane to fly to the next gig in Moorhead, Minnesota. The plane crashed with no survivors. Buddy Holly was only 22 years old. It was the day the musicians but not the music died.

With typical callousness, the management told the touring party to continue as a tribute show to those who had died. They used local radio to recruit extra performers for each performance and Bobby Vee and his group played on the first show on February 3 at the Armoury in Moorhead.

Robert Zimmerman was close to graduation. In Hibbing High's yearbook, Bob stated that his ambition was to join Little Richard's band, but why would Little Richard want a second pianist and anyway, Little Richard was studying for the ministry and had renounced the works of the Devil (that is, rock'n'roll music). Dylan must have known that he was being facetious.

Bob Dylan had disliked several school subjects including physics. In 1978 he said, 'I failed at school. There aren't really any mistakes in life. There's no success like failure', a rare instance of Dylan quoting his own lyrics, and it isn't really true. He did okay at school: he graduated and did better than John Lennon. Well, everybody did better than John Lennon.

In June 1959, his parents threw a graduation party which he attended with all the indifference of Dustin Hoffman in *The Graduate*. Abe told him, 'This is a milestone. You only graduate from high school once and you only graduate college once, so we have a party.'

It is surprising that his parents should celebrate his graduation: he had been rebellious; he had put a child in hospital and he had paid little attention to his studies. They must have known he would not behave well at the party. Still, an uncle gave him a collection of 78s by Leadbelly, which developed his passion for folk music and the blues.

During the late 50s, folk clubs were found in every major American city with Greenwich Village acting as the chrysalis and Chicago not far behind. This is where we will meet Dylan's manager, Albert Grossman for the first time.

The son of a tailor, Albert Grossman was born in Chicago in 1926 and came to be known as the Bear because of his bulk and argumentative manner. Although he claimed to have a degree in commerce from the University of Chicago, he was a clerk with the Chicago Housing Authority who had been dismissed for financial irregularities: start as you mean to go on. In 1956, Grossman opened the Gate of Horn folk club in Chicago with his friend Les Brown, later the TV critic for the *New York Times*. The resident singer and host was Bob Gibson, who played 12-string guitar and banjo and was funny and sarcastic. Its atmosphere is captured in a Roger McGuinn song. McGuinn says, 'The Gate of Horn was a wonderful folk club started by Albert Grossman. He'd been in Paris and he'd found a cabaret club with a listening room. He came back to Chicago and he started the Gate of Horn with a quiet room that was sealed off from the noisy bar. It became a wonderful folk and jazz club.' Also in 1957, the Liverpudlian Alan Sytner had been to Paris, seen a cellar club and copied it as the Cavern.

Grossman developed a negotiating strategy: he would stare and say nothing, leaving it to his opponent to back down. You can glimpse this in the film of Bob Dylan's 1965 tour, *Dont Look Back*.

For five years the Newport Jazz Festival was an important event in the music calendar and the 1956 festival with Duke Ellington had made the cover of *Time*. Its organiser George Wein discussed a folk festival with Grossman, who was managing Odetta. The first Newport Folk Festival was a two-day event held in July 1959 featuring Pete Seeger, the

Kingston Trio and the blues duo, Sonny Terry and Brownie McGhee. Thirteen thousand attended which was extremely good for the first time out. The age of those festivalgoers was about 20 years younger than the jazz fans.

When Bob Gibson performed, he introduced 'a young lady from Boston, Joan Baez and their duet of 'Virgin Mary' was a surprise success. Nobody coming into the festival would have heard of her but now everybody was talking about her.

Four months older than Bob Dylan, Joan Baez was born on Staten Island where her father Albert briefly worked. He was employed by UNESCO, teaching physics to military engineers. He had a wife Joan and three children – Pauline, Joan and Mimi. Joan's involvement in peace campaigns came from deep-rooted Quaker beliefs.

Joan started with the ukulele and Mimi the fiddle but after seeing Pete Seeger, they switched to guitars (mercifully not banjos). Joan often sang with her sister – Joan had the better voice but Mimi was the better guitarist. They could sing blues low and soulfully but Joan's voice was crystal clear. She had a ringing mezzo-soprano with a vibrato and sounded older than she was.

In April 1958 Joan attended Boston University. She started folk singing, encouraged by fellow folksinger Debbie Green. One night she sang Debbie's set and then introduced her. When Eric Von Schmidt was performing, he thought that there must be feedback but it was Joan adding harmonies from the audience. In May 1959, Joan took part in her first album, *Folksingers Round Harvard Square*.

I've an old vinyl album from the second Newport Folk Festival in 1960, recorded by Vanguard but released in the UK by Fontana. I am surprised that I bought it as it has the dullest cover known to man: it shows some young male folk singers from behind, practising on the lawn. The cover may be saying, 'This is the music of the people', but it doesn't reflect the quality of the contents. The performances are fine and it shows that the audience was happy with wacky novelties: Cisco Houston singing 'The Cat Came Back' and Ed McCurdy 'The Lavender Cowboy' are almost children's entertainers. Ewan MacColl and Peggy Seeger's 'The Ballad of Springhill', about a mining disaster in Nova Scotia in 1958, is the only track with any bite.

The liner notes were written by Stacey Williams, a pseudonym for Robert Shelton. He often used this alias, submitting liner notes for Carolyn Hester, the Clancy Brothers and Bob Dylan this way. It was because he didn't want to compromise his work with the *New York Times*. He praises Newport for presenting singers from around the world: 'There was a quality of a United Nations meeting about it with performers from six foreign countries and songs from a dozen other nations.' The album is certainly enjoyable but there's no excitement and no suggestion of anything that was going to rock Newport.

Bob Dylan had done sufficient work to enrol at the University of Minnesota. He could appreciate that learning did bring benefits, not least in keeping him out of the mines. Abe and Beatty wanted more application and didn't want him to waste his time.

It is possible that his parents sent him to Deveraux, a reform school in Pennsylvania, for a few months but it is highly unlikely and out of character for everyone. Even if they had thought it a good idea, why would Bob Dylan have agreed? The confusion is because Dylan met someone who had been there and he wrote 'Walls of Red Wing' about his friend's experience, not his own.

Instead, Bob spent the summer on the road. He went to Fargo and took a job clearing tables at the Red Apple Café. He played a couple of gigs with a local band, the Poor Boys, and then befriended Bobby Vee and his group, the Shadows, and told them that he had played piano for Conway Twitty (he hadn't). He could only play gigs where they had a piano and he would join Bobby on backing vocals and handclapping for Gene Vincent's 'Lotta Lovin", getting $15 a time.

Bobby Vee recalled, 'After we recorded 'Suzie Baby', we started getting out as a rhythm band with guitar, bass and drums. My brother Bill played lead guitar and I played rhythm guitar and we would switch round from time to time. We were looking for a piano player as we had seen Jerry Lee Lewis as the opening act on a country show and he tore it up. He was playing the piano wildly and rolling it to the edge of the stage and it was very exciting. Bill was in Sam's Record Land in Fargo and this guy introduced himself as Elston Gunnn and said that he had got off the road with Conway Twitty as his piano player. Bill took him to the radio station where there was a piano and he rocked pretty good in the key of C and we thought we would give him a try. It wasn't meant to be, he didn't have a piano and we didn't have enough money to buy him one. He stuck around for a couple of days and then he headed off to Minneapolis and then went to Greenwich Village where he became Bob Dylan. Years later he came to my hometown and I saw him then. I was amazed at how much he remembered as that was such a small slice of his life. He even remembered where my dad worked.'

A few weeks after leaving Bobby Vee, the single of 'Suzie Baby' got into the Hot 100, albeit only up to Number 77, but Bobby Vee was on his way. Maybe Bob should have stuck around.

Dylan's friend Monte Edwardson had told him that there was a thriving folk scene in Denver and, solely on this recommendation, Dylan hitch-hiked 900 miles. He had now decided to sing folk songs and he had traded his electric guitar for an acoustic Martin. The Smothers Brothers were making their name at the Satire Club, which was run by Walt Conley, who knew Pete Seeger and Earl Robinson. Conley gave Dylan an opening spot, but he sounded too rural for the audience. If they had to listen to folk songs, they wanted hit songs like 'Tom Dooley'. However, he did okay at another of Conley's venues, the Exodus coffee bar.

While in Denver, Dylan saw the 20-year-old Judy Collins and he was to take two songs from her repertoire for his first album, 'The House of the Rising Sun' and 'Maid (Man) of Constant Sorrow'.

Dylan witnessed the veteran, one-man band Jesse Fuller, who greatly impressed him. Jesse Fuller, born in Georgia in 1896, was abused and overworked as a child but he ran away from home and joined a circus and then became an extra in silent movies. He preferred his own company and became an extraordinary one-man band playing 12-string guitar, harmonica, kazoo, washboard, cymbals, drums and fotdella. The fotdella was his own invention, a six-string double bass, strung with piano wire and played with his big toe: 'I plays with my fot and it goes della, della, della' was how he described it. He was much more than a novelty act as he was a really good blues performer, noted especially for 'San Francisco Bay Blues'. Dylan was taken by Fuller having his harmonica in a holder rather than playing it with his hands. He saw how he could play guitar and harmonica and sing.

The Gilded Garter in Central City was short of a folk singer and Walt Conley sent Dylan. Dylan did five days there, bashing out 'Muleskinner Blues' in between the dancers. It had its compensations as he moved in with one of them.

Feeling he was not being paid enough, Bob apparently stole $20 and headed back to Denver. Then Dave Hamil and Walt Conley noted that some of Walt's records were missing. They went to see him and Dylan denied everything, tearful and swearing he was innocent. Hamil left the room to call the police and ask them to search his room and when he returned suddenly, he caught Bob flinging the records onto the street. They had been under his bed all along. Now they were mostly broken. Dylan said he was taking them back to Hibbing as a present for Conley's ex-girlfriend. Conley did not press charges. Dylan met him by chance four years later and pretended not to know him. Dylan later said, 'I was run out of Denver for robbing a cat's house.' For once, he was telling it like it was.

A fine singer Leon Bibb, who was performing in Denver, had to dash back to New York for a last-minute gig. Bob offered to come with him and share the driving and in that way, he would see New York. He was intrigued by all he heard about the city and especially Greenwich Village, but he decided he would have to leave that for the moment. He was 18 years old and it was time to enrol at the University of Minnesota. The university was highly rated and with 25,000 students, it formed 10% of the city's population.

We have had examples of Bob Dylan fabricating his history and now it goes into top gear as one story follows another and the press have had difficulty knowing who Bob Dylan really was. He had no American Indian blood; he had never toured in carnivals; he had never been a miner and he had never toured with Conway Twitty. In his prose poem, *My Life in a Stolen Moment,* he says that he ran away from home several times: more lies. Some of his fabrication matches the colourful life of Ramblin' Jack Elliott. Bob was telling tales but Jack had no need to invent anything: it had genuinely happened to him.

In November 1963, Dylan told *Newsweek*, 'I don't know my parents'. *Duluth News-Tribune* knew better and asked his father about it. He said, 'My son is a corporation and his public image is strictly an act. Playing around Minnesota, he developed his present stage character with his folk-style attire and accent. That is what we found so disturbing and still do.' If Abe had stopped speaking after the word 'accent', a reader might have said 'Fair enough', but clearly Bob had hurt Abe and Beatty with his careless remark. Looking at it from his side, he simply didn't want his private life in the public domain. After the *Newsweek* fiasco, Bob Dylan ordered his parents not to speak to anyone without his approval.

On 28 September 1959 and wearing a suit and tie, Robert Zimmerman enrolled at the University of Minnesota and joined the Jewish fraternity house, Sigma Alpha Mu. Dylan wanted to get involved in the folk scene. He was antisocial, singing and playing his guitar at all hours. He was asked to leave but he didn't mind – if he could find free lodging, he would be quids in. He later told Robert Shelton that he didn't have much in common with the other students, regarding them as privileged brats – all 25,000 of them?

Dylan stayed in a dump with Harry Weber and Spider John Koerner, so named because he was long and spindly. Koerner had dropped out of college and been in the Marine Corps and now he wanted to hang out in the folk music scene in Minneapolis, which had been praised in *Playboy*. Koerner played acoustic blues and was getting $5 a night at a beatnik café, the Ten O'Clock Scholar, owned by Melvin McKosh, who also ran a radical bookstore, and the café was managed by David Lee. It was in Dinkytown, a funky, hip district with such a ridiculous name that I am surprised it didn't make it into a Dylan song.

David Lee thought Bob was good and he would sing 'Sinner Man', 'St. James Infirmary' and 'The Golden Vanity' as well as songs from Hank Williams and the Carter Family. His current favourite was Johnny Cash. Sometimes he would play along with Spider John, who was grounding him in the blues. They created a blues duet from 'They Call the Wind

Maria' in *Paint Your Wagon*. This, incidentally, is a recurring theme. To make a generality, the US folkies would adapt songs from anywhere, but the UK folkies were more rigid in their choices.

The atmosphere suited Dylan fine. Koerner was talented but he lacked the ambition and drive that Dylan had. They weren't together long as they got evicted for not paying rent.

Dylan was to stay in several addresses in the area, sharing rooms with Dave Morton, Harvey Abrams, Max Uhler and Hugh Brown. When Dylan gave Brown a wedding present of a second-hand toaster and an iron, it turned out that Brown had owned them both originally at another address.

Dylan told Echo Helstrom that he was becoming a folkie, saying, 'That's the coming thing.' She thought it was 'hillbilly garbage'. Echo moved to Minneapolis herself in the autumn of 1959 and worked with a record distributor, Harold Lieberman. She saw Dylan perform but she no longer wanted a relationship with him. In December 1959 she married Danny Shivers and returned to Hibbing. Bob kept in touch with Larry Kegan, visiting him at the University of Minnesota Hospital.

In the late 1920s a young singer from New York, Ethel Zimmermann wanted to make it on Broadway. She had the voice and talent but she knew that her name was too big for a marquee. She had to change it, but she knew her father would not be happy, so she shortened Zimmermann to Merman and became Ethel Merman.

She became one of the famed Broadway stars and Cole Porter added the word 'terrifically' to 'I Get a Kick out of You' because he liked the way she rolled her r's. That song, incidentally, was controversial in the 1930s as Cole Porter had written 'I get no kick from cocaine'.

Dylan played with potential names: he thought of his first names, Robert Allen, but it sounded like a used car salesman. Soon he had Bob Dylan. This Bob Dylan would have no past, only a future, although he did say that he had an Uncle Dillon in Las Vegas (he hadn't). He tried it out on Echo Helstrom who said it was a good name.

Where had it come from? James Dillon was one of the founding fathers of Hibbing and there were Dillon families in the phone book. Indeed, Echo lived close to Dillon Road, and Bobby Dillon was a key member of the football team, the Green Bay Packers. Bob would have known of Matt Dillon in *Gunsmoke*. After all, Elston Gunn showed his interest in the TV crime series, *Peter Gunn*.

The most likely and obvious source is Dylan Thomas, although Bob has played this down, denying it at first. The Welsh writer was known in America and *Under Milk Wood* (1954) was a famous radio play, but possibly he thought that being compared to a great Welsh writer would affect the way the press wrote about him. Quite by coincidence, one of his subsequent associates, Richard Fariña wrote about having 'a copy of Dylan Thomas under my arm' for *The Cornell Writer* in 1958.

It was an apt name as there are many surreal images in Dylan Thomas' work. On the other hand, it could be a corruption of François Villon as Dylan admired this outlandish poet from the fifteenth century. There is a degree of intellectual responsibility if the name came from a literary source as opposed to a TV gunslinger. Bob said in 1983: 'If I were a fan of Dylan Thomas, I would have sung his poems or I would have called myself Bob Thomas.'

The country songwriter Guy Clark says, 'I only have one favourite author and that's Dylan Thomas – *"too gunned and cody bowled"* – after that, everything else is downhill. (Laughs). Just marvellous stuff. Every time Townes Van Zandt and I would get to thinking we were pretty slick, we'd put on a tape of Dylan Thomas reading his own work and it's like, "Oh, now I get it." I never know why people want to set his poems to music. It's the most musical stuff already.'

And why was Dylan Thomas called Dylan Thomas? Dylan Thomas' father was a school teacher and an authority on Welsh folklore. He was aware of Dylan being a Welsh god and the name meant 'son of the wave'.

By the time Robert Allen Zimmerman went to New York, he was Bob Dylan. 'Is that like Dylan Thomas?' he would be asked. 'No, like Bob Dylan,' he would reply. He was to say, 'I've done more for Dylan Thomas than he's ever done for me. Look how many kids are probably reading his poetry now.'

In his book *Chronicles, Volume One* (2004), Bob Dylan admitted that he took his name from Dylan Thomas and he chose Bob rather than Bobby as 'Bobby sounded too skittish to me.' In other words, he didn't want to be bracketed with the pop stars – Bobby Darin, Bobby Rydell and the up-and-coming Bobby Vee. Oddly, this sort of thing was an issue back then – once he was 21, Ricky Nelson wanted to be known as Rick Nelson, as if it mattered. In keeping with his new name, Dylan was casual about the spelling of it at first. Whatever; it was the perfect name.

Popular music too was being hit by the payola scandals, that is, cash for radio plays. To left wing students, pop was seen as corrupt while folk music was untainted. As we shall see, this was just a perception for there were many sharp practices in folk music. Still, folk music was viewed as pure and the finding and performance of songs was largely about authenticity.

A fellow student, a striking blonde, Bonny Jean Beecher was a month older than Bob. She went to the Ten O'Clock Scholar and he was impressed by her knowledge of an obscure blues record, asking 'How'd you know that?' She knew it because she had attended high school with Barry Hansen, later the DJ Dr. Demento. He introduced her to obscure blues records and she amassed her own collection from Sam Goody's in New York. She loved 'Stealin', Stealin'' by Gus Cannon's Jug Stompers and she put a verse by Richard 'Rabbit' Brown into one of Bob's own songs. Bonny bought Bob his first harmonica holder and suggested nail varnish to strengthen his fingernails: another friend suggested Vitamin E supplements.

Bob and Bonny attended classes on astronomy and theatre history together and she smuggled food out of the sorority house for him. Bonny is the 'actress girl' in *My Life in a Stolen Moment*.

When he was returning to Hibbing for Christmas, Bob asked Bonny to cut his hair. She cut it real short and he wrote 'Bonny, Why'd You Cut My Hair' which he sang that night. He was to record it in Bonny's apartment in May 1961: the song is based on 'Salty Dog' and the vocal, guitar and harmonica arrangement shows that the Bob Dylan style was coming into play. However, he broke down laughing after the first verse so if there were more lyrics, we don't know what they were.

Bonny was to marry Hugh Romney, later known as the performance artist Wavy Gravy. Bonny and Hugh were married by the blues singer, Rev. Gary Davis. He had them stand on a block of wood, so that their children would not be born mad.

In January 1960 Bob was back in the twin cities, securing a regular slot at the Purple Onion pizza parlour in St. Paul, which had been featuring calypso. He was starting to include his own songs like 'Greyhound Blues'.

In February a dancer called Gretel who had dropped out of university introduced him to David Whitaker. Whitaker had dropped out of school in 1957 and had ridden freight trains and known Jack Kerouac and other Beat writers. He had worked in a carnival and lived in a kibbutz. He recommended an early version of LSD, Heavenly Blue seeds known as Morning Glory, which only cost 15 cents a package. Whitaker had the background that Dylan wanted.

Whitaker passed him his copy of Woody Guthrie's memoir *Bound for Glory*, a first edition with untrimmed pages. Bob wanted to know what Guthrie sounded like. Dave played him a 10-inch album, *Dust Bowl Refugee*, on Folkways. Dylan learnt Guthrie's song about the main character in *The Grapes of Wrath*, 'Tom Joad' and would sing it over and over.

Bound for Glory gave Dylan a blueprint for life. Woody fought, cussed, sang, played jokes, campaigned for just causes and rode the freight trains. Dylan liked the way the hoboes talked in double negatives and clipped their words, something else he was to take on board. Sometimes Bob wouldn't speak to you unless you called him Woody.

Some weeks later Gretel met Bob on Fourth Street in Dinkytown and told him she had married David. Dylan said, 'Let me know when you get divorced.' Gretel and David had indeed married and they lived above Melvin McKosh's bookshop. However, this was no Positively Fourth Street as Bob did move in with them for a while. Bob met another key figure, Tony Glover, at a party at the Whitakers. A fine musician, Glover gave him tips for playing the harmonica and later commented, 'He was like a sponge. He was picking up people's mannerisms and accents.'

Bob Dylan said, 'I would blow out on the harmonica because everybody else sucks in.' In point of fact, he got that from Jimmy Reed. 'Did he ever get any better?' I asked Paul Jones from the Manfreds. He replied, 'Bob Dylan's playing is useless, utterly and incorrigibly useless but very endearing. He's one of my favourite artists of all-time, absolutely brilliant but he's certainly not an influential harmonica player.'

There was a pressing matter: the first-year exams. Bob got drunk with Bonny the night before. In the morning, he passed out in the street and threw up over his clothes. Bonny cleaned him up and got him to the exam. It was Music Theory and he got a C, which was unexpected however you look at it.

A new folk magazine *Little Sandy Review* started in spring 1960. It was edited by Paul Nelson and Jon Pankake. The magazine had started because the editors were so impressed with Harry Smith's *Anthology of American Folk Music*. One day Dylan was up to his old tricks, 'borrowing' 20 of Jon Pankake's albums while he was away including some UK albums made by Ramblin' Jack Elliott. Jon got most of them back but not Harry Smith's *Anthology* and then only after three people had threatened Dylan. Dylan said that someone had dropped them off to him for safekeeping which is like putting a mouse in charge of the cheese. Pankake extracted revenge by being the first publication to say that Bob had invented his name. In *Chronicles,* Dylan called him part of the folk police and didn't mention the stolen records.

Harry Smith's Anthology of American Folk Music had been released by Folkways at the height of McCarthyism in 1952 when Harry Smith from Portland, Oregon was 29. He had been raised in Seattle and because of childhood rickets, his growth was stunted and he had a hunchback. He had seen record production halted because shellac was wanted for the war effort. He collected as many old recordings as he could find and he had thousands of 78s. Moe Asch who ran Folkways wanted to release a compilation.

There were 84 old folk recordings in the set, which were split into three double-albums, Ballads, Social Music and Songs. The songs were not programmed chronologically, nor by race or genre, and they were largely picked for their strangeness. It brought people into contact with a lost music and so many folk musicians learnt the songs. Dylan was to record the first track 'Love Henry'. Smith supplied some bizarre sleeve notes such as 'Hattie Stoneman ought to be drowned' and 'Uncle Dave seems much too satisfied about the prospect of apocalypse'.

Greenwich Village musician Happy Traum says, 'Harry Smith was definitely eccentric, definitely not your average kind of guy. He was a friend of the poets and he lived a very minimalistic life but he collected different things including string shapes that were done by Eskimos, you know, the old cat's cradles which can be a very complex art form. He had boards all around his bookshelves with different string configurations. He was an alcoholic and it was hard to follow what he was saying. He made this fantastic *Anthology* which essentially is a bootleg. Some of these guys like Mississippi John Hurt, Clarence Ashley and Doc Boggs were just names and voices to us. We had never seen them and we never thought that we would see them, but in the early 1960s they were found by collectors and folklorists and brought to the city. It was fascinating to hear them on the records though where they were just voices from the past.'

Record producer Joe Henry: 'That folk boom in America wasn't about nostalgia. It was about authenticity and Harry Smith had that. Bob Dylan and all those in his shadow dug through his anthology like it was the Dead Sea Scrolls. They would listen to it and think that they had the keys to the kingdom.'

In May 1960, after playing the Purple Onion, Bob Dylan went to Karen Wallace's apartment in St. Paul. He recorded 27 songs, sounding like Hank Williams at times. 'The Twa Sisters' has some of his later phrasing and there is 'Gotta Travel on', 'This Land Is Your Land', 'The Great Historical Bum', 'Take this Hammer', 'Go 'Way from My Window' (recorded by Marlene Dietrich), 'Sinner Man', 'Wop Da Alano' (a Yiddish folk song), '900 Miles', 'Who's Gonna Shoe Your Pretty Little Feet' and his own 'One-Eyed Jacks'. He sang a Ewan MacColl song about British justice, 'Go Down You Murderers', and possibly he saw MacColl and Peggy Seeger when they played dates in Minneapolis.

In May 1960, Dylan was told to leave Ten O'Clock Scholar when he asked for a raise, but he was still playing the Purple Onion and the Bastille.

Actor David Soul: 'I just missed Bob Dylan. I started playing the Ten O'Clock Scholar the week after Bob left for New York. It was a small coffee house on the campus. That wonderful song of his, 'Positively Fourth Street', emanates right out of Dinkytown as Fourth Street goes right past the Ten O'Clock Scholar and a lot of those early songs also came from Dinkytown. Some great white city blues players like Spider John Koerner, Dave Ray and Tony Glover started in Minneapolis which was an urban centre for the blues. The Mississippi carried a lot of these guys up and down from New Orleans to Chicago and up to Minneapolis. There was a big Louisiana influence in those river towns.'

On 31 August 1960 Echo gave birth to a daughter. A day or two later Bob came to the hospital telling staff he was the father: another of his little games.

Around September 1960 Bob met the folksinger Cynthia Gooding in Minneapolis. He told her he wanted to be a rock'n'roll singer. He met Ellen Baker whose father had a large collection of folk records and sheet music. He played 'Those Brown Eyes' by Woody Guthrie and Cisco Houston over and over.

Bob Dylan: Outlaw Blues

In September, Bonny Beecher recorded Bob Dylan and you can sense how strongly he was now influenced by Woody Guthrie. Cynthia Fincher, a banker's daughter, plays banjo on the tape. He includes four talking blues including 'Talkin' Inflation Blues', written by Tom Glazer, and a song about the indolence of his roommate, 'Talkin' Hugh Brown'.

His 'I'm a Gambler' is sung well but carefully and could almost be any folk singer of the period. The song has been performed and recorded by many artists including Joan Baez (as 'I'm a Gambler, I'm a Rambler'), Odetta (as 'Rambler Gambler') and Simon and Garfunkel (as 'Rose of Aberdeen').

Bob Dylan played some Odetta albums and loved her choice of songs, some of which he learnt. Around October 1960 he met Odetta who was being managed by Albert Grossman. Odetta recalled, 'I was told that Bob Dylan learnt the Odetta repertoire and he started writing his own songs once he had met up with Woody Guthrie. It makes me proud when I hear of the brilliant people who have been influenced by me. All you can do is put it out there. You can't know who is going to respond and how they are going to respond and what they will do. They have been encouraged by what I've done and then they define themselves. It is beyond luxury to know that.'

Carolyn Hester, who was born in 1937 and had been discovered, like Buddy Holly, by Norman Petty in Clovis, New Mexico remembers, 'Don't remind me that I'm older than Bob and Joan! I was 21 years old when my first album came out and I was taken around different cities and I played a club in Boston called the Golden Vanity. A fabulous banjo player Sandy Ball was on the bill that night. Joan Baez came in with her mother and she was 17 years old. She asked if she could sing 'Virgin Mary'. She had a wonderful voice and as I got to know her, I didn't think that there would be anything holding her back because music is so important to her.'

Albert Grossman had first seen Joan Baez in Cambridge and he booked her for the Gate of Horn, offering her $200 a week. He appreciated that she had enormous potential because her voice was so beautiful.

After her unbilled performance at the Newport Folk Festival, Joan Baez had been offered a record contract by Jac Holzman at Elektra. Albert Grossman advised her not to sign as she could do better if he became her manager. Grossman thought that John Hammond at Columbia would love to produce her and he was right.

John Henry Hammond had been born in 1910 and came from the wealthy Vanderbilt family. They had a ballroom for 250 in their New York town house. Early in 1933 John Hammond went to hear the blues singer Monette Moore. She was unwell and Billie Holiday was singing in her place. He gave her a recording contract. When he heard Count Basie and his band, he did the same.

John Hammond worked for Columbia during the war years and then for a variety of other labels (Majestic, Mercury and Vanguard) before returning in 1958. Columbia wanted him to find major artists like Billie Holiday and Count Basie as he had done in the past. Mitch Miller was Columbia's big commercial producer with Tony Bennett, Doris Day and Rosemary Clooney. Miller didn't want to sign any of the new rock'n'rollers and told Columbia it would all go away.

The Dylan biographer Clinton Heylin feels that Hammond's reputation was overstated: 'Frank Walker discovered Bessie Smith. John Hammond wasn't around when Bessie Smith first started singing so he can't have discovered her. Again, Janis Joplin wasn't signed to Columbia until after Monterey. She'd made two records by that point. Hammond made a huge contribution in jazz – Count Basie, Billie Holiday – but I don't think he ever understood rock music.' There may be some truth in that but undoubtedly John Hammond was around when some major figures were signed.

Grossman introduced Baez to John Hammond at Columbia Records, but she didn't like the gold records on the wall and felt it was too commercial a label for her. She did not want to be commercial folk like the Kingston Trio or Harry Belafonte. On the other side, Hammond had just signed Carolyn Hester and thought the two artists were similar.

In 1949 the Solomon brothers, Maynard and Seymour, had started Vanguard in New York with $1,000 capital. They issued both jazz and folk albums and they were to sign several artists who had been blacklisted because of their alleged associations with the Communist Party. They recorded the Weavers, Paul Robeson, Odetta, Pete Seeger, Leon Bibb and Cisco Houston.

Joan Baez felt more comfortable with Vanguard, and Grossman negotiated a contract. Baez was not intending to make hit records – she felt that she could find a niche in a niche market. Grossman and Baez split up as they weren't right for each other. Grossman knew that folk music was making headway and with the right artist, he could conquer the world. The irony is that Baez was soon having hit albums as her purity and her integrity appealed to a large group of listeners. She says, 'I used to sing long and onomatopoeic murder ballads. I wouldn't sing a song unless there was someone dying in it. We reflect our surroundings all the time, consciously and unconsciously, and I didn't realise until we had finished recording the first album that the songs were so dark.'

Joan Baez's first solo album, simply called *Joan Baez*, was released by Vanguard in November 1960 when she was 19. It was a dark and serious collection of folk songs, one sung in Spanish and some British ballads. Robert Shelton wrote a glowing review for the *New York Times*: 'This disc sends one scurrying to the thesaurus for superlatives.' The album was on the *Billboard* charts for over two years and sold a million copies. Although she looked great, Joan Baez was not marketed sexily: indeed, it was akin to buying songs by the Virgin Mary. She looked mature and professional in stage photographs: very good posture, head back, gleaming eyes, long raven hair. Everything about her said, 'This is a serious performer'. She was not as virginally pure as her image suggests. According to her autobiography, she had teenage relationships with several men and experimented with women too.

Joan Baez's father was Mexican but her mother was born in Edinburgh: did this explain the large number of British songs in her repertoire? 'Not really,' said Joan when I asked her. 'It's not as though she sat down and taught me these songs, she didn't. They were new to her as well as me but it is most definitely in my blood. My feelings for the English, Irish, Scottish and early American ballads are tremendously strong, and they resound in me. Now I have to craft a song to suit my voice as I want it to sound perfect, but back when I was 18 to 30, I could sing anything that was put in front of me, which was a thrilling gift.'

In December 1960, Dylan returned to Hibbing. He told his parents that he was going to New York. He dated Judy Rubin, who had heard him in Minnesota. He bought her a dress but her parents made her give it back. They discouraged any relationship with him and they drifted apart. Dylan hitch-hiked down Highway 61 to Minneapolis. The stretch of road was going to have a section called the Bob Dylan Underpass but it never went through.

Bonny Beecher and Tony Glover recorded Bob once again and he sang 'Johnny, We Hardly Knew You' in an Irish accent. There is a drunk but fun 'Corrina Corrina'. Dylan said on hearing the tapes, 'I'm starting to learn timing.'

He was not happy with the tapes making the market, saying in the notes for *Biograph* (1985): 'The bootleg records are outrageous. They have stuff you do in a phone booth. If you're just sitting and strumming in a motel, you don't think anyone's there, you know. It's like the phone is tapped and then it appears on a bootleg record. With a cover that's got a picture of you that was taken from underneath your bed. It's got a striptease-type title and it costs $30. Amazing. Then you wonder why most artists feel paranoid.'

I can appreciate the arguments both for and against such releases, an argument that was lost in Dylan's case as the early performances are all over the internet. I'm for them being out there as we can learn so much about the formative years of a major musician. His early voice in 1960 is deeper, rather like the one on *Nashville Skyline* (1969). He is not snarling, nor particularly nasal. A good example is 'When I Got Troubles' in 1959.

During 1960 and possibly due to sleeping rough, Dylan had a cough and he did have a bout of bronchitis. It may have damaged his voice as it became rougher and more nasal. It could have been restored but maybe Bob liked the way it had changed; it added an authenticity and an edge to the performances.

He wanted to spend Christmas at Bonny's home but her family said no. Instead he left Minneapolis in a blizzard to go to Chicago. He looked up his friend Kevin Krown, and he played some coffee houses and slept on floors.

At a Christmas party at the Village Gate in Greenwich Village, Richard Fariña met Joan Baez for the first time. Like Dylan, he was extremely intelligent but had difficulty with organised education. In 1957 he sat a chemical engineering exam at Cornell University and instead submitted a poem as to why he shouldn't be studying this subject. He switched to English and then he organised student demonstrations which led to him resigning just before graduation. By meeting Joan Baez and her sister Mimi another piece of this complex story was falling into place, but Bob Dylan was not yet in New York.

Dylan knew he wanted to be in Greenwich Village. He was convinced that he had something to offer and that if success didn't happen within a year, he would return to college. There's no look back in anger about it. He liked Minneapolis and he wasn't unhappy in Hibbing.

CHAPTER 3
Talkin' New York

I. Hey, Hey Woody Guthrie

Of all the influences that Bob Dylan has acknowledged over the years, Woody Guthrie is easily on top. In terms of creativity and personality, Woody Guthrie stood apart from all the other performers of the day. He was stubborn, political and determined to do things his way. Even his most devoted followers recognised his faults except possibly Bob Dylan who has never said anything critical, possibly because he possessed similar traits himself.

Woodrow Wilson Guthrie was born into the farming community of Okemah in Oklahoma on 14 July 1912, and he was named after a Democrat politician standing for the presidency. By and large, Woodrow Wilson was a decent President, taking America into the First World War and then negotiating a peace settlement. He founded the League of Nations but couldn't get his own country to join. He had rock-solid opinions and didn't like to compromise so his name was appropriate for Woody Guthrie.

Woody's father Charley was a clerk of the County Court, but with another side to his personality. Woody wrote, 'Papa was a man of brimstone and hot fires and he was known all over that section of the state as the champion of all the fist fighters. He used his fists on sharks and fakers, and all to give his family a nice home.'

Okemah became the centre of an oil boom and, in a single stunning sentence, Woody described the scene. 'Okemah was one of the singingest, square-dancingest, drinkingest, yellingest, preachingest, walkingest, talkingest, laughingest, cryingest, shootingest, fist-fightingest, bleedingest, gamblingest, gun, club and razor-carryingest of our ranch and farm towns because it blossomed out into one of our first oil boom towns.' (This has been a terrible paragraph for spellcheck.)

However, Charley and his wife Nora had one misfortune after another. Their new home had been destroyed by fire in 1909 and their next was ruined by a cyclone. In 1919 Woody's sister Clara was killed when an oil stove exploded.

To make matters worse and despite Woody's testimony, Charley Guthrie was no match for the con-men who came with the oil boom and he lost what money he had. His hands were clenched from too much fighting and he himself was dreadfully burnt in 1924. Nora, who had a violent temper, was held responsible for the fire and placed in an asylum. Although not diagnosed at the time, she was suffering from the hereditary Huntington's chorea.

In 1927 Charley went to live 200 miles west in Pampa, Texas, while his sons, Roy and Woody, were left in Okemah. Roy had regular employment but Woody's ramblings began. 'I was a little past 16 when I first hit the highway and took a trip around the Gulf of Mexico, hoeing figs, watering strawberries, picking mustang grapes, helping carpenters and well-drillers, cleaning yards and moving garbage cans. Then I got tired of being a stranger, so I stuck my thumb in the air again and landed me back in Okemah.' By 1929 Pampa was an oil town and Charley managed the long rows of cots that the oil workers occupied on a Box and Cox basis. Woody helped him out and he was also figuring out how to write songs. In 1933 Woody married a local girl, Mary Jennings, and they had three children. They had little money and their home was only thirty feet by ten.

Woody was restless and throughout his active life, he was prone to drift away at a moment's notice. Jack Elliott, who has his own history of rambling, says, 'Woody was a tough little guy. He was a hobo; he rode on a hundred freight trains up and down the country, slept in a hundred jails. He liked to stay dirty a lot of the time. He could be on the road for a week without a bath and then he'd get in the bathtub and stay there all day.'

The definition as a hobo is usually that of a homeless tramp and yet Woody had a home and a family. Ramblin' Jack adds in his own laconic way, 'Woody really liked to ride those freight trains and I don't know why. I've only ever been on one freight train and I didn't like that. It wasn't comfortable and there were no cushions. There were no stewardesses and the only good thing about it was the price of the ticket.'

The word 'hobo' has gone out of fashion: you don't hear it at all these days. It has been replaced by 'tramp' and 'homeless person', and yet neither capture that. Being a hobo could be a lifestyle choice. Woody was a hobo, choosing to roam around, taking food and sleep where he could. He valued his liberty, his freedom.

It was one way of seeing the country. Burl Ives is seen now as much more of an establishment figure but he was also travelling: 'I hoboed in 46 states and I went to Mexico and Canada. There's an old joke that says a tramp is a tramp but a hobo is a tourist without funds. That's what I was. A lot of folk singers went travelling but I didn't lead a life of riding the rods. That was a dangerous, daredevil thing to do and not many people did it. I have a mark on my finger where a policeman brought his stick down on my finger to stop me riding on a train.' Ives' radio show, broadcast during the war years, was named after an American spiritual, *The Wayfaring Stranger*.

The dust storms evolved from overuse of the soil. The farmers had grown crops over and over until there was no nourishment left. The crops died, the soil eroded and the terrifying Black Sunday of 1935 was 1,000 miles long, 100 miles wide and a mile high. Huge black clouds of soil were swept along at 70 miles per hour and as one farmer put it, 'Why pay taxes in Texas when our farm is in Kansas?'

Will Kaufman, a university lecturer who tours with a Woody Guthrie stage show, says, 'The first of his great Dust Bowl ballads was 'So Long, It's Been Good to Know You'. It took place on Palm Sunday when the entire region was hit with the biggest dust storm that anyone had ever seen. It was like witnessing the end of the world and they felt God's judgment was upon them.'

The drought continued through 1936. There was no work, babies were dying and respiratory diseases were rife. The healthier migrants headed west on Highway 66 but promises of work in California didn't materialise. As Woody wrote, 'I saw thousands of stranded, broke, hungry, idle, miserable people.' The Los Angeles police had been overwhelmed by the influx of migrants and set up road blocks on the borders to California. Although the blockades themselves had been lifted by the time Woody reached California in 1937, he was still infuriated by this illegal act and he wrote 'Do-Re-Mi', advising people not to come to California without the right papers.

> *'California is a garden of Eden, A paradise to live in or see,*
> *But believe it or not,*
> *You won't find it so hot,*
> *If you ain't got the Do-Re-Mi.'*

Despite the tragic circumstances, his songs were packed with good but mordant humour. In 'Dust Pneumonia Blues', he said that he can't yodel for the rattling in his lungs.

Woody was fortunate. His cousin Jack lived in California and together they sang on KFVD and in bars. The radio station didn't censor his songs. When Jack went into construction work, Woody teamed up with a husky-voiced farm girl, Lefty Lou. They were earning $65 a week and Woody asked his family to join him.

The melody for 'Dust Pneumonia Blues' is based around Jimmie Rodgers' 'T for Texas', while 'I Ain't Got No Home' was Woody's answer to the Carter Family's 'This World Is Not My Home'. Many, if not most, of Woody's songs used borrowed melodies and he wrote several lyrics to the tunes of 'Wildwood Flower' and 'Goodnight Irene'. Ralph McTell justifies his behaviour: 'It didn't matter that Woody took his tunes from elsewhere. He was saying, "This is your tradition, this is your music, fellow Americans, this is your stuff." It's a valid approach but I haven't done it much myself as I like writing my own tunes.'

Woody's biographer Joe Klein sees it this way: 'Sometimes he'd change the notes of an old tune here and there to make the melody fit the words better, thereby creating a new tune – but the music was an afterthought. The words were always more important to him than the music. He wrote his songs at the typewriter. It was the instrument he played best.'

Tony Davis of the Spinners puts this in the context of Guthrie's life. 'If you are sufficiently erudite, you can recognise the sources of any composer, that is, the elements that they take from other songs. Woody didn't care. He had no clever lawyer, no manager. He had a Russian philosophy: tunes belong to everybody and anyone can sing them.'

Political songs were permitted at KFVD and Ed Robbin, a journalist for the Communist newspaper, *The People's World*, broadcast for the station. He invited Woody to sing at a rally. 'Left wing or chicken wing, makes no difference to me,' joked Woody. Country singer Stuart Hamblen, also on KFVD, criticised them both.

In May 1939 Woody began a daily column of homespun philosophy in *The People's World*. He performed for radical politicians and he toured the migrant camps with the actor Will Geer, later to be Grandpa in *The Waltons*.

Will Geer was recruiting performers for left-wing entertainments in New York. Burl Ives recalled, 'A whole bunch of us balladeers seemed to descend on Manhattan all at once. People like Leadbelly, Woody Guthrie and Josh White. We were like a flock of geese migrating. Leadbelly was a great artist who thrilled the ladies. The girls would flock around him and the men didn't like that. They'd get jealous. They'd start a ruckus and Leadbelly was good at defending himself. As for Woody, he could write brilliantly and he could give a new ballad the texture, the quality and the essence of a true folk song. He was the one true genius of all of us.'

On 3 March 1940 Woody Guthrie and Pete Seeger shared a stage for the first time at a benefit in New York for migrant workers in California. Pete had been born into an academic family in New York in 1919, his father being a musicologist and his mother a violin teacher. Pete learnt the banjo and ukulele when he was young and he connected with American folk music. At the time he met Guthrie, he was completing his degree at Harvard

University. Unlike more polished performers like Josh White and Leadbelly, the unshaven Woody would amble on stage and warble a couple of songs with an out-of-tune guitar. Pete was fascinated and wanted to know more about him. Woody liked the way that Pete communicated with an audience and could get everyone singing.

Josh White's voice had no rough edges and he sang blues like 'St. James Infirmary' more smoothly than other singers. He and Leadbelly found a niche in the supper club market where a more sophisticate clientele would meet for cocktails and entertainment. Josh White Jr says of his father: 'My dad was criticised because he spoke too well and he was too articulate when he sang. He didn't sound rural like the other country blues singers as he had improved himself but it wasn't going to change him. (Laughs) In 1949 I was nine and my father had a concert in Philadelphia at Orchestra Hall, I was there and I sang 'I Am Marching down the Freedom Road'; it was a poem that my father put to music and the reviewer called us both Communists.'

Billy Bragg: 'To songwriters of a political ilk like myself, everything goes back to Woody – Dylan went to see Woody, and Woody went to see Leadbelly. They are at the apex of the western-singer / songwriter tradition.'

Pete Seeger took Woody home and introduced him to his family. His half-sister Peggy, 15 years younger, remembers, 'Pete brought Woody Guthrie to the house when I was four or five years old. I have a memory of this small man putting his guitar on the floor and pushing it around with the strap by pretending it was a dog. My mother was baffled by him. She had strict rules of housekeeping and the people that Pete turned up with did not necessarily conform to that. They didn't have dirty habits: they were just too informal for her.'

One of Woody's skills was deriving humour from serious situations. The Office of War Information objected to Woody's song 'Take It Easy' because it advocated the use of bomb shelters for making love.

The folk song collector Alan Lomax recorded Woody in Washington for the Library of Congress. It was intended that these recordings would be heard only by students and library members but quite rightly, they have a wider circulation. Woody talks about his life and performs 28 songs. Several are traditional but many are his own compositions.

Woody never sought musical perfection: these were his songs and he sang them as he felt them. As Ramblin' Jack Elliott notes, 'Woody had a marvellous ability to sing in a minor key and play in a major, but they blended up together somehow.'

Ramblin' thought Woody's songs should also be available commercially he arranged for a 78rpm package with Victor called *Dust Bowl Ballads*, a precursor to the LP. Woody Guthrie received $300, and although the set was reviewed favourably, it only sold 500 copies.

It's worth comparing the different versions of 'So Long, It's Been Good to Know You'. Woody wrote it about the Black Blizzard and he refers to its background on the Library of Congress recordings. The narration was dropped by the time of the Victor recordings and we have a well-rounded song with the best set of lyrics. In 1950 Woody converted it to a pop song and the references to 'dusty old dust' were excluded.

Woody Guthrie was captivated by the outlaw Pretty Boy Floyd, who was killed by FBI agents in 1934. Rather as Bob Dylan approached John Wesley Harding, he turned him into a Robin Hood, but there is no evidence that Pretty Boy Floyd had any social conscience.

Think of Bob Dylan's famous line, 'To live outside the law, you must be honest.' Maybe Will Kaufman has nailed its source: 'Woody was out on picket lines and he saw working people getting their heads broken by the police or the vigilantes who could be in the hire of the police. He wrote in his notebook, "I love a good man outside the law as much I hate a bad man inside the law." The LAPD with their road blocks were bad men inside the law. Then he thought about good men outside the law and came up with Pretty Boy Floyd, although he had no justification for that. Woody took the tune from the old American outlaw song, 'Jesse James' and wrote about him as a great campaigner for social justice.'

Pete Seeger recalled that 'In 1940 John Steinbeck's best-selling novel of the Dust Bowl, *The Grapes of Wrath*, was adapted for a film starring Henry Fonda. Victor Records wanted Woody to write about the film and Pete Seeger watched him do it. 'Woody usually wrote in a hurry, in a flash of inspiration, no, that's too easy to say, he'd work at it. He'd sit down and say, "I want to write a song on this subject and I'm going to stick with it until it's finished." He'd pick up the guitar and sing a verse, see how it sounded, and then he'd put the guitar down and go back to pecking away at the typewriter. I happened to meet him in the streets of New York City and he said, "Peter, I've got to write a song. Can I borrow your typewriter?" I told him to come along with me. I was staying with a friend, six flights up, and he started typing, picking up the guitar, trying out a verse and putting it down. He had a big jug of wine, from which he'd take a swig now and again. Finally my friend and I got sleepy and we woke up in the morning and Woody was curled up on the floor under the table. The jug of wine was empty, and there was the completed song, 'Tom Joad', a long, long ballad, six minutes long and he'd finished it. Didn't do any rewriting on it.'

As well as the 17 verses of 'Tom Joad', Guthrie brought Reverend Casy's death into the mysterious 'Vigilante Man'. John Steinbeck recognised a kindred spirit: 'There is nothing sweet about the songs he sings. But there is something more important for those who will listen: there is the will of the people to endure and fight against oppression. We call this the American Spirit.'

Woody was writing himself into his depiction of 'Pretty Boy Floyd' but he was not sure he should be spending his time writing songs: Writing is no profession for a man these days with all these poor folks wandering around the country as homeless as little dogies. What I should do is strap on a couple of six-shooters, blow open the doors of the banks and feed the people and give them houses. The only reason I don't do that is because I ain't got the guts."Pretty Boy Floyd' contains the observation: 'Some will rob you with a six-gun, and some with a fountain pen.' In 'Talkin' New York' (1962), Bob Dylan said, 'Now a very great man once said that some folk will rob you with a fountain pen.'

Woody spoke his mind in his *Woody Sez* columns for the *Daily Worker*, the most influential of the Communist newspapers in the US. He lost a radio spot because he refused to give up his column; it was too extreme for them, and there are endless stories regarding Woody's individualism: 'I got disgusted with the whole sissified and nervous rules of censorship on all of my songs and ballads and drove off down the road across the southern states again.'

If Woody was turning his back on success, it never bothered him. Indeed, it wasn't anything he sought. He wrote relatively few love songs and doubtless, they would have found a wider audience than his topical work. It is difficult to appreciate 'Why Do You Stand There in the Rain' without knowing it was about a peace vigil on the White House lawn. Pete Seeger came to know Woody in New York and described his songwriting thus: 'Anything worth discussing was worth a song to him: news off the front page, sights and sounds of the countryside he travelled through, thoughts brought to him by reading anything from

Rabelais to Will Rogers. He composed for himself and his friends and he had a disparaging attitude towards the hit parade and any kind of commercial success.'

Woody hated the songs from Tin Pan Alley. He hated songs about the moon and June and he hated anyone using more than three chords – that was just showing off, in his opinion. He hated Cole Porter singing of privileged lifestyles. Woody said, 'I hate a song that makes you think you're just bound to lose.'

'Hard Travellin'' is Woody Guthrie's great ode to the working people, to people who wish they were working and to people who've lost their jobs. A central plank of Guthrie's work is poverty and he is giving voice to the disenfranchised.

New Multitudes, an engrossing collection of Woody's lyrics set to music by Jay Farrar, Will Johnson, Anders Parker and Yim Yames, was issued in 2013. Woody's daughter, Nora, says: '*New Multitudes* is a 2-CD project of Woody's lyrics and they are mostly skid row songs, end of the road songs. Woody wrote about what it was like to be a drug addict, to be a prostitute or simply to be homeless. Not a lot of people have written songs like that.'

Woody was unfairly harsh on Tin Pan Alley. Bing Crosby's massive hit 'Brother, Can You Spare a Dime?' (1932) was the greatest song to come out of the Depression. It had real social concern and yet it was written by an Alley writer, Yip Harburg. In 1939 Harburg wrote 'Over the Rainbow' and maybe there's a subtext in that song for anyone living in poverty and indeed, the song was written on the brink of world war.

In 1939 Woody Guthrie heard a Tin Pan Alley song that he loathed above all others. It was Irving Berlin's 'God Bless America', a gigantic success for Kate Smith. Berlin had written it 20 years earlier, but had decided there were enough patriotic anthems. When he dusted it off, he could see how appropriate it remained. It was now a positive song about the virtues of America while fascism and anti-Semitism were spreading elsewhere. Irving Berlin, a Jew and an immigrant, was making a personal statement, but Woody hated its jingoism, feeling that America was acting superior by claiming to have God on its side. He set out his own thoughts in 'This Land is Your Land', which was not an immediate commercial success but became a classic.

On the strength of this song, Woody was offered an intriguing commission. The Bonneville Power Administration in Portland wanted to make a documentary film to promote the sale of bonds for building dams. As a result, thousands of homes and factories would receive electricity for the first time. The project captured Woody's interest.

Acting against type, Woody accepted a full month's work. Although they gave him a car, he wrote, 'I pulled on my shoes and walked out of every one of those Pacific north-west mountain towns, drawing pictures in my mind and listening to poems and songs and words that would come and dance in my ears faster than I could ever get them written down.'

The Administration wanted songs to reflect the prestige of their project whereas Woody (naturally) was intent on glorifying the construction workers. Both requirements were met in his beautiful stately waltz, 'Roll on Columbia'. During that month Woody wrote 30 songs including 'The Grand Coulee Dam', which is Woody at his most poetic, and 'Pastures of Plenty'. He had been wonderfully productive but as usual, he was taking tunes from anywhere: 'The Grand Coulee Dam' was sung to 'Wabash Cannonball' and 'Ramblin' Round Your City' came from Leadbelly's 'Goodnight Irene'.

Filming was postponed because of America's involvement in the war but six songs were used when it was made in 1948. His achievement was officially recognised in 1966 when a sub-station was named after him.

Woody returned to New York and joined a new group, the Almanac Singers with Pete Seeger, Lee Hays and Millard Lampell, which was using music for social change. In August 1941, they performed at a fundraiser in Seattle for the Democrats. The event was called a hootenanny, a word which would gain popularity.

The Almanacs sang about the strength of the unions and advocated strike action when necessary. Woody's 'Union Maid' is their best-known song, which was updated by the Strawbs for 'Part of the Union' (1973). I'm fond of Woody's liberal interpretation of the Bible in 'Good Ole Union Feeling'. Indeed, I'd be interested to know exactly where Jesus said this:

'Jesus of Nazareth told his people one and all,
"You must join the union army
When you hear that union call
It's that good old union feeling in my soul".'

Woody wrote 'The Sinking of the Reuben James' and he put an ambitious slogan on his guitar, 'This machine kills fascists'. He said, 'This guitar makes me feel like beating the fascists and then that makes me sing about how much I hate them.'

Woody's personality and eccentric phrasing made it difficult for him to be a member of a group, no matter how much he sympathised with their aims. He left the Almanac Singers after a year and for a while he sang in the Headline Singers with Leadbelly, Sonny Terry and Brownie McGhee. In 1969 Ember issued two albums – *Cisco Houston and Woody Guthrie* and *Blind Sonny Terry and Woody Guthrie*. The packaging was appalling but the albums showed how Woody and his friends tackled old folk songs. Cisco and Woody's version of 'Take a Whiff on Me' is very entertaining.

For the most part, Woody was best as a solo performer, although he was certainly erratic. He drank too much, forgot his own words and rambled to an audience when he should have been singing. Oscar Brand is quoted in Joe Klein's biography as saying, 'He would test the audience. If he felt they weren't attentive enough, he'd start playing the wrong chords or just not change chords at all. I have heard him sing the same verse of 'Gypsy Davy' three, four times in a row. He'd go right up to the front of the stage and stare this wild stare and make everyone very tense and uncomfortable.'

Woody Guthrie's memoir, *Bound for Glory*, was published in 1943. It formed an excellent companion to *The Grapes of Wrath* and was illustrated by Woody's own drawings. Woody wrote about the Dust Bowl and the tragedies that had shaped his life, but he didn't regard the book as autobiographical. He called it 'my novel' and in essence *Bound for Glory* is Woody's life embellished by his imagination. A parallel with Jack Kerouac's *On the Road* can be made. Guthrie often wrote in dialect and Robert Shelton has remarked that much of Dylan's prose was inspired by Guthrie's 'folk talk and punk-tuation'.

There are many inconsistencies between *Bound for Glory* and Woody's life. Woody doesn't mention his marriage in the book, possibly because he was ashamed of his behaviour. He spent little time with his family and saw other women. He later admitted, 'And when my kids get counted, it will be a long list and all.'

Woody and Mary were divorced in 1941, and Woody married again, this time to a dancer with the Martha Graham Company, Marjorie Mazia Greenblatt. Their relationship was interrupted by his wartime service in the marines. He worked in the galleys and entertained the crew but his writings and his songs from that time are mostly unpublished. His ship was torpedoed twice and while he was in England, he called in at the BBC and appeared on *Children's Hour*.

Children's Hour was appropriate as Woody was changing his style. After the war, he lived happily on Coney Island and he wrote songs like 'Put Your Finger in the Air' and 'Riding in My Car' for his daughter Cathy. He said, 'I've sold two albums of phonograph records of kids' songs just by putting little tunes and guitar notes to the songs she sings.' Woody's songs can be heard on two albums he recorded for Moses Asch's Folkways label, *Songs to Grow on* and *Songs to Grow on for Mother and Child*.

However, tragedy struck again as Cathy was killed when her clothing caught fire: fire is playing a crucial role in Guthrie's story. Will Kaufman: 'Cathy's death almost destroyed him. He couldn't comprehend how someone so vibrant and so beautiful and so life-loving could be there one minute and gone the next. What had taken her away was really cheap wiring which had been produced in order to cut corners and the purchasers were the victims to such corner-cutting. He made a lot of comparisons between the loss of his daughter and the whole anti-capitalist movement.'

Songwriting royalties came his way for 'Oklahoma Hills', a song he had written and performed on KFVD with his cousin Jack Guthrie. Jack became a successful country singer and 'Oklahoma Hills' was his best-known record, topping the US country charts for six weeks in 1945.

Woody and Marjorie's son, Arlo, was born in 1947. 'When my mom was a little girl, she had to write about the book she was reading which was about a little Swiss kid called Arlo who got wood for his mother. She had to draw him too and she saved the picture. Years later she saw my dad walking down to the beach and he was wearing the same clothes as the kid in the picture. She was pregnant and so that's how I got my name.'

Lefty Lou's cousin, Mary Ruth, told Woody of Jack's sudden death in January 1948 when he was only 32. Woody wrote to comfort her but his letters became more and more erotic. She complained to the police and Woody was sentenced to six months in jail. Marjorie said, 'I wanted to say to the judge, "You can't do this. He'll go in there and have a fine old time. I'm the one who's going to suffer".' Marjorie was correct as he was annoyed when an appeal led to his release on 22 December 1949: he was organising the Christmas show.

Moses Asch, an enthusiast who had formed Folkways Records, suggested that Woody should write about Sacco and Vanzetti, two Italians who had organised union movements in Boston. In 1927, they had been arrested for murder and with scant evidence, they were convicted and executed. Woody's songs highlighted the absurdities of the case and 'Suassos Lane' and 'Root Hog and Die' are particularly good.

Woody worked with the up-and-coming Tom Paley: 'We started doing some bookings together and it was Woody who was being booked. I was the young kid who came along and played with him. I showed up at some union hall and he didn't. I called his home and asked Marjorie where he was and she said, "I don't know. He went out last Tuesday for cigarettes and he'll probably be back in a week or two." He would wander off. Some of that irresponsibility may have been a sign of Huntington's chorea, which does affect the brain, but he was never responsible about his commitments.'

Woody still performed his Dust Bowl ballads. The songs were pertinent as the Government still had to make good the damage caused by dust storms. Many migrant workers had found work during the war and settled in California, working in the orchards. Woody wrote 'Plane Wreck at Los Gatos (Deportee)' after hearing a plane carrying some labourers home had crashed. The newscaster's callous remark, 'They were just deportees' inspired the majestic chorus:

'Goodbye to my Juan, farewell Rosalita,
Adios mis amigos, Jesus and Maria,
You won't have a name when you ride the big airplane,
All they will call you will be deportees.'

It is sometimes said that Woody Guthrie rarely dealt with racial prejudice, but he certainly did there and also in 'The Blinding of Isaac Woodard', written after a demobbed, black man had been attacked by police.

One of Woody's greatest lyrics is '1913 Massacre', telling how a stupid prank caused the deaths of 73 children, but he should have made some changes to the melody to prevent the song being repetitive. In its original form, 'One Morning in May' was recorded by the Spinners and James Taylor.

When Pete Seeger was discharged from the army in 1945, he formed People's Songs to encourage radical protest songs and he started an agency, People's Artists. Primarily this was to help artists who had been blacklisted and find venues for them to play. This initiated a folk song revival and the magazine *Sing Out!* started in 1950. The agency was dropped in 1957 as the McCarthy era was over, and *Sing Out!* was broke. Moses Asch took it over. It became a properly funded magazine with a full-time editor and paid advertisements. The circulation increased tenfold.

Pete Seeger formed a new singing group, the Weavers: 'We started singing together in late 1948. We had a few bookings through 1949 but we were on the verge of splitting up but I didn't want to sing by myself. I went to a little nightclub in Greenwich Village that had once hired me for $200 a week but they said, "No, we don't want the Weavers." I said, "Would you take us if you didn't have to pay any more than the $200 that you pay me?" How could they lose, so we started working at the Village Vanguard. Six months later we were a well-rehearsed group and we had experimented with different kinds of songs. We'd go into the audience and start singing with them, so it was six months of improvisation and experimentation and rehearsing. At the end of it we had a record contract and a song called 'Goodnight Irene'.'

Their first record was 'If I Had a Hammer', but Leadbelly's 'Goodnight Irene' was a million seller. It wasn't a straight folk song arrangement as it was orchestrated by Gordon Jenkins who worked with Frank Sinatra. Then they revamped 'So Long, It's Been Good to Know You'. Woody shunned commerciality but he welcomed songwriting royalties.

Happy Traum: 'I don't know who persuaded the Weavers to have a big orchestra behind them but it really popped the songs up and made them slick and commercial. Then when they were blacklisted, everything dried up for them. They couldn't get jobs as radio stations wouldn't play their music and clubs wouldn't hire them. Pete said, "I'm going back to the roots with my banjo and my guitar and I will sing for the people." He was a fabulous musician, which is often overlooked, and he had charm and a way of bringing people into music. Before you were just a listener and an observer but when Pete came along, he made everybody a participant. The beauty of folk music is that you can participate at any level.

You don't have to be a great musician. You can strum a guitar and sing songs with your friends and have a good time.'

The threat from the Soviet Union was magnified once they had built an atomic bomb in 1949. Joe McCarthy, a senator from Wisconsin, began his infamous witch-hunt which was looking for 'reds under the beds'. The House Un-American Activities Committee was formed to expose the Russian threat. Charlie Chaplin was hounded out of America, and Paul Robeson told the Committee: 'You are the Un-Americans and you ought to be ashamed of yourselves.'

A publication *Red Channels* listed subversive folk singers and naturally Seeger was included. Guthrie was classified as 'prematurely anti-fascist' and he made no attempt to hide or change his beliefs, calling himself 'the most radical, most militant and most topical of the folk entrepreneurs'. In the *Sunday Worker*, Woody declared that 'The best thing I did in 1938 was to sign up with the Communist Party and start turning the pages of some thicker books.' That statement appears cut and dried but it was not true. Pete Seeger said, 'Woody never joined the Party. He tried but he had had too many strange ideas and they wouldn't take him!'

The House of Un-American Activities never called upon Woody to testify, perhaps because he was sick. He appeared much older than his 40 years and he was becoming even more impossible to live with. Marjorie left him, and after visiting her and attacking her, Woody was admitted to the Brooklyn State Hospital, ostensibly to be treated for alcoholism. They were divorced in 1953.

Although Woody was considered an alcoholic, the doctors diagnosed Huntington's chorea, a rare and incurable nervous disease inherited from his mother. Woody was fit enough to discharge himself in September 1952. He went to Topanga Canyon in California, an area favoured by victims of the blacklist, and shortly afterwards married 20-year-old Anneke Marshall. Woody worked on a new book, *Seeds of Man*, and made plans to visit Europe. The couple lived in an old bus at the edge of a swamp and Woody had an accident in which his arm was burned (fire again), making it difficult to play the guitar.

Woody and Anneke came to New York to have their baby, but Anneke left him because of his bizarre behaviour, which was probably caused by illness. Woody went on the road with Ramblin' Jack Elliott. In an attempt to cure Jack of his hero worship, Woody left him in California with a note, 'Dear Jack, Fuck you, Woody Guthrie'. Left to his own devices, Woody spent several months in and out of jails for vagrancy, drunken behaviour and trespassing on railway property. Woody was more than enough for Anneke and for a couple of years both Marjorie and Anneke were looking after him. In 1956 Anneke was granted a Mexican divorce.

Arlo Guthrie: 'I got my first guitar when I was six years old. My dad bought me an $80 guitar which was a lot of money for people who didn't have much. My mother just about shot him then and there. Not only that, he bought the neighbour's kid one too, also for 80 bucks. He said, 'Well, if you give a kid a lousy instrument, he won't play it and if you get him a good one, he'll keep on doing it.' I guess the proof is that the other kid and me are still playing. It was what they call a three-quarter size guitar which is about half the size of a normal guitar and as matter of fact, I gave it to my own daughter.'

In September 1954 and perhaps fearing another winter on the road, Woody checked himself into Brooklyn State Hospital. He said, 'This is the best damn place to be these days. It's the only place where I can get up on a stool and start screaming "I'm a Communist" and no one can do a damn thing about it.'

At the time Woody's songwriting royalties were around $1,000 a year but there was always the potential for a song to be revived and have commercial success. Some of his songs were already in schoolbooks and his Marxist vision of America, 'This Land Is Your Land' now means all things to all people, depending on which verses are sung. Indeed, it could appeal to Daniel Boone and his frontier spirit as much as Karl Marx, which is some achievement. Bob Dylan at the Carnegie Chapter Hall in 1961 gave it a slow, stately arrangement unlike any other: he knew the song said so much and there was no need to overstate it.

It is not a straight line from Woody Guthrie to Bob Dylan but it goes from Woody to Ramblin' Jack and then to Bob Dylan. Jack is the missing link. Jack had a wider repertoire than Woody's songs but he never wanted to shake that off. Ramblin' Jack Elliott: 'I used to look a lot like Woody. When I used to visit him in hospital, the other patients would announce, "Hey, Woody, your brother's here!"'

Ramblin' Jack Elliott had been born Elliott Adnopoz, in New York City, the son of a doctor, in 1931, but he had wanted to be a cowboy. He had been so rebellious that he refused a bar mitzvah. Dylan laughed when he heard that Jack was Jewish and Dave Van Ronk commented, 'That's when we knew that Dylan was Jewish too.' Like Dylan, Ramblin' Jack was to fictionalise his background and yet folk music is about authenticity. Jack loved talking and telling stories, tall or otherwise, for the sheer pleasure of telling them.

It's hard to say why Dylan was hiding his Jewish background and it is doubtful really whether he would have fooled anyone in the Greenwich Village folk scene which had many Jewish performers and followers.

Jack spent a lot of time with Woody but in 1955 he branched out and came to Europe, particularly the UK. A song associated with Jesse Fuller, 'San Francisco Bay Blues' became his signature tune. 'Woody wrote about 2,000 songs and I only know 50 of them. One that I did with a lot of enthusiasm was 'This Land Is Your Land' and it was strange that the audiences in England could join in without me even asking them. They loved the song and it was emotional to sing it in England.'

The Guthrie Children's Trust Fund was established in 1956 'for the purpose of collecting, publishing and protecting the rights and interests of the literary and musical works of Woody Guthrie'. The beneficiaries were the three living children of his marriage to Marjorie: Arlo, Joady and Nora. The Woody Guthrie Foundation was granted charitable status in 1972. The Foundation is responsible for Woody's archives and makes grants for research into Huntington's chorea.

By 1961 Bob Dylan was copying Woody Guthrie – his clothes, his hairstyle and his music. As Anthony Scaduto remarks in his biography of Bob Dylan, 'Guthrie was a ready-made image for a man in search of a strong image.'

Bob Dylan said in 1966, 'What drew me to Woody Guthrie was hearing his voice; I could tell that he was very lonesome, very alone and very lost. That's why I dug him.' Bob said something similar about Hank Williams.

Dylan played harmonica for the young Arlo in 1961 after the babysitter had let him into the house. He befriended Woody and sat by his bedside playing the guitar. Dylan's 'Song to Woody', which he recorded in 1962, is a lovely song about a vanishing lifestyle. Bob Dylan soon found his own personality, and Ramblin' Jack Elliott noted one big difference, 'Woody Guthrie wouldn't have wanted to experiment. Woody kept his music simple and basic, but Bob wanted new developments.'

Woody had many visitors while he was in hospital, and they included Tony Davis and Mick Groves from the Liverpool folk group, the Spinners in 1962. The very name, the Spinners, was a nod to the Weavers. Tony said, 'He had refused to take any money to help him as he said he was just an ordinary guy. So there he was in a state mental hospital, an old-fashioned lunatic asylum. There were metal bars and the doors were locked behind us. We went past these old guys slobbering and watching TV, and Woody was on a board in the balcony. He had a Linus comforter as he couldn't control his jaw muscles. Mick told him how much the young people of England appreciated his music and told him how much we had learned from him. When we mentioned Bob Dylan, Woody got quite agitated. He was semi-coherent and we had to listen hard to what he was saying. It was 'My son, my son', which we now take as a reference to Arlo. He was all spasms and twitches, but we got a tremendous feeling of strength from within him. He wore leather boots and he insisted on seeing us out. He stopped in front of the TV and all those creatures – there's no other word to describe them – said, "Get out of the way!" Woody hated TV as he equated it with moguls and big business. He gave them the finger as if to say, "Stuff the TV!" and it showed that there was still some spirit within that shell. As we went through the passageway, we passed a women's ward and we could hear somebody wailing the blues. Tears were streaming down our cheeks but we had met a fantastic man. I know it sounds sad and pathetic and horrible to describe but it wasn't like that at all.' Tony may be right but could the 'My son' comment relate to Dylan?

Mick Groves of the Spinners: 'In 1962 Tony Davis and I went over to America on a teachers' trip. Pete Seeger arranged some work for us and also for us to visit Woody Guthrie. We went to the hospital and we were taken into a room and it was like a plank with two seats and then they brought Woody in and he lay on this plank. Because of his Huntington's chorea, he was shaking, shaking, shaking, but able to talk to us so that we could understand him. He said, "Thank you for coming from Liverpool." We said, "No, it is amazing for us to actually be with Woodrow Wilson Guthrie." It culminated in Tony producing an EP that Topic Records had made of the Spinners at our club and he gave it to Woody, and Woody started reaching down to his boot, and it was awful seeing someone who had no control over himself. He pulled out a pen and he passed it to us and he asked us to sign the record for him. Can you imagine that? Tony and I giving Woody Guthrie our autographs. I am very pleased that we did go and see him but it was also very sad. He didn't seem to be in distress though as he was smiling and talking to us in his own way. It was terribly humbling to meet him but it was also magnificent because I saw in him, shambling wreck that he was, the urge and desire to live.'

Arlo Guthrie: 'I always remember my dad as someone who refused to give up on anything, let alone being sick. He was a real stubborn person and he changed that stubbornness into a quiet kind of persistence, and he refused to acclimatise himself to different hospitals. He refused to be a patient. Up until his last year, you could communicate with him. It was only in the last year that he had a lot of trouble talking and he couldn't write, so up to that point, although it was bothersome to some extent, it was still a two-way street and it wasn't too bad.'

The singer / songwriter Jonatha Brooke saw the lyrics he had written in hospital, but could only read them with difficulty. 'On some of them, I could barely read his handwriting. They were chicken scratches on legal pads. He wasn't in control of his limbs and yet he still had so much to say. Some of those later songs are the most yearning and simple and the most powerful and moving. I cried when I saw 'My Battle': (quotes) "Show me to how to win the battle in life." That was one that I could barely read and yet it said so much.'

Woody's condition grew worse. He was given 'Yes' and 'No' cards for communication and in the end, could only open and shut his eyes. He died in the Brooklyn State Hospital on 3 October 1967. He stipulated no funeralisin' and his ashes were scattered in the water off Coney Island.

Dylan says in *No Direction Home* that he wrote 'Song to Woody' out of gratitude and respect, and he also wrote his prose poem, 'Last Thoughts on Woody Guthrie'.

Woody Guthrie was too disorganised to be a star, and a touring schedule would never have been for him. Dylan, on the other hand, knew what he wanted. Dylan's volatile relationship with the press and public was part of the package and if Guthrie had had some major success, he would have acted in a similarly provocative manner. Woody Guthrie was more committed politically and he would have welcomed the opportunity to parade his views. Music was first and foremost a political weapon to Guthrie.

Nora Guthrie: 'It is like James Dean and Marilyn Monroe; you really only know Woody when he was young. They become stuck in time; held by a photograph, in Woody's case with "This machine kills fascists" on his guitar. My dad was true to that and that was his mission in life. There have been a lot of variations on that with Donovan and Joe Strummer and even Pete Seeger. Pete has on his guitar, "This machine surrounds hate with love". We did a show about Woody in Oklahoma with the Flaming Lips which is a big punk rock band and they had "This machine kills fascists" on the back of their iPads. It is something that people can adapt to their times and their instruments. Woody wrote, "Don't try to be me but take these ideas and spread them around with your own instruments and your own words".'

Oddly Dylan hasn't worked on any of the lyrics that Guthrie left although he has for Hank Williams. Arlo wrote the music for the beautiful lyric 'My Peace' which deserves more attention and Country Joe MacDonald did 'Woman at Home'. Nora Guthrie: 'Woody could write a song about anything. It could be a very simple lyric. The Dropkick Murphys saw one lyric with the word 'Boston' in it. They thought that this was so cool, that he should write something about Boston. These guys turned it into a major hit song and it was in the movie, *The Departed*. You can do so much with Woody's material. His work is not pigeonholed. He was a political songwriter but he could also write about baseball or flying saucers.'

Bob Dylan enjoyed Guthrie's commitment to radical causes, his impetuous attitude towards life and his refusal to compromise. Guthrie was even more irresponsible than the Beat writers, believing in total freedom…when it suited him of course. He was a prototype hippie and he had three wives and eight children – possibly more.

Many performers have acknowledged their debut to Woody: Phil Ochs (who paid tribute in a song called 'Bound for Glory'), Tom Paxton, Eric Andersen and Country Joe McDonald come to mind. Woody's songs have been recorded by Ry Cooder, notably 'Do-Re-Mi' and 'Vigilante Man', while the Boomtown Rats took their name from a phrase in Woody's book, *Bound for Glory*.

Two concerts were held in Woody's memory. The first at Carnegie Hall in 1968 featured Bob Dylan, Judy Collins and Arlo Guthrie. The second at the Hollywood Bowl in 1970 included Joan Baez, Country Joe McDonald and Arlo Guthrie. These magical nights can be heard on CD and DVD. An excellent double-album is *The Greatest Songs of Woody*

Guthrie, a 1972 compilation on Vanguard featuring Joan Baez, Ramblin' Jack Elliott, Cisco Houston, Country Joe McDonald, Odetta, the Weavers and six songs from Woody himself.

Woody's book, *Seeds of Man,* was published in the US in 1976, the same year as *Bound for Glory,* a feature film starring David Carradine as Woody Guthrie. The film concentred on a section of Woody's book and won much acclaim, not least from Marjorie Guthrie. 'There was a simplicity to Woody. He was not suave or sophisticated. He was a graceless, artless, kind of reticent guy. He loved the world and he identified with all the people, but he had a hard time loving people individually. David caught that in his performance.'

Woody Guthrie's influence on Bruce Springsteen is apparent in 'Born in the USA', a modern-day take on 'This Land Is Your Land' and equally misunderstood as it was misquoted by President Reagan. Springsteen even tried to set the public right about 'This Land Is Your Land'. Will Kaufman: 'It was a belligerent song – this is your country and don't let the big people take it. There weren't any recorded versions of those verses and they are not in school songbooks. In 2009 Pete Seeger and Bruce Springsteen sang them on the steps of the Lincoln Memorial for Barack Obama's inaugural concert. The next day the newspapers reported that Woody Guthrie had written that song.'

Martyn Joseph, whose own songs include 'The Good in Me Is Dead', says, 'Woody Guthrie was passing on information and trying to seek out the truth. Today we need a resurgence of songs that are meaningful and says something about these times. If you see despair and write about it, you can hopefully encourage others to make changes.'

Woody Guthrie's legacy is in his songs. And they keep on coming. He wrote thousands of lyrics and the Guthrie family often show them to other performers. In 1998 Billy Bragg's album with the alt. country band, Wilco, *Mermaid Avenue,* was particularly successfully, both artistically and commercially.

In Okemah when the house he had lived in was still standing, the walls were full of messages from people who'd looked in and perhaps slept there overnight. Maybe that's the most fitting testimonial of all. The house has now gone but there is a statue in Okemah of Woody Guthrie performing. A casual tourist might wonder what a statue of Bob Dylan was doing in Okemah.

II. So Much Older Then: 1961–1962

One of Bob Dylan's biographers, Bob Spitz, says: 'Greenwich Village is a tiny network, a rabbit warren of streets in lower Manhattan and it was a fabulous place when Bob Dylan was there. There were over 50 places to hear music within a three-block radius and many people were trying out music and comedy. Bob Dylan, Richie Havens, Peter, Paul and Mary, Dave Van Ronk, Tom Paxton and Phil Ochs were playing music and at the same time you could hear comedy from Woody Allen, Lenny Bruce and Richard Pryor – and all on the same night! After the coffee houses closed, these people would have a drink and talk about what they were doing and so there was amazing creativity. Right after that scene, there was Roger McGuinn, the Lovin' Spoonful, Jimi Hendrix, the Rascals, and the Mamas and the Papas, so it kept on going.'

That sounds fabulous, doesn't it – how spoilt for choice can you get? – but it didn't happen automatically or by accident. This northern suburb of New York has a remarkable history of its own.

John Sebastian of the Lovin' Spoonful was born in the Village but mostly the performers came from outside the area. Going back centuries, nearly everybody, it seems, was escaping from something in Greenwich Village. It had been an Algonquin Indian settlement and then a Dutch tobacco plantation. It became British in 1664 and Sir Peter Warren named it after an English town, Greenwich.

Washington Square Park was a duelling ground, hopefully not too often, and one of the Founding Fathers, Alexander Hamilton lost his contest in 1804. Little did he know that his story would become a Broadway musical. Aaron Burr, who had killed Hamilton, had a stable, which became the Café Bizarre on Third Street in 1957, being opened by Odetta.

In 1824 20 highwaymen were hanged in Washington Square Park. It was such a public event that the Marquis de Lafayette was invited as the main guest. In 1839 Edgar Allan Poe wrote *The Fall of the House of Usher* in Greenwich Village and he could be found happily arguing about the day's events over drinks with the poet Walt Whitman. In 1881 Henry James wrote *Washington Square* at Number 18 Washington Square.

Italian and Irish immigrants settled in the area and it was a bohemian centre attracting artists, sculptors, poets, playwrights and a few anarchists. Rather like Grosse Freiheit in Hamburg, which meant 'Great freedom', people could behave more freely in Greenwich Village than in the rest of the country.

When the First World War broke out, the avant-garde artist Marcel Duchamp moved from Paris and settled in Greenwich Village and he pioneered the idea of 'found art', the concept that everyday objects such as urinals could be art.

Rock musician Willie Nile, who is based in the Village, says, 'Greenwich Village has a long history of bohemia. In 1917 Marcel Duchamp and about six other people went to the top of the arch on Washington Square and put up Chinese lanterns and balloons declaring Washington Park a republic, a centre for artists.'

Kahlil Gibran, who wrote his famed mixture of prose and poetry, *The Prophet*, in 1923, lived and worked in Greenwich Village. Café Reggio, which opened in 1927, was the first café in America to have espresso machines.

A criminal court that had been built in Hudson Street in 1652 became the White Horse Tavern. In 1953 Dylan Thomas was at the White Horse. His doctor had told him to stop drinking. He set up a pyramid of 36 tumblers of whiskey and drank each one, though that number has probably been exaggerated. He collapsed, staggered out of the White Horse and died.

In the late 50s, the Clancy Brothers were regular performers at the White Horse, although the author James Baldwin objected to their bawdy shanties. Baldwin and Richard Fariña would read their prose and poetry, and Theodore Bikel performed Russian songs and read emotionally from the Old Testament.

In the late 40s and 50s, the Beat Generation and its spin-offs were in Greenwich Village, very much emulating Paris in the 1920s. You could hear Jack Kerouac reciting poems to jazz and the area was notorious for pot-smoking and, heaven forbid, 'living in sin'. Kerouac was thrown out of the Cedar Tavern for urinating in an ash tray, which was possibly not the best receptacle, but they had a bigger problem with Jackson Pollock who used the toilet but decided to rip off the door. It was in the Cedar Tavern that D.A. Pennebaker first discussed a potential film about Bob Dylan's UK tour of 1965 with Dylan's friend, Bobby Neuwirth.

Marlon Brando studied acting in Greenwich Village and other residents have included

Aaron Copland, Eugene O'Neill, F. Scott Fitzgerald, Leonard Bernstein, Norman Mailer and Jackson Pollock.

The music-based academic Liz Thomson says, 'Greenwich Village was the heart of the New York folk revival. It was anti-fascist and anti-Franco. It was home to Woody Guthrie and Pete Seeger and a lot of people who fell victim to Senator Joe McCarthy. Folk music was a reaction to the 40s and 50s and people gathered every weekend in Washington Square beneath the arch and by the fountain. It was a huge Mecca for folk music. In 1961 there was a freedom of speech demonstration after police tried to ban folk music from the square. The folkies prevailed.'

The Gaslight and Café Wha? were known for their folk and blues evenings, and the two genres had something in common: they decried rock'n'roll as a commercial product and in the folkies' case, it was a cynical rejoinder from a capitalist system.

The Gaslight at 116 MacDougal became a key venue, first for beatnik poets and then for folk performers. It was hot and crowded with condensation dripping from the walls and ceiling, but performers were paid and didn't have to pass the hat. Noel Stookey was a good MC, being as much a comic as a singer. The Gaslight wasn't licensed but you could always go next door into the Kettle of Fish.

The Kettle of Fish was known for its jukebox stacked with cool jazz records. Dylan once played 'The Man That Got Away' by Judy Garland and loved its bluesy mood. By then a lot of beatniks had moved to San Francisco as they preferred jazz to folk. There was sex tourism in the Village too. Tourists came, having heard about wild parties and free love. Let's hope that they weren't too disappointed if they found themselves locked into late-night political debates.

The folklorist Alan Lomax had left the US during the McCarthy era and settled in the UK. In 1959 he returned to Greenwich Village. His interest, as always, was in authentic folk music, whatever that is, and he and Pete Seeger presented a wide-ranging folk evening at Carnegie Hall in 1959 which included electric blues and black doo-wop from the Cadillacs. As Izzy Young was to write, 'The point Alan Lomax was trying to make was that Negro and white music were mixing and coming together, and rock'n'roll was that thing.'

There was, and never will be, no single, all-embracing definition of folk music. The folk clubs might feature shanties, prison songs, Cajun music, calypsos and doo-wop. Alan Lomax was full of praise for the Kingston Trio and the New Lost City Ramblers, while Izzy Young preferred the Highwaymen.

By 1960 Greenwich Village was an area of cheap rent and largely student accommodation. Although it had been an Italian area, the Mob largely left it alone: they preferred joints with liquor licences and Greenwich Village was full of coffee shops, not the trendy Costas of today, but low-rent dives that enabled residents to chat over hamburgers and coffee. Josh White Jr: 'When I started my solo career in 1961, there were a lot of coffee houses I could play. A lot of the owners would take advantage of my name and you would see in big bold 100 per cent type "Josh White" on the marquee and then in very small print you would see "Jr". We had to make sure in our contracts that the "J" in Junior was in 100 per cent type and the "r" no less than 60. Otherwise, it would be false advertising.'

In 1962 the playwright Edward Albee saw the question, 'Who's Afraid of Virginia Woolf?' scrawled on a bathroom mirror in Greenwich Village and wrote his controversial play of the same name. By that time, Bob Dylan was living in the Village: what would have happened if he had seen it first?

So let's get Bob Dylan into the Village. Early in 1961, Dylan hitchhiked the 350 miles to Madison, Wisconsin: no particular reason except the driver was going there. He met up with Marshall Brickman and Eric Weissberg, that is, Woody Allen's future collaborator and one of the two musicians in 'Duelling Banjos', featured in the film, *Deliverance*. While there he played at a coffeehouse with Danny Kalb on harmonica, who later formed the Blues Project. They did 'Worried Man Blues' together and Kalb says that Dylan was the first person he saw with marijuana.

On 24 January 1961, Bob Dylan came to New York via an 800-mile journey with co-drivers Dave Berger and Fred Underhill, whom he had met in Madison. He had been playing and singing for much of the journey and Dave and Fred had begged him to stop. He arrived in New York with a guitar, harmonica and sleeping bag – oh, and plenty of ambition.

His first task wasn't to find lodgings but to find somewhere to play. He made his way to Greenwich Village as he knew of their folk clubs. In the clubs, there was no need for a music licence so long as the instruments were acoustic and there were no drums. In most of the clubs though, you had to be in the musicians' union before you could be billed to appear.

That first night he went to Café Wha? a basement club owned by Manny Roth, David Lee's father. It was a training ground for new comedians – Richard Pryor, Joan Rivers, Woody Allen and Lenny Bruce. Dylan was in luck: that night was a hootenanny, which permitted anyone to perform, whether or not in the union. Dylan asked Roth for a slot. He sang two Woody Guthrie songs and asked if anybody could put him up for the night.

The next morning Dylan rang Greystone Park Hospital in Morris Plains, New Jersey and asked about the visiting hours for seeing Woody Guthrie. He took the bus and he heard someone say, 'There's a Mr. Dylan to see you Woody.' 'Send him right in,' rasped Woody. As simple as that – Bob Dylan was meeting his idol.

Guthrie was already very ill with constant twitching, uncontrollable spasms and slurred speech. Indeed, when Marjorie Guthrie heard Bob Dylan's first record, she thought he was picking up on the way he spoke.

Oscar Brand: 'Liam Clancy always said the reason that Bob Dylan sang the way he did up through his nose and halting was because he wanted to imitate Woody Guthrie but he only met Woody when Woody was ill, so he was singing an ill man's version of Woody's own music.' That's nonsense as Dylan knew his records but it's an interesting theory, nonetheless.

Woody's humour was still intact. He called the institution, Gravestone Park Hospital, and he scribbled Bob a note saying 'I ain't dead yet.' Bob showed it to everyone.

Later on when Bob went with Barry Kornfeld who had a car to see Woody, Bob took him a packet of cigarettes and Woody walked round the ward handing them out, hanging onto the wall as he walked; it was typical of Woody.

It had been the coldest winter in New York since 1933. Dylan found a job with the sanitation department clearing snow, but that only lasted a day and wasn't Bob's idea of fun.

On 27 January 1961 Bob Dylan went to Marjorie Guthrie's house in Mermaid Avenue, Coney Island. The babysitter rang Marjorie who said not to let him in but he and Arlo were already talking and Bob was showing him harmonica tricks. Nora Guthrie recalls, 'Bob Dylan came to our house in 1961. He came in, played some music and had dinner with us. My mom introduced him to some other musicians around town like Ramblin' Jack Elliott and he took off from there.'

It was fortuitous that Ramblin' Jack Elliott had returned to New York. He had been in Europe for five years, mostly in London, and he had promoted Woody Guthrie every time he sang. When he went to see Woody, he met Bob, and Bob told Jack that he owned his records – nicked, more like!

On 28 January 1961 Bob Dylan paid his first visit to the Folklore Centre. This had been started by a New Yorker, Israel (Izzy) Young in 1957, then 29, a loud, opinionated but ultimately big-hearted man. It was at the heart of the folk community as he sold records and instruments and had a noticeboard in which gigs could be promoted and musicians could learn of vacancies. There were regular performances on the premises and Dylan sang 'Muleskinner Blues' there. Izzy had a vast knowledge of folk music and Dylan was to celebrate his premises in 'Talkin' Folk Centre Blues', which Izzy sold as a broadside.

As far as I can tell, not many people went to visit Woody Guthrie in hospital but the music critic Ralph Gleason and his wife Sidel (Sid) took Woody to their home in East Orange, New Jersey most Sundays and several folksingers saw him there including Phil Ochs and Peter La Farge. If Woody was in the mood, he could play a little guitar, and everyone would sing for their suppers as the Gleasons fed everybody. Bob sometimes said to Jack Elliott, 'Play it slower' as he was clearly picking up on what he was doing. Ramblin' Jack had a cowboy hat with a wide brim and he told Bob he got a better echo that way.

Ralph McTell: 'I was into folk music then; it wasn't by chance. I started off with Ramblin' Jack Elliott who fused so many different styles and played the guitar in a very special way. He sounded authentic to me but he was copying Woody. Even though Bob says he was a Woody Guthrie acolyte and he knew all of Woody's songs, there is much of Jack Elliott's style in his work. We both fell for the Brooklyn cowboy.'

Liam Clancy: 'Bob was very influenced by Woody Guthrie, but he was more influenced by Ramblin' Jack Elliott who was a disciple of Woody Guthrie and older than Dylan, Dylan was imitating an imitator when he put on that voice but it was very effective. You could sing the most mundane song in that nasal whine and it would sound interesting.'

We can hear Dylan in February 1961 as he was taped by the Gleasons while singing 'Pastures of Plenty', 'San Francisco Bay Blues' and 'Remember Me (When the Candle Lights Are Gleaming)'. Sid Gleason gave him one of Woody's jackets, which he wore when performing.

One of Bob's early gigs had the billing, 'Son of Ramblin' Jack'. Jack told Bob, 'You've got to learn to be yourself but it can't happen overnight.' Jack was like Woody Guthrie musically, but he was not excitable and angry like him. He preferred dry, laconic putdowns. Dylan was much more like Guthrie himself, playing songs at twice Jack's speed.

Dylan biographer Howard Sounes: 'Bob Dylan was never really a Woody Guthrie clone, he was a rock'n'roll and Johnnie Ray and Hank Williams fan way before he had heard of Woody Guthrie. All his influences were important and he could be all these things at once, and the same is true to this day. The reviewers write about an album they have only heard twice: they think of something clever and then they go to the pub, and they define artists in this limited way. They are not thinking about it deeply and they are not thinking about it in the same way that the artist is. The artist is much more dynamic and exciting and doing things spontaneously on many different levels and that is beyond the imagination of the people who are describing him.'

Woody Guthrie influenced skiffle music in the UK in the mid-50s. The king of skiffle was Lonnie Donegan, who told me in his typically outspoken fashion: 'I am not a Dylan fan and never have been. I knew him from when he was an acolyte of Woody Guthrie – a Woody Guthrie impressionist. I didn't like that. It is fine to use somebody else's work but you should be adding your own personality to the song. Obviously, he did his own thing later but I don't think that musically he will be much remembered. He'll be remembered as a cult figure as he was the personification of the Flower Power generation and I didn't identify with them. I didn't like their excess. I think of the audiences who have paid to see a performer and they are not paying money to see him make a fool of himself.'

Fred Neil was starting afternoon sessions at Café Wha? His musician friends included Mark Spoelstra, Noel Stookey and Louis Gossett Jr, later in *An Officer and a Gentleman*. Fred Neil was sometimes backed by Bob on harmonica. Bob performed the Jewish folk song 'Hava Nagila' an unusual choice from someone denying his background. He would soon adapt this to a talking blues about the folk scene in the Village. In her autobiography, Nina Simone remembered Dylan as 'this very young guy who sang comedy parodies in the intermissions.' (Oddly, 'Hava Nagila' became popular in the UK in 1963 through instrumental recordings by Joe Brown and the Spotnicks, who performed in space suits.)

Mark Spoelstra, born in Kansas City in 1940, had travelled around, ending up in Greenwich Village. He was only 20 when Dylan met him and was already an excellent guitarist. He told Bob that although he enjoyed Woody Guthrie, Woody's guitar playing was poor and he preferred Leadbelly's. Spoelstra lacked Dylan's drive and most of his earnings came from driving Sonny Terry and Brownie McGhee to gigs. He enjoyed playing with Bob and they worked up 'Muleskinner Blues'.

Mike Porco came to America in 1933 when he was 18 and worked in his uncle's restaurant. After war service in a naval yard, he managed a jazz restaurant in the Bronx, but he returned in 1952 to the Village when his cousins bought Gerde's, owned by William Gerdes who was in his eighties. They kept the name of its previous owner as that was good for business, even when it relocated. It did okay in the daytime but needed evening trade.

Starting in January 1960, Izzy Young and Tom Prendergast offered to present folk nights called the Fifth Peg at Gerde's: the deal was simple: we do the publicity, we find the singers and we keep the door money and you make on the food and drink. It was successful and by April, Porco had dropped his new partners and taken over the events himself, putting on Cisco Houston, Judy Collins, the Clancy Brothers and Rev. Gary Davis. On a good night, Porco got 200 in the venue and he renamed it Gerde's Folk City. Robert Shelton never liked the venue, thinking the cash register too noisy and that Porco watered down the whiskey, but he liked the music.

Robert Shelton, known as a reviewer for the *New York Times* was mostly proofreading. He dated Carolyn Hester, dined her and took her to White Horse where they met Richard Fariña, who had plenty of magnetism.

Fariña's father was Cuban and his mother Irish and he was the last of 18 children. Richard claimed that, in the 1950s, he had been a gunrunner for Fidel Castro and following an injury, he had a metal plate in his head. He joined the IRA and he knew and idolised Ernest Hemingway. How much of this was true? In truth, he was raised in Flatbush, Brooklyn and had suffered from childhood asthma. In 1959, he was assigned to the Shell Oil account at the advertising agency, J. Walter Thompson. He didn't take his job seriously and he hung out at the White Horse.

On 30 May 1960 Carolyn Hester was booked for Gerde's Folk City and Fariña was very impressed. She looked great, not unlike Rita Heyworth, was charming and was an excellent entertainer. After a three-week courtship, Hester and Fariña married and Fariña quit his job and started transporting cars. 'Talk about mistakes!' says Hester of that marriage.

On 13 February 1961, Bob Dylan played a Monday night hootenanny at Gerde's. It was an entertaining performance with Dylan shuffling around like Charlie Chaplin's tramp. This was an amateur performance and although Mike Porco was impressed, he ran a professional club and couldn't feature Dylan as a billed artist until he was in the union.

We know that Dylan wrote 'Song to Woody' on Valentine's Day as he has dated his lyric. He wrote it in the Mills Tavern on Bleecker Street. It was a tribute to Woody and yet he was also seeing the world through his own eyes. It was his first serious song and he commented, 'I was writing it as I thought Woody would write it.' If Woody were writing it, he would steal a tune. It is close to Woody's '1913 Massacre' but less of a dirge. The line about coming with the dust and going with the wind is taken from 'Pastures of Plenty'. Dylan saw Guthrie most weeks and Bonny Beecher, who sometimes went with him, recalled a nurse bringing Woody his guitar. The nurse said, 'Oh, Woody, can you play it? That's so sweet.' He played 'Hard Travellin'' for them. Woody told Bob of his lyrics that had not been set to music. Bob did ask Marjorie about them but she was reluctant about passing them over.

In mid-February Dylan sent the Whitakers a postcard to say that he visited Woody four times that week. He had been playing The Commons 'where people clap for me'. The Commons at 105 MacDougal was opposite the Gaslight and featured Tiny Tim as a singing waiter, so Bob did not have much competition. He was regularly playing Café Wha?, the Commons and the Gaslight. Sometimes he would be playing for tips – that is, a basket would be passed around – but he did make a few dollars playing harmonica for Fred Neil, Mark Spoelstra, Ramblin' Jack Elliott and Dave Van Ronk.

Happy Traum: 'Dave Van Ronk was incredibly influential on a lot of musicians including Bob Dylan. He was a wonderful, very quirky and eccentric singer but he had an interesting approach to songs. He was at heart a jazz guy but he decided that folk music was easier. And cheaper too; all you needed was a guitar. (Laughs) He taught a lot of people the old blues songs but he never got the recognition outside of a relatively small group of folkies.'

White blues really started with Dave Van Ronk, whose favourite singer was Dinah Washington. He was nicknamed the Mayor of MacDougal Street. Elijah Wald recalls, 'Dave Van Ronk was not at all difficult to get along with. An analogy with Malcolm Muggeridge might be made. He was charmingly curmudgeonly, and he is remembered with great affection by almost everybody on that scene including people who arrived later. He acted as a mentor for younger players. As somebody who has taught and studied at universities, I know that I have never met anyone as widely knowledgeable and well-read as Dave Van Ronk. Dave's dream was to live in Greenwich Village and not be on the road all the time. He would rather have a regular gig running an open mic night at the Gaslight than schlepping his guitar all over the United States.'

Jim Kweskin: 'Bob Dylan and I were playing together at the Gaslight. The first set was Peter Stampfel from the Holy Modal Rounders, the second set was me, the third set was Bob Dylan and the fourth set was the three of us together as a little trio. Without a doubt, he was amazingly special. Most of the songs he performed were not his. They were ones he had adapted but he was constantly writing. He had a pad of paper and the songs were spewing out of him like water out of a fountain.'

On a free day, Dylan saw Ramblin' Jack Elliott at the concert room in Carnegie Hall. Marjorie and Arlo Guthrie were there and then they caught Cisco Houston's late-night show at Gerde's. Cisco had cancer: he performed well and travelled back to San Bernardino where he died on 29 April 1961. It took Arlo some time to appreciate Dylan's voice. He preferred to hear his father's songs performed by Cisco with his clear, rich tones.

Judy Collins: 'I saw Bob Dylan at Gerde's Folk City when he was still trying to be Woody Guthrie. He came to hear Cisco Houston who was playing with me. Bob was a jerky looking guy from Minnesota with this nondescript hat: he had a crummy voice and he sang bluesy songs, but in a way he was pretty funky.'

On Sunday 12 March 1961 on nationwide TV, *The Ed Sullivan Show* was celebrating St. Patrick's Day with the Clancy Brothers. Liam Clancy: 'It not only changed our lives but it changed the lives of the people who made sweaters as the sale of Aran sweaters jumped by 700% in a month. A big clothing company offered us $250,000 against a royalty on each sweater sold if we gave our name to them. I said, "We are making a great living, we have just got over $100,000 from Columbia. The people who are making these sweaters in Ireland have it as their only livelihood. Are we going to take the bit out of their mouths?" We turned it down.' Their manager Marty Erlichman was not happy with their decision but he had seen a new girl in the Village whom he thought could be the next Judy Garland. Her name: Barbra Streisand.

In March 1961 Dylan was visiting one of Marjorie's friends, Eve and Mac MacKenzie, to hear their Woody Guthrie records. There he met a dancer, Avril and moved in with her. Not for long. He just got up and left one day.

A few weeks later Bob turned up at the MacKenzies. He asked where Avril was and Eve said that she had moved to San Francisco. He stayed with the MacKenzies for a while and befriended their son Peter, who was already taking guitar lessons from Pete Seeger. Dylan would come in at 3am and sleep until noon and they tolerated his behaviour for three months. Eve told him to leave when Peter was coming up for graduation and shouldn't be distracted. Bob signed and dated his copy of *Bound for Glory* and gave it to Eve.

Dylan met 18-year-old Kevin, who had a dominant personality and came from a wealthy family. Dylan's verse about 'lots of forks and knives' in 'Talkin' New York' is about him. Kevin was into scams such as selling students oxygen shots for exams and printing the Lord's Prayer on a cent for a dollar. He submitted Dylan's tapes at the Gleasons to Vanguard Records, who turned him down.

Dylan wanted to be on Folkways but Moses Asch was not impressed. He ran a small but productive label from an office above a jeweller's shop in Greenwich Village. Dylan would have set him up for life, but there we are: he didn't spot his potential. Ironically, Asch released some recordings later, when he was signed to Columbia, using a pseudonym of Blind Boy Grunt for Dylan which fooled no one. Within the course of a few days, the three specialist folk labels – Vanguard, Folkways and Elektra – had said no to Dylan.

The Kingston Trio, the Limeliters and the Brothers Four were doing okay with big selling albums and even hit singles. Without Pete Seeger, the Weavers were also doing fine. On 27 March, Seeger's case for contempt on Congress was heard and he was found guilty two days later. On the same day, Dylan made his last weekly appearance at the Monday hoot at Gerde's as Mike Porco had booked him to support the blues musician John Lee Hooker. Porco acted as his guardian for union membership, which cost $46 and which he also paid. Dylan was going to earn $100 for two weeks' work.

Dylan had his first paid concert as a union man on 5 April, earning $20 at the Loeb Music Centre for the NYU Folk Society in Washington Square. Seventeen-year-old Suze (said Suzie) Rotolo was in the audience.

On 9 April 1961, there was a demonstration in Washington Square against the authorities' attempts to ban Sunday afternoon gatherings. Everyone was there and they sang a cappella as if they played instruments they would be arrested as minstrels. The headline in *New York Mirror* was *3,000 Beatniks Riot in Village*. Dylan wrote 'Down at Washington Square'.

Joan Baez and her sister Mimi had been at the protest. They stayed over and went to the hoot at Gerde's on Monday. Bob Dylan sang some Guthrie songs and he took Joan aside and played 'Song to Woody' to her. He said, 'You can sing it if you want.' Baez said, 'I was knocked out and amazed.'

On Tuesday Bob was playing the first night of his two-week stint supporting John Lee Hooker. Dylan had a five-song spot every night and he usually included 'Song to Woody' and the traditional 'House of the Rising Sun', although he was following Dave Van Ronk's arrangement. This was a special occasion – he wore Woody's jacket and clean blue jeans. Robert Shelton reviewed the show for the *New York Times* but he didn't arrive in time to catch Bob's act.

Around April 1961 Robert Shelton took Bob Dylan to see the Clancys and told him to notice how they put a show together. Liam sang a commercial about Donnell's sausages which amused Dylan. He was to call Liam Clancy 'the best ballad singer I ever heard'.

Liam Clancy: 'I remember walking in on a hootenanny night and seeing this pretty young boy – I thought it was a girl at first – and I was looking at him from the door and through the smoke. He came off stage and over to us and he was all excited and hopping around from one leg to another, and he and I became fast friends. We would hang out together, whatever that New York expression means. We used to go to parties and we courted two sisters and we used to sing 'Eileen Aroon' together and I would imitate him. I would do it like Bob Dylan and he would do it like me. (Laughs).'

It wasn't just Eileen Aroon. Liam Clancy: 'I had a girlfriend named Kathy and when I was out of town. Bob Dylan would take her out for a drink but it turns out that there was more to it than that, so we were sharing her, but that was common in the Village at the time.'

By the end of his two-week stint with John Lee Hooker, Dylan was bored with regular nightly gigs and left New York. While hitching on the New Jersey turnpike, he wrote 'Talkin' New York' about his first months in the city and how he earned a dollar a day. How come he found it so cold when he is from Minnesota? There is a very effective recording of 'Talkin' New York' with a little laugh: note how he blends his voice with guitar and harmonica and how he says Greenwich as 'Green-witch'.

Dylan loved the talking blues, which is speech set against a repetitive guitar accompaniment. They were mostly used for deadpan stories with sardonic asides, and they had started with Chris Bouchillon in the 1920s, also on Columbia. It seems that his producer preferred him talking!

Noel Stookey gave Dylan the story of a Father's Day boat trip to upstate New York that was oversubscribed and led to panic on the decks. This led to a deeply satirical composition, 'Talkin' Bear Mountain Massacre Blues' in which Dylan made the incident more serious than it was. It became a popular stage number with Dylan getting a huge laugh with the line, 'I almost lost my picnic spirit.' The song influenced the most famous of the talking blues of the 60s, Arlo Guthrie's 'Alice's Restaurant'.

Dylan's 'Talkin' Lobbyist' is really 'Talkin' Inflation Blues', which was written by Tom Glazer in the 1940s. It appeared in the *Fight to Save OPA* (Office of Price Administration) issue of *People's Songs* in 1946. Dylan, Phil Ochs and Tom Paxton improvised 'Talkin' Central Park Mugger Blues', but this was not recorded.

On 28 April 1961 Dylan sent a postcard to his parents from New York. He wrote, 'I've finished my time at Folk City and now I am at the Gaslight. My union costs were $128. I am now making $100 a week for five nights playing…that's not bad, considering that three months ago I was unknown. I am clean and I am brushing my teeth. Say hello to everybody for me. Love, Bob.'

On 6 May 1961 Bob Dylan played his first festival with Jim Kweskin and Mark Spoelstra, nothing too great but it was a start – the Indian Neck Folk Festival at Montowesi Hotel, Branford, Connecticut. During the festival, he jammed with Bobby Neuwirth – born Akron, Ohio in 1939 and playing in Cambridge folk clubs. Mark enjoyed Dylan's talking blues and now, while playing chess, Bob told him that he was writing seriously. Possibly it was to impress Woody Guthrie. He would play new songs to Woody and Woody would say, 'He sure as hell has got it.' When Bob was away, he was irritable and would say, 'When's the boy gonna be here?'

Dylan returned to Minneapolis and recorded 25 songs in two informal sessions at Bonny Beecher's apartment. Bonny had found somebody else, which he described as being 'kneed in the guts' in 'My Life in a Stolen Moment'. *Little Sandy Review* referred to his increased confidence and said that a star was being born.

During the summer Dylan associated with three people who would greatly influence his career – Robert Shelton, Albert Grossman and Suze Rotolo.

In June 1961, Dave Van Ronk and Bob Dylan shared a residency at the Gaslight and did Woody Guthrie's 'Car Car'. Robert Shelton introduced Dylan to Albert Grossman. Grossman preferred to handle new artists: if they did well for you, they would be indebted forever, plus he could get a higher proportion of the proceeds. For the moment, he stood watching Bob Dylan, offering him a little advice and seeing how he developed.

In July Dylan had a booking at the Kiwanis Club at the Fifth Avenue Hotel. He was distracted by some clowns and is said to have kicked one of them in the balls. Hence, Dylan was probably physically tougher than he is thought to be.

Suze Rotolo was part of a left-wing Italian-American family. Her father died when she was 14. Her mother Mary wanted her daughters to be activists. When Suze graduated, she had to sign an oath of allegiance to the flag. She had signed it but had written 'under protest': a born rebel then.

In February 1960 four black students in Greensboro, North Carolina had sat in a 'whites only' area at Woolworth's. This led to further sit-ins and protests. Suze had picketed Woolworth's in New York even though their northern restaurants were not segregated.

Suze had been on marches to integrate schools since she was 15. She had been to Washington Square Park; she had heard Ramblin' Jack and Pete Seeger, and she had seen Odetta and Tom Lehrer at Carnegie Hall. She loved the way Bob Dylan played harmonica with Mark Spoelstra and liked his humour.

Dylan met Suze on 29 July 1961 and was with her, on and off, until March 1964. Roger McGuinn knew them both and says that at first Dylan wrote political songs to impress her. It may be coincidence but once their relationship was over, Dylan largely stopped writing protest songs.

The event on 29 July was a blandly-named *Afternoon of Folk Music* at Riverside Church in New York, which was broadcast on WRVR. Dylan performed 'Handsome Molly', 'Deep Water' and 'Po' Lazarus' and spoofed teen music with 'Acne', written by Eric Von Schmidt and performed with Ramblin' Jack. He played harmonica with Danny Kalb. The Rotolos hosted the evening party after the event and Dylan improvised the satirical 'Beautiful People' with John Wynn.

Mary Rotolo, the mother, was a translator for medical journals, who lived in a penthouse at 1 Sheridan Square. Her husband had died and she planned to marry a teacher from New Jersey. She didn't take to Bob Dylan but her daughters, Carla and Suze, thought otherwise.

Carla, the elder, worked for Alan Lomax, but it was Suze who captivated him. Suze worked for the Congress of Racial Equality and an anti-nuclear organisation.

Café Society was also at 1 Sheridan Square. This was a courageous venue that had had John Hammond as a booking agent and had featured Billie Holiday, Lena Horne and Sarah Vaughan, supreme black cabaret in a white area.

Joan Baez was becoming the darling of the pacifist movement; her live album had her singing 'The Battle Hymn of the Republic' with students from Birmingham University.

In July 1961 Buffy Sainte-Marie had written the first of the anti-war protest songs, 'Universal Soldier'. She says, 'The Highwaymen were a big group and they had a big hit with 'Michael Row the Boat Ashore'. I was their opening act and they wanted to record 'Universal Soldier'. I said, "Yeah, that's great", and they asked me who published it. Some guy at the next table said, "I can do that for you" and, like a dummy, I signed on the dotted line. About 10 years later I bought the song back for $25,000 and I'm glad I did.'

In August Dylan was at Club 47 in Boston where he was introduced by Carolyn Hester. He spent a day on the beach with her and her husband, Richard Fariña. After seeing Jean Ritchie, Richard Fariña had taken up the dulcimer and he was joining Carolyn on stage. Carolyn did consider cutting a live album at Club 47 with Dylan on harmonica but changed her mind. Fariña made $50 from the literary magazine, *Atlantic Monthly*, and he used it to buy a cheap (very cheap) Dodge guitar. Fariña told anyone who would listen to him that folk music needed a beat. He picked up a waitress' metal tray and beat out some Cuban rhythms to prove his point.

John Hammond had missed signing Joan Baez for Columbia but he had Carolyn Hester and he hoped she would be the answer. Richard was very pleased about his wife's contract and he had his own ideas about what she should record.

In early September, Bob rented an apartment at 161 West Fourth Street for $60 a month, yet again a Fourth Street, and Suze moved in with him,

Carolyn Hester saw Bob at the Rotolo's apartment on Sheridan Square: 'Bob Dylan and I had met at Gerde's Folk City. He was sitting at the front and I played 'Lonesome Tears' and I explained how I had known Buddy Holly and what a great fellow he was. I thought he was a roots musician and Bob fell about at that thought. Odetta had played on my first album for Norman Petty, and my dad had played harmonica. I told him that I was doing an album for Columbia and I asked him to play some harp for me. He said, "How many songs do you want?" I said, "About three and I'm doing 'I'll Fly Away' and 'Swing and Turn Jubilee'." We had a rehearsal and he suggested (sings) "Come back baby, baby please don't go." He taught me the song and that was the third one. He was a very colourful harp player and I really liked what he did.'

On Tuesday 26 September 1961, Bob Dylan started his second residency at Gerde's, this time supporting the bluegrass musicians, the Greenbriar Boys, for two weeks. Robert Shelton noted his progression and wrote a review for the *New York Times*. Headed *Bob Dylan: A Distinctive Folk-Song Stylist*. Shelton called him a bright new face in folk music and praised his talking blues. You can sense that Shelton already twigged he was telling tall tales. 'It matters less where he has been than where he is going – and that would seem to be straight up', which echoed Dylan's own thoughts.

Suze and Bob were told of the review and bought an early edition of the *New York Times* at a news stand on Sheridan Square. They read it at an all-night deli and went back for more copies. The review was only 400 words but it was warm and friendly and as finely tuned as any song lyric: 'Mr. Dylan's voice is anything but pretty. He is consciously trying to recapture the beauty of a southern field hand musing in melody on the porch. All the husk and bark is left on the notes.' The Greenbriar Boys were annoyed that Dylan had eclipsed them in the review, which wasn't helped by Dylan quoting it on stage.

On 29 September Dylan went to the Columbia studio on 799 Seventh Avenue, the reason for the street reference in Paul Simon's 'The Boxer'. The session was for Carolyn Hester's album and Bob played harmonica on three songs. He held an impressive long note on 'Come Back Baby' and he got to know another influential figure, the session guitarist Bruce Langhorne.

When Bruce Langhorne was 12 and living in Spanish Harlem in New York, he had been experimenting with a chemistry set. He made his own rocket but he hadn't realised how quickly magnesium burns. There was an explosion in which he lost two fingers on his right hand and nearly lost an eye. Rather like Django Reinhardt, he had to develop his own way of playing guitar. He had met Dylan a few weeks earlier while working with Brother John Sellers at Gerde's and now they became friends.

At an opportune moment, Bob Dylan showed John Hammond the review in the *New York Times*, and Hammond was intrigued. Liam Clancy commented, 'Shelton really pushed Bob Dylan, probably more than anyone.' You can argue whether it was Robert Shelton, John Hammond or Joan Baz who put Dylan on the map, but when it comes right down to it, Dylan discovered himself.

Biographer Clinton Heylin: 'John Hammond was the luckiest man alive. He discovered Dylan before he wrote songs, so how could he have discovered Dylan the songwriter? He heard something of course, but what Dylan became, nobody could have foreseen. The same thing with Bruce Springsteen. Hammond signed him, thinking he was the new Dylan, and he had only heard him acoustically.'

On 26 October 1961 Bob Dylan signed with Columbia in what he has described as 'the most thrilling moment of his life'. John Hammond lived in a MacDougal Street townhouse and they met to discuss the contract.

John Hammond arranged for Bob Dylan to meet Lou Levy, who ran one of the music companies in the Brill Building: Leeds Music. Dylan would be assigned to their BMI subsidiary, Duchess, and they would collect the publishing royalties which would come from sheet music sales, record royalties (two cents a song per record sold), radio and TV plays and if lucky, film soundtracks. Two cents a record doesn't sound like much but if a record sold a million, then that was $20,000, split fifty-fifty to the publisher on the one hand and the performer and his manager on the other. Levy gave Dylan a $100 advance, which sounds tight but isn't. Dylan's first album sold 2,500 copies and he wrote two of the songs and that comes to $100, although Dylan's share would only be $50.

At the same time as signing Bob Dylan, Columbia signed Dion from Dion and the Belmonts, believing he had the talent to be an all-round entertainer like Bobby Darin. He had, but he had his own ideas and in the end was more Bobby Dylan than Bobby Darin.

'I liked the fact that Dion was signed to Columbia in the same year as Bob Dylan,' said Charlie Gillett, 'but by a different A&R man and he surfaced immediately with huge hits, while it took longer for Dylan to surface. Dion made some really good blues records like 'I'm Your Hoochie Coochie Man': in those days, a big label might indulge an artist and let him do what he wanted to do, the prevailing attitude was pretending it wasn't happening. Dion kept changing what he wanted to do as well, so he was very unpredictable.'

Harry Belafonte had been a huge star in the mid-50s, introducing the world to calypso rhythms. After conscription, he was in Greenwich Village and reviving his career. He was making a new album for RCA and Dylan was asked to play harmonica on the title track, Leadbelly's 'Midnight Special'. Bob was happy to oblige but Belafonte liked multiple takes so he could choose the best. To make matters worse, the microphone was picking up Dylan's toe-tapping, which called for more takes. Dylan said 'You've got enough' and walked out, the first of many such examples of Dylan's behaviour in a recording studio. His patience was easily tested and making records was top of the list.

As fate would have it, Izzy Young's first promotion had been with Albert Grossman and they had presented Peggy Seeger in the Chapter Hall at Carnegie Hall, a prestigious booking because of the name but this part of the building only seated 200. Izzy presented Bob Dylan in the same venue on Saturday 4 November 1961. Tickets were $2.

Izzy decided to interview Bob for the concert programme – good luck! Right from the start, Dylan had decided that formal interviews were not for him and he could only be interviewed on his own, ever-changing terms. His main trick was to answer a question with a question, which can be very unsettling for the interviewer. Still, the interview contained some classic moments. Asked about religion, Dylan said, 'Got no religion. Tried a bunch of different religions. The churches are divided, can't make up their minds and neither can I. Never saw a god, can't say until I see one.'

Elijah Wald: 'When Dylan was asked who his favourite singers were by Izzy Young, he said that the people he liked didn't have pretty voices. He mentioned Dave Van Ronk, Ramblin' Jack Elliott, Jim Kweskin and Peter Stampfel. These voices appealed to people who liked old southern field recordings. That prevented these people from becoming crossover stars and Dylan is almost a lone exception until it happened and then people like Neil Young could follow.'

Bob was on Oscar Brand's *Folksong Festival* on WNYC radio, plugging his Carnegie Hall performance, but only 53 people came to the show. Izzy Young said, 'The schmucks in the Village won't go uptown because they think it's the North Pole.' Did they avoid the concert because of jealousy? The following Saturday Joan Baez, with two Top 20 albums, was at Town Hall and 1,700 attended. It was only a few minutes from Chapter Hall.

Still, the concert did give Dylan valuable exposure and experience: he had often been nervous and unsure of himself and now he seemed more confident. Dylan didn't cut his strings and he said, 'This guitar needs a haircut.' Izzy gave Bob $20 as he felt he should have something.

On 20 November 1961 Dylan had a three-hour session to work on his first album, which was completed two days later. At first, Dylan popped his p's and hissed his s's and wandered off mike, but he soon picked up studio protocol. He may have been popping his p's accidentally but he was deliberately dropping his g's. Seven songs were to be used and he also recorded a rap about a Connecticut cowboy, 'He Was a Friend of Mine', 'Ramblin' Blues' (Guthrie), 'Milkcow Blues' and 'The Last Time I Saw Wichita'. The cost of Dylan's first album was said to be $402, but this was his union fee and didn't take into account studio expenses and the use of Columbia staff.

In 1927 Blind Willie Johnson combined his gruff voice with his slide guitar for 'Jesus, Make up My Dying Bed', which Josh White turned into 'In My Time of Dyin''. According to the album sleeve, Dylan recorded it, playing bottleneck guitar and using Suze's lipstick holder for a slide, although Suze discounts this in her memoir. This track influenced Led Zeppelin's 'In My Time of Dyin''.

'He Was a Friend of Mine' was taken from a prison song that Leadbelly had learnt from Shorty George in 1935. Eric Von Schmidt was playing the song and Dylan followed his adaptation. Both Dave Van Ronk and Eric Von Schmidt recorded it in 1963. The cover of *The Folk Blues of Eric Von Schmidt* is shown on the cover of Bob's *Bringing It All Back Home* so make what you will of that.

Perfect for his hoboing image 'Freight Train Blues' was taken from Roy Acuff's version in 1947 and, in his own way, Dylan copied his yodel. Acuff was a better artist than he is credited: on stage he would play with a yo-yo whilst he sang which rather undercut his performances. He founded the publishing company, Acuff-Rose.

A Columbia executive, David Kapralik thought that John Hammond had gone wrong and didn't want to release the album. He would rather the tapes were given or sold to a smaller label. Hammond had some job security as he and his wife played cards with the founders of CBS, William Paley and Frank Stanton, and he also knew the current president, Goddard Leiberson, known as God. The album was saved but Hammond was sidelining Carolyn Hester. She wouldn't topple Joan Baez but Dylan had enormous potential.

On 23 November, Bob and Suze had Thanksgiving Dinner with Eve and Mac MacKenzie. A few songs were taped including 'Hard Times in New York' which was based on 'Down on Penny's Farm' recorded by the Bentley Boys in 1929. Dylan ended the song very confidently.

Billy James had the unenviable task of interviewing Bob Dylan for Columbia's publicity. Dylan strung him along. There was another interview with wild stories for Robert Shelton, this time for use on the LP sleeve. Dylan told him that he wrote 'The Ballad of the Ox-Bow Incident' after seeing the film on TV. On recording the album: 'There was a violent angry emotion running through me then. Mr. Hammond asked me if I wanted to sing any of them over again and I said no.' Sounds like Bob:

In December 1961 Bob Dylan was back in Minneapolis for a concert at the University of Minnesota. He was still full of his review from the *New York Times* and he allowed Tony Glover to record him singing some songs at Bonny Beecher's apartment, which Dylan called the Beecher Hotel. This is his best-known home tape and part was included on the first bootleg album, *Great White Wonder*.

Dylan recorded 26 songs over 90 minutes including a brilliant 'I Was Young When I Left Home', of which he says, 'I sorta made it up on a train.' Well, he based it on the folk favourite '500 Miles'. It was a bonus track on the expanded edition of *Love and Theft* in

2001 and it sounds like a studio recording. Indeed, I would swap it for any track on Dylan's first album. Dylan performed a monologue he learnt from Lord Buckley as well as Woody Guthrie's sequence of songs about venereal disease: 'VD Blues', 'VD Gunner's Blues', 'VD City' and 'VD Woman'. Woody had written them for a public information campaign but they were not used. He was addressing the stigma of having the disease: it was bad enough to have it but you might be ostracised as well.

John Lomax had heard 'Dink's Song' from a plantation worker in Memphis. He had found Dink washing clothes by the Brazos River, Tennessee. Dink didn't want to sing on tape but given some liquor, she opened up. The song was picked up by Ramblin' Jack Elliott, Bob Gibson and Dave Van Ronk and was now sung by Bob Dylan. Later it was recorded by Jeff Buckley.

Dylan rewrote 'Song to Woody' as 'Song for Bonny'. Bob and Tony jammed on some Chuck Berry songs. Why did he make this tape when he had a recording contract? He had no concept of the trouble this could cause, but obviously it is good that we have so many examples of his formative years.

By now, Dave Van Ronk's partner, Terri Thal, was acting as Bob's agent and she got him bookings in Boston and Cambridge in Massachusetts and Saratoga Springs, New York.

While Dylan was in Cambridge, he befriended the singer, songwriter and painter, Eric Von Schmidt, who was 10 years older than himself. His father was a painter of the old west, Harold Von Schmidt. In 1948, Eric had heard Leadbelly on the radio and immediately become a fan, but he smashed his guitar when his girlfriend (an older, married woman) accused him of cheating. In 1956 Eric studied painting on a university grant and the following year, he moved to Cambridge, and befriended Jim Kweskin and Joan Baez.

Dylan put two of Eric's songs into his repertoire – 'He Was a Friend of Mine', which had come from a Library of Congress recording, and 'Baby, Let Me Follow You Down'. Eric had heard the song in different versions, notably as 'Mama, Let Me Lay It on You' by Blind Boy Fuller, recorded in 1936. Dylan may have also heard it from Rev. Gary Davis. On his first album he said that he had heard it in 'the green pastures of Harvard University', a gentle way of mocking the Lomaxes.

The Animals were to rework 'Baby, Let Me Follow You Down' as 'Baby, Let Me Take You Home'. The songwriting credit was 'Trad. Arr. Price'. Alan Price says, 'I nicked the chord sequence from 'Baby Let Me Follow You Down' which was on Bob Dylan's album. Mickie Most had brought the record back from America and we did the song our way. We hated it and it's a stilted version. We hated being controlled because we were our own bosses and we thought we were taking the blues to a public that hadn't heard them before. We were immediately put into a straightjacket and aimed at the charts, trying to make us nicey-nicey. We resented it. I was always at odds with Mickie Most but in retrospect he was good for us.'

Folk music in its many guises was on a rise at the end of 1961. Burl Ives was enjoying a Top 10 single with 'A Little Bitty Tear' at the start of 1962 and would have three more hits before the year was out. He had gone country and recorded in Nashville but the voice was still unmistakeably his and he was telling stories as he always did.

Pete Seeger is often depicted as the authoritarian, anti-commercial face of folk music and yet he was shown as the composer of three of the biggest hits of 1962, and two of them were protest songs ('The Lion Sleeps Tonight', 'Where Have All the Flowers Gone' and 'If I Had a Hammer'). All this before Bob Dylan even had a record out.

The story of 'The Lion Sleeps Tonight' is a book in itself. The fact that five composers were listed for this US Number 1 single suggests the complexity of this matter, especially when none of them was the original composer and one of them, Paul Campbell, was the four Weavers under a pseudonym, so the credit was acknowledging eight composers.

In 1939 Solomon Linda's Original Evening Birds recorded his song 'Mbube (The Lion)' for a small South African label and he sold his song outright to the record producer Eric Gallo for 10 shillings, thus forfeiting his right to royalties. Miriam Makeba recorded the song in the 1950s and it was picked up by the Weavers who changed the title to 'Wimoweh'. In doing so, they added a collective pen name, Paul Campbell to the songwriting credits. Their phrase 'seem-boom-beh' which became 'Wimoweh', had no meaning: it was equivalent of putting 'shooby-dooby-doo' in a doo-wop record.

In 1960 the RCA producers Hugo Peretti and Creatore Luigi loved the rhythm but thought the song needed an English lyric and asked Brill Building writer, George David Weiss, to supply it. He added 16 words and the song became 'The Lion Sleeps Tonight', which was ludicrous as lions don't live in jungles. The Tokens' version was a US Number 1 at the end of 1961 and in the UK it competed with Karl Denver who had recorded the Weavers' 'Wimoweh'. Poignantly, Solomon Linda died in 1962. The song grew in popularity with the years and it was a UK Number 1 for Tight Fit in 1982. Then came the big one: in 1994 it was part of the score for *The Lion King*.

This song represented big money and Solomon Linda's family wanted their share. Under the provisions of a 1911 copyright law, a song reverted to the original composer after 25 years and so the song belonged to Linda's estate by 1964. Eventually the Supreme Court in Pretoria ruled that Linda's daughters, who were living in poverty were the rightful owners and in 2004 the Disney Corporation was sued for $1.6m. for using the song without permission. By then, Disney must have been wishing they had commissioned Tim Rice and Elton John to write the entire score. The matter was settled with annual payments to Solomon Linda's family.

I give all this detail to show how complicated copyright can be and we will come across similar instances in Bob Dylan's work, albeit nowhere near as complex. Although a singer may use a traditional tune, he may have no idea how that song originated. It is fascinating too that Pete Seeger, such a firm believer in human rights, should be involved in this story, albeit on the wrong side, although 'Wimoweh' would not have found its way to America and the rest of the world without him.

In 1961 Seeger had taken a Russian folk song and turned it into a moving anti-war song, 'Where Have All the Flowers Gone', which was solely credited to Seeger. It had a very simple structure which was ideal for singing at concerts and in folk clubs. The Kingston Trio, by then Bob Shane, Nick Reynolds and John Stewart, made a commercial recording which was a US hit in 1962. Just listen to the wavering vibrato as John Stewart asks, 'Where have the soldiers gone?' Although the Kingston Trio were a middle-of-the road folk act, this song had clout and is really the first of the new protest songs to make the charts.

When John F. Kennedy was installed as the new President, he described the forthcoming changes as 'The new frontier', a phrase taken up by the Kingston Trio for an LP with a positive title song written by John Stewart.

After deciding Dave Van Ronk wasn't right, Albert Grossman had finalised the line-up for a two-boys-and-a-girl folk act – Peter Yarrow, Noel Paul Stookey and Mary Travers – collectively Peter, Paul and Mary as 'Noel' didn't sound cool. Grossman's contract was for

25% of their earnings. Like the Kingston Trio, Peter, Paul and Mary were the epitome for a commercial folk act – good-looking, white, smart, middle class: some angry songs but performed with sensitivity and no rough edges. Phil Ramone rehearsed Peter, Paul and Mary until everything blended seamlessly.

They were to record a cover version of 'Where Have All the Flowers Gone' for Atlantic but at the last minute, Grossman rang to say Mary had laryngitis and the session was scrubbed. This was untrue: Grossman had been offered a better deal by Artie Mogul at Warner. They recorded 'Where Have All the Flowers Gone' for their first album, which was released in May 1962, but the hit single from that album, a US Top 10 entry, 'If I Had a Hammer', had been written by Pete Seeger and Lee Hays when they were in the Weavers.

Pete Seeger: 'In 1949 Lee Hays sent me four brief verses and said, "Pete, do you think you can make up a tune?" Like the old gospel hymns, only one word changed each time and you had a new verse. If I had a hammer, if I had a bell, if I had a song. Well, I put a tune to it but maybe it wasn't as good a tune as it might have been because it never went anywhere. Then about eight years later three young people changed my tune. They kept the basic idea and some of the notes and their version went around the world. Most people sing it as Peter, Paul and Mary sang it and only a few the way that I wrote it. I then changed it a bit more to suit what I do.'

'If I Had a Hammer' was a catchy, singalong song on a serious subject, 'love between my brothers and my sisters', that is, human rights. In 1962 Peter, Paul and Mary were singing 'If I Had a Hammer' at the University of Mississippi as James Meredith was determined to become their first black student. The following year, the song went even higher up the charts in a cabaret arrangement for the Mexican-American Trini Lopez.

In February 1962 Bob Dylan was playing in Saratoga Springs. He was adept at pool, but he pretended he wasn't. The local shark played him and Dylan lost two games. His opponent raised the stakes and Dylan cleaned him out. He also was a fine and speedy chess player and he could remember the order of cards in a pack, so maybe he could have been a magician. It was hard to walk with him around the Village as he went so fast.

Dylan told friends that he had busked with the blues singer, Big Joe Williams, and they had ridden boxcars together: Big Joe had played guitar and Dylan spoons. Following Dylan's recommendation, Mike Porco booked Big Joe Williams for three weeks at Gerde's Folk City in February 1962.

Dylan's associates thought that he was bluffing and that he would be humiliated as Big Joe wouldn't know him. Dave Van Ronk and Bob Dylan went to Gerde's and Big Joe greeted him with 'Hey, Dylan, I've not seen you since that boxcar in Mexico.' Dave assumed that somehow Dylan had got there first.

Dylan made up tales and his friends enjoyed the stories even if they didn't believe them. Happy Traum: 'His accent sounded south-western. He sounded like Woody Guthrie and he could have come from Oklahoma. He spun this whole myth about himself. We all bought into it as we all wanted to believe that he was the reincarnation of Woody Guthrie, and that he had hopped freight trains and travelled around the country, working in carnivals. He said that he had been born in Gallup, New Mexico and we didn't know that he was a nice Jewish boy from Minnesota.'

Early in March 1962, Bob took part in a recording session with Victoria Spivey and Big Joe Williams. Four tracks were recorded, two appearing in 1964 on Spivey's own label. Dylan wasn't mentioned by name but billed as 'Big Joe's buddy'. Spivey claimed that the session was on 21 October 1961 so that she could argue for contractual reasons that it was before he signed with Columbia.

Maria Muldaur: 'I had the pleasure of getting to work with the great blues singer Victoria Spivey who was a contemporary of Bessie Smith and Memphis Minnie but had survived and made her way to New York. She was the first artist that I knew with her own record label and she saw John Sebastian and his friends fooling around with jug band music. She offered them a record deal and told them that the boys needed some sex appeal and she said, 'Go get that little girl I saw playing the fiddle.' This was in 1963, before women's lib, and I didn't consider it an insult. It sounded fun. She played me some wonderful stuff as she was finding songs I could record. She played me a tune by Memphis Minnie called 'Tricks Ain't Walkin' No More' and I was hearing her for the first time. It riveted me.'

On 11 March 1962, Dylan was on Cynthia Gooding's radio programme, *Folksinger's Choice*, broadcast in New York, and Dylan picked blues, country, folk and jug-band records. You could say it was his first shot at *Theme Time Radio Hour*. Even at this early stage, Dylan was not an easy interviewee.

The Canadian duo Ian and Sylvia Tyson released their first album, *Ian and Sylvia*, on Vanguard. The liner notes said they had worked out their arrangement of 'C.C. Rider' with Bob Dylan 'last summer'. Ian Tyson: 'The great acoustic songwriting thing was gathering momentum in 1961 and 1962 and I wrote 'Four Strong Winds'. It was covered almost immediately but its background came from my being in the rodeo and bumming around Canada. The song was about two people but it was really a combination of myself and several friends.'

On 19 March 1962 after much championing by John Hammond, Columbia relented and released his first album, simply called *Bob Dylan*. Bob is wearing a fake suede jacket on the cover as he couldn't afford a sheepskin like Ian Tyson. The album opened light-heartedly with Jesse Fuller's 'You're No Good', albeit misprinted as 'She's No Good'. Jesse Fuller's 'You're No Good' was very close to his 'San Francisco Bay Blues'. Dylan quickened it and modified its melody.

On the whole though, the songs were bleak and there is doom, despair and death. Bob Dylan was only 20 when he made the album but he sounds like a pensioner. Still, his vocals are great and he holds his notes both vocally and on harmonica in 'Man of Constant Sorrow'.

'Man of Constant Sorrow' can be traced back to a singer and fiddler in Kentucky in 1913, Richard Burnett. There have been many versions of this song, often with differences in the lyrics, and Bob's inspiration was 'I'm a Man of Constant Sorrow' from the Stanley Brothers in 1951.

When Alan Lomax was in the UK in 1951, he recorded John Strachan singing 'The Bonnie Lass o' Fyvie', which is about a frustrated romance between a soldier and a local girl. Lomax played this to the Clancys who recorded it as 'Maid of Fife-E-O'. This led to Bob Dylan's 'Pretty Peggy-O' in which he says he's been around the country and never come across a place called Fennario.

'Gospel Plow' is the liveliest track on the album and was taken from a gospel song 'Hold On' that Odetta performed with a choir at Carnegie Hall in April 1960.

Dylan admits that he took his arrangement of 'The House of the Risin' Sun' from Dave Van Ronk, but obviously not enough to merit a songwriting credit. The oldest known recording is from Clarence Ashley in 1933.

Josh White Jr: 'Woody Guthrie, Josh White and Leadbelly all sang 'The House of the Risin' Sun', which they had learnt from some hillbilly singer. At the time there was no minor chord in the song; it was all major. My father heard it more as a lament and so the very first chord is A minor. They were extra verses that turned it from the female first person singular to the boyfriend. My old man always kept it from the female's point of view; it did not bother Dad at all to take on the first person as a female.'

Eric Burdon of the Animals: 'I love the song. It strips away the glamorous side of being a hooker. When you see hookers at work, they are always projecting a bit of glamour, but there is nothing glamorous about it; it is desperation. It is a very desperate song. It has a great degree of empathy for enslaved people and the song has its own magic. My theory is that it was an English song and it went across the Atlantic with the immigrants. The reason I think that is because it's not a blues, it is certainly not black, and it was probably was an old hymn that somebody changed around. It has the same chord sequence as 'Amazing Grace'. It has made it into the 21st century via people like me and Bob Dylan interpreting it.'

Hughie Jones from the Spinners: 'I could certainly see Dylan's potential though I didn't particularly like what I heard. I thought the harmonica playing was diabolical. Tony Davis said in front of Sonny Terry, the wonderful blues harmonica player, when we were all having a meal, "Hughie can play the harmonica like Woody Guthrie." I was so embarrassed and I had to stand up and play a little bit of harmonica and that is when the great Sonny Terry said, "You are doing it completely wrong." He said it nicely but he taught me the principle there and then of the cross harp and it made me one of the few people in this country who had figured out the cross harp, instead of sucking you blow and vice versa.'

Did playing harmonica on a rack inhibit players as they couldn't get their hands to it? Hughie Jones: 'Well, I have heard a lot of players play a lot better than Bob Dylan with a rack. Me for a start!'

Tommy McClennan's 'New Highway 51' was released as a single by RCA in 1940, and Bob Dylan would have heard it on the Sam Charters' compilation, *The Rural Blues* (1960). Dylan had been performing 'Highway 51 Blues' in folk clubs but he sped it up for the album, adding a riff straight out of the Everly Brothers.

'See That My Grave Is Kept Clean' is a strange song for a 20-year-old but one of his favourite blues records was Blind Lemon Jefferson's version. Dylan's version is much starker than Jefferson's. Jefferson is making his request politely and Dylan is rasping it out.

The blues singer Bukka White was recording for Vocalion in 1940 when the label asked him if he had anything better. He went away and wrote 'Fixin' to Die Blues'. It wasn't a hit but was included on a highly-praised compilation, *The Country Blues*, in 1959. Dave Van Ronk sang it and then Dylan developed his own 'Fixin' to Die Blues'. Dylan's riff on 'Fixin' to Die Blues' came in handy when he wrote 'It's Alright, Ma (I'm Only Bleeding)'.

John Greenway, a teacher from Liverpool, ended up as a Professor of English at Denver University. In 1958 he released an album *Talking Blues*, which presented his takes on Woody Guthrie's talking blues, some of which had not been recorded by Guthrie. One was 'Talking Subway', which was probably the inspiration for Bob Dylan's 'Talkin' New York'. It's a pity his 'Hard Times in New York' was omitted, along with the one Woody Guthrie song he recorded for the album, 'Ramblin' Blues'.

Dylan's song for Woody is without political engagement – hey, you did some hard travelling, and that's about it. It's a good song but Steve Earle's 'Come Back Woody Guthrie' is better and more pointed. Happy Traum says, 'When I first heard Bob Dylan, he was doing traditional songs and doing them very well. We all loved 'Song to Woody' even though we recognised the melody. Very often he would take melodies from things we knew. 'Song to Woody' was Woody's '1913 Massacre'.'

The reviewer for *Village Voice* called his first album 'an explosive country-blues debut', but Dylan's favourite review came from Woody Guthrie who said, 'It's a good 'un, Bob!'

The album was not immediately popular as his voice was hard to take, and the folk community was split over the contents. There wasn't the dividing line between traditional and modern folk clubs in the US (as there was in the UK) but no one seemed sure where Dylan belonged. What's more: did listeners really want an album with such an obsession with death?

Tim Rose: 'Dylan's first album was just 'Turn on a mike and have him stand there'. Although John Hammond's name is on it, nobody produced it and that's what came out. It's an untrained singer with no record production, no studio production and no arrangements but it struck a nerve and we were willing to accept that. The singer / songwriter albums evolved from this and we all had very stylised voices.'

Dylan biographer Bob Spitz: 'John Hammond has been talked about as Bob's great producer but he was thrown off the project. John would say, "Go ahead, Bob, start singing", and he would sit in the control room and read magazines. Every once in a while, he would say, "That's great, Bob, go into the next one". Hammond didn't know about overdubbing and working for perfection or rather, John Hammond wasn't interested in perfection. He wanted performances and that helped the early Dylan albums. Bob hits some bad notes and is not a great guitarist, but those mistakes make the records spontaneous. When Dylan has produced himself, he has gone for first takes, so he likes rough versions himself. They are not gems of recording expertise and you're hearing real performances.'

In keeping with most song publishers at the time, Leeds Music asked their writers to record demos of their new songs so that they could copyright them and if needs be, transcribe the words and music for sheet music. Seven of Bob's demos for Lou Levy have survived. The best are 'Man on the Street' and 'Ballad of a Friend', both about hobo life, and the most entertaining is 'Poor Boy Blues', which shows Bob had been listening to Howlin' Wolf.

As well as writing his own songs, Bob was attracted to an old ballad he had heard from Joan Baez and Bob Gibson, 'House Carpenter', also known as 'The Daemon Lover'.

Joan Baez was making hit albums and then some. Her second album, *Joan Baez, Volume 2*, had rave reviews and was partly made with the Greenbriar Boys. It sold so well that it boosted the sales of the first album and both LPs were in the Top 20 US albums for most of 1962. They were joined by *Joan Baez in Concert* at the end of the year. Such beautifully pure singing wasn't for everyone (including Bob Dylan) but thousands of fans were devoted to her.

In April 1962 the Fariñas (Richard and Carolyn) and the Baezs (Joan and 17-year-old Mimi) went to Paris, but after Richard flirted with Mimi, Carolyn threatened to shoot him. He became besotted and he dedicated a poem to Mimi, 'The Field near the Cathedral at Chartres', which was published in *Mademoiselle*.

There are tapes of Bob Dylan singing a slave song, 'No More Auction Block for Me'. It was a song of liberation which had been written after Britain abolished slavery in 1833 in Canada. It had a variant 'Many Thousands Gone' and Odetta had recorded this at Carnegie Hall in 1960. Dylan worked on a new lyric: he called out chords and asked David Blue to strum them as he wrote the first and last verses of 'Blowin' in the Wind'. He would later add a middle verse. It was now a song about the struggle for justice.

Gil Turner, a folk singer and Baptist preacher, asked Dylan to teach him the new song and he performed it with the words taped to the microphone at Gerde's Folk City.

Happy Traum of the New World Singers: 'I first heard 'Blowin' in the Wind' when Gil Turner brought it in to Gerde's Folk City where we were playing that night and he said, "This is a fantastic song that Bob has just written. Let's do it." We quickly worked up an arrangement of it. We started singing it whenever we could and we ended up, at Bob's request, doing it on a Broadside album. It was the first recording of it. I am not saying it was the best but it was the first.'

On 16 April, Bob Dylan performed the song, still with two verses, publicly for the first time at Gerde's. He said, 'This here ain't a protest song or anything like that 'cause I don't write protest songs', so he hated this appellation from the start.

Not everybody was taken with the song at first. Tom Paxton called it 'a grocery list song where one line had no relevance to the next line.' Many other songs could be dismissed in that way – what about 'If I Had a Hammer'. Dave Van Ronk thought 'Blowin'' was dumb until he heard students singing a parody in Washington Square Park with the lyric now 'The answer my friend is blowin' out your end' and it hadn't even been recorded at the time. In November 2017, on *I'm Sorry I Haven't a Clue*, Graeme Garden sang the lyrics of 'I Am a Little Teapot' to the tune of 'Blowin' in the Wind'.

Over the years Bob Dylan has often dismissed 'Blowin' in the Wind' although he still sings it – and why not? It is an anthem up there with 'We Shall Overcome' and 'If I Had a Hammer'. Was it the American flag that was blowing in the wind? Is it another way of saying 'Well, maybe never'?

Bruce Dickinson of Iron Maiden: 'I like the words and the imagery of it. "How many times can a cannonball fly before they are forever banned?" was great. Cannonballs bounce and they are horrendous things – they don't go from A to B and go splot! – they cut a swathe through people, like a bouncing bomb. It takes a chunk off you and then takes a chunk off the next guy. That image has stayed in my head.'

At the end of April, Bob Dylan was headlining at Gerde's Folk City for the first time in a two-week residency.

At the same time he had sessions for his second album, *The Freewheelin' Bob Dylan*, though not all the songs were used. He worked with a jazz bass player, Bill Lee on some tracks.

The initial thought was to call the album, *Bob Dylan's Blues*, and have his modern take on the blues. Several of the songs like 'Goin' to New Orleans' and 'Sally Gal' were like old records but not quite as he was playing around with blues forms. This was soon dropped as he was writing more and more but the concept of rewriting the blues never left him and he returned to it big style with *Time Out Of Mind* in 1997 and subsequent albums.

His love for country music comes out in Hank Williams' 'Lonesome Whistle' but instead of modernising it, he is taking it back 20 years. He sounds particularly old on this track. If these sessions had been released, it would have still been a good album but it wouldn't have had such an impact.

When he recorded 'Worried Blues' he was finger picking as he had in 'Don't Think Twice, It's All Right' and 'One Too Many Mornings'. He abandoned this style after 1964.

After hearing of the building of bunkers, Dylan wrote about nuclear destruction in 'Let

Me Die in Your Footsteps'. He thought it was futile that schools should have instructions on how to dive for cover in a napalm attack. 'Let Me Die in My Footsteps' was passed to Happy Traum. Happy Traum: 'I think he was 21 at the time and he just knocked it out. It was still warm when I sang it. I loved it because it rang true because of all this craziness about the Bomb. Along with some other people, I'd been arrested for not going to a shelter during a drill. Going into a subway or a shelter during an atomic bomb blast was not going to help us. It was a much better idea to make sure that it didn't happen in the first place.'

Happy Traum watched Dylan writing and noticed his fear of the Cold War. 'I heard him try them out in little clubs and even in our living room. He would say, "Do you like this song?" He had a naivety about him and he really wanted our response to them.'

Unfortunately his song 'The Death of Robert Johnson' has either not survived or was never completed as that sounds a good one.

Pete Seeger introduced Bob Dylan to Agnes (Sis) Cunningham and her husband Gordon Friesen, who had been blacklisted for joining the Communist Party. Back in the day, they had promoted the Almanac Singers and now they were starting a mimeographed, folk magazine *Broadside,* which would be published in New York. The intention was to feature socially conscious singers. Sis had organised their own label, which would be pressed and distributed by Folkways. The magazine was to grow from its modest beginnings and print over 1,000 songs in its 30-year history. Bruce Springsteen was to record a song that Sis wrote, 'My Oklahoma Home'.

In May 1962 'Blowin' in the Wind' was published in the May issue of *Broadside* with three verses and Dylan performed the song on a *Broadside* show for WBAI. Dylan said he could write five songs before breakfast (but possibly not before delivery of the *New York Times*). Buffy Sainte-Marie said that so many of the new writers picked up the *New York Times* and then had something to write about.

Oscar Brand, an experienced broadcaster whose series *World of Folk Music,* was syndicated to 1,800 stations, got to know Bob Dylan. 'We had a good relationship, he came to my house, we had parties, he would eat and then one day this kid was performing at the Fat Black Pussycat which was a former strip joint where you had a runway and the runway ran sideways against the wall. The performers would get on that platform and they would sing their songs which were for the most part traditional. If the audience liked them, they would throw money on the stage; it was humbling but necessary. Bob was allowed to be on the platform and Dave Van Ronk, who had let him stay at his house, asked me to take a look at this kid. I had met him a few times but I had never heard him in front of an audience. This was a great test, especially an audience that had come mainly to scoff. We sat in the audience and we scoffed. He sang 'Blowin' in the Wind' and we shook our head sideways: kid didn't have a chance. It sounded very obvious, and didn't have a chance.'

Is there an underlining sense in such views that there was something about Dylan that was phony, something not quite right? Dylan knew this himself and I doubt that it bothered him. Also, he didn't look as authentic as the well-travelled singers but this probably gave him a greater sex appeal. He was already standing alone.

Like Brecht's play *Mother Courage,* 'Masters of War' attacks those who profit from war. 'Even Jesus would never forgive what you do.' The warmongers were not in the line of fire, an idea that can be heard in World War I songs such as 'Hanging on the Old Barbed Wire'.

In April 1962 Roy Silver started Campus Concerts with Bob Gibson and he managed Bill Cosby, Bob Dylan and Tiny Tim. He signed a five-year contract with Dylan but it was more as a booking agent than a manager. Silver shared an office with Albert Grossman. Grossman heard 'Blowin' in the Wind' and wanted it. It was time to move.

Judy Collins: 'I knew Albert Grossman because he hung around in the Village and in Chicago. He was never my manager but we were good friends. He wanted to put me in a female trio after he had started Peter Paul and Mary and I said, "No thanks." He brought me the first tape of Dylan, when he was considering managing him and looking for a record deal. I'd never heard anything like it. There was a Dylan Thomas influence in the early years. It was so fresh and so different. Albert said to me, "Do you think he can sing? Everybody thinks he's terrible." I said, "Don't listen to them – he's a wonderful singer".'

Albert Grossman was doing fine with Peter, Paul and Mary and now he wanted Bob Dylan. Grossman shared an office with Ray Silver and he offered him $10,000 and continued use of his office space. He signed him for seven years. Grossman wanted to keep his capital free and, unknown to Dylan, half the money was put up by Peter Yarrow. Peter, Paul and Mary thought that Dylan could become the most important songwriter in the country and that he 'had his finger on the pulse of America's youth'. That's an understatement – it was not just America.

Grossman loathed John Hammond. He claimed that Dylan's Columbia contract was null and void as he had been under 21 when he signed it. However, Columbia argued that he had used their studios six or seven times since turning 21 and so the contract was valid.

M. Witmark and Sons was a music publisher, formed in 1886, which had helped to create the industry. When Jack Warner went into sound pictures with *The Jazz Singer* in 1927, he knew it would make financial sense to own a music publishing company rather than be licensing songs from elsewhere. He bought Witmark in 1929 and Herman Starr was its manager. He was excellent at securing covers of the songs, a famous one being 'Stardust'. By 1960 Witmark had 30,000 songs on its books. One of his employees, Artie Mogull (you couldn't make that name up) told him of Peter, Paul and Mary, who were singing good, original songs, notably 'Blowin in the Wind'. Starr heard them and then invited Dylan to the office. He was given an advance of $1,000 on 13 July 1962.

Dylan would visit them to record demos for copyright purposes and for their use in writing sheet music. They were not intended to be perfect takes – for example, Dylan coughs during 'Blowin' in the Wind'.

Grossman collected an additional percentage of the royalties because he had brought Bob to them, a finder's fee if you like. As a result, Grossman would be earning more from Dylan's songs that Dylan was. I mentioned earlier that a million-seller could net $20,000 in songwriting royalties with $10,000 to the publisher and $10,000 to the manager and songwriter. Unknown to Dylan, Grossman would be taking $5,000 of each slice so he got $10,000, Witmark $5,000 and Dylan $5,000. Sharp practice but there was much worse in the industry.

When Grossman told Dylan he could make it professionally, he took him off Ray Silver by saying, 'Next year you can make $100,000 and your agent gets 20% or you can come with me and make $250,000 and I take 50%. Take your pick.'

Todd Rundgren, once managed by Grossman, said he was the person he would most like to hit in the nuts with a baseball bat. 'I pitied the people who had to work with him", said Pete Seeger. Yes, but it was worse for the people who had to deal with him. Dave Van Ronk commented, 'Albert Grossman got a perverse pleasure in being utterly unscrupulous.'

The managers of most folk artists like Harold Levanthal and Manny Greenhill behaved honourably and had political links to the music. Grossman was seen as a trickster: indeed, integrity bothered Grossman, who said that everybody had their price.

Grossman advised Dylan that it was a good idea to be inscrutable, but that was Bob's default position anyway. The more mystery the better. Maybe this is why Dylan dropped his funny songs: you can't be funny and have mystique.

A double CD of *The Witmark Demos* was officially issued in 2010 with 39 performances that have survived. Several of the songs were officially recorded for Columbia but there is much of interest here. Dylan is singing the songs so that Witmark can create the sheet music and even though he gave them the lyrics, he is taking care with his pronunciation. The publisher could forward songs with potential to other performers. Dylan chose not to include 'Tomorrow Is a Long Time' on his albums (an insane oversight) but Witmark secured covers from Ian and Sylvia, Odetta and Judy Collins. Judy cried when she first heard the song – she couldn't believe that Bob was giving such a good song away.

On 9 July 1962 Dylan had an official session for the second album at Columbia. He put down 'Blowin' in the Wind', 'Honey, Just Allow Me One More Chance' and 'Down the Highway', which all made the album. 'Down the Highway' starts off as a drifter's song but gets around to Suze and her trip to Italy.

Bob had taken 'Honey, Just Allow Me One More Chance' from the Texan blues singer Henry Thomas, who in turn had got it from Dorothy Scarborough. Bob took the chorus from Thomas' version and reworked the verses. Thomas did the original of 'Fishin' Blues', which the Lovin' Spoonful recorded and they recorded a song about him, 'Henry Thomas'.

Around July 1962 Richard Fariña and Carolyn Hester played the Edinburgh Folk Festival and were attempting a reconciliation. Todd Stuart picked up Mimi in Paris and brought her to the festival: she had told her parents she was going to a Quaker summer programme in Newcastle. Richard and Mimi were soon together and Carolyn wanted a Mexican divorce.

A teenage Greil Marcus in Menlo, California attended a writing class from Joan Baez's mentor Ira Sandperl to find Joan and Mimi entertaining kids with the Marvelettes' 'Playboy'. Joan often put a pop song into her act like 'Lil' Darlin'' and would have fun with it.

When Edwin Miller interviewed Dylan for the teen magazine, *17*, Dylan was already saying the first album was not representative of his work. It was an odd magazine to feature Dylan as he was not a pretty boy nor a macho hunk but then Roy Orbison was a major star. Dylan though was careful about how he looked in public. There are private photos of Dylan wearing spectacles, but he never had them on for performances or photoshoots, which has to be deliberate.

When Dylan was interviewed for *FM Stereo-Guide* in 1962, he again dismissed his first album and said Elvis Presley was 'a good singer…in the beginning.'

Gil Turner interviewed Dylan for *Sing Out!* It was a rival to *Broadside* but without the polemics, although Dylan said that songwriters have a duty to tackle social and political issues.

On 2 August 1962 Robert Allen Zimmerman at New York's Supreme Court changed his name legally to Bob Dylan. The following day the *New Musical Express* called him 'the most exciting new folk talent in years'.

A few days later he had another home taping session with Tony Glover in Minneapolis.

Dylan was ambitious so didn't he realise how these tapes might cause problems? Also why didn't he have his own tape deck by now? After all, he'd just been given $1,000.

On 8 June 1962 Suze Rotolo went on a trip to Europe as her mother took her to the University of Perugia for a summer course. Maybe her mother wanted to get her away from Bob. Bob saw her off at the docks and wrote the aforementioned 'Tomorrow Is a Long Time'.

A more famous song associated with Suze, is 'Don't Think Twice, It's All Right', but Dylan sings, 'You just kinda wasted my precious time'. Dylan said, 'It isn't a love song. It's a statement that you can say to make yourself feel better. It's as if you're talking to yourself.' Joan Baez introduced it by saying it was about a love affair that had lasted too long. Unlike Tom Paxton's 'The Last Thing on My Mind' which is a song of regret, 'Don't Think Twice, It's All Right' can be taken in two ways: the singer may be resigned to it.

Where did Dylan's ideas come from? In 'Don't Think Twice, It's All Right', the rooster crows at the break of dawn. Nothing wrong with that but who ever heard a rooster in New York? Well, Bob and Suze did: they lived in two rooms above a spaghetti parlour and across the road was a livestock shop selling chickens.

Suze had been working on an off-Broadway play, *Brecht on Brecht*. Dylan was impressed at Brecht's political songwriting and Suze was pressing him to write political songs. This was the basis for the second album.

At Bob's request, Dylan's publisher sent 'Don't Think Twice, It's All Right' to Roy Orbison, who had just recorded 'In Dreams'. He had no plans for it at the time but later wished he had accepted it.

The song was based on an early twentieth century song, 'Who's Gonna Buy Your Chickens When I'm Gone', which he had learned from Paul Clayton. Clayton had used that song for his own 'Who's Gonna Buy You Ribbons'.

Dylan wrote a great new lyric but Clayton didn't see it that way: it was plagiarism to him. He settled for $500 and that might have been the reason why Dylan left 'Percy's Song' off his next album as that was based on 'The Wind and the Rain', another traditional song he was doing. Paul Clayton has sold his writer's share on 'Gotta Travel On' for $500: he was Pete Seeger without the luck.

Also missing out were a folk-based cabaret trio, the Big Three, with Cass Elliot (Mama Cass), Tim Rose and Jim Hendricks. Jim had received his draft papers and Cass had married him as an escape. Bob Dylan heard them in the Village and offered them 'Don't Think Twice, It's All Right', but they went with a dramatic anti-war song instead 'Come Away Melinda', written by Fred Hellerman from the Weavers. It wasn't a hit for them but the song was recorded by Bobbie Gentry, Uriah Heep and, as a solo act, Tim Rose.

On 7 July 1962 Bob, Dylan recorded 'Blowin' in the Wind' although it would not be released until May 1963.

'Oxford Town' was about the first black student at the University of Mississippi and it summarised the Civil Rights struggle. The lyric was to be published in *Broadside*. Phil Ochs wrote 'The Ballad of Oxford, Mississippi'.

Dylan said an outtake 'Baby, I'm In the Mood for You' was 'probably influenced by Jesse Fuller'.

'Quit Your Lowdown Ways' was not used on the next album but given to Peter, Paul and Mary. It was a fun song based on blues that Bob had heard from Sleepy John Estes and Kokomo Arnold.

In September 1962 Suze Rotolo had the opportunity to remain in Europe with her mother and new stepfather, a college professor. Suze met her future husband Enzo Bartoccioli in Italy but didn't want to be involved as she was still with Bob Dylan. She was relieved to be away from him as he could be demanding and negative: it was hard for Dylan to accept anybody else's views.

Although Bob retained his fondness for Suze, it did not stop him from having other relationships. Mavis Staples and Bob Dylan were very fond of each other, so much so that Bob once asked Pop Staples if he could marry her, though this was probably in jest.

Joan Baez released her third album, *Joan Baez In Concert*, including her first topical song, a bewildering song about nuclear fallout, 'What Have They Done to the Rain'. Richard Fariña told Dylan that Baez was his ticket to fame: Joan could do his songs and bring herself into the twentieth century.

The theme of nuclear war was in Bob Dylan's poem, 'A Hard Rain's A-Gonna Fall', written on an old Remington in Hugh Romney's apartment: at the time Romney was the MC at the Gaslight. He later became Wavy Gravy and one of Ken Kesey's Merry Pranksters. Romney said, 'The words roared through him the way paint roared through Van Gogh.'

Tom Paxton might have dismissed 'Hard Rain' as another grocery list song, but he didn't. He recalled, 'Bob and I were sharing a little room above the Gaslight. You could hardly call it a changing room because no one ever changed. Bob was pounding away on a typewriter and he said it was "just a poem". I said, "Why don't you sing it?" and that's when he decided to put it to music.' Dylan sang it immediately at the Gaslight and the stunned reaction suggested he had written a masterpiece. Pete Seeger, Richie Havens and Hamilton Camp were all to sing it live before Dylan recorded it.

It is a conversation between a man and his son who has witnessed something terrifying and terrible. Happy Traum: 'I remember hearing 'A Hard Rain's A-Gonna Fall', and that was a moment of incredulity as I couldn't believe what I was hearing. It was based on an old English song but he had twisted it around and his poetry was staggering.'

'A Hard Rain's A-Gonna Fall' was based on the tune 'Lord Randall' and the first line came from that song. Townes Van Zandt: 'I don't put Bob down for writing new words on existing tunes because he was really good at it. It's a gift. "Where have you been, Lord Randall, my son" became "Where have you been, my blue-eyed son" and he took that and built upon it. He had learnt that from Woody Guthrie. I've never been able to do that.'

The singer / songwriter Julian Cope liked the advice in that same song, 'I'll know my song well before I start singing'.

'Pellets of poison' is about the lies told by the media.

The Rough Guide to Bob Dylan describes it as a 'long free verse poem in style of French symbolists'. Certainly there is the symbolism of Rimbaud in there, but it could just as easily been influenced by the Book of Revelation or Leonard Cohen's muse, Lorca. As with 'The Times They Are A-Changin'', Bob Dylan was favouring colloquial speech.

On 22 September 1962 Bob was part of the all-star hootenanny in Carnegie Hall. Pete Seeger was topping the bill and each artist had only 10 minutes. That was two songs to Bob Dylan: 'Ballad of Hollis Brown' and 'A Hard Rain's A-Gonna Fall', which showed his confidence in his new material.

Willie Nile: 'In 2016 they were celebrating his Bob's birthday in New York City and they asked me to play four songs. I didn't want to do it unless I could bring something to it. I thought I would do 'Hard Rain' like a bolero (sings). What struck me was how relevant many of the songs are to today's world. You could write 'Hard Rain' now. There are incredible images in that song: he was 21 years old when he wrote it. He's a kid and yet it's a masterpiece.'

I've always taken the line about the blue-eyed son to be about President Kennedy? Willie Nile: 'Could be but it could be Bob's own journey. His stuff can have so many meanings but I think he is talking about himself. Bob Dylan is the Greta Garbo of rock'n'roll and you need that, a crazy uncle, someone who doesn't obey the call, someone who doesn't do things to be on TV, it's refreshing. When he got the Nobel Prize, he didn't even answer his phone.'

In October 1962 Bob was back at the Gaslight on a double-header with the New World Singers. Around the same time, Dylan was recorded by Richard Alderson who did the sound at the Gaslight and cut 10 songs with him. He goes into falsetto for 'Rocks and Gravel' and gives us a foretaste of his *Nashville Skyline* voice on 'Barbara Allen' – the song Samuel Pepys called 'a perfect pleasure'. He sang 'Handsome Molly' with its line, 'I wish I was in London'. Soon he would be. In 2005 these 10 tracks were sold on a special release, *Live at the Gaslight 1962*, which was sold exclusively by Starbucks: HMV Canada was so disappointed with Dylan's decision that they removed his stock from the racks.

There is an earlier Gaslight session, possibly from 1961, which includes Lord Buckley's 'Hezekiah Jones (Black Cross)' He sings the slave song 'No More Auction Blok for Me', the melody he used for 'Blowin' in the Wind'.

In October 1962 the Beatles released their first Parlophone single, 'Love Me Do'.

On 26 October 1962 Bob Dylan was at Columbia Studios, rocking out on an electric session with Dick Wellstood (piano), Howie Collins and Bruce Langhorne (guitars), Leonard Gaskin (bass) and Herb Lovelle (drums). One track, 'Corrina, Corrina' is on *The Freewheelin' Bob Dylan* so that was not a completely acoustic album.

They cut Dylan's song 'Mixed up Confusion' and Elvis' first Sun single, 'That's All Right, Mama'. Bruce Langhorne's licks on the latter are similar to what he did in 'Maggie's Farm'. Dylan's rock roots were definitely showing but he later reflected, 'I played all the folk songs with a rock'n'roll attitude. This is what made me different and allowed me to cut through all the mess and be heard.'

He had completed 'Mixed up Confusion' in a taxi on his way to the studio. He was to cut it 14 times over three sessions. Such perseverance is unusual for Dylan and he was probably attempting his own Sun single. Dylan discussed his frustrations at getting 'Mixed up Confusion' right with Izzy Young, so he wasn't keeping it secret.

Dylan's second electric session was on 1 November 1962 with Dick Wellstood (piano), George Barnes and Bruce Langhorne (guitars), Art Davis (bass) and Herb Lovelle (drums). They recorded 'Mixed up Confusion' and 'That's All Right, Mama' again as well as Brownie McGhee's 'Solid Road' and 'Rocks and Gravel'. There is a snatch of Cyril Tawney's 'Sally Free And Easy' after 'That's All Right Mama': how had Dylan heard that one?

The third electric session was on 14 November 1962, this time with Gene Ramey on bass. There is 'Mixed up Confusion' and 'Corrina Corrina' as well as the definitive 'Don't Think Twice, It's All Right'. Blind Lemon Jefferson had recorded 'Corrina Blues' and Joe Turner had made the song an R&B hit. In 1960 it was a US Top 10 single for Ray Peterson and produced by Phil Spector. Dylan sang the plaintive 'Who's Going to Shoe Your Pretty Little Feet', which had been recorded by both Woody Guthrie and the Everly Brothers.

In October 1962 *Sing Out!* published the lyric for 'Blowin' in the Wind'. A student, Lorre Wyatt, read the lyric and passed it off as his own. He and his group, the Millburnaires performed their version of 'Blowin' in the Wind' at the Millburn High School thanksgiving assembly.

Dylan broke his recording contract with a session for *Broadside* including 'Ye Playboys and Playgirls', 'Oxford Town', 'Talkin' Cuban Missile Crisis' and 'Walkin' Down the Line'. At this stage in his career, he welcomed any visit to a recording studio.

The Cold War escalated in October 1962 with the Cuban Missile Crisis. The phrase Mutually Assured Destruction had the acronym, MAD. There was a feeling particularly amongst the left in America for songs about Cold War paranoia, Communist witch-hunts and civil rights martyrs.

British social commentator David Charters: 'To my generation the war hadn't really gone away. By 1962, Britain, France, the Soviet Union and the US had nuclear weapons, and there was a terrible fear of what could happen in the world. The Cold War was at its height and you had Kennedy who was the young prince of the new dawning age. Khrushchev was a sophisticated peasant if you like. He would take off his shoes and bang them on the table. He would express his anger in an earthy manner against this slick, smooth Irish-American. It came to a terrible clash with the Cuban Missile Crisis and the anxieties that everybody had at that time. Russia had got into space first a few years earlier with Yuri Gagarin and America was hard on their heels. The social movement that arose out of it came with the peaceniks. There was CND and a powerful group of young people. They looked pale and dressed in black and were looking very serious and carrying Jack Kerouac's *On the Road*.'

The threat of nuclear war is apparent in 'Blowin' in the Wind', 'A Hard Rain's A-Gonna Fall' and Malvina Reynolds' 'What Have They Done to the Rain', later a hit for the Searchers. The aftermath of nuclear war was conveyed in Nevil Shute's novel, *On the Beach,* filmed in Australia in 1959 with Gregory Peck, Tony Perkins, Ava Gardner and Fred Astaire. Later there was the banned TV documentary, *The War Game* and the Spike Milligan play and film, *The Bed Sitting Room*.

Bonnie Dobson: 'I saw the film *On the Beach* in 1959 and it made an incredible impression on me. We had a lot of gloomy conversations and I sat down with my guitar and remembered this scene with Anthony Perkins and his wife. They were discussing what the future was for them and for their child. They felt it was over, that the world was finished. The first time I sang 'Morning Dew' in public was at the Mariposa Festival 1962 I think, and a reviewer said it was a mournful dirge.'

On 23 November 1962, Joan Baez was featured on the cover of *Time* magazine. This was certainly an accolade but the cover painting by Russell Hoban was not flattering. Although the 5,000-word article was comprehensive and generally positive, 'all I thought about was how dreadful I looked on the cover,' says Joan. Even her mother said, 'Couldn't they have made you look prettier?' There were some snide remarks too: 'Anything called a hootenanny ought to be shot on sight.' Bob Dylan was described as 'a promising hobo', and some internal correspondence reveals that the editorial team found him 'a singularly unattractive man'.

Dave Van Ronk thought, 'Joanie's made the cover of *Time*. Now she's finished.' It was just too establishment. Not wanting to be bitten twice, in 1977 Joan Baez put her own feelings into 'Time Rag' and how unfairly she had been treated. "Deep in my heart, I don't give a damn where I stand in the charts.'

On 6 December 1962, there was a further session for the next album and some earlier songs were dropped. It would be the last time Dylan would work with John Hammond. The session, though it only lasted 90 minutes, worked well. Dylan recorded a brilliant 'Hard Rain' and he did 'I Shall Be Free'; the first take was used but he did two more with different lyrics. An outtake of 'I Shall be Free' refers to Huckleberry Finn hats. The final outing for his Huck Finn cap was the *Freewheelin'* cover. There was 'Oxford Town', 'Whatcha Gonna Do' and the introspective 'Hero Blues', a forgotten song dusted off for his 1974 tour.

On 13 December 1962 Suze Rotolo was sailing from Naples to arrive in New York five days later, but by then Bob had flown to the UK.

On 14 December 1962, Dylan's first US single was released – 'Mixed-Up Confusion' / 'Corrina Corrina'. It was Bob Dylan with a rock backing but no one was shouting 'Judas!' It was a strong week as Columbia released Dion's 'Ruby Baby', Eydie Gormé's 'Blame It on the Bossa Nova' and Johnny Cash's 'Busted'. The label would shortly have a Number 1 single with Steve Lawrence's 'Go Away Little Girl'.

John Stewart from the Kingston Trio: 'I'd heard about Dylan. We were in New York and Dylan was the *enfant terrible* of the Village. He came into this bar called the Dug-Out where everybody would congregate. Phil Ochs would say, "There's Dylan over there". He was keeping very much to himself and would slink around. He had a single out, 'Corrina Corrina', and we thought it was unbelievable. We were much aware of him and we knew Albert Grossman. He sent me a tape of some Dylan songs for the Trio to record. One of them was 'Mr. Tambourine Man' and I confess I sent it back. I said, "I have no idea what this guy is talking about".' What a mistake and fancy John Stewart not spotting its potential: that song could well have extended the Trio's chart success.

In December 1962 John Hammond Jr, the son of John Hammond, met the rock band Levon and the Hawks in Toronto. They were at Concord Tavern and he was playing at the Purple Onion. They recorded some songs together including Bo Diddley's 'Who Do You Love' and we'll be returning to the significance of that.

III. Film: *Inside Llewyn Davis*

Dave Van Ronk was known among his friends as the Mayor of MacDougal Street and he was working on a memoir with that title when he died aged 65 in 2002. The book was being ghost-written by Elijah Wald who completed it in 2006, making a controversial decision: 'It was supposed to be his book about the Greenwich Village of the late 50s and if he had been alive it would have been less about the music scene and more about the Village in general. He died early in the process and since I wanted to keep writing it in his voice, I had to call in all the interviews that people had done with him over the years and they were mostly about him and the music and so that ended up being more of a focus than he intended.'

Personally, I feel that was okay as Elijah Wald had integrity but there has been disagreement as to whether the book really is a first-hand account or not. Whatever, *The Mayor of MacDougal Street* is a highly readable account of life in Greenwich Village and is now available in an expanded 2013 edition.

Joel and Ethan, the Coen brothers bought the film rights and wrote a fictional story which became *Inside Llewyn Davis,* released in 2013. The central character was nothing like Dave Van Ronk as the fictional character is self-centred and manipulative, although you still root for him. Nevertheless, it is Llewyn Davis in the film who is considered for the fledgling

Peter, Paul and Mary by the tough-talking manager, Bud Grossman (played by F. Murray Abraham), who ran the Gate of Horn.

Jim Kweskin: 'I didn't like the film as it didn't portray what it was like back then. It made it out to be very dark and very lonely. To my mind and to my memory those times were very expansive and we were all learning and partying together, performing together, trading songs and learning from each other and from the older guys. We were all hanging out and it was a wonderful time to be alive. You can't get that from the movie as it does not portray what those days were really like.'

Elijah Wald: 'I wasn't in Greenwich Village in 1960 but the people I've talked to, the musicians who were there, say that the movie captures it very well, but I accept that it was too gloomy and the actual scene was more fun. On the other hand, the film is about one bad week in the life of one guy and the more fun the scene is, the gloomier he may feel, so I think it is pretty accurate in that regard.'

There is a superb recreation of the Clancy Brothers in their Aran sweaters, but Bonnie Dobson has reservations: 'I knew the Clancy Brothers and they were not po-faced at all, Tom Paxton was not like that, so it is a work of fiction. Llewyn Davis is based on Dave Van Ronk but he was not bitter like that: he was a large and funny man and we were all very supportive of each other.'

Roger McGuinn: 'Dave Van Ronk was running the hootenannys at the Gaslight when I was there. He was the resident singer. The movie looks depressing but it was not a depressing scene at all; it was a lot of fun. We had a great time in the Village but I don't think anybody has captured that feeling.'

Tom Paxton: 'Everybody assumes that I am the soldier in that film but I don't see any particular resemblance. I would have died before I would have worn my uniform in Greenwich Village, which he does in the movie, but they did a beautiful version of 'Last Thing on My Mind' and it was a great movie.'

The music was mostly played live and the Coens used actors who were also musicians. Oscar Isaac as Llewyn Davis had to learn Travis-picking and he played a 1929 Gibson just like Robert Johnson. In the final scene, he is booked for the Gaslight but an unnamed Bob Dylan is there too singing 'Farewell'. While he is singing, Llewyn Davies gets beaten up. In reality, Dave Van Ronk was beaten up by Jean Ritchie's husband. An alternative version of Bob Dylan singing 'Farewell' was included on the soundtrack album.

There is a very good 40 minute *Making Of...* extra on the DVD. They clearly enjoyed making it and T Bone Burnett is such an enthusiast that he was the perfect music producer. He suggested that the film itself is like a folk song. You come back to the same characters as at the start of the film but you know them so much better. As a Brit, I found it fascinating that there were so many songs from the British Isles.

One final point: Dave Van Ronk actually lived on Sheridan Street and it has been renamed Dave Van Ronk Street.

CHAPTER 4

'It's something I Learned Over in England.'

'Someone had to reach for the risin' star, I guess it was up to me.'
'Up to Me', Bob Dylan

I. Come Writers and Critics

No rock book has had such a chequered history as Robert Shelton's biography of Bob Dylan, *No Direction Home*, which was published in 1986, 20 years after Shelton had first suggested it to Dylan. It is flawed – Shelton, as we shall see, sabotaged his own work – but, without doubt, it contains the definitive account of Bob Dylan's formative years.

Bob Dylan began his career performing in the little clubs and coffee houses in Greenwich Village. Robert Shelton was entranced and wrote about him in the *New York Times* for 29 September 1961: 'He may need a bit of tailoring but when he works his guitar, harmonica or piano and composes new songs faster than he can remember them, there is no doubt that he is bursting with talent.'

That assessment can be placed alongside Bob Wooler championing the Beatles in *Mersey Beat* in August 1961 ('I don't think anything like them will happen again') or Jon Landau claiming the future of rock'n'roll was Bruce Springsteen in 1974. These writers are seen as visionaries, although perhaps in those cases, they were stating the obvious.

Robert Shelton died in Brighton in 1995, not quite 70 years old, his life changed forever – maybe even wrecked – by his association with Bob Dylan. Since the late 1960s, he had been living in the UK and he eked out a living by writing reviews for regional newspapers such as *Brighton Argus* and *Birmingham Post*. His sisters have given his papers, books and tapes to Liverpool University and they are stored in 40 large boxes. I've spent a day looking through them, although I could have happily stayed a week. The Dylan material is, as I expected, fantastic and it highlights a deeper story; how did a superb journalist for one of the world's leading newspapers lose his mojo?

The answer is sad. Robert Shelton had accepted an impossible challenge, that of trying to nail down the unpredictable and elusive Bob Dylan. True, Bob Dylan would talk to him from time to time but whether he would tell the truth was anyone's guess. Shelton had the measure of him: 'Dylan is such a moody cat that someone he growls at today (like Joan Baez), he may have as his duet partner tomorrow.' Dylan was an unreliable source for his own life, often deliberately so, but sorting out fact from fiction was only one of Shelton's problems. It is the story of one writer being sucked into the ever-changing world of another writer.

From reading the files, I can see that researching Bob Dylan took over Shelton's life; he was constantly reworking his text, either of his own initiative or because of a publisher's demands. Instead of finding his way through the forest to the other side, he got lost in the undergrowth. He told one publishing executive not to worry: he could write 3,000 words a week and then a few days later, Shelton sent her a letter 10,000 words long outlining his troubles and stating the difficulties in getting on with the job. Shelton desperately needed someone standing over him, telling him what to do and putting his own life in order, especially as he was drinking heavily. The rock biography that had the potential to be a milestone became a millstone around his neck.

What is doubly sad is that throughout the correspondence, Robert Shelton comes over as sincere and generous, although he could be tetchy and argumentative. Fuelled by alcohol, he wrote letters which should not have been sent but usually he was difficult for the right reasons as a principle was at stake.

Robert Shelton was born in Chicago in 1926, his father being a research chemist. He graduated in 1943, served in the US army in France and studied journalism at university. In 1951 he became a copy boy at the *New York Times* and his first by-line was on a feature related to hi-fi jargon in 1956. He was subpoenaed in the Communist witch-hunt and although they had the wrong journalist (they wanted Willard Shelton), he refused to co-operate and the *New York Times* moved him from news to arts and entertainment. For ten years from 1958, he was reviewing and reporting on rock, folk and country.

Shelton was living in Waverly Place in Greenwich Village and he encouraged the growth of folk music both in the Village and around New York itself, especially through the Newport Folk Festival. He told his readers about Joan Baez and Odetta and he noted the revival of interest in blues musicians like Lightnin' Hopkins.

Shelton saw Dylan at an all-night hootenanny in 1961 and then in September when he was supporting the Greenbriar Boys at Gerde's. This is the celebrated review which led to his contract with Columbia Records: it captured Dylan's uniqueness but acknowledged that his voice owed something to the pre-war country blues singers. He recalled in 1986, 'Dylan was fascinating to look at, a cross between a choirboy and a beatnik, a little like an Italian street musician. He was very engaging, he moved around a great deal with a lot of energy. When it came to singing and playing, he had a great deal of intensity. He had star quality. There was an Irish folk singer, Pat Clancy, having a drink at the bar. Pat exploded when he saw him, he said, "Well, what have we here?" We've been trying to answer that question for the last 25 years.'

Rock writer Elijah Wald: 'Robert Shelton's position is complicated. He was the *New York Times* folk music critic. He'd been blacklisted and he wrote for publications like *The Nation* which was a left-wing periodical. He latched onto Dylan as exemplifying all the things that he thought should be happening on the folk scene.'

In 1962 Shelton wrote the informative sleeve notes for his first album, *Bob Dylan*, but under the pseudonym of Stacey Williams. You can tell that Bob Dylan is playing him along – did he really have a residency at a striptease club in Central City, Colorado? Did he have a serious illness that gave him an insight into blues singing? Perhaps acknowledging this, Shelton referred to Bob Dylan's sense of humour and how he was influenced by Charlie Chaplin.

The liner note does acknowledge that Dylan was raised in Hibbing, Minnesota, but in a letter in 1969, Shelton confided, 'Dylan hates Hibbing and tries to pretend that he never was there and that it had nothing to do with him. He believes that he was born at the age of 19 in New York.'

Shelton picked up on Dylan's obsession with Woody Guthrie and in a subsequent letter, he noted, 'Woody Guthrie is so very, very central to an understanding of the Dylan of 1960–63 and even beyond.' Elsewhere he added, 'Drugs and women have a lot to do with the sort of person Dylan was from 1963 to 1965.'

As well as writing for the *New York Times*, Shelton wrote a biography of Josh White, *The Josh White Songbook*, published by Quadrangle in 1963. He was unhappy with the subtitle, *The Songs and Struggles of America's Greatest Folk Singer*, telling a rival publisher in 1970, 'Nothing I said or wrote indicated that he was America's greatest folk singer and Josh didn't think so either.' He said of the contents, 'The publisher wanted me to suppress the gutsy, grittier side of Josh White's life, although Josh didn't give a damn. He liked the romantic, swashbuckling story, despite his family and kids.'

In 1964 Shelton compiled and annotated a 4-LP collection, *Folk Box*, featuring many of the artists he had championed in the *New York Times*. Elektra Records paid him poorly, and in angry exchanges with its owner Jac Holzman, he wanted a better payment than $500 and virtually non-existent royalties for three months' work. In 1968, Shelton accused Holzman of 'falsifying royalties'. He wrote, 'Trying to get a redress of grievances from you is like the American people trying to get Lyndon Johnson to admit he may have made an error in Vietnam. They are greeted with smug arrogance and a set of pat answers that don't really get to the heart of the matter.'

Such tactics were hardly likely to work. Holzman denied the accusation and said, 'I have no intention of giving you the money you have requested. I will not buy off your paranoia.' He added, 'Don't destroy yourself with a hate that has no basis in fact and which only demeans you.'

Shelton supported Dylan when he went electric in 1965, writing in the *New York Times*: 'Facing a rude and immature audience, Bob Dylan gave a program Saturday night at the Forest Hills Music Festival in Queens in which he was a model of patient composure. Some 15,000 persons packed the tennis stadium for a program by the widely imitated and highly controversial young singer-guitarist-songwriter. Most of the audience's attitudes were concerned with Mr. Dylan's excursions into folk rock, a fusion of rock and roll with folk-based songwriting. The young audience's displeasure was manifested at the end of most of the numbers, by booing and shouts of "We want the old Dylan." The young star ploughed valiantly on, with the sort of coolness he has rarely displayed on stage.'

Shelton approved of his more imaginative songwriting. 'Desolation Row' was 'Another of Mr. Dylan's musical Rorschachs capable of widely varied interpretation, ranging freely from Cinderella to T.S. Eliot to "Einstein disguised as Robin Hood". It can best be characterized as a folk song of the absurd.'

That New Year's Eve, Dylan met Shelton at the Clique restaurant in Manhattan to discuss a biography. Dylan appreciated that there were going to be books about him so why not one by his friend and confidant, Robert Shelton? It would not be authorised by Dylan but he would cooperate and suggest those that Shelton could interview. Shelton offered it to the highly acclaimed Viking Books in New York. It was an easy sell. Dylan's unique and mercurial personality would be evaluated by a highly intelligent and informed journalist.

Dylan himself enjoyed writing and following the success of John Lennon's poetry book, *In His Own Write*, his manager Albert Grossman had secured a deal with Macmillan for a long experimental prose poem, which would be called *Tarantula*. Although finished in 1966, there was a long delay before publication and Shelton told his publisher that it would be no rival to his own book when it came out, 'Dylan took exception to Macmillan's editing changes and also had second thoughts about the book. Allen Ginsberg forecast that Establishment critics would pulverise it, and Dylan halted publication.'

In March 1966 Shelton accompanied Dylan on tour and was better placed than anyone to recognise what was happening. For Dylan, there was no direction home and he was confident of winning through. Shelton spoke to him at length and Dylan arranged for Shelton to talk to his parents, the only interview they ever gave together. When he returned from Hibbing, he wrote a short note to Doubleday: 'Fantastic. Unearthed all kinds of skeletons'. There was a downside: he hadn't anticipated that people might want money for their interviews; Dylan's former girlfriend Echo Helstrom cost him $200.

Shelton championed Peter, Paul and Mary, Joni Mitchell and Simon and Garfunkel and he wrote of the Mothers of Invention's first appearance on the East coast that they were 'the first pop group to successfully amalgamate rock'n'roll with the serious music of Stravinsky and others.' His reviews of Janis Ian and Janis Joplin paved the way for their recording contracts.

One of Shelton's close friends, the UK writer Liz Thomson says, 'Another of Shelton's discoveries was Janis Ian whom he propelled on Leonard Bernstein's TV show. 'At 17' is very personal. She is a fantastic, underrated writer. When she first sang it, she sang it with her eyes closed as it was so personal. It strikes a chord in teenage hearts around the world.'

Judy Collins says of him, 'Bob Shelton was so important, such a wonderful writer and such a wonderful man. He embraced this folk movement in such an impressive way and he knew how to get the music out there.'

Shelton sensed this himself as he reflected, 'I wrote a piece on Spanky and Our Gang which must have been worth thousands of dollars to them and months of time in developing the group.'

Although Shelton had Bob Dylan's tacit approval for a biography, he had to contend with Dylan's manager, Albert Grossman. Grossman hated anyone but himself making money out of Dylan. In February 1968 Shelton wrote to Viking: 'There is more resistance from Dylan and his management than I had ever anticipated. Dylan is evasive and totally unpredictable and will only go so far and no further. Grossman regards it as opportunism on my part. He threatens to sue and the book may become impossible to deliver.' A few months later, Shelton noted that Grossman has 'a virtual army of spies after me': that could be paranoia but on whose part?

Appalled at Nixon becoming President, the left-wing Shelton wanted to move to Europe, settling first in Galway and then Bromley. He thought he could complete his biography while away from the pressures of New York and all of its socialising. He described himself as 'a worn-out hulk' and he told a friend, 'Viking is bound to hear about this and I will be in a real jam with them.'

A literary agent and book packager, Peter Workman spoke to Viking on his behalf and there was talk of putting the book put up for auction, which could mean another publisher with a new advance.

Meanwhile, Shelton had to earn money. He thought he could freelance for UK publications as the occasions arose; he had a concept for a TV comedy series about the jug bands of the 1920s and for biopics about Woody Guthrie and Jimmie Rodgers.

In August 1968 a new deal was done with Doubleday. Shelton would deliver 150,000 words by 1 March 1970 for a $75,000 advance and 15% royalty, but he had to return his advance from Viking. They wanted a book that would outsell Hunter Davies' biography of the Beatles, but Shelton thought the comparison demeaning. 'There is no comparison,' said Shelton, 'This is absolutely no index of how our project will prosper. Dylan is much more stimulating to the imagination than the Beatles. The mystique of Bob Dylan grows daily and will last for centuries. I know this is a major bestseller that will be better, deeper, closer and of more literary-sociological value than *Papa Hemingway*. The advance orders for the biography of Tiny Tim are said to be 80,000. The Dylan book ought to do five times as well. Not that I don't like Mr. Tim, mind you, but really…'

Doubleday wanted the book to have a discography, but Shelton didn't compile it himself, which suggests his knowledge was not as comprehensive as might be thought. He agreed to pay Steven Goldberg, whom he didn't know, $750 for a discography, and told the publisher, 'He is not to be shown any of the manuscript I am working on unless I should meet him, here or in New York, and can decide that he is to be totally trusted. I am not paranoid. I know this is not Peter Maas' book on the Mafia.'

When Shelton spoke to Dylan in the UK for the Isle of Wight festival, he commented, 'Dylan spoke to me as though I was his psychiatrist.' He pitched his idea for a Woody Guthrie movie, presumably with Dylan as Guthrie but possibly he wanted Dylan on board as an investor. Either way 'Dylan was not impressed'.

Deadlines came and went on the Dylan biography. Shelton wrote in September 1971, 'I am within weeks of being absolutely dead, flat broke. I had no idea that the book would take so long.' Shelton could not hone the story down to 150,000 words. He suggested 'smaller type, less white space, narrower margins. The ones who want to read the book will still read it.' That may be true, but that surely is not the solution.

Shelton had married a 20-year-old singer and songwriter, Carol Crist, and he called himself her unofficial manager, mentor and adviser. He was impressed that the Major Minor label had two folk albums, both by the Dubliners, in the UK Top 10 and he told its owner, Phil Solomon, that it would be a perfect home for Carol. Shelton described her as 'a songwriting Julie Andrews' and said 'one song is easily as strong as 'Ode to Billie Joe'.' That song, 'I've Got Stairs to Climb', would be recorded with UK musicians.

As Shelton wanted £40 advance a week for Carol, he wrote, 'An important and new recording company like yours cannot fear it is unable to sell and promote enough recordings to cover such a small advance. Frankly, Philip, I do not think you have ever handled such a prodigious and multi-faceted performer as Carol Crist.' This to the man who discovered Van Morrison. According to Shelton, Solomon could earn $20,000 very quickly as Carol was perfect for the American market. 'Julie Felix would not dare appear in person in the United States and has prospered here only because there is a vacuum, a vacuum that Carol will fill and more so.' Felix was popular in the UK and there is no reason to suppose that they could not have done well in the US but Shelton was perhaps besotted by Crist and he was making these claims as a publicity agent.

Shelton soon fell out with Solomon, regarding him as devious as the folks he had left behind: 'We are not English or Irish and we had not any experience of your tricks. Therefore we could only assume you were an honest man. You have been rude in the extreme. You have built up the hopes of a talented young singer. Even if takes me 20 years, I will teach you a little bit about ethics.'

Shelton tried again, this time renaming Carol Crist as Suzanne Harris, He told Polydor: 'I feel the future for Miss Harris could be as great as Bob Dylan's although she is not at all the "mad poet" type. I stake my professional knowledge as an experienced music critic that she will be a major star within a year.'

Shelton initiated a bizarre PR stunt in which Suzanne busked her song on birth control, 'Go Out and Multiply (Are You Sure That's What God Said)', in St. Peter's Square in Rome. He told the press that she had been performing it for the Pope, which is hardly the same thing. It was released by Polydor in 1969 but Shelton called it 'a bad deal' and by then, he was 'church-mouse poor'. He wrote, 'By not getting behind this record, you jackasses, you are cowardly in refusing to take a chance. I haven't seen anyone churn out quality songs with such versatility, range of tone and meaningfulness since Bob Dylan.'

Suzanne appeared on the TV talent show *Opportunity Knocks!* and undertook a UK tour with Tex Ritter. In 1974 she recorded with the noted country publicist, Tony Byworth, but the proposed album for Westwood was never released. By 1977 Bob and Carol / Suzanne had split up and he sent her belongings to the States. It was a bitter fallout but he added, 'You did deserve then, and still deserve now, to be making a decent and secure living from your singing and songwriting.'

Trying to establish his wife as a star took time and the longer Shelton delayed his book, the more likely there would be rival volumes. Toby Thompson sent a 'guilt-ridden letter' to Shelton after interviewing Echo Helstrom and others. Thompson was about to give his research to Shelton but he changed his mind and wrote his own book, *Positively Main Street*, published in 1971.

There was the possibility of a book from Alan J. Weberman, a loose cannon who had been analysing Dylan's garbage and haranguing him in the street. According to Shelton, he was 'a freaked-out psychedelic of the worst sort and is driving Dylan up the wall.' Breathing with relief, Shelton said, 'After Dylan ran down Weberman in the *Rolling Stone* interview, I hear that no publisher is keen on taking a Weberman manuscript.'

Following the deal with Doubleday, Shelton had fallen out with Peter Workman and he considered Anthony Scaduto's *Bob Dylan: A Biography* (1972) 'should really be entitled *Peter Workman's Revenge*. No one has the data, the background or the insight to have written a better book on Dylan than me. This is a third-rate book from a fourth-rate publisher, so what mileage can I get?' The answer was, none at all if you don't finish it. Irrespective of how good or bad Thompson and Scaduto's books were, they were out there and adding to Shelton's woes.

In the press, even in his beloved *New York Times*, Scaduto gave the impression that he knew Dylan well. This incensed Shelton: 'Not the least of my joys is that Scaduto, having had one, or at the most, two, live encounters with Dylan, is now tabbed as "the Dylan authority". So much for the ethics of the New Journalism. The snideness in Scaduto's tone is clearly the sort of thing that has driven Dylan up the wall for years.'

Indeed, Shelton asked Dylan about this book and reported back to Doubleday. 'Dylan had told Scaduto that he was writing his own book and Scaduto said, "After I have spent 18 months on my biography, you are now going to ruin all my work." Dylan didn't like such a reaction from a total stranger who was acting in a proprietary manner towards his own life. When Dylan told me this, I said, "I know that there are parts of your life that nobody else could ever tell but you." That flattered him, apparently.'

But was Dylan really going to write his autobiography? 'Bob did say he was going to write about himself but he never used the words "autobiography" or "life story" to me. He said, "It won't be chronological – just some things that have happened to me that would show my feelings. I did get an insight into what Dylan's self-writing project might be. He freely answered most questions I asked about Hibbing, Minneapolis, New York and foreign tours. The only area where Dylan clammed up was when I enquired about a short trip he made in Greece with his road manager and friend, Victor Maymudes. Dylan gave me the name of the village – Vermilya – but he would not tell me what he saw or experienced there. He said, instead, "That's the sort of thing I want to keep for myself, for only me to write about. That is what I want to write about…those feelings." From all this I conclude that Dylan is planning a journal of fragments and episodic notations on things he's done and seen over the years. It could be like F. Scott Fitzgerald's *The Crack-Up*.'

These were shrewd observations: Dylan took his time but *Chronicles, Volume 1* (2004) was a series of unrelated incidents in his life. However, Shelton added, 'Another thought on this – since Dylan never announces what he is going to do, why announce that he is writing about himself to me and to Scaduto? Is it to keep us on our toes, to scare us into submission, to say that whatever we write, he will always have the last word? That could be an element in this strange game. It could even be a message to tell Joan Baez that he can write a better book than *Daybreak* in which she cruelly put him down. One thing is certain: he will never be a factually objective chronicler. He will still be the allusive / elusive poet. If he wasn't, it would mean unwrapping a mystique he has spent half his life in structuring.'

Bob Dylan was no longer with Albert Grossman, but Dylan wasn't going to talk about their working relationship, saying, 'Lots of people go out of their way to put Grossman down, but I wouldn't.'

Robert Shelton responded, 'Mary Travers said absolutely nothing good about Albert, except that he had good taste.'

Bob Dylan: 'Good taste? Albert Grossman has terrible taste and you can quote me on that. He has taken a beautiful old farmhouse and put a sophisticated French restaurant in it. He has put a recording studio in the woods of Mead Mountain.'

Shelton revealed: 'Dylan really hates Columbia for a long series of past injustices. They don't know how much Dylan has told me, and Dylan has not avoided calling them dishonest.'

In February 1974, Robert Shelton turned down an invitation from *Rolling Stone* to cover Bob Dylan's US tour. By now Shelton was drinking heavily and in no state to travel across America. He told Doubleday, 'I will finish the manuscript this year, come hell or high water, and you can publish it in 1975.' It was still on-going by January 1976 by which time his work had been 'butchered, revamped, brightened and tightened, but it will come in at 300,000 words.' This was a pre-PC world and corrected pages had to be retyped. Shelton did use typing services and he rented an electric typewriter for one lucky girl.

It got worse. Shelton grumbled in 1977: 'I have had to pay a small army of assistants. I was generous, perhaps a little too generous, with the dozens of kids who did the interviews and research for me, and now I have to be parsimonious on the picture budget. Even the bloody discography has cost me $2,000 with payments to Steven Goldberg, Roger Ford and Michael Gray. I have found at least six people who might have done it better than Goldberg.' No doubt wisely, Goldberg sent Shelton a note saying, 'I'm finished.'

Similar thoughts continued through 1978, his darkest year. 'This is a mess, a whole bloody mess. I am totally broke and deep in debt. I should never have paid so many people to assist me, but how can I expect people to help me for nothing?' Shelton heaped wholesome praise on the British Dylan scholar, Michael Gray. 'Michael Gray did solve several research problems for me, tying together a lot of loose ends which would have taken me weeks. Instead it has taken him weeks.'

Shelton was relatively happy with what he had drafted for Bob Dylan's life up to 1966 and he suggested to Doubleday that the biography should be published in two parts. That might have worked, but could there be any guarantee when Volume 2 would be ready? The answer was a flat no: a contract is a contract – we've been lenient with you, and now you finish the book. By way of assistance, they advanced another $5,000. He wanted more: 'I am exhausted, have a lack of money and few opportunities to freelance. I want $10,000 to finish what is 95% done. You'll get it back. I heard that the serial rights on Stephen Birmingham's sloppy book on Jackie Kennedy were sold for $84,000.'

Shelton added: 'I am stranded in Britain where the recession as it effects journalism is reaching catastrophic proportions. I am unable to find regular income. A British-style *Rolling Stone*, called *A M,* went into liquidation after three issues, owing me more than $1,000 for work done, not a penny of which I will see.'

Meanwhile, the book was becoming even more challenging as Dylan was writing, recording and performing songs that reflected his new beliefs as a born-again Christian. Shelton was surprised, 'He was one man who had been saying no to every establishment and every idea and concept for years. He suddenly turns around and accepts the biggest establishment of them all. It is a shock. I think what is difficult to absorb and accept from Dylan is that he is locked into a somewhat unforgiving, fundamentalist, fire and brimstone type of religion that does not seem to have a generosity or a warmth. It is a terrifying type of religious stance.'

Doubleday realised that they were getting nowhere with Shelton. They sold the book to the New English Library with the American rights going to Morrow in the US. Shelton told NEL that part of the problem 'was very poor editing from Doubleday, a shambles, a mess. They ask me what song Mr. Jones is in. I have lost seven years of my life due to their indifference. I wish I had been an academic like Tolstoy's biographer who took 30 years. Doubleday do not understand the work and want something akin to Albert Goldman on Presley.' The maximum wordage was now 230,000 and Shelton referred to it as 'abridged over troubled waters'.

Shelton had been communicating on and off with Dylan's office for years, asking questions and seeking contacts, and when Dylan saw the Scaduto book, he immediately granted Shelton the right to quote from his lyrics, subject to a suitable fee of course. His office wanted progress reports and by 1981, they too were fed up: 'Up to now this book has cost us inestimable time and energy. I now ask you to please do anything in your power to give us your final manuscript in a professional manner…with a clear list of quotes and proper copyright notices. The time spent from now on will be reflected in our fee for the use of those copyrights.' Another big expense was looming.

Rather like the protagonist in Samuel Beckett's play, *Krapp's Last Tape*, Shelton worked on his book, surrounded by his filing cabinets in a flat in Sydenham Hill. There was now pressure to get the book out fast. Shelton wrote, 'McGraw-Hill have signed someone called Bob Spitz to write a major biography of Bob Dylan. All I know of McGraw-Hill is that they published the nefarious Elvis biography by Albert Goldman, scarcely a contribution towards good taste, restraint or ethics in rock history.'

Amazingly, it happened. Twenty years in the making, *No Direction Home* was published in 1986. It sold 60,000 in the UK in its first year and did equally well around the world. The reviews were very good but reviewers pointed out that the final part was rushed. The last 15 years of Dylan's career were compressed into just 80 of the 500 pages. Some noted that he assessed Dylan as elusive. 'That's how he is,' said Shelton. 'Some critics assume that he has only been elusive to me which would mean I hadn't done my job. They miss the central point that I was making. I made it with subtlety but I made it repeatedly. The place where Dylan reveals himself most is in his music and in his lyrics so in a way everybody can get to know Bob Dylan. I was trying to present a context in which you can understand the music against the life or see it in the milieu of his life and a larger setting.'

Shelton met up with Dylan at a press conference in London for his film, *Hearts of Fire*. Dylan was amused that Shelton was 'going on tour' to promote his book. It was the last time they would meet: 'He had seen the book and he was cordial. If he hadn't been able to live with the book and not generally been pleased with it, I would have heard about it, loudly and clearly. I don't think it would have gone to the courts and I never felt that was an active danger, but publishers like to be careful with a mercurial subject like Dylan. He autographed a copy of the American edition for my discographer. He wouldn't have done that if he was against it and I understand privately that he likes it.'

He concluded, 'Writing this book has been a series of balancing acts for me. To what degree does being a biographer clash with that of being a friend? We have come to expect huge revelations in show business biographies. My book is perhaps not the thunder and lightning that people want. I wanted to draw a portrait of an intense and historically important man and I wanted to do it in a way that he could live with it and I could live with it. We had only one basic agreement about any matter that he felt should be soft-pedalled and that was about his wife and his children. He did not want them in the foreground. He felt this way while the marriage was good and later when the marriage went to pieces. I respected that and that is an area that I did not go into. He opened a lot of doors with other people so I can respect that.'

Robert Shelton said of his papers, 'My files on Dylan will stagger even the most earnest Dylanologist. I am a prodigious hoarder. I kept all my memorabilia and I had done tapes and they are in the archive in my house. Now I have some time I will unscramble them. I would like them to be in some place where they can be useful.'

In one letter, Shelton referred to being in the room, quite by chance, as Dylan taught Robbie Robertson 'Sad-Eyed Lady of the Lowlands'. He turned on his tape recorder so maybe that is amongst the numerous delights. I know that he spoke to Peter, Paul and Mary for 12 hours and I hope he recorded at least some of his interviews with Bob Dylan.

In 2011 a 25th anniversary edition of *No Direction Home* was published by Omnibus Press. Elizabeth Thomson and Patrick Humphries saw his many drafts and substantially improved the published book, restoring key passages and adding an unpublished Prelude. Liz Thomson says, 'Bob Shelton could be overwrought and use metaphors that went too far but there is a resonance about his prose which was often lost when it was cut. I think you get much more of a sense of Shelton now and it was hard to do as it was like a sacred text to me. I hope it is the book that he would have liked to have had published in 1978.'

Robert Shelton deserves to be remembered. I hope that Liverpool University will obtain the funding which will enable them to catalogue Shelton's papers. They can then be available to the public. The ideal time for the launch and perhaps a related exhibition of

Dylan in Liverpool and a conference would be in 2021, the year of Dylan's 80th birthday.

It seems to me that Robert Shelton missed a big story. His letters are so insightful and so colourful that there could be a wonderful book in that correspondence, suitably annotated, but maybe that's why he kept everything. I am certain that whoever compiled the book would find exactly the same problem as Shelton did with his biography of Dylan: how can you get all this into 150,000 words?

Judy Collins: 'The music was intersecting with the social relevance of what was happening and changing things, whether it was the music that was sung in Washington Square Park or the freedom riders going to Mississippi or the songs against the war and the marches that we did. There were record labels like Elektra and people like Robert Shelton who wrote about this and so it became public and the marketing of this wonderful amazing phenomenon actually happened. It wouldn't have happened if there weren't people who knew how to get the music out there.'

II. So Much Older Then: December 1962–January 1963

Around the turn of the last century, there were several dedicated individuals who were determined to collect folk songs from the older members of the UK population lest they died with them. The best-known collector was Cecil Sharp and today there is a large repository of their findings at Cecil Sharp House in London. By the 1950s many young performers would be researching the collection and putting songs into their repertoire. The collection is housed in the Vaughan Williams Memorial Library, so-called because the classical composer Ralph Vaughan Williams used many folk themes in his work as did Percy Grainger ('English Country Garden') and Aaron Copland in America.

After the Second World War, life took some time to get back to normal in the UK. There was a growing popularity for folk clubs, social as well as musical gatherings which took place weekly in the back or upstairs rooms of pubs with cheap entrance fees. Each club would have its resident singers and musicians who would perform a couple of songs each week: there would be space for floor singers, that is, anyone who wanted to perform a song or two and when the budget allowed, a guest group or performer. The better performers eked out a living by playing around the country, perhaps to audiences of 70 at a time. Martin Carthy has been doing precisely that for nearly 60 years and he owes his success as much to British transport as to the folk clubs themselves, because he does not drive and has performed all over the UK. In all that time, he has only missed two gigs and I suspect that folk performers with cars have missed a whole lot more. I have seen him about 15 times and it has rarely been in a theatre.

In the 1960s the Spinners were leading entertainers with their Christmas specials rivalling Morecambe and Wise in audience ratings, yet they maintained their weekly club in Liverpool. As well as connecting with their roots, it enabled them to test new material. One of the Spinners, Cliff Hall, came from the Caribbean and brought West Indian songs to their repertoire. The rise in World Music in the 1980s had its groundings in the folk clubs where songs from immigrants have been welcomed.

Playwright Willy Russell grew up around folk clubs: 'Sometimes in the folk club firmament you would have people who would want to give you some background to the song. It's like the way poets set up poems at readings. As long as they could do it with the right kind of informative patter, it was fine. A lot of folk clubs were run by teachers and they could become predominantly teacherly. If they spent half an hour telling you about the meaning and the derivation of 'Sir Patrick Spens' before they got round to singing it, the song was dead. My overriding memory of those folk clubs is of a massive amount of choral singing. You could learn harmony singing while sitting in an audience.'

Throughout the 1950s and 1960s, the folk song evenings would be defiantly acoustic. The emphasis was on traditional material but by the early 1960s, some performers were singing their own songs. Traditionalists were suspicious while newer clubs encouraged new material. The music would be a cappella or acoustic – usually guitars – but banjos, melodeons, accordions and violins were heard. The bass guitar came in during the late 1960s and by the 1970s, it was common for performers to have electric instruments.

The songs, new and old, were often about working people and the regular members were usually left wing and Labour supporters. Some would be communists but there was no hounding of them in the UK. From my own experience, I can say that the communists in the community were looked on as a little strange, but no more than that. At their core, the communists were against capitalism, and as America was the shining embodiment of that, it was the Devil. Hence, they thought that almost everything that came out of America was vilified.

The communists were very much against the Americanisation of Great Britain and they disliked American comic books, American TV shows, chewing gum, bubblegum, and worst of all, rock'n'roll. The Communist Party of Great Britain published *The American Threat to British Culture* in 1952 which referred to the 'violence and tawdriness of Imperial-American films'. Maybe they would have had my sympathy but denouncing rock'n'roll was never going to work for me.

So although communists were a concern to British society, there were no witch-hunts. Paul Robeson came here when he was hounded in the US and made a significant impression on UK culture. Eric Bibb who is Robeson's godson and wrote a good song with a clunky title, 'Put on Your Robe, Son', says, 'I recently played Porthcawl and there is a theatre there with a lobby full of photographs and text about Paul Robeson's time in Wales. This was like a holiday town for the miners and he gave them a voice. It was great to see him being celebrated so far from his home.'

The driving forces in the London folk scene were two communists – the folk song collector Bert Lloyd and the performer Ewan MacColl. You will have seen the photos of MacColl singing a cappella with his hand cupped over his left ear. The concept of the Singers Clubs stemmed from MacColl and Lloyd: it started in London but had a network of 1,500 clubs that abided by draconian rules. MacColl said, 'We had a whole generation who were becoming quasi-Americans and I felt that this was absolutely monstrous.' No prizes for guessing how he viewed rock'n'roll.

The Singers Clubs had inflexible rules. If the singer was English then the songs he performed had to come from the English tradition. The idea was that people had to be educated into their own tradition, but it was nonsensical and unworkable. Did MacColl expect potential floor singers to turn up with their birth certificates? MacColl, incidentally, was not all that open and honest – he had been born Jimmie Miller and strictly speaking he should have been restricted to Scottish songs, but who would have dared to tell him?

Willy Russell: 'If Dylan had not come to England and been to the Singers Club and seen Bert Lloyd and Ewan MacColl and been very taken by Martin Carthy, he would not have become the Bob Dylan we know. The effect of English folk song on his work is so marked. It's only hinted at in the first album but there are so many references on the second.' Willy is correct but over half that second album had been recorded before Dylan came to London.

As Dylan intoned in 'I Shall Be Free Number 10', 'It's something I learned over in England'. Elijah Wald: 'Dylan emerges from the month he spent in England with people like Martin Carthy and shifts from being a blues-oriented musician to writing songs that appealed to Joan Baez and Judy Collins who were already singing English ballads.'

Ewan MacColl's first wife was the explosive theatre director, Joan Littlewood, who was to revolutionise London theatre with her down-to-earth portrayals of working-class life. MacColl had his own background in theatre and in 1950 he wrote a play about the industrial north, *Landscape with Chimneys*: he got round a set change by writing a song, an affectionate look at Salford, 'Dirty Old Town'.

Now 40, Alan Lomax fled the communist witch-hunt in America and came to the UK, living in Highgate and striking up a relationship with a woman half his age, the singer Shirley Collins. He was an affable Texan with shaggy dark hair and he shared his home with his ex-wife and her partner. Alan's main concern was his hearing: it was deteriorating in one ear and he was worried about the other. His pet peeve was white boys playing the blues.

Once in the UK, Alan worked with Ewan MacColl on radio and TV programmes. In March 1956 Alan introduced him to Pete Seeger's half-sister Peggy, who was to become his working partner and wife. Peggy Seeger recalls, 'Those were the days when I more or less did anything I wanted and let the devil take the consequences. I hitchhiked and went to places on the spur of the moment. I'll go to Denmark with you, sure. That's how I came to England. There was part in a TV play, *Dark of the Moon*, on Granada and they needed a female who sang and played the banjo. They didn't know that I couldn't act, so I just got on a boat and came over and then I met Ewan MacColl.' The play, which was directed by Philip Saville and based around the folk song 'Barbara Allen', was screened on 5 April 1956.

In 1957 Ewan MacColl and Peggy Seeger worked with the radio producer, Charles Parker, on a series of 60-minute documentaries under the blanket title of *Radio Ballads*. It was a brilliant concept; they would tell the story of working men through their own words and through folk songs, both new and old, and the programme on fishermen, *Singing the Fishing*, included MacColl's much-loved 'Shoals of Herring'. Around the time that Dylan was in London, they were working on their sixth radio ballad, *On the Edge*, which was broadcast in February 1963. It looked at schoolchildren's aspirations and although it wasn't fully in MacColl's comfort zone, it worked very well.

Peggy Seeger: 'The *Radio Ballads* were seminal in their time and they still are because not even the later *Radio Ballads* have done what the original eight did. It was a serendipitous mixture of the songs, the instrumentation, the *actualité* and the sound effects. They had to be mixed like a recipe and the recipe is hard to follow unless you have someone who really understood theatre and that was Ewan. He was the driving force but we all knew when we had it right.'

Because of Musicians' Union restrictions, there had not been many American performers in the UK for 20 years, but now the rules were relaxed. Chris Barber was instrumental in presenting classic blues and gospel performers such as Sister Rosetta Tharpe, Big Bill Broonzy and Sonny Terry and Brownie McGhee.

Ramblin' Jack Elliott: 'I was planning to sing my way around the world with my first wife who was a movie actress, and she wanted to see the world. We got to England and we met some people in the music world and they invited me to a concert where Mick Mulligan was playing, plus a skiffle group and Chris Barber and they put me on as a guest. As a result, I got jobs in coffee houses and skiffle and blues clubs. I met Alexis Korner and Cyril Davies who ran upstairs sessions every Thursday night at the Roundhouse pub, and I used to sing there.' Ramblin' Jack did turn up for an appearance at the Bluecoat Chambers in Liverpool with his leg in plaster. He told the audience he had broken it at the rodeo but in fact, he had fallen off a skateboard. Skateboards were not known in the UK in the early 60s so that would have been equally exotic to an audience.

Lonnie Donegan played banjo with Chris Barber's jazz band and Chris formed a small group within the band to perform skiffle sets – acoustic blues songs with a cheerful down-home feel. In 1956 'Rock Island Line', attributed to Lonnie Donegan, became an international hit. Skiffle was only a brief phenomenon largely based around Donegan's success, but it led to teenagers forming acoustic groups and later, about 1958, going electric, the prime example being the transformation of the Quarrymen into the Beatles.

Skiffle was getting folk music to the masses but not in the way that MacColl and Lloyd had hoped: the British skifflers were all singing American songs! Woody Guthrie and Leadbelly songs were perfect for their singalong repertoires. In 1957 Lonnie Donegan topped the charts with a frenzied 'Gamblin' Man' and in 1958 he had a Top 10 hit with 'The Grand Coulee Dam'. In both cases the songwriting credit reads 'Guthrie / Donegan' and I asked Lonnie in the 1980s how he could justify that. 'I take your point but I made effective changes. I rewrote lyrics and changed the chords to the choruses. I think I'm entitled to the royalties. The Richmond Organisation, which is Essex Music here, was thrilled when I recorded 'Rock Island Line'. Ten per cent of what I made from them was put into trust for Martha Ledbetter and for Woody's children. I paid for Arlo's schooling.' When I met Arlo Guthrie, he wasn't impressed by Lonnie's assertion.

Billy Bragg: 'The guitar represented a bridge to the future. Unlike the New Lost City Ramblers or Bob Dylan who was finding a way forward through Harry Smith and those recordings, British kids were trying to break out from the post-war rationing. They were saying to the politicians, "Get on with it, hurry up, let's get into the 60s!"'

Folk songs became known through marches organised by the Campaign for Nuclear Disarmament. The Glaswegian folksinger, Alex Campbell would sing a song he'd learnt from an Odetta album, 'Freedom'.

In October 1962 the British director Philip Saville was in New York to put together the music for a TV play with the folklorist Alan Lomax. He went to West Fourth Street to see the English poet, W.H. Auden, and by chance he saw Bob Dylan at the club, Tony Pastor's Place. He was mesmerised and asked if he would be interested in coming to the UK for a TV drama, his next project which was a play for the BBC, *Madhouse on Castle Street*. He would play Bobby the Hobo, although the original script had no such character. As Dylan referred him to Albert Grossman, he wouldn't be cheap. Bob Dylan was contracted for 500 guineas (£525) plus his flight and accommodation at the grandiose Mayfair Hotel.

BBC expenses were no problem back then: a month or two earlier, the BBC had flown in the equally unknown Gordon Lightfoot from Canada to appear on *The Country and Western Show*. When he got back home, he recorded a song he had heard in England – 'Gossip Calypso', a whimsical hit for Bernard Cribbins. If these expenses had been revealed, would the newspapers have questioned why the BBC was spending all this money on unknown singers? Dylan and Lightfoot must have wondered too.

Although Columbia had reservations about Bob Dylan's first album, it had nevertheless been issued in the UK, although it had done little business. Mick Groves of the Liverpool group, the Spinners: 'When I was in New York I went on a riverboat shuffle with a lot of musicians and Bob Dylan was there. His manager said to me, "Hi, Pete Seeger tells me you are for England. Would you like to have a meal with Bobby and me as we would like to know how things are going in England with Bobby?" I went to O. Henry's steak house with them and I had to tell them that, no, there wasn't a big thing going for Bob Dylan at that time.'

Bob Dylan flew over in December while Lonnie Donegan was going in the opposite direction for a residency at the Village Gate in New York. Dylan was met by Pauline Boty who was known as the Wimbledon Bardot: she was at the Royal College of Art and was one of the founders of British Pop Art. She took him to the lavish Mayfair Hotel. He felt out of place in jeans and cowboy boots and soon moved out. As if to upset the protocol, he played his guitar in the lobby as though he were on a street corner.

Pete Seeger had told Bob that Anthea Joseph had been excellent at promoting his concert at the Royal Albert Hall. On the next day, he went to the Troubadour folk club in Old Brompton Road and Anthea recognised him from the cover of *Sing Out!* She told him he could come in for nothing if he sang. The audience was unsure about how to take his voice but many of them loved it. Dylan was introduced to the blues guitarist Alexis Korner.

Madhouse on Castle Street was a play written by the white Jamaican playwright Evan Jones. It was a bleak, kitchen sink drama about the fate of a lodger, who has locked himself in his room. (Shades of Paul Simon's 'A Most Peculiar Man'?) Dylan dutifully went to the read-through on December 19 and decided it was not for him. He could learn the lyrics of hundreds of songs but learning lines, even only a few, didn't interest him. He felt uncomfortable and he told Philip Saville, 'Why can't I just be a singer?' They reached a compromise. Evan Jones would split the role of Lennie into two. David Warner, then with the Royal Shakespeare Company, would say the words, leaving Bob with just one line, 'Well I don't know. I'll have to go home and think about it.' He would sing 'Blowin' in the Wind', The Cuckoo', which was on the Harry Smith anthology, 'Hang Me, O Hang Me' and a border song, 'Ballad of a Gliding Swan' with an updated verse about the Thalidomide scandal: 'The doctor gave Sally a sad surprise, A Thalidomide baby with no eyes.'

Saville realised that Dylan was a loose cannon: if he moved from the Mayfair Hotel, would he lose track of him? As a result, he put Dylan up at his own house in Hampstead for the next three nights. His wife was the playwright Jane Arden. Dylan admired her anarchism but not her feminism.

Bob enjoyed wandering around London and was taken with the trendy fashions emerging from Carnaby Street. Saville found him a hotel that was more to his liking, the Cumberland Hotel by Marble Arch.

On 21 December, Bob Dylan appeared at the King and Queen in Foley Street by Goodge Street station and met Martin Carthy who was part of the Thameside Four. He sang both 'Ballad of Hollis Brown' and 'Talkin' John Birch Paranoid Blues', an interesting choice as it was such an American subject.

On 22 December Dylan performed at the Singers Club Christmas Party in the Pindar of Wakefield, now the Water Rats theatre, at 328 Gray's Inn Road. It was named after an old folk tune, 'The Jolly Pindar of Wakefield'. There is a plaque to commemorate the first gig by Oasis but the one for Dylan, put in place in 2013, is not on display. There is however a photo of Dylan performing on a dais with Ewan MacColl and Bert Lloyd watching. MacColl is scowling but Lloyd seems happy enough. Years later, Dylan met Kirsty MacColl and said, 'Your daddy didn't like me at all.' He was right. MacColl was once asked if he had disliked Dylan from the start. 'Yes,' he replied, 'tenth rate drivel.' So long before he went electric, Dylan was regarded with suspicion for reworking and sometimes rewriting old folk songs. Dylan had to work hard to be heard as MacColl ran his club on voice and instruments alone and hence, Dylan had to perform without a microphone.

Karl Dallas, the folk specialist for *Melody Maker*, recalled, 'The first time I heard Bob Dylan perform in the Singers Club, I thought he was awful. He sang "Hey, Hey, Woody Guthrie I wrote you a song", and everybody said, "Big deal. Who cares?"' Later, Dylan asked Karl Dallas, 'Are you for me or against me?' to which Dallas replied, 'Frankly, I don't know you.' We'll take that as a no then.

Liz Thomson: 'The folk musicians had always been holier than thou. Ewan MacColl was outraged and he held very much to the puritanical, finger-in-the-ear scene of singing songs about northern travellers and the like. They felt that Dylan wasn't being true to the movement. But what is folk music? Folk music should be something that means something and it should be sung with some kind of mass sentiment – and in that sense you can say that Bob Dylan has always been a folk singer, but the roughness and down-home quality that characterises his first album soon vanished. Maybe he saw folk music as a bandwagon on which to jump and when he found success, he was no longer interested in being part of a movement.'

Because of a technicians' strike, the recording of *Madhouse on Castle Street* was delayed and Dylan was asked to stay until the new year. It is a shame that we have never had Bob's take on British culture: he was surely impressed by the iconoclasm of *Private Eye* and *That Was the Week That Was*. We know that he went to Peter Cook's *Establishment* night club but he didn't perform. Sometimes he asked strangers, 'Where's Christine Keeler?', but surely his satire was sharper than that.

Ramblin' Jack Elliott had recommended Bob to Max Jones of the *Melody Maker*. He went there hoping to catch him, probably not knowing that Karl Dallas had already seen him. Mr. Jones was not there but then it was December 28. He did however give an arrogant interview to the British magazine, *Scene*.

The next day he was at the Troubadour and met Bob Davenport, almost certainly hearing him sing 'Nottamun Town', an old spelling for Nottingham. He went to the *Ballads and Blues* club at the Roundhouse in Wardour Street, accompanied by Martin Carthy but Dylan was ordered to leave for smoking pot.

The first day of filming for *Madhouse* was on December 30. Dylan recorded four songs plus some instrumental music and had a photo session.

Dylan sang in 1963 at the King and Queen with Martin Carthy and was best received in this club. Dylan was singing 'Auld Lang Syne' with the rest of them, or at least what he knew of it.

Nigel Denver was not the most popular folk performer. He was a bitter Scottish nationalist quick to deliver his opinions. When Dylan saw him perform an unaccompanied song at the King and Queen, he shouted out, 'What is this shit?' He was told to keep quiet and he said, 'I don't have to keep quiet. I'm Bob Dylan.' He left the club which was just as well as Denver was a tough little guy. However, despite heckling, Dylan was definitely listening to what Denver was doing – see the next chapter.

Rory and Alex McEwen were the sons of the wealthy politician Sir John McEwen. In 1956 they had been in New York and met Leadbelly's widow, Martha Ledbetter. She allowed Rory to play his 12-string guitar and she encouraged them to perform his songs. They performed club dates in America, recorded an album of Scottish ballads for Folkways and even had a short appearance on *The Ed Sullivan Show*.

In the UK, they were best known for appearing on the TV news programme, *Tonight*. In 1962 they met Richard Fariña and Carolyn Hester when they appeared at the same event in Scotland. The Fariñas were living in Paris but Richard was coming back early in 1963 to discuss his novel with a publisher. Called *Been Down So Long, It Looks Like Up To Me*, it was the story of Gnossos Pappadopoulis, and the book was influenced by Beat writing and was full of sex and drugs. Rory gave Richard a front door key to their opulent townhouse in Tregunter Road, Chelsea and said the family would be away over Christmas. Bad move.

Richard Fariña had asked Eric Von Schmidt to illustrate his text. He told him that he had a meeting with Weidenfeld and Nicolson early in January and Eric should come along.

While in Paris, Richard had met an American lawyer, Tom Costner. Richard wrote a sleeve note for Jim Connor and Richard Lockmiller, a duo he represented, and Costner arranged a £250 budget for an album to be made by Fariña and Von Schmidt in London. Were they interested?

Eric was divorced and feeling lost, so he thought 'Why not?' He flew into London on New Year's Eve and met up with Richard who had arrived from Paris.

Richard knew Dylan was in London but didn't know where. He left some messages and Dylan arrived at the townhouse. At first he ignored Richard and spoke to Eric. Dylan writes about pretending not to know someone in 'I Don't Believe You': it sounds unreasonable behaviour but it's typical, and indeed Albert Grossman was employing this tactic long before Dylan.

Here two huge egos were meeting – Richard Fariña and Bob Dylan – and Bob had to spray his territory. At first he didn't want to know about Fariña's novel but some drinks and pot changed all that. Dylan played a new song, 'Don't Think Twice, It's All Right' and Richard said it was great. Richard performed Buddy Holly's 'Oh Boy!' on which he played his dulcimer like a guitar.

Rory McEwen returned to find them stoned and the house in a mess. He ordered them to leave. Richard and Eric booked into a nearby hotel and then went to the Troubadour. Ewan MacColl probably wouldn't have approved but Richard could pretend he was Irish when he performed in England.

On January 2 Dylan attended the Surbiton and Kingston Folk Club where the Strawberry Hill Boys featuring Dave Cousins were performing.

Rory McEwen did meet up with Dylan again as he had promised to introduce him to the poet and writer Robert Graves. Dylan had read at least some of his study of myths, *The White Goddess*, but the meeting did not go well. Graves complained about his rudeness.

Madhouse was completed on January 4 and the next day Dylan flew to Rome, not knowing that Suze had returned to America. He met up with Albert Grossman who was accompanying Odetta on tour. They went to a nightclub where Bob attempted to dance and he performed at the Folkstudio Club. He was working on 'Girl from the North Country'. When he returned to London, he went to Odetta's show at the Prince Charles Theatre on January 10.

On January 12, Martin Carthy was joined on stage by Bob Dylan, Eric Von Schmidt, Richard Fariña and another American folkie, Ethan Signer. By now, they were mocking the city in 'The London Waltz' to which they all contributed. Dylan said that he would like to be a part of their album.

Making sure Carthy was listening, Dylan said, 'Hey, here's 'Scarborough Fair' and proceeded to sing 'Girl from the North Country'. Carthy recalled, 'He was laughing and he knew what he was doing, and I was delighted. It was lovely and a new song.' Who though was the girl from the north country? Was it Bonny? Was it Echo? Was it someone else or, as seems more likely, a composite picture?

Roy Harper: 'When I did 'North Country', I put 'Traditional' on it. We expected a libel suit and we got one but it was dropped because they realised that we had sufficient ground to stand on. Dylan was nicking tunes, especially ones from England and Ireland. 'Masters Of War' is 'Nottamun Town'. A lot of people knew where he was getting the stuff and they didn't think he should be getting the acclaim he was getting: it was sour grapes from us, I guess. I think he did it because he wanted to identify with the folkies. He wanted to be in with the folk crowd in New York, who knew the tunes anyway. The one I regret him stealing is 'Lord Franklin' which is a really beautiful, really wonderful English song but it turned out (Imitates Dylan) "While riding on a train going west." Oh dear.'

At 9pm on 13 January 1963, *Madhouse on Castle Street* was screened in the *Sunday Night Play* spot.

Doug Dobell was a specialist record seller in London. He had Dobells Folk Music Shop at 75 Charing Cross Road and Dobells Jazz Record Shop at 77, which had a basement for second-hand records but it could also be used for making recordings. He had another folk shop at 10 Rathbone Place.

Dobell had his 77 label for jazz records (his main interest) and Folklore for folk. His latest idea was to record Richard Fariña and Eric Von Schmidt and they recruited Ethan Signer, who was from Massachusetts and had been captivated when he heard a programme about English folk music on Harvard University's radio station. Ethan secured a scholarship to Cambridge University and he was eager to explore the scene. He could play mandolin, fiddle and guitar. Tom Costner came to the session with Dylan and a crate of Guinness. Dylan was used to Bud and light lager. Dylan took a swig of Guinness and shouted, 'My god, what's this?' tipping the contents onto the floor, which annoyed Doug. The drinking was so hard that Gordon's Gin was to get a credit on the sleeve.

Although 'The London Waltz' was included, the music was mostly familiar folk material with Bob adding backing vocals and playing harmonica. He would use his Blind Boy Grunt alias. Doug Dobell thought that Dylan sounded terrible and was unsure about using him. Look at the sleeve which was designed by Eric Von Schmidt – note the alternating heavy lettering, displaying his last name as 'Shit'.

Later that night, the musicians went to the Troubadour and saw an Israeli singer, Judy Silver. 'Now there's something you don't see every day,' said Dylan, 'a Jewish folksinger.' Richard Fariña sang 'Cocaine', which they had just recorded, and Dylan, high as a kite, asked 'Are we underwater?' before singing 'Don't Think Twice, It's All Right'. Nigel Denver was in the audience and if he barracked Dylan, as he had every right too, Dylan would have ignored it.

On January 15, there was a second session at Dobell's and then a jam at Bunjies coffee house. The next day he and Eric flew back to New York.

Gil Turner had recorded some songs with Dylan at his home. Dylan had changed 'The Leaving of Liverpool' to 'Farewell'. Although he did not record it, a typewritten lyric for 'Liverpool Gal' was up for auction in 1991. He had probably written it in London. If we take the lyric as being true, Dylan had met up with a Liverpool girl in London or else he was fantasising about one, and why not?

Aside from Bob Dylan's involvement, *Madhouse on Castle Street* would be forgotten today. The BBC wiped the tapes and the Corporation shouldn't have clear outs as valuable archive material is lost. Even without Dylan, it involved several people who went on to greater things. David Warner made an impact in the film *Straw Dogs* and also played the title role in *Morgan, A Suitable Case for Treatment*. Evan Jones wrote the screenplays for *King and Country, Modesty Blaise* and *Funeral in Berlin*. Philip Saville directed the groundbreaking TV series, *Boys from the Blackstuff*.

In 2005, a TV documentary was made about *Madhouse on Castle Street* called *Bob Dylan in the Madhouse* but they had little to draw upon, a sound recording of a few extracts. Michael Gray comments, 'The TV programme was very disappointing, a waste of time, and 50% of it was taken up with London having bad weather. My wife Sara said, "What would they have done if it had been an ordinary winter?"'

There was a loophole in the law which allowed Doug Dobell to press up to 100 copies of an album without paying purchase tax. Even though there were only 99 copies, it took Doug Dobell a year to sell them and he wouldn't have recouped the costs.

It was not good news for Richard's novel either. Weidenfeld and Nicolson rejected Richard's book on the grounds of being too expensive to print.

The real legacy is the effect that London and in particular Martin Carthy had on Bob Dylan's songwriting. 'Bob Dylan's Dream' was 'Lord Franklin'. Martin Carthy recalls when he first heard 'A Hard Rain's A-Gonna Fall', 'I thought he was doing 'Lord Randall' at first but then we were sent somewhere else completely.' Dylan's interest in English and Celtic folk music drew others to the source and possibly to Ewan MacColl, but Dylan's verdict on him, 'Ewan MacColl. He's the worst, I think.'

The Beatles' first Parlophone single, 'Love Me Do', was in the charts and the British beat explosion was about to take place. So many of the musicians, including the Beatles, had come out of the skiffle craze, and at the end of 1962, there was one last blast from Lonnie Donegan with Leadbelly's 'Pick a Bale of Cotton'. There was a terrific feel to it: it was folk music becoming rock, although Lonnie would have never said that. This was the changing of the guard and Bob Dylan was there.

CHAPTER 5

A Lone Guitar and a Point of View

'I always thought a lone balladeer could blow an entire army off the stage if he knew what he was doing.'
Bob Dylan, 1985

I. The Cruel War

When we hear the phrase 'protest singer', we immediately think of Bob Dylan. True, the phrase became popular during his acoustic peak of 1963, but there were many protest singers and protest songs before him, several contemporary performers who followed his lead, and many more since. Indeed, I have come across the very phrase 'protest songs' in a newspaper article from 1953. Dylan himself has never acknowledged the term. The most he will admit is to writing 'finger-pointing songs', but, unlike the songs themselves, that phrase never caught on.

In 1992 Buffy Sainte-Marie told me, 'Protest songs go back to who-knows-when, way back in British folk music. There were broadsides and little treatises and songs carried around by the balladeers. In those days, you could get your head chopped off for singing the wrong song in the wrong place about the wrong guy. Nowadays your record is just put to rest and isn't played.' Buffy said that over 25 years ago and the world has moved on again: now anybody can put a protest song on the internet: nobody may hear it but it has the potential to be heard by everyone for free.

On the whole, protest songs are a sign of a democracy although there have been examples in oppressive regimes where protesting against the government can cost someone his or his freedom or even life. Think of Victor Jara who was executed in Chile in 1973 or more recently, Pussy Riot who criticised Vladimir Putin. Bob Dylan was never under threat of legal action or imprisonment for any of his songs, although he was accused of defamation of character when he wrote about robbery and murder in 'Hurricane'.

Dylan's theme, if there is one, has to be pacifism or non-violence, which is why the songs resounded so strongly with Joan Baez and her Quaker upbringing. It was nothing new: the spiritual 'Down by the Riverside' goes back to the American Civil War, maybe even further back as the singer wants to lay down his sword and shield. The much-repeated refrain is that the singer doesn't want to study war no more, an unusual use of the word 'study'. When it is sung today, I don't think anyone pays attention to its content.

It is a different matter for another gospel song with an identical message: 'We shall live in peace, We shall overcome one day.' 'We Shall Overcome' owes its popularity to Pete Seeger, who gave me this vivid example of the folk process at work: 'A black preacher in Philadelphia around 1903 wrote a song, "I'll overcome someday, I'll overcome someday. If in my heart, I do not yield, I'll overcome someday." The song became well-known in black churches but Afro-American people carry a great tradition which says that a song is just a basis for improvising and down in the Deep South, they started changing it. It got a new tune and the words changed slightly. In 1926, tobacco workers in Charleston, Carolina went out on strike and some pickets were walking up and down, singing old hymns and changing this one still further. It was now "We'll get higher wages, we'll get higher pay, We will overcome someday." They taught this song to a white friend, a union organiser, and he taught it to me and I taught it to others up north and I added some new verses. I taught it to Guy Carawan who took it back down South and taught it to the students who were sitting in the restaurants and demanding a cup of coffee, no matter the colour of their skin. They'd be taken to jail and in jail, they would do a lot of singing. In two or three months this song went across the southern states and everybody realised it could be the theme song for the civil rights movement.'

As a 45rpm single, 'We Shall Overcome' was never more than a minor US success for Joan Baez (Number 90, 1963) but you can't overstate its importance. It was quoted by President Johnson when he was announcing civil rights legislation.

Nearly all the protest songs in the western world are left wing. I've got three CD collections of protest songs and all three have bright red covers. The Industrial Workers of the World (known as the Wobblies) was formed in 1905 to encourage workers to join unions. In 1909 they published the *Little Red Song Book*, which featured new words to traditional hymns.

Pete Seeger said, no doubt humorously, that all songs are political songs and even a lullaby is a protest song in that you want to effect change: you want the baby to be quiet and go to sleep. We have seen from Chapter 3 that Woody Guthrie wrote protest songs: his whole perspective was political and maybe the political content of each song is only a matter of degree.

Woody had much to complain about because the working men and their families in the Dust Bowl had been treated shamefully, but his songs did not have much political effect. His most successful campaign was to encourage workers to join the unions.

Hundreds of blues songs described the conditions of the downtrodden, but few of them asked the Government to do something about it. The performers knew that wasn't going to happen but the songs helped to share experiences. It is often overlooked that blues songs are more than gritty slices of reality: there is humour and pathos and plenty of X-rated lyrics.

The fallout from the Wall Street Crash was clearly displayed in Bing Crosby's poignant 'Brother, Can You Spare a Dime' (1932), written by Yip Harburg and Jay Gorney. Many years later, Johnny Cash put some childhood experiences in 'Five Foot High and Rising' (1959): when I first heard this song I thought, 'Can this really be true?' but of course it was.

In 1939 Abel Meeropol, an English teacher in the Bronx, was haunted by a photograph he saw of a lynching down South. He wrote a brilliant poem, 'Strange Fruit', which didn't refer to the lynching itself but to the smell of burning flesh and the bloodied 'fruit' hanging from the trees. After it was published in a teachers' magazine, he set it to music. He wrote a haunting melody and a club owner passed it to the jazz singer Billie Holiday. She injected it with raw emotion and the song, after its première in Café Society in Greenwich Village, brought her both fame and notoriety.

Meeropol wrote the song under the pseudonym, Lewis Allan, and he was asked officially whether the Communist Party had paid him to write it. He was a communist but the feelings had come from his heart. He used the pseudonym after his two children Lewis and Allan had been stillborn. When the married couple Julius and Ethel Rosenberg were executed for spying, Meeropol brought up their children as his own.

'Strange Fruit' was also sung by Josh White, and his son recalls the intensity with which he sang it. 'My father witnessed what that song was like because for nine years, he had led blind, black street musicians for a living. When he was only eight years old, he was sleeping in a field with Blind Man Arnold and he was awakened by Blind Man putting his hands over his mouth to keep him quiet. Some white people had found two black men and had hanged them. They were swinging from the trees and throughout the night they had a bonfire and were drinking. Every now and then somebody would come up with a poker and burn the bodies and my father knew that they dare not move. If they had made a noise, there would have been four people hanging from that tree. They stayed there very quietly until the sun came up and the lynching party scattered. They then knew it was safe to go, so my father saw first-hand that strange fruit hanging from the tree and it affected him whenever he sang the song. He was reliving his experiences.'

Some say that protest songs are not the purpose of music and the issues should be left to politicians. In 1953, Liverpool-born author and singer, John Greenway wrote that 'Protest songs are unpleasant and disturbing', a clear indication of favouring the *status quo*.

Going back to the turn of the nineteenth century in Britain, there were many music hall songs which commented satirically on the issues of the day. Similarly, Gilbert and Sullivan's comic operas contained political satire.

There is a strong tradition of socially aware songs in musical theatre, both on Broadway and in the West End. Oscar Hammerstein's plea for racial tolerance, 'Carefully Taught', in *South Pacific* (1949) is a brilliant song, which actually says the opposite of what Hammerstein thought in order to make the point.

Stephen Sondheim was mentored by Hammerstein and you can see that same approach in 'America'. His satire on New York policing, 'Gee Officer Krupke!' could never have had radioplay in its own right but as part of a Broadway musical, *West Side Story* (1957), it was permissible.

Noël Coward was writing about his gayness in 'Mad about the Boy' (1932) and so was Lorenz Hart in 'My Funny Valentine' (1937) but neither wanted that to be exposed.

In 1943 Noël Coward was controversial when he wrote the very witty 'Don't Let's Be Beastly to the Germans', which was banned by the BBC as the Corporation felt that listeners might not realise he was being sarcastic.

The French and Belgian writers were commentating on life as they saw it, often with a radical outlook. Georges Brassens criticised the judicial system in 'Le Gorille' (1952) and wrote about his revolutionary views in 'La Mauvaise Réputation' (also 1952). Boris Vain released 'Le Déserteur' (1954): the soldier refuses to fight and 'if you come looking for me, I will be unarmed and you can shoot'. Definitely not a record to be played during the Indochina war. Léo Ferré's 'Paris Canaille (Dirty Paris)' is no travelogue as he is attacking the pimps who make their money from exploiting young girls. Jacques Brel mocked the middle class in *Les Bourgeois* (1962), later reworked by Tom Robinson as 'Yuppie Scum'.

Tennessee Ernie Ford's US and UK Number 1, 'Sixteen Tons' (1955) was a new song by Merle Travis but it revealed the unfair practices before the coalminers had a union. The mine owners owned the stores and as the miners were paid in tokens, they were cheated at every turn.

Taken as a whole, rock'n'roll can be seen as protest music as the music was generally made by teenagers for teenagers. Chuck Berry was telling it like it was but the teenager in 'Too Much Monkey Business' (1956) is more frustrated than angry and the song was Dylan's template for 'Subterranean Homesick Blues'. Eddie Cochran's 'Summertime Blues' (1958) can be seen as a protest song and contains a telling observation when he complains to a Congressman: 'I'd like to help you, son, but you're too young to vote.' Although the lyric is not so astute, Helen Shapiro's 'Don't Treat Me Like a Child' (1961) is in the same territory. You could argue that Danny and the Juniors 'Rock and Roll Is Here to Stay' was at least a call to arms if not a protest song.

We are now moving up to Bob Dylan but he didn't suddenly burst onto the scene with protest songs. Pete Seeger had done the groundwork. Pete Seeger wrote many songs on his own but he liked to find an old song, perhaps from another country like 'Wimoweh' or 'Guantanamera', and then adapt it for his own purposes. He was brilliant at this. 'Guantanamera', for example, was used at the time of the Cuban Missile Crisis. A very good example is 'Where Have All the Flowers Gone'. Pete Seeger told me, 'I wrote down three lines that I read in a book, *And Quiet Flows the Don* by Mikhail Sholokhov, the Soviet author. He describes the Cossacks galloping off to join the Czar's army, singing an old Ukrainian song. Well, I tried to locate the song but I didn't try hard enough. Bert Lloyd did some research and sent the original to me and these three lines were from the middle of a long, long song – "Where are the flowers, the girls have plucked them. Where are the girls, they've all taken husbands. Where are the men, they're all in the army." I was in a plane riding over Ohio on my way to sing for some college students and I pulled out these lines. You know how it is when you're sleepy: your subconscious goes to work and the song was put together in 20 minutes. The line "long time passing" had been with me for several years. I had wanted to use it in a song but hadn't figured how. I just knew it was a good line. The three extra verses were added by kids at a summer camp, actually the same camp where I learnt 'Guantanamera'. They were kidding around, "Where have all the counsellors gone? Broken curfew everyone", and so on.'

Seeger's words and melody were first published in *Sing Out!* in 1955 and the additional verses in 1960 turned it into a round robin where it cleverly came back to the opening verse. When Seeger recorded the song, produced as it happens by John Hammond, it did not sell beyond the folk market. Seeger felt that Hammond did not have as much interest in folk as he had for jazz.

Then the song was 'covered' by the Kingston Trio. I put 'covered' in inverted commas as they believed it was traditional and could claim authorship. Seeger's publisher told them otherwise and their record reached Number 21 on the US chart. It was hardly 'Easy Listening Folk' although it was branded as such. Just listen to John Stewart's wavering voice: records hardly come with more of an emotional punch.

Peter, Paul and Mary included the song on their début album, which topped the US charts for several weeks in 1962. The intensity was increased when Marlene Dietrich recorded three versions – English, French and German. She sang it in French at a UNICEF concert and then went to Israel and sang it as a German-born actress singing in German. This might have seemed extreme provocation but it was a conciliatory gesture with a song of peace and it worked fine.

Pete's half-sister, Peggy Seeger, says, 'Popular songs tend to be of the same length, about three minutes long, but folk songs can be very short and very concise or can be long, long,

long, and work just as well. Length is no way to judge a song. 'Where Have All the Flowers Gone' works because of the simplicity of its words and Pete's excellent tune which is very easy to sing along to. The fact that it is a circular song where you go back to the beginning makes it an intriguing thought.'

Happy Traum: 'Pete's songs had simplicity but they had depth. That is the beauty of them. 'Turn! Turn! Turn!' is a fabulous song and Pete took the words from the Bible. Then there's 'Where Have All the Flowers Gone' and 'If I Had a Hammer' but there are many songs of his that are not that well-known but are tremendously moving and beautiful. 'Sailing Down that Golden River' is about the Hudson River where he lived most of his life and he fought to clean it up. Arlo grew up with Pete Seeger and sang a lot of his songs really, really well.'

I don't think Dylan has ever commented on Pete Seeger's voice or banjo playing: the performance style was not for him. Seeger was a generous sort, encouraging new talent and indeed, wanting a new generation of committed folk singers. The irony was that most of those singers would grow away from him.

So it can be seen that before Bob Dylan got going with his protest songs, Seeger was making headway, one way or another, with 'The Lion Sleeps Tonight', 'Wimoweh', 'Where Have All the Flowers Gone', 'Guantanamera', 'If I Had a Hammer' and 'We Shall Overcome': many a full-time songwriter would have wished for a CV as strong as that.

In 1960 Ed McCurdy, a Greenwich Village folk singer, wrote 'Last Night I Had the Strangest Dream', a dream in which all the world leaders were committed to peace. The Weavers recorded it in 1960 and the best-known recording (and the best) is by the Kingston Trio. McCurdy was known in the US for his cigarette commercials and starting in 1956 he made three albums of bawdy Elizabethan songs.

The building of the Berlin wall threw up a love ballad about lovers trapped on either side, 'West of the Wall' by Toni Fisher, a US Top 40 hit in 1962. It was written by Wayne Shanklin, the composer of 'Jezebel' and 'The Big Hurt'. It didn't make sense if you didn't know about the Berlin Wall.

The Crystals had a US top 20 hit with 'Uptown' (1962), which like 'West of the Wall', showed a couple apart, this time separated by social class. Songwriter Cynthia Weil: 'I was into writing these sociological lyrics before Dylan came along. We thought that we could change the world if we wrote a song that everybody could sing and it said the right thing. 'Uptown' was one of those songs, I wanted to tell everybody what it was like and I wanted to change the world.'

In December 1961 the first American soldier was killed in Vietnam, which was to prompt a wave of political songwriting. Pete Seeger and Joan Baez were seen as figureheads for the peace movement, which wanted to bring the American soldiers home. Dylan did not specifically refer to Vietnam in his songs and he teased one journalist by saying, 'How do you know I'm not for the war?'

Singer / songwriter Eric Andersen: 'The confluence of things came from so many directions and reached a critical mass between the Ban the Bomb movement, the Civil Rights movement and the nascent war in Vietnam. Things were cooking up in Southeast Asia and people in the Village were sensitive to that. It was left wing politics and also had the influence of the Beat Generation. A lot of Bob's early songs were probably because he had read *Howl*. The Beats liberated language.'

US music writer Robert Santelli: 'We had two important events which didn't impact on the UK. The first was the Civil Rights movement, which was a very bloody stain on American history but it ended in a great triumph, at least from a legislative viewpoint. Then you have the socially conscious songwriting from the Vietnam era. There were protests and the songs were about being Americans. A lot of American kids wanted to stay in college as long as they possibly could so that they would not be called up.'

Jon Savage: 'There were four dissolving agents in the 60s – the threat of nuclear war, the Vietnam war, civil rights and drugs. Civil rights made black people a major force in American life and was a template for other liberation movements: the women's movement and the gay movement too. David Bowie comes along five years after this and the climate was right for him.'

There was a wave of protest songs emanating from Greenwich Village. Buffy Sainte-Marie. 'I saw what a lot of the songwriters were doing. They would get the *New York Times* in the morning and they would look for stuff to write songs about. It was a very commercial approach to writing protest songs but it can work.'

Is there anything wrong in that approach? Tom Paxton: 'Whenever I talk about songwriting, I tell people to pick up a newspaper and find something in there that moves them in any way – anger, disgust or hilarity – and then write a song from the point of view of a participant in that event or an eyewitness. It has the great benefit of getting us out of our boring lives and into the world where things are going on.'

Tom Paxton alone wrote over 100 songs in 18 months in the early 60s. 'I should have written three times as many but really I write a lot of songs and most of them are unrecorded because they are bad songs. I write about five songs to get one good one. Now I write songs the same way that porcupines make love – very carefully.'

Buffy Sainte-Marie: 'Some of the things that the early protest writers were writing about were the obvious headlines and one thing I have always loved about Bob – and it's a way that I work too – is that he likes to give people songs that are informative about things that they don't know about. I am not writing a song about the bad leadership of Donald Trump because everybody knows that and there would be no point to it. I am writing songs about the way that I look at things because people haven't been looking at them in the way that I have.'

Indeed, you had to be sure that people heard your song correctly. Buffy Sainte-Marie had written 'Universal Soldier' in 1961 but it found fame when Donovan recorded it in 1965. Buffy Sainte-Marie: 'Donovan heard it when I came over to do a concert at the Royal Festival Hall. He recorded it but he got the words wrong. He didn't quite understand what I was saying. The last verse is "He's the universal soldier and he really is to blame, His orders come from far away no more, They come from him and you and me, And brothers, can't you see, this is not the way we put an end to war." Those are the correct words. Donovan sang "They come from here and there and you and me". I tried after that to improve my diction. (Laughs)'

Liz Thomson: 'I was ten years old playing a guitar and listening to records by Judy Collins and Joan Baez. My parents didn't mind hearing them but were much less keen on Bob Dylan. I can see why but he is a fantastic interpreter of his own work and even occasionally of other people's work.'

In 1965 Eric Andersen wrote 'Thirsty Boots', which was recorded by Judy Collins. 'There was a protest writer called Gil Turner who worked in Mississippi organising voter registration and things, and he wrote 'Carry It On'. I met him for the first time in the

Kettle of Fish, an old bar in McDougal Street where Phil Ochs, Bob Dylan, David Blue and myself would hang out. He had almost been killed, been thrown in jail and he had been marching. I was looking at him in his denim jeans and dirty old coat and he was relaxing. I looked at his old boots, which were scuffed with knife scars and had the heels falling off. He was drinking beer and I thought, "Boy, I bet his old boots must be thirsty too." Even when people are struggling or working hard, you have got to stop for refreshment and have a beer or whatever.'

Brill Building had broken the mould by writing teenage songs. Then Gerry Goffin was amazed by Bob Dylan and what he wrote in his songs. He heard 'Ballad of a Thin Man' and felt 'like a dwarf'. Although Brill Building was only a few blocks from Greenwich Village, there was little connection.

A Brill Building couple Barry Mann and Cynthia Weil wrote 'Home of the Brave', a US hit about nonconformity for Jody Miller. Barry Mann: 'That was a controversial song for Jody Miller and for Bonnie and the Treasures, which sounded like a Phil Spector record. They were chart records that I would have liked to go higher. It wasn't as deep as a Dylan song and it was adolescent. Dylan's stuff was deep on so many levels. He was fantastic and he changed society. He was the ultimate reflection of what was going on in the 60s.'

In 1965 the teen idol Bobby Vinton made the US Top 40 with 'What Colour Is a Man' – 'If you colour him red, someone may steal his land' and 'If you colour him black, he may never be free'.

Ralph McTell wrote about what he saw on the streets of Paris but he changed it to the UK with 'Streets of London', recorded acoustically on his second album in 1969 but a hit in an electric version in 1974. 'A lot of people are under a misapprehension about that song. I wouldn't purposefully set out to write a song about homelessness. The most important part of that song for me is the chorus, "Please don't tell me that you are down and oppressed and alienated because there's this forgotten war hero who walks the street." The central part of the song is the character I am addressing, but the world picked up on the four characters who illustrated my argument. It is not a song about homelessness: it is a song about alienation.'

Another Mann and Weil song with a substantial social message is 'We Gotta Get out of This Place', a hit for the Newcastle group, the Animals in 1965. It had been written about New York, but in 1974 the former Animal, Alan Price made the Top 10 by writing about his hometown in 'Jarrow Song'. BBC presenter Stuart Maconie: 'The Jarrow March was very much part of the popular culture of the north. My grandma used to say that the Jarrow marchers were brave and wonderful men, and their story had passed into folklore. The march was very much a part of Alan Price's background as he had gone to Jarrow Grammar School. The song is a lot more radical than the actual march. The marchers were very compliant – they went cap in hand to London and their attitude was "Please Mr. Baldwin, can we have some work?" In the song, the wife says, "Well, if they don't give you anything, you can, with my blessing, burn them down." The marchers were nothing like as radical as that and the song is much more hard-line. Alan Price at first identifies with the marchers by saying he is Geordie McIntyre and then he becomes Little Alan Price. He is saying, "I am a Jarrow lad, I identify with the marchers and the struggle still goes on." That continuity is really clever and it shows that this is not just heritage.'

Bob Dylan was the one who brought protest songs to the fore in a classic era where there was so much to write about: civil rights, nuclear arms race, the Vietnam war and social issues such as the generation gap. What made Dylan so special is that he did two albums largely of protest songs and so many other songwriters picked up on this.

It was not always clear what Bob was protesting against. 'Blowin' in the Wind' is said to be a protest song, but what is Bob Dylan advocating? Probably the end of war but that is idealistic. Some writers such as Phil Ochs would have said it much more strongly but that was a perfect entrée for him into the public market.

The west coast songwriter, Phil Sloan, wrote and performed as P.F. Sloan. He had been writing lightweight surfing and hot rod songs when the music publisher, Lou Adler, gave him a Bob Dylan album in 1965 and told him to come up with something similar. That night he wrote 'Eve of Destruction', which looked at the horrors of the day rather like a man with a placard saying 'The end of the world is nigh'.

The confrontational song was given to the Turtles. I asked Howard Kaplan of the Turtles why they turned it down. 'Come on, man, you would have turned it down too. That song would have been the kiss of death for the Turtles and we knew that. We were young kids from middle class families in California and we had nothing to protest about and if we had sung that song, the authorities might have carted us off to Vietnam. It was such a strong statement that we would never have been able to follow it up with anything that wasn't political. When Phil Sloan sang the song to us backstage on Sunset Boulevard, we knew we were listening to a Number 1 record but we also knew that it would be the only hit record that person would ever have. Once you put out something that inflammatory, there was no way you would ever be able to have a successful follow-up. I don't think Barry McGuire had another hit record so we were right.'

'Eve of Destruction' was a US Number 1 for Barry McGuire and many now think it was a Bob Dylan song. The former Cavern DJ Bob Wooler said, 'Talking of conmen, what about Bob Dylan? I can think of no better example of the Emperor's new clothes, but there are many people whose opinion I respect who think he is tremendous. I did like some of the protest records, but I thought Barry McGuire's 'Eve of Destruction' was better than any of his.'

Barry McGuire, who now sings 'Eve of Destruction' with verses about climate change, told me, 'That song was banned in England and America. I know it was played on your pirate ships but I think it would have broken through anyway because it was a heart cry for a whole generation. It wasn't a protest: it was holding a mirror to society. It is saying, 'Hey, let's look at ourselves.' That is not protesting, but people didn't like that they saw and so they wanted to break that mirror. No one expected it to do what it did, but it knocked the Beatles off Number 1 in America and John Lennon was a little upset with me for that (laughs) He told a reporter that 'Eve of Destruction' was a very negative song and that I had recorded it for the money. He was wrong. When I'm in the studio, the last thing I'm thinking is whether it's going to be a hit. All I think about is whether I like the song and can I do it justice. When I sang 'Eve of Destruction', I knew that we had a terminal case of greed and moral decay. We needed to wake up and smell the flowers. We are now 50 years later and look what is happening between the East and the West and the Christians and the Muslims and the world is just crazy. We are on a collision course with oblivion and I feel 'Eve of Destruction' song is more valid today than it was 50 years ago.'

Jonathan King wrote his response to 'Eve of Destruction' with 'It's Good News Week', a Top 10 single recorded by British servicemen, Hedgehoppers Anonymous. It ended with a nuclear explosion, a sound effect also used in the Hollies' 'Too Many People' and Tim Buckley's 'No Man Can Find the War'.

There were many songs about Vietnam, sometimes told with humour. Phil Ochs' 'Draft Dodger Rag' is a very funny song which was covered by Pete Seeger. Tom Paxton wrote about wounded soldiers in 'Jimmy Newman', a song which packed an emotional punch in its final line. Although Mel Tillis said he had written 'Ruby, Don't Take Your Love to Town' about the Korean War, the song wasn't copyrighted until 1966 so I suspect he was trying to avoid a ban on US radio. It told of the plight of a wounded veteran in a surprisingly complex story for a three-minute song. Even more harrowing was John Prine's 'Sam Stone' in which the soldier returns home a junkie: 'There's a hole in daddy's arm where the money goes.'

Mike Harding: 'I thought Woody Guthrie was a great writer and a great man of the people, but I've never been into Bob Dylan and he's never meant a light to me. I don't really believe in him. I don't even think that he actually believes in what he is doing and he has never convinced me. I would rather hear John Prine and Leon Redbone. 'Sam Stone' is a wonderful song about someone coming back from Vietnam as a heroin addict. I love Harry Chapin's 'WOLD', which shows how good Americans are at using their own musical history in their songs.'

Unexpectedly a song supporting the troops, 'Ballad of the Green Berets' by S/Sgt. Barry Sadler was a US Number 1 in 1966 and his companion album topped the LP charts. His combat days were over when he was hit with a poisoned spear in the jungle and he had to operate on himself. He was shot whilst sitting in a taxi in 1984 and never fully recovered, dying in 1989.

Pete Seeger wrote about the horrors of fighting in the jungle in 'Waist Deep in the Big Muddy': 'I saw some photographs of American soldiers slogging through the rivers and swamps down there in Vietnam, and I thought of the line, "Waist deep in the big muddy, the big fool says to push on." I've sung enough songs to know that was a good line but it took me three weeks to get the song written. I am not a quick songwriter. How I envy Bob Dylan, Woody Guthrie and Phil Ochs as they could dash off songs in a hurry.'

Famous for the Fish Cheer at Woodstock, Country Joe McDonald came from an activist family – indeed, he was named after Stalin and he fell comfortably into the role of a left-wing singer and songwriter. He used humour to make his point in 'I-Feel-Like-I'm-Fixin'-to-Die Rag': 'It is poking fun at the top brass like *HMS Pinafore* and because of my socialist background, I could blame Wall Street as I knew that war was good for the economy and for the war industry. So I wrote the song in that sarcastic style with a happy little melody. The count-in posed the radical question of the era, "What the hell are we fighting for?" English people compare the song with *The Charge of the Light Brigade*. "Ours not to reason why, Ours but to do and die." Until that time, that was the attitude that a soldier had to have. If you questioned the authority in times of war, you could get imprisoned or shot.'

But did the song do any good? Did it help to end Vietnam? 'Yes, I have met hundreds of people who have told me that it saved them from joining the military, and many veterans have told me that it saved them from going completely mad. It became a rallying cry, an anthem, and with the cheer, it was a very powerful psychological operation for the anti-war movement. It was a very bonding experience. Many families had fights over the song and then to combine it at Woodstock with the cheer really separated us from the World War II generation. It was the beginning of the New Age, the first Global Age.'

Pete Seeger: 'I look upon Vietnam as an endlessly important one for the American people. It ended in a victory for the American people. It might have been a defeat for the

Pentagon and a defeat for Richard Nixon but it was not a defeat for the American people. It was victory to get out of Vietnam. There are only a minority of Americans who think that we should have fought harder, stayed and dropped the bomb.'

The US government refused to classify Vietnam as a war: it was just a conflict. Buffy Sainte-Marie: 'For me it got very pointed when I was on a flight that was going through San Francisco and stops in the middle of the night and you can't get on another flight until the morning. In the dead of night, there came a stretcher and several wheelchairs with returning veterans who were all bandaged and their faces were shot up. I was talking to the people who were with them and I felt overcome with the need not only to speak out against the war but the fact that we were being continually lied to by politicians who thought that if we knew the truth, the public might panic. It is the duplicity that goes on in most governments.'

In recent years there has been a new development with servicemen returning home and speaking about their experiences. Mary Gauthier's album *Rifles and Rosary Beads* (2017) is a superb but disturbing example.

Many comedians have shown social concern through laughter – Lenny Bruce, Mort Sahl, Jackie Mason and Dick Gregory. Putting wit into protest songs can work effectively, the masters being Tom Lehrer and Randy Newman. Phil Ochs, who was usually more intense than Bob Dylan, wrote a very witty song about American politics, 'Love Me I'm A Liberal'. Tom Paxton says, 'I haven't the slightest qualms about making my songs humorous. There's more than one way to skin a cat.'

Tom Lehrer made his famed albums in the 1950s but preferred to continue as a professor of mathematics at Harvard University. He sang about the drug culture, advertising and nuclear war ('We'll All Go Together When We Go'). His return to public life in *That was the Year That Was* (1965) was as a full-blown topical songwriter including songs of civil rights ('National Brotherhood week'), ecological disasters ('Pollution), Catholicism ('The Vatican Rag') and again, nuclear war ('Who's Next').

Randy Newman started life as a jobbing songwriter ('Just One Smile', 'Simon Smith and the Amazing Dancing Bear') but he soon developed a low-key performing persona, writing about civil rights ('Rednecks'), nuclear war (Let's Drop the Big One'), victimisation ('Davy the Fat Boy') and the plight of the working man ('Mr. President').

In 1978 Neil Innes of the Bonzo Dog Band parodied protest songs in 'Protest Song'. 'Protest songs are a genre and if it's not Dylan, there is a whole bag of other people who do it. It always seemed odd that people who were rolling in money were writing songs about being poor and oppressed. I did it on an Amnesty International show and it was released following that. Poor Donovan was on the show, doing something with a mouth organ, and he came into the dressing room and said, "My friends say you're sending me up." I said, "No, I'm not," but that is the kind of thing that can happen.'

Then there was Sam Cooke with 'A Change is Gonna Come', Curtis Mayfield (both solo and with the Impressions) and Marvin Gaye, all writing about civil rights from the black perspective.

But overall did it work? Did protest songs make a difference? The fact that we still need protest songs today may be evidence that they didn't. Buffy Sainte-Marie disagrees: 'We are never going to get rid of greed forever. There are always individual issues like corruption. That doesn't mean that protest and our temporary solutions to greed and oppression and war count for nothing. It doesn't mean that our actions were in vain. We did help to stop the Vietnam War and we have been powerful in counterbalancing those people who use the military for their own greedy purposes.'

Undoubtedly, Live Aid and USA for Africa work well and they highlighted a humanitarian issue. The whole world became aware of the problems, but there was controversy over the distribution of the funds.

Joe Boyd: 'I got to be a very good friend of Phil Ochs. He was very talented and he made some great records in the early days but he had a complicated and intense personality and ultimately it led to his very sad end. Very few people have realised that his singing style is always totally derived from the country singer Webb Pierce. If you listen to a Webb Pierce record and then a Phil Ochs one, you will find that the mannerisms are almost identical.'

Tom Russell: 'Bob Dylan moved on and Phil Ochs and all the others didn't. Phil Ochs thought he was supposed to do that all the time. Dylan did it for five minutes and then he moved on to love songs and everything else, but the world of folk music never recovered. Pete Seeger never recovered from the revolution at Newport. I applaud Dylan because he has been growing since day one and if the folkies don't understand him, that's not his problem. He is a huge writer with a very deep repertoire and we have precious few people like that.'

Joan Baez: 'Lots of people have written about the world's problems but you have to do more than that. You have to capture people's ears so that they can sing with it. There are a lot of very clever songs that are oriented to what's going on around us but you have to find someone with genius so that people really want to hear the music.'

Michael Gray: 'I try to be fair to everyone but in some ways Joan Baez is a complete pain, full of self-regarding virtues. Dylan is very polite to almost everyone in *Chronicles*, but he complains about her song 'To Bobby'. There is nothing attractive about someone waving a political flag and telling someone else off because they are not on the march. 'Diamonds and Rust' on the other hand is a beautiful love song.'

The Listener magazine asked in 1969: 'Can Bob Dylan have forgotten entirely the horrors that gave such a fine edge to his protest music?' That question is equally valid 50 years later.

John Prine: 'Why should Bob Dylan have to write any more protest songs? The ones he has written are going to stand for a long time.'

Michael Gray: 'He lost interest in it because a lot of people took it up in a fatuous way. He was excited by electric music, he was excited by the Beatles and he was suffocated by the worthiness of the milieu around Greenwich Village, all that leftier-than-thou people telling him what he ought to think and what he ought to say and he got into trouble for that early on. Look at the Tom Paine speech.'

Buffy Sainte-Marie said in 2018: 'I will always be a Bob Dylan fan. He is just brilliant – always has been, always will be – but I don't know where his new songs are today. Are people deaf and blind? How can they not be writing songs today when they have the ability to do so?'

II. So Much Older Then: 1963–1964

It is wrong to assume that Bob Dylan's first album was buried by Columbia. It didn't sell well but it was nominated for a Grammy and issued in the UK. The Grammys were in their infancy and no one had realised that it was nonsensical to have albums competing against singles in some categories including Best Folk Recording. What's more, Bob was in there twice as the nominations included *The Midnight Special* album by Harry Belafonte on which he played.

Also nominated were *Presenting the New Christy Minstrels*, *Joan Baez in Concert* and the Kingston Trio's *Something Special*. Remarkably productive, that was the Trio's 13th album in four years and it was something special in that the tracks were orchestrated. Again, nobody cried 'Judas!' and it was a Top 10 album in the US. These five albums were joined by two singles: the TV theme from *The Beverly Hillbillies*, 'The Ballad of Jed Clampett' by the bluegrass duo, Flatt and Scruggs, and Peter, Paul and Mary's hit single, 'If I Had a Hammer'. Peter, Paul and Mary won the Grammy although they had to wait until May 1963 for the results. The Grammy for best country recording went to a folkie in Nashville, Burl Ives with 'Funny Way of Laughin'', a nondescript choice in a strong year: I'd have backed Marty Robbins' 'Devil Woman'.

After his time in London, Bob Dylan returned to Greenwich Village with renewed confidence and several new songs. He was testing them out at Gerde's Folk City and he made a home tape with Happy Traum at Gil Turner's apartment.

Bob's main task was to finalise the second album. Dylan had recorded enough songs before he left for London and he approved a 13-track listing. The title was *The Freewheelin' Bob Dylan*, thereby implying he was free of restrictions and rules; devil-may-care you might say.

Side 1 – Blowin' in the Wind / Rocks and Gravel / Let Me Die in My Footsteps / Down the Highway / Bob Dylan's Blues / A Hard Rain's A-Gonna Fall

Side 2 – Don't Think Twice, It's All Right / Ramblin' Gamblin' Willie / Oxford Town / Corrina Corrina / Talkin' John Birch Paranoid Blues / Honey, Just Allow Me One More Chance / I Shall Be Free

Nothing wrong with that listing at all except that it is not *The Freewheelin' Bob Dylan* as we all know it. Some promotional copies were pressed and are now collectors' items. In error, some copies of the real *Freewheelin'* album were released in Canada with the original track listing on the cover except the second track was called 'Solid Road'. 'Solid Road' is a phrase in the song, 'Rocks and Gravel', another song he had recorded in 1962.

In March 1963 a version of 'Blowin' in the Wind' by the Chad Mitchell Trio was included on their *In Action* album. If they had released it as a single, they might have stolen Peter, Paul and Mary's thunder.

There was a fear of nuclear war and this is behind much of Dylan's writing. Dylan commented, 'I'm only 21 years old and I know that there have been too many wars. You people over 21 should know better.'

Izzy Young was requesting contributions for a poetry book on the Third World War, and although the book was never completed, Bob Dylan gave him 'Go Away You Bomb': 'I want that bomb, I want it strapped to my belt buckle. Then I walk into the White House and say "Dig yourselves".'

Dylan was singing 'Masters of War' at every opportunity. He played a young man who questioned being at war, presumably Vietnam though never articulated. 'There's one thing I know and I'm younger than you, That even Jesus would never forgive what you do.'

Martin Simpson: '"Masters of War" is a song that still needs to be sung. I hadn't heard it for a long time and then I was wandering around a Greek supermarket in London and it came over on the tannoy, following some Tamla-Motown. It killed me. I'd heard it as a child many times but to hear in that context was amazing. I thought that I had to sing this. It's a frightening and very, very brilliant song.'

Dylan said that it was not an anti-war song and he is right as it is about people profiteering from war, particularly arms dealers. It could be twinned with Bertolt Brecht's play *Mother Courage*.

On 12 April 1963, Dylan made his first appearance at the New York Town Hall on West 43rd Street in front of an audience of 900, which was two-thirds full, so the buzz was spreading. Dylan was superb despite an argument with Suze just before the show. Harold Leventhal, who promoted the concert and managed Pete Seeger, hosted a party afterwards.

This show was professionally recorded although not released at the time. It is just Bob Dylan, his voice, guitar and harmonica for two hours. Dylan had only been professional for a year and yet here he is with a complete show of his own material. He is so confident and often so shrewd and funny: '"I am the Lord thy God." That's a great commandment so long as it is not said by the wrong people.' The songs are not yet known and yet there is tumultuous applause for 'With God on Our Side'. Dylan says that he hasn't got a set list: 'I don't believe in lists'. Maybe he should have done: he overlooked 'Girl from the North Country'.

There are three songs from the first album including 'Highway 51 Blues' which he didn't write, five songs from *Freewheelin'*, which had yet to be released, three songs from *The Times They Are A-Changin'*, which wouldn't come out for a year, and 12 songs he didn't release at the time.

Dylan referred to Big Joe Williams and 'a 1930s ragtime tune I just wrote this week', 'All Over You', which showed that ragtime had much in common with British music hall. It's a typical Dylan theme in that he is the one who is moving on, rather than his girlfriend. Some listeners are uncomfortable with the treatment of women in his songs and this is typical, 'If I had to do it all over again, I'd do it all over you.' Yes, well…You can see how this song will morph into 'If You Gotta Go, Go Now'.

Dylan included 'With God on Our Side' and as an encore he read his seven-minute poem 'Last Thoughts on Woody Guthrie', an odd title as Woody wasn't dead yet. His programme note was another poem, 'My Life in a Stolen Moment', which was the usual partly fact and partly fiction. Dylan's misspellings and deliberately poor grammar showed the influence of the Beat writers and the rebellious tone of his poems can be more revealing than his songs.

We have the only professional recording of 'Who Killed Davey Moore'. Three weeks earlier, Davey Moore had died following a fight with Sugar Ramos after his neck had hit the ropes. He gave an interview before collapsing into a coma and being pronounced dead. As Dylan loved boxing, his song is not an attack on the sport but it is about everyone denying guilt and is a clever twist on 'Who Killed Cock Robin'.

Singer and songwriter Jackie DeShannon: 'I cherish my history as I was often in the right place at the right time. Randy Newman and I were at Metric Music at the same time and I met Bruce Springsteen when his *Greetings from Asbury Park, N.J.* album was coming out. I got to know Bob Dylan through Peter, Paul and Mary and I went to his first concert in Town Hall and I could see he was going to be the new guy.'

Another new song at Town Hall was 'Tomorrow Is a Long Time', based on a folk song, 'Westron Wynde'. It has been recorded by Elvis Presley and Judy Collins. It is a beautiful love song, but somehow Dylan didn't appreciate its potential as he didn't put it on an album or single at the time.

Albert Grossman instilled him with the idea of regularly touring, perhaps 100 concerts and club dates a year. In April he did some dates in Boston, Cambridge and Chicago. While in Cambridge with Ramblin' Jack Elliott and Eric Von Schmidt, Bob got to know the musician Bobby Neuwirth. Neuwirth became one of Dylan's best friends, although the journalist Al Aronowitz says, 'Neuwirth was about as charming as a mugger.'

The two Bobbys worked on his image together. They went to funny films to train themselves not to laugh. They enjoyed putting people down: Bobby Neuwirth said of Joan Baez: 'She has one of those see-through blouses that you don't even wanna', a cruel line but actually reprising one of Lenny Bruce's jokes.

Tom Russell: 'I remember seeing Dylan for the first time at the Santa Monica civic auditorium and there were only 100 people in the audience. He was a lot funnier back then. It was a Charlie Chaplin routine on stage with lots of rapping, the real hobo humourist. After the show he was sitting in his car behind the auditorium, waiting to get paid, and we sat there talking with him and he asked us where the nearest liquor store was and he danced round and signed harmonica boxes. He took off in his car and we were prepared to follow him right through the States. For some reason he stopped on the Santa Monica Freeway and he saw us and laughed. We all jumped out and laughed and danced amongst the cars on the Santa Monica Freeway. We had a little mini-party and then he took off and the next time he came to town, 'Blowin' in the Wind' was out and he was a star and we didn't have access to him.'

The Freewheelin' Bob Dylan could have been released in that earlier format, but Dylan was writing new songs and it was agreed that the album could be improved with a further recording session, which took place on 24 April 1963. Even though he had written 'With God on Our Side', he did not record it: possibly he felt that it wasn't ready.

Columbia's lawyers had decreed that 'Talkin' John Birch Paranoid Blues' would have to be replaced. It might be actionable and the equivalent today would be writing a song mocking the National Front. They mightn't win but it could give them publicity. Dylan didn't object. He liked the idea of a further session as he had better material which would strengthen the album.

The 'John Birch' song was different every time he performed it. In the recording, he included a reference to *Hootenanny*, to Albert Grossman and to George Lincoln Rockwell who ran the Society and picketed the film, *Exodus*.

Through Grossman's manipulations, John Hammond was no longer Bob's producer and he had been replaced by Tom Wilson. An African-American, Wilson was born in 1931 and raised in Waco. He graduated from Harvard in 1954. He had been the president of their jazz society so it was logical for him to produce jazz records for Savoy including John Coltrane. When he joined Columbia, he was asked to produce Bob Dylan without having heard him. Tom Wilson later commented, 'What he had to say astounded me but his music didn't excite me.'

Five songs were recorded on 24 April 1963 at Columbia's studios in New York, four of which made the *Freewheelin'* album: 'Girl from the North Country', 'Masters of War', 'Talkin' World War III Blues' and 'Bob Dylan's Dream'. The four songs replaced 'Rocks and Gravel', 'Let Me Die in My Footsteps', 'Ramblin' Gamblin' Willie' and 'Talkin' John Birch Paranoid Blues'. The playing time of the new album, released on 27 May 1963, was 50 minutes which was exceptional and possible because it was largely voice and guitar, so the grooves could be compressed.

Paul Simon was taken with 'Girl from the North Country': 'Here was Dylan writing about subject matter that is neither teenage nor traditional folk. He was travelling on his own and writing about what he saw.' Paul Simon knew that Dylan had based the song around 'Scarborough Fair' but that wasn't going to inhibit him.

Throughout this book, there are comments on the originality of Bob Dylan's melodies. In many cases, the criticisms are justified, but it all depends on what you have heard. I know I have not heard an earlier song like 'Mr. Tambourine Man' but that doesn't mean there wasn't one. There are so many mysteries around Bob Dylan. Still, Judy Collins thought it was original. 'Dylan wrote wonderful melodies of his own like 'Mr. Tambourine Man' but he also knew how to absorb the best part of the folk process. He could find those traditional songs and give them new lyrics. 'Bob Dylan's Dream' came from a song Martin Carthy was singing. It was a wonderful tradition and he had the added genius of developing the melodies.'

Howard Sounes: 'Leonard Cohen has a humility that you don't find in Dylan but I don't think he is as great a songwriter. 'Girl from the North Country' has a sentiment that has really endured and it still sounds fresh and real. 'Bird on a Wire' has a similar sentiment but it's mawkish and stuck in its time. When I hear it, I think of hippies and bangles and people blowing bubbles.' Mawkish? Surely not?

'Talkin' World War III Blues' was a talking blues about ducking and diving with some classic asides: 'Great car to drive…after a war.' It was wittier and less specific than 'Talkin' John Birch Paranoid Blues'.

That fifth song, 'Walls of Redwing' was recorded again for the next album and also not used. Buffy Sainte-Marie: 'That is a pretty obscure song. That was about a reform school and it was largely Native American kids who were imprisoned there. He is one of the reasons that I have the guts to put out my albums – I did feel that these songs were wanted and needed.'

Dylan was back with Suze Rotolo and they were photographed by Don Hunstein in the snow on Jones Street facing West Fourth Street for the cover of *The Freewheelin' Bob Dylan*. It had to be shot quickly as no one wanted to be outside for long. It led to a great cover picture. Bob had the spot-on crumpled look for the cover and to put it crudely, every young boy wanted a girl like that. The playwright David Hare said in his memoir, *The Blue Touch Paper*: 'The photograph of Dylan with his arm round the artist Suze Rotolo was, for me, a definitive image of romance, one I had stared at longingly more times that I cared to admit. It represented a perfect fantasy of everything I might wish my life to be.'

Dylan is not wearing the same jacket as on the first album, much to Joan Baez's relief: She said that old one had 'throw-up all over it'. Bob himself loved the cover and was to say 'the cover's the most important part of the album'. Suze liked being on the cover too, a nice boost to her ego.

Paul Simon loved the cover of *Freewheelin'* too, thinking it had real attitude, 'It felt so daring, so new.' Bob Dylan would be in jeans but Simon and Garfunkel in suits. Their name was square and they looked square.

Here's a potential *Only Connect* question: What have the covers for *The Freewheelin' Bob Dylan*, *Sticky Fingers*, *Little Criminals* and *Two Virgins* in common? Bob Dylan's fly is half-open, the Stones' cover featured a zip and a pair of underpants, Randy Newman's impressive genitalia is outlined on *Little Criminals* and John Lennon went full frontal on *Two Virgins*.

Shortly after the album was released, Rob Mori challenged Dylan to a game of chess in a Greenwich Village café. Dylan offered his jacket as the stake and lost the game. Rob's wife took the sleeves off the jacket to make a purse.

The jazz journalist Nat Hentoff interviewed Bob for the sleeve notes: as Hentoff liked to refer to him as 'the wild Jewish boy', he knew Dylan was taking him for a ride. Dylan said, 'Nobody's gonna kill traditional music. All those songs about roses growing off people's brains and lovers who are really geese, and swans that turn into angels – they're not going to die.'

Although not for the second album, Dylan had written possibly his greatest song, a pragmatic look at American history, 'With God on Our Side'. It continues Woody Guthrie's theme about the nationalism of 'God Bless America'. His father Abe recalled, 'When I saw the title 'With God on Our Side', I thought it was going to be a beautiful song, but it was a sarcastic song.' Abe should have known his son better than that. Bob was recounting one historical event after another and the victors always had God on their side. It is a song about how the strong exploit the weak with the questionable justification of having God on their side. It contains the thought-provoking line, 'I can't think for you, you'll have to decide, Did Judas Iscariot have God on his side?'

The melody for 'With God on Our Side' was not original. Bob Dylan heard Nigel Denver sing 'The Patriot Game' at the Troubadour in London. Not only does Dominic Behan's song, which was written in 1957, share the same melody, the theme is similar: in Behan's case, the traitorous actions of politicians have led to the formation of a rebel army who want a united, independent Ireland. Many of Behan's original lines are not sung by more commercial performers. Later in the year, it was revived by the Kingston Trio on their thought-provoking album, *Time to Think*.

Dominic Behan attacked Dylan in *Melody Maker*, accusing him of plagiarism and denouncing his writing: 'Dylan's songs say nothing and if you want to sing Woody Guthrie songs why don't you sing them in your own accent?' In short, 'Dylan's songs say nothing at all.' It was a minefield and Dylan needed God on his side to get him out of it.

After such a tirade, Albert Grossman was in no mood for a cash settlement and fortunately, the perceptive *Melody Maker* readers pointed out that the tune was not Behan's. He had taken it from 'The Grenadier and the Lady', 'The Shores of Loch Earne' or 'The Merry Month of May'. In retaliation, Dominic Behan said that 'The Patriot Game' was one-third his own creation, one-third a traditional tune and one-third a Kay Starr hit. He could hardly claim ownership after that.

Joan Baez wanted to sing about peace and equality. She didn't fancy what was in *Sing Out!* as they were more like chants than songs. However, 'With God on Our Side' was perfect. She liked the idea that not everybody could be forgiven, but thought the tune was similar to 'Magyar Himnusz', the Hungarian national anthem. (It isn't).

Jim Kweskin challenged Bob as to who knew a song with the most verses and Bob simply sang his own 'With God on Our Side'. Joan Baez said, 'It was beautiful and devastating' before adding, "I never thought anything so powerful could come out of that little toad.'

Howard Alk, who had made the documentary film *The Cry of Jazz* in 1958, knew Albert Grossman. Grossman had moved out of Chicago and Alk took over his club, The Bear. Dylan appeared there two nights in April 1963 and he met the local blues guitarist, Mike Bloomfield. Bloomfield was very taken by 'The Walls of Redwing'. They jammed after the show. The following day Dylan appeared on *Studs Terkel's Wax Museum* on Chicago

WFMT radio, performing a variety of songs and saying he was writing a novel. In the liner notes for *Freewheelin'*, Dylan says he was working on three novels.

The interview with Studs Terkel on a Chicago radio station is entertaining as Dylan performs several little-known songs such as 'John Brown' and 'Who Killed Davey Moore'. Terkel tries to get him to explain 'A Hard Rain's A-Gonna Fall' but he does say Big Joe Williams is an old friend and an uncle took him to see Woody Guthrie when he was ten. Terkel admonishes him for 'mountain talk' and Dylan says he has been travelling in France and Mexico.

Richard Fariña divorced Carolyn Hester and married Mimi Baez in Paris. Many thought he married Mimi to get to know Joan better. Joan regarded him as an opportunist, but they were all to live closely together in Carmel. Biographer David Hajdu: 'For most of Joan's life she felt that she was in the shadow of her little sister who was regarded as the more beautiful one and Joan was haunted by feelings of inadequacy because of her dark complexion, her Mexican heritage and growing up in a white environment. She never felt that she could match up to her little sister Mimi, the angelic beauty. She originally pursued the spotlight in public life as a way of compensating for these feelings of inadequacy.'

In April 1963 there was a new ABC TV folk programme, *Hootenanny*, hosted by Jack Linkletter and filmed on university campuses. They refused to book Pete Seeger unless he signed a loyalty oath. The producers had been forced into this by advertising agencies and sponsors. Seeger did not want anyone to turn down the show on his behalf but Baez, Dylan, Paxton, Ochs, the Kingston Trio and another 30 performers said no. Grossman wouldn't allow Peter, Paul and Mary to appear anyway as he felt that TV exposure could harm their college bookings.

Carolyn Hester: 'We told the network that we were regarded as the children of Pete Seeger and if he wasn't going on the programme then we weren't going on. There was no doubt that Pete Seeger was responsible for us and our opinions. The criticisms of him were unjustified. He is one of the most American people I have ever known and he has made American folk music really stand for a lot.'

It is amazing that the show could keep going with such a backlash, but there were a substantial number of well-known performers on *Hootenanny* including Trini Lopez with guitarist Glen Campbell and drummer Mickey Jones. the Brothers Four, Hoyt Axton, Jimmie Rodgers, Josh White Jr and his sister Beverly, Bob Gibson and the New Christy Minstrels with Barry McGuire. Under the influence of something, Johnny Cash sang 'Busted'.

Long before the Byrds and the fame of Carly Simon, the Simon Sisters performed 'Turn! Turn! Turn!' It was written by Pete Seeger, this time with help from the Book of Ecclesiasticus, while Leon Bibb sang a song associated with Pete Seeger and written by Malvina Reynolds, 'Little Boxes', a criticism of suburbia and an unlikely choice for a black singer.

Woody Allen did a famed routine about analysis. Gospel, country, bluegrass and African music was included. At its peak *Hootenanny* had ten million viewers and it lasted until September 1964, when it was replaced by a beat programme, *Shindig!*

On 11 May 1963 the Chad Mitchell Trio performed 'The John Birch Society', a clever comic song and in view of its topicality and its left-wing bias, a surprising choice for *Hootenanny*. The group had previously been told by WCBS and WOR in New York that they could not perform it, so in this case, good for *Hootenanny*.

The Chad Mitchell Trio performed their song the day before Bob Dylan was due on

The Ed Sullivan Show. It is possible that Sullivan's team heard this song and pulled the plug. Sullivan had the biggest variety show of the day with up to 60 million viewers.

Ed Sullivan's son-in-law, Bob Precht, lived in the Village and had seen Dylan perform. He had recommended him to Sullivan, who despite his staid appearance, wanted to keep up with the trends. Bob Dylan was given a two-song slot which would be live. Dylan knew that 'Talkin' John Birch Paranoid Blues' had been removed from the album but he wanted to perform it. It was hardly what Columbia would have wanted but Dylan was always his own man.

Ed Sullivan thought it was wry and funny and he liked the joke of somebody who ends up investigating himself. Stowe Phelps, whose job was to check the legal content of the show, said it could not be performed. The argument was that the song criticised every single person in the John Birch Society and therefore was potentially libellous. By the same argument you could equally argue that's why it wasn't libellous.

Dylan was ordered to choose something else, but that isn't Bob Dylan's way. He walked. We don't know what Grossman thought about it, but Izzy Young was so taken with Dylan's action that he sold the lyric of the John Birch song as a broadsheet in his Folklore Centre.

Peter, Paul and Mary and Joan Baez were among the headline acts at the Monterey Folk Festival, though Joan Baez was the star. Bob got to Los Angeles and was taken to Monterey by Jac Holzman and Jim Dickson. Bob had a short unbilled set at the Festival on May 18 but he did well with his John Birch narrative, 'A Hard Rain's A-Gonna Fall', 'Masters of War' and 'With God on Our Side' for which he was joined by Joan Baez. He went back with Joan to Carmel for a couple of days.

Bob Spitz: 'I first saw Bob Dylan in 1964 when Joan Baez trotted him out in the middle of her concert. Nobody knew who he was. He blew me away and at the time I was only 14 years old. I recognised that here was somebody singing to me for the first time with songs that were full of content, full of meaning. They weren't songs about cars and high school and girls as I had been used to hearing, they were songs that made me think, made me think to myself, "Well, maybe I don't have to grow up to be like my parents".'

At long last *The Freewheelin' Bob Dylan* was released on 27 May 1963. Perhaps the dropped g in the title indicated that Bob was playing hard and loose with language. Dylan was fighting war and prejudice and showing you how to be wistful about someone who has dumped you. It was the first great bed-sit album, paving the way for Leonard Cohen, Joni Mitchell and Al Stewart's *Bedsitter Images*. The album was reviewed in *Time*, albeit somewhat missing the point. 'Hard-lick guitar, whooping harmonica, skinny little voice, beardless chin, porcelain pussy cat eyes.'

Although they were credited in the liner notes, there was a critical review by Paul Nelson and Jon Pankake in their *Little Sandy Review*, published in Minneapolis. According to them, 'Corrina, Corrina' was a pallid attempt at rhythm and blues and 'Talkin' World War III Blues' was an 'absurd concoction', although that was surely its intention. On the other hand, 'Oxford Town' is 'a pleasant surprise: a protest song that ironically implies its grimness through common sense and good humour rather than baldly stating it.' According to them, 'Dylan bases everything here on his own personality' and they preferred the first album. A 'Judas!' review before its time.

John Bauldie: 'Bob Dylan said on the notes for *Freewheelin'* that he was really into the blues but he hadn't yet learned to carry himself like the old blues singers did. It is hardly surprising – he was a middle-class Jewish white kid from the middle of nowhere in Minnesota, and he had only been playing real blues music for a few months when he recorded that. Bearing that in mind, it was a pretty spirited effort.'

Playwright Alan Bleasdale: 'I go back and think of my lack of maturity when I was 22. He flew so high but he did get his wings burnt. He sang them with such feeling and then he threw it all away.'

Woodstock in the Catskill Mountains is a two-hour drive north of New York City. It had been a hunting ground for the American Indians and its original name was Waghkunk (a place near a mountain). There are imposing views of the Overkill Mountain.

Timber mills flourished there in the eighteenth century and an art colony was established in the early twentieth century. The maverick artists and craftsmen enjoyed their own company and Woodstock festivals were held as early as 1915. Generally speaking the artists worked inside during the winter when it was cold and enjoyed mixing outside in the summer. The old-time favourite 'Down by the Old Mill Stream' was written near a mill stream in Woodstock.

In June, Bob and Suze spent a couple of weeks in Woodstock, staying at the cabin owned by Peter Yarrow's uncle. They loved the tranquillity of the place after the mayhem of New York. Bob called it a hip Hibbing and no one bothered them. Suze and Peter Yarrow painted in the mornings while Bob wrote songs including 'Only a Pawn in their Game', a chess analogy.

When Suze returned from Italy, she was treated rather unfairly as the girl who had abandoned Bob Dylan. In a folk club, someone sang 'Don't Think Twice, It's All Right' and directed it at her. She felt that she had lost Bob to his growing fame. She witnessed all these 'bloodsuckers' around him. She never felt hurt by his songs but she declined to see him again in the mid-70s as she felt it might hurt her husband's feelings.

In 1909 the National Association for the Advancement of Coloured People was formed by a white lawyer from Boston, Moorfield Storey. In 1955 the lawyer Medgar Evers was its field secretary in Jackson, Mississippi, a potentially dangerous job at the time. The state of Mississippi was 45% black but most of them were not eligible to vote. Medgar Evers wanted to resolve the murder of Emmett Till and he had supported James Meredith as the first black student at the University of Mississippi. In 1963 Medgar Evers was killed.

Dylan told the story in the first verse, then stated why it happened and concluded that the killer can't really be blamed because he's only a pawn in their game. This was a controversial thought as Dylan has some sympathy for the assassin, making him sound like a foot-soldier doing his job, and it is not careless writing as it is in line with his remarks at the Tom Paine awards. Effectively, Dylan is saying that we are shaped by the forces around us and so the system is to blame. Phil Ochs and Bob Gibson wrote about Evers in 'Too Many Martyrs', a much more straightforward composition.

It wasn't until 1994 that a fertiliser salesman, Bryon de la Beckwith, a white supremacist, was convicted for killing Evers. He had previously been freed by two all-white juries.

Woodstock, New York was named after Woodstock, England, although the first settlers were Dutch. It was founded on 11 April 1787 and the Delaware and Hudson Canal was finished in 1828, which improved communications. By 1900, Woodstock was a fully formed rural village, about 100 miles from New York City. Landscape artists congregated in the area and became known as the Hudson River Painters.

Ralph Whitehead, the son of a wealthy mill owner from Yorkshire, who had studied in Oxford under John Ruskin, established a home for independent artists that he called

Byrdcliffe. The colony was completed in 1903 on 1,500 acres of land after he had purchased seven farms and put them together. There were 40 artists' cottages and studios, but would experimental artists like being herded like this? As it happened, Whitehead had seen this work in the UK with artists who objected to machinery and the dark satanic mills. It was a peer group for sharing ideas. Woodstock became a sleepy town with heavy duty thinking (and drinking!).

The Byrdcliffe School of Art was the first permanent art school in the Hudson Valley. Aaron Copland, Edward G. Robinson, John Cage and Lee Marvin all lived in Woodstock. Later it was ideal for holiday homes for busy New Yorkers. There were lots of rattlesnakes in the area.

And Albert Grossman.

Milt Glazer brought Albert Grossman to Woodstock, who bought 120 acres in Bearsville. Grossman bought his property from John Striebel who created the comic strip, *Dixie Dugan*, and it had large rooms which he filled with antiques. Grossman built a brilliant new kitchen: his main interest was food and he was to open restaurants in Woodstock as well as a recording studio. It was an ideal escape from New York with its forests, clean air and privacy, although there was still a thriving artistic community of painters and writers.

On 21 June 1963 Richard and Mimi Fariña left Paris to sail to New York. Mimi's parents didn't know that they were married. They were met by Pauline Baez and her husband, the painter Bruce Marden. They saw Richard's family in Brooklyn and then travelled to Carmel.

Peter, Paul and Mary had reached Number 2 on the US charts with 'Puff the Magic Dragon', a children's song but a record that achieved notoriety as some US radio stations said it was about drugs. Apart from the title, there was no evidence of that but it didn't harm sales as it climbed to Number 2, losing out to Little Peggy March's 'I Will Follow Him'. They followed it by releasing 'Blowin' in the Wind' on June 18 and it sold 300,000 copies in the first fortnight and again stalled at Number 2, this time losing out to Little Stevie Wonder's wild harmonica in 'Fingertips, Part 2'. When they appeared in concert, they acknowledged that it was written by Bob Dylan and this record more than any other got his name across to the public.

Happy Traum: 'I can remember riding in my car and listening to the radio. I heard the normal pop music stuff on AM, which was very carefully controlled. Suddenly 'Blowin' in the Wind' came on with Peter, Paul and Mary and I thought it was a new world. I had known Peter and Mary in Washington Square and it was mind-blowing that the song would be on pop radio. It was a huge hit as they did a beautiful rendition of it. Peter, Paul and Mary had a dynamism about their music. Mary was so charismatic and beautiful and she looked great alongside the two guys and their little beards. It was a package that worked really well.'

Liz Thomson: 'There is a quiet intensity about that recording and also 'If I Had a Hammer'. They were a Kingston Trio-imitation but they were better. Ralph Gleason described them as two rabbis and a hooker which is amusing but unfair. In that footage of Newport in 1963; the wind is getting up and Mary's long blonde hair is blowing around and she puts her hand up to pull it back and the two guys are very tight to the mic on either side of her. It looked great and they worked really hard on their harmonies. Pete Yarrow was one of the organisers of the March on Washington – the 'I Have a Dream' moment – so they have a significant part to play in music and social history. They were acceptable to radio stations in a way that Dylan never was.'

Theodore Bikel paid Dylan's fare so that he could see at first hand what was happening down South. On 5 July 1963 Bob Dylan flew to a voter-registration rally in Greenwood, Mississippi. Pete Seeger was the main performer, but Dylan sang 'Only a Pawn in their Game', which is shown in *Dont Look Back*. He joined hands with the campaigners for 'We Shall Overcome'.

Peter, Paul and Mary followed their single with 'Don't Think Twice, It's All Right', another Top 10 entry, and both songs were included on their Number 1 album, *In the Wind*, released in October 1963. It topped the US album charts for five weeks and was Number 1 the week John F. Kennedy was assassinated. Who knows but maybe Peter, Paul and Mary's attractive sound and the Singing Nun provided some solace to American record buyers?

Both 'Blowin' in the Wind' and 'Don't Think Twice, It's All Right' were widely covered and became buskers' favourites. This was a turning point for folk as youths were finding out that there was something with more substance to listen to. 'Blowin' in the Wind' retained its popularity and Peter, Paul and Mary always sang it. Peter Yarrow said, 'We interpret the lyrics in terms of the challenges of the day.'

Although Peter, Paul and Mary's records were produced by Milt Okun, he was only credited as musical director: the producer was given as their manager Albert Grossman, a nice little earner.

In 1999 an internet group was discussing 'Blowin' in the Wind' and someone said it was a naïve political plea from a callow youth. The contributor was asked how he had come by this view. He replied, 'Because I'm Bob.' Asked to prove it, he said, 'Okay. I'll sing 'Highlands' tomorrow night at San Diego' and he did.

'Blowin' in the Wind' asked questions but Dylan's next big song was about taking action, 'The Times They Are A-Changin'', which was full of powerful words like 'sink' and 'accept'. John Stewart of the Kingston Trio: '"Blowin' in the Wind" was the first Dylan song that really caught our attention and then we heard 'The Times They Are A-Changin'', which I still think is one of the most powerful records ever made by anyone, just one guitar and one voice.'

Simon and Garfunkel were asked to cover the song on their first album *Wednesday Morning, 3am*, also on Columbia in 1964. Paul Simon said he would have preferred to cover 'Don't Think Twice, It's All Right' and 'Girl from the North Country'. 'The Times They Are A-Changin'' was too direct for Simon: 'I am not a fan of songs that tell you, "And my point is…".'

Scott Walker: 'Folk music was never that interesting for me and that was Bob Dylan's starting point. It was too limited in its musical content for me.'

Del Shannon: 'I didn't get into Bob Dylan initially. It was just him and his guitar and it used to drive me nuts. I said, "That guy is never gonna make it without drums." A lot of people praised him for writing personal songs, but all of my songs are personal too. They come from when I was a kid or a teenager. Most of them are taken from that.' Already Bob was enjoying a complicated love life. Joan Baez sent a copy of *The Freewheelin' Bob Dylan* to Mimi with a note that he was 'my new boyfriend', an odd comment when Bob was with Suze on the cover! Richard Fariña took the album as a challenge. He hoped Mimi's guitar playing was up to Bob Dylan's as he wanted to form a duo as a showcase for his own songs. They might be able to cross over like Peter, Paul and Mary.

In July 1963 Dylan's own version of 'Blowin' in the Wind' was released as a single by Columbia and in publicity he was called 'a rebel with a cause'. The UK sheet music for 'Blowin' in the Wind' drew attention to the cover version from Marianne Faithfull.

While in Las Vegas of all places, Johnny Cash heard *Freewheelin'* and loved its commitment. He sent a note to Dylan and they exchanged several letters before they met in New York. His image like Bob's was a little fanciful – was he really part-Cherokee and a former jailbird? Johnny Cash was in Greenwich Village in late 1963 to look around and was with Peter La Farge and Ramblin' Jack Elliott. He recorded songs by both of them.

A new French singer, Hugues Aufray was brought to New York by Maurice Chevalier for a charity gala about French singers. He represented the new generation. He appeared on *The Ed Sullivan Show* and at the Blue Angel night club, which had a French owner. Whilst in New York, he heard Bob Dylan and commented that he was as good as Rimbaud. He asked Albert Grossman if he could translate his songs. Aufray made an album to show Dylan was a genuine singer / poet, although Aufray felt that the backings were wrong. Dylan applauded his intentions but was unsure of the results. He told Aufray, 'You don't just blow into a harmonica. You suck and breathe to bend the notes.' Later Dylan sent him a Clifton Chenier album with the note, 'See, the French language really can swing.'

In mid-July 1963 Dylan with Suze and Carla attended a Columbia Records convention in Puerto Rico aimed at salesmen from the South. Dylan performed 'With God on Our Side' and 'Only a Pawn in Their Game'. Many walked out, unable to take his harsh voice. He was refused admission to the restaurant for not wearing a tie. The head of Columbia Goddard Lieberson (known as 'God') intervened on his behalf. This prompted him to write 'When the Ship Comes in'.

The Newport Folk Festival went through administrative changes in 1963 with Pete Seeger taking over from George Wein. Elijah Wald: 'The folk festivals in 1959 and 1960 were modelled on the jazz festivals. Then in 1963 Pete Seeger had a new model, which was a non-star festival. He said, "We will invite popular names but we will pay them the minimum, so everybody gets $50 plus lodging whoever they are." Because Pete Seeger, Bob Dylan, Joan Baez and Theodore Bikel were working for $50, this enabled the organisers to invite little-known musicians from the rural South such as Mississippi John Hurt and Doc Watson. That was the dream of Newport, there are no stars and all we care about is the music.' It worked too as the festival grossed $70,000 and drew nearly 40,000 people. The profits were used to encourage folk music in schools.

Elijah Wald: 'Pete Seeger had already brought Dylan on stage at two of his concerts at Carnegie Hall and Pete was spreading the word by singing 'A Hard Rain's A-Gonna Fall'. Pete felt that Dylan was the great young voice and the heir to Woody Guthrie. He loved Dylan as much for the fact that he was trying to play real, authentic folk music rather than trying to pretty it up for an urban audience. He loved that as much as his writing.'

There was a workshop where Bob and Pete Seeger sang a new song together, 'Ye Playboys and Playgirls'. The next day Bob joined Joan Baez for 'With God on Our Side' and joined Peter, Paul and Mary for 'Blowin' in the Wind'.

He was also in charge of Arlo Guthrie: 'Dylan didn't really babysit for me but he was responsible for me the first time I went to the Newport Folk Festival. My mom handed me over to him and said, "Take care of him." I can remember that. Bob was taking me around and saying, "This is Woody's kid".'

It sounds like Bob was accommodating and friendly at Newport but he was carrying a bullwhip most of the time: he didn't use it and who knows why? Loudon Wainwright: 'I saw him at Newport at the time 'Masters of War' came out and I thought he had balls.'

'Ye Playboys and Playgirls' is little known but a live recording of it was made by

Carolyn Hester in New York: 'I sang it at Town Hall in 1965 and that is one of the few live recordings of a woman singer in the 1960s. It was a protest song and it has a verse about civil rights and the burning crosses. The "light my way" line is totally powerful. I had a new verse to pitch in and this was about one of Bob's friends anyway – "Ringo just got married, now he'll never marry me".'

Bob Dylan had another recording session on August 12 including a Scottish ballad 'Moonshine Blues' and 'Only a Hobo', which was based on Aunt Molly Jackson's 'Poor Miner's Lament' and Woody Guthrie's 'The Great Divide'. A copy was passed to Witmark, which made more sense than doing separate recordings for his publisher.

On August 17, Bob was Joan Baez's guest in front of 15,000 fans at Forest Hills. Their version of 'Troubled and I Don't Know Why' was recorded. Baez returned to Carmel and met up with Mimi and Richard, who were living close at hand. Dylan was a guest on *The Tonight Show* with Johnny Carson but looked uncomfortable.

In late August, Suze moved out of Dylan's apartment because of his affair with Joan Baez. She moved in with Carla who thought Dylan was manipulative, selfish and immature. Suze was pregnant and was to have an abortion.

'One Too Many Mornings' could be about their relationship – 'You are right from your side and I am right from mine', that is, I'm not really taking the blame. When it was recorded in October, it was a rare example of Dylan fingerpicking. The song sounded perfect for Rick Nelson, who was to record it. Rather delightfully, Ralph McTell was to call it 'a goodbye song for a whole generation'.

On August 24 there was a second wedding for Mimi and Richard in Portola Valley where Big Joan and Albert Baez spent the summer. At the reception Mimi and Richard performed a whimsical song about a dog, 'Old Blue', their start as a performing duo. Fariña had plans to write Bob a western about a peace-loving cowboy. Maynard Solomon gave him a publishing contract. Joan Baez was performing his song, 'Birmingham, Sunday' about the deaths of four schoolgirls following a racially-motivated arson attack. It was based on the folk tune, 'I Once Loved a Lass'.

But it was Dylan's songs that captured Baez's attention. She said, 'I feel it but only Dylan can say it. Bob is expressing what all these kids want to say. He speaks for me.' It's odd that Joan never had a big hit single with a Dylan song, but she was considering an album.

Ramblin' Jack Elliott: 'I think Bob did offer me something, but I didn't really notice, I was into other things – sailboats, diesel trucks – and I probably could have made it any time I wanted but I wasn't interested. I knew Bob was heading that way and I knew that from the minute I met him. I didn't envy him or dislike him for that. I thought it was exciting. Here was a guy who had the drive and the desire for success and he also had the talent. Therefore I figured he was going to be a big star.'

A.J. Croce, the son of Jim Croce: 'Dylan to my ears was copying Woody Guthrie and it wasn't until we had the same management that I saw him in a new light. 'Hard Rain' is a cool song but I had seen it as a take-off on Woody Guthrie. Woody borrowed from a lot of people too and that's just the folk tradition. My dad was doing it too and 'Time in a Bottle' is influenced by the folk music of the British Isles. The only difference between singer / songwriters and folk singers is that the singer / songwriters have lawyers. They want their name on the song and they want to make money from it. The folksinger is just adding this or that to an existing song. With them, it is about sharing and anybody else can take it on.'

The Appalachian singer and dulcimer player, Jean Ritchie, had revived the English song, 'Nottamun Town' and because her publishers claimed Dylan had taken her arrangement for 'Masters of War', she was given $5,000 in settlement, doing somewhat better than Paul Clayton. Roll on another ten years and you have John Lennon's 'Working Class Hero'.

Later in the month there was the taping of a two-hour *Songs of Freedom* TV show in New York starring Odetta. Dylan performed 'Blowin' in the Wind' and 'Only a Pawn in Their Game': his two main stands, racial injustice and anti-war. Joan Baez was not on the show but could be seen in the audience.

Dylan was not one for sitting on his laurels and on August 6 and 7 he was back in Columbia's Studio A working on his third album with Tom Wilson producing. He put down five songs that were to appear on that album and plenty more besides. At last we had 'With God on Our Side' and 'Only a Pawn in Their Game'.

'Boots of Spanish Leather' was to be the one light moment on *The Times They Are A-Changin'* album. It was a loving song to Suze asking her to bring him back a gift from her trip. The song contained very few accurate rhymes, showing that Dylan was ploughing his own furrow.

Carolyn Hester: "Boots of Spanish Leather' will definitely go down as one of his classics. It could have been written a couple of hundred years ago and I heard Bob Dylan sing it in concert in New York. I called him the next day and said, "I love that song and I would like a copy of it." He said he would send one but it never came. He was already moving away from all the rest of us (Laughs). That was my first real clue that this was happening.'

Dylan recorded a trenchant song about the mines being closed in Minnesota, 'North Country Blues'. Dylan liked calling songs blues that weren't blues. It was a bleak song, telling of poor conditions in a mining community 'where the miners work almost for nothing'.

'The Ballad of Hollis Brown' was a murder ballad set in South Dakota, taking its melody from 'Pretty Polly' by Dock Boggs. Dylan concluded the tragic song optimistically with seven new people being born.

On August 10 Joan Baez appeared in a tent concert at Asbury Park and introduced Bob Dylan. He sang a couple on his own and a couple with Joan. A young Greil Marcus was there and said to Dylan, 'You were terrific' to which he replied, 'I was shit.'

On 8 February 1963 a 51-year-old waitress at the Emerson Hotel in Baltimore, Hattie Carroll, who had 11 children, was slow in serving William Zantzinger. He was the 24-year-old son of a wealthy farmer and he shouted, 'When I order a drink, I want it now, you black bitch!' and hit her on the head with his cane. She died from the injuries. Zantzinger was charged with murder but was found guilty of manslaughter and given a six-month sentence. It inspired Bob Dylan's song 'The Lonesome Death of Hattie Carroll', which never mentioned that Carroll was black and Zantzinger white, but maybe it was obvious. Zantzinger did not comment on the song for many years and then he said, "Dylan's a no-account son of a bitch. I should have sued him and put him in jail".' Dylan's song was hardly defamation of character: he rented out shacks with no running water and he was arrested for not declaring income.

This song followed the standard journalistic approach: who, what, when, where and why, which is Phil Ochs' default position. The lyric reads like a news report but Dylan was inspired by the narrative in Brecht's 'The Black Freighter'. Tom Waits was staggered by Dylan's song and wondered if the story was true. Martin Carthy: 'I couldn't believe a narrative song could be that powerful.'

Judy Collins: 'I used to go to his concerts with Jac Holzman, the president of Elektra Records, and we would see him in the Village and sit in the front row. Jac would sometimes go, "That one's for you." He said that of 'Hattie Carroll' and he was right.'

On 28 August 1963 there was the Civil Rights March on Washington which included Dr. Martin Luther King's speech, 'I have a dream'. Both Joan Baez and Bob Dylan performed and Dylan sang 'Only a Pawn in Their Game' and 'Blowin' in the Wind'. The comedian Dick Gregory was not so sure about this, saying, 'What's a white boy doing up there? Stand behind us but not in front of us.'

During September Bob Dylan was with Joan Baez in Carmel with Richard and Mimi close to hand. The men would spend the day writing and as well as songs, Dylan wrote a prose poem for Joan's next album, *In Concert, 2*. When in the Village, Baez and Dylan would stay at Hotel Earle, 'that crummy hotel in Washington Square': *Trip Advisor* had nothing on Joan's views. Bob wrote a poem celebrating the Village for the *In the Wind* LP for Peter, Paul and Mary.

Dylan wrote the notes for an LP by the New World Singers on Atlantic and Bob mentions Happy Traum's daughter, Merry. 'I think we were among the first of our group to start a family,' says Happy. 'Phil Ochs had a little girl about a year afterwards. Bob was quite taken by the fact that we had a daughter.'

Dylan was asked to contribute to Robert Shelton's new magazine, *Hootenanny*, for $75 an issue. Dylan dutifully did this at first but got fed up. Then Shelton got fed up and the magazine folded.

At Joan's house, Bob heard a Scottish ballad on the bagpipes. He wanted lyrics with the same feel and wrote 'Lay down Your Weary Tune', which could be a drugs song. It sounds like a prototype for 'Mr. Tambourine Man'. Joan Baez: 'He could never resist singing what he had just written, and when he sang 'Lay down Your Weary Tune', it sounded like it was 45 minutes long.' There are only five known verses.

Joan Baez invited him to join her for a northeast tour – four big concerts. The press had commented on Dylan's scruffiness and she attempted to smarten his image: as the song says, 'I bought you some cufflinks.' Even *Sing Out* derided his 'sloppy dress and slob-like appearance'. At Forest Hills Dylan sang two solos and they did three duets. Their voices didn't match but they worked well together with some amusing comments.

Country Joe McDonald: 'I had been discharged from the navy and I was going to Los Angeles State College and I went to see Joan Baez at the Hollywood Bowl, and she introduced Bob Dylan, who came out with jeans and a harmonica rack and sang some of his songs. It blew my mind, and I decided that whatever he was, I wanted to be. The songs he was writing, the clothes he was wearing, the harmonica on the rack, and the acoustic guitar. He was a modern Woody Guthrie, a minstrel, a poet, and he struck my fancy. I was writing protest songs and doing folk music, but this motivated me and I became obsessed with him for a decade. I wanted to be Bob Dylan and I became Country Joe. Same with Phil Ochs. Bob can influence you but you have to find yourself.'

While at the Hollywood Bowl, they visited Henry Miller at Pacific Palisades and Dylan and Miller played table tennis. He met Lawrence Ferlinghetti and discussed a book of poems for his City Lights press, although this never materialised.

The jazz musician Barney Kessel was intrigued to hear Bob Dylan even if he didn't appreciate it. 'I didn't think he had a voice; I didn't think he could play the guitar or harmonica; and I thought his melodies were very poor, but I did recognise that there was something there. It wasn't for me but I wished him well. The meaning was in his words, and the words mean something for people of his age. Since I was older than Bob Dylan, the words were not speaking to me. That is what Bob Dylan had to offer – he had words of relief, words of comedy and words to make them understand what they were going through."

On October 26 Dylan played Carnegie Hall itself, this time not the concert room. A reporter from *Newsweek* was annoyed by his lack of cooperation. Dylan told the reporter that he didn't know his parents and yet they were sitting in the audience. He had paid for them to come. He opened with a new song, 'The Times They Are A-Changin'', which was about the generation gap, and had another new one, 'Lay down Your Weary Tune'. Abe and Beatty were very impressed by the turnout at Carnegie Hall. Abe said, 'He had mannerisms that were meant to attract attention and separate him from the ordinary.' Spot on there, Dad.

Shortly after the concert, Dylan wanted to record a new song for the next LP, 'Restless Farewell', possibly a response to the *Newsweek* journalist, possibly a response to his fans who wanted more of the same. He was moving on. In addition, he wrote 11 epitaphs for the album sleeve, one of them about *Newsweek*. Graham Nash owns the original manuscripts. Why epitaphs? He is remembering something past.

On 4 November 1963 came the bombshell, a bitter feature in *Newsweek* by Andrea Svedburg which revealed his real background and called him a phony. She said that she had interviewed Dylan but had mistrusted his answers.

The feature suggested that Lorre Wyatt from New Jersey had written 'Freedom is Blowin'' in the Wind' and Bob Dylan had copied it. Lorre performed it with the Millburnaires, a Kingston Trio-styled act from his school. In reality, Lorre had seen the lyric of 'Blowin' in the Wind' in *Broadside* in October 1962, changed it slightly, written his own tune and performed it at Millburn High. He included it on his group's album, *A Time to Sing*. *Broadside* had published a letter in which he said that his song was being mistaken for Dylan's. The story had been picked up by *Newsweek* who accused Dylan of plagiarism and they said the Millburnaires' version was available nationally on an album, *Teenage Hootenanny*. Dylan would rarely trust journalists after this. He tore up *Newsweek* and used it for cigarette papers. He wrote a poem about it for the sleeve of his next album. In 1974 Lorre Wyatt admitted to the *New York Times* that he had only written his song after reading 'Blowin' in the Wind' in *Broadside*.

Dylan blamed Grossman for the *Newsweek* feature and was annoyed that Grossman didn't have a press officer to resolve it, although it was not to lead to any lasting harm. Grossman gave him books by the Jewish philosopher Martin Buber as a peace offering.

Many people in Greenwich Village thought Dylan was getting his come-uppance. Happy Traum: 'There was a lot of competition. There was a finite number of record companies and venues and it is probably the same today. You are fighting for your little spot of fame and some people rose above the crowd because they were more talented and other people didn't get the recognition that they felt they deserved. Sometimes they got bitter and sometimes they went off and did other things. It's very easy for people to get jealous.'

Dylan indeed was distancing himself from his associates; Pete Seeger, Ramblin' Jack Elliott and Carolyn Hester were part of an album of western songs, *The Bad Men*. Dylan was expected to contribute, especially as it was on Columbia but he decided against it.

On 22 November 1963 President Kennedy was assassinated in Dallas. Bonnie Dobson: 'I was in Chicago when Kennedy was killed. I had gone out to have lunch with a few other people at a television station and the chap I was seeing said, "Bonnie, can you just wait because the President has been assassinated?" I thought he meant the president of the television station at first. The lunch was cancelled and they put us in a cab and I remember driving back into the centre of Chicago listening to the radio and you could see people in other cars on the road and they were weeping. It was horrendous and I still get a chill now thinking back. It really did change America.'

Bob and Suze watched the TV reports all night. The next day Dylan was playing, somewhat reluctantly, in Princeton, New Jersey, opening with 'The Times They Are A-Changin". Dylan wondered if he might be next. Dylan: 'Jesus got himself crucified because he got himself noticed. So I disappear a lot.'

In December Bob Dylan was given the prestigious Tom Paine award, and the previous recipient had been Bertrand Russell. Dylan attended the presentation at the Hotel Americana, New York, but found that he had nothing in common with middle-class, middle-aged radicals. He got drunk and offended the audience by saying he saw something of himself in Lee Harvey Oswald. He told the audience, 'You can boo but booing's got nothing to do with it.'

Some members resigned in disgust and the fundraising for the night was poor. The next day Dylan offered to make good the shortfall, and he wrote a poem in apology, 'A Message to Emergency Civil Liberties Commission'. He wrote a song about it too, 'As I Walked out one Morning', and he said, 'They thought I was saying it was a good thing that Kennedy got killed.' He wasn't but it was a similar thought to 'Only a Pawn in Their Game'.

Eric Bibb, the son of Broadway performer and folk singer Leon Bibb, was a few years younger than Arlo: 'I met Bob Dylan a couple of times. We lived in a big house in Queens as my dad was doing great at the time. He figured it was time to have a big showbiz party. Mary Travers and Peter Yarrow came around and at two in the morning on this cold December night, Bob Dylan showed up. I came downstairs in my pyjamas and met him. It was in a crowded living room and he looked out of place, but he was talking about writing songs and playing guitar. He said to me, 'Keep it simple and forget all that fancy shit.' I guess he was referring to some of the people in the living room who were not real folk musicians in his eyes. He was into guitars and fingerpicking and he liked Mance Lipscomb but his image was that of the Dust Bowl Okie with an elementary guitar style.'

At the Grammys, Peter, Paul and Mary's 'Blowin' in the Wind' beat Pete Seeger's 'We Shall Overcome' as the folk record of the year. However, the song of the year was 'Days of Wine and Roses', recorded by Andy Williams.

Judy Collins: 'In 1964 Albert Grossman had me come up to his house in Bearsville, near Woodstock for a little gathering with Suze Rotolo, Bob Dylan, Sally Grossman and the reviewer Al Aronowitz, who had invited me. We were staying in this big stone mansion. After dinner and a great festive evening, I went to sleep and I woke up at 3am and I heard a melody coming up the stairs from the basement. It was not very loud and I was drunk. I went downstairs about three flights and Bob Dylan was behind a closed door and writing 'Mr. Tambourine Man'. I heard this melody over and over again. I was mesmerised and I sat there and just listened. It was a spectacular experience. I fell in love with it straightaway and of course I recorded it.'

Eric Andersen: 'I thought Bob Dylan was great. He had a lot of attitude, a lot of edge, even though he sounded like Woody and Jack Elliott at first, but there was so much humour in his songs. I met him in Gerde's Folk City but I first saw him at the Gaslight singing a couple of numbers. Then I saw him at Phil Ochs' house, he came in an old station wagon. He had been playing concerts and Victor Maymudes was with him. He sang 'When the Ship Comes In' and 'Mr. Tambourine Man' and he had paper all over the coffee table – he had been writing in the car. He was very excited – it was like somebody with a new baby. The song was sparkling and gleaning and the images were wonderful.'

There are so many stories connected to 'Mr. Tambourine Man' as Dylan wrote the song over several days and in different places. The initial impetus might have come from the Mardi Gras in New Orleans and a possible literary reference is Arthur Rimbaud's 'The Drunken Boat'. Dylan has said he was inspired by the film *La Strada* and by Bruce Langhorne's large tambourine, 'as big as a wagon wheel'. Liam Clancy: 'When he sang "My ancient empty street's too dead for dreaming", I knew he was writing about Sullivan Street on a Sunday.'

Dylan had not broken through in the UK, but the Beatles played and listened to *Freewheelin'* in January 1964. George Harrison recalled, 'We got a copy of *Freewheelin'* in Paris and we wore it out. The content of the song lyrics and the attitude was incredibly original and wonderful. We recognised some vital energy, a voice crying out somewhere. We got a lot of pleasure out of it and it made us want to be more funky again, but Brian Epstein had told us we would get more work if we had suits.' Paul McCartney: 'We all liked his early talkin' blues.'

Al Stewart, then a member of a beat group: 'I started learning Dylan songs as a little side venture. I did a lot of stuff from *Freewheelin'* including 'Masters of War'. We would play two or three sets a night and when they took a break, I would get up and do a couple of Bob Dylan songs. When we played rock'n'roll, people just mooched about and talked and danced and paid no attention, but when I did the Bob Dylan songs, everybody stopped and listened. I thought that there might be something to this. There was only me and about three other people in Bournemouth at the time buying Bob Dylan records but I went up to London and started playing in coffee bars which is where that kind of music was played.'

Former England cricket captain Bob Willis: 'I first heard Bob Dylan in 1963. A colleague at school had been to a Peter, Paul and Mary show at the Royal Albert Hall and they had told the audience to listen to Bob Dylan. He had his second album which he lent to me. We had a big radiogram at home and my parents made me lie down with my ear to the loudspeaker and the volume turned down as they hated it so much. They thought he sounded like a strangled cat but I manged to convert them both in about five years. They realised that I was completely besotted by Bob Dylan and they bought me a portable record player so that I could play them in my bedroom. Instead of doing my homework, I was listening to Bob Dylan, so my educational progress at the Royal Grammar School in Ilford came grinding to a halt. All I did was play his records and play cricket.'

Bernie Taupin in Lincolnshire heard 'The Times They A-Changin'' on the BBC: 'To me, folk music had always meant tunes you heard on *Children's Favourites* like Burl Ives or 'English Country Garden'. This voice was like broken glass. The words were like arrows being shot straight into the heart of the Establishment. That was what made me realise what the words of a song could do.'

Steve Harley: 'I remember being in hospital when I was 12 and 'I Want To Hold Your Hand' was Number 1 that Christmas. Dylan came along about the same time and he was really saying, "You can have pop music and proper words too." I was reading serious literature when I was 12 and that all sounded good to me.'

Although he is hated by rock'n'rollers, a lot was made in the press about Pat Boone having a degree. Elijah Wald: 'The position of intelligent pop musicians had always been complicated but the Beatles and Dylan changed that. As it happens, Mick Jagger was far better educated than Dylan or any of the Beatles and yet his act was that of being a working-class lout.'

Music writer Robert Santelli: 'Bob Dylan is a really interesting character in the British Invasion. Was Dylan of more importance to the Beatles than the Beatles were to him? It was a two-way relationship. The Beatles are a large part of the reason for Dylan going electric in 1965.'

Bob Dylan was unsure about the Beatles. He called their music 'bubblegum' but soon changed his mind. He said he heard the phrase 'I can't hide' in 'I Want to Hold Your Hand' as 'I get high' and wondered what the Beatles were taking. When Dylan heard the Beatles on a car radio, he realised that 'their chords were outrageous and their harmonies made it all valid. I knew it was pointing the direction where music had to go.' However, the record that really got him going came from Tamla-Motown: he loved Marvin Gaye's 'Can I Get a Witness', a secular update on a gospel theme.

Bonnie Raitt: 'I was very lucky to come from a very musical household and I was exposed to all kinds of music. I am a child of my era which included the folk revival which all the counsellors sang at my summer camp. I went to camp in upstate New York and I caught the folk fever and I was singing Joan Baez and Bob Dylan songs and I fell in love with folk and eventually country blues. The Stones and the Beatles and Motown and the whole British invasion were the music of my era and it was just an incredibly rich time to be going into puberty.'

'The Beatles shut us down,' says a fellow folkie, Ian Tyson 'The only one who had the guts to challenge the rock'n'roll guys on their own terms was Bob Dylan.'

The album, *The Times They Are A-Changin'*, was released in the US on 13 January 1964. It had a stark, black and white photograph of Dylan on the cover as if to say this is a modern-day Woody Guthrie. The photograph was taken by his friend Barry Feinstein who was married to Mary Travers. It is a stark contrast to the photograph on *Freewheelin'* as he had lost his puppy fat. This was the most significant of all protest albums, though no one would believe that senators and congressmen would heed the call and change the world. It is stark, uncomfortable listening.

Bob Dylan got the Mersey sound in a way he didn't expect from Burl Ives: 'I felt that Bob Dylan hadn't sung 'The Times They Are A-Changin'' in the right way. The text required something more dignified and solemn. Bob Mersey wrote a very nice arrangement and that was exactly what I wanted'

There were ten songs on Dylan's album, six of them over four minutes long and again Dylan had strong songs that he omitted from the final cut – 'Lay Down Your Weary Tune', 'Percy's Song' and 'Only a Hobo'.

Arlo Guthrie: 'I remember somebody playing "Percy's Song" for me and I just loved it. I almost learned it the first time I heard it. There is something Shakespearian about it that made you want to remember it.'

At the end of January 1964 Dylan was in Toronto to film a half-hour programme for the CBC-TV series, *Quest*. It is a bizarre programme in which he performs in a log cabin to some card-playing workers. He told the *Toronto Telegraph* that he was working on a novel and a play.

In light of what happened next, Dylan sent a revealing letter to the February issue of *Broadside* indicating that the pressure was getting too much for him. He called Pete Seeger a saint, which would seem to be putting too much pressure on Pete Seeger.

On 3 February 1964 Dylan set out on a road trip with Victor Maymudes (road manager), Pete Karman (writer) and Paul Clayton (folk singer) in a station wagon. Paul had been going out with Carla Rotolo; he had made several albums but without much success. They had an itinerary as Dylan had several concerts to perform but there was plenty of time for diversions. There were unscheduled performances such as one at Tougaloo College, Mississippi.

The travellers took some clothes that had been collected in New York for the striking miners in Hazard, Kentucky. Many jobs were being replaced by machinery, wages were being reduced and the community was being decimated.

They wanted to visit the poet Carl Sandburg in Hendersonville, North Carolina. He had collected 300 traditional songs in his book, *American Songbag* (1927), but he was 86 and had never heard of Bob Dylan. Dylan told him that he too was a poet: Sandburg was unimpressed. They had a more successful meeting with the civil rights campaigners Bernice Johnson and Cordell Reagon in Atlanta.

On 9 February 1964 – the day the Beatles were first on *The Ed Sullivan Show* –Bob Dylan drafted 'Chimes of Freedom' on notepaper from the Toronto Waldorf Astoria, an indication that the party was not skimping on accommodation. The critic Paul Williams has called it Bob's Sermon on the Mount. Could the chimes of freedom really be the songs of freedom? I say this because we hear chimes, we can't gaze upon them.

Dylan played 'Chimes of Freedom' for the first time at the Civic Auditorium in Denver on 15 February. While he was in Denver, he revisited coffee houses he had played. In Dallas he visited the site of the Kennedy assassination and visiting famous sites was to become a Dylan fixation.

Several unreleased songs were performed at Berkeley Community Theatre including 'Walls of Redwing', and Joan Baez joined him for 'With God on Our Side' and 'Blowin' in the Wind'. The students loved him and so did Ralph J. Gleason in the *San Francisco Chronicle* and Richard Fariña (hardly an unbiased reviewer) in *Mademoiselle*. The four travellers went to Carmel with Joan, Mimi, Richard and Joan's mum. The following day, February 24, they headed to Los Angeles in their station wagon.

Dylan sang 'The Lonesome Death of Hattie Carroll' on *The Steve Allen Show*, broadcast by CBS from Hollywood. Steve Allen found the song monotonous and Dylan uncooperative. The party stayed at the Thunderbird Motel for a couple of days and met up with friends.

In March 1964 Carla Rotolo introduced Bob Dylan to Paul Simon, but they were very guarded with each other. The next night the harmonies of Simon and Garfunkel sounded out of place at Gerde's Folk City. Simon thought a drunk Bob Dylan and Robert Shelton were laughing at them.

It was in March 1964 that Bob Dylan broke up with Suze Rotolo and he talks about the night in question in 'Ballad in Plain D', although it is also behind many of the songs on his next album, *Another Side of Bob Dylan*. All the Rotolos are put down in 'Ballad in Plain D'. Dylan has said that he doesn't write emotional songs: 'I did write one once and it wasn't very good – it was a mistake to record it.' Almost certainly, that was 'Ballad in Plain D', which incidentally is played in C. Dylan only performed it live once – in Ann Arbor, Michigan in July 1964.

Suze Rotolo, who had never seen herself as becoming Dylan's wife, said, 'I never felt hurt by the songs. I understood what he was doing. They were the way he saw the world.' There is a belated apology in the *Biograph* notes, 'I must have been a real schmuck to write that…it was a mistake to record it and I regret it.'

In March 1964 Robert Shelton wrote about Judy Collins in the *New York Times*. Liz Thomson: 'He wrote about Judy and about almost everyone who came out of that scene. It was the closest America had then to a national paper as it was before *USA Today*. He reviewed Judy's first concert in New York.' Indeed, and Shelton wrote, 'Judy Collins, a 23-year-old native of Denver, established herself without delay in the front rank of American balladeers. She was greeted with polite enthusiasm at the start, and by the end she had raised her large audience to cheers, whistles and bravos, all heartily deserved.'

Judy Collins: 'That was an amazing time and an amazing review. Robert Shelton was such a support. He was very important to Dylan and to everyone making music. If you sing something in a closet and nobody hears it and nobody talks about it, you are the Van Gogh of your age as nobody appreciated his work.'

In April 1964 Joan Baez sent in her tax return; 'I am not going to volunteer the 60% of my year's income tax that goes to armaments.' A press release was published and she was now a radical figure.

Joan Baez: 'I refused to pay taxes in 1964 and for the ten years following that. They put a lien on the house and the land and they would come to concerts and take money out of the cash register: they got it but they had to work for it. It was very gratifying for me that it was public knowledge that I had refused to donate to the war in Vietnam, where so much of the money was going. What I went inside for was aiding and abetting the draft resistance, supporting the men who refused to go and fight in Vietnam. We sat in at an induction centre and got ourselves arrested on their behalf. The first time 60 men and 30 women were arrested and then the second time 80 men and 60 women and that is when Martin Luther King came to visit me in jail. I was so honoured: the black women sneaked out and broke the rules just to touch him. Later on, they were reprimanded by the white sergeant who said, 'You can't go to the movies tonight', and they were rolling on the floor laughing, as if they cared after that.'

In April 1964 Bob Dylan was in Boston for a concert at Symphony Hall but also made a surprise appearance at Club 47. That same day the future record producer Joe Boyd met Mary Vangi who was working as a waitress and whom he had known at college. She said he could stay with her. She would be home at midnight, she told him, so come round after that and the key would be under the mat. Joe rolled up at 12.30, looking forward to some fun and found a note and the bedroom door shut. The note said, 'Change of plan, you'll never guess who's here!' Joe slept on the couch and in the morning he had breakfast with her and Bob. She said, 'Sorry, Joe, but I couldn't turn down that opportunity.' Joe found Dylan 'medium size, wiry, sarcastic and funny'.

On 30 April 1964, while celebrating Mimi Fariña's birthday in a restaurant, Dylan lashed out at Joan, mocking her appearance. Mimi grabbed his hair and said, 'Don't ever treat my sister like that again.' Next day he saw Joan off at the train station and Mimi heard Bob making a call, 'Don't worry, she just left.' He was ringing Sara.

Shirley Noznisky was born in Wilmington, Delaware on 28 October 1939. Her grandfather came from Odessa. Her father, Isaac, had a scrap metal business in the US, but he was killed in a hold-up in 1956. Shirley worked as a bunny girl at the Playboy Club in 1960, but it is not correct that her first husband was the Playboy executive, Victor Lownes. She was married to the fashion photographer Heinz Ludwig Lowenstein (Hans Lownds), who was 25 years her senior, and he changed her name to Sara. Their daughter Maria was born on 21 October 1961 but their marriage fell apart the following year.

Sara gravitated to the Village and worked in film production for Time-Life as a secretary and she knew the documentary filmmaker, D.A. Pennebaker. She met the waitress Sally Anne Buehler, who was dating Albert Grossman at the Bitter End. She had dropped out of school after being fascinated by Jack Kerouac's film, *Pull My Daisy*. Sally told her to watch Albert's client Bob Dylan on TV. She misheard and thought she was going to see Bobby Darin.

By all accounts, Sara was well read, good-hearted and a good listener, but like Bob, she could do an icy burn if she wanted to. Sara was slim and dark-haired like Joan Baez and Dylan met her and her daughter in 1964.

It is around this time that Bob first tried LSD in the company of Victor Maymudes and the record producer Paul Rothchild. From time to time, Dylan said he was against chemical drugs but even if he believed it, he didn't follow it.

When Bob Dylan came to the UK for a major concert and promotional visit: his UK promotion was handled by Ken Pitt. Ken Pitt says, 'People equate Bob Dylan with an ordinary pop singer who's all out for publicity. Dylan never was that and he's never understood that mentality. You might ask Dave Dee what he's done to his hair and he'd tell you where he had it done, who did it and how much it cost. A question like that throws Dylan completely.'

There was talk of Bob Dylan doing the BBC's teen programme, *Saturday Club*, but it did not materialise. On 12 May he was on the early evening news programme *Tonight* on the BBC singing 'With God on Our Side'. His oddest appearance was on ATV's religious programme, *Hallelujah*, hosted by Sydney Carter. It was filmed in Didsbury and he refused to rehearse. A security guard Neville requested 'Don't Think Twice, It's All Right', so he performed that and 'Chimes of Freedom'. Between the songs, Dylan said, 'That was a love song and this is an hallucinatory song', hardly appropriate for *Hallelujah*. Dylan gave Neville a white label copy of *The Times* album.

He was interviewed by Maureen Cleave for the *Evening Standard* while the *Daily Mirror* said he had earned £85,000 in the past year. He spoke to the editor of *Melody Maker*, Max Jones at the Mayfair Hotel. He said he was working on a play and a book of photographs with Barry Feinstein, but 'I don't really care to define what I do.'

Also for *Melody Maker*, Eric Winter had little luck with him as Dylan only replied 'Yup' or 'Nope' to a series of questions. Winter wrote his feature using the notes on the sleeve rather than reporting what had happened.

The main purpose of Dylan's visit was to appear at the Royal Festival Hall in London on 17 May 1964. It was an afternoon concert promoted by John Coast and all 2,700 seats were sold. Dylan played a two-hour concert and included 'Bob Dylan's Dream', 'Masters of War' and 'Girl from the North Country', which all had origins in the UK. *Freewheelin'* was in the UK charts and he did several songs from the album including 'Down the Highway'. Dylan gave the first public performance of 'Mr. Tambourine Man'. Oddly, he did not perform 'Blowin' in the Wind' but the concert was very well received. He was in good humour as he told a funny story about a movie, *Hootenanny*, which featured muscle men and girls in bikinis. Dylan signed autographs at the front of the stage and was mobbed at the stage door. The *Daily Sketch* had the headline, *No Voice but some Singer*.

Syd Barrett of Pink Floyd saw the concert and wrote a cynical but humorous song about him, 'Bob Dylan Blues'.

Pete Frame: 'I saw Dylan at the Royal Festival Hall in London in April 1964 and he totally blew me away. I was immersed in his music anyway. His first three albums had come out and he ambled onto the stage dragging his heels with his harmonica harness and he enraptured me and the rest of the audience for the whole of the show. He didn't have a capo with him and he borrowed one from someone in the audience, and everything he played was sensational. He made a huge impact on me.'

On 21 May 1964 Dylan went to Paris with another singer / songwriter Ben Carruthers. Dylan met Françoise Hardy in Paris and was to dedicate a poem to her on *Another Side of Bob Dylan*. He learnt about Jacques Brel and found him writing about a world that was not in other songs – death, prostitutes and the human condition.

Dylan asked Hugues Aufray to show him around. He bought a leather jacket on Boulevard St. Michel, which he wore in hundreds of photographs. Dylan started wearing Hugues' Cuban-heeled boots. He met Mason Hoffenberg who wrote the screenplay for *Candy* and was married to Hugues' cousin. He and Mason rented a Volkswagen and went to see the Berlin Wall.

He met the singer Nico, who was part of Andy Warhol's Factory. He played her a new song, 'It Ain't Me Babe', which she loved, and he gave her one that she could record 'I'll Take It with Mine'. There has been some debate as to how this song arose:

Judy Collins: 'On the *Bootleg Series* Dylan says that he wrote it for me and I believe him. There was a little argument about it as Joanie thought he had written it for her. We got him on the phone and Joanie said, "Okay, who did you write this for? Me or her?" He said, "I wrote it for Judy." I got it so it proves the point, I suppose, and he talks about it in his *histoire de Dylan*. To be honest, I didn't think it was a good song. I never put it on an album and I only recorded it for a single. Everything else of his was at such a high level, but at least it was my song.'

When Bob Dylan was in Vouliagmeni outside Athens in early June, he concentrated on writing songs for the next album. The songs were personal and he was dismissing his past in 'My Back Pages', sneering at his old self (from earlier in the year!). He was to say, 'There ain't no finger-pointing songs in here.'

Dylan was among the signatories to a letter supporting the comedian Lenny Bruce in his hounding by the media and the police for obscenity.

On 9 June 1964 Dylan recorded a whole album (plus more!) in a long session at Columbia studios, produced by Tom Wilson. This became the album, *Another Side of Bob Dylan*. The whole session was observed by a leading journalist Nat Hentoff for *The New Yorker*. Amongst other things, he obtained Dylan's side of the Tom Paine fiasco.

Hentoff was never kind to Ramblin' Jack Elliott, writing about him here as the person who brought in the wine. He was around because he was visiting his ex-wife Patty, who was staying with Sally Buehler, who was to marry Albert Grossman. Patty had sung him what she knew of 'Mr. Tambourine Man'. At the session, Dylan said to Jack, 'Let's do it' but he only knew the chorus. 'I know the words!' said Dylan and off they went. He stumbled over a few lines but it was a decent recording. They didn't try again as Dylan decided to leave it for another day.

This time Dylan was writing songs of love and was clearly writing about real relationships. His wit had returned as it was missing from the previous album, obviously deliberately.

Dylan didn't use 'Mama, You Been on My Mind' although it was an excellent song. Dylan tended to ham it up in concert with Joan Baez and it sounded better without her.

Although it is great to hear an album that was recorded at one session, it does have its drawbacks as you have to make do with what is there. For example, Dylan sniffs in 'All I really Want to Do' and at another point is about to break into laughter, possibly because he isn't sure of the lyric. You can tell that Dylan is having fun singing, 'I don't want to knock you up.' Pete Townshend was taken with this song and would play around with it a lot, getting inspiration.

'To Ramona' is a beautifully sensitive love song. Dylan said, 'That's pretty literal. That was just somebody I knew.'

Loudon Wainwright: 'If I got to choose one Bob Dylan song, I'd pick "To Ramona". I just love that song.'

Ralph McTell: 'I've spent a long time over Bob's lyrics and they reveal themselves in different ways and they don't follow a logical process either. Both 'To Ramona' and 'Love minus Zero / No Limit' are tangential. One thought doesn't unwrap the next. It is like each line is the first line of a new song. The lines are so great and yet he throws them away in a declamatory way. I emphasise my good lines and my good words in a song but they flow out of him. I still love listening to his early songs.'

'I Shall Be Free Number 10' is a continuation of 'I Shall Be Free' from *Freewheelin'* and an indication that Bob could write stoned nonsense whenever he wanted. Were there another eight versions? Certainly that is what he would like us to think. The inspiration for these songs is 'We Shall Be Free', a goodtime record made by Leadbelly, Woody Guthrie, Cisco Houston and Sonny Terry.

'Spanish Harlem Incident' is a strong love song about a one-night stand. What does 'Make my pale face fit into place' mean?

Dylan played piano on 'Black Crow Blues', a song of disillusionment that doesn't add up to much.

'I Don't Believe You' is a song about not recognising people who meant a lot to you. Strange behaviour but very much a Dylan trait.

'My Back Pages' is one of Dylan's most important songs as he is saying that he is moving away from protest songs. Roger McGuinn said in *Sing Out!* 'That protest song wasn't effective as a means of psychological warfare so he dropped it.'

A goodbye song, 'It Ain't Me Babe' was the final song of the album. Dylan is saying that he doesn't owe anybody anything and nobody should trust him as 'I will only let you down'. Perhaps this was his goodbye to being the spokesman of the generation. Was 'No, no, no' his answer to 'Yeah, yeah, yeah'?

Dylan hated Tom Wilson's title for the album, *Another Side of Bob Dylan*. He felt it was a negation of the past and yet Dylan himself is far more negative about it in 'My Back Pages'. Dylan looked like one of the Beat Generation writers and the album is about a 23 year old who is having trouble with girlfriends. Maybe that was the other side of Bob Dylan.

Dylan wrote some poems for the sleeve. Columbia couldn't fit them all onto the sleeve, but couldn't they have created a gatefold sleeve? In any event, the full complement was published in Dylan's *Writings and Drawings* (1973).

The first poem is the precursor to 'Subterranean Homesick Blues'. The fourth poem was adapted by Ben Carruthers for the song 'Jack O'Diamonds'. Carruthers was in the UK in 1965 for a TV play *The Man Without Papers* and he cut the song as a single with Jimmy Page on guitar.

Bob Dylan: Outlaw Blues

Despite Dylan's reservations, *Another Side of Bob Dylan* is a fine album which stands up today and it's a pity it was criticised at the time. The fans were upset by what wasn't there (goodbye to protest) rather than being pleased at what was there. Such stark, personal songs were something new for popular music, certainly in the US but he was probably inspired by Jacques Brel's frankness.

In July 1964 Bob Dylan went to Ondine's, an exclusive club on the East Side, to see Ronnie Spector. The house band was led by Jimi Hendrix, but they didn't meet that night. Hendrix said in 1969, 'I love Dylan. I only met him once about three years ago back at the Kettle of Fish on MacDougal Street. That was before I went to England. Both of us were pretty drunk at the time, so he probably doesn't remember it.'

When Dylan went to the Newport Folk Festival in July 1964, he had become the major performer, the hippest of the hip, and over 70,000 people had bought tickets for the event.

On the first day, he took part in a topical songwriting workshop where he sang 'Mr. Tambourine Man' and 'It Ain't Me Babe' and he sang 'With God on our Side' with Joan Baez. Later he joined Joan on stage for 'It Ain't Me Babe' so she had picked it up fast.

The next day he performed to a huge crowd introducing them to songs from *Another Side of Bob Dylan* but the fans were expecting protest songs. *Sing Out!* was unimpressed and called his new songs maudlin. Robert Shelton called his set lacklustre, but it wasn't. Pete Seeger felt he was no longer one of them, but Dylan said, 'Politics is not my thing at all.' Dylan was insisting he wasn't a protest singer, despite all the evidence to the contrary. Joan Baez remarked, 'Nobody could have written those songs and not meant it.' I think that's true but it's possible that Dylan may have felt that he had exhausted that well. It is very hard, if not impossible, to top 'Masters of War' and 'With God on Our Side'.

Sing Out! also said that José Feliciano 'needs to curb his exhibitionistic tendencies'– he's José Feliciano, for heaven's sake. Also, both Johnny Cash and Muddy Waters were playing electric sets.

In June 1964 'The Ballad of Ira Hayes' was released by Johnny Cash, written by Peter La Farge. It received little airplay as it implied the founding fathers were wrong. Elijah Wald: 'Pete Seeger introduced Johnny Cash in 1964. It was the first time that Cash had come to Newport and they were suspicious of him because he was a pop star. He wanted to tell people who Dylan was. From the point of Newport and New York, Dylan was the known quantity and Cash was the outsider. It is a reminder that Dylan who had never had a real radio hit was unknown in the rest of the country.'

Rodney Crowell: 'Johnny Cash had told me the story of the competition between himself and Bob Dylan. Bob Dylan had recorded 'Don't Think Twice, It's All Right' and John had done 'Understand Your Man'. They had the same melodies and there was an ongoing stalemate about who had the melody first. I think that it was some old folk song melody that had been going round for years that they had both pilfered.'

Newport Daily News printed many critical views of the festival. Possibly some of these came from locals who had been given free seats. Dr. John Carr commented that 'some of the lyrics advocate the overthrow of all parental, church and police authority.'

While the Newport Folk Festival was being staged, a famous folk song was on its way to topping the US pop charts – 'The House of the Rising Sun' by the Newcastle band, the Animals. The Animals had picked up the song from Bob Dylan's first LP. It now had a macho lead vocal from Eric Burdon and an organ solo from Alan Price.

Alan Price: 'It is a Jacobean folk song, originally about a brothel in Soho, and it was taken by the emigrants to America and it became an Appalachian folk song and then some black artists picked it up and Josh White made it his own. It came full circle with us – from white to black to white.'

John Steel, drummer with the Animals: 'Eric Burdon had heard 'Rising Sun' long before the Dylan version but it was the Dylan version that inspired us to do it. We followed the same chord sequence and just made it electric.'

Ramblin' Jack Elliott: 'I remember sitting in Bob Dylan's car at Newport, Rhode Island at the end of the festival in 1964. That record had just come out and they were playing it on the radio as we were saying goodbye. Bob was going in one direction and I was going someplace else and the record came on of the Animals doing 'The House of the Rising Sun' and at the same time we both exclaimed, "Hey, that's my arrangement." We couldn't help laughing.'

Back to John Steel: 'We wanted to meet Dylan. 'The House of the Rising Sun' was on his first album and that is what inspired us to experiment with it. We went to Al Grossman's apartment and had a bite to eat and Bob took us on a little tour of his favourite places in Greenwich Village. We had a big drinking session and ended up in Dave Van Ronk's apartment. He said that when he heard our version of 'Rising Sun" he knew what he wanted to do next. He played us an early mix of 'Subterranean Homesick Blues', so we influenced each other on 'Rising Sun'.'

Hilton Valentine, guitarist with the Animals; 'Pricey's name went on it only because our manager said that there was not enough room to put "arranged by Price, Burdon, Valentine, Steel and Chandler". They put Pricey down and it was understood that the royalties would be shared equally. As soon as he got the first royalty cheque, he left the band.'

Alan Price: 'Al Grossman told me that the greatest thing that the white groups did was to give white players in America their self-respect because they had always been under the shadow of the black players. The blues musicians told us that they appreciated what groups like the Stones and the Animals were doing as they had been living on pennies. They were playing hellholes and they achieved their proper place in American music. B.B. King became a major star but he was playing in out of the way places until we came along.'

Protest songs were entering the supper club world and Bobby Darin was putting Dylan songs into his shows for Vegas. Duke Ellington was playing 'Blowin' in the Wind' with three trumpets in unison. Sam Cooke was singing the same song with a big band at the Copa, although he did it so fast that he was not dwelling on the lyric. He was amazed that a song that addressed civil rights could go to Number 2 in the pop charts, but why were the songs being written by white kids in Greenwich Village? He put his feelings into 'A Change Is Gonna Come', which he hoped would speak to everyone. It crossed musical barriers – gospel, blues, nightclub and protest.

The first Big Sur Folk Festival took place in 1964, run by a resident Nancy Carlen. Just 1,000 attended despite Joan Baez headlining. Jac Holzman offered the Fariñas a record contract at Elektra but they preferred to sign with Vanguard and they shared the same manager as Joan Baez, an older man Manny Greenhill. Mimi wouldn't contemplate Albert Grossman as a manager as she had heard so many bad things about him.

In August 1964 Bob, Joan, Mimi and Richard moved to Woodstock for the summer. Although they valued their privacy, Daniel Kramer took some excellent photographs and would continue to do so.

Mimi and Richard worked on their album, *Celebrations for a Grey Day* which they recorded in Manhattan. They had two travelling songs with rock backing, 'One Way Ticket' and 'Reno, Nevada', which was progressive for Vanguard. Bruce Langhorne played a rocking solo in 'Reno Nevada' with some bluesy licks. It's a good track but Fariña had a nondescript voice. The UK cover version by Fairport Convention is far better but hey, they had Richard Thompson.

Their version would have been improved if Mimi had taken the lead vocal but Richard was said to have 'Cuban jealousy'. In other words, he didn't want Mimi in control, either artistically or socially. He didn't want her to be independent and he didn't want her to drive.

Richard bought a Triumph 350 motorbike from Barry Feinstein. He, Bob and John Sebastian enjoyed riding around Woodstock. Joan didn't like Bob out on the road at all and certainly didn't like being driven by him: she said, 'I always feared that he was trying to drive and write a song at the same time.'

Bob Dylan took Joan Baez to meet Bob Markel at Macmillan's New York office to discuss a book. A possible title was *Side One*, but it became *Tarantula*. The advance was for $10,000 and the book was to be delivered within a year. Richard Fariña was jealous of the ease with which Bob had the contract, but now he had to write it. He worked on the book while he was with Joan, ramblings really with no message.

Bob joined Joan Baez in Forest Hills and they did 'With God on Our Side' and 'Mama, You Been on My Mind' together, but it was a poor performance by Dylan who had drunk too much and vomited over a fan. (Who was this fan? Did he remain one? Another Judas moment!) Dylan scared everybody by driving back that night. Robert Shelton wrote a review referring to 'the declining nature of Dylan's new compositions'. Joan wrote a letter to her mother, 'I've got very close to Bobby in the last month. Wow, he takes baths and everything.'

Mort Sahl joked that Baez and Dylan were the Burton and Taylor of the self-righteous set. The front cover and lead story of *Hootenanny* magazine had them as a couple. Izzy Young commented, 'They would get married if they could only agree on whose last name to use.'

Al Aronowitz was born in New Jersey on 20 May 1928. He wrote the Pop Scene column for the *New York Post*. He met Dylan mid-1963 when writing for *Saturday Evening Post*. He said, 'Dylan was doing more to change the English Language than anybody since Shakespeare.' But he recognised that Dylan could be cranky and nasty. 'I consider Bob to be one of the greatest artists ever born, but he's not the kind of guy I would trust with my wife. Unfortunately, I once did.'

At the end of August 1964 Bob Dylan with Al Aronowitz met the Beatles at Hotel Delmonico in New York. Dylan brought some pot. He was not introducing the Beatles to pot as is often claimed, as they had previously smoked it with the comedy actress Cherri Gilham in London. In September he saw them on stage at the Paramount and was with them afterwards. He said, 'There was no way you could hear them.'

In September 1964 the Byrds made their first stab at recording 'Mr. Tambourine Man', but it wasn't quite right. Roger McGuinn went to see the Beatles' film, *A Hard Day's Night* and immediately watched it again as he wanted to check what George Harrison was playing: it was a 12-string electric guitar. He wanted one.

In September 1964 Miles Davis threw a party for Robert Kennedy, who was running for office in New York and Bob Dylan attended. Shortly after that, Robert Kennedy picked up a Dylan album and said, 'This is what young people are thinking.' Kennedy was unimpressed by Dylan's voice but when he heard Bobby Darin sing 'Blowin' in the Wind', he got what Dylan was saying.

On 31 October 1964 Dylan played the Philharmonic Hall in New York, which was part of the Lincoln Centre. He said, 'It's Halloween. I have my Bob Dylan mask on. I'm mask-erading.'

Despite plenty of serious songs ('Hard Rain', 'Hattie Carroll'), the show is full of jokes, raps and getting things wrong. Someone calls out for 'Mary Had a Little Lamb' and he says deadpan, 'Is that a protest song?' (Actually, it was!) He laughs at his falsetto on 'All I Really Want to Do' and when he switches on the radio in 'Talkin' World War III Blues', he hears Martha and the Vandellas and it is the poet Carl Sandburg 'who said that'. When he starts playing 'I Don't Believe You', he asks if anybody knows the first line.

'Who Killed Davey Moore' is greeted like a hit song; possibly it was based on a big news story from the previous year and the audience could relate to it. Mind you, they also clap the announcer saying, 'No smoking, no pictures'.

The show included his only public performance of 'Spanish Harlem Incident' – heavens know why he didn't include this song more often. Joan Baez joined him for four songs, taking a solo on 'Silver Dagger' with Bob on harmonica. He is making it difficult for Baez to harmonise on 'Mama, You've Been on My Mind': listen to the way he draws out the first syllable of each verse – it is hilarious but you feel sorry for Joan. It reveals how awkward he can be.

And that's not all. In the programme, Dylan included a new poem. 'Advice for Geraldine on Her Miscellaneous Birthday', the advice being to be a radical and when asked to give your real name, never give it.

The concert was recorded by Columbia for a live album and even given a catalogue number but it was not released as Dylan's career was moving so fast. Indeed, Dylan's first official live album wasn't released until 1974 but he has made up for lost time ever since.

It would have made a fine album including 'If You Gotta Go, Go Now' and several songs not on studio albums. Robert Shelton was back on side calling him 'the brilliant singing poet laureate of young America'. Irwin Silber wrote an open letter to Dylan in his magazine *Sing Out!* saying that Dylan was influenced by his hard-drinking cronies but wasn't it ever thus?

On the other hand, few artists have had Dylan's determination. He is going to do what he wants to do no matter what. He didn't mind that audiences weren't going to get it and he wouldn't listen to those who wanted him to drop something. He also knew that he had a very distinctive but somewhat limited voice: he paved the way for Lou Reed and Tom Waits, artists who have learnt to live and work with their voices and turn them into assets. Joan Baez had a wonderful voice and I think Dylan would have hated to have a voice like that. It was all part of his uniqueness.

In November 1964 Johnny Cash released an early folk-rock single, his version of 'It Ain't Me Babe'. It was spoilt by strident backing harmonies from June Carter.

On 12 November 1964 Albert and Sally Grossman were married with Bob and Sara among the guests. Dylan gave up his apartment on West Fourth Street and moved into the Grossman's apartment while they were honeymooning in Europe. Then they moved into Room 211 of the Chelsea Hotel on West 23rd Street. They had three-year-old Maria with them. Her first husband, Hans, died in 1995 and he never saw his daughter again.

Dylan moved a piano into the room and wrote songs there. Dylan was still seeing

Joan Baez and she didn't know about Sara for six months. While Dylan was in the UK, he propositioned both Dana Gillespie and Marianne Faithfull. In 1980 there was a headline in *News of the World*, *I Was Dylan's Cuddly Teddy Bear*, and it was Dana Gillespie's memories. Let's say Bob's hormones were raging.

Dylan went on some concert dates around the US and a 15-year-old Tom Waits saw Dylan at the Peterson Gymnasium at San Diego State University. He commented, 'Here's a guy on stage with a stool and a glass of water and he tells these great stories in his songs. It helped unlock the mystery of performance.'

In December 1964 Tom Wilson overdubbed instruments on Dylan's version of 'House of The Rising Sun', but it was not issued until 1995 on CD-ROM. It hadn't really worked but Wilson was experimenting. He called 'The House of the Rising Sun' by the Animals the first folk-rock record and was keen to take this forwards.

The model Edie Sedgwick met Bobby Neuwirth at the Gaslight. She had a relationship with Bobby Neuwirth and she was then introduced to Dylan at the Kettle of Fish. There was talk of her making a record but she couldn't hold a tune. Both men were fascinated by her connection with Andy Warhol's Factory.

Bob Dylan put surprise presents under the Christmas tree for Joan Baez: an African scarf, a yo-yo, a seashell, a pogo stick, some *Batman* comics, Lorca's *Gypsy Ballads*, a coonskin cap and Blind Lemon Jefferson's 'Bedbug Blues'.

In 1964 Phil Ochs wrote a prickly, end of year piece for the male magazine, *Cavalier*. Part of *That Was the Year that Weren't* ran:

COVER: A dungareed, half-smiling, long-haired boy walking down a snow-covered street with Suze Rotolo.

TITLE: *The Freestealin' Phil Ochs*

COVER: A dungareed, half-smiling, long-haired boy leaning over the body of a dead Negro woman with a cane.

TITLE: *Still Another Side of Bob Dylan*

Music writer Terry Hamblin: 'It is very hard to understand Dylan's psychology. Dylan might have been uncomfortable with protest songs but he didn't shy away from them either. Maybe Dylan didn't like being a spokesperson but he embraced it as well.'

Bob Stanley: 'Some artists do want to be the spokesman for a generation – Michael Stipe and Bono spring to mind. Dylan didn't want to do that. Having read *Chronicles* and listened to his radio shows, it is much easier to put his work in perspective. He wasn't solely a political songwriter and he became very uncomfortable about it.'

Bob Spitz: 'When Bob caught on, people followed him everywhere. When he sat down, they would grab the napkin off his plate; they would grab his scraps because the great Dylan had touched it. We have encountered that with Beatlemania and the Stones and Bruce Springsteen and Michael Jackson and Madonna. Dylan didn't know what was happening and he thought everybody was crazy but not him. It made him very wary and to this day people camp outside his house wanting to touch him and wanting him to explain his songs. They have become a nuisance in his life.'

We will see how Bob Dylan's success affected his contemporaries, notably Paul Clayton, Peter La Farge and Phil Ochs but it also had positive outcomes as recording managers wanted to sign acts from the Village. José Feliciano says, 'I was playing at Gerde's Folk City and this feller from RCA Records came to see a group called the Wanderers Three. It was a Kingston Trio-type group. I opened for them and he didn't sign them but he came over to me and said, 'How would you like to be on RCA?' We talked and he produced my first album which was *The Voice and Guitar of José Feliciano* and then *A Bag Full of Soul*. I was only about 19 years old at the time and it was a wonderful thing to sign with him.'

III. I Can't Help If I'm Lucky

A recurring question when writing the last few chapters has been why didn't Bob Dylan receive his draft papers or if he did, how did he avoid serving in the US forces and perhaps being sent to Vietnam?

Judging by what we know of him, there would have been no reason for exclusion at the time he graduated in terms of physical fitness or mental ability, but his service could have been deferred because he was attending the University of Minnesota from the age of 18. If he had received his call-up papers, he would have had a good reason to apply himself to his studies.

In 1958 Elvis joined the US army in what was seen a recruitment drive. Colonel Parker would have never agreed to Elvis doing regular service instead of entertaining the troops if there had been a war on with a possibility of his valuable client being killed. Elvis left the army in 1960 just before the Cold War became a physical war under the new President, John F. Kennedy. The first American casualty in Vietnam was in December 1961.

My guess is that Dylan received no call-up papers and it is significant that Dylan never aligned himself to the youngsters who were burning their draft cards or fleeing to Canada. Dylan told *Playboy* in February 1966: 'Burning draft cards isn't going to end any war. It's not even going to save any lives. If someone can feel more honest with himself by burning his draft card, then that's great; but if he's just going to feel more important because he does it, then that's a drag.'

Also, Dylan never, at the time, came out against the war in Vietnam. Indeed, he told one reporter, 'How do you know I'm not for the war?'

In 1965 the number of men being conscripted increased to 35,000 a month but by then Dylan was 24 years old and it was usually younger men who were conscripted. In November 1965 Dylan was married and he adopted Sara's daughter, Maria, and both events would push him further down the line. He had his motorcycle accident in 1966 and it would be relatively easy to find a doctor who would say he was unfit for service. By the time of the big draft in 1969, Dylan, at 28, would have been too old to fight.

It is possible that the US military might not have wanted him anyway as he would have been seen as potentially disruptive and this could have weakened their cause. Indeed, there would be a media circus around him.

If he had been conscripted, he might have avoided active conflict with concerts for the troops though the press might have viewed this as a cop out.

IV. There but for Fortune: Phil Ochs

It is always fascinating when writing a biography to contrast the subject with a fellow performer who might have been equally talented but somehow took the wrong turnings or made the wrong decisions: Dick Haymes with Frank Sinatra or Gene Vincent with Elvis Presley, for example. With Bob Dylan, the most pertinent comparison can be drawn with Phil Ochs.

Phil Ochs was born in El Paso on 19 December 1940, the son of an army medical officer. He grew up in many places, including six months in Scotland, but the family eventually settled in Columbus, Ohio. Ochs studied journalism and political science at Ohio State University. His chosen subject became Dylan's line of mockery, calling him a journalist rather than a songwriter.

Ochs shared digs with folksinger Jim Glover and they were soon performing together as the Sundowners, the name coming from a 1960 Robert Mitchum film. They described themselves as 'the singing socialists'. The strong negative feedback to a pro-Castro article he wrote for the university's magazine led to him being relegated to record reviewing.

During vacations Ochs travelled with his guitar and, after being jailed for vagrancy, he was in further trouble for befriending black prisoners. He began writing songs about the problems of the day and in 1961, he went to Greenwich Village, intending to perform in folk clubs. He said, 'I looked around the folk circuit and found a lot of amateurs but as soon as I saw Dylan, I knew that I could never match him.'

Ochs and Dylan were as much rivals as friends. The love-hate relationship between Dylan and Ochs spanned many years and Ochs is as well known for his part in Dylan's career as he is for his own music. Both singers visited the sick. Woody Guthrie and Ochs' tribute, 'Bound for Glory', is the equal of Dylan's 'Song to Woody'. Other early songs such as 'Links in the Chain' and 'Power and the Glory' are in the Guthrie tradition.

Ochs performed at the Third Side coffeehouse in Greenwich Village but only received payments by passing the hat around. He married a young actress Alice Skinner and they lived close to poverty. Eventually Phil was booked at the Gaslight and in 1963 he recorded 'The Ballad of William Worthy' for *Broadside Ballads, Volume 1* – an album that featured Bob Dylan as Blind Boy Grunt and then he had 'The Ballad of Medgar Evers' and 'Talking Birmingham Jail' on a live album from the 1963 Newport Folk Festival, again with Dylan on the same album. Vanguard recorded Phil for the *New Folks* album, which also featured Eric Andersen, and this album marked the first recording of 'There but for Fortune'.

In the programme for the 1963 Newport Folk Festival, Phil Ochs comments, 'I wouldn't be surprised to see an album called *Elvis Presley sings Songs of the Spanish Civil War*.' This thought was to stay with him and was to manifest itself in a unique manner.

In 1964 Phil Ochs joined Elektra and he made *All the News That's Fit to Sing* with 'The Power and the Glory' and 'Talking Cuban Crisis'. Then *I Ain't Marching Anymore* (1965) with 'Draft Dodger Rag' and 'Here's to the State of Mississippi'. The albums are superb examples of protest writing and the second is opinionated on everything in sight (segregation, Cuba, Vietnam, religion and capital punishment) and Phil commented that the title song, 'I Ain't Marchin' Anymore' combined the best qualities of pacifism and treason. It can be compared to Buffy Sainte-Marie's 'Universal Soldier', though both songs would be trumped by Dylan's 'With God on Our Side'. When folk-rock came into fashion, Ochs released a band version of 'I Ain't Marchin' Anymore' which looked like opportunism and didn't sell. He wasn't helped by such Dylan remarks as 'I have no respect whatsoever for Phil Ochs', but they enjoyed winding each other up.

Ochs alienated the authorities in Alabama with 'Talking Birmingham Jail' and in 'Here's to the State of Mississippi', he chronicled the state's many evils concluding:

"Here's to the land you've torn out the heart of,
Mississippi, find another country to be part of."

Unfortunately, truly controversial songs don't get airplay and so it was the more generalised protest ones ('Blowin' in the Wind') which picked up sales. However, Joan Baez hit the charts with Ochs' song for the homeless, 'There but for Fortune'.

Dylan was moving away from protest so Phil Ochs became the political song champion. Ochs cleverly likened Dylan to a frog, hopping around while we are trying to dissect him.

Phil Ochs in Concert in 1966 is a superlative record, showing how good he was as a live performer and how engagingly he spoke. It was a live album of all new material and the album included 'There but for Fortune' (recorded the previous year by Joan Baez), 'Changes', 'Love Me, I'm a Liberal' and the prophetic 'When I'm Gone'. His introductions were very humorous and those moments were often when he was being his most serious.

Although the sentiments of most protest singers are to be applauded, their music is often hard going and Ochs' saving grace was his wit. 'Love Me, I'm a Liberal' is the best example but there are sardonic overtones in most songs. The faux Pepsodent commercial in 'Talking Cuban Crisis' says, 'Have whiter teeth, Have cleaner breath, When you're facing nuclear death.' He adapted poems he knew from school ('The Bells' and 'The Highwayman') but it never distracted from his real aim: 'I want to build a career in which a truly controversial song can become a hit single.'

Phil Ochs made a tactical mistake: he didn't write love songs. Dylan and Ochs wrote about morality, mortality, politics and religion but Dylan also had sex in there.

'Changes' shows how tender Ochs could be but he never developed his more lyrical aspects. He was capable of following Tom Paxton and touring for life, but this didn't interest him.

Shortly after Joan Baez had a hit with 'There but for Fortune', Phil Ochs toured the British folk clubs. In Liverpool he said he would not sing 'There but for Fortune' if the hosts Jacqui and Bridie joined in, while at Manchester he introduced it as 'a song written for me by Miss Joan Baez'. He performed 'Talking Airplane Blues' in which the airsick traveller turns out to be the pilot.

There but for fortune indeed.

V. Hawk-eyed: Ronnie Hawkins and the Hawks

"It's Wednesday. Let's get drunk."

Ronnie Hawkins' opening words on meeting Spencer Leigh, 1986

Life on the other side....

Bob Dylan and The Band is one of the most inventive musical collaborations of the twentieth century, but where did they come from? Like Bob they were raised on rock and roll, but they had far greater practical experience and they learnt their trade from Ronnie Hawkins who was out where the buses don't run. As a result, we had two parties – Bob and The Band – who were really up for anything.

The wild men of rock like Little Richard, Gene Vincent and Ronnie Hawkins were characters who would never have made it in earlier decades. Ronnie Hawkins says, 'Dave Brubeck was playing to a few people in a little jazz place in Arkansas that was really elegant and I was in a funky old club and they were lining up to get in. He came to see what in hell was going on and I was doing the back flips and screaming at the top of my lungs. He called it a monkey act and said I was the abortion of music.' Maybe but Ronnie Hawkins had one of the tightest and most disciplined bands in the early days of rock'n'roll, the Hawks.

Ronnie Hawkins was born in Huntsville, Arkansas in 1935, two days after Elvis Presley. He grew up in Fayetteville, Arkansas and when he was only 12, he had a 20-year-old girlfriend and in his words was 'learning about life'. By 1952 he knew that he wanted to form a country band but he also ran a bootleg whisky operation. He did his national service and worked with the Hollywood star, Esther Williams, on some personal appearances at swimming pools.

By 1957 Ronnie knew that he had to have a rock'n'roll band and he recruited Levon Helm on drums. The son of a cotton farmer, Mark Lavon (sic) Helm was born near Marvell, Arkansas, 70 miles from Memphis on 26 May 1940. His name was often mispronounced and so he became Levon. His father played the mandolin and Levon and his sister would play alongside him. Unlike Bob Dylan, Levon really did play drums for Conway Twitty and then he moved over to Ronnie Hawkins. Conway had a band that was as wild as Ronnie's: one of the band members bit off a girl's nipple in an excited moment in the back of a van as they were travelling.

When Levon joined the Hawks in 1957, he had to be hustled in and out of clubs in case the authorities were around as he was too young. They were signed to Roulette Records in New York, not realising it was a gangster operation run by Morris Levy. They cut some fine singles including 'Forty Days, 'Ruby Baby', 'Mary Lou' and 'Southern Love (Whatcha Gonna Do)'. Ronnie Hawkins told audiences, 'There ain't no difference between me and Elvis except maybe looks and talent.'

One of their songs 'Odessa' was about a prostitute friend of both Ronnie and Levon. Ronnie though didn't like paying for sex and his standard chat-up line was 'C'mon here, you pretty young thing, and give me some sugar.' I'm sure if I tried it, it would be disastrous but Ronnie would say it with a nod and a wink and draw the girls in.

By 1959 they had Fred Carter Jr as lead guitarist and he would become one of Nashville's top session musicians. Ronnie would annoy him by stealing his girlfriends. The bass player Lefty Evans didn't like their wild living and left to become a preacher.

Early in 1960, Jack Good was producing a Saturday teatime beat show for ATV, *Boy Meets Girls*, hosted by Marty Wilde. Good wanted American acts on the show, largely because it would increase viewing figures and also show the British acts how rock'n'roll should be performed. A bit costly perhaps but a win-win situation as nobody else was doing it. Larry Parnes was bringing over Gene Vincent and Eddie Cochran, who were featured regularly and he also invited Johnny Cash, Ronnie Hawkins and Brenda Lee.

Jack Good hadn't got the budget for the whole band and in any event he wanted Hawkins to work with local boys. It was agreed that Ronnie would come over early in 1960 with just his drummer Levon Helm. Ronnie was won over by Joe Brown and offered him a job with the Hawks, but Joe decided to stay in the UK. 'Who knows,' says Joe today, 'I might have ended up in The Band.' Ronnie and Levon had a good time in London, perhaps too good a time as Levon returned with a souvenir of London, venereal disease.

Known as Robbie, Jaime Robertson was born in Toronto on 5 July 1943. His father was a Jewish gambler connected to the Mob who got killed in a shoot-out, and his uncle did time for a diamond robbery. His mother was a Mohawk who remarried and they lived in the impoverished Cabbagetown area of Toronto. He played with a group called Caesar and the Consuls and then the Suedes, getting to know Ronnie Hawkins when he was 15. The pianist in the Suedes, Scott Cushnie, was to join the Hawks before Robbie did.

By now Ronnie Hawkins and the Hawks had become a showband. Quite often Ronnie Hawkins would leave the stage for a drink or a quick fuck and the others would take over. Levon had a solo with Larry Williams' 'Short Fat Fanny' and he had a hawk motif on his drums. Ronnie's absences would irritate them as he was taking the bulk of the cash.

When the rhythm guitarist Jimmy Ray Paulman left in April 1960, Ronnie invited Robbie to join the band. Ronnie told him, 'Son, you won't make much money but you'll get more pussy than Frank Sinatra.' A tempting offer indeed, so Robbie was soon travelling from Toronto to Fayetteville, Arkansas to join the Hawks. He had never been this far before and he was told not to mention at the border that he was going to a job.

At first Fred Carter was unhelpful, saying to Robbie, 'Nobody ever showed me nothing. Why should I show you?' Then he changed his mind and he showed Robbie how to get a better sound by using a banjo string for a high E. Robbie met the modest Carl Perkins who gave him good advice, 'I'm just trying to get a bit better than I was yesterday.'

Ronnie's sales pitch to Robbie had been true but he stole Robbie's first girlfriend. 'She might not have been ready for you,' said Ronnie, 'but she was ready for me. She just wanted someone a little more grown-up.'

Poor Robbie. When they did some dates with Bo Diddley, Bo went into Robbie's hotel room and sang a love song to his girl: 'When this young man's gone, Bo Diddley move in. Patricia gotta know, Real loving ain't no sin.' Bo got the girl.

As Fred Carter wanted to settle down to session work in Nashville, Ronnie Hawkins invited Roy Buchanan to take over on lead guitar. He was a brilliant guitarist who was into fast runs and extreme string bending and he didn't mind showing Robbie his tricks. However, he was a very odd character, calling himself half human, half wolf and he felt he would only be settled if he married a nun (which he did!). Even by Ronnie Hawkins' standards, Roy was too weird and he couldn't be a full-time Hawk. When Roy had a guitar battle with Robbie on stage, Ronnie Hawkins realised that Robbie was good enough to take over and Robbie established himself with his Fender Telecaster.

When Morris Levy saw Robbie Robertson, he said to Hawkins, 'Nice looking kid. I bet you don't know whether to hire him or fuck him.'

Offered shorter working hours and getting more money, Ronnie Hawkins and the Hawks moved to Canada. He told me, 'An agent came to New York looking for acts to play in the clubs he looked after in Hamilton, Ontario. He thought he would try some rock'n'roll and Conway Twitty went there and it worked. He chiseled out a good following and stayed. When 'It's Only Make Believe' hit the bigtime, Conway had to leave Hamilton and he started touring the States.'

In a bizarre moment in 1960, Ronnie Hawkins recorded a folky single, 'The Ballad of Caryl Chessman', the true and current story of a killer on Death Row. It led to Hawkins wanting to record folk and country and Hawkins paid two visits to Nashville to make the albums, *Folk Ballads* and *The Songs of Hank Williams*, using session musicians and the ever-faithful Levon Helm.

Ronnie said he was looking for new songs. Robertson wrote 'Hey Boba Lou' and 'Someone like You' which Hawkins recorded. Robbie said, 'The worst record I made with Ronnie Hawkins was 'There's a Screw Loose' but I was too young to tell him not to do it.' Nevertheless, Hawkins would often show him songs that others had written as he wanted his comments.

Morris Levy, true to form, had a gravelly gangster voice. He told one performer, 'See that Cadillac convertible parked down there. I can drop you onto it or you can walk down there with the keys and drive away. All you have to do is sign the papers.'

When Robbie's songs were released, he noted that they were credited to Robertson and Magil. He asked Ronnie who it was and was told it was an alias for Morris Levy. 'But he didn't write them,' said Robbie. Ronnie Hawkins replied, 'Son, there are some things in this business that you don't even question.'

Robbie on the Hawks: 'We got to one of those places that Hank Ballard and the Midnighters had just left. We had to follow them and they had a routine where for some extra dollars, they'd play naked except for little gold jockstraps.'

The band was not paid for a residency in Tulsa and the next band in was fronted by Leon Russell. After the first night, Ronnie and the Hawks returned to the club, removed Leon's equipment and then burnt the club down. They worked some low dives for Jack Ruby, who was to kill Lee Harvey Oswald. He had them working in a club with a one-armed stripper.

They were also booked into New York's hot spot, the Peppermint Lounge, which then was Twist Central. They were told, 'If you don't do more Twist music, we're going to fire you.' They started twisting.

When the Hawks were playing in Stratford, Ontario early in 1962, they heard an outstanding pianist and singer in Richard Manuel of the Rockin' Revols. Richard Manuel was known as Beak because of his long nose. He had been born in Stratford in 1943 and he sang 'Little Boy Blue' (Bobby 'Blue' Bland) and 'Georgia on My Mind' (Ray Charles) with a lot of soul. They sensed he might have a drink problem but he was invited to join the band and became best friends with Robbie. Together they did a great version of 'Bring It on Home to Me'. In Ontario, they were impressed by an 18 year old who could sing like Sam Cooke, Rick Danko. He had a girl he planned to marry and he was training to be a butcher. Encouraged by Levon and Robbie, he learnt bass and so by 1963, Robbie, Rick, Richard and Levon were in the Hawks. Ronnie wanted to add singer Bruce Bruno from New York to the Revue. He often had a bad throat and was too fond of middle of the road songs for the rest of them and he didn't last.

Ronnie Hawkins had fallen out with his agent Colonel Kudlets but with his connections, he could easily find the Hawks some work and they had a residency in Le Coq D'Or in Toronto and Ronnie started his own after-hours club, the Hawk's Nest, also in Toronto. Ronnie banned girlfriends from Le Coq D'Or as he felt the band had to mingle with the crowd. Levon demanded higher wages as sometimes Ronnie Hawkins would hardly perform. This led to the Hawks leaving Ronnie Hawkins.

In order to avoid the draft, Levon married one of his girlfriends, Connie from the Concord Tavern. It was at the Concord in December 1962 that they met John Hammond Jr for the first time. He was the son of Bob Dylan's record producer and was a promising blues singer. He got up with the Hawks and they played some exciting electric blues together.

Ronnie Hawkins had been performing 'Hey Bo Diddley' for years and in January 1963 he recorded it in New York with the Hawks – then Robertson, Danko, Manuel and Roy Buchanan on bass. He combined it with Bo Diddley's 'Who Do You Love' as one long track, but it was split into two for a Roulette single. It was seriously good, a great rave-up which deserved to be a big hit. In the jargon of the day, it was 'Bubbling under the Hot

100' but it was too aggressive and in your face for its time: five years later it could have been a heavy rock classic. Still, a mass murderer from Phoenix cited it as one of his favourite records. This wild, wild single certainly sounded like nothing else from 1963.

Over in Canada, Garth Hudson was becoming a competent musician: 'My roots came from rhythm and blues. I first heard it on the radio from the Alan Freed show from Cleveland, Ohio. It would come across Lake Erie to London, Ontario and I heard these recordings at 5.05 every day. I didn't know that they were all black, but I knew that someone over there was having more fun than I was. I learnt all the tenor sax instrumentals that were on every jukebox in the black community. Every tenor sax player had to play 'Honky Tonk' and so I got together with some guys and a girl singer in London in 1957 called the Capers. Membership changed a little bit and I went with the group to Windsor and Detroit and played there for a couple of years and that was Paul London and the Capers.'

The Hawks met Garth Hudson in London, Ontario. He had a new gizmo that could make a piano sound like an organ which intrigued them. He was quiet and classically trained and Ronnie Hawkins had to explain to his parents what a good career opportunity this was. He would also give the rest of the band music lessons. Robbie says, 'Garth could run rings round the rest of us.' One odd feature: he had narcolepsy and could fall asleep at any time. All five members of The Band were now in place and in May 1963 they recorded 'Bossman', 'High Blood Pressure' and 'There's a Screw Loose' with Ronnie Hawkins. That is the only time all five members of The Band recorded with Ronnie Hawkins until *The Last Waltz*.

The Hawks and Ronnie Hawkins were falling apart. Ronnie wasn't paying them enough and he didn't like them spending their money on grass.

When the Hawks left, Harold Kudlets became their manager. Levon assumed leadership, calling the group Levon and the Hawks. They copied Booker T and the MG's who worked at Stax and didn't go for exciting instrumental solos between the verses; it was better to build on the atmosphere and then crash in with the next verse. They recorded a single, 'The Stones I Throw', which was inspired by the Staple Singers. You can hear how Garth's organ is developing into The Band's sound.

They met the bluesman Paul Butterfield in Chicago. Levon didn't like him and thought him unhygienic but he had the best weed around. When they knew he was out, Levon and Robbie went to his place and stole the weed. Butterfield was to accuse the guitarist in the Paul Butterfield Blues Band, Mike Bloomfield.

Meanwhile, John Hammond Jr had determined that the guitarists Mike Bloomfield and Robbie Robertson would sound great together. He invited Levon and the Hawks to join him in New York for an album which worked out fine but not in a way that Hammond had anticipated. Bloomfield was overawed by Robertson's technique and would only play piano. The resulting album, *So Many Roads*, was a hot, bluesy record, although Greil Marcus was to criticise Hammond's 'blackface vocal'. The Hawks had clearly enjoyed their earlier arrangement of 'Who Do You Love' as they reprised it for this LP.

Hammond was so pleased with the sessions that he gave them some Panama Red to celebrate. They were taking it back to Canada but unfortunately Rick Danko had fallen out with his girlfriend, who informed the police. He was arrested at the airport and given a 12-month suspended sentence.

Mary Martin, who worked for Albert Grossman, came from Toronto and she knew Levon and the Hawks from their residency at Tony's Mart and was very impressed. She had to be circumspect in recommending them to Grossman as he loathed John Hammond and thereby by extension, his son John Hammond Jr.

We will see how all this comes together in the next chapter and how Ronnie Hawkins had, unknowingly, created the perfect group for Bob Dylan, that is The Band. Do we have to feel sorry for Ronnie Hawkins? Not really as he has lived a rocking, rollicking life and never really had the application to further his own career. He is an extraordinary, larger-than-life character and when I asked him about one of his more dubious exploits he said, 'Everybody does stuff they don't want the world to know about.'

CHAPTER 6
Electricity + Eccentricity / No Limit

I. Big Bang Factors

Bob Dylan's appearance at the Newport Folk Festival in June 1965 is legendary and is detailed in the second part of this chapter. Dylan only sang three songs with a band, the previous acts had used electric instruments, and the concert wasn't televised but no matter, this performance had consequences that resonate even today. What's more, we don't really know whether Dylan expected this controversy and whether he was happy about it, but it is among the most controversial appearances ever by an entertainer.

Dylan had done two things to alienate his folk audience: he had gone electric and he had stopped writing protest songs. I think, and I may be wrong, that at Newport and on the following tour, he was going out of his way to be provocative. Just look at his press conferences; if Dylan didn't want this reaction, why didn't he explain himself and just dress and behave normally? Not a chance: everything he did during 1965/6 was confrontational and was bound to alienate a significant proportion of his earlier fans, albeit gaining new ones in the process. The concerts themselves had degenerated into Punch and Judas shows.

Here's an audacious thought that may be quite off the wall, but Dylan's approach in press conferences is not too far removed from Jesus talking to his critics in the Gospels. When Pontius Pilate asked him if he were the Son of God, he replied, 'Thou sayest', and he often answered a question with a question, both approaches typical of Dylan. Next time you hear a preacher quoting Jesus, think what it would sound like in Dylan's voice. I draw no conclusion from this other than they had both decided this was the best way to approach your detractors.

Dylan was fully aware that many people had a singular view of him, that they regarded him as the new Messiah. He played along with this by evading answers and being cryptic, which added to his mystique. He was a smart cookie and knew exactly what he was doing.

Looking at his previous behaviour, we have seen that Dylan enjoyed being provocative and taking a different turning whenever he could. We will try to understand this in the second part of the chapter, but first, let's put Dylan into context. What key events challenged an audience's expectations before Bob Dylan and indeed, what has happened since?

There are many examples from creative people who have challenged their audiences. This is unusual in popular music because it is a commercial business and most artists don't want to give their audiences something that they don't want to hear. But there are individuals who are non-showbiz as it were, and who want to map out a new terrain and they can get a hostile reception.

Dylan was never comfortable with praise. 'The songs are not meant to be great,' Bob Dylan told *Saturday Evening Post* in 1965, 'I'm not meant to be great. I don't think anything I touch is destined for greatness. Genius is a terrible word, a word that they think will make me like them. A genius is a very insulting thing to say. Even Einstein wasn't a genius. He was a foreign mathematician who would have stolen cars.'

The painter Henry Fuseli who pushed the envelope in the 19th century with paintings like *The Nightmare* said, 'It is the lot of genius to be opposed, and to be invigorated by the opposition.'

Larry Beckett, who wrote imaginative songs with Tim Buckley, said that they never intended to bow to commercial pressures. 'The problem was that neither Tim nor I were ever interested in music as commerce. We were only interested in making music as art. Because of the success of the Beatles and Dylan, some record labels were making lots of money and had money to invest in new talent. That was how Tim Buckley got a contract with Elektra. We don't know what their thinking was but ours was "If they are going to pay us money to make art, we are going to do it." We never looked at the sales figures or the charts or even tried to write a song for a single. We didn't care about any of that. We were true 60s dropouts. FM radio yes, and no to AM. We were only listening for the artistry.'

Bob Dylan wasn't far away from this thought when he told *Rolling Stone* in 2006: 'The stuff that trained me to do what I do was all individually based. The individual crying in the wilderness. That's kind of lost – who's the last individual performer you can think about? I'm talking about artists with the willpower not to conform to anybody's reality but their own – Patsy Cline and Billy Lee Riley. Plato and Socrates. Whitman and Emerson. Slim Harpo and Donald Trump. It's a lost art form. I don't know who else does it beside myself.' (Yes, he did say Donald Trump, but he did fall in with Dylan's definition.)

Dylan was seeing himself as the voice crying in the wilderness, although his list of fellow rebels is bizarre. Very often rebels are seen as troubled individuals but I don't think this ever applied to Bob Dylan. He was doing what he intended to do and no one was going to stop him. It was not so much Dylan who was troubled but those with the bad luck to get in his way.

This part of the chapter is about people who were ahead of their time. In 1966, when John Lennon asked Bob Dylan if he was ahead of his time, he replied, very wittily, 'I'm only 20 minutes ahead so I won't get far.'

Most musical changes have been gradual: they weren't big bangs. The concepts of symphonies, ballets and operas evolved over time. I am concentrating on the big events – one day it's not there: the next day it is.

Let's consider some of the events that created a stir and see how they compare. We can justly give Bob Dylan top marks for the way he shook things up. When asked about his 1966 tour in 1987, he said, 'Every night was like going for broke, like the end of the world.' This is an extreme example of the so-called 'shock of the new' and so Big Bang Factor 10.

Briefly talking about the tour in 1983, Dylan said, 'Deep down inside I think that people enjoy whistling, like at a ball game.' That's true. If you go to a football match, you automatically jeer at your opponents, but then sporting fixtures are intended to be confrontational. It is more fun if you are a partisan.

Let's start with a musical work written under psychedelic drugs and about sexual obsession – a symphony written in 1830!

Hector Berlioz was born in France in 1803 and his father wanted him to be a doctor, but he had other ideas, rejecting his studies and becoming passionate about composing music. He saw an Irish actress Harriet Smithson playing Shakespeare but she rejected his advances. He dedicated *Symphonie Fantastique* to her, which had no words but came with a programme note in which Berlioz explained what the music represented. It told of Lélio who was consumed by love and when he lost out, he took opium. The symphony relived his nightmarish fantasies about being marched to the scaffold and being part of a voodoo ceremony.

The audiences at the first performances had heard nothing like it but according to contemporary reports, many loved it. Franz Liszt was so impressed that he transcribed a piano version. Leonard Bernstein said, 'This symphony tells it like it is. You end up screaming at your own funeral.'

If the symphony was intended to win Harriet over, it didn't work. He gave up on her and doted on a 19-year-old pianist Marie Moke who turned him down in favour of a piano manufacturer. Berlioz planned to murder both her and her mother but thought better of it and turned his attention to Harriet again. This time they were married but it was unhappily ever after. Berlioz was writing until his death in 1869, often shattering established forms but he never got as outlandish as *Symphonie Fantastique*.

Berlioz had broken with tradition and it would be 130 years before other composers wrote under psychedelic drugs. However, there wasn't an outcry when he was so different as the public rather liked it, hence Big Bang Factor 4.

Similarly, Samuel Taylor Coleridge and Lord Byron were both writing under the influence around the same time as Berlioz. It seemed entirely appropriate that Coleridge's coffin should be discovered in 2018 in an old wine cellar.

Despite everybody thinking otherwise, none of the 60s hit-makers have admitted writing their songs on drugs, possibly because they thought it would take away from their creativity. It wasn't the land of dope and glory. Dylan told a friend, 'Amphetamines do not help me to write songs. It just helps me to stay up longer to write more of them.'

Richard Wagner was only a teenager when Berlioz wrote *Symphonie Fantastique*, but even though he is so controversial today, he was a hero in his time. There are many anti-Semitic characters in his operas but then Shakespeare had Shylock as a central character in *The Merchant of Venice*. Wagner expressed strong, negative views about the Jewish race. His reputation would have been secure had not Adolf Hitler named him as his favourite composer.

The annual Bayreuth Festival was established to carry out Richard Wagner's artistic legacy and was attended by Adolf Hitler each year from 1933 to 1939. He drew upon Wagner's own ideas about racial purity and anti-Semitism for his doctrine in the Third Reich.

Wagner's music was banned in Israel but there have been several attempts to play it, always facing controversy. In 2011 the Israel Chamber Orchestra was threatened with funding cuts if they played Wagner as guests at the Bayreuth Festival. The orchestra's conductor Roberto Paternostro said that Wagner's ideology was terrible but you had to separate the man from the music. As there was no outcry at the concert itself, it is Big Bang Factor 3.

Having said that, I attended a performance of the musical *Cabaret* at Paul McCartney's performance arts school, LIPA, in 2019. The audience which had been applauding enthusiastically didn't know what to do when the first half ended with 'Tomorrow Belongs to Me' and Nazi salutes. I could even sense their thinking: 'We can't applaud a Nazi salute, but this is only within a play that will move on, so okay, let's clap.' The applause came about five seconds late, a fascinating experience.

Igor Stravinsky was born in Russia in 1882. He planned to be a lawyer but he was a gifted pianist and encouraged to compose by Nikolay Rimsky-Korsakov. His short orchestral pieces were heard by Sergei Diaghilev who had formed Ballets Russes in Paris, really because he knew France would be more receptive to new ideas than Russia. He invited Stravinsky to write a ballet on the legend of the Firebird. Both *The Firebird* (1910) and *Petrushka* (1911) were critical and popular successes.

Stravinsky rather like Dylan said that his work was born from his unconscious. Well, not quite. Stravinsky and Diaghilev had the concept of a ballet about the rebirth of the earth during spring and wanted to combine this with pagan rituals, hence *Le Sacre du Printemps (The Rite of Spring)*, which had its première at the Paris Opera House on 29 May 1913.

Stravinsky admitted that when Diaghilev first heard the discordant start of *The Rite of Spring*, he said, 'Will it last a long time like this?' Rather offended, Stravinsky said, 'To the end!'

The ballet was to be choreographed by Vaslav Nijinsky, who was already working on Debussy's ballet, *Jeux (Games)*. The plan was to perform this ballet at Théâtre-des-Champs-Élysées in May 1913 and follow it with *Le Sacre du Printemps* a fortnight later. *Jeux* itself was controversial. The concept had been to have three young men in a sexual encounter while searching for a tennis ball. This had been changed to two girls and one man but even so, it was hot stuff.

Diaghilev had told the press that *The Rite of Spring* would cause an impassioned debate, so even if he was not expecting a riot, he did think it would be controversial.

The ballet was in two parts: *The Adoration of the Earth* and *The Sacrifice*, so you can see where this is going. The elders in a Russian village choose a young virgin, who whips herself into a frenzy and dances herself to death. *The Wicker Man*, really. The music was difficult and ear-splitting as it built up to the girl's death.

The performance began with the overture and as Stravinsky was getting outlandish sounds from familiar instruments, the scene was being set for a disturbing production. Although the audience was sophisticated, many felt embarrassed and uneasy at watching primitive emotions. Stravinsky said that the trouble started 'when the curtain opened on a group of knock-kneed and long-braided Lolitas jumping up and down.' Were some audience members offended by knock-knees?

At first there were catcalls and whistles and objects were thrown at the stage. The policemen who were on duty intervened and this only encouraged the protestors. The police averted a riot and the production continued to its conclusion.

Following newspaper reports, future audiences knew what to expect and with good policing, the rest of the performances passed without incident although many concertgoers were unhappy. Meanwhile, Nijinsky eloped with one of the ballet dancers which caused a rift with Diaghilev that was never repaired.

In an attempt to avoid a repeat at its first London performance, the ballet was preceded by a lecture to prepare the audience for what was in store. It passed off uneventfully as did concerts in Russia, which featured the music on its own.

Stravinsky wrote many other works including settings for the poems of Edward Lear and Dylan Thomas and he revisited *The Rite of Spring* on occasion. In view of all that has happened since, it does not seem revolutionary, but what has happened since is partly down to the influence of *The Rite of Spring*. For that first night, Big Bang Factor 7.

In 1917, Pablo Picasso designed the costumes and scenery for Diaghilev's company and the audience threated to attack him, the choreographer and the performers when *Parade* was presented in Paris. Picasso was delighted with the reaction to his colourful backcloths and promised more outrageous efforts to annoy the bourgeoisie. Many didn't understand his abstract paintings and his famed painting of the bombing of a Spanish town, Guernica, had very mixed reactions in 1937 but is now regarded as his masterpiece. Big Bang Factor 6.

Sir Arthur Conan Doyle wrote his first Sherlock Holmes novel, *A Study in Scarlet* in 1887. The detective was fictional and so popular that Doyle wrote a second novel, *The Sign of Four* and published short stories in *The Strand*. By 1891 he had tired of Holmes and he and his nemesis Professor Moriarty fell to their deaths over the Reichenbach Falls in Switzerland. There was so much mourning for a fictional character that Doyle resurrected him. He had not been killed in the fall but it was a good idea to lie low to fool his other enemies. The impact of Holmes' supposed death merits a Big Bang Factor 5.

The Irish writer James Joyce was a teacher who established his reputation with *Dubliners* (1914) and *Portrait of the Artist as a Young Man* (1916). He decided to set a novel over one day in Dublin, 16 June 1904 (now called 'Bloomsday', though the novel is *Ulysses*), but every time he received the proofs, he added more details. The book grew and grew and as the day was to be comprehensively covered, it included sexual actions and thoughts. The book ended with Molly Bloom's soliloquy, which alone would have prevented publication in many countries. It was published in Paris on Joyce's fortieth birthday in 1922. Those who read it reported that it was lewd and obscene. In 1933 an American judge determined that it could be published: it was foul, he said, but not an aphrodisiac. There were new words and deliberate grammatical mistakes that made it hard to read, but critics came to realise that this could be the greatest novel of the twentieth century. Big Bang Factor 5.

Joyce retreated into himself with the story of a single night and its dreams, *Finnegans Wake*. It took 17 years to complete, partly because he was going blind, but also because the text was so dense, impenetrable and perhaps only fully understandable to himself. James Joyce had found a new way to write but he died in an asylum in 1941. Big Bang Factor 2.

D.H. Lawrence's novel, *Lady Chatterley's Lover* could not be published in the UK in 1928 because both the author and the publisher would have been arrested for obscenity. It had a feeble plot: Sir Clifford Chatterley has war wounds and is impotent and his wife, Constance, has an affair with their gamekeeper, Mellors. The sexual scenes were graphic and although other writers had used four-letter words, this was a novel from a leading literary figure. The book was published privately in 1928 in Italy and then France and Australia. It became notorious, although an expurgated version, which didn't amount to much, was widely published.

In 1960, after Penguin Books had published the original text in the UK, it was the subject of an obscenity trial. The book was deemed to have artistic merit and was not obscene. This allowed many other controversial books to be published and future authors would have more freedom.

The freedom of the 1960s starts here. Whatever the merits of the case, this novel harmed Lawrence's reputation. For many, he was a pornographer rather than a major literary figure. His novels, *Sons and Lovers* and *Women in Love*, are set in industrial England in the early part of the century and are studied in schools. The indignation caused by Dylan's switch to electricity was short-lived and his new music was soon accepted. Lawrence's reputation though was permanently tarnished by *Lady Chatterley's Lover*, but the result of the trial affected society as a whole, probably for the better. Big Bang Factor 7.

In 1940 Gracie Fields lost much of her popularity by marrying an Italian film director, Monty Banks. If they had lived in the UK, he would have been interned by the British, so they moved to America and Gracie raised money for the war effort. She returned to the UK in 1948 for a comeback concert at the London Palladium, certain there would be protests. The concert passed without incident and was regarded as a triumph.

Marlene Dietrich was jeered when she returned to Germany after the war because she had fraternised with the Americans. It had been very tricky for her as there had been a possibility that Germany would respond by arresting her mother and sister.

Born in India in 1903 and educated at Eton, Eric Blair became the writer George Orwell, a noted literary critic, essayist and novelist. His 1937 book, *The Road to Wigan Pier*, is a telling picture of poverty and working-class life in the north-west of England. Orwell wrote about his experiences of fighting in the Spanish civil war in *Homage to Catalonia* (1938).

At the end of the Second World War, Orwell published *Animal Farm*, an allegorical tale about the threat of totalitarianism and the different ideologies of Stalin and Trotsky. The slogan, 'All animals are equal' becomes 'All animals are equal but some are more equal than others'.

Orwell was a socialist but his conclusions did offend some socialist readers, but his papers show that Orwell had no time for many of his 'leftie' readers: Change that to 'folkies' and you have Dylan.

Animal Farm was a huge success in the western world, although when it was filmed by a US company in 1954, the ending was changed so that the American way of life prevailed.

Orwell worked for the BBC during the war and their bureaucracy inspired his most famous and controversial novel. He wrote it in 1948 and he changed two digits to take the world forward to 1984 by which time everything was controlled by the State. The book introduced new phrases into the language – newspeak, hate week, thought crimes, double think, Big Brother and Room 101, the last two paradoxically being used as titles for high-rating entertainment series.

There had been no book like *1984* before and it was more chilling than, say H.G. Wells' *War of the Worlds* (1898) because it was so grounded in reality. The book was not published until 1949 by which time Orwell was seriously ill, but it was not highly acclaimed as it was seen as too pessimistic. Orwell died in January 1950, little knowing the impact that it would have. The book can be seen as a warning: if some political actions are not taken in 1948, then its seeds could give us *1984*.

David Bowie wanted to write a musical based on the book but he could not get Orwell's estate to approve it. In the end, he recast the songs that he had already written and released the album, *Diamond Dogs*, in 1974. It was a Number 1 album but it was not what Bowie had intended. A comparison can be made with Dylan's *New Morning* (1970) which had its origins in an abandoned musical.

Nightmarish visions of the future are inevitably linked to *1984* and the inauguration of President Trump immediately led to a revival of *1984* on Broadway. Trump doesn't have the discipline or ideology of a dictator but he has the same passion for power and he dismisses anyone who stands in his way. Right from the start of his presidency, we have seen 'alternative facts' and Trump's dismissal of negative stories about him as 'fake news'. Orwell had said it all first with 'newspeak'. Big Bang Factor 5.

There was controversy from both sides over the Communist witch-hunt during the McCarthy era in the States. Burl Ives, to save his own career, gave the names of many fellow-sympathisers. This cut him adrift from the left-wing, folk song performers and he was to head to right-wing Nashville and have chart success with country songs.

For some years Samuel Beckett acted as James Joyce's secretary and Joyce's writing had a marked effect upon his own work. He wrote a series of intense, psychological novels, *Molloy*, *Murphy*, *Watt* and *Malone Dies*, which you could say describe life on Desolation Row. Beckett wrote *Waiting for Godot* in 1952, a play set in a wasteland where nothing happens for two hours. Maybe Godot was God and the play was about religion or the lack of it, but Beckett wasn't saying.

Waiting for Godot had its champions as otherwise it wouldn't have been staged but it struggled to find an audience. It was vilified when it first appeared but then both public and critics began to appreciate it. During all this time, Beckett said little to justify his writing or to court favour: the work had to speak for itself and if it said nothing to you, then so be it.

When Beckett was photographed, he would stare at the camera like a man facing execution. Occasionally we got a glimpse of hell as he wrote, 'No, I regret nothing – all I regret is having been born.' Yet people who knew him talk of his sense of fun and his love for cricket.

Like Joyce with *Finnegans Wake*, Beckett's work became even more intense with theatrical conventions being abandoned: there were long periods of silence because the characters had nothing to say. In *Happy Days*, the central character Winnie is buried up to her waist in sand with no indication as to how she got there.

Beckett's advice to writers was 'Have the courage to fail and then fail better.' Doesn't that resemble Dylan's 'There's no success like failure and failure's no success at all.' Big Bang Factor 4.

The jazz pianist Thelonious Monk deserves a special mention. He would take a standard such as 'Smoke Gets in Your Eyes' and define and redefine how he would play it. If he didn't feel inspired, he might not play at all and on several occasions, he left the stage early. He even left the stage in London and went back to his hotel while the audience was waiting for him to return. Because his followers regarded him as a genius, this highly eccentric behaviour was accepted and I don't know of any instances where he was booed.

In 1955 a little-known poet called Allen Ginsberg read his new epic poem, *Howl* to a small audience in the Six Gallery in San Francisco. It caused a sensation as he was so frank about his sexuality, about America today and about the Cold War. *Howl* was published by the City Lights bookshop and it was controversial at the same time that Bill Haley and the Comets were shaking staid America with 'Rock around the Clock'. *Howl* was banned for obscenity and the publisher jailed but the ban was later lifted as a judge agreed it did possess redeeming artistic values. Big Bang Factor 6.

In 1956 Elvis Presley was infamous for his pelvic thrusts. He told his mother that it was just how he felt the music, he wasn't trying to be sexy, but of course he was: that was the whole point. So Steve Allen had him on TV in a tuxedo where he had to sing to a real hound dog and to emphasise the controversy, he was filmed from the waist up on *The Ed Sullivan Show*. His manager Colonel Parker saw it as a brilliant opportunity for creating publicity. It widened the gap between teenage rock'n'roll and adult pop in a way that Bill Haley couldn't imagine. Big Bang Factor 8.

Around the same time, Ray Charles was taking black gospel music and turning them into popular songs – 'I Got a Saviour' became 'I Got a Woman' and 'Hallelujah I Love Him So', the Him being Jesus, became 'Hallelujah I Love Her So'. He was heavily criticised for it by ministers in the US, but everybody else thought it was a fine idea and the gospel catalogue has been plundered ever since. Big Bang Factor 2.

Bob Dylan: Outlaw Blues

The Newport festivals had seen controversy before Bob Dylan. In July 1958 Chuck Berry appeared at the Newport Jazz Festival. The organiser George Wein knew Chuck Berry would be controversial and in his introduction he acknowledged Chuck's debt to Big Bill Broonzy and Chuck, most out of character, began by saying what an honour it was to play Newport. He was working with a pick-up band as usual but this one included Buck Clayton (trumpet) and Jack Teagarden (trombone). You can see that Jack Teagarden was amused by Chuck Berry's duckwalk. Chuck did say in 'Sweet Little Sixteen' that he got no kicks from modern jazz, a line he should possibly have rewritten. The younger element in the audience liked Chuck but the older traditionalists jeered or booed. All taking place in Newport, seven years before Bob Dylan. Big Bang Factor 1.

Muddy Waters' electric set at the Newport Jazz Festival in 1960 was recorded for a live album. It was not jazz nor blues as the audience knew it and it wasn't too far from Bob Dylan at Newport in 1965 but the audience loved it. He closed his set with the improvised 'Goodbye Newport Blues'.

In May 1965 Mick Jagger and Keith Richards saw Muddy Waters with an electric band in Manchester. Keith told *Rolling Stone* that Muddy had a hostile reaction. Maybe he was playing too loud. In that same month, Muddy recorded 'My Dog Can't Bark', which has a slide guitar part similar to 'Highway 61 Revisited', which Dylan recorded in August. You can see the connections here. The magazine *Rolling Stone* was named after a Bob Dylan song, which in turn took its title from a Muddy Waters record. As did the Rolling Stones. Dylan's debt to Muddy Waters is substantial. In 1969 Mike Bloomfield worked with Muddy Waters on the album *Fathers and Sons*. Big Bang Factor 2.

In 1959 another Beat writer, William Burroughs, found that US publishers were reluctant to touch his novel, almost a memoir, *The Naked Lunch*. Its twin themes were drugs and homosexuality. It was published in the USA in 1962 and the Beatles chose to include him on their *Sgt. Pepper* cover. The book is famous for being infamous but it is difficult to read as Burroughs shuffled the order of his pages before publication. Big Bang Factor 3.

Andy Warhol is among the most significant artists of the 20th century but there are many who do not rate his talent. He was brilliant at drawing attention to his work and indeed to himself, as Warhol could be considered his own work of art. His obsession with consumerism was at the heart of his work, but there was an irony about it that you never knew what he was thinking: was he being deliberately kitsch? What is the point of a ten-foot flower? He is best known for his tins of Campbell's Soup (1962) and boxes of Brillo pads (1964), but surely it was the original designers who deserved the millions and not Warhol. You can see Warhol's influence in more recent *cause célèbres* such as Damien Hirst's shark in formaldehyde and Tracey Emin's bed. Warhol made controversial films and discovered the Velvet Underground. One of his great quotes was that the 1970s were too empty and the 1960s were too full. Big Bang Factor 5.

Although West End theatre productions have to be commercial because of the high staging costs and tenancy rates, they have often been controversial. In 1966 I saw *US,* produced by the Royal Shakespeare Company directed by Peter Brook. It questioned America's involvement in Vietnam and called on the cast to go to the circle and spit on the audience in the stalls. I have been spat upon by Glenda Jackson! Naturally this play caused much controversy and presumably dry cleaning bills. Big Bang Factor 4.

The National Theatre is officially the Royal National Theatre but it does not use the regal prefix because it wants to be seen as cutting edge. Its plays have included *Saved* by

Edward Bond (1965), part of a Theatre of Cruelty season in which a baby was stoned to death on stage; *Soldiers* (1967) in which Churchill was said to have ordered Sikorski's death; *The Romans in Britain* (1980) which included male rape; and *Cleansed* (2016) in which some audience members fainted or left during every performance because of the explicit torture and rape scenes.

Rather than a Judas moment, the Beatles had a Jesus moment when John Lennon had told a London journalist that they were bigger than Christ. Nobody took much notice when this was originally reported in the UK but it was taken wildly out of context in the Bible belt and led to the public destruction of their records. The Beatles were starting a US tour and John Lennon, very much out of character, was persuaded to apologise. We can see that he was upset as he spoke poorly for someone who was so good with words. The tour went ahead without trouble and it didn't damage their reputation. But what if Lennon had been defiant, what if Lennon had dismissed his critics as stupid? It might have led to John and Paul going their separate ways, but Lennon would have been okay as the growing underground movement in the US would have taken him to heart. Big Bang Factor 5.

With one exception, the Beatles were not risk-takers in the Stravinsky style. They advanced from album to album but they always released infectious hit singles and confined the experimentation to a few tracks. This even applies to *Sgt. Pepper's Lonely Hearts Club Band* in June 1967 where the lavish packaging and head-on promotion might have been seen as pretentious. There were very catchy songs that the public could hardly ignore and its darkest moment, 'A Day in the Life', was banned by the BBC for its promotion of drugs. The dissonant arrangement at the end rivalled Stravinsky. Big Bang Factor 3.

Always keen to put their own spin on what the Beatles were doing, the Rolling Stones made their own psychedelic album, *Their Satanic Majesties Request*, which had uniformly poor reviews and lacked the bite of their earlier records. Their blues base had gone completely. It sold enough to go gold but I doubt if it was played much. The Stones had made a mistake and quickly sought to cover their tracks. Big Bang Factor 1.

Their Satanic Majesties Request was released for Christmas 1967, the time they Beatles miscalculated with their TV film, *Magical Mystery Tour*. Paul McCartney can be held responsible but on the other hand, the other Beatles would have chosen to do nothing after Brian Epstein's death which might have led to their break-up. The film was plotless and silly rather than funny and although its standing has increased with time, it had appalling reviews and I can't remember anyone saying it was any good at the time. Big Bang Factor 2.

The Monkees had found fame through aping the Beatles in a light-hearted TV series. They switched to a feature-length film for the spaced-out *Head* (1968), written by Jack Nicholson. It didn't really affect their career as they wanted to split up anyway and the film had such poor reviews that nobody went to see it anyway. Big Bang Factor 0.

By 1968 the Byrds were long-haired hippies and they encountered redneck opposition when they recorded *Sweetheart of the Rodeo* in Nashville. They were invited to perform on the radio show *Grand Ole Opry* where they were booed by the audience and ridiculed by the MC, Ralph Emery. It heralded country-rock, the cult of Gram Parsons and Americana. Big Bang Factor 4.

The Rolling Stones restored their equilibrium with a brilliant single 'Jumping Jack Flash' and a very strong, bluesy album, *Beggars Banquet*. The original sleeve of graffiti on a toilet wall was replaced with an almost white cover, which meant that once again they were following the Beatles.

Mick Jagger went public about their original sleeve, openly criticising Decca Records for duplicity as they had issued Tom Jones' *A-Tom-Ic Jones* with Jones standing in front of a nuclear explosion, possibly the most tasteless sleeve of the 60s.

On 8 June 1969 Brian Jones left the Rolling Stones. He was in poor health, largely on account of drug use and everybody knew that neither Mick Jagger nor Keith Richards had much time for him. On July 3, he was found dead in his swimming pool after taking a midnight swim. The coroner recorded misadventure, that is 'drowning while under the influence of alcohol and drugs'.

The Rolling Stones were due to play a free concert on July 5. They had a new guitarist, Mick Taylor. The public expected them to cancel the show but instead it became a tribute to Brian. They took a risk by choosing to play and Mick Jagger opened their performance by reading part of Percy Bysshe Shelley's *Adonais: An Elegy on the Death of John Keats* and releasing 3,000 butterflies in Brian's memory.

This could easily have gone totally wrong. Everybody knew that Mick and Keith had fallen out with Brian and the spectators could have viewed this as supremely hypocritical. It could have ruined their performance and their reputation. It turned out to be the right thing to do but they weren't to know that.

As it is, for all their bad boy reputation, the Rolling Stones were hardly controversial. What misdeeds immediately spring to mind? Peeing on a garage wall? Well, I ask you. Big Bang Factor 2 really but in terms of public perception, 5.

Talking about the 60s, Miles Davis said in his autobiography: 'All of a sudden jazz became passé, something dead that you put under a glass in a museum. I was already moving towards a guitar sound in my music because I was beginning to listen to a lot of James Brown and I liked the way he used the guitar in his music.'

Miles had long been at the cutting edge of modern jazz and he became infatuated with funk and what could be done with a couple of chords. He introduced his new stripped-down sound at the Fillmore West – he played long improvised pieces with Chick Corea and Keith Jarrett, which displeased many of his long-standing fans but he had wisely chosen to appear at a rock haunt.

This led to the double-album *Bitches Brew* (1970) with its highly questionable cover. Indeed, I never bought it because I found the title, the sleeve and indeed the punctuation so offensive. Many of his jazz fans hated it – what was Miles Davis doing with wah-wah pedals? – but he was bringing jazz into rock. It was his first US Top 40 album. With *On the Corner* (1972), Miles was playing organ as often as his trumpet. Miles Davis said, 'People who don't change will find themselves like folk musicians, playing in museums.' Big Bang Factor 4.

In 1970 the folk songwriter Phil Ochs wore a gold lamé Elvis suit for two concerts at Carnegie Hall but at first A&M refused to issue the tapes: 'I can't believe it. I thought it was great,' said Ochs, 'You can hear the whole audience thing. At first they're booing me, then I win them over and they come round. At the end, they're cheering. But Jerry Moss came back from Europe and said, "Terrible". They didn't see the point of putting out rock'n'roll medleys when people can buy *Buddy Holly's Greatest Hits*.'

Ochs was as ambitious as Dylan but not as talented and his ways of alienating an audience were somewhat crass. He performed Merle Haggard's right-wing anthem, 'Okie from Muskogee', which was bound to annoy his hippie following.

The album, *Gunfight at Carnegie Hall*, was eventually released in 1974 and it's an enjoyable, good-time record where Ochs is clearly enjoying his Dylan moment, which was surely his intention. To be fair, he said he was doing it because he wanted Elvis to come out against Vietnam. His repartee is first-rate: 'Let's not be like Spiro Agnew. Let's not be narrow-minded Americans' is his answer to the hostility. Big Bang Factor 2.

There have been several concerts in which a performer has rejected what an audience wants. In 1973 I saw Neil Young at the Liverpool Empire perform a set consisting solely of his forthcoming album, *Tonight's the Night*. After he had finished the audience was calling for 'After the Goldrush' and 'Heart of Gold'. He returned to the stage and said, 'Here's something you've never heard before.' The audience cheered but he went into the opening number of *Tonight's the Night*. He was being deliberately provocative, perhaps hoping for a 'Judas' moment, but that's Neil Young for you. And what's wrong with that? Why should an artist feel obliged to perform his best-known songs? If you had gone to see Laurence Olivier in a play, would you be disappointed if he didn't recite the soliloquy from *Hamlet*? Big Bang Factor 2.

Another contrary fellow Lou Reed brought out a double-album of feedback, whines and whistles, *Metal Machine Music* in 1974. Nobody understood what he was doing and it was vilified by fans and critics alike. What he was doing was planning his exit from RCA and a move to Arista and he was deliberately giving RCA a product that they couldn't sell. This album now has legendary status but don't believe anyone who says he enjoys it or indeed plays it. Big Bang Factor 4.

Neil Young had a son with cerebral palsy who was quadriplegic. In 1983 he made an album in which he was trying to express what was in his son's head. He didn't tell anyone what he was doing and nobody understood *Trans* and thought he was aping *Metal Machine Music*. David Geffen considered suing him for breaking his contract by not delivering a Neil Young record. He told Neil that he wanted a rock'n'roll record next and so Neil took him literally and made a rockabilly record, *Everybody's Rockin'*, which worked fine.

In 1975 Charlie Rich presented the Entertainer of the Year Award at the Country Music Association's annual ceremony. He opened the envelope, read out 'John Denver' and set fire to the envelope. It was seen as a comment on the vacuity of current country music as Mr. Sunshine on his Specs was such a big star. Charlie however told me it was no such thing and no big deal: he was simply drunk.

The country scene had always been self-contained but in the 1970s Dolly Parton went pop with a Brill Building song, 'Here You Come Again'. It was a huge hit but she was at pains to say that she wasn't deserting her audiences. In more recent times, artists like Miley Cyrus and Taylor Swift have started in country and switched over, caring little about the fans they left behind. In 2018 after making a rock album, Kacey Musgraves was careful to point out, even in her UK performances, that she would always love banjos and steel guitars.

Formed in 1975, hardly anyone outside of a few London clubs had heard of the Sex Pistols, but it looked like they could make a sizeable killing by being accepted by a record label and then being sacked for unacceptable behaviour. I would not be surprised if their manager Malcolm McLaren had planned it that way. At different times, EMI, A&M, Polydor and Chrysalis wanted the Sex Pistols. EMI gave them £40,000 for not releasing 'Anarchy in the UK' and walking away from the deal. It was even better at A&M as many existing stars including Rick Wakeman and the Carpenters objected to them being on the label and the Sex Pistols pocketed £75,000. Over £100,000 for doing nothing!

The crowning glory came in December 1976 when they appeared on a regional news programme in London, *Today*, hosted by Bill Grundy. The veteran broadcaster saw no need to swot up on a punk group and he made the mistake of provoking them, taunting them to be controversial. With Grundy being called 'a dirty fucker' on a teatime programme, television history was made. It cost Grundy his job, but Richard Branson saw the merits of the Pistols. He signed the band to Virgin and they soon had hit singles. It is now known that their 'God Save the Queen' would have been Number 1 during Silver Jubilee week, but the chart compilers patriotically changed the positions so that Rod Stewart was top. The Sex Pistols weren't untalented but they were all about image and anti-charisma and were at the forefront of the punk explosion. Big Bang Factor 9.

In 1977 Cat Stevens embraced Islam and became Yusuf Islam. He retired from performing and recording in 1979 although he was to return on his own terms in 1995.

In 1988 Salman Rushdie published *The Satanic Verses*, which was partly inspired by the life of Muhammad. He must have known that such a controversial book would not be welcomed by Muslims but he had no idea that the reaction would be so extreme. The book was well reviewed and nominated for awards but many Muslims regarded it as blasphemous. Ayatollah Khomeini issued a fatwa calling for Rushdie's death and following failed assassination attempts, he was placed under police protection. Hitoshi Igarashi, the Japanese translator for the book, was murdered. *The Satanic Verses* made Rushdie famous but most readers (myself included) found the book as impenetrable as anything by Stephen Hawking. Rushdie is now out of hiding but the fatwa could not be rescinded as Khomeini had died. He was knighted in 2007. Big Bang Factor 8.

Clearly a troubled performer, Sinéad O'Connor brought out strong feelings on both sides in her audience. Many thought that she should use her remarkably good voice to entertain but she was passionate about many political issues, even supporting the IRA early in her career. She endorsed many causes including women's rights, the prevention of child abuse, and opposition to organised religion, especially Roman Catholicism. In 1992 O'Connor was a guest star on NBC-TV's *Saturday Night Live*. She sang a solo version of Bob Marley's 'War' and she tore up a picture of the Pope, proclaiming 'Fight the enemy'. She was then booed at a Bob Dylan tribute concert by an audience who should have known better. Despite criticism she refused to apologise and angry fans gathered in New York where a steamroller ran over her albums. Now that we know about child abuse within the Catholic church, we know that she was right. Sinéad converted to Islam in 2018, changing her name to Shuhada' Davitt. Big Bang Factor 5.

Bob Dylan would have known that many of his heroes had courted controversy including Allen Ginsberg, William Burroughs and Elvis Presley and I think he enjoyed what happened at Newport in 1965 and not knowing how it was going to be resolved. It is surprising that since that time he hasn't done anything else equally outrageous but if ideas aren't forthcoming, there is not much you can do about it. For example, we know that Dylan liked the way Burroughs cut up *The Naked Lunch*, how Charlie Parker improvised, and the fact Jackson Pollock and Mark Rothko threw paint at canvas. Could not Dylan have pioneered a cut-up approach to music and lyric writing?

Nevertheless, Dylan has not stayed still. He has made several significant changes but those changes would not be controversial. In his own way, he is still on the outer edge. I would say that he is a maverick in the best sense of the word. Allen Ginsberg said, 'It was an artistic challenge to see if great art can be done on a jukebox and he has proved it can.'

Al Kooper goes a step further: 'I think Bob is, historically speaking, akin to Shakespeare and will last as long as the earth does.'

Dylan hated being put in a bag – he didn't like the term 'protest music' and he was equally opposed to 'folk-rock'. It is to Albert Grossman's credit that he recognised that his client's wish to change had to be respected. Bob Dylan was giving audiences something that they hadn't heard before, neither folk nor rock songs had contained many ideas and images. It was a turning point in popular music, no doubt about that.

Others followed Dylan and it is arguable as to whether they would have done it without him, but both Fred Neil and Tim Hardin made electric recordings before Bob Dylan. Eric Andersen said in 1966: 'I'm an artist. I can do whatever I want. The rock'n'roll thing that Bob Dylan did was no big deal. There were a few of us – Phil Ochs, Bob Dylan, David Blue – who had learned to play guitar from Elvis Presley, Buddy Holly, the Everly Brothers and Little Richard, and the idea of playing with other musicians was not a weird thing to us. My first album *'Bout Changes & Things* was released and it was just me acoustically. I then did a couple of concerts with musicians and it was such fun that the record company said, 'Let's record these songs again.' The guy who recorded it was Bill Szymczyk who produced the Eagles and the mixes that he did were much hotter than the ones that came out. The old guys at Vanguard watered it down.'

Ewan MacColl in *Sing Out!* took an opposing view towards Dylan: 'I am still unable to see in him anything other than a youth of mediocre talent. Only a completely non-critical audience, nourished on the watery pap of pop music, could have fallen for such tenth-rate drivel.'

I should think that Bob Dylan was secretly pleased with that assessment but on the whole he wasn't concerned about other people's opinions. The question he asked himself was 'How does it feel?' and most of the time, the answer was 'Pretty good'.

Bob Dylan was not the first artist to confront his audience but he was the loudest. And where, I ask you, are the Big Bang moments of today? Maybe it's a sign of the times that we don't have them.

II. So Much Older Then: 1965–July 1966

So many singers were now seeking Bob Dylan's songs and Bob was pleased about *Odetta Sings Dylan* which was released on New Year's Day, 1965. She included a song that Bob hadn't released 'Walkin' Down the Line' but such was Dylan's following and Witmark's promotion that it soon had six covers including Jackie DeShannon, Hamilton Camp and the Dillards. It is worth catching Rick Nelson's version on *The Mike Douglas Show* in which Rick is interrupted by his brother doing a soft shoe dance.

When the Grammy nominations for 1964 were announced, *The Times They Are A-Changin'* LP was included for Best Folk Recording alongside Woody Guthrie's *Library of Congress Recordings*. They both lost out to Gale Garnett's album, 'We'll Sing in the Sunshine', a song that was the antithesis to Dylan and was more middle of the road pop (or pap) than folk.

In 1964 Albert Grossman had bought an estate in the Bearsville district of Woodstock from the family of the cartoonist John H. Striebel. He created the *Dixie Dugan* strip and he often featured Woodstock as the town Stoodwock. Grossman had a sign, 'If you have not telephoned, you are trespassing'.

Dylan found he could get away from the city by going to Woodstock and he would write songs above the Café Espresso in Bearsville: 'hang around an inkwell' as he would put it.

That phrase comes from 'Subterranean Homesick Blues', which was heading in a new direction and could never be a blues. Dylan liked calling songs 'blues' even when they weren't. Townes Van Zandt, Guy Clark and Steve Earle followed him on this by adding 'blues' for no valid reason to a song title. Its very title suggested an underground movement and appeared to be mocking American society and even his own generation. There is a touching line refuting formal education, 'Twenty years of schooling and they put you on the day shift'.

The song was inspired by two others, 'Too Much Monkey Business' by Chuck Berry and 'Takin' It Easy' by Woody Guthrie, which was recorded by the Weavers with Pete Seeger narrating the verses, a very polite rap. When you hear Pete say, 'Papa's in the cellar mixing up the hops, Brother's at the window watching for the cops', you realise that this isn't far from 'Johnny's in the basement, mixing up the medicine.'

The lyric included street talk and aphorisms, the final one being 'You don't need a weather man to know which way the wind blows'. In all probability, Dylan is referring to TV weather reporters but some have said it is a reference to the left-wing terrorist organisation, The Weathermen, which orchestrated a series of riots, jailbreaks and bombings. However, they were not formed until 1969 and indeed, took their name from Dylan's song.

I have listened to this track for over 50 years and it is only now I realise that 'Don't try No Doz' is a reference to the pills that truck drivers took to stay awake.

It's not clear as to what it all means. The reference to Johnny mixing up his medicine could relate to drugs but is he in the basement or could it be debasement? Jack Kerouac did write a novel set partly in Greenwich Village called *The Subterraneans* (1958). In Smackeroo's terminology, the Beats were the subterraneans and the underground movement was underlined with references to the basement and manhole covers.'

The images came frantically and the song seemed entirely new but Bob Dylan also had 'Too Much Monkey Business' is mind. He would record this track as a hyped-up Chuck Berry. It is often said that Dylan was not a great rock'n'roller but he was. He knew his limitations and as such was able to turn them into strengths.

Tom Wilson had booked sessions from 13 to 16 January 1965 at Columbia's studio in New York. He appreciated that Dylan was offering something new and that the standard approach of four songs in a three-hour session was not a discipline which appealed to Dylan. Wilson decided that the first day should be simply to hear new material and then they could work on the songs with other musicians. Dylan brought John Sebastian with him, nothing wrong with that except Dylan wanted him to play bass, an instrument that was new to him. It was not the way George Martin organised things: he also wouldn't have cared for one session which was full of friends and their noisy children. The musicians included Bruce Langhorne (guitar), Will Lee (father of Spike, bass), Al Gorgoni (guitar), Kenny Rankin (guitar) and Bobby Gregg (drums). During those four days, Dylan would make one of the rock world's legendary albums and have some good songs to spare.

Andy Gill aptly called the album, *Bringing It All Back Home*, 'a distorting mirror to modern life'. It was certainly a distorting mirror to Bob Dylan's life. The songs were cryptic and mysterious: there were no directly political songs and one side was, heaven forbid, electric. On the whole though, the electric touches are fairly light.

The album opened with the very track that would alienate folkies and show a new dawn and a new Dylan, 'Subterranean Homesick Blues'. The lyrics were funny and mysterious and performed with great commitment.

The second track was the wistful 'She Belongs to Me', a gentle and sensual 12-bar blues with sexual overtones. It is a love song where the singer is clearly under somebody's spell. Is Joan Baez the enchantress? Lou Reed was more limited technically than Bob Dylan and he might have based his whole career around this track.

Tony Crane of the Merseybeats: 'I like his simple songs and "She Belongs to Me" has a lovely lyric. You can play it over and over and get different things from that song. You don't really know what is going on. It is obviously about a girl but just what is happening?'

These days the title seems politically incorrect and indeed, never appears in the song. Joan Baez did have an Egyptian red ring and with her repertoire of old ballads, Dylan may have seen her as 'a walking antique'. The idea of possession might have been ironic: Joan Baez was assertive so would never have belonged to anyone.

Americans were brought up to be patriotic but then the Vietnam war threw that into question. The lyric could be about that. The phrase, 'Don't look back' would be purloined for a documentary film about Dylan himself.

'Maggie's Farm' is another rocker, this one based around a grouchy song that sharecroppers used to sing, 'Down on Penny's Farm'. Both this and 'All I Really Want to Do' have been criticised for being one note, but it doesn't matter because that one note is a great one.

A mysterious fraction, 'Love minus Zero / No Limit' is another title that doesn't appear in the song. It is about undying love. On tour later in the year, he said in Newcastle, 'I made the title before I made the song.' On other days he called it 'a painting in purple' and 'a painting in maroon and silver'.

The lyrics are as beguiling as its title. His love is like 'a raven with a broken wing'. Carolyn Hester: 'I can remember being crazy about "Love minus Zero / No Limit" when I first heard it.'

'Outlaw Blues' is a Chicago blues with wacky lyrics. It is the most inconsequential track and yet it is very entertaining and it foreshadows punk rock. No, it is punk rock.

Getting in on the act, Tom Wilson called the next song 'Alcatraz to the Ninth Degree'. Dylan: 'No, that's not the name of it.' Wilson: 'That's what you told me.' Dylan: 'I switched songs, this is 'Bank Account Blues'.' The song in question was 'On the Road Again', which has a Bo Diddley beat. The listed title, which doesn't appear in the song, could be a nod to Jack Kerouac's *On The Road*.

When Bob stumbled as he started 'Bob Dylan's 115th Dream', everybody laughed and the cheerfulness was included on the record. The song is a pastiche of American history with some great pronunciation: 'Captain Ay-rab'.

There are just four songs on the acoustic second side but they are all brilliant – 23 minutes of perfection. One of the changes that Bob Dylan wrought along the way was that the pop song no longer had to be over and out in three minutes.

This time he redid 'Mr. Tambourine Man' and got it right.

The title, 'Gates of Eden' could have been prompted by James Dean's *East of Eden*. It is a long song about what is not in Eden. Ralph McTell: 'What is a better title than *Gates of Eden* because Gates are a door into something and Eden is a beginning, so that's what it was for me. It showed me that music was more than something to jump up and down to. It could contain poetry and politics and messages and all those other wonderful things.'

In his own way, Bob was still writing protest songs. 'It's Alright, Ma (I'm Only Bleeding)' is Bob Dylan's State of the Union address, containing the much-quoted line that even the President of the United States must sometimes have to stand naked. Dylan has revisited the song over the years and there are lyrical changes in *Writings and Drawings*. It is a sophisticated song with 15 verses and five choruses (all different except for the title line) about the perils of capitalism and consumerism.

Maybe Dylan didn't realise he was doing it, but he liked to close albums on a goodbye note. This time the title 'It's All Over Now, Baby Blue' could be a nod to two records that Dylan would know well – 'It's All Over Now' (Rolling Stones) and 'Baby Blue' (Gene Vincent). Dylan has said that he sang 'Baby Blue' in high school. It could have a connection to David Blue and it has been suggested that the song is about Paul Clayton or about Joan Baez. Is there a reference to singers who are copying him in 'the clothes that you once wore'? He doesn't care: he's starting anew.

Not only did Dylan complete the album in four days but there were tracks which were used elsewhere including 'I'll Keep It with Mine' and 'Farewell, Angelina'. 'Farewell Angelina' is a companion to 'It's All Over Now, Baby Blue'. Its melody comes from 'The Wagoner's Lad', which Joan Baez recorded in 1961 and is also used for 'Farewell to Tarwathie', written by George Scroggie in the 1850s and recorded by Judy Collins in 1970 with an accompaniment of humpback whales – I kid you not. 'Farewell Angelina' is an overlooked song that was a minor hit for Joan Baez. Dylan's original recording has since been released but it has a lifeless vocal as though Dylan is simply putting down the song with a view to working on it later, possibly with other musicians. He does sing an additional verse about 'camouflaged parrots' and the images are not far from 'Desolation Row'. That may be why he didn't return to it.

In February 1965, Bob Dylan agreed to appear on *The Les Crane Show* on WABC-TV with Nancy Sinatra and Allen Ginsberg. Les Crane dressed like Dylan and asked him questions which made Dylan uncooperative but his crazy answers were good entertainment and left him in charge. His message was 'Eat…Be'. Dylan performed two songs with Bruce Langhorne 'It's All Over Now, Baby Blue' and surprisingly for national TV, 'It's Alright, Ma (I'm Only Bleeding)'.

In February and March 1965 Bob Dylan and Joan Baez did a handful of dates together. Eric Von Schmidt created an effective poster in the style of Toulouse-Lautrec. They were presented as the King and Queen of Folk, a billing that both would have hated. Dylan got a better deal than Baez because Baez's manager Manny Greenhill was more of a gentleman. At one soundcheck, they sang 'You've Lost That Lovin' Feelin'' and they took turns in being the opening act. Among their duets, they sang the traditional 'Wild Mountain Thyme'. After the final concert in Pittsburgh, Bob said to Joan, 'Let's do Madison Square together' but it didn't happen.

In February, Brian Epstein was offered the promotion of Dylan's 1965 UK tour but he turned it down so his usual foresight wasn't working. Tito Burns picked it up instead.

Bringing It All Back Home was released in America on 22 March 1965. After the starkness of the *Times* cover, Columbia wanted one that had the magic of *Freewheelin'*. Suze Rotolo was out of the picture and Bob suggested Sally Grossman. The photograph was shot in Grossman's home in Woodstock. Dylan and Sally had fun deciding on the props. She bought a red dress and they wanted the cat in the shot. It had been a wedding present from Mary Travers to the Grossmans and had been named Lord Growing by Bob.

Dylan and Sally looked well-off and sophisticated in a well-stocked living room. The contents were discussed with the photographer Daniel Kramer and indeed, this unusual cover with all its memorabilia could have been an inspiration for the *Sgt. Pepper* sleeve. Certainly, a CD reproduction doesn't do it justice.

There are many artefacts in the picture: Dylan's collage, *The Clown*, was made of coloured glass and was given to Bernard's Café; *Time* magazine with President Johnson on the cover; LP sleeves from Eric Von Schmidt, Lotte Lenya, Robert Johnson, the Impressions, Françoise Hardy and I think Mahalia Jackson (on the mantelpiece). There is the *Gnaoua* magazine associated with William Burroughs, which folded after its first issue. Bob is wearing the cufflinks that Joan Baez gave him.

Dylan was among the first artists to lay claim to the whole package and his notes on *Bringing* are his best non-lyric writing. It is a surreal narrative rather than free-form verse. When Bob wrote his novel, *Tarantula*, he wanted a similar cover using his wife Sara but then decided he would be repeating himself.

Dylan got to know Kramer well, supplying cryptic comments for his book of photographs. Kramer photographed him in a colourful tie for his *Positively Tie Dream* interview with Maura Davis for a male's magazine, *Cavalier*. Dylan devised a news conference for *Village Voice* to answer the questions he had been avoiding – the start of Fake News.

The film-maker D.A. (Donn) Pennebaker had been born in Illinois in 1930. He had been an electrical engineer and had worked on the first computerised airline reservations system. He modified the hand-held camera to give it a handle and he wanted to make documentary films. Sara had worked with Pennebaker at *Life*. Grossman suggested a film on Dylan, although Pennebaker thought Baez might be better. He tried to get finance from Columbia for Dylan – half the film for $5,000 – but they said no, and so Dylan and Grossman financed it themselves. Pennebaker met Dylan and Bobby Neuwirth to discuss making a feature-length documentary on 16mm around the UK tour. Just by saying yes, Dylan thought it would be a cheap way of learning about making films.

This would be a documentary about a musician on the road who had to deliver every night and although Pennebaker would film some songs in full, he didn't plan to use complete songs in the finished work. It was a modern *On the Road* as Pennebaker saw Dylan as 'the Kerouac kid.'

Pennebaker was known for his top hat, a useful prop for a filmmaker as he could always be spotted. He had two people working for him: Jones Alk was on sound and her husband Howard Alk on camera.

The Alks introduced Bob to Andy Warhol. Andy Warhol was a leading modern artist, infamous for turning everyday objects into artworks. Was he conning the public? No one was sure but he was certainly making money. He had established The Factory on 47th Street where he encouraged creative young people to be themselves and during the 60s, that would include Lou Reed with the Velvet Underground. One of the snapshots on the back cover of *Bringing it All Back Home* is of the filmmaker Barbara Rubin massaging Bob's head at Warhol's Factory.

Bringing It All Back Home was a great title but what is 'It'? Dylan was merging folk and rock so that didn't quite fit, although it was later used for a BBC-TV series which merged Celtic music with American. Maybe it is a reference to the Beatles and their freshness in the current music scene. Indeed, Dylan had joked that he wanted the cover for *Another Side of Bob Dylan* on the sleeve and a caption, 'This is what I no longer am.' Well, maybe he wasn't joking, but it was a brilliant idea.

There was some advice for record stores from Columbia: 'Put Bob Dylan displays in shop windows with displays of men's boots (he wears them all the time), sunglasses (he wears them all the time) or ANYWHERE they will attract attention.' The promo men could be 'contacting radio personalities in your area that have Americana-type shows and pointing out to them the merits of featuring Bob Dylan in an American heritage theme.'

Oddly enough, Columbia didn't address the real selling point. This was the first album on which Dylan was having fun. There were some downbeat songs but on the whole this was cheerful, upbeat and positive, not your standard Bob Dylan package at all.

In an ad Columbia called Dylan 'the new cult leader', the sort of marketing he would come to despise although he didn't denounce it at the time. The press release even called his music Americana, a term that would be used for a new genre 40 years later. Another Columbia slogan was 'Be Different – He Is!'

Their marketing was hyper as one ecstatic term followed another. Columbia called it 'folk-rock' but Dylan recoiled at the term. He declared, 'Folk-rock? I've never even said that word.' You just did, mate. But Dylan, I think, was regarding himself as rock. Trying to be helpful I suppose, he said it was 'vision music' and that certainly didn't catch on.

Neil Young says in the biography, *Shakey*: 'Early on, when Bob decided to play with a band, everybody else perceived it as a radical change. I thought it was great. I was fuckin' knocked out. I had already played rock'n'roll and folk music. I was going back and forth from one to the other, so to me it never made any difference. I couldn't see what the big deal was.' (Neil was already on his fourth band and I suspect he's really saying – 'Dylan was great but I was there first.')

Jim Dickson who managed the Byrds passed 'Mr. Tambourine Man' to Clarence White who was with the Kentucky Colonels. White wanted to give it a bluegrass treatment but Dickson then thought it would sound better with the Byrds. Roger McGuinn of the Byrds had a knowledge of folk music and had played on *Judy Collins Number 3*. Indeed, the Byrds were to record three songs from that album; 'Deportee' (Woody Guthrie) and 'The Bells of Rhymney' and 'Turn! Turn Turn!' (both Pete Seeger).

Roger McGuinn had worked with Bobby Darin: 'I had a conversation with Bobby Darin asking him how to make it in the business and he used to call me Skinny McGuinny. He said, "Well, McGuinny, you get into rock'n'roll, that's what you have to do first and from there, you can do anything you want. Also, get up in front of audiences as much as you can. You can be great in front of your mirror but it is under fire that counts. The adrenaline shift is what's gonna throw you and you have to learn to control it. And stick with it." That is all good advice. I followed that.'

Dylan attended a promotional party for his LP and there is a photograph of him with the Byrds. Dylan knew Roger McGuinn and liked the band he had formed. On 20 January 1965, the Byrds recorded one verse and two choruses of 'Mr. Tambourine Man' for a single, produced by Doris Day's son, Terry Melcher. 'I was playing the Rickenbacker electric 12-string and George Harrison played one in the Beatles,' says Roger McGuinn. 'I had been using a 12-string since the late 50s and it was merely a shift from acoustic to electric. Now I use a Rickenbacker electric 12-string and a Martin acoustic 12-string. Both are now signature models with my name on them and I am very pleased about that.'

McGuinn was unsure of what to make of the lyric. He was to say, 'At the beginning it's me speaking to God and saying "Hey, Mr. Tambourine Man", but I don't know what Dylan meant by it.' McGuinn was seeing it in a similar light to George Harrison's 'My Sweet Lord', or even 'The Pied Piper'. Dylan didn't explain his songs but he certainly enjoyed the Byrds' record, saying, 'Wow, man, you can dance to that!'

Chris Hillman, who played bass for the Byrds, says 'As a folk singer, Roger McGuinn had learnt to play the long-neck banjo and he had used Pete Seeger's instruction book – and I had it too. Pete had recorded some Bach on the banjo and if you think about it, that intro to 'Mr. Tambourine Man' is very Bach-inspired. It's close to 'Jesu, Joy of Man's Desiring', which was also in the middle of 'She Don't Care about Time', and it worked brilliantly.'

Roger McGuinn: 'Dylan never expressed any displeasure with our version of 'Mr. Tambourine Man'. I think he liked it and I know that he told Joan Baez, 'There's nothing happening on the radio, man, except maybe the Byrds.' He liked what we were doing and he gave us his full endorsement. He heard our arrangement of it in a rehearsal hall before we recorded it and he liked it. We had changed the time signature and we cut out three verses. The reason we put in the verse that we did was because it had 'boot heels' in it and the Beatles wore boots.'

Chris Hillman: 'On AM radio in the States, you had singles that were maybe two minutes thirty seconds and they certainly didn't want them over three minutes. We had to cut the song down and just sing one verse and we missed out some beautiful lines.'

Music writer Johnny Rogan: 'McGuinn says that he programmed his voice to come out somewhere between Dylan and Lennon. All their early material was a transition from folk to rock, and their early demos are very folk-influenced. They wanted to change to electric guitars and Beatle-style harmonies.'

Back to Roger McGuinn: 'Once we saw the Beatles in *A Hard Day's Night*, we wanted to be like them and that included getting suits with velvet collars. We went to Mr. Parker's Closet in South central Los Angeles and we bought black suits with black velvet collars. We wore them on stage and we had them at Ciro's. Instead of taking them home every night, we would hang them on the racks at Ciro's and went home in our jeans. One day we returned and the suits were all gone. I told John Lennon later on that somebody had stolen our suits. He said, "I wish somebody had stolen ours." (Laughs)'

But wouldn't a better comparison be with the Searchers? Roger McGuinn: 'If you listen to 'I'll Feel a Whole Lot Better', you can tell it was influenced by the Searchers' 'Needles and Pins'. They weren't using 12-strings though, it was two six-strings in octaves to get that sound. That sound was influential and we did take that from them, so thank you, Searchers. I loved a lot of those British acts – the Searchers, Dusty Springfield especially and the Seekers, who were Australian and did kinda folky things. Later, I loved Fairport Convention.'

'Mr. Tambourine Man' had yet to be released but on March 8 they had recorded another Dylan tune, 'All I Really Want to Do' and now their first single as the Byrds and their first album, both called 'Mr. Tambourine Man', were ready for release. On 26 March 1965, Dylan went to see the Byrds at Ciro's and guested on harmonica when they played 'All I Really Want to Do'.

There was an off the wall interview with Paul Jay Robbins of the *Los Angeles Free Press*, and Dylan commented, 'Sure, you can make up all sorts of protest songs and put them on a Folkways record, but who hears them?' A little unfair perhaps but Folkways was a specialist label.

Bob Dylan: Outlaw Blues

In March 1965 Martin Luther King led a four-day march covering 54 miles. There were 3,000 marchers and the musicians included Pete Seeger and Guy Carawan. There were tense encounters and the marchers kept going by singing 'We Shall Not Be Moved' and 'Lonesome Valley'.

Having had no luck selling his book in England, Richard Fariña had contacted Random House in New York and they had accepted his novel *Been Down so Long It Looks like Up to Me*. They didn't want illustrations, just conventional text with the raunchy passages deleted. He got an advance of $1,800. It had taken a long time but at last he would be a published novelist.

The album he had made with Mimi, *Celebrations for a Grey Day*, was being released, the cover photograph being taken in a tunnel in New York's Central Park. One of the songs, 'Pack up Your Sorrows', was picked up by Judy Collins for her *Fifth Album*. Richard played dulcimer on her version and wrote liner notes.

'Pack up Your Sorrows' was written around a saying in the Baez family and Joan was to record it. Biographer David Hajdu: 'Richard's best-known song is 'Pack Up Your Sorrows' which is a standard to this day. Judy Collins recorded 'Hard Lovin' Loser' which passes any test of greatness and is unique among songs of that period for its irony and humour. There was much stridency and self-righteousness in the writing and pretentiousness of Fariña's peers. Here is a song that is not afraid of being funny and it has a winking savviness that is more akin to Ira Gershwin than to anybody in the folk-rock milieu.'

Bob Dylan commented, 'Richard Fariña is the best of all the bullshitters, that's really where it's at with him. I have heard all his songs and I didn't like any of them.' So, no love lost there then.

Baez paid for the Fariñas to join her in California and help at the Institute for the Study of Non-Violence which she had established with her guru Ira Sandperl. Another singer / songwriter, Tom Rush, took over the Fariña's apartment and found that Richard had left behind his gun and an X-ray of his head.

Bob Dylan's *Bringing It All Back Home* was well received in the UK press, although the reviews could be bitter-sweet. *New Musical Express* gave it four stars but said, 'He punctuates his rather tuneless singing with his wailing harmonica.' Jeremy Rundall in *The Guardian* did an overview of his career so far: 'His subjects are war, intolerance and the deprivation of liberty. "Blowin' in the Wind" would not be the first song which has precipitated a revolution.'

CBS in the UK had a catalogue of Dylan product to promote; he had now made five albums, all offering something different. The first stirrings were towards the end of 1964 when both *The Freewheelin' Bob Dylan* and *Another Side of Bob Dylan* made the Top 10 albums, but fell back. *Another Side of Bob Dylan* returned in February 1965 and then in April 1965 *The Freewheelin' Bob Dylan* narrowly failed to knock *The Rolling Stones Number 2* off the top, despite being two years old. It bounced back and displaced *Beatles for Sale* in May 1965 (which is amazing really) to be followed by a five-week occupation for *Bringing It All Back Home*. The soundtrack from *The Sound of Music* took over but *Bringing It All Back Home* had a further three weeks at the top. *The Times They Are A-Changin'* had several weeks in the Top 10.

The ITV pop show *Ready Steady Go!* had discovered a young Scottish singer and songwriter, Donovan, so clearly modelled on Bob Dylan. In March 1965 he had a Top 10 hit with 'Catch the Wind', a decent enough song but musically inspired by Dylan's 'Chimes of Freedom'. Indeed, I won't damn it with faint praise as some of the lines ('When sundown pales the sky', 'When rain has hung the leaves with tears') are good. The 'diddy di diddy' adds to its charm.

Al Stewart: 'Don and I both played acoustic guitars and came from Scotland, but he wasn't playing folk clubs in the 60s. He was much more in the popular wing of music than me. He did *Thank Your Lucky Stars* and programmes like that and was being marketed as a pop star, Britain's only folk star, and he had that little niche until Cat Stevens came along.' Donovan's album, *What's Bin Did and What's Bin Hid* (good title) climbed to Number 3.

The Ministry of Labour Permit said 'Bob Dylan Employment: Variety Artiste', which meant that Bob could have a UK tour. He would be playing two acoustic solo sets of 40 minutes at each show, and he had flown over with Joan Baez who was expecting to make an unbilled appearance each evening. This was a strange idea: why should an artist who had had her own Top 10 album the previous year (*In Concert, Volume 2*) not be touring in her own right? As it happens, she was about to enter the singles chart with 'We Shall Overcome' and have another hit album with *Joan Baez 5*. What would she gain from the tour and why would Albert Grossman want her around – he didn't manage her. She liked what Bob was doing and had an idea for doing an electric album herself.

Dylan's biographer Bob Spitz: 'The UK tour was Bob's biggest achievement in tormenting Joan Baez. She wasn't a fixture in the UK in 1965 but Bob was already well known. Joan thought, "Good, he is bringing me along and he will do the same for me as I did for him: he'll introduce me in the middle of his shows", and every night Joan stood in the wings with her guitar and Dylan would shake his head and keep on performing. He delighted in doing that.'

Why didn't Joan just walk on stage one night? How could that have made it any worse? Finally she broke down crying and left the tour. Biographer David Hajdu: 'That was the darkest period of their relationship. He was suffering from a variety of demons – drugs being the most invasive and the worst. He was already seeing the woman who would become his wife and Joan didn't know about this. Joan had no business being there really, but it is not my place to ascribe moral judgments, He had moved on but not told Joan. That happens in a lot of relationships'

There were issues regarding work permits for foreign performers but surely a couple of TV appearances and some concerts could have been arranged at short notice, especially when it was clear that Bob Dylan was not going to let her anywhere near his stage. She did have one solo concert on May 23. Of course Bob owed her one and she was his girlfriend for want of a better word, but that didn't count for anything as Dylan was promoting himself as a single entity.

Bob had another musician, Bobby Neuwirth, with him but only as a buddy and he wasn't expected to join Bob on stage. As they flew into London on April 26, they were singing 'London Bridge is Falling Down'. The night club singer Lena Horne was on the same flight but nobody took any notice of her when the plane landed. Dylan came out with jokey one-liners, which he rarely repeated, to the pressmen. Asked where he was living, he said, 'Right here' and he even said that he replied to all his fan mail. He didn't and indeed in most cases, it wouldn't be forwarded to him.

Ray Coleman of *Melody Maker*: 'I met Bob Dylan at Heathrow Airport and he was carrying a plain, ordinary lightbulb. I said, "Hello, I'm from *Melody Maker*" and he said, "Keep a clear head and always carry a lightbulb." That's all he would say for the entire journey from Heathrow Airport to the Savoy Hotel. I thought it was very, very funny but it was frustrating; I was trying to get an intelligent interview from the man but that's the game he played.'

Patrick Humphries: 'I love that remark. Dylan is so often depicted as a sackcloth and ashes poet who is terribly earnest and whining about the wrongs of society, but he also had a very good sense of humour and there is some very good stand-up comedy in there. 'Tombstone Blues' is one song that will always have me chuckling.'

When Dylan was first asked about Donovan, he said, 'Donovan who?' but he soon found out and said, generously, 'I liked 'Catch the Wind'. It's a good song and he sang it well.'

Albert Grossman hosted a cocktail party for the media. Dylan sat on the window ledge and was bored. I say this because Maureen Cleave wrote 'Dylan is very, very bored'. He said, 'I have no message for anyone. I don't want to influence people in any way.' One of the guests, Alan Price of the Animals, became a friend throughout the tour.

Dylan was more animated that evening as he was driven to Weybridge for a meal with John and Cynthia Lennon. The two musicians were cynics who enjoyed belittling others and were masters of wordplay and they got on well together. Bob stayed until 4am.

The next day Bob was meeting selected journalists and he walked around Carnaby Street with Joan Baez and bought three pairs of boots. They visited Regent's Park Zoo and he was fascinated by the hippopotamus.

Dylan again met John Lennon, this time with the rest of the Beatles. During the next few days, he would get to know the Rolling Stones. He had fun with the musicians and once when he sang a song and nobody clapped, he sang, 'Nobody wants the clap in this room' which made everybody laugh.

He got to know Donovan who sang him a new song, 'Tangerine Eyes', which shared the same melody as 'Mr. Tambourine Man'. Donovan had thought it was an old tune but Dylan said, 'I haven't written all the tunes I am credited with but I did write that one!' It is clear from *Dont Look Back* that Bob got on well with Donovan. He liked his song, 'To Sing for You'.

Joan Baez gave Donovan a ring. When I was looking at old photographs of Donovan with him at Tate Liverpool, he said, 'Lewis Morley took this photograph in 1965 and I am in my finery. I went to Liberty's and I bought silk paisley-patterned fabric and they tell me that I pioneered it as I started making clothes with this pattern. I was a bohemian wishing to present an artistic image to the world which would be an illustration of my music. Look, I am holding a Sun disc above my head in this photograph and in this one I am looking very clearly, very slowly at the camera, and what I am doing is meditating as the photograph is taken. On that finger is a ring that Joan Baez gave me. She said, "You must take this chalice I give you" – she called the ring a chalice – "and you will accept this mission to take to the world freedom of expression and freedom of thought." The whole world is a brotherhood of man. There was a mission of peace to the world in all this.' (Is it just me or do you think they're all bonkers too? One thing is certain: they have very high ambitions.)

When Dylan reviewed the singles for the *Blind Date* column in *Melody Maker*, he praised 'Catch the Wind'. The *NME* sent him their *Lifelines* to complete and he responded hilariously with answers about his dog. When Dylan heard he was getting an award for the Best Folk Music Record of 1964, he said, 'Give it to Donovan.'

The folk singer Dana Gillespie invited herself to Dylan's press reception: 'I was 16 and I can't say it was love because I was too young to know what love was but it was awe-inspiring to be carrying his guitar and see girls screaming and trying to climb into his limo. You can see me in *Dont Look Back* with my blonde hair and bursting out of a shirt as usual. Every night the Stones and the Beatles came to the Savoy and they would play their latest recordings. Everyone was in awe of Dylan and he was one person that both the Stones and the Beatles held in great admiration. When he held court in his hotel room, everyone sat and listened. John Lennon got legless one night and fell asleep on my bed while I was in it. He didn't know I was there, he was so out of it.'

One day Bob borrowed Dana's pants decked with pink and orange roses and told her to wear his while he went out for a couple of hours. Dana couldn't get into them and so she was stuck in his room until he returned – 15 hours later. Dana Gillespie revealed that she would spend the night with him and then slip back to her parents. She had a 44-inch bust and said that 'I was his substitute teddy bear.'

The Beatles' chauffeur, Alf Bicknell, recalled: 'I met Bob Dylan on a couple of occasions. I went with Paul McCartney to the Savoy Hotel one night. There was Bob Dylan, Allen Ginsberg, Paul and one or two others sitting around talking and my job was to take Paul home when he wanted to go. I remember getting so smashed that I was sitting inside a wardrobe in Bob's bedroom. He had plied me with vodka. Another time I drove the Beatles to the hotel to see a film that Bob had made. Bob came down the stairs with a copy of *Time* and he said, 'Alfie, look what I got' and he had a picture of me running across the stage at the Cow Palace in San Francisco. I was pleased he had remembered me.'

Ken Pitt: 'Bob was very amused when I told him that *Vogue* magazine had agreed to interview him. It did seem incongruous but he was so thrilled that the night before, he put his faded, crumpled jeans under the mattress so that there was a crease in them when the photographer came.'

Ah, such fun but in the midst of this activity, you might have overlooked that Bob Dylan was here to work. Starting on 30 April 1965, he had eight concert dates around the country. He was sometimes appearing at Odeon cinemas, which did have occasional touring shows.

The Guardian reported that Dylan was earning £85,000 a year (about right, I would think) and their reviewer Dan O'Neill said, 'With his voice, his lyrics are astonishing: without it, in print, they are poetry.'

When Mike Hurst of the Springfields interviewed him for *Teen Scene* on the BBC Light Programme, Dylan said that 'Subterranean Homesick Blues' was 'early authentic folk music'. So now you know.

The tour has been very well covered. There is not only the film, *Dont Look Back* but also all the outtakes. Not at all the recluse, Dylan was socialising and enjoying himself.

Pennebaker shot whatever was happening: 'Dylan was going to do things in a different way but I wasn't sure how. I knew that totally by chance I'd fallen right where I should be. You couldn't get people to act funnier than Albert Grossman and Tito Burns.' That is a wonderful scene where the two agents are hustling for a deal as they played Granada TV against the BBC. Such incidents inspired Dylan's later song, 'Dear Landlord'; 'Dear landlord, please don't put a price on my soul'.

Film-maker Tony Palmer: 'You remember the scene with Tito Burns in *Dont Look Back* where he is trying to get Dylan's fee up to £2,000 and you can see the shiftiness and deviousness in the way that those old-style shysters fixed the market. Eddie Rogers was a party to that too and he is in the film because he represented what Tin Pan Alley pop music had been. It is important to show what Dylan wanted to get away from.'

Johnnie Hamp from Granada TV recalls, 'I knew of Bob Dylan but he wasn't a big name at that time. I met him at a press conference and I wanted him to do two programmes. There is a discussion about the fees in *Dont Look Back* where Tito Burns is on the phone to me. He was acting as the agent and trying to get more money out of me. I went to my bosses but they said, "Well, what are you going to do with a folk singer?" They thought I would be showing films of cotton fields and I couldn't convince them that Bob Dylan would be the guy he would turn out to be so I lost that one.'

Willy Russell: 'You see the great and the good and the dignitaries in *Dont Look Back*. They were just getting hip to the fact that if you strung onto the coattails of some pop singers, it might do you some political good.'

The tour started at Sheffield City Hall and Harry Goodwin, the photographer for BBC-TV's *Top of the Pops,* was determined to get some photographs he could use for their chart countdown. Ken Pitt told him that Dylan was unpredictable but there was no harm in trying. Harry was taking photographs but Dylan was smoking a cigarette (the nicotine on his fingers was apparent) and keeping his eyes shut. Harry double-flashed him so that his eyes opened and he got his shot.

Dylan didn't say too much between songs but after a modest reception he said, 'It's mighty quiet, where are you all?' and the audience became livelier.

Bob Spitz: 'We always have high expectations of Bob Dylan because he is such a great poet and we would expect him to be a great conversationalist, but they are two different things. He can perform and he can sing because he has the crutch of his music. He doesn't know how to address people and that is why he has never really talked in concert. He never says what he has been doing during the day. He plays his songs and gets off. He thinks you have come to hear his songs and not what's on his mind. You hear what's on his mind through the music and Dylan does not want any relationship with his audience past his talent.'

On Saturday 1 May 1965 Dylan crossed the Pennines to appear at the Odeon in Liverpool. F.A. Cup Final day, as it happened. The Odeon, around the corner from the Empire Theatre, showed films but there was the occasional stage show and I saw Brook Benton and Dion there in October 1963. Dylan was booked into the Adelphi Hotel and enjoyed their Cheshire cheese.

Liverpool DJ Norman Killon: 'Joan Baez had walked from the Adelphi Hotel to the stage door and I got both volumes of *In Concert* autographed by her. Bob Dylan drove up in his limo and went straight in. There were a couple of girls there, and Joan took them in through the stage door. They were later seen with Bob in his hotel room.'

Only a few weeks earlier, I had attended a poorly-attended Tamla-Motown package at the Empire Theatre with Stevie Wonder, the Supremes and Martha and the Vandellas, so within a month, I saw Stevie Wonder, Diana Ross and Bob Dylan. I had no trouble in purchasing the Dylan tickets – the *NME* said when tickets would be on sale and I simply walked across town to the Odeon in my lunch hour: there wasn't a queue. Couldn't have been easier. I've seen a reference in the music press to ticket touts – £1 tickets being offered at £5 – but I never saw any of that.

I bought two tickets, one for myself and one for my girlfriend, Diana. I wasn't sure that Diana would like it. She'd heard me play Bob Dylan's albums, especially *The Times They Are A-Changin'*, and she didn't care for him. She hated his voice, his songs, his stark instrumentation – in fact, the whole enchilada. I told her that he would be quite different in person and she would love him. I realise now how naive and stupid I was – you don't force your tastes onto other people. Mind you, I play records I like on local radio each week so maybe I haven't changed much.

We went into Liverpool on the bus, got off at the terminus and walked down Lime Street towards London Road. As we turned the corner we saw the lettering above the entrance: 'The Sound of Music, 2.30' on the top line and 'Bob Dylan, 7.30' on the bottom.

The cinema's plush curtains were shut and in front of them on a small stage, a platform really, were two microphones, one head-high, one waist-high, a stool and a table which contained harmonicas, a carafe and a glass. Minimalism, but strangely exciting. If the show had been at the Empire, the curtains would have covered the stage, but this was great – the anticipation of knowing that my hero was about to appear, stand there and play his songs. If there was a programme, I wouldn't have bought one – in my arrogance, I would have told Diana that I knew it all already: I was insufferable and I'm embarrassed to write this but it's true.

The place was full and Dylan did two sets, but everything didn't go to plan. Dylan started with 'The Times They Are A-Changin'', or at least I think he did, as his vocal mic wasn't working. A technician came on stage to sort it and Dylan just hung around. Surely the man who was so good with words could have said something to us through the good mic. As it turned out, he didn't say one word to us all night. When the technician got it working, there was a huge cheer from us all, and Dylan started on his rallying song, opening with a quick burst on his harmonica. It was followed by the beautifully sensitive 'To Ramona'. He was singing his lyrics much clearer than on record as if he wanted to get every word across to a UK audience.

The lengthy and complex 'Gates of Eden' was next but he lightened the mood with the humorous 'If You Gotta Go, Go Now', which we'd never heard before. He played up the absurdity of 'It's Alright, Mama (I'm Only Bleeding)' but I'd noticed Diana had stopped clapping – did she ever start? The wonderfully lyrical 'Love minus Zero / No Limit' was next and he closed the first half with 'Mr. Tambourine Man'. 'Don't worry,' I told Diana, 'The second half will be better.' I don't remember anything about the interval except that it was awkward.

The funniest moment of the night occurred in the opening song from the second set, 'Talking World War III Blues'. He changed a line so that when he turned on the radio, it was no longer Rock-a-day Johnny but 'Donovan' (pause, laughter from audience), 'whoever Donovan is' (more laughter). He changed the line, 'I think Abraham Lincoln said that' to 'I think Robert Frost said that'. A friend told me that he said, 'I think T.S. Eliot said that' in Newcastle so he was testing variations.

'With God on Our Side' was chilling and I still think that the line about Judas Iscariot is the most surprising, the most thoughtful and the most provocative line ever written in a popular song. It was followed by the cheerful mysteriousness of 'She Belongs to Me' and the bitterness of 'It Ain't Me, Babe'. I had a friend with an active sex life and we had written a new version for him, 'It Ain't My Babe', and the alternative and much feebler words were going round in my head. Sorry, Bob.

Then there was the tragedy of 'The Lonesome Death of Hattie Carroll', one of the few protest songs in which he named names. Dylan had a coughing fit when he started 'All I Really Want to Do' and after drinking water, he started again, almost yodelling the title line. Everything about Dylan was anti-showbiz so why did he close with 'It's All Over Now,

Baby Blue'? But it was all over now, baby blue, as there was no encore. You knew an artist wasn't coming back when the National Anthem started. I'd been hoping for 'Subterranean Homesick Blues' as it was in the Top 20 and even though he had recorded it with rock musicians, surely he had composed it on an acoustic guitar. Not to worry, the concert had been great, superlative even. Somebody said, 'I don't how he remembers all those words' to which the reply was 'I don't know how he wrote them.' Amen to that.

There was a euphoric feeling on Lime Street as Liverpool had beaten Leeds at Wembley and had therefore won both the League and the Cup. The supporters who were coming off the London trains or out of the pubs were as happy as his audience. Did Bob Dylan think Liverpool was always as happy as this? Did he appreciate that Liverpool had won the Cup?

I'd love to add that Diana was converted but she complained that I had wasted two hours of her life. She finished with me there and then. We did get back together and in 1966 we were again having a threesome with Bob Dylan, but more of my love life later.

After the Liverpool show, Dylan was at the late-night club, the Blue Angel, owned by the Beatles' first manager, Allan Williams and he met up with Merseyside personalities including Roger McGough and Mike McGear (Paul McCartney's brother) from Scaffold, who went back with him to the Adelphi.

Roger McGough: 'I was down at the Blue Angel and Allan Williams said, "Bob Dylan is coming" and a buzz went around. He introduced us and I had a group of girls called the Poppies, whom I was thinking of managing with a friend called Clive Goodwin. We all went on Bob's invitation to the Adelphi. Bob Dylan sat in the corner talking. We were talking about Liverpool and this, that and the other. I was in awe of him and I found him to be very nice.'

The next night Bob Dylan was playing the De Montfort Hall in Leicester and he was driven back to the Savoy after the show. He received a gushing letter from Nico who wanted to sing 'Mr. Tambourine Man' on *Ready Steady Go!* but it didn't happen.

In *Dont Look Back*, Dylan was working on *Alternatives to College* (rejected by *Esquire* but in his *Lyrics* book) and Joan Baez was playing her guitar as Dylan typed. She was singing a song that Bob had given her, 'Love Is just a Four Letter Word', the title coming from a line in *Cat on a Hot Tin Roof* as Paul Newman says, 'You don't know what love is. To you, it's just another four-letter word.'

The film and its outtakes show how Dylan taunted Baez. At one stage he held up a glass and challenged her to break it with her shrill voice. However, they had much in common: they sang Johnny Cash's 'Bad News' together and several old-time country songs – 'I Forgot More than You'll ever Know', 'Remember Me (I'm the One who Loves You)', 'More and More' and 'Blues Stay 'way from my Door' as well as some Hank Williams songs – 'Weary Blues from Waitin", 'Lost Highway' and 'I'm So Lonesome I Could Cry'.

Taking a lead from Kerouac, Dylan was seen typing his lyrics on a roll of toilet paper. Ken Pitt: 'He would put a roll of toilet paper into his typewriter and start writing. When he was at the Savoy, I tried very hard to get my hands on the original typescripts but I didn't succeed.'

On May 5, Dylan, accompanied by Joan Baez and John Mayall, made his way to the Grand Hotel, Birmingham to play at the Town Hall. He met the vintage folk singer Derroll Adams: he had been born in Portland, Oregon in 1925, an old salt who had moved to Europe and was a great mate of Ramblin' Jack Elliott. Jack and Derroll would go into a studio with marijuana and whisky, sing whatever they wanted and *voila!* a new album was ready.

During the day, Joan wrote to Mimi, 'I'm leaving Dylan's entourage. He has become so unbelievably unmanageable that I can't stand to be around him.' She voiced the same opinion to Pennebaker. Bob preferred to be with Marianne Faithfull and Dana Gillespie. Joan was being teased by Dylan and Neuwirth and she flew to Paris to be with her parents.

On May 6, Dylan played the City Hall in Newcastle. He was seen admiring musical instruments in a shop, a reverse from the normal attitude as many American models were not available in the UK. There was a terrific exchange with Terry Ellis for the university magazine. 'Why should you want to know about me?' said Dylan, 'I don't want to know about you.' Dylan was playing games, but no harm done as Terry Ellis went on to found Chrysalis Records. He could have been one of the inspirations for 'Ballad of a Thin Man', but there are many candidates.

On May 7, Dylan played the Free Trade Hall in Manchester and was driven back to London.

Dylan had seen a video jukebox, the Scopitone, in France and he wanted to make a video of his own. He had bought some shirts and so he used the cardboard inserts to write key words. Bob Dylan, Alan Price and Donovan wrote the placards, Donovan's being the most flowery, no surprise there.

Dylan filmed the video for 'Subterranean Homesick Blues' in an alley at the back of the Savoy Hotel off the Strand in London. Dylan was holding up the cards to emphasise the lyric and Allen Ginsberg made a guest appearance. They had no permission to film: they just did it. They also filmed in a park but a policeman asked them what they were doing and they had to stop.

Noddy Holder of Slade: 'My favourite track of his, mainly lyrically, even though it doesn't make a lot of sense, is 'Subterranean Homesick Blues'. It's just the force of the song and the words that he uses, People talk about videos being a modern thing and yet he made a promotional film for that song and he is holding up the hook words of each line and throwing them away. It's a really good idea and a really good video.'

Music writer Johnny Rogan: 'In 1965 on my twelfth birthday, I remember hearing 'The Times They Are A-Changin'' and knowing that I'd never heard anything like this before in both the lyrics and the way he sang them. That was followed by 'Subterranean Homesick Blues' which was so fast and so surreal, and then finally by 'Like a Rolling Stone', making it a wonderful year. I couldn't believe that 'Like a Rolling Stone' was six minutes long and the B-side 'Gates of Eden' was equally long and equally extraordinary. I was saving up the money from my paper round to get the album.'

Mike Evans: 'When Dylan did the film for 'Subterranean Homesick Blues' with the flashcards, Allen Ginsberg was in the background with his kaftan and his shepherd's crook. It was just after Allen had been in Liverpool. It was in the days before cash machines and the banking system was very creaky, and the only American Express office was down by the docks and it opened peculiar hours. Allen kept running out of money but he discovered that you could get money sent to you at a Post Office if a person in another part of the country wanted to send you some money. It was very handy as he was phoning this friend in London for money and it turned out to be Bob Dylan. Dylan's entourage would put the money in the Post Office for Ginsberg.'

There was another evening party which included an argument as someone had thrown a glass shelf from the bathroom into the street. 'Who threw the fucking glass?' Dylan ranted. Quite right too; he didn't want anyone to be injured. The culprit was probably Brian Pendleton of the Pretty Things.

On May 9 and 10, Bob Dylan played two nights at the Royal Albert Hall. Tim Rice: 'I was knocked sideways by his first concert at the Royal Albert Hall.'

There was a party after the first night at the Savoy which all four Beatles attended. Dylan insulted Judson Manning of *The Times* – he was still wary of the quality press following the negative features in *Time* and *Newsweek*. In the film, Dylan tells Horace Judson from *Time*: 'I'm as good a singer as Caruso. You have to listen carefully but I hit all those notes.' This is similar to Eric Morecambe's comeback to André Previn in 1971: 'I play all the right notes but not necessarily in the right order.' Dylan was to repeat this claim in his *Playboy* interview.

Two of Dylan's poems 'Jack O'Diamonds' and 'Go Joshua Go' were set to music by Ben Carruthers (Benito Carruthers), an actor from Greenwich Village, who had worked in Albert Grossman's office. He had been in a film, *Shadows* in 1960. Dylan gave permission for them to be used in a BBC-TV play, *The Man without Papers*, which was filmed during the week and shown on June 9 in *The Wednesday Play* slot, written by Troy Kennedy Martin (*Z-Cars, The Italian Job*). The tall, handsome Carruthers was playing the central character in the play.

Dylan was having fun with Laurie Henshaw of *Disc*, but Henshaw enjoyed the challenge. Dylan said that John Hammond discovered him in 1935 sitting on a farm. In another interview with Ray Coleman of *Melody Maker*, he returned to the lightbulb.

Hughie Jones of the Spinners: 'We were performing in the Troubadour in London, which gets mentioned in a Tom Paxton song. The show went well into Sunday and Mary Travers and Bob Dylan were there. Bob was matey with Martin Carthy who was also there. He asked us about hiring rock musicians for a session but we were the wrong people to ask. We did give him and Mary a lift in our van.'

On 12 May Dylan had a session at Levy's recording studio in New Bond Street, which was owned by CBS, with Tom Wilson producing. On paper it looked good: Tom Wilson had flown in to record Dylan with John Mayall's Bluesbreakers but it was a disaster as both Wilson and Dylan were drunk. The musician Hughie Flint, said to Dylan, 'You haven't worked much with bands, have you?'

'If You Gotta Go, Go Now' is a light-hearted, funny song, but that day neither Dylan nor the musicians were up to it. John Mayall had 'Slow Train to Nowhere' that they planned to record but no satisfactory take was produced. Eric Clapton had left the Yardbirds and joined the Bluesbreakers and he and Dylan got on okay. At the time, Eric dismissed white folk music, largely because Paul Samwell-Smith of the Yardbirds liked it so much. Well, they were all young.

On May 13, Bob went to see the Lennons again in Weybridge and Dylan thought of owning a proper home. He liked Lennon's stuffed gorilla and suit of armour. The next day he met Sara in Paris and took her on holiday to Portugal. (This is mentioned in his song, 'Sara').

Dylan had met an American rock'n'roll singer from Hounslow who was now a star in France, Vince Taylor. He had spent over £200 on LSD on the night he met Bob Dylan. The next night he was in Paris and went on stage with a bottle of Mateus Rosé and said to the band, 'My name is Mateus. I am the new Jesus, the son of God.' Vince Taylor almost made my Big Bang list.

Dylan was in London on May 21. He was taken ill at the Savoy (same intake as Vince Taylor?), and two nurses (sisters of mercy?) were employed to look after him. He could not be stabilised so he was admitted to St. Mary's Hospital, Paddington on May 26.

While he was ill, Dylan wrote a story, 'this long piece of vomit, about 20 pages long, and out of it I took 'Like a Rolling Stone' and it made it as a single. I'd never written anything like that before.' It could be that the song was so venomous because he was ill. Dylan loved his opening assonance of 'kiddin' you' with 'didn't you'. Dylan wrote the melody on piano and transferred it to guitar. He first saw the song as a waltz and an early take is in that tempo.

The song when recorded would last six minutes – in reality, a tirade like this would never last so long as the subject would interrupt. Hank Williams' 'Lost Highway' starts 'I'm a rolling stone, all alone and lost' which could have been an inspiration. Muddy Waters had written and recorded 'Rollin' Stone' in 1950 and it had been a standard part of his act.

Clive James has stated that Arthur Rimbaud's 'The Drunken Boat' is perfection but 'Like a Rolling Stone', it has slipshod organisation, missed opportunities, easy rhymes and unfocused images, but this awkwardness can be 'certificates of authenticity'. The order of the verses does not matter so a whole dimension is missing. James says that it would help if Dylan's songs were shortened and more concentrated. I'm not sure: I like the long, rambling verses with images that can go anywhere and then you get the punch of the title line.

On May 23 Joan Baez was back in London, playing her own concert but Dylan was too ill to attend. Joan saw him in hospital and met Sara for the first time. Dylan was discharged three days later and returned to the Savoy.

By now, Bob Dylan had five albums in the UK Top 20 LP chart, with *Bringing It All Back Home* at Number 1 (and Number 6 in the US) – and all this while Beatlemania and the British Invasion were happening. Even the first album, *Bob Dylan*, reached Number 13 on the chart.

On 1 June 1965, Bob Dylan filmed a concert for the BBC, two 35-minute sets that would be broadcast on June 19 and 26. A similar concert with Joan Baez was broadcast on June 2 and 12. *Radio Times* in mixed-up confusion, said there would be commentary from the boxing specialist Harry Carpenter. The Polish artist Felix Topolski drew sketches for the credits. Dave Cousins from the Strawbs was in the audience and recalls, 'He had bright red bloodshot eyes.' Dylan was concentrating on newer songs. Manfred Mann and Tom McGuinness realised that 'If You Gotta Go, Go Now' was a potential hit song.

On the next day, Bob and Sara flew back to New York. They went to a cabin in Woodstock and Bob invited Mike Bloomfield to hear new songs. He had been writing in England but this time his songs weren't based around traditional tunes.

Donn Pennebaker had shot about 20 hours. He decided on the title *Dont Look Back* with no apostrophe. That resonated with several areas of Dylan's life, although it had come from the baseball player, Satchel Paige who offered the advice, 'Don't look back: he may be gaining on you.'

John Lee Hooker had recorded a song called 'Don't Look Back' and the phrase occurs in 'She Belongs to Me', although that song was not included in the film. It could also refer to John Osborne's play, *Don't Look Back in Anger,* which was at the forefront of the kitchen sink dramas. It could refer to Bob Dylan in interviews – how does he respond to the same old questions?

Pennebaker had seen how perverse Dylan could be and he couldn't predict how he would react to the rough cut of *Dont Look Back*. Dylan's only comment was that he didn't want a scuffle in his hotel room to be shown. Bob lost his temper in the film and treated Baez badly but he was okay about that. Dylan enjoyed baiting journalists and even Donovan didn't mind the wind-ups. On the whole, Dylan came across well. *Dont Look Back* doesn't feel like it is being staged for the cameras.

Grossman was unsure about the film. He disliked the *cinéma vérité* style – that was giving it intellectual pretensions when it was a home movie to him. He found the dialogue muffled as Pennebaker had sometimes shot on 8mm. There was the fade to black at the end as though they had run out of film.

Dont Look Back was rejected by distributors and said to have been badly made. It had its first public screening at a porno cinema in San Francisco. It was never called a documentary because that word was box office poison. It could have had a great strapline as Dylan told Pennebaker, 'It's a great movie. Too bad it's not about me.' Fairly early on it was recognised that this provided a unique insight into one of the most mysterious people on the planet and its stature has grown with the years. The way the camera follows Dylan from the dressing-room to the stage was parodied in the mock-doc, *This Is Spinal Tap*.

When Dylan returned to America, he found that the Byrds' single of 'Mr. Tambourine Man' was about to top the charts. His own 'Subterranean Homesick Blues' was a Top 40 hit, albeit only Number 39, and the Byrds' single was Dylan's first rock hit. It is frustratingly short and it is annoying that they didn't record a longer version for the album. David Crosby said, 'Most people couldn't get past Dylan's voice. We took the song and made it pretty. We put Bob on AM radio.'

Chris Hillman: 'Bob had written it originally in a straight country groove, almost bluegrass, and the original demo is with Ramblin' Jack Elliott. We changed it to 4/4 where you could dance to it. Bob was definitely excited that it was such a big hit. It could have helped to push him forwards but he probably had that intention anyway. Bob Dylan is a brilliant man with a very high intellect and he knew he had to expand on just using a guitar and harmonica.'

Bob Spitz has described the Byrds' record as 'a mousy whitewash', but Hunter S. Thompson disagreed, 'To me, this is the hippie national anthem. It's an acid or LSD song and like much hippie music, the lyrics don't make much sense to anyone not into the drug scene. Dylan's lyrics became increasingly drug-oriented with double-entendres and dual meanings that were more and more obvious until his 'Rainy Day Women' which was banned from coast to coast.'

The Byrds came to the UK on the success of 'Mr. Tambourine Man', now a transatlantic Number 1 but it fell to Number 4 while they were here. Their appearance on a pop package with Donovan, Kenny Lynch and Elkie Brooks was not well received and the NME criticised them for playing everything with that 'chiming whining effect'.

Some gigs were cancelled which were attributed to McGuinn having a virus, but the Byrds' UK publicist, Derek Taylor, had his work cut out as the band was playing badly with poor equipment. The Musicians' Union blocked them from appearing on *Saturday Club* and *The Joe Loss Show* as there were no similar US shows that British acts could appear on.

The Byrds' follow-up single, 'All I Really Want to Do', did well but suffered from competition from a rival version by Cher, produced by her husband, Sonny Bono. Roger McGuinn: 'We didn't know that Cher was doing it as well but Sonny and Cher used to come to Ciro's when we were performing and take notes. They copied some of our ideas (chuckles). She did a more Dylanesque version of it with the 3/4 time and we changed the time signature to a 4/4 beat. I don't know why theirs did better – well, maybe it was just a better record!'

When Dylan heard Cher's cover of 'All I Really Want to Do', he said to Roger McGuinn, 'They beat you, man.' McGuinn said, 'He had lost faith in me and his material had been bastardised. We'd let Sonny and Cher get away with it.'

Sonny and Cher's initial breakthrough hit 'I Got You Babe' was a classic teen song but it can be seen as folk-rock. Sonny Bono copied Dylan's nasal vocal and aped Phil Spector's production techniques. The song, 'I Got You Babe' is not far from Donovan's 'Catch the Wind'.

The success of the Byrds gave Bob Dylan encouragement. It made him want to strap on an electric guitar and turn the 60s inside out. When he heard the Rolling Stones' 'Satisfaction', he knew that he could have written 'Satisfaction' but the Stones could never have written 'Mr. Tambourine Man'. This quote got back to Mick Jagger who said with a laugh, 'It's true but I'd like to hear Bob Dylan sing "Satisfaction".' Actually, I am sure Dylan could have done a great version of 'Satisfaction: 'I'm driving in my car' could have been made for him.

The most unlikely songs were being taken up by the beat groups as 'With God on Our Side' was performed by Manfred Mann. Lead guitarist Tom McGuinness: "With God on Our Side' was a good anti-war song to be doing and there was a strong CND element within the band.'

The lyricist Tim Rice saw Manfred Mann perform 'With God on Our Side' on ITV's *Ready Steady Go!* 'I had probably heard Bob Dylan's "With God on Our Side" but it hadn't sunk in, but when I saw Manfred Mann do it, I thought that this was fantastic. It had a good tune but the lyric was brilliant – "I can't think for you, you'll have to decide, Did Judas Iscariot have God on his side?" I had been to very religious schools, and I had always had this interest in Jesus' story. I used to wonder whether Pontius Pilate and Judas Iscariot were just unlucky to be around at the time. They are now damned for all time. I thought that if I were Judas, I might have reacted that way as it is hard to believe that your boss is actually God. On hearing that line sung by Paul Jones, I thought that this is really interesting. That was in 1965 which was when I met Andrew and I suggested a musical about Judas, but it seemed ludicrous. We went down a more conventional route and we wrote a very naïve musical about Dr. Barnardo. Then we wrote *Joseph* and its success led to the opportunity to write a modern pop or rock musical. We went back to Judas Iscariot and it worked, as you know.'

On 15 and 16 June 1965 Bob Dylan was back in Columbia's Studio A on 7th Avenue and this time it was all-out rock. This was the start of the sessions for *Highway 61 Revisited* and he had with him with Paul Griffin (keyboards), Bobby Gregg (drums), Mike Bloomfield (guitar) and Russ Savakus (bass).

Plus Al Kooper, whose father had changed the family name from Kuperschmidt. Al was establishing himself as a Brill Building songwriter, mostly writing teen songs with Bob Brass and Irwin Levine. In 1965 they were coming good with 'This Diamond Ring', a US Number 1 for Gary Lewis and the Playboys, and 'I Must Be Seeing Things' for Gene Pitney, but changes were coming in with groups writing their own songs. Bob Brass left to work in a fish market. Al Kooper had married his childhood sweetheart Judy Kerner, but had his problems as he was on mescaline.

Bob Dylan: Outlaw Blues

Al Kooper had done some prom gigs with Paul Simon and his father Lou, and Paul had turned him on to Dylan. Al Kooper wrote '38 People' about a crowd who stood by in Forest Hills while someone was killed. He found that the folkies were united in their contempt for rock'n'roll and so Kooper wrote 'Talkin' Radio Blues'. When '38 People' was to be featured in a CBS documentary, Tom Wilson agreed to produce a single of it with Al singing. It wasn't released but he now knew Wilson and he got invited to a Dylan session. This one.

But Al Kooper didn't want to be a spectator: he wanted to play. He could play guitar and if pushed, a little piano. The session was scheduled for 2pm and he arrived at 1pm with his guitar and plugged in. The other session men drifted in and as he knew them, they didn't give any indication that anything was wrong. If Tom Wilson questioned him, he would say sorry, he had misunderstood the invitation.

Dylan arrived with a wild-looking guy carrying a Telecaster. It was raining hard but it didn't have a case. When Mike Bloomfield wiped it down and started playing, Al realised he was out of his depth and he slunk away to the control room.

They started loosely with 'Sittin' on a Barbed Wire Fence', nothing special but it was followed by the bluesy 'It Takes a Lot to Laugh, It Takes a Train to Cry'. Kooper thought Dylan was difficult and rude but what the hell, he was Bob Dylan.

Dylan wanted both a piano and an organ for 'Like a Rolling Stone' and Paul Griffin couldn't play both at once. Could somebody else play the organ? Al Kooper chanced his arm and said he could play, although he hadn't played one before. Fortunately, Paul Griffin had switched on the Hammond B3 so Al didn't have to work out how it started. The band began playing and he could hardly be heard. Dylan said, 'Turn the organ up'. Dylan liked what he heard and everybody applauded.

Dylan said of 'Like a Rolling Stone': 'My wife and I lived in a little cabin in Woodstock which we rented from Peter Yarrow's mother. I wrote the song there, in the cabin. We had come up from New York and I had about three days off up there to get some stuff together. It just came, you know. It started with that 'La Bamba' riff.' And as Phil Spector remarked, 'Rewriting 'La Bamba' is always a lot of fun.' As if to make Spector's point, there is an outtake on *Bootleg 12* in which the 'La Bamba' riff is to the fore.

It opened like a pistol shot and had a bluesy feel akin to Bukka White. Then after a fairy tale opening ('Once upon a time') came the scornful, disdainful lyrics. Dylan has said that the song was more about revenge than hatred. Dylan knew he had something with the phrase, 'How does it feel?' He had originally written it in waltz tempo but that changed with Kooper on organ. Because he was not used to the instrument, he had inspired a new way of playing organ.

They spent the rest of the day and all of the next on 'Like a Rolling Stone'; they knew they had something but weren't sure what. After a couple of takes, there is a silence as if they are saying, 'What did we just do?' They knew they had it right but they wanted it better, an unusual mind-set for Bob Dylan. Perhaps he didn't hear what he wanted. As it happens, the track they issued as a single, the definitive cut as it were, was the second take on the second day, but there were 13 takes after that.

At the end they felt they had made an extraordinary six-minute track but they didn't see how it could be a single. When one of the production team was asked to test it at a local disco, Arthur's, everybody stopped talking and wanted to hear it. The sound spread through the room.

Clinton Heylin: 'Paul Williams the rock writer went backstage at a Dylan show and he brought with him a book with a series of sketches by Picasso. In the book, you could see Picasso working towards finishing a painting. Dylan pointed at the third sketch and said, 'He should have stopped there'. Then he looked at the fourth sketch and went, 'Ah, I see why he continued'. When Dylan recorded 'Like a Rolling Stone', he didn't realise that he already had the master take near the beginning. The takes are all inspired as you can hear Dylan experimenting with different keys, tempo changes and time signatures. The song had started as a waltz, and clearly he didn't realise when he had recorded a perfect take.'

The engineer Roy Halee's first session with Bob Dylan was 'Like a Rolling Stone', which was before he worked with Simon and Garfunkel. He recalled, 'It was not an enjoyable experience with Dylan. The standard of recording was low and you had to be drunk.'

'Like a Rolling Stone' cut across what the Beatles, the Stones and the Byrds were doing and then some: it marked the birth of art rock. It was emotional and full of cynicism. As Steve Van Zandt has said, 'The classic rock artist's image is dour, serious, frustrated, confused, controversial, political, spiritual, isolated and a threat to society's status quo.'

After originally being in a cabin on Grossman's estate, Bob and Sara bought their own property in Byrdcliffe in July 1965: another misspelling of Byrds. The chalet on Camelot Road was surrounded by pine trees. It cost $12,000 and was two miles from the centre of Woodstock and a mile from Grossman. Dylan's home was called Hi Lo Ha, not an Indian name but the first letters from the mother and two daughters who had lived there. It had belonged to the theatre director, Ben Webster.

On 20 July 1965, 'Like a Rolling Stone' issued as a US single. It was split into two parts for radio stations and juke-boxes. No juke-box proprietor wanted a six-minute single as you would only get ten plays an hour.

The single combined 'Like a Rolling Stone' with 'Gates of Eden' from the previous album. The initial reaction suggested it was going to be a major hit, much more so than 'Subterranean Homesick Blues', which had been regarded as a novelty. He was already a top songwriter with several songs in the US Hot 100 and this would be his breakthrough single.

Bruce Springsteen likened the opening drums to 'somebody kicking open the door to your mind,' When issued in the UK, *Record Mirror* called it, 'The six longest minutes since the invention of time.'

Donovan was heading for controversy as two of his songs were banned by the BBC for commenting on Vietnam. Donovan wrote 'Ballad of a Crystal Man' while Mick Softley, another British writer, wrote 'The War Drags On'.

Acting somewhat out of character, Paul Simon made humorous jabs at Dylan's expense on 'A Simple Desultory Philippic'. He was mocking Dylan's writing style with his cultural imagery and slapdash rhyming. He said to his biographer, Robert Hilburn, 'I couldn't be Bob Dylan any more than I could be Elvis Presley.'

Dylan was scheduled to appear at the Newport Folk Festival on July 24, and I don't think that he had any plans for rocking the boat in the days beforehand. He had however offered a surreal story for the programme, *Off the Top of My Head*, which suggested that things were going to be different. Dylan showed up with his acoustic guitar and played a standard set on the Saturday afternoon. Admittedly, he was wearing a polka-dot shirt with puffed sleeves, dark glasses and had a plentiful head of hair. He was no longer singing protest songs but the audience related to the quality of the songwriting and there were no issues. 'All I Really Want to Do' got a fine reception.

Even Joan Baez was messing with the genres. She sang 'A Satisfied Mind' with a vintage act from Boston, the Lilly Brothers, and had fun with the Supremes' US Number 1, 'Stop! In the Name of Love', but this was now a political statement. The number of troops in Vietnam had risen from 25,000 to 150,000 within a year and she dedicated the song to President Johnson and 'his marvellous foreign policy'. Think it over, indeed. Joan didn't sing with Bob Dylan but she did perform 'Colours' with Donovan.

President Johnson was ordering air strikes on North Vietnam. Teenagers did not want to be enlisted and Pete Seeger saw that this would be a year of mounting protest. As an organiser of the festival, he wanted to reflect this in some way.

Elijah Wald: 'A lot of people coming to Newport were very upset about the world in general. The weekend that Dylan went electric is the weekend that Lyndon Johnson doubled the military draft and firmly committed the US to the war in Vietnam. Many festivalgoers hoped that Dylan and the other artists would do what they did in 1963. Everybody would join arms and the crowd would sing 'Blowin' in the Wind' and 'We Shall Overcome' and it would make them feel that they were not alone and were part of something that was going to change the world. Instead Dylan was blasting out electric music and shouting, "How does it feel to be on your own?" (Laughs). Pete Seeger was extremely angry and as he had made chopping a log part of his stage presentation, it was easy for people to believe that he wanted to break the leads with his axe.'

One thing was certain: Dylan didn't want to lead anything. He did not want to be seen as the new Pete Seeger or the male Joan Baez. He only wanted to answer to himself.

It wasn't just an acoustic festival and the definition of folk was wide. Why else would the Paul Butterfield Blues Band and the Chambers Brothers have been invited? When the Paul Butterfield Blues Band had been signed to Elektra earlier in the year, Paul Rothchild told him that Elvin Bishop was not a strong enough guitarist to hold the band together and Joe Boyd had recommended Mike Bloomfield. Now Paul Rothchild had recommended the band to Albert Grossman with a view to representing them. Dylan told a journalist, and presumably Grossman, that his three favourite groups were Butterfield's, the Byrds and the Sir Douglas Quintet.

The lead track from Butterfield's first album, 'Born in Chicago', was about gun crime and the easy access to weapons. Butterfield wasn't advocating change as he was a tough cookie who carried a gun himself.

Geoff Muldaur, who later played with the Butterfield Blues Band, says, 'Butterfield is better than people think. I was in a hotel room in Cleveland with Cannonball Adderley and when Paul left for some cigarettes, Cannonball said, "Do you know who the hell you are playing with, do you know how good he is?" He was a big fan. If Paul came up to the mic and hit three notes, everything got better right away. He knew how to put a hook it in there. He was brilliant and he taught me a lot.'

Because of the varied nature of the performers, the festival organisers wanted more experienced technicians working on the sound and they had hired Paul Rothchild and Joe Boyd.

The festival was growing annually with 70,000 attending the 1965 event, a definite success, and a film was being made, which was released in 1967 as *Festival*, directed by Murray Lerner. Elijah Wald: 'Newport had been getting bigger. There were people who had regarded it as their own little world and as it got bigger, the tensions became dramatic. The people who were most disappointed with the diversity were not the hard-core folkies.

It was the people who liked Peter, Paul and Mary and Donovan and who wanted beautiful, intelligent, poetic stuff. They didn't want rowdy, noisy music. On the other hand, people who liked John Lee Hooker and Muddy Waters wanted just that.' In short, nobody was going to please everybody.

A young Eric Bibb saw Bob Dylan: 'I saw Dylan at the top of the stairs in a big grey top hat – that was his freaky period! I saw Son House, the Chambers Brothers and the Paul Butterfield Blues Band and then I had to go back to the city as I was only 14, and I missed the booing for Bob Dylan. They were very purist at the time. My father would have supported him. He would say, "Hey, where the spirit moves you, you've got to go." He was like that himself.'

Alan Lomax wrote in the festival programme, 'Money and prestige count for nothing compared to honesty.' Lomax was presenting a history of the blues and ending with the Paul Butterfield Blues Band. He hadn't heard them before but Peter Yarrow had recommended them. They were electric. Lomax gave them a lukewarm introduction causing Albert Grossman to confront him when he stepped off stage. They pushed each other around and ended up fighting. We can see this as symbolic – progress versus tradition, commercialism versus idealism – and it was the appetiser for Dylan's performance.

The folksingers who knew Grossman didn't like him, thinking him furtive, underhand and untrustworthy. Some thought he had an underground trade in drugs and this scuffle was a good reason to ban him. However, the organisers caved in as Grossman said he would take his performers with him including Bob Dylan, Odetta and Peter, Paul and Mary. So Bob Dylan at Newport in 1965 might not have happened at all!

Potentially, the climate was a bigger problem as it threatened to ruin the festival. John Lee Hooker, who was playing 'Highway 13' with John Hammond Jr, said 'it rained so hard, I could hardly see the road.'

When Dylan learnt that Al Kooper was at the festival, he thought he would perform an electric set on the Sunday. Dylan spoke to the Butterfield Band and as well as Mike Bloomfield, he recruited their bass player Jerome Arnold and their drummer Sam Lay. In a rerun of Al Kooper's behaviour, the Chicago musician, Barry Goldberg, offered to play piano. Richie Havens watched them rehearse and was impressed.

That Saturday night Pete Seeger introduced the Texas Prisons Worksong Group. They had axes on stage and were hacking away at a tree stump, narrowly missing a cable, as they sang Leadbelly's 'Linin' Track' with Pete. Surely that was far more precarious than anything Dylan did. Seeger played the sound of a baby crying and asked what sort of world he would grow up in: Seeger could have been a preacher.

Richard and Mimi Fariña were performing on Sunday afternoon on the New Folks stage and opened acoustically. The plan was to invite Al Kooper (electric guitar), Fritz Richmond (bass) and Kyle Garahan (harmonica) to join them and they would shake the festival up a little bit with 'Pack up Your Sorrows' and a lively 'Hard Lovin' Loser' with harmonies from Maria Muldaur and Joan Baez. However, their set hardly got going when the sky darkened and there was a downpour. They had to leave the stage. Celebration on a grey day, indeed.

It was not a good weekend for Mimi Fariña as she did not know until she read the programme that they were represented by Albert Grossman, whom she detested. Richard had signed with Grossman without telling her.

So much of what happens in life depends on luck, either good or bad, and nobody can say what would have happened if the Fariñas had completed their set. I doubt that it would have made much difference one way or the other as there were no real expectations with the Fariñas.

The rain could have continued and wiped out the rest of the day but the sun came out. The New Lost City Ramblers with Tom Paley and the vintage country performer, Cousin Emmy, were on before Bob Dylan. Bob Dylan was introduced by Peter Yarrow at 9.15pm. He said, 'The person who is going to come up now has a limited amount of time.' This odd remark related to the show being cut back but surely they would have wanted Dylan to do a full set in any circumstances. The audience jeered before he even played a note. No wonder; the set started shambolically as Dylan and his five musicians took their time in setting up.

The P.A. system was rudimentary with no stage monitors or direct feed. There were microphones in front of each amplifier and the levels had been marked on the mixing desk. They opened with 'Maggie's Farm', a song that Pete Seeger loved as it had a strong socialist message. Dylan wanted it loud and it was, by the standards of the day.

Alan Lomax, Pete Seeger and Theodore Bikel were backstage together. They wanted the speakers turned down, but Peter Yarrow said it was just right. Theodore Bikel said, 'You don't whistle in church and you don't play rock'n'roll at a folk festival.' It is said that Seeger wanted to cut the cables with his axe but this is fanciful. The axes may have been around from the previous night but you could kill yourself and possibly others if you severed live cables.

Sam Lay's drumming was wayward and Jerome Arnold could have been tighter but it was okay. After 'Maggie's Farm' came 'Like a Rolling Stone' and 'It Takes a Lot to Laugh, It Takes a Train to Cry'. Bloomfield was playing some scorching electric guitar, making the performance a partnership with Bob.

Geoff Muldaur: 'When Dylan went electric at Newport, he had already recorded an electric side of an album, so too much is made of it. The electric instruments weren't the problem. It was the bad sound system, and it wasn't managed well. He didn't have the same brilliance as the record.'

Elijah Wald: 'There had never been a rock festival at that point. Nobody had ever had the experience of sitting in a field with 18,000 people and having a full-scale rock band blasted at them. Some loved what they were hearing and some felt the Newport Folk Festival was being overrun by those who had come to see Dylan. Some people were horrified because they were so loud."

By 9.30pm, it was over. The band had only rehearsed three songs. It can't have been too much of a surprise for his audience as they would have known the electric side of *Bringing It All Back Home*. Some wouldn't have liked Dylan flaunting it. He wasn't respecting the tradition. Some were booing because they wanted more. As Al Kooper said, 'If James Brown had been headlining at the Apollo and played only three songs, they'd fucking boo.'

Peter Yarrow said, 'Do you want some more?' Dylan was shaken as you see him wipe a tear from his left eye. He returned on stage with his acoustic guitar, which could have been Johnny Cash's Gibson. The strap was certainly too big for him. Dylan said, 'Anyone got an E harp' and about six harmonicas were thrown onto the stage. He did 'Mr. Tambourine Man' and 'It's All Over Now, Baby Blue' and left to mixed applause. The sense of betrayal was very acute for some listeners but Dylan knew he was on to something.

What happened next was quite moving. Mel Lyman from the Jim Kweskin band who had lectured Bob about his responsibility to folk music, sat on the edge of the stage in the dark and soothed the emotions by playing 'Rock of Ages' on harmonica. He was about to leave the band for a new job – marijuana curator on Albert Grossman's estate. Later he would start an avatar cult in Boston.

A succession of acts followed: the Moving Star Singers (who sang 'Been in the Storm too Long'), Oscar Brand, Josh White, Ronnie Gilbert from the Weavers and finally Peter, Paul and Mary. The festival ended with Pete Seeger leading everyone in 'Down by the Riverside'.

After the festival, Pete Seeger resigned from the board of the Newport festival, stopped writing for *Sing Out!* and stopped being a director of the Woody Guthrie Trust. He blamed Albert Grossman for encouraging Bob Dylan to go commercial – ignoring the fact that some years earlier he had annoyed the *status quo* with the hit-making Weavers. Pete sought solace with some dates in Russia.

And what of the aftermath? Donovan told *Melody Maker:* 'The audiences were beautiful. They mobbed Dylan and me – or maybe I should say they mobbed Dylan and I was with him.' Yes, you should.

George Harrison: 'There were these people who'd never heard of folk music until Bob Dylan came around and two years later they are walking out on him, which is so stupid.'

When an unconvinced Robert Shelton discussed the performance, Dylan said, 'Whoever was in charge of the sound at Newport didn't know what was happening.' This suggested that the sound could have been better and he has also said, 'I thought we did rather well for the equipment we had to use.'

Bob Dylan had had a highly productive session with Tom Wilson in June and 'Like a Rolling Stone' was on its way to becoming his biggest-selling single in the US, only being kept off the top by 'Help!' However, 'Like a Rolling Stone' would be the last record that Tom Wilson would make with Dylan. Wilson was just another person who could not tolerate Albert Grossman and Grossman wanted him out.

Wilson did okay. He took an acoustic album track by Simon and Garfunkel, 'The Sound of Silence' and added instruments so that it became highly commercial, topping the US charts in January 1966 – something Bob Dylan never did. Wilson moved to MGM, discovering the Mothers of Invention and causing Frank Zappa to comment, 'Tom Wilson was a great guy who really stood by us.'

After 'Like a Rolling Stone', Frank Zappa wanted to make records that would change the face of music and perhaps society too. To him, making a surreal six-minute single hit was a major musical breakthrough. Music could breakthrough in both what was said and how it was expressed. Zappa was abstemious about drugs, although you wouldn't think so from listening to the records. Then there was the Velvet Underground's first album, which Wilson co-produced.

The next producer for Bob Dylan was Bob Johnston, who was born in Hillsboro Texas on 14 May 1932 and raised in Fort Worth. His great-grandfather invented the railway coupling and his grandmother wrote 'When Irish Eyes Are Smiling'. His mother wrote 'Miles and Miles of Texas' (Asleep at the Wheel). His wife Joy Byers wrote songs for Elvis Presley including 'It Hurts Me'. After an uncomfortable career as a performer and working in the Brill Building, Johnston became a staff producer for Columbia. His first success was a Number 1 country single for Marty Robbins, 'Ribbon of Darkness', written by Gordon Lightfoot. He resurrected Patti Page's career in Nashville and produced her film theme, *Hush, Hush, Sweet Charlotte* (1965).

Bob Johnston supported his artists: 'I never had a cross word with Dylan. There was never any of that with any artists I ever had. They knew I hated the fucking company and I hated the goddamn people at the top.' Johnston said he only got paid $3,000 for *Sounds of Silence* and *Highway 61 Revisited* combined even though they were million-selling albums.

Starting on July 29 and ending on August 4, Bob Johnston produced four sessions with Dylan, which with 'Like a Rolling Stone' would make up the album, *Highway 61 Revisited*. There were two other songs that would be singles; 'Positively 4th Street' and 'Can You Please Crawl out Your Window', though Bob was to re-record the latter before release.

The musicians were the same as for 'Like a Rolling Stone' but with the addition of Sam Lay (drums), Frank Owens (piano) and Charlie McCoy (in this instance, guitar and vibes). Russ Savakus was a good bass player but couldn't take Dylan's sarcasm and left. Al Kooper suggested a friend from his bar band, Harvey Brooks. This was his first real studio job. He was influenced by Motown and would later be on Miles Davis' *Bitches Brew*. Brooks was to record 'Just Like Tom Thumb's Blues' with Dylan and then the cover version from Gordon Lightfoot.

The first session started with the lengthy 'Tombstone Blues' which Bob had been thinking of recording with the Chambers Brothers. He wrote the song because he had played in a bar where off-duty cops said things like, 'I don't know who killed him but I'm sure glad he's gone.'

The song is about confrontation but how do the images hang together? Is the title a western reference as there had been gunfights in Tombstone? Could there be a reference to Vietnam with the King of the Philistines (President Johnson) sending soldiers to the jungle? Possibly but it hardly qualifies as a protest song, just a cock-eyed look at the American dream. Were the lyrics nonsense? Possibly. Certainly Dylan attached no specific importance to them as the locations for Mama, Daddy and himself vary from take to take.

The song is a Chicago blues with several great lines including 'The sun's not yellow, it's chicken'. That could be a reference to Sun Records, but who knows with Dylan? He sensed that the song was special: 'I felt like I'd broken through with this song and that nothing like it had been done before' It was helped as always by some energetic guitar playing from Mike Bloomfield.

Next up was another go at 'It Takes a Lot to Laugh, It Takes a Train to Cry'. He had nailed the lyrics and dropped the original title, 'Phantom Engineer'. Allen Ginsberg said, 'His interest was in improvised verses which he would sometimes blurt into a microphone without knowing what the next word was going to be. That song was a composite of what was going on in his mind.' Dylan also recorded a fast take: Al Kooper liked this version and used it as a basis for his *Super Session* album in 1968.

The third song could have been inspired by Newport. 'Positively 4th Street' was even more vitriolic than 'Like a Rolling Stone'. Joni Mitchell said that once she heard 'Positively 4th Street', she realised that you could write about anything. After 'Ballad in Plain D', 'Ballad of a Thin Man', 'Like a Rolling Stone' and now this one, Bob Dylan was becoming an expert in unpleasant material. There was a vengeful streak in Bob Dylan's character. David Blue said, 'Dylan was very hostile, a mean cat, very cruel to people' but then he could be a recipient. When people impersonate Bob Dylan, they often pick this track as his words are so forcefully underlined.

In 12 critical verses with no repeated lines or title, Dylan is putting down someone or some people who have annoyed him. Muddy Waters had recorded some vicious blues, so that could have been an inspiration. Oddly enough, you can write a put-down with affection, the best example being Carly Simon's' You're so Vain' (1972).

Dave Von Ronk: 'It was a contest to be Bobby's target. I should have sold raffle tickets.' Who'd want to be a winner?

Izzy Young said, 'Dylan comes in and takes from us, uses my resources and then he leaves and gets bitter.' In that sense, 'Positively 4th Street' would be like a curse on you.

David Hajdu: 'Dylan has never explained 'Positively 4th Street'. He doesn't see it as his responsibility to explain his songs. The title leads us most obviously to Washington Square but there was a West Fourth Street in Dinkytown in Minnesota. That song is Dylan's valedictory to the folk scene. Whether it was intended to one individual or to the whole group at large is irrelevant. It was the site of many key events in his life and of so many key events in post-war popular music. Gerde's Folk City was on West 4th Street which is where he made his debut. It was on West 4th Street that Bob and Joan met in the company of Mimi.'

Michael Gray: 'Some of the titles have more of a relationship to the song than others. 'Rainy Day Numbers 12 & 35' is a classic example of a completely meaningless title. 4th Street was an area of Greenwich Village when he had lived with Avril the dancer and his photo was taken in a booth for his union card on 4th Street. The folkies who were against him hated the fact that he had been successful and gone onto something else. It is a venomous song and if you were positively 4th Street, you were one of his targets. Dylan has always taken it very slowly and doesn't beef it up for live audience. He does it with a delicacy and intensity that is unrivalled.'

The second session started with 'From a Buick 6' and curiously the US mono and stereo versions of *Highway 61 Revisited* featured different takes. It is Bob having fun with a Bo Diddley riff with images that could have come from 'Who Do You Love' and there is a passing reference to Bo Diddley. It's odd that Bob never did this song with The Band.

On August 2 Dylan had one mad burst to complete the album and one glorious performance followed another. Maybe he had already decided that the album would be called *Highway 61 Revisited* as his song was so powerful. Highway 61 ran from the Gulf of Mexico to the Canadian border and Dylan knew the section from Duluth to St. Paul very well. Is it coincidence that the biblical Abraham and Bob's father shared the same name? Abe is about to kill Bob on the road out of Hibbing so it has to be a joke.

Al Kooper had a police whistle on a cord around his neck. He occasionally blew it as a joke when friends were taking drugs. He passed it to Dylan, who put it on his harmonica holder. The take used on the album includes the siren. It sounds tacky but it was all part of the fun.

Oddly, Dylan was doing more rock than folk-rock. 'Highway 61 Revisited' sounds more like the Rolling Stones than the Byrds, although there are too many words and uneven lines for rock music. Despite the title, it is not road music. On the other hand, the Beatles were going in the Byrds' direction as the next thing they did was *Rubber Soul*, which has several folk-rock moments.

Howard Sounes: 'Al Kooper said that Bob came up with titles off the top of his head. Al said that stream of consciousness and silliness had a lot to do with it. Dylan is so clever and so creative that he has the ability to have a song full of fascinating stuff and then think of a title which isn't even in the song. It is like an extra bit, a bonus, and then the album title is clever again. Even *Blood on the Tracks* is a great line. It perfectly sums up the album and what he is trying to do and yet that line is not in that album. Leonard Cohen said all the other songwriters are many floors below Hank Williams in the tower of song, but in my opinion, Dylan is at the top of that penthouse.'

Far more serious is 'Just like Tom Thumb's Blues', one of six tracks on the album not to have its title in the song itself. Originally called 'Sittin' on a Barbed-Wire Fence', the song has no title line, no chorus and is six lengthy verses. It is about someone in Jaurez, Mexico trying to free himself from drug addiction and the lyric is often, but not always, in the first person. Over the years Dylan has offered clues in stage introductions. In Vancouver he said, 'This song is about a painter. Not too many songs are about painters. This one lived in Mexico City. He lived with the Indians in the jungle.'

In Melbourne he was more expansive. 'This is about a painter in Mexico City who travels from North Mexico up to Del Rio, Texas all the time. His name is Tom Thumb and right now he's about 125 years old but he's still going. Everybody likes him a lot down there, he's got a lot of friends and this is when he was going through his blue period.'

Neil Young: 'I love that song. I like the melody and I like images of sweet Melinda and Housing Project Hill. It's like a movie.' Arthur Rimbaud's poem, 'My Bohème', refers to Tom Thumb, which is unlikely to be coincidental.

In 1964 Joan Baez recorded 'The Death of Queen Jane', a folk song about the death of Henry VIII's wife, Jane Seymour. Possibly 'Queen Jane Approximately' is about Joan Baez but Dylan is so cryptic that we have no way of knowing. Clinton Heylin puts his money on Andy Warhol, particularly because of the line, 'When you're tired of yourself and all of your creations'.

None of these tracks though compare to the speculation over 'Ballad of a Thin Man', which appears to be about an incompetent journalist – does 'thin' in this context mean 'shallow'? And Bob Dylan physically is a thin man.

We know from *Dont Look Back*, there is no end of candidates. When he finished the song, the drummer Bobby Gregg said, 'That's a nasty song, Bob', which Dylan took as a compliment.

In 1978, Dylan said in concert, 'I wrote this for a reporter who was working for the *Village Voice* in 1963.' Another possibility is Max Jones of *Melody Maker*, but is using his surname too obvious? Dylan has said on stage: 'Mr. Jones lives in Lincoln, Nebraska. He hangs around bowling alleys there. He owns watermill rights. But we don't talk about that when we're in Nebraska. We just let Mr. Jones have his little way.' Make what you will of that.

Chris Charlesworth from *Melody Maker*: 'I never got to interview Dylan but I met him once when he was drunk backstage at a Rolling Stones concert at Madison Square Garden. He was swigging wine through a big flagon. I asked someone to introduce me and he said to me, "How's Max Jones?" He was *Melody Maker*'s jazz critic and he had been sympathetic to Dylan way back to him in 1962. Dylan remembered those who treated him well.'

There's Jeffrey Jones, the student reporter for *Time*. Jeffrey Jones was writing about harmonicas and spoke to Dylan and other artists at Newport. Dylan teased him and he is certain he is the subject of the song.

There are literary antecedents too. Mr. Jones is the farmer in George Orwell's *Animal Farm*. There is a Mr. Jones who hates women in Joseph Conrad's *Victory* and he is played by Cedric Hardwicke in the 1940 film. This is a possibility because 'Black Diamond Bay', which we will come to, has a Conrad connection.

There may be a gay connection: could the sword swallower be about a heterosexual at a gay party? Maybe it was just an attack on upright squares, which is the way it was used in the film, *I'm Not There*. The song appealed to Procol Harum who were minded to write their own 'A Christmas Camel'.

The most surprising musician at the New York sessions was Charlie McCoy, who was visiting from Nashville. Charlie McCoy was the same age as Dylan and building a reputation. He played harmonica on Ann-Margret's 'I Just Don't Understand' and Roy Orbison's 'Candy Man', a 1961 hit written by Fred Neil. Dylan knew 'Harpoon Man' and 'I'm Ready', a Monument single by Charlie McCoy and the Escorts from January 1965. Charlie had gone to New York for the World's Fair and Bob Johnston had given him Broadway tickets. He invited him to the sessions and there is a version of 'Desolation Row' on which he played acoustic guitar.

Just as 'A Day in the Life' was the perfect way to finish *Sgt. Pepper's Lonely Hearts Club Band*, so 'Desolation Row' seemed to sum up *Highway 61 Revisited*. There are carnivals in 'Desolation Row', 'Like a Rolling Stone', 'Queen Jane Approximately' and 'Ballad of a Thin Man', so it is a familiar image. 'Desolation Row' had ten long verses, each of which ended with the title phrase but with a different connotation every time.

Dylan had put down a semi-electric version of 'Desolation Row' on August 2 and was intending to be at a mixing session for the LP two days later. However, he thought 'Desolation Row' might sound better acoustically and he cut a new version, which then became the final track of the album. The guitars are played by Bob Dylan and Bruce Langhorne on the issued take.

On the first take, Dylan sings, 'They are spoon-feeding Casanova the boiled guts of birds.'

Dylan is looking down on 'Desolation Row', mocking everything and describing a bizarre cast of characters. T.S. Eliot and Ezra Pound are fighting, calypso singers are laughing, and Dr. Filth keeps his world in a leather cup, whatever that means.

The young Tom Waits was so amazed by the richness of its images that he would paste parts of 'Desolation Row' on his bedroom wall. He has acknowledged that it got him started.

The song opens with the brilliant but mysterious line, "They're selling postcards of the hanging", which as we have seen may relate to an incident in Duluth before he was born. Bob Spitz: 'I think Bob Dylan often wrote to shock people. Just take that scene, "They're selling postcards of the hanging." It was Dylan's way of saying that we are getting very crass in our culture and we will make a buck on anything.'

Tim Rice: 'I think "Desolation Row" is about the end of the world. He's very careful about what he writes and I think it is deliberate that there are many interpretations. Take that famous line in 'Love Minus Zero', "She knows there's no success like failure, And failure's no success at all." I'm not sure what it means but when you hear it, you think "Hey, that is brilliant!" I don't think he can be bothered to explain what the songs are about. He may not even know himself.'

The poet Philip Larkin revelled in jazz but he was intrigued by Dylan. 'I poached Bob Dylan's *Highway 61 Revisited* out of curiosity and found myself well rewarded. Dylan's cawing, derisive voice is probably well suited to his material – I say, probably, because much of it was unintelligible to me – and his guitar adapts itself to rock ('Highway 61 Revisited') and ballad ('Queen Jane Approximately') admirably. There is a marathon 'Desolation Row' which has an enchanting tune and mysterious, possibly half-baked words.'

Bruce Robinson, film director: 'I heard a radio programme where some poets were calling 'Desolation Row' facetious nonsense. I remember thinking, "You complete fucking idiots!" If only somebody had given Rimbaud a harmonica. There's a Dylan line that describes the essence of every despair one's ever been through. "I awoke in anger so alone and terrified, I put my fingers against the glass and bowed my head and cried." Just that one line puts him in the genius department for me.'

The penultimate verse is about the Titanic but surely if you are aboard that ship, it doesn't matter which side you were on. Although there is a section on cultural references in the Titanic Museum in Belfast, this song is a careless omission.

In 1999 the J. Paul Getty Museum published a book *The Superhuman Crew* which combined James Ensor's *Christ's Entry into Brussels in 1889*, with the lyrics of 'Desolation Row'. This is an official publication with Sony so Dylan must have approved it. This book was said to bring together two visionary works of art: "Two visions of modern life as a swirling, grotesque carnival. The circus is in town." Dylan 'sardonically set forth his depiction of a depleted but strangely vital place'.

Tom Russell: 'My favourite Dylan record is *Highway 61 Revisited*. I remember seeing him at the Hollywood Bowl and hearing 'Desolation Row' for the first time. I thought, "That's it! This is the high point of music; it goes upwards from here." 'Desolation Row' is a landscape, like a Sam Peckinpah movie.'

Al Stewart: 'I loved everything on *The Times They Are A-Changin'* and almost everything on *Another Side of Bob Dylan*. Needless to say, everything on *Bringing It All Back Home*. There was a time when Dylan was making all the right moves. I learnt 'Desolation Row'. It came out on a Friday and I had an advance copy the day before. I actually played it in two separate clubs in London on the day it was released. (Laughs) All 11 minutes of it and I learnt it all too. (Sings) I still know it now.'

Joni Mitchell: 'Dylan will write a song and it will have abstract passages and then it will have a direct phrase – like Bam! – direct communication, and then he'll go back to something more surrealistic.'

Billy Joel: 'I remember everybody sitting around smoking pot trying to figure out what the hell Dylan was talking about. I always had a deep-seated suspicion that a lot of what Dylan was talking about wasn't anything – it just sounded good. He was using words like a musician would use notes to create a certain mood. A guitarist would use a fuzz-box to get a distortion and Dylan found his fuzz-box in the English language. I think a lot of it is nonsense, creatively well done but nonsense.'

In August 1965 Dylan wanted a band for two up-coming shows – one at Forest Hills and one at the Hollywood Bowl – with possibly a tour after that. Mike Bloomfield declined as he wanted to stick with Paul Butterfield. He was to comment, 'Bob's a cool guy but he doesn't know much about playing with other musicians.'

Bob wondered about some of the musicians who worked with Johnny Rivers in LA: Joe Osborn and Mickey Jones, but nothing came of that. He fancied using James Burton, but he was too involved in the session scene. Mary Martin who worked for Albert Grossman told him of Levon and the Hawks They had been playing at Tony Mart's on the Jersey shore and Friar's Tavern in Toronto.

Levon and the Hawks had been working with the blues musician Sonny Boy Williamson who told them that they were much better than the bands he had heard in England: 'They want to play the blues so bad and they play it so bad.'

The band had a summer season at Tony's Mart in Somers Point, New Jersey but Dylan was impressed and wanted them as his touring band.

'You wanna play the Hollywood Bowl?' asked Dylan.

'Who else is gonna be on?' said Levon.

'Just us,' said Dylan.

The notion that Bob Dylan could fill the Hollywood Bowl seemed incredible to Levon Helm. They didn't want to lose their regular work so it was agreed that just Levon and Robbie Robertson should do the dates with Bob and the others could hold down the residency. Dylan added Harvey Brooks and Al Kooper. Levon Helm had thought of Dylan as a strummer but then heard the blues in his music.

On 13/14 Aug 1965 Dylan met the Beatles at the Riviera Hotel near Kennedy International Airport. Now if they'd agreed to back him…

Sonny and Cher had been imitating Dylan's style and now the Turtles were making the US charts with a rocked-up 'It Ain't Me Babe', clearly inspired by the Byrds. Howard Kaylan admits, 'Totally. We were thieves in the night. If the Byrds could record a Dylan song with a 12-string guitar, we could go into the studio a week later with our own Rickenbacker knock-off. Bob Dylan had already written scores of great songs and we easily found one to suit us.'

And what about the name, the Turtles? Howard Kaylan: 'My favourite artist was Colin Blunstone. I was totally into the way he sang but I loved the production on the Zombies' records. We wanted to be the Beatles and we wanted an animal name with a '–tles' ending.'

'It Ain't Me Babe' had changes in tempo so you couldn't dance to it. Howard Kaylan: 'It was never meant to be a dance record. It was a very angry interpretation of a Bob Dylan song. It is a plaintive, pleading song but I didn't understand that as a 17-year-old kid. To me it was like he was yelling, "It ain't me, babe, get away from me, I don't need you anymore."'

Arlo Guthrie was gathering the experiences that would come together in his 18-minute 'Alice's Restaurant': 'I got out of high school in 1965. I was 18 years old and I came to England and was touring around. Then I went to college in Billings, Montana which is out in the west. Left there, went to visit some friends who were living in Massachusetts, dumped some garbage in the wrong place and kept singing about it. Not only was the song real and the incidents true but the people who were in it decided that they didn't mind being in the movie about themselves even though the film was fictionalised. Officer Obie was a real guy and he played himself, the blind judge was real too, and the people at the draft board were real too. They all had a good sense of humour about it.'

Arlo was fortunate to avoid the draft: 'I'm not sure what it was that got me out of the draft, they never told me. They gave me a medical discharge and I don't know whether that is a political medical discharge or some other kind of medical discharge.'

In late-August Dylan was in a rehearsal hall with Robbie Robertson and Levon Helm, plus Al Kooper and Harvey Brooks. After rehearsals. Kooper would go the Village with Dylan and Bobby Neuwirth, who would be the road manager. They liked the Kettle of Fish on MacDougal Street and eating at the Limelight. Kooper saw Dylan and Neuwirth being cruel to other performers by taking their work apart.

The rehearsals had gone well but on 28 August 1965, the day of their gig at the tennis stadium, Forest Hills in front of an audience of 15,000, Robbie Robertson woke up with stage fright. He got over it but the feeling stayed with him and was channelled into one of his best songs, 'Stage Fright'.

The weirdest part of the show was in getting the rock and roll DJ, Murray the K, to officiate. He told the audience, 'It's not rock, it's not folk, it's a new thing called Dylan. It's a new kind of expression, a new kind of telling it like it is, and Mr. Dylan is definitely what's happening, baby.'

As Murray the K was rabbiting away, baby, Albert Grossman groaned, 'Who let Murray the K up there?' There was booing for Murray the K but he was the antithesis of what the crowd liked: someone who was phony, arrogant and ridiculous.

Dylan did 45 minutes solo and then 45 minutes with the band, which set the template for the next year's shows. The solo set went fine and included the first public performance of 'Desolation Row', which received a tremendous reception. Dylan enjoyed playing songs that audiences had not heard before and he must have been very gratified about this.

Dylan knew that there could be a repetition of Newport for the second set and he told the musicians, 'Just go out and keep playing no matter how weird it gets.'

The authorities had said that the audience could not be near the stage as they might damage the grass but they just ran onto the courts and some reached the stage. Dylan hadn't anticipated that.

Elijah Wald: 'Dylan had been startled at Newport but by the next concert which was in Queens a month later, the booing was much louder and he seemed to be totally enjoying it. The booing was absolutely vital to the way that we understand Dylan. The fact that that they were booing and that he kept on doing it challenges all the charges of him selling out. When he went electric, all sorts of people said that he was selling out to the pop scene. The fact that he was sticking to his guns proved that he wasn't selling out and that it was a serious artistic decision.'

Film director Todd Haynes: 'Dylan met with such antagonism when he went electric and he just fucking went for it. He used that energy to fuel himself further, crank up the music louder and basically invite violent dissent. That is punk rock in 1966, before anybody did that. Dylan is so canonised, so worshipped, so approved nowadays that you forget his genuine weirdness.'

Bob Dylan played the opening notes of 'Ballad of a Thin Man' over and over trying to get them to be quiet and then he gave up. There were plenty of boos, but Dylan's only comment to the audience was 'Aw, come on now.' The sound was excellent, so the crowd was hearing Dylan as he intended. There was an after-show party at Albert Grossman's flat in Gramercy Park and it was clear that Dylan had loved the show.

Dylan told Levon Helm that he wanted them to do 15 gigs with him abroad. Levon in his sardonic way said, 'I thought you would have learned your lesson by now.'

On 30 August 1965 there was a speedy release for *Highway 61 Revisited*. The cover photograph from Daniel Kramer showed the contemporary Dylan with Bobby Neuwirth, although we only saw Neuwirth's lower half. Dylan's hair is fluffed up and he is wearing a Triumph motorcycle T-shirt. It was a brilliant album which spoke to its generation. Dylan had got away from the folk and pop clichés of the day and added surrealism with nods to Arthur Rimbaud, William Burroughs and Jack Kerouac.

With songs like 'Like a Rolling Stone' and 'Ballad of a Thin Man', this was as defiant as punk rock. Phil Ochs called *Highway 61 Revisited* 'the most important and revolutionary album ever made'. Why wasn't the title track a single – it has astonishing power and great drumming, but admittedly they should have lost the whistle. It could have been a Number 1 single but no matter, this was his best-selling album to date, by far.

The UK acts wanted to record Dylan songs. Joey Molland of the Liverpool band, the Masterminds: 'Andrew Loog Oldham came to the Blue Angel one night and saw us. He invited us to London and that was when the Masterminds started recording. I didn't hear a lot of bands doing Bob Dylan songs and we picked 'She Belongs to Me' which was pretty routine for Bob Dylan but it was a nice thing with easy guitar parts.'

Chris Farlowe: 'Mick Jagger picked out 'It's All Over Now, Baby Blue' for me and said to put it on the album. It wasn't my own choice and if it had been, I would have been singing blues songs, but that wasn't commercial.' The Rolling Stones' 'Sympathy for the Devil' (1968) was strongly influenced by Bob Dylan.

On 1 September 1965 Dylan visited Sonny and Cher recording at Atlantic. He even thought of writing them a single.

Sonny Bono's 'Laugh at Me' (1965) is like a child's take of Dylan but it does hold a mystery worthy of Dylan. When Bono sings, 'I'll do everything the man upstairs says to do' is Bono talking about God or the man in the upstairs apartment? It was a US Top 10 hit and despite its ridiculousness, I would favour this Bono over the other one any day.

Ian Hunter: 'I didn't think 'Laugh at Me' was a joke record. I liked Sonny Bono: he couldn't really sing but they were having monster hits. I was using him as much as I was using Dylan to come up with some kind of unique sound as I didn't think I could sing either."

Al Kooper: 'I only had a rudimentary knowledge of the keyboard at that stage. We used to go to Bob's house and listen to records by people like P.F. Sloan and laugh ourselves silly. They had top session guys like Larry Knechtel trying to imitate what I had done on 'Like a Rolling Stone'. The irony of that was not wasted on me.'

In September 1965 Manfred Mann had a hit single with 'If You Gotta Go, Go Now', which reached Number 2. Tom McGuinness: 'Manfred and I were watching the BBC concert of Bob Dylan in England where he was just acoustic and playing 'If You Gotta Go, Go Now' which he hadn't released. We were at my mother-in-law's and we both said, 'We've got to do that'. Our manager Ken Pitt had been Dylan's publicist in the UK. Dylan was to praise our cover versions and we were knocked out that he had even heard them.'

Jon Savage: 'It was still seen as a teenage market and all these people were rising to the top of their game vying with each other and influencing each other. A very good example is 'Reach out I'll be there' by the Four Tops, which was one of those unstoppable records that changes everything and sweeps everything before it. Lamont Dozier said that they were influenced by the phrasing of Bob Dylan. It's the dragging of the phrase "If you feel that you can't go oooooonn".'

In September 1965 another group with Village connections, the Lovin' Spoonful broke through, although Zal Yanovsky was Canadian. Happy Traum: 'John Sebastian was a folk guy and he grew up a few blocks from Washington Square. He loved that old jug band music. Even the name the Lovin' Spoonful comes from a Mississippi John Hurt song, (sings) "I love my baby by the lovin' spoonful". I have a tape of John playing harmonica behind him. John's a little younger than I am, and by the time he started, the very traditional folk music had started to morph into something else because of the Beatles and the Stones. John took that music into the electric realm. I heard them play in a little club on 3rd Street called the Night Owl café. John is a very creative songwriter so many of his songs left the folk realm but quite a proportion of the Lovin' Spoonful records are influenced by jug band music. There is even a song called 'Jug Band Music'.'

Bob Dylan: Outlaw Blues

On September 3 Bob Dylan had a concert at the Hollywood Bowl. Al Kooper wanted to fly commercially to Hollywood and not take Albert Grossman's private plane. It would be his first ever flight and he had visions of Buddy Holly's final flight. When he did fly with them, the two Bobbys (Dylan and Neuwirth) kept pretending that the plane was going to crash to shake him up.

Dylan held a press conference at a hotel in Beverly Hills. Dylan arrived with David Crosby from the Byrds and announced that *Tarantula* will be 'a book with words'. You can't argue with that. The show at the Hollywood Bowl went down really well because the west coast audience was much more liberal. For one song, Bob wanted a C harmonica as his wasn't working and several were thrown on stage.

Gregory Peck, Johnny Cash and Dean Martin were in the audience and Dylan met Marlon Brando privately. Brian Wilson went to the Hollywood Bowl concert to keep up with Dylan. This was the hippest place to play as he was not performing for folk purists and the audience would be too cool to boo. They were enthusiastic.

Tom Russell: 'I saw him at the Hollywood Bowl singing 'Desolation Row'. He had come a long way in a short time. I was being returned to my seat as I had moved closer to the stage and they were putting me back. He was starting that song and it drilled its way through my head. It is the high point of modern lyricism; it's never gotten better than that.'

At the end of the show, Kooper's ulcer was playing up and he wanted his pills. He thought he would escape from the Bowl with Bob: 'Boy, that little fucker could run!' They ran to a car driven by Victor Maymudes, who almost drove them into a wall.

Al Kooper left Dylan as he wanted to join the Blues Project, who were being produced by Tom Wilson. Harvey Brooks was told after the show that they would be using the Hawks, which was hard on Harvey as he had done nothing wrong.

Everybody wanted a Dylan sound on their records and Al Kooper was soon in demand. John Court who was Grossman's partner asked him to do a session for the Simon Sisters and many of the Count Basie band were there. Al formed a studio band for Tom Rush and the album, *Take a Little Walk with Me*, worked out really well. He played on Judy Collins' 'I'll Keep It With Mine' with Mike Bloomfield as well as Dion's blues singles and an electric 'I Ain't Marchin'' no more' for Phil Ochs. On the sleeve note for the multi-artist album, *What's Shakin'*, the critic Nat Hentoff wrote, 'Al Kooper may be a New York legend, but based on his track record, certainly not for his singing or piano playing.'

On 15 September 1965 Dylan flew to Toronto to rehearse with the Hawks, who now had a residency at Friar's Tavern. Among the songs they played around with were Fats Domino's 'Please Don't Leave Me' and the Delmore Brothers' 'Blues Stay Away from Me'. Dylan would jam with them after the show for two nights, sometimes playing until 6am. When he was interviewed by Robert Fulford of the *Toronto Star*, he said that imitators like Barry McGuire are 'not very honest'.

Bob Dylan had done three electric shows and Albert Grossman now booked a tour. He had played at Newport and had a mixed reception, which might have been down to the quality of the sound. The sound was fine for Forest Hills but there were still detractors. There were no problems at Hollywood Bowl, but it was a more sophisticated audience. How could anyone predict what would happen next?

Although Dylan supported the *Sing-In for Peace in Vietnam* at Carnegie Hall, he decided not to appear. There was a full house for Joan Baez, Pete Seeger and the Fariñas. If

Dylan had gone electric, it might have detracted from the message of the event. If he had played acoustically, it might have been a backwards step. Better not to be around.

For the tour, Dylan was often advertised as 'Bob Dylan with band' and this over time meant that they called themselves The Band. Garth Hudson laughed when I said it was amazing that no one had called a group, The Band, before. 'When we were ready to go and play the second half of the shows with Dylan, someone would say, "Okay, get the band backstage", and that stuck.'

The tour started well in Texas – I know this because Dylan referred to the enthusiasm of audiences in Austin and Dallas three months later. He was playing 'Maggie's Farm' on piano. At the press conference in Austin, he said, 'God is a woman…you take it from there.' This is a few months before John Lennon's controversial 'bigger than Jesus' remarks.

The band was tight by the time they got to Carnegie Hall, and they performed 'Can You Please Crawl out Your Window'. There was some jeering and some insiders were advising Grossman to get rid of the band.

On 5 October 1965 Dylan recorded with The Band for the first time. He wanted to rework 'Can You Please Crawl Our Your Window' with added bile, but he should have been thinking more about the arrangement, which needed to be more creative.

'I Don't Want to Be Your Partner' was redone a fortnight later as 'I Wanna Be Your Lover'. It was a blatant copy of the Beatles and the Rolling Stones with the title being a nod to 'I Wanna Be Your Man'. That would upset the folkies and it was just Dylan having fun.

Dylan was sometimes booked into university gigs which were the most receptive of all. The press reviews were good except for one in Boston at the end of October which said, 'Get rid of the band!'

In October 1965 Jimi Hendrix was playing some records in a black club and when he put on 'Blowin' in the Wind', the club owner said, 'What are you doing? Are you crazy?' Jimi said, 'These people in Harlem have to learn. They can't go around without knowing what's going on.'

Nat Hentoff was commissioned to interview Bob for *Playboy* magazine. *Playboy* wasn't happy with the results, sending Hentoff a revised piece which was heavily edited. Dylan was annoyed and suggested that they worked on an interview full of daft opinions, jokes and wordplay with Hentoff as the straight man. It was brilliant. Dylan said, 'I guess everybody's smoked pot', the first rock star to admit it when it was published in March 1966.

And how about this: 'Folk music is a word I can't use. Folk music is a bunch of fat people. I have to think of all this as traditional music. Traditional music is based on hexagrams. It comes about from legends, Bibles, plagues and it revolves around vegetables and death.'

After a show in November in Buffalo, Dylan joined the Rolling Stones at the Phone Booth club in Manhattan. He took Brian Jones around Greenwich Village and they ended up at a night-time session with Wilson Pickett. Dylan and Jones apparently worked on some lyrics together: results unknown.

There was the east coast blackout on November 9. Bob, Robbie Robertson, Brian Jones and Bobby Neuwirth were jamming in the City Squire Hotel in New York as the power failure hit. The event inspired 'Visions of Johanna', which was originally called 'Seems like a Freeze Out'. In the song, hippies are wandering from one corner of a loft to another, doped up, drunk and half-asleep. There are crazy rhymes and cartoon characters but just what is happening? Because of its lyrical content, the arrangement should be languorous, even lethargic but on an early attempt to record it in New York, he rocked it up. It's great fun but it is much better slow and mournful. The former Poet Laureate, Andrew Motion, has said that Dylan was the best lyricist of all time and this was his best song.

Blues songwriter Chris Smither: 'It is on my list of the best Dylan songs. It is an unbelievable song. I have no idea what Bob Dylan meant by it but I have no problem in building a concept out of what he hands me. I see a guy sitting there thinking about another woman while watching yet another woman involved in another relationship. His sense of word play, his sense of the inherent sound value of words and his phrasing is absolutely gorgeous. What a start, "Ain't it just like the night to play tricks when you are trying to be so quiet".'

It is a wonderful song, providing descriptions of Johanna while he has a different girl is on his mind as he is thinking in the middle of the night. One amazing phrase followed another – 'Name me someone who's not a parasite', 'Jeez, I can't find my knees'.

Where is Johanna, who is she and why isn't she there? Some say Johanna is Gehenna, the Hebrew term for the underworld. Then again Johanna could be another way of referring to Joan Baez.

In mid-November, Dylan did a photo session with Jerry Schatzberg, which led to the iconic gatefold cover for *Blonde on Blonde*. Not that it was very practical as the second record fell out if you held the sleeve up. Eric Clapton loved Dylan's curly frizzy hair and had his own hair permed. It still couldn't be anyone other than Bob Dylan and his name was not even given on the front or back covers.

Jon Savage: 'Bob Dylan had one of the best pop looks ever. Look at the cover of *Blonde on Blonde*: the huge oriole of hair which looked like a bird's nest and went out and out and out, the very chunky Ray-Ban shades, the beautiful shirt with the collar that goes round in a little circle, not a tab, plus the suits and the boots and he just looked fantastic. Garfunkel's hair was too tightly coiled, it wasn't wild enough. Simon and Garfunkel were still wearing preppy wear and they looked too straight." Tim Buckley, it must be said, had wonderful hair and ran Dylan a close second.

The title possibly came about because Suze Rotolo had worked on a theatre show, *Brecht on Brecht*. Also in *The Diaries of Paul Klee*. there is an entry during 1905, 'Everything is a bit blond on blond.'

On 22 November 1965 Bob and Sara were married on Long Island with only Albert Grossman, a lawyer Pete Pryor, Robbie Robertson and a bridesmaid attending. The wedding breakfast was at the Algonquin restaurant. It was a secret marriage and it didn't make the press until Christmas. Bob guarded his privacy and they were rarely seen at public events.

Both Glen Campbell and Donovan were on the US chart with Buffy Sainte-Marie's song, 'Universal Soldier'. Clearly influenced by 'Like a Rolling Stone', the Rolling Stones wrote and recorded 'Get Off of My Cloud'. Most unlikely of all, the Byrds had a US Number 1 with verses from the Bible, 'Turn! Turn! Turn!', put into song by Pete Seeger. Whatever Pete Seeger really thought of folk-rock, he had now written one of its key records.

Pete Seeger: 'That was a little poem that I had kept from the Book of Ecclesiastes and I thought it would make a good song one day. I got a letter from a publisher who said he couldn't publish my protest songs. He wrote, "Give me a song like 'Goodnight Irene' – I can really sell that." I wrote him an angry letter saying I didn't know how to write songs like that and all of a sudden, I pulled out that little poem and improvised a melody, adding a few lines of my own. I sent him the tape and he said, "Wonderful, just what I'm looking for." He went out and sold it, and the Byrds recorded it. I like their recording with all those clanging steel guitars but the song has proved itself as you can do it in half a dozen different ways."

Roger McGuinn: 'Pete Seeger did a wonderful job on that. He got the Book of Ecclesiastes and then made up a melody that was so simple and yet so touching that it moves you. It is truly my favourite song in the world. It made me look in the Bible to see where it came from. Pete had recorded the song in 1959 and then I recorded the song in 1963 with Judy Collins when I was the musical director for her third album. We did it as the Byrds in 1965 and Pete sent us a letter when it got to Number 1. He wrote, "Dear Byrds, I really enjoyed the way you performed 'Turn! Turn! Turn!' with all those chiming guitars. My only musical query is why did you not repeat the chorus?" It would have been too long as the radio back then was very tight on time. We could only get by with a couple of minutes and 'Turn! Turn! Turn!' was already three minutes thirty seconds. That would have been pushing the envelope.'

Dylan was enjoying another hit single with 'Positively Fourth Street' but the *NME* said, 'Compulsive listening for all Dylan fans though it seems to go on a bit.'

Levon Helm was having his own problems. He felt he was no longer the leader of the group and of course Dylan was singing lead vocals. He was fed up with the booing, which some nights was louder than others. After the concert in Washington on 28 November 1965, he left and returned to Arkansas. From there, he went to work on an oil rig in the Gulf of Mexico.

On November 30 with Bobby Gregg on drums, Bob and the Hawks recorded their first attempt at 'Visions of Johanna'. It was a fine cut but Bob would return to it. Bobby Gregg remained with them for some concert dates, but he did not want to be a permanent replacement.

Early in December, Dylan had an evening with Allen Ginsberg, Peter Orlowsky and Lawrence Ferlinghetti in San Francisco. He met Ken Kesey of the Merry Pranksters and so it was a week of counter-culture. The following day (December 3) he played the Community Theatre in Berkeley. There is a film of the press conference, presided by Ralph J. Gleason, with Dylan in good form but only answering what he wanted. He came out with the famous quote, 'I think of myself as a song and dance man.'

On December 5, Dylan played the Masonic Memorial Auditorium, San Francisco with Michael McClure and Allen Ginsberg in the front row. They were trying to guess what Dylan had been reading when they heard the new songs – Arthur Rimbaud and William Blake, they concluded.

In December 1965, the second album by Richard and Mimi Fariña was released, *Reflections in a Crystal Wind*. It contained a variety of sounds including a very Dylany 'Hard Lovin' Loser', which could easily have come from *Blonde on Blonde*. *New York Times* said it was one of the albums of the year.

Dylan was socialising in Greenwich Village, attending a party at Paul and Betty Stookey's and visiting the Clique club with Phil Ochs, David Blue and Robert Shelton.

Bob and Brian Jones had visited Andy Warhol's Factory when he wasn't around. Barbara Rubin then coordinated a proper visit with a film crew and Andy being there. Warhol wanted to shoot a screen test with Dylan. Dylan agreed in return for one of his pictures, which put Warhol on the spot as he rarely gave anything away. Dylan chose a large silver screen of *Double Elvis* – a picture of Elvis' image as a cowboy in *Flaming Star* duplicated. He gave Warhol his screen test and then he and Bobby Neuwirth put it on the roof of a station wagon and drove away. Dylan deliberately hung it upside down. Later, he swapped it with the Grossmans for a sofa. In 1988 Sally Grossman sold it at auction for $720,000.

Andy Warhol moved jerkily, probably a legacy of St. Vitus Dance. He once invited journalists to a new exhibition and when they got there, there was nothing on the walls. He said that the journalists would write about 'no art', and they did.

Bob Dylan was as sceptical about Andy Warhol as many listeners were about him. He wasn't sure about the value of Warhol's work and possibly Warhol was in his mind when he wrote some of his diatribes. Warhol had no doubts: he certainly approved of Dylan as someone who was shaking the establishment.

Warhol's screen test of Bob Dylan is now in the Museum of Modern Art in New York. Dylan is wearing dark glasses and smoking a cigarette and seems uninterested. It is unlikely that he was seriously considering an appearance in one of Warhol's films.

Unlike Edie Sedgwick.

Edie Sedgwick's relations signed the Declaration of Independence and she came from a family of high achievers: lawyers, ranchers and the man who invented the elevator. She was raised on a huge ranch where all eight children had their own horses, but her mother went insane and two of her brothers killed themselves. Edie came to New York from Boston and met Warhol, who had created an insular world of his own in the Factory, so named because hats had been manufactured there. Edie was a beautiful girl and a great model with large eyes. The miserly Warhol wouldn't pay Edie for being in his films as he didn't want to set a precedent.

Edie hoped that Dylan might make a record with her but she had no singing voice. Warhol who was homosexual was only interested in her as a friend. She became Bobby Neuwirth's girlfriend. She was taking diet pills when she was with the Factory and got into hard drugs with the Dylan set. She died from an overdose in 1971.

A film about her life, *Factory Girl*, was released in 2006 with Sienna Miller as Sedgwick and is worth catching on DVD in view of the bonus material. Hayden Christensen (Quinn) is obviously Dylan and there is a recreation of the screen test and the way that they played games with each other. He says to Edie, 'Your heart is as empty as your friend's soup-cans.' Warhol comments, 'It's not what they say about you, it's how they measure it in inches.'

In the winter of 1965, Johnny Cash and Ramblin' Jack Elliott were together on a show in Boston and then Johnny wanted to pick up a Gibson that he had lent to Dylan which had belonged to Gene Autry. Dylan was staying at Grossman's house and he met them at a coffee shop as it was late and he didn't want to wake the Grossmans. Ramblin' Jack was dropped off in Greenwich Village and Johnny Cash went to Virginia.

In January 1966 the poet Leonard Cohen heard a Bob Dylan album for the first time at a party. He listened intently and solemnly to *Highway 61 Revisited* and declared that he would become the Canadian Bob Dylan, and everybody laughed.

On 6 January 1966 Bob and Sara's first son, Jesse Byron, was born in New York, and note the poetic name, while they were living at the Chelsea Hotel.

Dylan and The Band with Bobby Gregg on drums returned to Columbia's studio and cut 'She's Your Lover Now', an excellent song with a sarcastic vocal, but why did they give up on it? It would have been fine on *Blonde on Blonde*.

Al Kooper played on 'Leopard-Skin Pillbox Hat' and 'One of Us Must Know (Sooner or Later)'. The former, a Chuck Berry styled song, was given a string of sound effects but they were dropped. 'We're spending too much time on it. It's just a natural song,' said Dylan. 'One of Us Must Know' could be about Joan Baez or his relationship to the folk world, but I tend to think not as he had already used those subjects: 'I never really meant to do you any harm' might have no bearing at all on his life.

There was not much drive in these sessions, which included Dylan returning to 'I'll Keep It with Mine', the implication being that Dylan had little new material.

Bob Johnston thought that Dylan would benefit from a move to Nashville and Bob agreed if he could bring Robbie Robertson and Al Kooper. Al Kooper said, 'Going to Nashville was Bob Johnston's idea. Dylan wasn't sure about it. He brought me and Robbie Robertson along to have some part of his past there. I was glad I went because the Nashville musicians were fabulous.'

The world tour was starting in February 1966 with some US dates and yet another drummer, this time Sandy Konikoff, an older guy, too influenced by jazz for the Hawks. Dylan gave a few wacky interviews. When asked about Bob Lind's 'Elusive Butterfly', he laughed.

There was a break on Valentine's Day for three days in Nashville. They were hippies in a redneck city. They knew that the rednecks wouldn't go for them – well, they might, that was the trouble. Lamar Fike was hired as a bodyguard as there might be trouble. Bob Dylan and Al Kooper were in a bookshop and narrowly avoided a pack of angry rednecks. Al Kooper: 'Dylan was the quintessential New York hipster. You put these two elements together and it just exploded.'

Bob Johnston had got rid of individual booths for musicians. He had invited a crack team of players: Wayne Moss (guitarist on Tommy Roe's 'Sheila' and Roy Orbison's 'Oh Pretty Woman'), Jerry Kennedy (guitar), Charlie McCoy (guitar), Joe South (an excellent bass player and soon a hit-maker in his own right), Hargus 'Pig' Robbins (piano) and Kenny Buttrey (drums). These were experienced session men but not veterans – Hargus, the oldest was 28.

'Fourth Time Around' was Bob Dylan's take on 'Norwegian Wood', a song about a one-night stand with unlikely details – the wheelchair, the chewing gum. Why had he done such a blatant copy of 'Norwegian Wood'? Was he implying that John Lennon had used a folk tune – if so, I don't know what it was. It's a good arrangement with Tex-Mex leanings.

The second song was 'Visions of Johanna' and nothing like this had been attempted in Nashville before. The musicians knew instinctively what to do and it was a perfect recording.

The third song was another stab at 'Leopard-Skin Pillbox Hat' with Dylan playing lead guitar, but the new setting helped and they had a fine version. The song is possibly about Edie Sedgwick, who could be the blonde of the album title.

Julian Lloyd Webber: 'I rate Bob Dylan very highly as he is one of the great originals. I liked him best when he was a hard rock'n'roller. He played guitar on 'Leopard-Skin Pillbox Hat' and it is really great. Same with 'Highway 61 Revisited'. That guitar is angry-young-man stuff and I love it.'

They were staying at Roger Miller's new *King of the Road* motel. Al Kooper: 'We'd record all night then he'd sleep, get up and call me over to his room. He had a piano in his room. He'd teach me a song and I'd play it over and over again and he'd write down the lyrics. Then I'd go to the session an hour before he did and teach the songs to the band. They'd be ready to go when he came in.'

The session men were used to Jim Reeves, not the 'ghost of electricity'. Ian Whitcomb: 'Any thinking rock fan would have told you that Nashville was capable of producing only plastic-coated oily whine'n'slide sludge. What did country music have to do with rock?

The South was beyond the pale, but here was the modern bard with some good-old-boys, pickers who picked for Patti Page and her ilk. The results were mind-boggling.'

Charlie McCoy: 'We were booked in for 6pm and he said, "Can you wait? I haven't finished writing the song yet." We started recording at 4am. We had been doing four songs in three-hour sessions and the hardest thing that night was staying awake. That was bizarre behaviour for Nashville.'

When Dylan came in with 'Sad Eyed Lady of the Lowlands', they did it in three complete takes. Dylan was to have it standing alone on Side Four as 'the best song I've ever written'. In 'Sara' he says that he wrote it in the Chelsea Hotel. Kenny Buttrey: 'It kept going on and on. We'd never heard anything like it before.' Dylan slept for the rest of the day and the next session went from 6pm to 7am. A thirteen-hour session and very productive.

Adrian Henri: 'Bob Dylan is self-indulgent from time to time but he does have a great genius for making the words work. He writes things that I wouldn't and he has the gift of making them sound simple and musical. He has some odd surrealistic images. Some of his work doesn't work on paper but when you hear him sing them, they sound absolutely incredible. 'Sad Eyed Lady Of The Lowlands' is my absolute favourite and it is wonderful. He doesn't explain things but that style of writing is meant to be ambiguous. It is up to you to form your own opinion as to what it means and it may mean something different to everybody.'

There was a long session for 'Memphis Blues Again'. Musically, it wasn't very exacting as it is the same backing for each of the nine verses, but this rigidity was contrasted with its wild imagery. There is fine playing though, especially the interplay between Al Kooper's organ and Joe South's bass. You could imagine the song being recorded by Curtis Mayfield.

Howard Sounes: 'In one sense he is stuck in Mobile which is a place he would have been to on tour. Maybe he is thinking of a girl in Memphis or a bad show he had there. It could be as simple and as literal as that, but it means everything else as well. On some levels, the songs are very simple. There is a song called 'I Want You' which is a simple and straightforward direct love song about a guy lusting after a woman. There is no mystery in that. Maybe they are more straightforward than people think.'

Ralph McTell: 'I thought 'I Want You' was Bob's attempt at writing a pop song.' That could be right as this is one of the first of Dylan's songs to have a middle eight or a bridge.

Dylan had recorded five songs in three days in Nashville and planned to return when he had more. Going to Nashville was good for Dylan and good for the musicians as it opened their minds. Numerous musicians decided to follow Dylan's lead and record there.

The Fariñas were promoting their second album with concerts and a TV appearance with Pete Seeger. Back in Carmel, Richard and Joan played games in restaurants by pretending to be other people and it could get out of hand.

Richard had persuaded Joan Baez that she could make a rock album. They picked 'Yesterday' (Beatles), 'Homeward Bound' (Simon), 'My Little Red Book' (from *What's New, Pussycat?*), 'One Too Many Mornings' (Dylan), 'Pack Up Your Sorrows' and 'A Swallow Song' (both Fariña). Baez put music to Fariña's 'All the World Has Gone By'. Richard wanted to produce her album but Maynard Solomon wanted a professional rock producer, Trade Martin. Baez did some sessions, which went well. Joan: 'It's folk-rock with some hard rock in it.' Dylan told Shelton: 'Hard rock! She's not that kind of person.'

Travelling on a Lockheed Lodestar, Dylan did more dates in North America and the pilot ordered the passengers not to smoke drugs on the plane as air circulates and could affect his judgment. Dylan met Anthony Quinn in Miami, which could have prompted 'The Mighty Quinn'. It may be coincidence but Marlon Brando's girlfriend was Pat Quinn.

On March 8, Bob Dylan, back in Nashville, cut eight new songs in three days. He used the same musicians plus Henry Strzelecki on bass. The musicians now knew how Bob worked and played table tennis matches while Bob finished his songs. The first day started with 'Absolutely Sweet Marie', which featured a dominant, playful organ and was a close cousin to 'Memphis Blues Again'.

Up to now Dylan had been writing in the folk tradition – verse, chorus, verse, chorus or verses with title lines. He appreciated Tin Pan Alley bridges or middle eights and among the first was the 'You have many contacts' section in 'Ballad of a Thin Man'. The bridge was used to perfection in 'Just like a Woman'. The songwriter Jimmy Webb has said, 'We all live for the moment when words fall together like that.'

'Just like a Woman' was another put down, but quite affectionate. It's gentle and regretful although he did sing it maliciously on the *Before the Flood* tour in 1974. This and 'Leopard Skin' may be about Edie Sedgwick and it was used in her biopic, *Ciao Manhattan*. This song has been called chauvinist with the female a victim. Note how sorrowfully Roberta Flack sings her version, which is like an answer version to the original. Even if true, this does not condemn Bob Dylan. He is writing a song: he does not have to be the male character.

Hazel O'Connor: 'I love "Just like a Woman". I did it about 1984 and changed it to a white soul vibe. It had more of a bounce to it. His songs are so elastic that they can be made to suit every singer. I love the bit that they were lovers and are no longer lovers, and they're to keep quiet about it.'

The arrangement includes Joe South on a classical guitar. He also adds the 'Yes she does' to the chorus. They had several takes until they hit the right one and *Bootleg 12* has a take in which Dylan performs the song to an arrangement rather like Elvis Presley's 'Suspicion' but it doesn't fit and Dylan says, 'We lost, man.'

'Pledging My Time' was a fun, blues workout with the fine line, 'If it don't work out, you'll be the first to know.' The track is driven by Bob's harmonica. Listen to the instrumental break: Bob is improvising like Miles Davis!

On the second day he did a fun rocker, 'Most Likely You Go Your Way and I'll Go Mine'. Bob didn't want overdubs on *Blonde on Blonde* so Charlie McCoy offered to play bass and trumpet at the same time, and he did. Bob said, 'I thought you were kidding.'

'Temporary like Achilles' – well, what does that mean? Did Dylan really mean 'Temporarily like Achilles'? It's a routine song that works okay in the context of the album, but doesn't really take hold.

The third and final day (or his sixth) in Nashville featured 'Rainy Day Woman Numbers 12 & 35', 'Obviously Five Believers' and 'I Want You'.

Bob Dylan and Phil Spector had been in a coffee shop when they first heard Ray Charles' 'Let's Go Get Stoned', which was about drinking gin. They were surprised to hear such an explicit song on air and Dylan wanted to do the same, a really joyous drinking or drugs song. Actually, Dylan has said, 'I never have and never will write a drug song.' Well, could have fooled me. Bob Dylan told Nat Hentoff: 'Opium, hash and pot they just bend your mind a little. Those things aren't drugs.'

Dylan thought, 'I'm not going to do this with a bunch of straight people' so booze and grass were available. Charlie McCoy said, 'We can play pretty dumb if we put our minds to it.' Dylan performed with slurred vocals and much laughter and it sounds like the craziest of parties. In keeping with the session, Henty Strzelecki on bass was so drunk that he couldn't stand up. He lay on the floor and played the bass pedals of the organ with his hand while Wayne Moss played bass.

Charlie McCoy: 'The night we cut 'Rainy Day Women', Dylan said he wanted a kind of Salvation Army sound and they asked me if I could find a slide trombone player. I recommended Wayne Butler. He came over at midnight and 20 minutes later we sent him home because we had finished it in one take.' Robbie Robertson went out for some cigarettes. When he came back 20 minutes later, the track had been completed.

At first Dylan said 'Rainy Day' was called 'A Long-Haired Mule and a Porcupine Hare', but who knew what he was thinking? Dylan said that he once saw a mother and daughter in a doorway sheltering from the rain, one about 35, one about 12. Hence the title but he was putting someone on.

Fred Dellar: "Rainy Day Women' is about as vague as you can possibly go. If you look at an Impressionist painting, you can say what you feel about it or you can say what you think the artists felt about it. None of us needs to be correct. Even on *Nashville Skyline*, which people think is Dylan's simplest thing, the lyrics are often vague.'

Al Stewart's *Love Chronicles* album is said to be the first to put a four-letter word on vinyl. 'I used it in its literal sense, it wasn't a swear word. I have a feeling that Bob Dylan beat both John Lennon and myself as if you listen to 'Rainy Day Women', Dylan says, "They stone when you're trying to have a..." and you can't really hear what he is saying next but it rhymes with "good luck". I strongly suspect he might have been the first.' Dylan's book of lyrics rhymes 'good luck' with 'make a buck'.

When Dylan was asked about the song, he said it was about 'cripples and Orientals and the world in which they live'.

At a rough guess Bob had a copy of Bo Diddley's 1955 single, 'She's Fine, She's Mine' and he worked it up for 'Obviously Five Believers'. When Dylan was asked what the song was called, Robbie Robertson chipped in with 'Obviously Five Believers'. 'Yeah,' said Dylan, 'that's good.'

After trying 'Leopard-Skin Pillbox Hat' with some doorbell noises, he stuck to an earlier version for the album. Dylan had a new song with surreal words and the simplest of titles, 'I Want You'.

Pete Frame: 'How do you pick one song out of a million but I love 'I Want You'? It is a surrealist, bizarre lyric with a brilliant backing. Just wonderful. I've never stopped to analyse the lyric and I'd have great difficulty trying to do so.'

Bob Spitz: 'Every time I think, "That is his greatest song", I realise that there are many other candidates. I am a very big fan of *Blonde on Blonde* and *Highway 61 Revisited* and every time I hear 'I Want You' with that trenchant passion, I love it. He is singing from the heart and I am bowled over by it.'

Al Kooper: 'I had the opening guitar lick in my head and Wayne Moss came up with that amazing sixteen-note run that comes out of it. I almost fell off the chair when he did that. Nobody in New York could have even have thought of doing that.'

It's a funny lyric. Everything is happening to Bob Dylan and he just knows what he wants. Maybe it's a love song to Sara. Note the passing reference to the Rolling Stones and 'Time Is on My Side'.

All the studio tapes for *Bringing It All Back Home, Highway 61 Revisited* and *Blonde on Blonde* were preserved and there is now an 18CD set of them, nine of them being for *Blonde on Blonde*. It includes a session in a hotel room in Denver on 13 March 1966 with Bob Dylan and Robbie Robertson and even more new material: 'Positively Van Gogh', anyone?

That session in the hotel room had been taped by Robert Shelton and we are fortunate to have it, but if Shelton had thought ahead, he should have gone to Nashville and sat in on some sessions. Dylan told Shelton that he had been on heroin and had shaken it. Dylan commented that the acoustics in Vancouver and Ottawa were terrible and he didn't want to play arenas.

Sandy Konikoff was not working out as the road drummer and Dylan brought in Mickey Jones to replace him. Mickey Jones was born in Houston in 1941 but raised in Grand Prairie, Texas. He had been playing drums since 1956. He had been in a band whose leader had killed himself playing Russian Roulette. Mickey met Trini Lopez in Dallas and was his drummer for eight years. Trini was managed by Bullets Durban, who had brothers, Buckshot and BB: clearly not people to mess with. Johnny Rivers formed a trio with Mickey and Joe Osborn and offered him $500 a week. Lopez said, 'You're making a mistake, I'm a million-dollar property.' Mickey said, 'I know you are but even if I stay, I'm not going to see much of it.' Dylan saw Johnny Rivers at Whisky a Go Go and said that he wanted Mickey. Albert Grossman invited him on a world tour. He was offered $750 a week but had to pay for his food and hotels. As he was married with a son, he negotiated for hotel expenses but couldn't get the food. 'Doesn't matter,' he thought, 'I can eat at McDonald's.' He admitted that he ate 'one too many double cheeseburgers, so loose clothes worked for me.'

The rehearsal at the Columbia studio on Sunset Boulevard was chilly as Mickey was an extrovert and the rest were quieter. Dylan wanted an eight-note build-up for 'One Too Many Mornings', which Mickey did perfectly. He was an aggressive drummer, playing the bass drum like a cannon. They had the biggest speakers and monitors that Mickey had seen. It was expensive to take this equipment around the world but it was what Dylan wanted.

Once again a strange track was chosen for a single, 'One of Us Must Know', which was lacking a strong melody and had little chance of being more than a specialist success. There was a rooftop photo session on Sunset Strip where Bob looked skeletal and ill.

Mickey told Dylan that Otis Redding was performing at the Whisky a Go Go and Dylan gave Otis an acetate of 'Just like a Woman'. He hoped that Otis would record it but Otis told his manager Phil Walden that it had too many words. Otis couldn't get his head around 'her amphetamines and her pearls'. Is it possible that the song inspired 'Sittin' on the Dock of the Bay'?

The entourage flew to Honolulu for April 9 where Mickey Jones had his first gig with Dylan. They performed in the concert hall that Elvis Presley was to use for *Aloha from Hawaii*. The audience was unsure sure about the electric set and after the show, Dylan went looking for a hot dog stand.

The next day they flew to Australia. Both the Kingston Trio and Peter, Paul and Mary had done well in Australia before Bob. Garth Hudson slept for the whole of the 14-hour flight to Australia. Dylan was reading *An American Dream* by Norman Mailer. Bob was keen to play his black Telecaster, which looked good next to Robbie's white one. Dylan authority Derek Barker says, 'Dylan did get off on alienating audiences. Mickey Jones said that Bob was never more animated or excited as when he put on an electric guitar. He did his thing and if people didn't get it, then so be it.'

When in Australia, the reporters said that the first half was good and then the band came on and ruined it. Or worse. The Australian magazine *The Bulletin* had a feature by

Charles Higham: 'His voice is a monotonous drone like the sound a man makes after sea-sickness. The songs go on and on as inexorably and tunelessly as water dripping down a drain.'

Dylan met the press at Sydney Airport and seemed bewildered. He said his songs were about the Second Coming. He was asked, 'Is that a band with you?' and he responded, 'No, they're all friends of my grandmother.' The most surreal moment came from the fans when he was given a fifty-foot fan letter (shades of Jack Kerouac?) They hated performing at Sydney Stadium which had a revolving stage. Dylan joked about performing for brand new people all the time and said, 'Tell me when I get there.'

Dylan added a new song for his live shows, 'Tell Me Momma', a punkish rocker. When he sang 'I Don't Believe You', he said, 'It used to go like that, now it goes like this.'

His show at the Festival Hall in Melbourne was broadcast. The show started late and was 'monotonous and untuneful' in the first half. His version of 'Rainy Day Women' was very stoned. He coughed and spluttered into the mic. Some of the audience didn't care for the electric set. The beat poet Adrian Rawlins took Dylan around Melbourne's slum area, Fitzroy, and invited him to play pinball.

After a raid at a pot party in Melbourne, Victor Maymudes was deported. Mickey Jones' home movies were ruined by the police by being exposed to light. They had to stay in Perth six extra days as the Australian government had requisitioned planes to send troops to Vietnam. To fill the time, Garth and Mickey went to four films in one day.

In Perth, Dylan met the actress Rosemary Gerrette who hung around for a couple of days. She was part of an all-night session with Dylan and Robertson who wanted to stay awake so they could sleep through on the plane. Dylan had been working on and off on *Tarantula* and he showed her some of it – and that keeps you awake?

At the end of April, Dylan and his musicians had gone to Europe. At a press conference in Copenhagen, Dylan answered questions with questions and asked, 'Where is the nearest cow?' He saw Kronborg Castle, the model for Elsinore in *Hamlet*. Mickey got invited to a party with a bunch of Swedes who were shooting heroin. This was scary stuff as the country was just changing to driving on the right. The show in Copenhagen went well but Dylan didn't mind if he was received badly. He liked to challenge an audience. It was always another side of Bob Dylan.

Columbia had come to its senses and released an ultra-commercial track as a single, 'Rainy Day Women Numbers 12 and 35', although it brought troubles of its own. In terms of sales, the marketeers regarded it as a novelty. It was a Dylan record that was not for listening but for driving or doing housework. A young Eva Cassidy would sing 'Rainy Day Women' over and over without realising what it was about.

Willie Nile comments, 'It was so great to hear it on the radio as it was banned in some places, but they certainly played it in Buffalo, New York. It was all good fun, but Dylan was always pushing the limit.'

Colin Beardwood, a Birmingham councillor, asked the Home Secretary Roy Jenkins to ban 'Rainy Day Women' and the Byrds' 'Eight Miles High' as they encouraged drug taking. 'I'm not a fuddy-duddy but these songs encourage drug taking which can't be good for young people.' The BBC, which had disbanded its listening committee, said the decision was left to individual producers.

No creative person is going to admit it but without some of the drugs in the 1960s, especially LSD, I doubt if we would have had so many strange songs filled with fantastic metaphors. There was a rare admission in the present tense from a top rock musician in 1968: David Crosby said, 'I don't know any good guitar players who haven't taken speed. I play most of the time high and I always write high.'

Barry Feinstein, who was married to Mary Travers wanted to do something with his photographs. He had an idea for a book *Hollywood* with text from Bob Dylan.

Unlike Leonard Cohen who had started as a literary figure, Dylan felt he had to work for recognition. David Hajdu: 'Bob Dylan and Richard Fariña were in a race in 1966 to have their books published. They both wanted a literary reputation: Bob wasn't sure that his songs were enough for that. Fariña had been working on a novel for a decade, *Been down so Long It Looks like Up to Me*. It was published on Mimi's twenty-first birthday: 30 April 1966.' At the time, Joan Baez was in Paris with their parents.'

There was a book-signing party at the Thunderbird bookstore and café in Carmel. Richard was looking good with a deep tan from the beach and was considering a second book, a memoir about Dylan and the Baez sisters, although Dylan would probably block it. Fariña likened Dylan to James Dean by saying, 'Catch him now. Next week he may be mangled on a motorbike.'

Richard seemed to have forgotten Mimi's birthday. Pauline invited them to her house afterwards. When they arrived, they found that Richard had organised a birthday party. A friend of Pauline's husband had come on a motorbike. Willie Hinds took him for a ride – going to a place where mountains tumble to the sea, ideal for bike riders. They were going at 90mph around sharp bends. Hinds knew the roads well, but they crashed. A motorist was injured and Fariña was thrown off and killed. There was a funeral and a burial near the ocean, and Judy Collins sang 'Amazing Grace'.

David Hajdu: 'Bob and Richard set out to do something similar from different vantage points. Richard was a writer who wanted to merge folk and rock with literature. Bob was a rock'n'roll pianist who went into folk and took on poetry, and then tried merging the three. A couple of months before *Bringing It All Back Home*, Richard had some tracks with Mimi that were rock tracks. There is also a bit of a world music vibe.'

Joan continued performing and told audiences about Richard. She cancelled her rock album, calling it a lapse of judgment: 'Rock'n'roll does not elevate my spirit.' Two songs, 'Pack up Your Sorrows' and 'Swallow', were issued as a single. Mimi put Joan's version of 'All the World Has Gone by' on an album of unreleased material by the Fariñas. Was Richard's song about the dysfunctional 'Morgan the Pirate', about Dylan? It could be his response to 'Positively 4th Street'. The song was later recorded by Iain Matthews.

On 2 May 1966 Dylan and his crew arrived in London and straightway went clubbing with Paul McCartney, Keith Richards and Brian Jones. The next day he gave a press conference at the Mayfair Hotel and said that *Tarantula* was about spiders, which figures. Then he went to see John Lee Hooker at Blaises club with McCartney and Dana Gillespie. Macca played him an acetate of *Revolver* and Dylan said, 'Oh, I get it, you don't want to be cute anymore.' Dylan played him some acetates from Nashville. Dylan said, 'Why don't you guys write a song and I'll record it, and I'll write a song for you?'

Dylan was in Dublin on May 5. The acoustic set was well received but there was trouble in the electric. Someone shouted, 'Leave it to the Rolling Stones' and one review was headlined *Night of the Big Let Down*. According to Bob Geldof, he announced every song as 'Mr. Tambourine Man' and then didn't sing it. If this is so, shouldn't alarm bells have been ringing in Mr. Geldof's head as he subsequently booked him for Live Aid? Some objected to Dylan giving up on protest songs and were holding placards saying 'Stop the War'. Ken Pitt was given a tape of the Dublin show, which he played to Manfred Mann. They wanted to do 'Just Like a Woman'.

The entourage then went by train to the ABC Theatre in Belfast, next to the Grand Opera House, later damaged in an IRA attack and now apartments.

Then it was over to the mainland. During his appearance at Colston Hall in Bristol, there were cries of 'Turn it down' and the local paper called it, *Day of disillusionment for Dylan fans*.

Bob Dylan met up with Johnny Cash when he was in Cardiff and Donn Pennebaker filmed them rehearsing 'I Still Miss Someone' with Bob on piano. Dylan had a look around the medieval Raglan Castle.

On 12 May 1966, Dylan was at the Odeon, Birmingham. He reacted to hostility with 'Baby Let Me Follow You Down' by saying, 'If you want some folk music, I'll play you some folk music. This is a folk song my granddaddy used to sing to me. It goes like this....'

Dylan met the Spencer Davis Group backstage just before his show in Birmingham and said, 'Britain reminds me of ghosts.' They knew of a big house in its own grounds in Kidderminster: it had burnt down and an old man and his dog had perished. After the show Steve and Muff Winwood took Dylan to Kidderminster. There was someone living in the gatehouse and so they had to drive up quietly. They walked around and they heard a dog – well, this is the country – and Dylan was convinced he had heard the ghost. He had a wonderful time.

We now come to Saturday 14 May 1966 and another personal note as I was seeing Bob Dylan for the second time and again in Liverpool.

Although Bob Dylan's first tour had been a runaway success, I don't recall it being any harder to obtain tickets. As before, I had bought my tickets from the Odeon Cinema in Liverpool during my lunch break and I had bought two, taking along my hapless girlfriend, Diana, who so loathed him the first time round. Maybe I genuinely believed it would be different: maybe I was being pig-headed, but I did know from the music press that Dylan had been performing with a rock band and that the fans hadn't liked it. 'Probably folkies,' I thought and because I liked rock bands more than acoustic folksingers, I knew that I'd be happy.

It was again Cup Final day and again a Lancashire v Yorkshire match, in this case, Everton v Sheffield Wednesday. Unlike most people in Liverpool, I didn't support Liverpool or Everton. I supported both local teams as I felt that if either did well, it was good for the city.

Although I didn't know it at the time, Bob Dylan and the photographer Barry Feinstein were wandering around Liverpool in the early morning and they had gone to the Dock Road and into an abandoned area which had not been rebuilt after the war. A group of children followed them and Barry had filmed Bob with the kids in a doorway. Forty years later the Dylan archivist Chris Hockenhull traced as many of them as he could for a recreation of the event (*sans* Dylan) for the BBC-TV regional programme, *Inside Out*. By all accounts, Dylan was pleasant and friendly and the photographs give that impression too.

That evening I told Diana that I had a surprise for her in Liverpool. I took her to Reece's bar and grill: I didn't do much eating out back then – no one did: we relied on our parents to feed us – so maybe I was serious. More likely, I was sweetening the pill for what was to follow.

Again we turned the corner into London Road and again she saw 'The Sound of Music 2.30 – Bob Dylan 7.30pm' on the marquee. That film was still popular and it ran almost two years at the Odeon. 'Oh no,' she moaned, 'not him!' 'Don't worry,' I replied, 'he's changed – he's got a rock band with him. You're going to love him.'

As we went into the auditorium, we could see the instruments on stage and at the front, those two microphones, and a table for harmonicas and water. Resting on the floor on either side of the stage were two large speakers, much larger than any I had seen before.

For the first set, it was Bob Dylan on his own.

And he was stoned.

Really stoned.

Dylan sang, spoke and played his guitar and harmonica at a ponderously slow pace. Some of the songs were new to me but for the ones I knew, it was like playing a single at LP speed. The first half was not really to mollify the folk fans as it was unlike any folk concert that they would have heard. My conclusion now is that he was stoned out of his skull but back then I just thought it was very odd.

Michael Gray was also there: 'I don't think we thought he was stoned. We just thought that he sounded American. He slurred and drawled and we just assumed it was American. My own awareness of drugs at the time was absolutely zilch, so I wouldn't have known.'

Right from the start, which was 'She Belongs to Me', he had that measured phrasing which has been mocked so much. It is ironic that such a serious performer has, unknowingly, prompted so much laughter. In 1966, nobody else was singing like that.

'Fourth Time Around' was even slower. *Blonde on Blonde* had not been issued and so this was a new song. Again it was incredibly slow and we wondered what it was about – was his girlfriend in a wheelchair – and what was that tune? Wasn't it 'Norwegian Wood'? Most of us would have been confused, but not Diana who was on the road to hell.

In a rambling introduction, Dylan criticised the music press for saying he wrote drug songs: 'I wouldn't know how to write a drugs song. This is not a drugs song. It is vulgar to think so.' He was introducing 'Visions of Johanna' which he sang with nearly every syllable emphasised. It was brilliant but I was thinking, 'Oh please sing something that Diana will even half-like.'

No chance. The ten-minute 'Desolation Row' put paid to that. The harmonica break was like a slowed-down sailor's hornpipe. He sang another new song, 'Just like a Woman', but what was that about? 'She breaks just like a little girl' sounded dodgy to me. He closed the first set with an acoustic 'Mr. Tambourine Man' although by now, it had been a transatlantic Number 1 for the Byrds. Dylan still chose to perform it acoustically. There had been no protest songs and his delivery had been strange but by and large the audience approved and he left the stage to warm applause. However, those instruments were on stage, so what was coming next?

Michael Gray: 'We had never heard 'Visions of Johanna' before, which he did as an acoustic solo, and we had never heard anything like it before. This transcendent poetry soared up through the hall, yet it was mixed with this strangely unsettling jokiness. Some of it is clearly rhapsodically wondrous stuff and then you get to things in the middle like "The jelly-faced women all sneeze" and the audience had to think, "Is this still poetry? Is it okay to like this?" This is an example of the way that Dylan changed the culture, which can be easily forgotten. It was a riveting solo performance where you could hear a pin drop. We applauded politely at the end, not like now where it doesn't matter how indifferent the performance is, the crowd will go mad for it, completely over the top regardless of the standard of performance. It was a drawing room atmosphere, no doubt disheartening and deadening for the performer, but it was breath-taking.'

Willy Russell: 'The 1965 gig in Liverpool was the big one for me. The following year he brought The Band over and I wanted to walk out of it, not because I'm a terrible old reactionary or objected to The Band, but because his first set, his acoustic set, was so dull. He had none of the drive from the year before and he was going through the motions. Presumably there was a managerial decision – 'Look Bob it's causing a hell of a lot of fuss, so why don't you keep the punters happy by doing an acoustic set?' He was loath to do it – he really wanted to be blasting his 10,000 watts out and the second set was so much better.'

No one in the audience really knew what would happen next. The 1960s weren't like today where ardent fans follow their heroes on tour. I didn't know anyone who went to more than one venue. I knew a girl who went to both houses of a Cliff Richard show in Liverpool, sitting in the front row each time. She took a change of clothing just in case Cliff recognised her and thought she might be a stalker.

Norman Killon: 'The word was already out. He had been performing in America and Australia and there was a sense of "This is what you do, you boo." It was a ritual which you see later with the Beastie Boys, say. The press had it in for him. Some didn't do it for that reason – they were mortally offended to see Dylan with a group, but it sounded good to me.'

Dylan fan, Hugh Douglas: 'Dylan was the voice of rebellion and protest and I didn't want him as just another rock star. When The Band came out, I thought it was time to leave. I left in the second number and I threw my programme at Dylan. I had nothing against the musicians: it was at Dylan. There were a large number of us in the lobby asking for our money back but we didn't get it. What I did was a sign of youth, I regret doing that now. I thoroughly enjoyed his set at the Isle of Wight.'

Norman Killon: 'That was the loudest thing that we had heard in Liverpool. We were used to the small speakers that the Beatles and other groups had. They were minuscule. These were on the floor resting against the stage and I was on the front row to the right and it was really loud.'

The tension was high as The Band came on stage with Bob Dylan for the second half. The volume was up as they launched into a new Dylan song, the bluesy 'Tell Me Momma'. The loudness was clearly deliberate and I had no idea if Dylan had written good lyrics as I couldn't make out anything but the title. Perhaps Dylan had thought that if he was going to wind up his audience, he might as well go the whole hog. Whereas the audience had been mostly as one 20 minutes earlier, there was now a marked division. An older, definitely male contingent was jeering. Some would leave noisily, banging their seats, shaking their fists at the stage and throwing down their programmes. The diehards went across the road to the Washhouse Folk Club which met in Samson and Barlow's building. Pete McGovern ran the club and he had written the singalong favourite 'In My Liverpool Home' for the Spinners. Like Robert Johnson at the crossroads, you had old music on one side and new on the other.

Frank Sellors was already in the Washhouse: 'My Dylan period was over by then. It seemed to be showbiz when he got a band, but I can see I was very naïve to hold these views. I didn't buy a Dylan album after *Bringing It All Back Home*. I was anti-electric and I would have been chopping the wires with Pete Seeger. I was persuaded by the electric Dylan in the end and The Band became my favourite group.'

The famed criticism of 'Judas!' was at Manchester three days later, but Liverpool was up there too. When Dylan said, 'You don't have to be like this', a guy close to me responded, 'Nor do you!' Before 'Ballad of a Thin Man', Dylan said, 'There's a feller up there looking for the Saviour. The Saviour's backstage, we have a picture of him.' He then went straight into 'Ballad of a Thin Man'.

Michael Gray: 'There was a serious divide between high culture and pop culture, and people booed because they were serious-minded young people. They saw his electric guitar as a sell-out to some capitalist cheapness. They would be folk fans or student-politico types. They had latched onto Dylan not because of folk music but because of the political content of his protest. That divide between what was serious and what wasn't, what was poetical and what wasn't, this was a challenge, and it was in both halves of the concert.'

The Liverpool concert was recorded by Bob Johnston for Columbia but the only song released at the time was a harsh version of 'Just like Tom Thumb's Blues', a brilliant set of surreal lyrics about beatniks in Mexico with a blistering accompaniment. For some years, it was the only track by Bob Dylan and The Band to be officially released. It was a great B-side too as well as being historic.

Johnston also recorded full sets at Manchester and the Royal Albert Hall. The sound is very good but they have been taken from the mixing desk and maybe the sound was not as good in the hall.

It was not a long set, 45 minutes, and it included 'I Don't Believe You', 'Baby, Let Me Follow You Down' and 'One Too Many Mornings', all of which he had recorded acoustically. The closer, 'Like a Rolling Stone' already had the stature of a rock anthem and it has become the one constant in Bob Dylan's tours. The final number, 'God Save the Queen', was sadly not played by The Band.

Diana thought the National Anthem the most musical moment of the evening. By this time, there were many empty seats – a third of the audience had left early, a third was clapping politely and a third was on its feet, applauding loudly. I was on my feet but I knew that my time with Diana was well and truly over. I couldn't come back from this, couldn't even try. I hardly saw her again and I wonder if she appreciates that she saw a genius musician at the height of his powers or if it is still a nightmare. When we meet again, introduced by friends...

It was an astonishing concert, all the more so for containing so many songs that had not been released in the UK. Nobody would do it now as those songs would find their way to YouTube before the official release.

After we left the Odeon, there was again euphoria on Lime Street as this time Everton had claimed the FA Cup. Playwright Alan Bleasdale: 'I first saw Bob Dylan on the night that Liverpool had won the cup for the first time and then the next year was the day that Everton won the cup. I was walking out of there and my dad was coming off the train at Lime Street as part of the biggest conga I'd ever seen. I'd actually given my ticket to my dad. It was a big conflict within me but it was a great day for him too.'

A passing word about Mr. Dylan's appearance – he was broomstick thin, dressed in a black suit and a black-and-white polka dot shirt with a wide collar and cuffs – maybe the cufflinks were a present from Joan Baez. Everybody talks about the many recorded tributes but they overlook the biggest tribute of them all – the man who copied his 1966 look and still does – the Salford poet, John Cooper Clarke. Dylan looked fantastic on this tour and he was surprisingly animated in the second half, waving his arms like Mick Jagger as he pranced around to 'Leopard-Skin Pillbox Hat'. He dedicated the song to all the people who read *Time* magazine, but none of them would be in a Liverpool audience.

Looking back to 1966, that show seems even more remarkable with hindsight, easily the most extraordinary night I have spent in a theatre. Since that first appearance with a band at Newport, Bob Dylan knew that many were coming to boo him but he took no prisoners and made no compromises. Those audience members were the losers as they had paid for their seats and Bob Dylan wasn't offering refunds.

Michael Gray: 'Dylan said it was a luxury to buy a ticket for something when you were planning to walk out. This was someone who only two years earlier had not really performed with a band, who was associated with the folk scene, and here was in the heartland of Merseybeat and doing something so much more challenging than those musicians including the Beatles.'

Around this time, I was promoting a young folksinger from Formby, Stephen Murray, then known as Timon and later Tymon Dogg. I was greatly impressed by Bob Dylan doing a whole concert of his own songs and I thought Timon should do the same. Timon was writing new songs every day and he did a few shows around Liverpool, mostly of his own material but also with a full version of 'Desolation Row'. He was good too – he recorded for Apple, cut singles for Pye and Threshold and played for years with Joe Strummer. Great guy and still going today.

Dylan followed Liverpool with a show at De Montfort Hall, Leicester and then the Gaumont in Sheffield, where a bomb hoax delayed Dylan's performance for two hours. After the show, they listened to a playback at the Grand Hotel.

That day, 16 May 1966, was when *Blonde on Blonde* was released in the USA, the same day as the Beach Boys' *Pet Sounds*. Things were not so coordinated back then and both took a few weeks to make the British shops. *Pet Sounds* cost £1.12.6d (£1.63) while the 70-minute *Blonde on Blonde*, being one of the first double-albums, was £2.10s (£2.50). It was the first double-album that most of us had ever bought (me included).

The album could have been even longer as it could have included 'I'll Keep It with Mine', 'She's Your Lover Now' and 'I Wanna Be Your Lover' and perhaps a studio version of 'Tell Me Momma'. Phil Spector didn't like Dylan's production and wanted to make a Dylan opera with him. It never happened but rock operas were just around the corner.

On May 17, it was anarchy in the UK as Dylan played the Free Trade Hall in Manchester. The Free Trade Hall was on the site of the Peterloo Massacre, so Bob Dylan's concert was not the most notorious event on this site.

The people who went to the concert could have stayed home and watched *Double Your Money* and *Emergency – Ward 10*.

IBC had been hired to record live shows with Bob Johnston for a potential LP. The soundcheck was at 4pm. The manager at the theatre could have blocked the recording as he had not been given notice of this.

Who actually shouted 'Judas!' at Dylan? When the banker Keith Butler, who had lived in Toronto since 1975, saw a review of *Live 1966* in 1998, he realised that this was at Manchester and not the Royal Albert Hall. He remembered the barracking, the slow handclaps and that he had shouted 'Judas!' He was a second-year student at Keele University. 20-year-old Keith was also interviewed for *Eat the Document*. He said, 'Any pop group can produce better rubbish than that. It was a bloody disgrace. He's a traitor.' The other candidate is John Cordwell from County Durham. Cordwell, a teacher at a training college, died in 2001 and said he was fully repentant. Butler died in 2002.

After the shout, Dylan went into his muttering routine and then 'You're a liar, a fucking liar', saying to the band, 'Play it fuckin' loud'. Mickey Jones came crashing in with the drums and they delivered a blistering 'Like a Rolling Stone'.

To follow up 'Judas!', somebody threw some silver on the stage. Robbie said to Dylan, 'I'm gonna pick it up' and Dylan laughed.

Geoff Speed ran the Widnes Folk Club and when he had Paul Simon as a guest, Paul was working on a new song, 'Homeward Bound'. When Dylan was at the Free Trade Hall, Geoff fell asleep. I told him that he had been even more critical than the guy who shouted 'Judas!' The most infamous moment in rock history and Geoff Speed was asleep.

The next day the manager of the hall sent Tito Burns a strong letter saying that they had not been given advance notice of the recording. A fire officer had to check the equipment and he had been insulted by the sound engineer, 'If we can't do the recording, there will be no concert tonight'. Some patrons were given different seats and others had their view impaired. The staff had to be at the hall until midnight and the manager submitted an invoice for £65.

Dylan moved onto the Odeon, Glasgow (*Scottish Daily Mail*: 'Folk fans walk out on Dylan') and the ABC, Edinburgh (*Scottish Daily Mail*: 'Dylan faces second night of cat calls'). At Edinburgh some fans brought along their own harmonicas to drown him out. The Scottish branch of the Communist party had deliberately barracked him but they had to buy their tickets first, and really they were spoiling it for other people.

Dylan didn't do pleasantries on stage: never has, never will. You just get the odd great comment like 'They're all protest songs, come on.' 'Dylan has difficulty in that he refuses to do the traditional show-biz things so if he does get stuck, he doesn't have the ordinary professional tricks to fall back on,' says Michael Gray. 'He used stage announcements in a masterful way at the Royal Albert Hall and he mumbles. He gets them silent and then he says, "If only you wouldn't clap so hard." The mumbling technique always worked and it was really funny.'

Bob Spitz: 'When he performed in London in 1966, he told the audience that he would never come back again. He said that they did not know how to listen to his music, that they did not appreciate him and walked off the stage. Every once in a while, Bob Dylan will explode but not often.'

Biographer Howard Sounes: 'That was some of the best music he ever made. It was stunning music, beautiful music, powerful music, and you look back and think, "These people in the audience were moronic." They were so mired in their own preconceptions as to what they thought Bob Dylan should be, what folk music should be, that they got on their high horse and jeered. What a wretched bunch of people they were and that silly man who stood up and said "Judas!" was a spotty teenager from some provincial university showing his ignorance. Bob Dylan was singing wonderful music, he was reinterpreting his songs in a brilliant new way like "Baby, Let Me Follow You Down". It sounds fabulous when you listen to the tapes now. He was right, The Band was right, history has proved them right, and the people that slow handclapped were a bunch of Dumbos. This is true of all great art: if it is really good, it is a long time before the mass of the public, the middle-minded middle-England, catches up with it. They haven't got the imagination to make that leap that Bob Dylan can. To my mind, he was entirely right, they were entirely wrong. However, the controversy made him even more successful, popular and famous and so no one lost out.'

But it was also an example of a major artist deliberately alienating his audience. Paul Morley: 'The great thing about the 1960s artists was their ability to change very quickly: they could be releasing a couple of albums a year and it all relates to a sense of context of who and what they were and how people responded to them. They made adjustments because they had so much that they wanted to say. That Judas heckle at the Free Trade Hall is like a tweet. Everybody does that kind of thing now, but back then it was very unusual to have an outrageous comment about what you were doing. Dylan was carrying on with the spirit of being Dylan but certain fans didn't want him to do that. They wanted him to be the Dylan in their head, not the Dylan in Dylan's head. It was the Dylan in Dylan's head that they had originally fallen for and some fans wanted him to stay as he was. Dylan was moving fast as he had a lot he wanted to achieve.'

Jazz singer George Melly: 'It is amazing that someone with a voice like a corncrake could succeed. But there was something about what he sang and how he sang that produced a very, very powerful magic. In the 60s I thought he was remarkable and I loved his – what I should call it – his poetry. I didn't mind, not being a purist, when he turned from folk to rock.'

After a show at the Odeon, Newcastle, Bob Dylan and his superhuman crew flew to Paris. France's top star, their Cliff Richard if you like, Johnny Hallyday was jealous of Hugues Aufray's friendship with Dylan and met him at the airport in his Rolls-Royce, giving him grass and wine as they drove to the plush George V Hotel. Five months later Johnny Hallyday would be playing the Olympia backed by the Jimi Hendrix Experience. Dylan saw Mike Porco again and Robbie Robertson met a journalist, Dominique Bourgeois, who became his wife.

The concert was at the Olympia on May 24. At the press conference, Dylan arrived with a puppet he called Finian. He said the puppet had followed him here and would be telling him the answers. Asked if he was certain of anything, the puppet supposedly replied, 'Yes, ashes, doorknobs and windowpanes.'

Dylan had trouble tuning his guitar which was greeted with hostility from the audience. He had not been heckled during an acoustic set before. He told the hecklers, 'Go to the bowling hall until I'm finished.' But it was a bad first half. The *Le Figaro* review contained a highly combative accusation: 'Bob Dylan should stop singing altogether or stop taking barbiturates.' There was a long intermission as Dylan spoke to Hugues Aufray and the effortlessly cool Françoise Hardy. She found him looking sickly. They were photographed holding a James Brown album.

Bob had seen an American flag backstage. He knew that the French were always criticising the Americans – Coca-Cola, racism, napalm for starters – and so as an act of defiance he wanted it draped across the back of the stage. This may have been his motive but Bob never says. It may have been his way of celebrating his twenty-fifth birthday or even his comment on the anti-American protests over Vietnam as France had negotiated a ceasefire that the Americans opposed. Possibly Dylan's view was 'You can love your country but you can criticise it at the same time.' In any event, hadn't France started the Vietnam war? The flag was a hostile gesture and a bit unfair on the musicians as only Mickey was American. The audience jeered and this was before Dylan had started singing. The concert was recorded for French radio but Dylan said it could not be broadcast.

After the show he went back to the George V Hotel 'speaking to some French girl' as he went with Françoise Hardy and Hugues Aufray. He played them his recordings of 'Just like a Woman' and 'I Want You'.

Dylan was back in the UK the next day for concerts over two nights at the Royal Albert Hall. Someone shouted at him before 'Leopard-Skin Pillbox Hat' and he snarled back, 'Come up here and say that!' 'Like a Rolling Stone' was dedicated to Taj Mahal (the mausoleum or the blues singer?) and he introduced the musicians for the only time on the tour.

The Seekers went and they had recorded some of his songs. Judith Durham remembered, 'The importance of Bob Dylan's lyrics never struck me at all at the time, but I didn't evaluate song lyrics much at the time.' She was surprised at how informally he was dressed.

The critics were divided: Ray Coleman said in *Melody Maker* 'Dylan insults his own talent with a shambles of noise.' *The Times* thought the acoustic set was best and said, 'Now you know how many holes it takes to fill the Albert Hall', a remark that would soon find a new home.

All four Beatles saw Dylan at the Royal Albert Hall. George Harrison was amused by him saying, 'It used to go like that, now it goes like this' before singing 'I Don't Believe You'. George added, 'All these people who had never heard of folk music two years before were now walking out, which is stupid.' Bob had been on a world tour and he looked like he'd been on a world tour.' Indeed, he was so physically depleted that he was 'practically unconscious' when the Beatles came round to see him. According to Robbie Robertson, he put Dylan in the bath to freshen up, but leaving the musician nearly proved fatal. 'I hurried back into the bathroom, only to find that Bob had sunk down into the water and it was starting to bubble. My heart stopped for a moment. I thought he could really drown here.'

Dylan went to the Cromwell Club with some of the Beatles and the Stones. Bill Wyman speaking for the Stones said, 'We all enjoyed it.'

The tour was over and Rick Danko spoke for everyone when he said, 'The hotels were great, the food was great and the audiences yelled and booed and cheered, but nobody threw anything.' Robbie Robertson: 'We had to tell ourselves they were wrong and we were right.'

There is a bootleg CD set of all the 1966 live concerts, some professional recordings and some audience recordings but there are 296 songs over 36 CDs.

On May 27, Bob Dylan and John Lennon were filmed by Pennebaker for 20 minutes in a London cab, stoned off their heads, though possibly Dylan was ill and Lennon stoned. They talked about the Mamas and the Papas and Dylan said, 'You're just interested in the big chick.' They mock 'Barry McGuire and his 'rock-a-boom'. He and Pennebaker put him on his bed in the hotel and John says, 'I think we just said goodbye to old Bob.'

When he got back to the US, Dylan watched the rushes of what Pennebaker had shot. Robbie went to Woodstock with the intention of helping with the documentary. The theme of *Eat the Document* is of an artist against the crowd, and at times Dylan felt like there was a fatwa on him. The film is disconnected with no commentary or captions to say what we are watching. It is assumed that viewers will know what it is all about. There is an opening scene of Bob Dylan taking something (cocaine?) twice, perhaps by way of explanation of the mess we are watching – to be fair, Johnny Cash seems even more wrecked.

Dylan's face is inscrutable. They are some fine scenes such as when he is singing 'What Kind of Friend Is This' with Robbie Robertson in a hotel, which is rather like the Everly Brothers' 'When Will I Be Loved'. There is an amusing sequence outside of a pet grooming parlour.

Eat the Document was eventually screened in a 50-minute version at the Academy of Music, New York in February 1971. Pennebaker wanted a longer version and Dylan withdrew the film. The film with outtakes is on YouTube.

Dylan had turned down another appearance at Newport. It would have been interesting to know what he would have done and what would have been the reaction. As it is, the Lovin' Spoonful appeared and did well, singing rock with no opposition. There was a larger young contingent at the festival which helped.

Albert Grossman had introduced Carly Simon to Bob Dylan and The Band. The idea was to make an album, *Carly and the Deacon*, the Deacon being Richie Havens. Dylan rewrote 'Baby Let Me Follow You Down' for her the day before his accident and she recorded it with The Band. According to reports, Bob Johnston said, 'If you're nice to me, I'll make you a nice record.' Carly Simon replied, 'I'm not that hungry' and the LP was abandoned.

By any standards, Bob Dylan was having a tumultuous year. He and his musicians were playing great but a faction of the audience regarded his switch to rock as a betrayal. Possibly the adversaries thought that by voicing their opposition, he would recognise his error and revert to what he was doing in 1964 – acoustic, political songwriting.

I can understand how the pressure of that could have made Bob want to change. In 2017 I was backstage with Billy Bragg and he had been handed a large file of information about someone who might have been wrongly imprisoned and he had been asked to help. How do you deal with such requests? Just imagine the number of appeals that Bob Dylan must have had, especially when so many people had been conscripted for Vietnam. I suspect that Bob partly dropped political songwriting so as not to encourage requests for help.

For now he had a few weeks to think about things. *Blonde on Blonde* was on release and in August he would tour again. The first show was on August 6 at the Yale Bowl in New Haven – capacity 60,000 – and there would be 64 dates. Like the Beatles, he was playing the 50,000-seater Shea Stadium in New York. At Shea, Peter, Paul and Mary would be the opening act and Dylan, for the first time, would be solely electric. The world tour would continue including some dates in Russia: these would not be financially viable but the kudos would be enormous: Dylan would be the first major western star to play in the Soviet Union.

For the moment, it wasn't exactly a holiday in Woodstock.

Bob Markel at Macmillan wanted a book from Dylan. They had published Milt Okun's first book *Something to Sing about* and Milt had produced Peter, Paul and Mary. The meeting between Bob Markel and Albert Grossman was a disaster as they hated each other on sight. The contract did get written and an advance for $10,000 was agreed which was small considering the author's reputation.

Bob had to finish *Tarantula*, originally called *Side One*. In 1965 he had submitted 12 typed, single-spaced pages of dense text to Macmillan. It was not an easy read but there was a fine section on Aretha Franklin. Allen Ginsberg had warned him off writing a book, telling him that the literary mafia was waiting to shoot him down: did Dylan care – just look at the popular success for John Lennon's prose and poems? Whatever, now he hated *Tarantula*, was bored with the project and feeling that it was only being written to fulfil a contract.

There were other issues. Dylan appears to have been taking amphetamines and this can be heard in his performances. Just contrast the difference between his introductions in 1965 and 1966. At Dublin and Manchester in 1966, he is sounding like a clock that is running down. Some say, 'Nonsense, his drawled introductions were part of the act.' That could be true but why would anyone want to speak so ridiculously? I'd put it down to drugs: there is no other valid explanation. Maybe he needed the drugs to keep going. His world tour had a punishing schedule and in July he had time off before it started again. Some consider that Dylan's main problem at the time was drug use and it looked as though something dramatic would happen to break the chain.

Jack Elliott had left a Triumph 55 motorcycle on Albert Grossman's estate before ramblin' off and Albert told Bob he was welcome to use it. On July 29, Grossman was away and Bob went over to collect it, going with Sara in their car. He would take it into Woodstock for a service and they would return home in the car.

They were driving along a narrow back road and Bob was blinded by the sun, Bob hit the brake too hard: the rear wheel locked and he was thrown off. He told his father that he had feared the worst. He was heading towards the Gates of Eden.

III. Reviews: *World's Fair*

A little light relief: I've been looking at reviews and articles from all over the place. I never saw the UK fairground and jukebox newspaper, *World's Fair*, in the 1960s. I'm glad I didn't as I might have been put off a whole pile of great records. Here's how *World's Fair* saw folk-rock in 1965.

Catch the Wind – Donovan
'This pop-folk field is beyond me: it would seem that anyone with a mediocre voice can meander through a dreary song, label it 'folk', and then wait for the hysterical acclaim. This is getting a lot of publicity which will have some effect on the demand.'

Subterranean Homesick Blues – Bob Dylan
'Bob Dylan's cynical lyrics are sung in a hard, not really pleasant voice, but one which commands the listener's attention.'

San Francisco Bay Blues – Jesse Fuller
'He sounds like a 60-year-old Bob Dylan. It might just be bad enough to happen.'

Don't Think Twice, It's All Right – Heinz
'A very good version of the Bob Dylan number which moves along with gusto.'

Baby Won't You Tell Me – John Hammond Jr
'Sounds like Mick Jagger on an off-day.'

Ye Playboys and Playgirls – Carolyn Hester
'Miss Hester sings the Dylan songbook with her talented little tongue in her talented little cheek. This happiness, gaiety, call it what you will, is most infectious and could catch on big.'

Colours – Donovan
'A shade more melodic than 'Catch the Wind'. If his girlfriend's hair was yellow at night, what colour is it in the morning?'

Maggie's Farm – Bob Dylan
'Too messy for my liking.'

There but for Fortune – Joan Baez
'Simply and beautifully sung.'

I'm A Rock (sic) – Paul Simon
'Yet another young man on a diluted Dylan kick. It would appear that this boom has rather subsided so tread wearily.'

All I Really Want to Do – The Byrds
'Doesn't engender any wild enthusiasm from me. All right but a typical follow-up disc.'

All I Really Want to Do' – Cher
'Many of the words are unintelligible on this Bob Dylan number.'

Laugh at Me – Sonny Bono
'Very definitely on a Dylan kick using a rather thick backing. Sonny and Cher have more talent than their kinky discs would have you believe.'

Like a Rolling Stone – Bob Dylan
'There has been a lot of talk about this one. Dylan uses quite a heavy backing and it carries his special message for teens.' (We aren't told what this message is.)

Eve of Destruction – Barry McGuire
'Dylanish and rather sick.'

It's All Over Now Baby Blue – Leroy Van Dyke
'Is it about forsaken love or is it about after the bomb?'

If You Gotta Go, Go Now – Manfred Mann
'An outspoken version of 'Baby It's Cold Outside' and I am left breathless at the sheer audacity of it all, but oh, it's fab!'

Sins of a Family – P.F. Sloan
'Bob Dylan played sideways.'

Positively 4th Street – Bob Dylan
'More acceptable than most Dylan discs.'

What a World – Benny Hill
'Very, very funny. A protest disc about protest discs.'

And a little more light relief: Ray Davies was heckled when he was appearing at the Royal Albert Hall in 1993 and he responded with 'Are you the guy who heckled Bob Dylan?'

CHAPTER 7
Life in the Country

I. Illegal Smile

> *'To live outside the law you must be honest.'*
> 'Absolutely Sweet Marie', Bob Dylan, 1966

> *'Some of these bootleggers, they make pretty good stuff.'*
> 'Sugar Baby', Bob Dylan, 2001

When I talk to twenty-somethings today, I find that nearly everything they want to hear is available on the net, usually on Spotify, and for free. They may be music fans but they have no intention of paying for it. This illustrates how things have changed with the years and indeed how difficult it is for musicians to make money outside of concert appearances. You still see stalls offering bootleg CDs at record fairs but even they don't do much business these days as most of the bootleg material is also on the net.

And yet, whether Bob Dylan liked it or not (and often he didn't), the illegal bootleg albums set him apart from other performers and established him as someone who was utterly unique. I can remember the difficulties I had in finding a copy of Bob Dylan's famed 'Judas!' appearance from 1966: now such an occurrence would be all over the net within minutes.

A bootleg recording is an illegal recording, something that has been issued without the permission of the artist or his record company. The very term sounds exciting: it sounds like smuggling, as indeed it is. In times of prohibition, bottles of whiskey were smuggled inside tall boots, hence, bootleggers.

Bootleg recordings are not be confused with counterfeit recordings, though both are illegal. A counterfeit recording is simply a copy of an officially released record, but a bootleg features unissued live or studio recordings.

Before the 1960s, it was very different. We knew nothing of outtakes and rejected songs and all we knew was what we were given. There were occasional instances where an alternative take got onto an album by mistake and we had two versions of the same song, which happened with Elvis Presley ('Doncha Think It's Time') and the Everly Brothers ('Poor Jenny'). It made us wonder what else was out there.

Joanie Sommers released an album, *Behind Closed Doors at a Recording Session* on the new Warner Brothers label in 1959. It promised recording secrets for the first time. There were only two tracks, 'What Is this Thing Called Love' and 'Am I Blue' and you got studio chat with Sommers, the conductor Carl Brandt and the producer Alvino Rey. Everyone was very polite but there wasn't much room for improvisation as we were dealing with an orchestra with written arrangements, Furthermore, Joanie Sommers was the wrong artist for this experiment. Nobody was bothered about what she thought – a similar session with Elvis would have been much more interesting.

Or Bob Dylan.

Bob Dylan had an unorthodox approach to recording sessions from the start. The Dylan authority John Bauldie said, 'Artists often recorded more tracks than they could use and then they had to choose what they wanted to release. Bob Dylan often missed off great performances of great songs. Maybe they represented something that he didn't want exposed at that time and usually we don't know the reasons for his decisions.'

Good material was often held back by Dylan and several lesser songs were nevertheless recorded and released. We are fortunate that Columbia kept their tapes and didn't destroy them or record over them so we know exactly how Bob Dylan approached recording.

After his motorcycle accident, Bob Dylan worked with The Band in Woodstock and they recorded several new songs which were passed to other artists as publisher's demos, often in the UK, to record. Dylan fans learnt of these *Basement Tapes* but usually had never heard them, although occasional tracks had been played on radio.

Although *Nashville Skyline* in 1969 was a big-selling album, many fans were disappointed. Dylan had gone country; his lyrics were straightforward, and the album didn't even play for 25 minutes. One track was an instrumental and another was a remake, so what was Bob Dylan up to? Fans would discuss *Blonde on Blonde* for hours and here there was little to debate.

Two keen fans, Ken Douglas and Mike Taylor (who was known as Dub) worked in the record industry. Ken's father owned a record distribution company, Saturn and he was concerned that 20,000 copies of *Nashville Skyline* had been returned on a sale-or-return basis, despite containing a Top 10 single 'Lay Lady Lay'.

Ken had a copy of the *Basement Tapes*, which he had recorded from the radio, while Dub had a hand-me-down cassette of the Minnesota Hotel recordings. With a few other bits and pieces, they had enough for a double-album. They pressed 100 copies, keeping ten for themselves, and when their friend Jim sold 90 to the first store, they knew they were onto something. There were no album notes, no artist name or no contents. This was because the pressing plant was doing them a favour and if they had designed a sleeve, they might have been pushing their luck.

They pressed more copies and when a potential stockist referred to it as the *Great White Wonder*, they knew they had their title. They had a rubber stamp made up and they put it in the top right-hand corner of each double-album.

Tom Waits says, 'I like my music with the rinds and the seeds left in. The noise and grit of the tapes becomes inseparable from the music.' One of his favourite bootlegs was *Great White Wonder*.

The album sold throughout California but its success opened the floodgates. They could hardly complain when other underground businessmen tried their luck by re-pressing their album and selling their own copies. This has happened through the world of bootlegging and so it has been very difficult for anyone to make money out of it. It is estimated that 350,000 copies of *Great White Wonder* were sold in 1969, probably at around $12 a copy, but who pressed them? I had one myself and part of the thrill was in owning something that was so clearly criminal.

New labels cropped up every week and a purchaser was buying a pig in a poke as he had no knowledge of the sound quality. Wisely, one company called itself TMQ (Trade Mark of Quality) and had recognisable sleeves featuring William Stout's artwork. That label also started with Bob Dylan, in their case *Troubled Troubadour*. A label clearly less sure of guaranteeing its product was Double Cross.

People didn't buy bootlegs to snub the official releases as most of the purchasers would already have all a particular artist's work. I don't think I ever bought a bootleg of someone that I didn't already collect. They were bought to appreciate everything about an artist's career, certainly one as changeable as Bob Dylan's.

In June 1968 *Rolling Stone* ran a feature, *Dylan's Basement Tape Should Be Released*. Then it had a cover story about *Great White Wonder*, the first bootleg success. They said it had been manufactured by two draft dodgers who took their profits to Canada and opened a petrol station.

In 1969 *Rolling Stone* published a hoax review of a bootleg album by the Masked Marauders. Mick Jagger, Bob Dylan, John Lennon, Paul McCartney and George Harrison were said to be involved with the tracks produced by Al Kooper. *Rolling Stone* foxed some readers with this and indeed, there was even a band that recorded the song titles listed under that name.

In January 1970, Columbia Records issued a statement that *Great White Wonder* was a fake and the artist was an impersonator, which was untrue and a ridiculous statement to make. They did issue a subpoena but as they put the wrong names on it, Ken and Dub survived.

Ken and Dub followed *Great White Wonder* with another Dylan collection, *Stealin'*, a double-album with outtakes from *Blonde on Blonde* which was definitely chancing your arm. The UK price, rather quaintly, was six guineas. Ken and Dub released a Rolling Stones concert from Oakland, California, *Liver than You'll Ever Be*. The Beatles' Abbey Road tapes somehow got onto the market and a recording at the Star-Club in Hamburg was issued as *The Beatles vs. The Third Reich*.

A number of radio concerts recorded for FM stations found their way onto bootlegs and, exploiting a legal loophole, are often on low price CDs today, despite the fact that the artist would have been contracted to another label at the time.

The customers for the Dylan collections had been mostly male and now bootleg albums appeared across the board with the Beatles and the Rolling Stones. Keith Richards unwisely told the press that he collected Rolling Stones bootlegs which suggested he endorsed the practice.

Newsweek reported in October 1970 that the record industry was declaring war on bootlegs calling it 'plain theft' but the American legislation was a grey area. Just by sheer luck, the bootleggers kept ahead of the game. It was discovered that the laws in Italy and Australia were fairly weak, so many bootlegs were pressed there.

The success of the bootleg albums prompted legitimate releases designed to combat them such as the Rolling Stones' live album, *Get Yer Ya-Ya's Out* and the Who's *Live at Leeds* which was packaged like a bootleg. The Who also released an album of unissued tracks, *Odds and Sods*.

Maybe some studio performances were never meant to be released. Carolyn Hester told me that she recorded a couple of Beatle songs just so technicians could get the right balance and levels and she was surprised when they ended up on a Bear Family album. This was not a bootleg, far from it, but it was not a product she endorsed.

The record company started to copy the bootlegs. Bob Dylan's *Self Portrait* sounded like he was just having fun with a few favourite songs in the studio and his 1973 album *Dylan* was a collection of outtakes. Like Carolyn Hester, this may have included a few warm-ups.

Columbia even purloined the name for their Bob Dylan archive collection, *The Bootleg Series*. John Bauldie said, 'Although I wrote the booklet notes and my opinions rather than my advice were sought, I didn't have any hands-on experience of putting *The Bootleg Series* together. It was put together by Jeff Rosen who works for Bob Dylan and takes care of his business matters. It was his initiative to do *The Bootleg Series* and he compiled the tracks. My part in it was relatively minor. He sent me a list of songs and asked me if I had any suggestions for tracks that had not been included.' After Dylan did *The Bootleg Series*, Scorpio responded with *The Genuine Bootleg Series*.

Some committed fans wanted every live performance by their favourite bands and there was a growing market in everything by Led Zeppelin. Bruce Springsteen and the E Street Band changed their repertoire every night, hence the Springsteen market in bootlegs rivals Bob Dylan's.

Frank Zappa loathed bootleggers. On the other hand, the Grateful Dead encouraged bootlegging and even set aside a special area for them in their larger shows. They were ahead of the game as most artists today have accepted the position and have turned live tapes into a marketing tool. Some artists sell fans a copy of the show on a USB stick some 15 minutes after the performance, and I have even seen that at a classical concert. In 2018 Duane Eddy appeared at the London Palladium and that concert was recorded and immediately released.

Obviously Dylan has not benefitted financially from the sale of bootlegs but artistically it has been very beneficial. It has set him up as this extraordinary performer who has more songs and recorded performances than he knows what to do with. He has been ambivalent about bootlegs and in 1979 he received a UK High Court undertaking that two bootleggers from Leicester would desist.

By the 1980s the quality of bootlegs had improved considerably and the major manufacturing was done in Germany. There was a Dylan bootleg, *Spanish Boots*, which was pressed in 1984 but then had to wait two years for the bootleggers to get out of jail.

Dylan's show at the Hammersmith Apollo in 1990 was available on cassette for £5 and on VHS for £22. The seller had a 90-page mailing list of other Dylan products.

As far as I know there are no instances of Bob Dylan signing a bootleg, but Johnny Cash has signed bootlegs of his album with Bob. Jerry Lee Lewis is very particular about what he signs: he never signs bootlegs and never anything on Sun Records as he believes they cheated him.

It's hard to tell what Dylan really thinks of bootlegs as there are comments on both sides of the argument. You could argue that Dylan had a bootlegger's mentality as throughout the years he has taken bits and pieces from old songs and books to create his own material.

Michael Gray: 'Dylan hates the trade in bootlegs. At the same time he often encourages it. He knew that *The Basement Tapes* would get out. At one time, the bootlegs were like a subsidiary to his recorded work but in the post-religious period, he released indifferent stuff and held back much better material. 'Blind Willie McTell' is a marvellous blues song with an inventive melody and the lyric running backwards to the slave ships, and yet he didn't release it at the time.'

In 1989 Prince caused a bootlegging sensation with *The Black Album*, which he withdrew just before release but not before a few copies had been distributed.

Around 2010, whenever you went to the cinema or bought a DVD, there would be a public information advertisement asking you not to support illegally obtained films. There were several reasons why you shouldn't do so but the industry only gave one: you would be supporting drug barons. This weakened their case as I don't know of any bootleggers who were using their profits to set up drugs supplies. It didn't really make sense. These were separate entities.

Some of the first bootleg DVDs were comical. Someone had taken a video camera into a preview screening and filmed what was on the screen. If someone walked out of the screening room, then his silhouette would be on the DVD as he crossed the screen. Copying facilities got better and eventually the bootleg was indistinguishable from the real thing: it might even contain that public information ad.

Today the copying of copyright material is sophisticated, but most people do not want physical copies anymore. Once something is officially released, it is streamed and downloaded and the major companies have a continual fight in closing down rogue suppliers. Security has to be tight to prevent the results of recording sessions getting onto the market before release and the outtakes from getting onto the market at all. Whether artists like it or not, their live performances are often on line the next day.

Even though Dylan's voice is faltering and he continues to do 100 shows a year, the demand to hear Dylan's performances hasn't abated.

II. So Much Older Then: August 1966–August 1969

Bob Dylan's accident on 29 July 1966 wasn't the motorpsycho nightmare that some newspapers reported, but it was still bad. He was taken to Middletown hospital, some 60 miles north-east of Woodstock, with cracked vertebra and a fractured neck. He had concussion as he was not wearing a helmet, so from that point of view he was lucky that there was nothing more serious. The papers reported that he had broken his neck: as Robbie Robertson said, 'When someone says "broken neck", you fear the worst.'

It seems likely that Bob took stock of his life: he knew that he would not be fit to start his tour in August and rather than postpone the dates, he preferred to cancel them all.

Did Albert Grossman go along with the pretence that the accident was more serious in order to give Bob more breathing space? That would be out of character as he wanted to make as much money from Dylan as possible, but it was much easier to abandon commitments if the other parties believed he was seriously injured. This might avoid penalties for cancellations.

Bob was to tell Robert Shelton, 'It happened one morning after I had been up for three days.' This is fairly close to admitting drug use and maybe there is an element of rehab in this.

Certainly, his old friends in the Village thought his symptoms were being exaggerated and with a nod to James Dean, David Blue sent Dylan a note, 'It's been done already.'

Bob Dylan had been living a pressure cooker life. Music writer Peter Doggett says, 'Dylan was driven faster and faster until – like the merry-go-round in *Strangers on a Train* – he exploded out of his moorings and collapsed in a mesh of twisted metal.'

At the time, Bob Dylan was winning through: he would never get the diehard folkies back but the later shows indicated that most people were accepting the new Dylan and his new album, *Blonde on Blonde*, despite being more highly priced than single albums, looked as though it was going to be successful. It entered the US Top 40 album chart the first week in August and reached Number 9 during its four-month stay. It climbed to Number 3 in the UK, only *Revolver* and *The Sound of Music* keeping it from the top.

As a single, 'Rainy Day Women Numbers 12 and 35' had got to Number 2 in the US, but 'I Want You' (Number 20) and 'Just like a Woman' (Number 33) were only moderate hits in the US. Considering that 'Just like a Woman' is acknowledged as one of his finest records, it is surprising that it didn't do better.

There is a misconception amongst the general public that Bob Dylan is a recluse but what recluse goes on stadium tours? Oddly enough, these are the only months in his career that Bob Dylan was a recluse and anyway, he was recovering from an accident. Columbia issued a statement that Bob would not be performing before March 1967.

Bob was generous to his musicians. He rang drummer Mickey Jones to say that the world tour was off but he would still be paid. Mickey joined Kenny Rogers and the First Edition and loved their four-part harmonies, playing with them for ten years.

Bob Dylan did not stay in hospital which suggests that his injuries were not severe. He was treated by Dr. Ed Thaler who lived in Middletown, and he may have had Dylan in his home for a couple of weeks. That is certainly unusual behaviour for a doctor and why should Dr. Thaler have done this? What about his other patients? It is plausible, but it is also plausible the physical injuries were not the main problem and this was a cover for rehab.

Possibly if anything was going to turn Bob Dylan's habits around, it would have been the death of Lenny Bruce from a drug overdose on August 3, five days after Bob's accident.

Happy Traum: 'John Herald of the Greenbriar Boys suggested that my wife Jan and I should come to Woodstock and we spent the whole summer there in 1966. We re-established our relationship with Bob. He had become a world-famous guy but now he had decided to be a family man in Woodstock. We had a friendship that lasted for a number of years after that. There were rumours that he would never play again; that he was a vegetable; that he was really dead but nobody wanted to say so. He didn't want to correct it at all. He wasn't talking to the press, but a handful of us knew him, and the photographer Elliot Landy took fabulous photographs in this period. We were privileged to just call him up and go over. There was a local painter that Bob liked to study with and he knew a local carpenter and he got into the local life of Woodstock.'

Some have doubted that Bob Dylan even had an accident and that it was a ruse to get out of commitments. Even his biographer Bob Spitz believes that. 'I think that Sara Dylan saved Bob Dylan's life. When Bob met her, his life was spiralling out of control. He couldn't cope with the fame. It was rushing at him and turning his head around, and nor was he able to cope with the drugs. He was taking handfuls of amphetamines daily and some harder drugs too. If he had not met Sara, he would have self-destructed but Sara was a very intelligent woman who did not take drugs. She demanded that he got off them and that is why they concocted the motorcycle accident. It was really to get Bob out of the public eye.'

Michael Gray: 'He did fall off his motorbike but it was not a serious accident. He wanted to get out of a lot of contracts and so it was blown out of proportion. He had to make a TV movie, write a book and carry out 60 dates. He was in no state to fulfil his obligations and one reason was probably drugs. Pennebaker did film some drug-taking on the 1966 tour. Dylan said, "They didn't help my writing but they did help me to pump it out and get through." There is a line, 'I'd taken the cure' in 'Sara', although songs don't have to be autobiographically accurate.'

Maybe it was getting too much for everyone. On 29 July 1966 Bob Dylan came off his motorcycle. Exactly one month later, after playing Candlestick Park in San Francisco, George Harrison got on the plane and said, 'That's it, I'm not a Beatle anymore.' He remained a Beatle but there would be no more touring. The pressure was immense and it was harder for Dylan as he stood alone as opposed to being one of four.

Unquestionably, whether planned or not, the crash increased the mystique. Dylan's parents had not been given his new telephone number and although they rang Grossman's office, neither Dylan nor Grossman returned their calls. To make matters worse, Abe Dylan had a heart attack. Abe would tell his neighbours that Bob came to Hibbing in his private plane at night and so no one else saw him, but there's no evidence of this visit.

As well as the news reports of his accident, *Saturday Evening Post* published a cover story and interview by Jules Siegel entitled *King of Rock'n'Roll*. While Dylan might have enjoyed the title, he certainly didn't like the text: 'Bob Dylan is the least likely king popular music has ever seen. With a bony, nervous face covered with skin the colour of sour milk, a fright-wig of curly brown hair teased into a bramble of stand-up tangles, and dark-circled hazel eyes usually hidden by large prescription sunglasses, Dylan is less like Elvis or Frankie than like some crippled saint or resurrected Beethoven… Yet, Bob Dylan, at the age of 25, has a million dollars in the bank and earns an estimated several hundred thousand dollars a year from concerts, recordings, and publishing royalties.' Dylan sent an angry message that he was sure would get to Siegel but although you may disagree with its tone, it is a good summary of Dylan.

As Dylan's shows were cancelled, The Band planned to return to Toronto and work out a new repertoire. Robbie and Dominique were staying at the Chelsea Hotel and Dylan invited them to Woodstock so he could work on *Eat the Document*, which was planned for TV. D.A. Pennebaker was also there and he recalled Dylan walking around in a neck brace. The very title of the film implied concealment.

Robbie commented, 'Bob's okay apart from the cast on his neck.' They stayed in a cabin on Grossman's estate. It seems odd that they should be working on this when no one had yet seen *Dont Look Back*, which would have its première in May 1967: it was way too late as Dylan had effectively moved on twice. Another film, *Festival*, directed by Murray Lerner, was released around the same time to cover three years of the Newport Folk Festival including Dylan going electric.

At the time of the accident, Macmillan were taking a draft of *Tarantula* to a book fair in Atlantic City. Some at Macmillan said it could be published anyway but Grossman told him that Dylan had difficulty reading after the accident, which wasn't true. Bob Markel said, 'We have to have integrity and we can wait.'

These though were gentler times and there was not massive security. Barry Cunningham of *New York Times* got into Bob's house as his front door was unlocked. He saw Sara and was then thrown out by a security guard. Nevertheless, he had enough for an article.

Bruce Dorfman was Bob's next-door neighbour and Bruce had a baby girl, about five years old, as did Bob with his adopted daughter Maria. Each day both men would take their daughters to the school bus for Woodstock School and they started chatting. Bruce knew very little about Bob Dylan as he was not interested in popular music, but he was a painter and he invited Bob to his studio. Over the next two or three years, Bruce taught Bob to paint and that became his primary hobby.

Howard Sounes: 'Bruce had this studio in the woods by Bob's house. These were big houses with lots of land between and Bob came up first with his dog. His wife had bought him some paints and an easel for his birthday, and Bruce said, 'What are you interested in painting?', and Bob said, 'I would like to paint like Vermeer' as Bob had a book of his reproductions. He tried and gave up and the next day he had a book of Monet. He was trying something new each day. Finally, he brought in a book of Marc Chagall and his work matched Dylan's songs from that period: rabbits with green faces, old women flying through the sky. Bob painted something based on 'All Along the Watchtower' which he had just recorded. It clicked and he has been painting ever since.'

Mike Bloomfield saw Jimi Hendrix and John Hammond Jr in a house band at Café à Go-Go in Greenwich Village. Bloomfield got to talking with them and Hendrix was asking him about working with Dylan. Dylan had enjoyed seeing how his music worked with rock musicians and Hendrix would be offering something else again.

On 15 September 1966 Andy Warhol's film *Chelsea Girls,* which was set in and around the Chelsea Hotel, was released. It would never have more than a cult following but it wasn't designed for mass acceptance. It lasted four hours and well, it's four hours of my life that I will never get back.

In October 1966 the Beach Boys released 'Good Vibrations'. Like Dylan, this was a vision of the future but this one was sweet and sophisticated. Like Dylan, they had a new sound: they were also amused by Dylan's as they did some parodies on *Beach Boys' Party – Uncovered and Unplugged.*

In November 1966, Judy Collins released her influential album, *In My Life,* which touched so many bases. She says, 'At that point my own background began to gel. On that album was the music from *Marat / Sade,* Kurt Weill's 'Pirate Jenny' and a mixture of theatrical things and surprises. My first Leonard Cohen songs were on that album, 'Suzanne' and 'Dress Rehearsal Rag'. I met him when he was starting to play songs and figuring out if they worked. From then on, I have presented an eclectic mix of music. It's not all one thing, it's not all another. I was trained as a classical pianist and as an interpreter. The songs you choose to sing can be as personal as the songs that you write.'

Leonard Cohen, however, soon had his confidence. In an interview with a Montreal newspaper, he said that pop music would be the future of poetry, and added, 'Dylan's a Picasso – he has an exuberance, a range and an assimilation of the whole history of music.'

Prompted by Bob Dylan, songs were becoming longer. Up to the end of 1966, performers were paid royalties according to the number of songs on an album. The Grateful Dead realised that they would be losing out as they recorded lengthy, spaced-out songs, which were ideal for folks who were high. A new royalty deal was devised for songs that were over three and a half minutes, and the Dead signed with Warner Brothers. The Dead had done everyone who sang long songs a favour.

Albert Grossman had signed Richie Havens, a black folksinger based in Greenwich Village. His debut album, *Mixed Bag,* on the Verve Folkways imprint included 'Just like a Woman'.

Dylan's contract with Columbia expired at the end of 1966 and he was free to go where he pleased. At the start of 1967, the businessman Allen Klein was trying to take control of MGM and he thought the best way was to secure Bob Dylan for the label. The music executive Mort Nasatir visited Dylan to see if he would sign with MGM. He found Dylan in good health, keen to move on and saying he had new songs. Dylan was offered the excellent terms of $1.5m cash and 12% royalties.

MGM announced that they had signed Bob Dylan, which they hadn't, but they did have his former producer Tom Wilson who was now producing Eric Burdon and the Animals. Wilson found them 'Help Me, Girl' which was a hit, and then they turned to psychedelic music.

But we are dealing with alpha males here. Clive Davis who ran Columbia played a bold but dangerous game by showing Allen Klein Bob Dylan's actual sales figures. They were much lower than the public was led to believe. MGM wouldn't be gaining a Beatles. There's no accounting for taste but MGM's Top 40 act, Herman's Hermits, were selling far more than Bob Dylan.

Davis, incidentally, played a completely opposite game when trying to get Harry Chapin on Columbia telling him that it was the label of legends and giving him Dylan and Simon's sales figures, which he had doubled. Nevertheless, Chapin went to Elektra.

Dylan and his lawyers also attended a meeting with Warner but Dylan was so bored that it went nowhere.

As if to ensure that MGM would go away, Clive Davis told Dylan and Grossman that Columbia were still owed 14 tracks under the existing contract, which seems hard to credit as Dylan had been recording at a fast rate. They negotiated a new album with Dylan but it would be ready on Dylan's terms and with an increased royalty to 10% of the retail price. Nice work if you can get it.

For the record, Albert Grossman and Robbie Robertson (and their wives) lived on Tinker Street (a surprisingly good but unused name for a song) and Dylan's property was behind them.

Garth Hudson rented a rambling ranch house for $275 a month known as Big Pink up a mountain road in West Saugerties, which was to the left of Bob Dylan's property. It was so named because it looked like a strawberry milkshake. Rick Danko and Richard Manuel shared the property with him. Quite possibly, Dylan was paying the rent and keeping them on a retainer. He would drive to Big Pink in a Ford station wagon or a blue Mustang. Its basement was a garage with the house on top of it, so the basement recordings are really the Garage Tapes.

Tiny Tim and four of The Band were involved in a hippie movie, *You Are What You Eat*, which was co-produced by Peter Yarrow. They recorded tracks with Tiny Tim, both at Big Pink and at Barry Feinstein's studio, backing him on strangled falsetto versions of 'Be My Baby' and 'I Got You Babe'.

They took Tiny Tim to Bob's house where they discussed crooners like Rudy Vallée. Bob enjoyed hearing Tim sing 'Like a Rolling Stone' in Rudy Vallée's voice and he sang Rudy Vallée's 'My Time is Your Time' as though he were Bob Dylan. Bob Dylan offered him a banana and went to bed. As for *You Are What You Eat*, the film was so bad that it looked like a case against the hippies rather than one for them. Even in this internet world, the film has disappeared – possibly the best solution.

In February 1967 and in the absence of new product, Columbia issued the first Bob Dylan compilation, *Bob Dylan's Greatest Hits*, which was marketing him like a pop star. It was a diverse collection but it did enable the public to purchase his best-known tracks in a single package. It was one of the first albums with a giveaway poster, this one by Milton

Glaser of a black silhouette of Dylan with multi-coloured hair. It was a Top 10 album and sold well for many years. But most people were wondering what Bob Dylan was up to now.

Inspired by 'Rainy Day Women Numbers 12 & 35', Donovan wrote and recorded 'Mellow Yellow', which was arranged by John Cameron and John Paul Jones and produced by Mickie Most. Paul McCartney added backing vocals. They wanted to capture the burlesque of 'Rainy Day Women'.

Today Donovan's record sounds suspect as he sings 'I'm mad about 14' and repeats it as though we didn't get it the first time. Donovan: 'All my fans were four years younger than me. They were honest and they weren't the folk crowd. A lot of the folk crowd were very upset that I was popularising the folk tradition to pop audiences, but I knew what I wanted to do. I wanted to popularise the subjects in the songs that I had heard in the coffee houses. I thought that the wider generation should hear them. I said, "I'm mad about 14", because they were listening honestly to songs. All they had had before was pop lyrics and now they were getting conscious lyrics from the newly emerging folk-rock world, and it was important for them. When I mentioned 'electrical banana' in the song, there was an uproar and it was banned in Boston because they thought it was about abortion. Don't know where they got that from. Then it got round that it was about smoking bananas which I have never tried, but we can't lightly talk about drugs. In those days it was a soft drugs culture; there were junkies and heavy users of hard drugs but they were not encouraged by me. Maybe some soft smoking was encouraged by me, but today the problem is extreme, nobody should try anything. We all smoked grass but those days have gone. It is very different out there now.'

In perhaps the most famous drugs bust of all, Mick Jagger and Keith Richards were arrested on 12 February 1967. They were imprisoned which led to the famous editorial by William Rees-Mogg in *The Times, Who Breaks a Butterfly on a Wheel?*, the title coming from Alexander Pope.

Daniel Kramer had taken photographs of Bob Dylan during his transition from folk singer to rock star. They were very visual as Dylan played with his looks as much as he played with his music. Dylan had posed for many of the photographs but he felt that the book invaded his privacy. His legal plea was rejected and the book was published in March 1967. Bob himself had a new look of short hair, small trimmed beard and rimless glasses

Moses Asch had decided to leave his stock in the folk magazine *Sing Out!* and a new board was constituted in May 1967 including Paul Nelson, Happy Traum and Izzy Young. The existing directors Irwin Sibler and Pete Seeger wanted to take the magazine back to its original concept, that is, to encourage radical songwriting and to promote amateur singing.

The first revamped issue was published in August 1967 and included features on Leonard Cohen, the Newport Folk Festival, war songs and Pat Boone with his views on draft-dodging, 'Wish You Were Here, Buddy'. The changes worked and with better distribution, the circulation soared to 16,000.

Paul Clayton had moved from Folkways to a more commercial label, Monument, where Roy Orbison had had success. Unfortunately he had problems confronting his homosexuality and he was arrested for drug abuse. On 30 March 1967 he took an electric heater into a bath and killed himself.

The so-called *Basement Tapes* started in March 1967, first in Dylan's Red Room but because of the interruptions of family life, they relocated to Big Pink. He would play with Robbie Robertson, Rick Danko, Richard Manuel and Garth Hudson at Big Pink, usually between taking his stepchild Maria to and from school. He would write at the Café Espresso in Tinker Street and would play chess there. Its owner Bernard Paturel was, on occasion, Dylan's chauffeur. No one bothered him and it was a pleasant and idyllic situation for creating music.

Garth Hudson was taping the sessions on an Ampex 602 reel-to-reel recorder, borrowed from Peter Yarrow (remarkable how useful this guy was!). As there are very few half-takes, he only kept the completed ones. Al Aronowitz visited Dylan who explained he was writing ten songs a week. It may not be accurate, as at first they were mostly recording old songs. Indeed, there was a wide selection of American music and many of their recordings were infused with the spirit of Harry Smith.

Hugues Aufray came to Woodstock as Mason Hoffenberg was living there and sharing an apartment with Richard Manuel. Hugues spent a day with Dylan. When Sally Grossman gave him a cigarette, he didn't realise it was grass.

By May, Dylan was enthusiastically back into making music. Even if he was reluctant to tour, Albert Grossman wanted new songs that he could tout to other performers. This amused Dylan. Robbie Robertson, said, 'The mood was never real serious. Bob would say in fun, "OK, that's a great one for the Everly Brothers".'

There could easily have been a strong Dylan album for official release:

Side 1: You Ain't Goin' Nowhere / Tears of Rage / Nothing Was Delivered / I'm Not There / Too Much of Nothing / The Mighty Quinn
Side 2: Goin' To Acapulco / Lo and Behold / Odds and Ends / Down in the Flood / This Wheel's on Fire / I Shall Be Released

In terms of quality there would have been few complaints, but the country was in turmoil, largely because of Vietnam. Bob Dylan, the spokesman of his generation, was not addressing the issues of the day. The songs were moving towards simplicity and were often presenting a cartoonish vision of the world. They were more about community than alienation, which was certainly true of The Band's own songs. The music was also going against the current trend for psychedelia.

In June 1967 the Beatles upped the game with the heavily orchestrated and produced *Sgt. Pepper's Lonely Hearts Club Band*. The sleeve was designed by Britain's leading modern artist, Peter Blake. Among the many faces on the cover, there were just two contemporary musicians, Dion and Bob Dylan as well, incidentally, as Dylan Thomas. Peter Blake says, 'I chose Dion and John Lennon picked Bob Dylan. Looking back I think there must have been a veto on musicians as I know I would have suggested Chuck Berry but I suspect that the Beatles didn't want too much musical competition on there.'

Howard Kaylan of the Turtles: 'On the first night we were in London, Graham Nash played us a tape of *Sgt Pepper* after getting us into the right frame of mind. We were gobsmacked. We had no idea that there was music this powerful on the planet. Within an hour we were in the Speakeasy meeting the lads themselves. That was the most mind-blowing thing of the entire trip. We were talking to the Beatles about a record that wasn't even in the shops yet.'

As for Bob Dylan, he called *Sgt. Pepper* 'self-indulgent'.

June 1967 also marked the release of *The Doors*, their first album and an immediate seller, making an overnight star of Jim Morrison. It was heavy rock with pretentious lyrics and far too much posturing for me. Morrison's influences included Arthur Rimbaud and the Beat writers but the results were very different to Dylan's – and Dylan knew he could never wear leather trousers like Jim Morrison.

This was the Summer of Love but from 5 to 10 June 1967 there was the Six Day War. There was the possibility that Jews who were not living in Israel would be conscripted, though I don't know how this could have worked. Fortunately for Bob, he had family commitments and their second child, Anna Lea, was born on 11 July 1967.

Now that Richard Fariña had died, Joan Baez was touring and sometimes singing with Mimi. They harmonised on 'Catch the Wind' and 'I Am a Poor Wayfaring Stranger'.

The Big Pink sessions ran through until August. It was a simple, straight-forward production with no Beatles' trickery and some of the new songs were improvised. Bob Dylan: 'At the time psychedelic rock was taking over the universe and we were singing these homespun ballads…or whatever they were.'

Sid Griffin: 'When they started the sessions in Dylan's house in Woodstock, the Hawks were still a rootin', tootin' R&B band playing up tempo, highly-caffeinated R&B with Robbie Robertson going up the neck of his guitar. We hear this on their 1966 live record from Manchester. They backed John Hammond Jr on a couple of his records and you hear it there. They are doing that in February 1967 but by September they are no longer the Hawks but mutating into The Band with slow country, soulful versions of 'Tears of Rage', 'Ruben Remus', 'Katy's Been Gone', 'Lonesome Suzie', 'Yazoo Street Scandal' and so much of the stuff on the first Band album. This is where Americana starts. They had changed entirely and Robertson had moved from this fanatic, up tempo, chomping at the bit, Mike Bloomfield R&B guitar to a more laidback, tasteful Nashville country-rock setting. Levon Helm had been playing that style since 1959 but Dylan had an amazing influence on those guys.'

Robbie Robertson: 'We used to get together every day at 1 o'clock in the basement of Big Pink. Dylan wrote a bunch of songs and we wrote a bunch of songs. Bob would be running through an old song and he'd say, "Maybe there's a new song to be had here." 'Silent Weekend', for example, was just a bit of fun, which was even funnier when you've had a joint or two. The tracks were often without drums as Levon was still not with us.' As with several tracks, 'Silent Weekend' is performed like a 50s rocker, but Robbie said, 'If a song is going to live, it must live in a contemporary setting.'

Kim Fowley said, 'If you put two songs together like the Miracles' 'Tracks of My Tears' and Patsy Cline's 'Walkin' after Midnight' and then merge them, you come up with something that has pathos and heartbreak and no one would ever suspect that you got the new song from them. That is what Dylan and The Band did time and time again on the *Basement Tapes*.'

Robbie Robertson described the tapes to Greil Marcus as 'reefer run amok'. There was heavy drinking, especially with Richard Manuel. Dylan gave Richard Manuel his lyric for 'Tears of Rage' and Richard wrote the melody and then made some refinements. Rick Danko was teaching himself piano. Dylan liked a lick he heard and gave him the lyric for 'This Wheel's on Fire'.

There were familiar folk songs like 'Bells of Rhymney' (Pete Seeger) and 'Four Strong Winds' (Ian and Sylvia) and country standards like 'You Win Again' (Hank Williams), 'I Forgot to Remember to Forget' (Elvis Presley) and several songs associated with Johnny Cash – 'Belshazzar', 'Big River' and 'Folsom Prison Blues'.

Sid Griffin: 'Quite a lot of that stuff is like Buddy Holly. They would play a rock'n'roll song and out of that would grow another song. It wouldn't be the same chords or the same subject but it would have the same theme. They did some songs about floods done by the old country and R&B guys because floods were a popular topic back then in the 1920s and 30s. They were playing those things and then came up with a wonderful song, 'Crash on the Levee'. Even Flatt and Scruggs have done that so there was cross-pollination going on.'

Unlike most bands, there wasn't much disagreement. They all respected each other's talents and could contribute whatever was needed to complete the tracks. But, as Barney Hoskyns observed, 'Dylan knew he was too much of a loner for a regular band.' Whatever they had was unlikely to last.

In August 1967, fourteen of the songs were put onto promotional acetates which would be played by music publishers in Britain and America to potential performers. It seems that not all the acetates were the same, perhaps because some were geared for certain performers. There was little security over them and often the original Dylan tracks were played on the radio. Here is what is known of the songs recorded during the basement sessions.

'Ain't Got No Cane' (Traditional) – The Band almost a cappella.

'All American Boy' – A parody of the Bobby Bare hit where being conscripted was seen as an unnecessary chore.

'All You Have to Do Is Dream' – Farming imagery.

'Apple Suckling Tree' – The melody is 'Froggy Went A-Courtin''. When this was officially issued in 1975, Robbie Robertson tidied up the ending.

'Baby Ain't That Fine' (Dallas Frazier) – Originally a duet for Gene Pitney and Melba Montgomery.

'Be Careful of the Stones that You Throw' – Written by Bonnie Dodd, Tex Ritter's guitarist in 1952, and recorded by Hank Williams as Luke the Drifter.

'Belshazzar' – Johnny Cash song mixed with Rufus Thomas' 'Walking the Dog'.

'Bessie Smith' (Rick Danko, Robbie Robertson) – Could only be a Band song and Garth Hudson plays outstandingly. Although this appeared on the official *Basement Tapes* album, it was an outtake from The Band album, *Cahoots* and not a basement tape at all.

'Blowin' in the Wind' – A rare excursion into Dylan's back catalogue and given a gospel-funk arrangement.

'Bonnie Ship the Diamond' – Old Scottish song.

'Bourbon Street' – Rick Danko on trombone.

'Clothes Line Saga' – 'It was the third of June, another sleepy dusty Delta day' – remind you of anything? 'Ode to Billie Joe', which was Number 1 in the US for Bobbie Gentry from Chickasaw County. This was a jokey response.

'Confidential to Me' (Dolinda Morgan) – Originally recorded by Sonny Knight in 1956.

'Crash on the Levee' (aka 'Down in the Flood') – The 'sugar for sugar' line is taken from 'James Allen Blues' by Richard 'Rabbit' Brown (1927). The new song was given to the bluegrass duo, Flatt and Scruggs.

'Don't Ya Tell Henry' – Excellent Levon Helm vocal.

'Down in the Flood'– See 'Crash on the Levee'.

'Down on Me' – Cover of an Elmore James record.

'Edge of the Ocean' – Dylan ballad.

'Ferdinand'

'Folsom Prison Blues' – How Dylan might have performed it on the 1966 tour.

'A Fool Such As I' – Associated with Hank Snow and then Elvis Presley.

'The French Girl' – Ian and Sylvia had released this in 1966. The theme of love with a language barrier is very Canadian.

'Get Your Rocks Off' – Plenty of innuendo on these tapes and Dylan is full of laughter.

'Goin' to Acapulco' – Slow tempo song about crossing the border for the whores. It may be a dirge and possibly a song for a funeral but they're having fun. Jim James and Calexico did this song in the film *I'm Not There* very well.

'Gonna Get You Now'

'The Hills of Mexico'

'I'm All Right'

'I'm Not There (1956)' – Brilliant song but not used until the film of the same title in 2007. Dylan is low-key and mumbling. This song developed into 'Going Going Gone' but the original is very powerful. Dylan said, "I'm Not There' is a song that's not there.'

'I Can't Make It Alone' – R&B ballad.

'In The Pines' – Levon Helm: 'We would try and come up with harmony blends that we could put behind Bob's voice – we certainly weren't Crosby, Stills and Nash.'

'I Shall Be Released' – Influenced by Curtis Mayfield's work for the Impressions, 'I Shall Be Released' was intended for *John Wesley Harding* but dropped. Striking falsetto harmony from Richard Manuel on *Basement Tapes*. It would have been perfect for *John Wesley Harding* as it is hymn-like with its spiritual message. It has become the most covered *Basement* song and is an anthem for Amnesty International. It is the go-to song for protesting about wrongful arrest. Both the Beatles and Elvis Presley have sung snatches of it and Van Morrison turned 'I Shall Be Released' into 'Brand New Day'. David Crosby wrote 'I shall be released' on his prison wall. The title could refer to the Basement Tapes themselves.

'I Was Young but Daily Growing' – Dylan had sung this at his first solo concert in 1961.

'Johnny Todd' (aka 'Theme from Z-Cars') – Did Bob pick this up when he was first in London?

'Joshua Gone Barbados' (Eric Von Schmidt) – Dylan: 'That's enough. It's a very long song.'

'Katie's Been Gone' (Robbie Robertson, Richard Manuel)

'King of France' – Odd and incomplete.

'Lo and Behold' – Similar delivery to 'Million Dollar Bash'. Would have suited Johnny Cash.

'Lock Your Door'

'Long Distance Operator'

'The Mighty Quinn' – It possibly relates to the Eugene O'Neill play *The Iceman Cometh* (1946), which is about death (the iceman coming!), especially as the play was based around a bar that O'Neill knew in Greenwich Village. And/or it could refer to *The Savage Innocents* (1960), a film featuring Anthony Quinn among the Eskimos. Then there is Samuel Beckett's classic play about *Waiting for Godot* but Godot never comes: had Dylan got this in mind?

Could it be about Roger McGuinn? Could the reference to pigeons relate to the other Byrds? This is nonsense but it is easy to devise these explanations. Again, when Quinn gets there, you will either want to jump or doze, so is it about drugs? The song was a UK Number 1 for Manfred Mann and Dylan was surprised it was a hit. 'I don't know what it's about. It's some kind of nursery rhyme.'

Pete Townshend: 'To me 'The Mighty Quinn' is about the five Perfect Masters of the Age, the best of all being Mehar Baba. To Dylan, it's probably about gardening or the joys of placing dog shit in the garbage. Maybe his silence is a good idea. Maybe if he told you what it means, you would think he was taking himself too seriously.'

Manfred Mann has another take: 'The Eskimos are the only people who haven't waged war on each other or others. The song is like a modern painting which can mean so many things.' Whatever, Bob Dylan was happy with their version as Manfred says, 'It is very satisfying to hear Dylan saying that we did his songs better than anybody else.'

German rock writer Bernd Matheja: 'An Englishman who worked with Casey Jones and the Governors, Dave Coleman, left the group and worked as a Schlager singer and he did a song in German called 'Alaska Quinn' and it was Bob Dylan's 'Mighty Quinn'. The German translation is about a park you can have fun in and there is somebody running around clad like an Eskimo. If Dylan had heard a re-translation, I think he would have killed them!'

'Million Dollar Bash' – Jokey country blues, not far removed from 'Memphis Blues Again', and Dylan is parodying himself.

'Minstrel Boy'

'My Bucket's Got a Hole in It' – Rock'n'roll started with Hank Williams.

'Nothing Was Delivered' – A new song but like an R&B ballad from the early 1950s.

'Odds'n'Ends' – Both Buddy Hollyish and Beatleish, so what's not to like? Some of the basement tracks are rough but this could pass for a studio recording.

'Ol' Roisin the Beau' – A gypsy sound anticipating *Desire.*

'One for the Road' – Drunken waltz, not the Sinatra song.

'One Man's Loss' – Sample lyric: 'One man's joy is another man's pain'.

'One Single River' (Ian and Sylvia Tyson) – Sometimes known as 'Song for Canada'.

'Open the Door, Homer' – The original title was 'Open the Door, Richard' and surely they should have kept that as Richard Manuel was around. It's a Dylan song, very much in The Band's style.

'Ruben Remus' (Robbie Robertson, Richard Manuel)

'Santa Fe'

'See That My Grave Is Kept Clean' – Robbie Robertson on autoharp, Levon Helm on harmonica and Dylan singing in his *Nashville Skyline* voice.

'See You Later Allen Ginsberg' – Bill Haley meets the Beats. Robbie: 'Nobody was supposed to hear that.'

'Sign on the Cross' – Christianity causing anxiety – 'That old sign on the cross still worries me.'

'Spanish is the Loving Tongue' – Dylan probably heard Ian and Sylvia do this.

'Tears of Rage' (Dylan, Manuel) – It's about how people come to terms with childhood problems. Barbara Dickson: "Tears of Rage' was a great song. It had such a great sentiment and I liked what he was saying.'

'This Wheel's on Fire' (Bob Dylan, Rick Danko) – Could the title refer to Bob Dylan's accident? Dylan had the lyric and he worked on the melody with Rick Danko. Robbie Robertson played drums and it was taken up by The Band for their first album. Tony Visconti's former wife Siegrid cut it for a single and wrote a cryptic message to Dylan for the B-side, but it was never released.

Brian Auger: '*The Basement Tapes* were sent to London and were distributed to several different managers. 'This Wheel's on Fire' suited our style of playing and it had a very moody, psychedelic lyric. It was Bob and a walking jazz bass line. Julie Driscoll said that she would love to sing it but I didn't know how we were going to do it as a pop thing. I tried a rock beat and then a funk beat but neither worked. I decided to leave it as it was and have a marching rhythm. I laid down the piano with bass and drums and then overdubbed organ and strings. We had a phaser for a swirling sound, which was very out there for the time. Julie put a tremendous vocal on it and it was very atmospheric. I thought of it as an album track but I was happy to be proved wrong.'

Julie Driscoll had a distinctive Joan of Arc look and became the Face of '68. Julie Driscoll: 'I cut my hair on a whim because I got fed up with it, it was getting in the way and it looked untidy. I kept it short because it was so easy to maintain. If I hadn't liked the look of it, I would have let it grow immediately. As time went on, I realised that I was making some sort of impact but I had to stop this silly thing of covering my face with make-up. Fourteen year olds would come to me and say, "We want our eyes like your eyes", and I felt a responsibility and I thought I would stop it. It was just a mask for me to get through my commitments. It was only a surface thing, but when it became the important thing, it was time to knock it on the head.'

'Tiny Montgomery' – Inspired by 'Big Bad John'.

'Too Much of Nothing' – A fairly tuneless take was used on *The Basement Tapes* when there were better ones. Peter, Paul and Mary did it very slickly and then Ian and Sylvia, both managed by Grossman. It was the first *Basement* song to be recorded; which was fair enough as they were using Peter Yarrow's equipment. UK cover in 1968 from Spooky Tooth.

'Try Me Little Girl'

'Waltzing with Sin' – Hank Wangford: 'This is a wonderfully dark apocalyptic song, rather like "I Didn't Know God Made Honky Tonk Angels", being sung by a really bitter man whose woman has turned him over and broken his heart. He is going to get back at her.'

'Wild Wolf'

'Yazoo Street Scandal' (Robbie Robertson) – The Band with a Levon Helm vocal.

'Yea! Heavy and a Bottle of Bread' – Not a song many would want to cover: 'nose full of pus'.

'You Ain't Goin' Nowhere' – There are various versions of this: the first one has 'You ain't no head of lettuce' and another refers to feeding the cat.

'You Say You Love Me'

A friend of Richard Manuel, Eric Clapton went to Big Pink and met Bob with Van Morrison. Clapton jammed with The Band and loved them. Bob Dylan gave him a lyric, 'Standing around Shoeing a Horse', but Clapton lost it on tour.

In 2014 *The Basement Tapes Complete: The Bootleg Series Vol 11* was issued, the deluxe edition featuring 6CDs, put together by Garth Hudson. Thirty of the 140 tracks had never even been mentioned before. We never know what else will turn up but so far as is known, Columbia have now released everything they have which is salvageable.

Around the same time, a batch of lyrics that Dylan had tucked away and ignored were discovered – initially sixteen and then a further eight. Dylan had written the lyrics in 1967 but had done nothing with them. He could have written the music and released them for his next album but he decided to pass them over. He gave them to T Bone Burnett and told him that he could distribute them as he thought fit. Burnett liked the lyrics very much and assembled a group of musicians who would work through them. There was Elvis Costello (of course), Rhiannon Giddens (Carolina Chocolate Drops), Jim James (My Morning

Jacket), Taylor Goldsmith (Dawes) and Marcus Mumford. The idea was that they would be gathered in a *Big Brother* fashion where they would work on the songs, individually and collectively, and then record them for an album, *The New Basement Tapes – Lost on the River*. There would be a TV special about the project. Dylan didn't have to approve the results and the writers were free to amend his words if thought fit.

As a back-up, Jim James and Elvis Costello worked on some of the lyrics in advance, but much of the album was improvised. Apparently, 44 songs were recorded in 12 days in 2014 so there could be a second album. The album included 20 tracks but only 18 songs as you could take your pick on the title track as to whether you preferred Elvis Costello's melody or Rhiannon Giddens and Marcus Mumford's. Similarly there were two versions of 'Hidee Hidee Ho', the title line coming from 'Minnie the Moocher' but also a nod to his home, 'Hi Lo Ha'.

The best tracks are the rather spooky 'When I Get My Hands on You', sung by Marcus Mumford and the ultra-quirky 'Married to My Hack', sung by Elvis Costello. Rhiannon Giddens treats 'Spanish Mary' and the fiery 'Duncan and Jimmy' like an old folk tune. Marcus Mumford asks 'How long can I keep singing this same old song?' in 'Kansas City', a track with Johnny Depp on electric guitar.

Many people have been sceptical about this project as the obvious question is 'Why didn't Dylan do anything with these lyrics at the time?' That is a valid question as these songs could have improved *Self-Portrait* and it does demonstrate that Dylan was certainly not short of his own material.

On 21 August 1967, Bob Dylan signed a new deal with Columbia for a 10% royalty on each record sold, although of course these deals are never as simple as they sound because offcuts, promo copies and returns are taken into account.

Albert Grossman saw Stanley Gortikov at Capitol who offered Dylan's musicians a contract, subject to hearing them. It was October 1967 and at the time they were calling themselves Crackers. Once they got this news, they knew that they had to have Levon Helm back.

Rick Danko: 'When Capitol gave us a record contract. I got in touch with Levon. He was working on a boat in New Orleans. I told him what the deal was and in traditional Levon fashion he said, "Well, the contract sucks, but I'll be on the next plane".'

Levon would say that but the advance for the album was $50,000. He didn't like the idea of being in Woodstock – he was a southern boy through and through, but as it happened, he liked Woodstock immediately and thought it had much in common with other places he knew. Because both Dylan and The Band had new projects, the sessions that produced the Basement Tapes finally wound up after a couple of sessions with Levon.

The Band had this extraordinary, old-time pioneer look. Levon Helm said, 'We didn't want to have anything to do with that psychedelic stuff. We thought it was all bullshit.'

Happy Traum: 'Bob had gotten the Band to come up to Woodstock and they were recording at Big Pink. They looked great; they looked like they had come straight out of the old west. Before that, they had been rock'n'roll guys touring with Ronnie Hawkins. Mostly I was friendly with Levon Helm and Rick Danko, whom I played with frequently and was a lot of fun. I did go to Big Pink a couple of times, not while they were recording but just sitting around and that was fun too.'

In September 1967 Bob Dylan had rewritten 'Baby Let Me Follow You Down' for Carly Simon who was now working on her own. She recorded it but felt it was in the wrong key and blamed the producer. She was going to be managed by Albert Grossman but she turned him down after he came on to her. In her autobiography, Carly described how she and her sister set out to seduce Sean Connery.

In September 1967 the Hawks went to New York to cut their own demos for Capitol and while they were away, Dylan was completing new songs – 'Tears of Rage,' 'The Mighty Quinn', 'Nothing Was Delivered' and 'Odds and Ends'. They were recorded with Dylan when they returned.

Bob Johnston visited Bob Dylan regarding his next album. After producing *Blonde on Blonde*, he had made an instrumental album *Mouldy Goldies* by Col. Jubilation B. Johnston and his Mystic Knights Band and Street Singers, playing hits like 'Rainy Day Women, Numbers 12 and 35' with several of the *Blonde on Blonde* musicians. It was a self-indulgent romp and didn't sell.

Brian Epstein died at the end of August. He was planning to work with the singer / songwriter Eric Andersen: 'I knew that everybody in the folk world would hate me for having anything to do with Brian Epstein, and the only person I told was John Denver. I was going to keep it quiet until Brian made an announcement. He died when I was at the Philadelphia Folk Festival. The guy who ran the festival got on stage and said, "I have good news for everybody – Brian Epstein has died." The implication was that he had never done anything for folk music and that the Beatles had done nothing for folk music, and this is the day that I hated folk music. I rued the day that anybody called me a folk singer as they were so narrow-minded, so self-righteous and so bigoted. I had to play that night and I felt like walking off into the woods.'

The Greenwich Village folkies had been horrified by Dylan at first, and although Phil Ochs supported Dylan's right to do what he liked, he didn't follow suit at first. By 1967 he knew he'd have to change. He moved to Los Angeles and made his first album for A&M, *Pleasures of the Harbour* which combined personal poetry with a fuller sound. The arrangements by the experimental musician Joseph Byrd sometimes put the songs into settings that were not wholly appropriate.

In October 1967 *Disc* published this letter; 'Can you please, for the sake of my sanity, tell me what is happening in the world of Bob Dylan? Is he ill, well or in jail? (Elaine Batten, Whitmore near Leeds).' It's an indication of how slowly news travelled back then: very few people knew what was going on.

Woody Guthrie died on 3 October 1967. Arlo Guthrie: 'My dad did hear *Alice's Restaurant* some weeks before he died. My dad died in October 1967 and the record came out in late August.' Hopefully, he could recognise that his legacy would be safe with Arlo.

Sid Griffin: 'Bob Dylan was doing no live concerts at the time: he wanted to be with his wife and family. Dylan had become uneasy with people staring at him as he walked down the street. He was off the road and he wanted to live in an idyllic rural retreat. Chip Carter, the son of Jimmy Carter, was such a Dylan fanatic that he went there to shake his hand. In January 1968 he did a live gig but it was only because his great mentor Woody Guthrie had died. He called up Harold Leventhal and said that he would do the tribute. He played very well with the Hawks backing him up but he didn't do a regular live tour for years.'

In November 1967 Albert Grossman brought some of the *Basement Tapes* to the UK and several acts recorded the songs. Marianne Faithfull had a copy which she loved and this in turn influenced Mick Jagger – just listen to 'Dear Doctor' from *Beggars Banquet*, but the whole Rolling Stones album has the feel of the *Basement Tapes*.

Allen Ginsburg had invited the Indian musicians, the Bengali Bauls, to America and Grossman put them up in one of his cabins. They recorded an album, the sweet and gentle *Bengali Bauls at Big Pink*, which was released by Buddah in 1968. Bob Dylan would be photographed with two of them alongside Grossman's gardener, Charlie Joy, for the cover of his next album, *John Wesley Harding*. It is said that there were photographs of the Beatles in the tree bark; a nod to *Sgt. Pepper*. Dylan had a beard on his chin and his jaw, rather like Abraham Lincoln. The cover was a $1 Polaroid photo, a little different from the lavishness of the *Sgt. Pepper* sleeve.

Dylan had liked the way that the Nashville musicians had played on *The Way I Feel* by Gordon Lightfoot so he returned to Music Row for his next album on October 17 and 18. Gordon Lightfoot had used Charlie McCoy (bass) and Kenny Buttrey (drums) and that would be enough for him, except he added Pete Drake on steel guitar for 'Down along the Cove' and 'I'll Be Your Baby Tonight'. Unlike *Blonde on Blonde*, Dylan had come to Nashville with his songs prepared, in most cases writing the lyrics before the melodies. The new songs did not have choruses so are in line with traditional ballads and folk songs. Only 'I'll Be Your Baby Tonight' had a bridge. The songs were unadorned, austere and much calmer than the ones on *Blonde on Blonde*. For the first time Dylan was conforming to a standard LP of three-minute songs with six on each side.

However, unlike Gordon Lightfoot, Bob Dylan was not playing a 12-string guitar. That Lightfoot album produced by John Court included 'Song for a Winter's Night' and 'Crossroads', which would have sounded right on *John Wesley Harding*. Gordon Lightfoot: 'I was working as a single performer for a long time and I was using the 12-string just to get the variety and you can get an extra sound out of a 12-string. I started doing it around 1964 – Roger McGuinn might have been playing it all his life for all I know. He's a very good guitar-player and it gives you a very distinctive sound. When Bob Dylan was recording *John Wesley Harding*, he did say he was trying to get a Gordon Lightfoot sound.'

Sid Griffin: 'It is extraordinary. Why is there no cross pollination between *John Wesley Harding* and *The Basement Tapes*? Dylan is working on both projects at the same time but at no time does The Band tackle 'All Along the Watchtower' and at no time do the boys in Nashville perform 'This Wheel's on Fire' or 'You Ain't Goin' Nowhere', which would have made sense with the type of production on *John Wesley Harding*.'

Sid Griffin is both right and wrong. There is no direct crossover of songs but the themes are similar: the Old Testament and the old west, songs about oddballs and drifters, misery and suffering, and a lost America. Possibly it stemmed from Dylan having a Bible on a lectern in his home and a book of Hank Williams' lyrics. Most of the songs were quiet, serious and modest: Dylan was not playing word games and was moving towards country music. Dylan said in 1985, 'Maybe it was better than I thought', which suggested that he had been wary about it: he shouldn't have been. It is very different from his previous album, *Blonde on Blonde*, but isn't that Dylan just being Dylan?

Perhaps not deliberately, *John Wesley Harding* offered a commentary on myths and legends. It wasn't a concept album but it did sound like a collection of songs which belonged together. It is odd that Dylan didn't use The Band but it might have confused things as their solo album was coming out.

Dylan played the results to Robbie and Garth and asked whether The Band should enhance some of the music. They said it sounded fine the way it was.

Dylan had never played so much harmonica. This is a plus as it gives the songs a lonesome feel without much effort. It was recorded well but some popping of the p's had to be taken out of 'The Ballad of Frankie Lee and Judas Priest' which led to the bass being taken out by the compression: this added to the mellow sound. Dylan's voice is smoother than before and ironically, this is the first Bob Dylan album that could be used as background music.

The title song was a tribute to a gunslinger with a great name, John Wesley Hardin – for once, Bob Dylan was adding a 'g'. Hardin was one of Tim Hardin's ancestors and he was the son of a minister, hence the Christian names, born in 1853. He was jailed in 1877 for around 25 killings. He wrote his autobiography in prison. He received a pardon in 1893 but returned to his old ways and was killed in a gunfight in El Paso in 1895. In short, a nasty piece of work.

Not that you get that from the song. Bob Dylan turns him into a Robin Hood figure and he must have known that this was wrong. He would have known Johnny Cash's song, 'Hardin Wouldn't Run' (1965). Nevertheless, the song contains some great lines – such as 'He was never known to make a foolish move' – but is there such a term as a milk-white steed and when he says Hardin had a gun in every hand, just how many hands did he have?

The transformation of John Wesley Harding is wrong but Americans often like to glamorise the west. Dylan however was doing it at a time when the folk singers were concentrating on the massacre and resettlement of Native Americans. In a couple of years' time, you can see Dylan continuing his western theme with 'Knockin' on Heaven's Door'.

Tom Russell, who lives in El Paso, says, 'John Wesley Hardin is in a graveyard in downtown El Paso, and he worked a while as a lawyer but he wasn't a very good one. I love the western songs like 'Jesse James' and 'Sam Bass' as they are so well written and very much in the folk tradition and Mexican corrido, which means a long story. The Mexicans have a very deep tradition of story-songs which I am picking up on more and more. I enjoy having a plot and creditable characters who have lived through something.'

Laurie Lee's memoir *As I Walked out One Midsummer Morning* is sometimes cited as the source for 'As I Walked out One Morning', but Lee's book didn't appear until 1969. Possibly they are both quoting from a similar source and that is W.H. Auden's 1937 poem, 'As I Walked out One Evening'. Once again Dylan is referring to the abolitionist Tom Paine, although in this song, he appears to be owning a slave.

'I Dreamed I Saw St. Augustine' is not a dream at all but a rewrite of a union song, 'I Dreamed I Saw Joe Hill'. Joe Hill was executed in 1915 and the song was written in 1936, and Dylan probably heard it by Pete Seeger or Joan Baez. 'That song speaks for the workers,' says Joan, 'and whenever a song is really popular, there is usually something of genius in the writing of it. I love the way that Dylan adopted it for St. Augustine.' Maybe but St. Augustine was not martyred: he died peacefully as a bishop.

A song of fear and betrayal, the idea for 'All along the Watchtower' came to Bob Dylan in a storm. The title was probably inspired by Jimmie Rodgers' All around the Watertank'. Contrast it with the empathy of 'I Pity the Poor Immigrant'.

Eric Bogle: 'I would pick "All along the Watchtower" as my favourite Dylan song. I like everything about it. You can interpret it in about three or four different ways, and each one would be valid. I am incapable of writing on that level. If I try and be mysterious, I just become obscure. (Laughs) He is a master craftsman and even if he was unsure of what he was saying himself, it doesn't make the song any less valid. His songs are like modern paintings. You get out of them what you see in them. I'm more of a black and white songwriter. Anybody who misinterprets my songs tends to do it deliberately.'

Bob Dylan had met Jimi Hendrix and seen him in the Village. Hendrix was taken by Dylan and performed several of his songs, 'All around the Watchtower' being the classic. Dave Mason from Traffic played on Hendrix's version: 'I was in the Speakeasy one night and I started talking to him. He was a fan of Traffic so we stuck up a relationship and I spent some good times with him. I finished up in the studio with him and I sang on 'Crosstown Traffic' and played acoustic guitar on 'All Along the Watchtower'. We both heard *John Wesley Harding* at the same time. He had an idea about what he wanted to do and I knew his tempo. There is only me, Hendrix and Mitch Mitchell on that – Jimi plays the bass on that too. He was very innovative: there have been a lot of great guitar players but there are no more Jimi Hendrixes.'

Bob Dylan's is the black and white original, Hendrix's the full, giant screen, Technicolor treatment. Jimi's is the one that begins to howl. He plays three great guitar breaks – blues (slide guitar), rock (wah-wah) and R&B (treble with top three strings). As a result Dylan started playing 'All Along the Watchtower' like Hendrix and sometimes gave 'Masters of War' the Hendrix treatment too.

Jimi Hendrix's version was a big single in September 1968. Toyah: 'I love 'All along The Watchtower' most of all of Dylan's songs, especially in Hendrix's version. It was so very soulful and so very modern. Lovely. I've never really listened to the lyric as I'm so honed in on Hendrix's playing.' The best of the Dylan fanzines, *The Telegraph*, took its name from the song's title.

'The Ballad of Frankie Lee and Judas Priest' is a frontier ballad with references to the west and the Bible. Judas is taking someone (possibly Jesus) to a whorehouse and the song demonstrated that no good will come of being in the wrong place. Was the Judas prompted by his own experiences in 1966 and indeed could Judas Priest be Albert Grossman? Within a few months, the Beatles would release 'Rocky Raccoon', which went for a similar effect but McCartney was overdoing the humour.

'Drifter's Escape' has neat flamenco touches and as the song is about being tried for no offence; it could be related to Franz Kafka's novel, *The Trial*, or Lewis Carroll's *Alice's Adventures in Wonderland* where Alice tells her accusers, 'You're nothing but a pack of cards!'

'Dear Landlord' is Bob on a barroom piano and sounding good. Dylan said he woke up with 'Dear Landlord' on his mind and the song wrote itself. At the time, Dylan owed things to Columbia, Macmillan and the TV channel, ABC, so it could be about that. Grossman is a strong possibility as he had said it was one of the few Dylan songs that he didn't like, but if Dylan felt this strongly about Grossman, why didn't he warn The Band?

Cross the Rolling Stones with a folk song and you could have 'I Am a Lonesome Hobo'. Listen to the Triffids' cover from 1983 and you will see what I mean.

The tune of 'I Pity the Poor Immigrant' is 'Come All Ye Tramps and Hawkers' and Dylan may have heard the Dubliners' version from 1964 or the rewrite about a lumberjack, 'Peter Amberley', recorded by Bonnie Dobson.

'The Wicked Messenger' is about the role of the messenger and possibly the singer's duty to tell the truth. It could be Dylan talking about his protest years but when asked about this by Paul Krassner, he responded, 'No, it is about stupid Jews I have known, the really stupid ones.'

'I'll Be Your Baby Tonight' was a straight, simple country song and indeed Hank Williams sang of mockingbirds too. Bob Johnston said, 'I just loved 'I'll Be Your Baby Tonight'. He mentioned going in on a steel guitar and so I brought in Pete Drake. I loved the song. I think it's beautiful.'

Tony Crane of the Merseybeats: 'Dylan's most commercial song is 'I'll Be Your Baby Tonight' and I am surprised that it hasn't been Number 1 for somebody. It is really early country and it could have been recorded by somebody in the 1950s.' Though possibly not with the innuendo. When I told Maria Muldaur that her version sounded sexy, she said, 'Well, thank you. If you are going to say "I'll be your baby tonight", you might as well sound sexy.'

Chris Simpson from Magna Carta: 'Dylan was pandering to the fact that he was an enigma and everybody expected him to be a little strange. You know, what is 'Can You Please Crawl out Your Window' about? The richness of Bob Dylan's imagery can be exquisite, but I love 'Lay Lady Lay' and 'I'll Be Your Baby Tonight' which have nothing strange about them.' Indeed, 'The big fat moon is gonna shine like a spoon' is deliberately corny.

The final two tracks, 'Down along the Cove' and 'I'll Be Your Baby Tonight', preview Bob Dylan's next album, *Nashville Skyline*. There's not much to say about 'Down along the Cove': it's a cheerful country song that could have been knocked off any afternoon during the Basement sessions.

The record was not released in the US for Christmas but on 27 December 1967, a strange release date, especially for a comeback. However, there was another notable album issued by Columbia on the same day. The first album by Leonard Cohen, *Songs of Leonard Cohen*. It was the first time we had heard that hypnotic, off-beat voice.

Gretchen Peters: 'I think the thing that intrigued me about Leonard Cohen's songs were the things he didn't say, all those layers of mystery and things that were implied but not really stated. I aspired to write like that, although living in Nashville, it was the opposite approach that was knocked into your head. You have to tell the story and it has to be linear and very clear, and I got a healthy dose of both. I aspire to write songs that have a layer of ambiguity about them. In Nashville, I would have been out of a job if I had written 'your warehouse eyes, my Arabian drums', but the songs that have that mystery about them last and develop layers that you didn't know were there. I can still listen to 'Famous Blue Raincoat' and have new thoughts about it.'

The release date may have been Dylan's own doing as he had stipulated no advance publicity for his album. It was released when there was public hostility to what President Johnson was doing in Vietnam by escalating the 'conflict'. The US authorities never called Vietnam a war, although it obviously was.

The reviews were good for *John Wesley Harding* if a little odd. Jon Landau in *Rolling Stone* said, 'Bob Dylan manifests a profound awareness of the war and how it is affecting all of us.' There was a sleeve note from Bob Dylan in which three critics are arguing over his new record and it suggests that Dylan had come across Spike Milligan.

John Wesley Harding reached Number 2 on the US album charts. In the UK, it was on top for ten weeks straight and then a further three. There was no UK single from the album. The song, 'John Wesley Harding', was up for a Grammy as Best Folk Performance but lost out to Judy Collins' 'Both Sides Now', but did Dylan even like being in this category?

When the journalist Hubert Saal spoke to Dylan in Woodstock, he said, 'I am sure I will give concerts again. If you take a show on the road, you might as well be out there for six or eight months and the test is if it will hold my interest for that long. Right now, it couldn't. It's hard out there. One plane to another, bad food, motel rooms, they herd you around. Europe is even worse. They have no heat. You have to sleep with hot water bottles to keep warm.'

Commenting on *Tarantula,* he said, 'I'd been so embarrassed at the nonsense I'd written that I want to change whole thing. And all the time they had 100,000 orders.'

On 20 January 1968 Bob Dylan and The Band took part in the Woody Guthrie Memorial Concert at Carnegie Hall. There was a second concert in Los Angeles in the autumn which did not involve Dylan.

Odetta: 'The folk musicians were very supportive; we were all tuning our guitars together. When we did that concert, Bob Dylan was a part of the family again. A family can be dysfunctional too! He came to serve Woody Guthrie, the same as we all had. We did it like a hootenanny. We sat in a circle and each stood up when it was our turn. We all participated.'

Except for Ramblin' Jack Elliott who found himself excluded. I'd read that he threatened to busk outside the concert. 'I'd driven all the way from California to be on the concert. I called up to say I was on my way and Harold Leventhal said, "Didn't you get our letter? We're going to put you on the one in Hollywood." I was living with Woody years before we ran into Harold. I was singing with Woody and I was the only one in that whole shebang that had sung with Woody, apart from Pete Seeger who had known him longer than me. There were quite a few who never even saw Woody and I felt that I should have been at that concert. I don't remember talking about busking but that would have been a cute thing to do. (Laughs).'

Judy Collins: 'That was an extraordinary event. I read a poem on that concert and I did 'Union Maid' with Pete Seeger. I was in on it from the beginning. Harold was my manager and so I could pick 'Roll on Columbia'.'

There was both an afternoon and an evening concert at Carnegie Hall. There was a huge media buzz because it was Dylan's first public appearance for 20 months. This was also the first major outing for Sara Dylan. She was never cold or rude but she rarely attended his music shows. She always looked great with her deep, large eyes but she was often ill at ease.

Dylan performed three songs – 'I Ain't Got No Home', the little heard 'Dear Mrs. Roosevelt' and 'The Grand Coulee Dam', which had been a 1950s UK hit for Lonnie Donegan. They are good versions but not very exciting as though Dylan did not want to offend anyone when Woody was the star of the show. His version of 'Dear Mrs. Roosevelt' was so Woody that any dissenters were won over. After the show, Dylan briefly attended a party at the actor Robert Ryan's apartment in the Dakota.

On 4 February 1968 Graham Nash left the Hollies: 'They wanted to make an album of Dylan tunes. I thought that was sacrilege because we were doing them like Las Vegas.'

Musicians were starting to go to Nashville. Buffy Sainte-Marie made the album, *I'm Gonna Be a Country Girl,* in 1968. She recalled, 'It was the middle of the winter and Chet Atkins called my record company and said, "Send Buffy down and we will make some music." At the time I believed that Chet Atkins had six fingers on each hand as he was so good. He was very nice to me and he introduced me to some songwriters – Kris Kristofferson who was just starting off, Mickey Newbury and Boudleaux Bryant, which was a treat for me. The first album that I made in Nashville was with Grady Martin playing guitar and Floyd Cramer piano. They were the big boys in country music. Chet Atkins had invited all his best musician friends to come into the session and see what we got.' Also the bass player Norbert Putnam became her partner.

During the second week in March 1968, the Byrds, encouraged by their new recruit Gram Parsons, recorded at the Columbia studio on Music Row. They made the classic country-rock album, *Sweetheart of the Rodeo*, released in September 1968 and produced by Gary Usher. When the Byrds were cutting Bob Dylan's 'You Ain't Goin' Nowhere', they asked Lloyd Green to join them on steel. 'How do you want me to approach it?' said Lloyd. They replied, 'Play everywhere!'

Roger McGuinn: 'We didn't think about what would happen if we did a country album when we did *Sweetheart of the Rodeo*. We loved the music so much that we wanted to do the best job that we could possibly do on it. We had the sincerest of intentions, we wanted to record this wonderful music and we were hoping that the people would like it just as much as we did. It turns out that they do, but it took about 30 years for it to catch on. (Laughs)'

On 15 March 1968 the Byrds were on the *Grand Ole Opry*. It turned out to be their Judas moment! The *Opry* audience was not ready for long-haired rockers and gave them a hard time despite the fact that they were doing a beautiful new song from Gram Parsons, 'Hickory Wind'. Soon Gram Parsons was to leave the Byrds on the verge of going to South Africa, citing political reasons but really because he wanted to spend time with the Rolling Stones.

Joan Baez married anti-war activist David Harris. They had a son Gabriel in 1969. Joan had been in jail twice for being on protests and was marrying a draft resistance leader.

On the other hand, Bob Dylan had to deal with family problems. Abe Zimmermann was disturbed that his second son David was planning to marry a Catholic girl, Gale Jurenes. The wedding was set for June but postponed because of Abe's health. Then on 5 June 1968 Abe had a fatal heart attack. Bob flew to Hibbing for the funeral on June 7. He was uncomfortable afterwards with so many people being around him but Beatty said it was the mourning tradition. Abe was buried in Duluth. On June 11, Bob was back in New York. David later married Gale.

Life goes on. Samuel Abram Dylan was born on July 30 in New York. Bob and Sara were now raising four children.

Later in the year Beatty decided to sell the 2425 house. The beige stucco house had been built in the early 1940s and had three bedrooms and two bathrooms. Bob wanted it to go to a young couple. He said that he would make up the price difference and an ad went in *Rolling Stone*. It was bought by a first-time buyer Angel Marolt for $22,000. In 1969 and completely out of character, Bob returned for a high school reunion and showed Sara around and in 1984 he came again, this time with his dog. In 1990 a local couple Gregg and Donna French bought the house for $57,000. Bob Dylan advised the young couple to 'check the furnace'.

On 4 April 1968 Martin Luther King was assassinated, and two months later Robert Kennedy was assassinated. The first date happened to be the day of release of *Bookends* by Simon and Garfunkel. Its melancholy songs were right for the moment.

For the summer edition of *Sing Out!*, Bob Dylan agreed to a major interview with John Cohen and Happy Traum, which was spread out over 13 pages. Dylan asked for the songs, 'The Weight' (Robertson) and 'Penal Farm Blues' (Scrapper Blackwell) to be included.

How times change. The big hit of the 1968 Newport Folk Festival was the rock band,

Big Brother and the Holding Company, managed by Albert Grossman and featuring Janis Joplin. Grossman was now managing Janis Joplin, Bob Dylan, Peter, Paul and Mary and The Band. He had 25 people working for him on East 55th Street.

On 30 August 1968 the Byrds' trailblazing *Sweetheart of the Rodeo* was released. It included two *Basement* songs, 'You Ain't Goin' Nowhere' and 'Nothing Was Delivered'.

Early in 1968, Bob Dylan had come clean with Macmillan. He was unhappy with *Tarantula* and proposed something different. At the time of the accident, his book was at galley stage and plastic bags and promotional badges saying *Tarantula* had already been manufactured. Albert Grossman arranged a meeting with the publisher in Woodstock. Dylan eventually turned up in good spirits, saying he would get back in touch but he didn't.

Then Dylan went to New York to see Bob Markel to discuss the next stage. Still, it was nothing he couldn't resolve if he wanted. He could tell the publisher that he was now planning a different sort of book and because he was Bob Dylan, the publisher would go along with it. One thing was certain: if you tried to force Bob Dylan to do something, it wouldn't happen: he was stubbornness personified, and then some. He was chopping and changing the title; *Ho Chi Minh in Harlem* was a possibility. He was planning to include 'Here lies Bob Dylan. Murdered. From behind. By trembling flesh.' Paranoid, moi? Whatever – it would not be a book for badges, sweatshirts and shopping bags. He told Markel he had a new title, *Fuck You*. Markel said, 'It's not really in keeping with what you're doing' and Dylan said, 'Fine'. He was just testing him.

When bootleg copies of the book appeared, Macmillan took action. As Dylan hadn't amended what he had written or offered anything new, Macmillan eventually decided to publish it. Dylan said, 'That's the way I did it. That's it.' He approved the cover and all was well. It sold 100,000 copies in hardback and the paperback rights were sold to Bantam for $200,000. It should have remained a bootleg. The text did resemble stoned ramblings. It had a preoccupation with midgets, which is another link with John Lennon. His reference to 'a sheriff in the machinery' surely alludes to *A Spaniard in the Works*.

In September 1968 Leonard Cohen started recording *Songs from a Room* in Nashville, this time produced by Bob Johnston. Gordon Lightfoot was in Nashville to make his next album, *Back here on Earth*. The sessions with Charlie McCoy and Kenny Buttrey didn't go to plan and they were paid off and he used different musicians at Bradley's Barn. The songs included 'Bitter Green', 'The Circle is Small' and 'Affair on 8th Avenue'. An early outtake, 'Station Master', sounds like it was written after listening to *John Wesley Harding*.

In November Bob Dylan was the cover story in *The Saturday Evening Post*. Elliott Landy took the photographs of the clean-shaven Dylan, looking fit and healthy by his woodstack in Woodstock. Landy shot the covers for *Nashville Skyline*, and Van Morrison's *Moondance* and had total access to The Band. Because their surnames are anagrams, many thought that Landy didn't exist and Dylan was using a pseudonym, Bob Landy.

Also in November George Harrison visited Bob and Sara in Woodstock for Thanksgiving. George said to Bob, 'Hey man, how do write all those words?' and he replied, 'How do you get all them chords?' The dreamy 'I'd Have You Anytime', which opened George's *All Things Must Pass* (1970), came out of that. There were two other songs they wrote at the time, 'Nowhere to Go' and 'When Everybody Comes to Town', which have not been officially released.

Happy Traum: 'I met George Harrison on three different occasions. One time was a Thanksgiving dinner and he showed up at my house with Bob and The Band and I found him a lovely guy. My late brother Artie and Bob and George Harrison and I spent an entire afternoon just playing folk songs. It would have been fabulous if there had been some tapes or photographs from that. Nowadays there would be selfies but then you could respect the privacy. It was fabulous – three or four hours of just sitting around with them playing folk songs. It was fun. Some of the songs George didn't know but some he did. We were playing anything that came to mind really including some Buddy Holly songs.'

George heard 'I Threw It All Away' which he sang to the other Beatles in January 1969 in the *Let It Be* sessions at Twickenham. He sang a snatch of 'Please Mrs. Henry' and said to Ringo, 'Did you play those tapes?', indicating that he had been passing them around. George wrote 'Behind That Locked Door' about Dylan, wishing he would perform again.

In January 1969 Joan Baez's tribute to Bob Dylan, a double-album *Any Day Now*, was released. The musicians included Pete Drake, Kenneth Buttrey, Norbert Putnam, Stephen Stills and Jerry Reed. The album included several songs that he had not released himself. 'Love Is just a Four Letter Word' was issued as a single and she said, 'I can't sing his nasty, hateful, ugly songs'.

Joan Baez: 'Dylan could get up for five hours and most people would recognise the songs. He resonates in people and he certainly does it for me. It was like a goldmine when I made the Dylan album. I had sheet music all over the floor and I would say, 'That one' and 'This one'. I did that and the country album *Help Me Make It through the Night* within five days in Nashville. I've never gone all-out country but I do like to be a little country, although country itself is so all-encompassing now.' Joan Baez wrote a memoir *Daybreak*, which had a chapter *The Dada King*, but never mentioned Dylan by name.

In June 1969 Joan released *David's Album*, dedicated to her husband who was in jail for resisting the draft. Joan drew the cover picture and it was a US Top 40 album. She was starting to write songs: 'It took me ten years to even try and the first song was 'Sweet Sir Galahad'. It is very difficult for me to write songs and it is much easier to sing.' 'Sweet Sir Galahad' was written about the record producer Milan Melvin, who had married Mimi but the marriage would only last two years.

In February 1969 Manfred Mann topped the UK charts for two weeks with 'The Mighty Quinn' and it was a Top 10 hit in the US.

Bob Johnston arranged further sessions for Bob Dylan but until he met up with him at the Ramada Inn in Nashville on 12 February 1969, he had no idea what his songs would be like. The next day they were in the studio with old friends Pete Drake, Charlie McCoy and Kenny Buttrey plus Norman Blake and Charlie Daniels on guitars and Bob Wilson on piano. Everything went fine with six songs recorded the first day, but Dylan felt he could do 'Lay Lady Lay' better. It was sorted the next day along with three more songs and on the 17th, an instrumental 'Nashville Skyline Rag', 'Tonight I'll Be Staying Here with You' (which he had written on Ramada Inn notepaper) and a jam session with Johnny Cash who had arrived early for his own time in the studio. They hurriedly agreed to work together the next day.

With Cash's band, Bob and Johnny covered 20 songs but it was too loose and they sounded like two singers after a night on the tiles. In 2019, the sessions were officially released on *Travellin' Thru*. Johnny Cash's repertoire dominates and when Cash starts 'I Still Miss Someone', Bob goes into a harmony and then changes his mind as though he was thinking of being June Carter. Admittedly we are only hearing impromptu takes of these songs and we don't know what would have happened if they had tried to work on something else. The likelihood is that the results wouldn't be very different.

By way of contrast, Hank Thompson's famed country single, 'The Wild Side of Life' was cut in one take. There is one amusing idea that they could have developed. Bob Dylan's 'Don't Think Twice It's All Right' and Johnny Cash's 'Understand Your Man' have the same melody and they decided to sing their own lyrics at the same time. It sounds a mess but these two songs could have merged in a very entertaining way.

In 'Careless Love', the 'son of a gun' becomes the 'daughter of a pistol' and surely they could have done better than that. 'Girl from the North Country', however, was very entertaining as their voices sounded so different, like they are arguing over whose true love it was. Asked about that duet in 1988, Johnny Cash said, 'Musically, it's really inferior. It's not up to par for either of us. I think he was embarrassed over that and I don't blame him.' Still, he put it on *Nashville Skyline* and had Johnny Cash write the sleeve note.

Liz Thomson: 'Dylan made *Nashville Skyline* at a time when country music was quite unhip and it seemed a redneck thing to be doing, but in the early 1970s that changed with the Eagles, Linda Ronstadt and then Emmylou Harris.'

Another duet, 'One Too Many Mornings' was filmed for a documentary, *Johnny Cash – The Man and his Music*. Bob gave Johnny a new song, 'Wanted Man', which would have sounded fine on *Nashville Skyline*; what's more, the album needed it as there are only ten tracks and 25 minutes playing time, although that was typical of country LPs of the period. Dylan told *Rolling Stone*: 'The new songs are easier to sing as there aren't too many words to remember.' 'I Threw It All Away' was released as a single and described as a country equivalent of 'When a Man Loves a Woman'.

The late Rory Gallagher told me, 'I love Doc Watson, who plays acoustic country bluegrass and is a superb player. He does a great number called 'Deep River Blues' and he does an instrumental called 'Doc's Guitar' which is like 'Nashville Skyline Rag', the instrumental on that Dylan album. It is almost the same tune.'

While in Nashville, Bob Johnston introduced him to Jerry Lee Lewis who was recording nearby. 'I said "Jerry, this is Bob Dylan" and he said, "So?" Bob said, "Well, maybe you and me could get together sometime and cut something", and Jerry Lee said "No" and started playing the piano. Dylan said, "Let's get out of here!"' A pity as Bob had written the blues-tinged and highly commercial 'To Be Alone with You' for Jerry Lee.

Despite its brevity and its lightness, there are stellar moments on *Nashville Skyline*. There are three excellent ballads: 'Tonight I'll Be Staying Here with You' builds marvellously with piano, organ and steel guitar; Nick Cave has called 'I Threw It All Away' his favourite Dylan record; and 'Tell Me that It Isn't True' is typical of Hank Williams' love triangles.

On the lighter side there is the country rock of 'One More Night'; the playful 'Peggy Day' which was inspired by the Mills Brothers; and the sheer fun of 'Country Pie'. When *Rolling Stone* asked him if it was anything like the Beatles' 'Honey Pie', he said, 'No, I wish it was.'

Dylan had been asked to write a theme for the film *Midnight Cowboy* but he delivered 'Lay Lady Lay' too late for inclusion. The director John Schlesinger used Fred Neil's 'Everybody's Talkin'' as sung by Nilsson instead. Perhaps Dylan was wondering what to do with it when he saw the Everly Brothers in New York. Don Everly: 'We met Bob Dylan at the Bitter End. We were looking for songs and he was writing 'Lay Lady Lay' at the time. He sang parts of it and we weren't sure if he was offering it to us or not. It was one of those awestruck moments. We wound up cutting the song about 15 years later.'

Bob Dylan: Outlaw Blues

Bob had been going 'la la la' as he played a new melody and it led naturally into 'Lay Lady Lay'. This is a romantic song with Bob as Teddy Pendergrass and it has become his best-known love song. Kris Kristofferson was still working as a janitor at Columbia when Bob Dylan cut this song. He held the cowbell that Kenny Buttrey played to add a light, jokey touch to the song.

Norma Waterson, perhaps taking her stance from *Lady Chatterley's Lover,* thinks that 'his clothes are dirty' might relate to a gardener. On his *Rolling Thunder* tour, Dylan added, 'Let's go upstairs, who really cares?'

Raul Malo of the Mavericks: 'I have all his records on my iPod and I love *Nashville Skyline,* I listen to it quite a bit. I wish we had more of that in contemporary music in Nashville. He doesn't write the same thing over and over again. I could do 'Lay Lady Lay' as that phrasing is so relaxed and easy. Anyone who wants to write songs should study Bob Dylan and study his lyrics. It is art.'

Dylan was happy with the album but wasn't sure about how to market it. At one stage he told *Rolling Stone* that he was keeping out of people's hair by cutting country. Later he said, 'Clive Davis wanted to release 'Lay Lady Lay' as a single. I pleaded with him not to. I never felt too close to the song or thought it was representative of anything I do. He won the argument. He thought it was a hit single and he was right. Pete Drake played steel guitar on the record and that's what made it sound different.'

Perhaps taking the lead from 'Lay Lady Lay', Kris Kristofferson was soon pioneering a new style of country song with 'Help Me Make It through the Night', 'For the Good Times' and the ultimate drinking song, 'Sunday Mornin' Comin' Down'. Prior to Kristofferson, the country songs tended to stop at the bedroom door. Now Kristofferson and Bob Dylan would be offering a similar frankness. 'Kris came along with a new way of looking at country music,' says Donnie Fritts who worked with him, 'bringing ideas in from soul music.' Maybe, but a good deal of it was from Kristofferson's own life.

The back cover photograph of *Nashville Skyline* was originally going to be the front cover, but they went with a photo of Bob outdoors wearing the same jacket as in *Blonde on Blonde* and *John Wesley Harding.* Same hat too! This time Dylan looked as though he were in a good mood and about to say hello. Bob was holding George Harrison's guitar on the cover and that guitar is now owned by Chris Simpson of Magna Carta.

On the front of the *Bringing It All Back Home* LP, there is a picture of *The Folk Blues of Eric Von Schmidt.* That stance has been copied for the *Nashville Skyline* cover. Dylan wrote the liner note for Eric Von Schmidt's 1969 album, *Who Knocked the Brains out of the Sky?* One of Eric's songs, 'Catch It', was about Richard Fariña.

Bob knew that going full country could alienate his fans. Look at how the Byrds were booed at the *Grand Ole Opry.* It didn't bother him: he might lose some fans but he would pick up new ones.

Roger McGuinn: 'I thought *Nashville Skyline* was a good direction for Dylan and it was a really good album. He was still recuperating from that motorcycle crash and he was looking for something else to do. I don't think he wanted to do anything complicated and he wrote some good stuff.'

At the end of April, Bob Dylan was back on Music Row. It was the usual musicians but without Bob Moore and with Bill Pursell on piano and Fred Carter Jr on guitar. They recorded six songs in two days but only 'Living the Blues' was an original and that was much like a Jerry Lee Lewis country ballad. He recorded 'Take Me As I Am', 'I Forget More than You'll Ever Know', 'Let It Be Me', 'Spanish Is the Loving Tongue' and 'A Fool Such As I'. Dylan had no plan in mind at the time but this was the start of his double-album, *Self Portrait*.

Oddly enough, Dylan agreed to promote *Nashville Skyline*. Johnny Cash was not a country star like Jim Reeves or Eddy Arnold. He was rough-hewn and had gravitas and was always his own man. He insisted on having Pete Seeger on his TV show, thereby ignoring the unspoken ban. *The Johnny Cash Show* though was a corny summer replacement show with tacky sets and Dylan drew the line at performing in a country shack. He became friendly with the Cajun fiddler, Doug Kershaw.

Doug Kershaw: 'I did a song with Dylan in 1969 for *Self Portrait*. He said to me "Do you know 'Blue Moon'?" I said, "Sure." He said, "Can you play it in D?" I said, "Sure." He said, "Be there tomorrow morning" and I was. I love the guy; he is so authentic.'

On 1 May 69 Dylan recorded *The Johnny Cash Show* at the Ryman Auditorium, doing 'I Threw It All Away', 'Living the Blues' and 'Girl from the North Country' with Johnny Cash. He was not looking comfortable though he loved working with Cash's band. Drummer W.S. Holland: 'Bob came into Nashville. Now I know it is a big honour to have done that, but it just seemed to be something to do that day. His singing and his voice were locked into what he always did. I had a ball working with him and I loved 'Lay Lady Lay'.'

Graham Nash: '*The Johnny Cash Show* was done from the Ryman in Nashville. It was an incredible place – Hank Williams and Elvis had been at the *Opry*. After the show, he invited everyone to his house for dinner with gold and silver and beautiful plates. After dinner, he said, 'Here at the Cash house we have a tradition. The tradition is that you sing for your supper, so who's first?' Nobody moved, and nobody moved because Bob Dylan was there and it had been his first TV appearance since his motorcycle accident. He is sitting there with Sara and I was there, Joni Mitchell was there and Kris Kristofferson was there. I can't stand a vacuum. I have to fill it. I sang 'Marrakesh Express'. I got to the end and I put my guitar down; I'd done a great job and I turned and knocked over a standing lamp, which crashed to the ground and that broke the ice. I have courage and I thought it was a song everybody would understand and they did.' Dylan sang for his supper by singing 'These Hands'. This song, made popular by Hank Snow and recorded by Dylan with David Bromberg, was one of the outtakes from his next album, *Self Portrait*.

Before he left Nashville, Dylan had a further session in which he recorded the Everly Brothers' prison song 'Take a Message to Mary' and the Broadway standard, 'Blue Moon', which had been recorded by Elvis. Pete Drake was on steel and he was going full country with the Anita Kerr Singers.

Charlie McCoy: 'History tells us that Dylan coming here was one of the biggest things that ever happened to Nashville. At the time, nobody realised it, but it opened the door for all these other people to come down.'

Nashville Skyline was a Number 3 album in the US and Number 1 in the UK. Three singles made the US charts with 'Lay Lady Lay' reaching Number 7. Glen Campbell and Johnny Cash had big albums but on the whole the rock fraternity liked to mock country music. By bringing country into the mainstream, did Bob Dylan turn that around a little bit and in so doing pave the way for the Eagles?

Michael Gray: 'In 1969 Dylan was one of the hippest people on the planet at a time when hipness was very important. The counterculture was very strong. He moved into country music which was strange and *John Wesley Harding* was a statement against the excesses elsewhere. He went into bland country music next. Nothing was treated with more contempt than country music at the time. Dylan was being defiant, really. Cash had a solemn sober voice and Dylan was running vocal rings beautifully around him.'

At the same time as Bob was in Nashville, John Stewart from the Kingston Trio was there making a solo album, *California Bloodlines*. 'It was a lot of fun to make the record. Nik Venet can take full credit for that. He said, "Let's go to Nashville and get a live feel – the players are better down there." It was his vision and it was the first emergence of folk becoming country-rock, done before the Eagles, but I can take no credit for it. Nik's a very intuitive guy. As a producer, he's excellent at getting the best out of you. He has no real ideas in the studio. He lays out the format for you and that album was mostly done live. We made a two-track as we were doing the album and when we went back to mix it, we couldn't get it as good as the two-track and we stuck with that, so it's pretty much a live album.'

During 1969, Peter Fonda and Dennis Hopper had been making their biker film, *Easy Rider*, and they had wanted Crosby, Stills and Nash to come up with the title song. However, Dennis Hopper fell out with Stephen Stills over the use of a limousine and that was that. They wanted to end the film with Bob Dylan's 'It's Alright, Ma (I'm Only Bleeding)'. They screened the film for Bob but he didn't care for the ending in which Dennis Hopper was killed and then Peter Fonda. He said, 'You shouldn't end it like that. Peter should go back and blow those guys away.' He said that his song wasn't suitable as the film was negative enough as it was.

Roger McGuinn: 'Peter Fonda was a friend and I knew him from the days when I was playing with Bobby Darin. He made films with Sandra Dee who was Bobby's wife. We would hang around together and even fly in Lear jets and have a good time. *Easy Rider* was a low budget film and he put tracks from his record collection on the soundtrack. This was only meant to be temporary but he ran it a few times and got to like it as it was. Even though he liked the soundtrack being his record collection, he wanted one song that would be custom-made for the movie. He took the movie to New York and he screened it for Bob Dylan. Dylan wrote a few notes on a piece of paper. He then said, "Peter, give this to McGuinn." Peter flew back to Los Angeles and gave me a cocktail napkin with some ballpoint pen scribbling on it – it said, "The river flows, it flows to the sea, Wherever that river goes, that's where I want to be, Flow, river, flow." I got out my guitar and wrote the melody and finished off the words. I called it 'The Ballad of Easy Rider' and I gave Dylan a credit for it. About three weeks later, I got a call at 3am, "Roger, this is Bob" and he said, "Take my name off that, I don't need the money." It was very generous of him. I liked the *Easy Rider* movie very much. I thought it captured that culture, that hippie thing, very well.'

Because of the dubious accounting practices of the film industry, Roger McGuinn reckons that he only got one fifth of his royalties from 'The Ballad of Easy Rider'. They said that he was one-fifth of the Byrds and as the other four didn't write it, the producers held the rest back.

In April 1969, the Dylans left Byrdcliffe and moved to a much bigger property, a 40-acre farm on Ohayo Mountain Road in Woodstock, which had belonged to the politician, Walter Weyl. He had founded the magazine, *The New Republic*. Dylan bought a further 80 acres of surrounding woodland, all of which he sold in 1973. He and Sara had got fed up with the fans: they had even found one in their bed. Now the fans were fewer as they had an uphill trek up to his house. One girl came from New York to Woodstock by bus every weekend and walked up to the property hoping for a sight of her hero.

Maria was troubled because everybody was talking about her father and wanted to see him. Dylan allowed Landy to take photographs but said that the photos could only be used when the children were older. He was worried about kidnapping.

Released at the same time as *Nashville Skyline* was the second Leonard Cohen album, *Songs from a Room*, produced by Bob Johnston. I can remember buying both of them on the day they were released at NEMS in Liverpool and wondering which I should play first: it was so exciting. I favoured the Leonard Cohen album as the song titles were so mesmerising, but *Nashville Skyline* was still money well spent.

They both drew heavily from the Bible and Hank Williams. Dylan has said that he would not mind being Roy Acuff, Walter Matthau or Leonard Cohen. The *New York Times* said, 'On the alienation scale, Cohen rates somewhere between Schopenhauer and Bob Dylan, two other prominent poets of pessimism. Whereas Mr. Dylan is alienated from society and mad about it, Mr. Cohen is alienated and merely sad about it.'

The 1969 Newport Folk Festival featured the Everly Brothers, Pete Seeger and Johnny Cash but lost money. On the other hand, 80,000 people came to the Newport Jazz Festival to hear Jethro Tull, the Mothers of Invention and Led Zeppelin. Nevertheless, the promoter George Wein called it 'four of the worst days of my life' and really the precedent was set for the title of a festival having little to do with its contents.

In July 1969 Richard Thompson of Fairport Convention thought that 'If You Gotta Go, Go Now' could have a Cajun setting. Acting on a whim, when Fairport Convention were playing in London, they asked if there was a Frenchman in the house. Three people came backstage and the French lyric was written by a committee and ended up not being very Cajun, French, Dylan or Fairport. Still it was a UK hit, their only one.

In August 1969 and acting way out of character, Bob Dylan took Sara to Moose Lodge in Hibbing for a ten-year reunion for his year from Hibbing High School. They met Echo Helstrom but generally speaking, he was not social and most people wondered why he was there. But that is Bob Dylan – complex, difficult and hard to understand and with much more to come.

CHAPTER 8

Help Bob Dylan Sink the Isle of Wight

I. Festival Life

The concept of an open-air musical festival took some time to develop. Although there were many major musical attractions in the 1930s, nobody thought of putting several of them in a field on a summer weekend to entertain the public. Bing Crosby never sank the Isle of Wight. Even if a festival had been booked, would the public have turned up? Would the fans have wanted to spend the weekend in a muddy field and would the transport links have been good enough? Plus there were the problems of mass catering, bathroom facilities and unpredictable weather. The issue was really a non-starter.

During the Second World War, British and American entertainers were used to boost the morale of the fighting forces and they often found themselves performing on makeshift stages outdoors, often in the middle of a field. So, open-air music festivals were an unexpected consequence of the Second World War.

The Newport Jazz Festival in Rhode Island began in 1954 when two well-heeled residents had sought the cooperation of John Hammond and George Wein in organising the event. Hammond persuaded Billie Holiday to star at the first one.

There were enormous logistical problems: they couldn't just hire a field and hope that people would turn up. How many were expected, how big a field, what camping facilities, how to avoid traffic gridlocks and how to reassure the residents that this was good for the community? After all, beatniks might attend.

The concept of an open-air festival was so novel that it formed the background to Cole Porter's 1956 film, *High Society*. The film was set at the Newport Jazz Festival featuring Louis Armstrong, but the plot revolved around the socialites Bing Crosby and Grace Kelly, dogged reporter Frank Sinatra and photographer Celeste Holm. *High Society* had a sparkling score and was more about the rom-com than the festival itself.

The 1958 Newport Jazz Festival was filmed in colour for the feature-length *Jazz on a Summer's Day*, which included Louis Armstrong, Mahalia Jackson, George Shearing and Dinah Washington. The festival was controversial through Hammond's suggestion for having an R&B show on Saturday night with Ray Charles, Big Joe Turner, Big Maybelle and one of the new rock'n'roll stars Chuck Berry. There is a marvellous album, *Ray Charles at Newport*, covering his 1958 set.

Jazz is a broad church and the fans who like Dixieland, for example, are unlikely to have much time for modern jazz or Chuck Berry. The Newport Jazz Festival is known for several mind-blowing appearances by Miles Davis, Dave Brubeck and Thelonious Monk, but they weren't for everyone.

By 1960 the audience was 12,000 but there was a problem that year with drunk students that the police had to resolve. The Board decided that this would be the last festival. Muddy Waters and his band were the final act and as they finished the poet Langston Hughes gave them his poem, 'Goodbye Newport Blues', as an encore. They worked out the melody and the arrangement as they went along and George Wein was crying as they finished. You can hear it on the live album *Muddy Waters at Newport* (1960) and also from that year there is *Nina Simone at Newport* (1960).

The festival did return in 1961, but under new organisation. Sid Bernstein, who later presented the Beatles at Shea Stadium, thought the best way to combat local opposition was to star Judy Garland and give the residents free tickets. A clever move and it worked a treat.

The festival returned to George Wein the next year and everybody was more tolerant. The audience figures reached a high when Frank Sinatra appeared on 4 July 1965, a tremendous success and only three weeks before Bob Dylan's electric appearance at the Newport Folk Festival.

When the folk musicians in Greenwich Village were showing an interest in the old blues performers, George Wein thought there was a possibility of having a folk afternoon at the 1959 jazz festival. After sounding out interested parties, he realised that it would be better to have a separate festival and so the Newport Folk Festival was born in 1959. He asked Albert Grossman to help him and they tried the first on a 'not for profit' basis to see if it was viable. Performers would get accommodation and travelling expenses and any profit would be ploughed into the next festival.

The first festival featured Pete Seeger, the Kingston Trio, Odetta, Earl Scruggs and the duo Sonny Terry and Brownie McGhee, so like the jazz festival, there was a range of styles – blues, bluegrass and commercial folk among them. Bob Gibson brought along a special guest to perform with him, the 18-year-old Joan Baez, who caused a sensation.

The hit-making Kingston Trio went down exceptionally well and their full set has appeared on CD. Shirley Collins, who worked for Alan Lomax, commented, 'I despised them but the audience loved them.'

In 1960 the Newport Folk Festival included Ewan MacColl and Peggy Seeger as well as John Lee Hooker. There was no festival in 1961 and 1962 but it returned in 1963 with Joan Baez expanding its scope with a civil rights march through the streets of Newport. This was topped by Michelle Shocked who asked a Newport audience in the 1990s to lie down as though they had been killed by a nuclear bomb: the naval college in Newport was having to remember the end of war in Japan 50 years earlier.

We have already discussed Dylan's role at the festival – first with Joan Baez (1963), then on his own (1964) and then going electric (1965).

The Monterey International Pop Festival, which was held on 16 to 18 June 1967 in Monterey, California is seen as the first rock festival, but that isn't true, although it was the first to make an international impact.

Strangely enough, the UK can claim to be first, albeit by accident. Clearly wishing to establish a UK equivalent to Newport, Lord Montagu of Beaulieu set up a jazz festival on his estate in Hampshire. The Beaulieu Jazz Festival ran from 1956 to 1961. It was surpassed by the National Jazz Festival which started outside London in Richmond in 1961. The organisers planned an annual event and, to expand the audience, it became the National Jazz and Blues Festival, thereby bringing in the R&B-slanted beat groups. By 1965 the festival had moved to Windsor with jazz taking a back seat. Eventually this became the Reading Festival.

No matter how well organised they are, festivals in the UK always have a question mark hanging over them as they can be wet and windy or even worse. We have all seen the news footage of participants wading through mud in their wellingtons at Glastonbury, which had started in a small way in 1970. The likelihood of good weather has increased with climate change but that is small consolation. Coping with bad weather has become part of the community spirit.

Belgium and Yugoslavia staged rock festivals in the early 1960s, and it is extraordinary that a communist country should have been leading the way in something that was potentially anti-establishment.

Monterey wasn't the first rock festival in America or even in California. A week earlier there had been a festival in California with the unwieldy name of the Fantasy Fair and Magic Mountain Music Festival. It was held in a stone amphitheatre that held 4,000 on the face of Mount Tamalpais in Marin County, California, some 120 miles north of Monterey.

The radio station KFRC in San Francisco had the idea for the a rock festival and although the line-up included Dionne Warwick (well, San José was close by), it was mostly the alt. rock acts from the area who were beginning to break through – the Doors, Canned Heat, Jefferson Airplane and Captain Beefheart with a major chart name in the Byrds. This was the dawning of the Age of Aquarius.

The executive board for the Monterey festival included Paul Simon, John Phillips from the Mamas and the Papas, and the record producer, Lou Adler. Although chart acts were featured, this was not a Top 40 festival and it highlighted the underground movement, FM radio or if you like, thinking man's rock. It was rumoured that Bob Dylan might appear but that was never on the agenda. Still, the Byrds sang 'Chimes of Freedom' and Jimi Hendrix performed an electrifying 'Like a Rolling Stone'.

It was decided that, with the exception of Ravi Shankar, the participants would not be paid and that the money raised would go to good causes. Although the festival took place in June, the month that *Sgt Pepper* was released, none of the Beatles took part, but there were 32 rock acts including the Who, the Byrds, Jimi Hendrix and Otis Redding. Paul Simon secured the Grateful Dead who had fallen out with Phillips. Not only did the Mamas and the Papas perform but John Phillips wrote the anthem for the festival, 'San Francisco', which he gave to his fellow Journeyman, Scott McKenzie. It was a hippie anthem that said no to Vietnam and yes to flower power.

One of the most popular paperbacks was Norman Mailer's *Why Are We in Vietnam* and the boxer Muhammad Ali was resisting the draft and facing five years in jail. Many young men were burning draft cards and some were moving to Canada, the singer Jesse Winchester among them. At one stage, the crowd was chanting, 'Hey hey LBJ, how many kids did you kill today?'

Rock music, love and flowers was the festival's ingredients and the hippies were encouraged to bring their children. There was a nearby fairground. California dreamin' was becoming a reality.

It was the first time that many of the acts had performed before such a large audience and everyone did well. Record company executives were signing new acts that they liked and Clive Davis of Columbia secured Laura Nyro and Big Brother and the Holding Company which featured Janis Joplin.

Rather like Newport on the east coast, Monterey on the west had been a sleepy town where nothing much happened with a population of 25,000. With the festival, the population suddenly became 90,000. Only 7,000 could fit into the arena but the others were camping happily outside, soaking in the vibes.

The artists included the Byrds, Country Joe and the Fish, the Blues Project, the Paul Butterfield Blues Band and Jefferson Airplane. One of the compères was Micky Dolenz from the Monkees. The Who, playing much louder than Dylan at Newport, were a sensation and became a 'go to' act for any festival organiser. Eric Burdon and the Animals had gone hippie overnight with 'San Franciscan Nights' and they also performed Donovan's 'Hey Gyp'.

David Crosby in a wild stage rant with the Byrds declared, 'I believe that if we gave LSD to all the statesmen and politicians in the world, we might have a chance of stopping a war.' LSD was not illegal in the USA until the end of the year. Some people got high on simply smoking dried banana peels and you could never ban bananas.

Bob Dylan: 'The flower generation, is that what it was? I wasn't into that at all. I just thought it was a lot of kids out and around wearing flowers in their hair, taking a lot of acid. I mean, what can you think about that?'

Despite the preponderance of drugs, there were few arrests and the crowd was well behaved, much to the relief of Ronald Reagan, then Governor of California.

Although the organisers had liberal values, the acts had been chosen to appeal to a white hippie audience. They often performed with psychedelic lighting which heightened the experience. The most significant black act was the soul singer, Otis Redding, backed by Booker T and the MG's. Otis knew that it wasn't his crowd but he stormed the festival with an electrifying set. Ravi Shankar was building a new career for himself at rock festivals and maybe the stoned hippies were attracted to his peaceful, repetitive mantras.

Simon and Garfunkel closed the first night but you wouldn't know that from D.A. Pennebaker's film *Monterey Pop* or the 4CD set. According to Simon's memories, Lou Adler and John Phillips were in control so 'history is written by whoever writes it.' Still, they scored well with the crowd who clapped along to 'Feelin' Groovy'.

Backstage, Jimi Hendrix and Paul Simon had a jam session, although Simon says he was only playing rhythm, feeling somewhat intimidated. 'If he'd said to me, "Take it, Paul", I wouldn't have been able to take it anywhere.'

The musicians had agreed to play for expenses and accommodation. Following the festival, Simon was given $50,000 to supervise the buying of instruments and tuition for teenagers in the ghettoes.

Since his now legendary appearance at the Newport Folk Festival in 1965, the organisers had been trying to tempt Bob Dylan back, even offering him and The Band $150,000 in 1969. He wasn't interested, largely I suspect because he didn't know how to top such a performance. Would it seem right if he deliberately set out to alienate the new audience and anyway, a hip audience might well lap up anything they were given.

On 14 July 1969 The Band was playing at the Mississippi River Festival at Southern Illinois University, Edwardsville, in front of an audience of 4,500 when Bob Dylan made an unscheduled appearance. The Band had finished their set with 'The Weight' and then they returned with Bob Dylan for four songs including Little Richard's 'Slippin' and Slidin'. Newport had offered him all that money and he was doing this for nothing.

Because of his songwriting revenue, Bob Dylan could afford to turn down the biggest festival of the decade, Woodstock. He hated the idea of a festival on his doorstep but logistics forced the organisers to move to Max Yasgur's dairy farm in Bethel some 50 miles away, although they retained the original name. Dylan dismissed the festival calling it 'just an excuse to sell tie-dye'.

Ray and Ronnie Foulk had the idea of creating a music festival in the South of England, off the mainland on the Isle of Wight, another quiet, small community that was about to be invaded. Their first event took place on 31 August 1968 and featured Jefferson Airplane, the Crazy World of Arthur Brown, the Move, the Pretty Things and Fairport Convention. It went well – an audience of 10,000 and no trouble – and they planned a much bigger event for 1969, two days of music with the Who, the Moody Blues, Joe Cocker and much more. Bob Dylan would be appearing on 30 August 1969 and no one really knows why he said yes, but isn't that what we love about him?

There were hard negotiations with Albert Grossman: he got $50,000 for Bob Dylan, $20,000 for The Band, who would also play their own set, and $7,000 for Richie Havens. Richie Havens was originally booked as a favour to Grossman but it became a bonus as he had opened the Woodstock festival and increased his reputation with that performance.

Dylan and his entourage got over half the performance fees for the festival. No one else topped £1,000, the Who getting £950, despite their talent for getting more. Joan Baez was paid £750 and Tom Paxton £700.

On 11 August 1969 the journalist Al Aronowitz went to see Dylan in Woodstock. The Woodstock festival was about to start but Dylan was not interested in making a surprise appearance. He was more concerned with the water supply to his home and with his dog Buster, a Great Dane, which had bitten a neighbour's child.

On August 14 Bob and Sara were about to go to New York to board the QE2 to sail to England but Jesse had an accident. They had to postpone their travel and would fly instead.

There was difficulty in keeping to the running order at Woodstock because the huge crowds often prevented the performers from reaching the stage on time. Country Joe McDonald who had arrived early found that he was on twice. 'The festival was well managed, but there were problems, like if you had prepared for 100 guests and 500 arrived. It was incredibly peaceful and creative and it was wonderful musically. I'd come early to watch as many acts as I could and they found me a guitar and pushed me out there. I was the second act on stage, after Richie Havens. I said, "Should I do the Fish cheer or save it tomorrow for the band?" They said, "Go ahead, what difference will it make?" I walked out and said "Give me an F" and they all screamed back, "F". Then they were singing along as you see in the movie.'

Although Dylan had said no to Woodstock, The Band thought it would be a good idea to promote their album and they were the only act on the bill who lived in the area. They went on just before Jimi Hendrix and they wisely ignored Wavy Gravy's industrial-strength LSD.

Bob Spitz, who wrote *Barefoot in Babylon* about Woodstock, reveals, 'It wasn't built on peace and love but on backstabbing and blackmail and people ripping others off. The artists were ripping off the promoters by blackmailing them, saying they would not go on unless they got more money and that would start a riot. On Saturday night, they needed the Who to go on and the Who heard that the promoters were flush. Their manager said, "We want double the amount of money. We are on in an hour and if you don't give us the money, they will go up there and say, 'They won't pay us', and that will start a riot." They would only accept cash and the promoter had to wake up the president of the bank and tell him to pay the money. The Who got their double fee.'

Arlo Guthrie had an audience far greater than anything his father knew: 'There were three-quarters of a million people and it was pretty scary. I got there at 11 in the morning of the first day and they had already run out of cigarettes and they had nothing to eat or drink except 147 cases of champagne, which were waiting backstage for the end of the festival. By two o'clock in the afternoon, all that champagne had gone. I don't know how many cases I was personally responsible for but by time I came to play at midnight, they had to point me in the direction of the stage. I walked out and did my best under the circumstances. I don't think I'll ever forget it either.'

Arlo was followed by Joan Baez, who says, 'Sometimes being famous is more trouble than it is worth, but there are times when it is marvellous. Woodstock was one of those times. I sang in the middle of the night and they accepted my songs. It was a humbling experience. I'd never sung to a city before.'

British writer Ray Connolly: 'I had just finished interviewing Elvis in Las Vegas and I knew that Dylan was coming over for the Isle of Wight. I thought I would call in on his manager and ask about an interview. He said, "Okay, let's get Bobby on the phone now." I hadn't planned anything like that and there I was talking to Bob Dylan. I told him that I had been to see Elvis. He wanted to know what he was playing and who was on stage with him. We were both Elvis fans. When I got back to England, I told John Lennon that I had been to see Elvis and he asked exactly the same questions. We were all the same age and we had all begun with the same record, 'Heartbreak Hotel'.'

On 25 August 1969 Bob and Sara Dylan flew to London. Al Aronowitz accompanied them as Bob's road manager. Effectively, he was looking after seven suitcases. One of the organisers Rikki Farr drove them to Portsmouth where they boarded a hovercraft for the Isle of Wight. They were based at Forelands Farm, Bembridge. The Band were staying nearby at the Halland Hotel, Seaview with their road manager, Jonathan Taplin.

The next day Bob Dylan gave a press conference at the Halland Hotel. He said that his 1966 tour was 'all for publicity, I don't do that kind of thing anymore', which sounded good but what did he mean? And why was he on the Isle of Wight? 'I want to see the home of Alfred, Lord Tennyson.'

Dylan told the *Daily Mirror*: 'I'm happy with my new songs. They make me feel good.' Chris White of the *Daily Sketch* got a personal quote: 'The English are the most loyal fans I have and that was one of the reasons I wanted to come to England to make my comeback.' Was Dylan really talking of a comeback?

The Beatles were not playing the festival but John, George and Ringo had come. Paul was not on the island as his wife Linda had just given birth. George had two important roles – he brought the pot and he lent Bob a guitar. They met up with The Band for tennis and a jam session in a barn. As Dylan had forgotten his harmonica, a Beatles' employee Christine O'Dell brought him new ones by helicopter; such were the excesses of 1960s rock.

On August 31, Tom Paxton and then Richie Havens did early evening sets. Richie Havens included both 'Maggie's Farm' and 'Strawberry Fields Forever'. He finished at 8.30pm but then the sound system broke down and The Band was not on stage until 10pm. This might have been due to Jonathan Taplin's fastidiousness as the Band had brought their own 2,000 watts system. Taplin wouldn't be swayed and Dylan was annoyed, 'I wanted to catch the crowd when it was still at the peak of its psychic energy.' Maybe Taplin was right as The Band were excellent with a sound that merged country, gospel and rock. Taplin later worked as a producer on *Concert for Bangla Desh* and *The Last Waltz*.

Bob Dylan: Outlaw Blues

Bob Dylan came on stage at 11.10pm. He wore a white suit and was largely singing country and so he resembled Hank Williams. He did three songs with The Band and then performed some acoustic song solos. The Band returned but Dylan was only on stage for 65 minutes, just over the minimum specified in the contract. The public was disappointed as they had been hoping for two hours with a jam session at the end – and they deserved it because of the long wait. In his defence, Dylan was used to short sets on festivals but it was a long way to come for 17 songs and certainly he didn't match the impact of the Who, who had towered over both Woodstock and the Isle of Wight within a month.

Despite predictions, Dylan hadn't sunk the Isle of Wight. John Lennon said, 'He gave a reasonable, albeit slightly flat performance, but everybody was waiting for Godot to appear.' Everybody said that Garth Hudson excelled himself on 'I Threw It All Away'. After the show, Dylan, the three Beatles, The Band and their friends returned to the hotel for a party.

Michael Palin wrote in his diary: 'On the Isle of Wight, 150,000 people gathered to hear Bob Dylan – the gutter press are having their work cut out to track down smut in a gathering which seems to have been happy and peaceful.'

On 1 September, Bob and Sara Dylan were back on the mainland and George Harrison drove them to the airport. Dylan saw the front-page news that Robin Gibb had left the Bee Gees and said, 'They make too much of singers over here.' On his return to America, he said he had no desire to play in the UK again.

Despite that, the Labour MP Marcus Lipton thought we made too much of American singers. His £30,000 fee was ridiculous and he wanted to stop him visiting the UK again. The Ministry responded that this would not be in the interests of British artists who wanted to work abroad.

Bob had asked for his performance to be recorded so he knew he was going to give a good performance and that he might use some of the tracks. Four cuts were on his next project, *Self-Portrait*.

The vibes from Woodstock and the Isle of Wight were very good but everything took a turn for the worse on 6 December 1969 when the Rolling Stones topped the bill at the Altamont Speedway in Northern California. For some crazy reason, the organisers employed Hell's Angels as security guards. The Grateful Dead refused to play as they thought the event was getting too violent, which only made a bad situation worse. The festival is notorious as the stabbing of Meredith Hunter was captured on film. There were two deaths caused by a hit-and-run driver and a death from drowning of someone who thought he could walk on water. There was damage to property and many cars were stolen. In short, don't invite Hell's Angels to your party.

In August 1970 the Isle of Wight festival had another major scoop with the Jimi Hendrix Experience. The country songwriter Kris Kristofferson played his cards badly: 'Blame It on the Stones' was heavily ironic, but stoned audiences don't do irony as he was booed for criticising the Rolling Stones. I asked Kris Kristofferson what went wrong. 'It would be easier to say what went right. (laughs) Nothing went right! They hated me and it was only my third gig in show business. They were tearing down the outer wall and making so much noise that most people couldn't even hear us. Billy Swan was on the stage and he thought that they were going to shoot us.'

Kris was a former soldier and he stood firm. His pianist Billy Swan put his arm around his shoulder and said, 'They love you, Kris.'

Kristofferson told me: 'It was a tough audience. They hated Jimi Hendrix, they hated everybody, except on the last night when Leonard Cohen charmed them at four o'clock in the morning. They were burning down the concession stands and burning trucks and he went out on stage in his pyjamas and took 20 minutes to tune up. I said, "They're gonna kill him." They were brutal to Jimi Hendrix, to Joan Baez, to Tiny Tim for crying out loud, but Leonard Cohen won them over.'

II. So Much Older Then: August 1969–1971

On 19 August 1969 Bob Dylan's contract with Albert Grossman was up for renewal and Grossman was hoping he would reconsider and renew. There was little chance of that. Dylan had found out too much about Grossman's practices, in particular with regards to publishing royalties. He didn't think it was right that Grossman was making more money from his songs than he was.

Even though Dylan moved away, Grossman was still entitled to royalties on earlier songs with a publishing agreement running through to1976. Dylan wanted to be rid of him completely but he would have to prove sharp practice. It was agreed that Grossman would share the publishing royalties up to 1973 and would get a 50% share of some earlier compositions indefinitely. This could be why Dylan held back on new songs in the early 1970s. The conflict rumbled on for years and was settled in 1987 when Grossman's widow Sally received $2m.

Dylan was asked in court in 1981 how long he had known Albert Grossman. He replied, 'I don't think I have ever known the man.'

Grossman often worked in his kitchen for good reason. He liked eating so he combined his interests and opened a gourmet restaurant. Also, food didn't talk back. His restaurant was called The Bear and had an office upstairs. He also opened a Chinese restaurant and a fast food eatery. He had the concept for a sandwich glue in which nothing would slip out.

He developed and extended his Woodstock estate – he collected antiques and had enormous greenhouses.

Building on what was around him, Albert Grossman wanted to promote an artists' community in Woodstock and make it a cultural Mecca. He wanted all-purpose buildings where musicians could work, record and socialise but it was never realised. His idea for a theatre didn't work out but he did open two recording studios in Woodstock, which Sally ran. She continued with the Turtle Creek Studio for many years after his death. Grossman also had the Bearsville record label and the artists recorded included Todd Rundgren, Paul Butterfield, Jesse Winchester and Bobby Charles.

Geoff Muldaur: 'Bobby Charles was a great songwriter and I travelled with him in Better Days. He was really behind the sun. That's a Muddy Waters reference and Bobby was a very funky character. I did his 'Small Town Talk' which he wrote with Rick Danko.'

Losing Dylan was bad news for Grossman and he was hit again when Peter, Paul and Mary split up in 1970. The good news, albeit a brief respite, came in signing Janis Joplin

A beneficiary of The Band was English folk-rock with Fairport Convention's *Liege and Leaf* and Traffic's *John Barleycorn Must Die* (1970), and Steve Winwood has admitted he was very influenced by The Band. For their annual festival at Cropredy, Fairport sang Ashley Hutchings' new words for 'Million Dollar Bash':

*'You can meet all your friends, you can meet on the ledge,
You can meet at the bar, you can meet Percy Sledge,
Well, maybe not this year, but see the stars flash,
They're all going to be there at that million dollar bash.'*

In the early 1970s, there was a great boom in singer / songwriters, propelled by Joni Mitchell's *Ladies of the Canyon* (1970) and *Blue* (1971) and Carole King's *Tapestry* (1971). Bonnie Dobson: 'The whole singer/songwriter phase was kicking off. I didn't really have the confidence to do that and then Joni Mitchell came along and she is one of the great writers of all time. Most of my songs are pretty personal but they are not as up front as hers.'

Judy Collins: 'I discovered Joni Mitchell by great good fortune. She had no contract but she wasn't like Leonard Cohen who had no real understanding of what he wanted to do. Joni was singing in the Village, she was divorced from Chuck Mitchell and on her own. She started writing these wonderful songs. Tom Rush loved 'The Circle Game' and kept asking her to sing it. I loved 'That Song about the Midway' and one night Al Kooper – funny how Al Kooper comes into everything, isn't it? – called me at three o'clock in the morning and he said he was sitting with Joni Mitchell and she had a song I had to hear. She came on the phone and sang 'Both Sides Now' and I said, "That's it. I have to sing this song." I recorded it a few days later. The song has held up beautifully and I still love singing it. It is a remarkable composition.'

Bob Dylan had inspired this remarkable run of new singer / songwriters who were to include James Taylor, Kris Kristofferson, John Prine and Jackson Browne, and it is odd that it did not propel him to up his own game. Why did he release *Self Portrait* at the very time when he should have had an album of great new songs? Maybe that dispute with Albert Grossman was holding him back. Possibly he was getting older: did he want to keep up with the new generation?

What's more, John Lennon himself was inspired by Dylan for 'Give Peace a Chance' and 'Working Class Hero', which borrowed the same melody as 'Masters of War'. On his first solo album, John Lennon performed 'God', a rant in which he stated, 'I don't believe in Zimmerman' as well as 'I don't believe in Beatles'.

Dylan was astonished by the bad-tempered but illuminating John Lennon interview in *Rolling Stone*. 'Did you see the Lennon interview? Whew! John is making a mistake, revealing so much of himself. If he keeps it up, he's not gonna have anything left for the fans.'

Pete Seeger: 'I happened to hear 'Give Peace a Chance' from a young female guitar-picker just two days before I went to Washington for a peace demonstration. I thought, "That's a namby-pamby song, it doesn't have enough bite or militancy for me", but I was faced with half a million people and I needed a slow, slow song. I hadn't learnt anything but that one phrase, and I tried it and by gosh, it worked better and better and I had the sense to keep it going. We sang it over and over – Brother Kirkpatrick and me, Peter, Paul and Mary and Mitch Miller. Before we knew it, we had half a million people like a huge ballet swaying back and forth, with children on their parents' shoulders. I'll never forget it. Just for that one occasion, it's a special song for me.'

On 9 December 1969 Bob and Sara's son Jakob Luke was born.

On 29 December 1969 Bob Dylan saw Janis Joplin in concert at Madison Square Garden. There was a party afterwards in Clive Davis' apartment and Bob chatted with her. Lacking self-confidence, she said to Albert Grossman, 'I know I'm not The Band or Bob

Dylan but care about me too.' Grossman did care about her to the tune of $200,000, the size of a life assurance policy on her life. Grossman demanded payment when she died from a drugs overdose in 1970. Grossman argued in court that it had been an accident so that the monies should be paid out. The parties reached an agreement and Grossman received $112,000.

At the Grammys for 1969, Bob Dylan was nominated for Best Country Instrumental Performance for 'Nashville Skyline Rag', which was unlikely to have been heard on country radio as disc-jockeys avoided instrumentals. He lost out to an LP by *Danny Davis and the Nashville Brass*. (Nashville Brass was an oxymoron at the time). Johnny Cash won a Grammy for Best Album Notes for *Nashville Skyline*.

Still the recognition may have prompted Bob to write another instrumental, 'Wigwam' and a song with just a repeated, short verse, 'All the Tired Horses'. Possibly it was a deliberate joke to release 'Wigwam' as an A-side, but it sold okay, making Number 41 on the US Hot 100. Professor Christopher Ricks has likened the 16 words of 'All the Tired Horses' to Keats and Tennyson.

In 1970 Dylan was the front-runner for playing Woody Guthrie in a film of *Bound for Glory* but eventually the role went to David Carradine and the film was completed in 1976. Burt Bacharach and Hal David wrote 'Raindrops Keep Fallin' on My Head' with a view to Bob Dylan singing it on the soundtrack of *Butch Cassidy and the Sundance Kid* but it went to B.J. Thomas and was a US Number 1.

Bob Dylan was putting together a book of his lyrics. This was no easy task as he had rewritten songs, added new verses and dropped others. It would have been best if had written commentaries and made notes on what we were seeing, but he was not that kind of guy. At first the book was to be called *Words* but as he began to illustrate them, it became *Writings & Drawings*.

Between 3 and 5 March 1970 Dylan was recording in New York with David Bromberg among the musicians. Dylan had seen him with Jerry Jeff Walker at the Bitter End. Dylan had copies of *Sing Out!* in the studio and was choosing songs to perform on *Self Portrait*. He did include a new song, 'Went to See the Gypsy'.

'Went to See the Gypsy' was written after Bob had seen Elvis in Las Vegas and gone backstage to say hello. The song is about the impossibility of having a sensible conversation with someone in those circumstances: '"Hello", he said to me, and I said it back to him.'

When I spoke to Keith Emerson of Emerson, Lake and Palmer, I saw the same situation from the other side. Keith Emerson: 'I got to meet Bob Dylan at the end of a concert and we were playing there the next day. The promoter invited everybody back to the hotel for a party. I got to the hotel suite and everybody went for the booze. Bob Dylan arrived and went into the back room. When a performer comes off stage, he needs time and space to unwind, but the promoter thought it would be a great idea to introduce Keith Emerson to Bob Dylan. I said that I had to get back to my hotel. He said, "No, no, Bob, come here." We were introduced and said hi. He asked where I came from and I said, "From England." We looked at each other and shrugged. Nice meeting you, bye. (Laughs).'

Brief meetings between celebrities can be fun. In November 1970, Dylan and some of The Band saw Elton John at Fillmore East. Elton said to Dylan, 'You can't keep going around in clothes like that: I'll give you a few clothes.' Dylan didn't mind the ribbing as he also went the next night with Sara, though possibly he went to collect the clothes.

It has been suggested that Elvis Presley and Bob Dylan had a session in Nashville but

US postage series on folk musicians, 1998.

Arlo Guthrie on the set of Bound For Glory, 1975. David Carradine, getting ready for the road, was playing his dad.

At first Bob Dylan wanted to keep his background hidden, but you can't escape from public records.

Carnegie Hall was an important venue for many folk performers including Bob Dylan. His first performance there was in the small Chapter Hall and 53 people turned up.

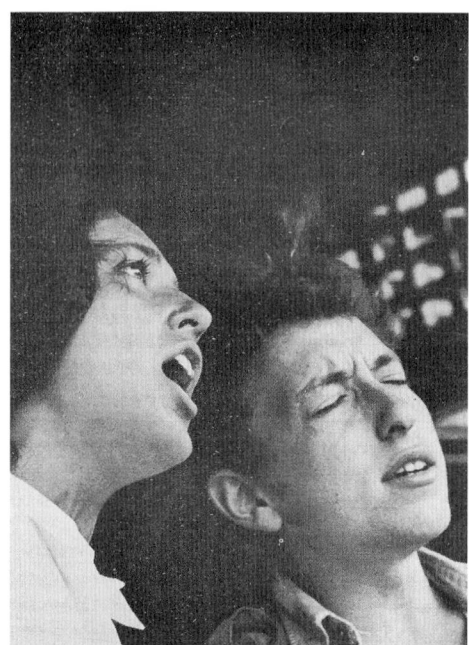

Bob Dylan got his first big break singing with Joan Baez and their on/off relationship runs through this book. The relationship between Bob, Joan, her sister Mimi and her husband, another folksinger Richard Fariña was analysed in a book by the noted music writer, David Hajdu in 2001.

A *Top Of The Pops* chart from early June 1965. Notice the competition: there were some brilliant records around and I bought Burt Bacharach, the Everly Brothers, Roger Miller, the Beatles and Bob Dylan.

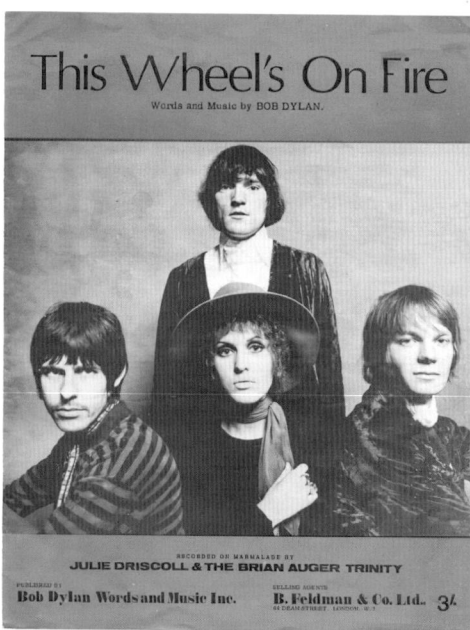

Collecting sheet music is a relatively cheap and enjoyable hobby throwing up many surprises. Who would have thought that 'Blowin' In The Wind' would have been published with Marianne Faithfull on the cover? The UK chart debut for 'Blowin' In The Wind' wasn't until 1966 when Stevie Wonder rocked it up.

IDEAS ... IDEAS ... IDEAS .

We have all tried "different" avenues of exposure in promoting our artists and artist product. You have probably done some of these "different" types of promotion on Bob Dylan, but have you tried. . .

- Getting your accounts to position Bob Dylan product in other areas of their stores besides in the folk music section, such as with The Byrds, Sonny & Cher, etc. This will afford the customer a better chance to do some impulse buying.

- Contacting musical instrument outlets and persuading them to use Bob Dylan display pieces in conjuction with their guitar, harmonica and sheet music displays.

- Contacting radio personalities in your area that have "Americana"-type shows and pointing out to them the merits of featuring Bob Dylan in an American Heritage theme.

- Getting in touch with the casual wear buyers in department stores and men's stores and convincing them to use Bob Dylan display pieces in their clothing displays. His dress may be considered "kooky" by conventional standards, but kooky or not he is a motivating force of the youth of today, and they like to emulate their leaders.

- Contacting the little theater groups and drama groups in your area to convince them that readings of the lyrics of Bob Dylan songs would be presenting modern poetry in its finest form.

- Getting in touch with the local newspaper culture editors and showing them the merits of doing a piece built around Bob Dylan, using a changing times theme.

- Putting your ads in your local newspapers on Bob Dylan is unusual areas of the paper such as on the sport page, the women's section or even the financial section...after all, he does mean money...for us at least.

- Putting Bob Dylan displays with displays of men's boots (he wears them all the time), sunglasses (he wears them all the time), or A N Y W H E R E that they will attract attention.

Be Different - He Is!

In 1965 Columbia sales staff in the US were told how to market Bob with an early use of 'Americana' for this music.

Note all the cryptic clues on the cover shot for *Bringing It All Back Home* (1965), taken by the New York photographer Daniel Kramer. It was the first major sleeve to be debated and would be followed two years later by *Sgt Pepper*.

Bob Dylan recording in 1965.

Only a pawn in the game, Bob Dylan plays open-air chess.

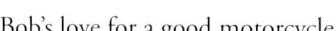

Bob's love for a good motorcycle.

Bob Dylan in 1972.

Bob Dylan on tour in 1974 (Island Records).

Bob and his top hat at Blackbushe Aerodrome, 1978.

The Last Waltz concert, filmed by Martin Scorsese. Ronnie Hawkins (centre) reunited with two of his Hawks, Robbie Robertson (l) and Rick Danko (r).

Rupert Everett, Fiona and Bob Dylan appeared in the UK film, *Hearts Of Fire*, in 1987.

Bob Dylan with his spiv moustache, 2005. It was known as a Boston Blackie after the crime fighter played by Chester Morris in the 40s and Kent Taylor in the early 50s.

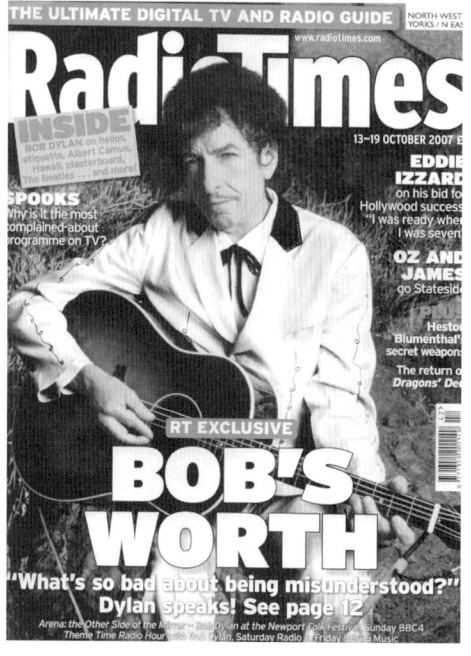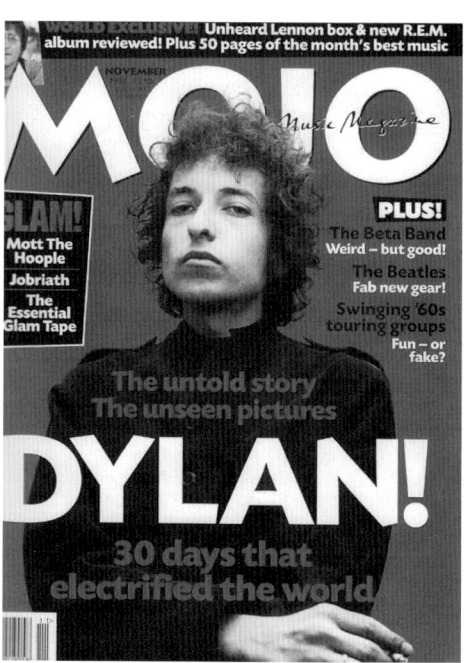

Bob Dylan on the cover sells magazines.

no details have ever emerged. Elvis recorded two of Dylan's songs, an excellent 'Tomorrow Is a Long Time' and 'Don't Think Twice, It's All Right', which is a jam session around a few lines as Elvis doesn't know the song well. Dylan called Elvis's 'Tomorrow is a Long Time' one of his proudest moments.

Dylan had asked the Byrds to join him in the studio but they never received a call and flew back to the west coast. They left New York at noon, not knowing the session was at 2.30pm. Because Bob Johnston had forgotten to tell them, they stopped working with him.

In April 1970, a spin-off from the Byrds, the Flying Burrito Brothers with Gram Parsons and Chris Hillman, released *Burrito Deluxe*. All the media coverage of country-rock following *Nashville Skyline* was good for bands like this but they made a mess of 'If You Gotta Go, Go Now'. Dylan in *Rolling Stone* praised their 'Hippie Boy'. It was country music but aimed at baby boomers.

On 8 June 1970, the double-album, *Self Portrait*, was released. Dylan painted his own portrait for the cover, but he can do better than this shapeless picture, especially now. The face, reduced from a canvas four feet square, looked more like Shaun Ryder than Dylan. Some songs were dropped to make a single album for release in Peru, which has become a rarity, worth $2,000 in mint condition.

Why do other people's songs and call the album *Self Portrait*? Are you being yourself through others' work? Does it show an absence of ego? Did he record it to get the fans off his back? In my view, *Self-Portrait* is not so much a bad album as a wrong one. Perhaps it was as mystifying as Dylan wanted it to be. It was around the time that the Beatles split and *Self-Portrait* is as indifferent and yet illuminating as *Let It Be*. Bob Dylan joked, 'The way it turned out, the album became a concept record with a title that could be taken a ton of ways.'

Some tracks on *Self Portrait* were big productions, but on others, Kenny Buttrey and Charlie McCoy overdubbed drums and bass to what Bob had done on a demo. On the whole, it felt like indifference.

At the time, rock stars didn't make covers albums – it was three years to David Bowie and Bryan Ferry. In its defence, Bob Willis: '*Self Portrait* is a wonderful album with all those old Nashville songs being revamped. He is taking the mickey out of an audience waiting for something really significant. It is one of the most endearing parts of Dylan: he never gives the people what they want.'

Greil Marcus: 'I once said I would buy an album of Bob Dylan breathing hard. I never said I'd buy an album of Bob Dylan breathing softly.' Greil Marcus' review in *Rolling Stone* opened with the question, 'What is this shit?' MOJO said that Dylan was trying to shake off his fans and 'a single album wouldn't be enough to lose them for good.'

The album was uniformly panned but it sold. Bob Stanley: 'Dylan now seems to be proud of *Self Portrait* and so he keeps changing his mind. It is a patchy record but there is some lovely stuff on it.'

Exactly. It is not a disaster. It was not like Van Morrison's contractual obligation album for Bang Records or Lou Reed's *Metal Machine Music* or Neil Young who was almost sued by David Geffen for making 'wilfully uncommercial' records. Personally I feel that Dylan was enjoying himself, doing one song after another and sometimes it works and sometimes it doesn't. They are nearly always decent songs. He loved 'Blue Moon' and later he was to record many MOR standards. Dylan often sang 'I Forgot More than You'll Ever Know' with Tom Petty and the Heartbreakers.

Paul Simon was pleased that both Bob Dylan and Emmylou Harris have recorded 'The Boxer'. However, Dylan's version is not a good one: it was the first time he had tried double-tracking and it didn't sound right. The song is taken a little too fast.

Derek Barker: 'Although 'The Boxer' is a hideous version the song is very interesting. When Paul Simon wrote it CBS was on 7th Avenue, they then moved to 8th Avenue.' Simon has pointed out that the song is about him and not Bob Dylan but they were both on Columbia.

Dylan probably took 'Days of 49' from Hedy West. John Cooper Clarke took the term 'chicken town' from this song. Since 1963 Dylan had been careful to use songs in the public domain but he was challenged by Alan Lomax and Ludlow Music over 'Days of '49'.

There are some good outtakes. The skiffle favourite 'Railroad Bill' was very good but one clunky line could have been improved by changing 'the brakeman's hand' to just 'brakeman's hand'. Tom Paxton's poignant 'Annie's Going to Sing her Song' has empathy with its pitiful subject.

In 2002, when Ryan Adams was asked if he feared burning out and making *Self Portrait*, he replied, 'I hope so, man, because it's a great album.'

Fully aware of the bootlegs, Dylan said, 'I figured I'd put all this stuff together and put it out, my own bootleg record, so to speak.' *Self Portrait* can be compared to albums of cover songs by David Bowie (*Pin-ups*), John Lennon (*Rock'n'Roll*) and Bryan Ferry (*These Foolish Things*). Dylan was, unsuspectingly, the first major songwriter to make a covers album and now everybody does it.

In May 1970 Bob Dylan had a day of sessions at the Columbia studio with George Harrison and Charlie Daniels on bass, Bob Johnston on piano and Russ Kunkel on drums. They started in the afternoon and went on until 1am. Really they were having fun together and playing each other's songs. They could never have wanted their version of 'Yesterday' to be released. You have to hear the 20 song session as a whole to realise what a good time they were having. Their version of Carl Perkins' 'Your True Love' is given the swing of a music hall song.

These sessions were only for fun because occasionally they aren't even singing on a live microphone. Fancy jamming on 'Just like Tom Thumb's Blues'? Let's do it. Why not add a lyric about the days of the week to 'Da Doo Ron Ron'? Dylan returned in the evening and cut five new songs for *New Morning*. They were songs about everyday life.

Al Kooper: 'I produced *New Morning*. Bob Johnston got the credit and he wasn't even there. It was a nerve-wracking job as Dylan changed his mind from second to second and we were lucky to get what we got.' When Kooper tried Stax-like horns on the title track, Dylan didn't like it, but it is a fairly disjointed song. The strings and the harp are an unusual mix for 'Sign on the Window'. Dylan plays piano on that track and Kooper says that Dylan was a good pianist. The academic Christopher Ricks has called it 'one of Dylan's most perfect songs'. Dylan's special thanks to Al Kooper was originally omitted from the proof cover for *New Morning*. Dylan asked if it was all right. He said no and it had to be redone.

'The Man in Me' is a wonderful tribute to Sara. Dylan probably wrote the warm, simple and charming 'If Not for You' for Sara. Dylan envisaged a Tex-Mex arrangement but it came out folk. George Harrison played harmonica on 'If Not for You', although he never played harmonica with the Beatles. It has been taken as light pop but it has gravitas. Liz Thomson: 'There are little intricate chords in that song. You think there are three chords but there are seven.'

Maeretha Stuart adds a jazz-rap to 'If Dogs Ran Free' which is unlike anything Dylan had done before, while 'Three Angels' is beat poetry with a choral arrangement. His waltz, 'Winterlude', is a perfect pastiche of 1940s pop. His little joke of 'winterlude, this dude' can be compared with the 'moon' and 'spoon' of 'I'll Be Your Baby Tonight'. Dylan is enjoying himself.

The poet and playwright Archibald MacLeish wanted Dylan to write songs for a play based on *The Devil and Daniel Webster*. Dylan did write some songs, but MacLeish didn't care for 'Father of Night'. Three songs went on *New Morning* – 'Father of Night, 'Time Passes Slowly' and 'New Morning'. They both realised that the project wasn't right. The play did get on Broadway but only for two days.

On 9 June 1970 Bob Dylan was awarded an honorary doctorate in music from Princeton University, New Jersey. He and his guest David Crosby were driven there by 'One-legged Terry (Noble)', a tough Bronx guy who was Bob's chauffeur and taught him Hebrew. When Bob was asked why he was learning Hebrew, he said, 'Because I can't speak it.'

When they arrived, the authorities wanted Dylan in a cap and gown. He refused but David talked to him and he agreed on the gown but not the cap. The ceremony was delayed because Coretta Scott King, the widow of Martin Luther King, was being honoured and arrived late. Dylan became the first rock star to receive an honorary degree, although they are commonplace today. On August 12, he completed *New Morning* with a song about the ceremony, 'Day of the Locusts'. 'The man with his head exploding head' was his guest, David Crosby.

On 10 September 1970 the Federal Communications Commission published a list of songs which appeared to eulogise the use of narcotics. It included 'Rainy Day Women, Numbers 12 and 35'. As if to make the point, Jimi Hendrix died a week later. Then on October 1, Janis Joplin released 'Mercedes-Benz', written by Bobby Neuwirth and Michael McClure, but she died from her excesses three days later.

Around this time, Dylan wanted a base in New York City. His new address was 94 MacDougal Street in the Village. He had commented that there were 'too many flower children in Woodstock' so why come to Greenwich Village? However, he had a point: some of the flower children in Woodstock liked the area so much that they stayed in the area. Dylan also had a home in East Hampton on Long Island that had belonged to Henry Ford.

A very intense enthusiast A.J. Weberman started looking through Dylan's rubbish for scraps of discarded lyrics and evidence that he was a drug addict. Literally, he was dishing the dirt. He would take Dylan fans on tours of the Village which would end up outside his townhouse. It was a huge invasion of privacy and you don't need a Weberman to know which way the wind blows.

Bob Spitz: 'A.J. Weberman is the strangest character in the Bob Dylan story. He was a teenager when he encountered Bob Dylan and he was swept away by his lyrics. Dylan became his philosopher king. He started to go through Dylan's garbage looking for clues and at first it was funny. He entertained people but he was looking for syringes. Weberman interpreted his songs as drug songs and he formed tours outside his house and disrupted his life. A.J. Weberman is no different from Mark David Chapman in the John Lennon story; he is just a man without a gun. We have to protect ourselves from people like that.'

Dylan mentioned him in *Rolling Stone*, so he knew he was needling Dylan. On 6 January 1971 Dylan confronted him outside his house. He offered him an interview if he had the right to see it before publication.

Weberman recorded a phone call from Dylan. Weberman said that Dylan was saying 'Don't expose me' when you play *New Morning* backwards 'Oh fuck me,' said Dylan, 'why don't you play an Andy Williams record backwards?' Dylan ended by saying, 'You don't have my permission to do any of this shit.'

In October 1971 Dylan obtained an order for A.J. Weberman to desist but he soon broke that. Dylan attacked him in the street after he was spotted going through his garbage. In December, A.J. Weberman called Dylan and recorded the conversation. Folkways wanted to release it but Dylan filed an injunction. Weberman wrote about Dylan in *East Village Other*. They refused to publish Dylan's response as they said it was libellous. Dylan went round to their office and was told to leave. John and Yoko and Jerry Rubin wrote an open letter in *Village Voice* saying Weberman should apologise.

If only Weberman had known… While Dylan was in Greenwich Village, he rented the ground floor of 124 West Houston Street and he was to leave a couple of boxes of acetates in a closet, nearly 150 of them! Years later, the new owner Jeff Gold sold them. Mostly they related to *Self Portrait*, often without overdubs and some different mixes.

New Morning was released in the US on 21 October 1970. The cover had Dylan's photograph surrounded by a frame as though this were the real self-portrait. On the back of the sleeve, there is a photo of Bob and Victoria Spivey in 1971 and he is holding Big Joe Williams' nine-string guitar. Possibly it was released too soon after *Self Portrait* but this may have been damage limitation. *Self Portrait* had sold well but had damaged his standing. It is a pity he omitted 'Tomorrow Is a Long Time' as it had yet to make an official appearance.

Harvey Brooks was back for *New Morning*. Harvey played chess with Dylan several times during the making of the album. He found him mellower and wanting to paint. By and large, it was an optimistic album about domestic bliss. Others had been doing that but Dylan gave it an edge. The songs followed on from each other, even though three had been written for a musical play. Dylan was fond of putting locations into his songs: he wants a cabin in Utah and it's wet tonight on Main Street. Most of all, *New Morning* had a rural feel and sounded like a Band record even though they were not on it.

The outtakes and alternative versions on *Bootleg 10* are especially good. There is a lovely 'If Not for You' with Bob's piano and a violin and an excellent string arrangement for 'Sign on the Window'. He amends Leadbelly's 'Bring a Little Water, Sylvie' so much so that it is almost a different song. Well, he's taking the songwriting credit, anyway.

In 1970 Dylan had invested in a tax shelter Home-Stake Oil Production Company in Tulsa but it was fraudulent and he lost $120,000.

In December 1970 Dylan played with the Scruggs family (Earl, Randy and Gary) for a TV documentary *Earl Scruggs Performing with his Family and Friends*. Dylan played both harmonica and guitar on 'Nashville Skyline Rag' and then sang with Earl on 'East Virginia Blues'.

There is a fascinating anecdote in a biography of screenwriter William Golding by John Carey. In 1971 Andrew Sinclair put up William Golding in Hanover Terrace. Golding got drunk and argumentative and during the night he destroyed Sinclair's puppet of Bob Dylan believing it to be Satan and buried it in the back garden. Sinclair retrieved it.

In February 1971 there was a showing of *Eat the Document* at the New York Academy of Music, with proceeds to combat strip mining. The credit was 'Directed by Bob Dylan and Howard Alk'. There were two more showings and then it was dropped.

During March 1971, Bob spent a couple of days recording with Leon Russell at Blue

Rock in New York. The line, 'What's the matter with me, I don't have much to say' in 'Watching the River Flow' suggests he may have had writer's block, but he's content to watch the river flow. For that, the song could be compared to 'Sittin' on the Dock of the Bay'.

Leon Russell: 'I took Jim Keltner, Jesse Ed Davis and Carl Radle up to New York to a studio called Blue Rock and I cut some tracks and some changes and then Bob wrote the songs to go with the changes and he allowed me to follow him around. I looked over his shoulder and watched him write both songs. I was a fan and he allowed me to see how he worked. 'When I Paint My Masterpiece' refers to that event. "You'll be right there with me when I paint my masterpiece", that's about me looking over his shoulder.'

Did he pick up any songwriting tips? 'Yeah, when we were walking down a street in Manhattan, he said, "Yeah, I get ideas from whatever, I got one from those angels up on the church hall." He was trying to help me and I thought that was going beyond the extra mile.'

In May 1971 Dylan and Sara flew to Jerusalem and they visited the Wailing Wall. They visited a kibbutz and did consider moving to Israel but that soon passed.

Dylan employed Naomi Saltzman, a music publisher and lawyer, who used to work for Albert Grossman. Around September 1970, she told Bob Markel at Macmillan that they could publish *Tarantula*, but she advised them to lose no time as Dylan might change his mind. *Tarantula* was finally published in May 1971 and the book is like a long edition of his sleeve notes. There is a vague story involving both historical and fictional figures. The influence is *The Naked Lunch* but Bob Dylan had not written a masterpiece.

Disc reported that there were more Dylan bootlegs around than official releases. They knew of 18. One was said to be Bob Dylan at the Royal Albert Hall with the 'Judas!' shout, so there was even confusion back in June 1971.

On August 1971 the first of the big charity rock concerts took place: *Concert for Bangla Desh*, at Madison Square Garden. The Monterey Festival though had also been for good causes. Michael Gray: 'George Harrison of the Beatles was the most decent human being in the Beatles. Dylan responded to that and he liked his modesty and his single-minded musicianship.' Dylan wasn't keen though on George asking him to do 'Blowin' in the Wind'. He said, 'And are you going to do 'I Want to Hold Your Hand'?'

The concert was a joint undertaking between Harrison and the US fund for UNICEF and included Eric Clapton, Billy Preston and Leon Russell. Bob would be backed by George and Leon, who told me, 'George Harrison was a friend of mine and Ravi Shankar had asked him to mount some relief effort for that famine in Bangla Desh. George was living in the Hollywood Hills and he asked me to help him figure out how to stage it. Bob Dylan was a good friend of George's and at that time he was very reluctant to perform. He is a very reticent guy but when he hits the stage, he gets very bright and big. Then he comes off stage and he is able to disappear. We were trying to get a band for him rather than have him play by himself. He said, "When it's just me, I do fine but when I have anybody else, it all goes haywire." We had Ringo to play tambourine and George to play guitar and me to play bass, of all things. We rehearsed one of the songs and we had it all figured out but when he started to play on the show, he turned one of the songs into a waltz and everybody was confused for a few seconds.' So when it goes haywire, it's all Bob's fault.

The best moment is George saying, 'I'd like to bring out a friend to us all, Mr. Bob Dylan' and hearing the incredible reaction. The perfect introduction. There were two houses: for the afternoon show, Bob performed 'A Hard Rain's A-Gonna Fall', 'Blowin' in the Wind', 'It Takes a Lot to Laugh, It Takes a Train to Cry', Love Minus Zero / No Limit' and 'Just Like a Woman'. In the evening, he dropped 'Love Minus Zero' and added 'Mr. Tambourine Man'. He did 'Blowin' in the Wind' because he knew that it was his most appropriate song.

It was Dylan's first gig since the Isle of Wight and it won a Grammy as Album of the Year. Surprisingly, this did not lead to a spate of big charity concerts. The next big one was *No Nukes* but that was not until 1979.

In September 1971, Dylan had a session with Happy Traum. Columbia wanted to issue a second volume of *Greatest Hits* and the label wanted his own version of some of his songs. Happy Traum: 'There were some well-known songs from *The Basement Tapes* that Bob had not recorded himself like the Byrds who had had a hit with 'You Ain't Goin' Nowhere'. The Band had done 'I Shall Be Released' beautifully on *Music from Big Pink*. We did 'Down in the Flood' and 'Only a Hobo', which Bob had only recorded as Blind Boy Grunt and that was the first song he wanted to do. It was just us and an engineer and we did two takes and Bob said, 'Okay, let's move on.' He didn't say it was good or bad and I thought I must have been terrible. I didn't hear that song again and I didn't know it had been preserved because the three other songs came out on the *Greatest Hits*. That was great for me, three songs on an album with Bob Dylan. Then in 2013 this compilation came out called *Another Self Portrait* and there was 'Only a Hobo' with me singing and playing banjo. I was shocked that it had finally seen the light of day and when I listened, it wasn't bad (laughs).'

Was it hard to harmonise with Dylan? Happy Traum: 'Oh, this was very loose. We were not trying to be the Everly Brothers! People do moan about Bob's voice but I've always loved it, and when he does sing well, he is right in pitch. It's not difficult to create harmonies to go along with that. This was loose and easy and we weren't trying for perfection, which was just as well as there is no perfection about it (laughs).' A key moment is Dylan's little dig at Roger McGuinn for singing wrong words on 'You Ain't Goin' Nowhere'.

The double-album was issued with a poster of Dylan with rainbow hair by Milton Glaser. It included live performances, new songs and rarities. Not really a *Greatest Hits* at all!

George Jackson was the same age as Bob Dylan and when he was 18, he was jailed for driving a getaway car. He became a Black Panther while in prison and his letters home were published in 1969 under the title of *Soledad Brother*. He studied Marx and Lenin. In 1970, there was a racial fight. The guards opened fire and three black prisoners were killed. It was deemed 'justifiable homicide' which led to the death of a white guard by way of retaliation.

On 17 August 1970 when George Jackson was about to be tried, his brother Jonathan took a judge and three jurors hostage during a different trial. In an attempt to regain control, Jonathan Jackson, the judge and two jurors were killed. George Jackson's trial was postponed but just before it took place, he was shot dead by a guard in San Quentin for attempting to escape. (Escaping from San Quentin? That's unlikely.)

Dylan was moved by the story and recorded 'George Jackson' on 4 November 1971. In the song he was arrested and taken to San Quentin on a trumped-up charge. Dylan wanted it rush-released even though the death was in August. His solo version was on the A-side and on the B-side was the same song with accompaniment from Ben Keith, Leon Russell (bass again) and Kenny Buttrey. The acoustic version works best as the 'big band version' (it isn't) is perfunctory but does speed up neatly in the fade-out ending. The line 'He wouldn't take shit from no one' gave the radio stations an excuse to ban it. It was Dylan's first overtly political song in years.

Dylan cut 'Wallflower', continuing his interest in country music, and John Prine's 'Donald and Lydia'. 'Wallflower' was later recorded for *Doug Sahm and Band* with Dylan on vocal.

When Dylan attended an evening of improvised poetry by Allen Ginsberg, Bob said to him, 'What about improvising poetry and music?' As a result, Dylan met at Ginsberg's apartment with Peter Orlovsky and David Amram and they worked on improvised poems and music. Dylan said, 'Let's book a studio.' At the Record Plant in New York, Dylan sang 'Gimme My Money Back' and Ginsberg offered him, 'September on Jessore Road' as he wanted to 'offer Dylan a text equal to his own genius and sympathy'. Another offering was 'CIA Dope Calypso' and 'Vomit Express' so they were having a good time. Three tracks were released in 1983 on the album, *First Blues* by Allen Ginsberg.

Meanwhile Eric Von Schmidt had hooked up with Rick Danko and Garth Hudson for *Living on the Trail*, recording at Bearsville Studios and produced by Jim Rooney. The musicians included Geoff and Maria Muldaur, Paul Butterfield and Amos Garrett. It included 'Joshua Gone Barbados' about a union boss who accepted a bribe and betrayed the workers he represented. The album should have been released in 1972 but was held back for 30 years.

The Band were doing a residency at the Academy of Music on 14th Street in New York from December 28 to 31 with a horn section under Allen Toussaint and the concerts were being recorded for a live double-album, later called *Rock of Ages*. A union problem prevented Howard Alk from filming more than a few songs. Bob Dylan joined them on New Year's Eve and they performed 'Down in the Flood', 'When I Paint My Masterpiece', 'Don't Ya Tell Henry' and 'Like a Rolling Stone'. It was short, and pithy and it sparked what would happen next – Bob Dylan and The Band, billed equally, together in concert.

CHAPTER 9

Framed

I. Musicians Making Movies

Bob Dylan is not like any other music star. You'll know that, if you didn't already, from reading this book. But in one way, he is the same. He has wanted to establish himself in films and over the years, he has acted, contributed to soundtracks, written screenplays, and directed and produced with varying success. Later in this chapter, we'll look at his contribution to an expensive western *Pat Garrett and Billy the Kid*, where the backstage story was as dramatic as anything on screen. There have been films about the making of movies (*The African Queen, Psycho, The Birds, Mary Poppins*) and there is enough drama and comedy to make one about *Pat Garrett and Billy the Kid*.

The first successful 'talkie' was *The Jazz Singer* starring Al Jolson in 1927. Because Jolson performed in black face, he is dismissed today but he introduced many famous songs ('Alexander's Ragtime Band', 'Swanee', 'Sonny Boy', 'California Here I Come') and uttered the immortal phrase, 'You ain't heard nothing yet!' Larry Parks played Jolson in *The Jolson Story* (1946) but instead of singing, he mimed to Jolson performances.

Bing Crosby was an easy going singer who acted in many films, winning an Oscar as a Catholic priest in *Going My Way* (1944), a role in which he was also typecast. With a slight build and protruding ears, he was not an obvious leading man but he was perfect for roles which called for warm and gentle homilies. The comedy in his *Road* films with Bob Hope seems hopelessly unfunny today but times change and the series was massively successful in its day. He starred alongside Frank Sinatra in the Cole Porter musical *High Society* (1956) and in later years he was part of the ensemble cast for the remake of *Stagecoach* (1966).

When it comes to combining acting and singing, Frank Sinatra has been extraordinarily successful and his celluloid CV is more impressive than many full-time Hollywood A-listers. He won an Oscar as a supporting actor for his role as Maggio in *From Here to Eternity* (1953) and he must have been close to winning another for the title role in *The Man with the Golden Arm* (1955), but possibly some voting members shied away from the subject of drug addiction. He played a night-club comic whose throat was cut by the Mob in *The Joker Is Wild* (1957) and starred in a series of Rat Pack adventures, notably *Ocean's 11* (1960), which has survived much better than it deserved as the actors didn't take it seriously. It didn't matter: their lack of commitment tied in perfectly with the Rat Pack image.

Elvis Presley acquitted himself well in his early films playing a troubled youth in *King Creole* (1958) and a half-breed cowboy in *Flaming Star* (1960). He then made a series of popcorn movies which were ideal for dating and not much else. The only fun in *Fun in Acapulco* (1963) was in the title. Colonel Parker saw these films as the easy option and the King of Rock'n'Roll was wasting his time and his talent, but making a lot of money. Parker rejected both *West Side Story* and the remake of *A Star Is Born*. His concert documentaries were good and the recently compiled film on the *'68 Comeback Special* is top drawer Elvis.

Many pop stars wanted to follow Elvis into the movies but it wasn't easy. Look at Heinz in *Live It Up*. He should have had the main role but the producers soon realised that the guitarist in the group, David Hemmings, was a far better bet. Roy Orbison looked uncomfortable in *The Fastest Guitar Alive* (1966) and Ricky Nelson read his lines without emotion in several films. Bobby Darin could play both comedy and drama and was nominated for an Oscar as a shell-shocked GI in *Captain Newman MD* (1964).

The Beatles' natural charm and wit carried them through *A Hard Day's Night* (1964) where they were little more than cartoon versions of themselves – no wait, that was *Yellow Submarine*. *Help!* (1965) was like a pantomime and John Lennon was okay in an ensemble piece *How I Won the War* (1967). Paul McCartney was stuck in a gormless film *Give My Regards to Broad Street* (1984) but George Harrison made some astute decisions as a film producer (notably, *Monty Python's Life of Brian*) but did not pay attention as to where the money was going. One of George's disasters was *Shanghai Surprise* (1986) with Madonna and Sean Penn.

The experimental French director, Jean-Luc Godard, filmed the Rolling Stones for *One plus One* (1968). It was later retitled *Sympathy for the Devil*, but it fooled no one. The Stones are shown in a recording studio alongside footage from Vietnam, and your point is...

An even bigger mistake was made by Tony Richardson when he cast Mick Jagger as an Australian outlaw with a ridiculous beard in *Ned Kelly* (1970). Mick Jagger did move into film production with *Enigma* (2001), a decent enough wartime espionage film set in Bletchley Park.

Top marks to Jagger's girlfriend, Marianne Faithfull. Even if her acting could have been better, her look in *Girl on A Motorcycle* (1968) made her iconic. Her black leather outfit is zipped from neck to crotch and she says to her boyfriend Alain Delon, 'Skin me.' Dear me, I'm getting horny just thinking about it.

Mick Jagger has never been captured right on screen, perhaps because his speaking voice didn't match his rock star image, but he gave his best performance in Nicolas Roeg's *Performance* (1970) in which he played Turner, a rock singer getting away from his fame who is thrown together with a gangster Chas, played by James Fox. The film rates highly in the Stones' mythology as Anita Pallenberg is the love interest.

As we applaud authenticity in a performer, it is surprising that David Bowie was so successful as his whole career was built on artifice. He changed his look and his style so many times, his most famous role being Ziggy Stardust. He was ideally cast as the alien in *The Man Who Fell to Earth* (1976) and then he was on Broadway as *The Elephant Man* (1980), curiously playing the circus freak without grotesque make-up. Neither Sinatra nor Presley had the discipline for a theatre run, and it illustrates that Bowie was comfortable as an actor. Not sure how convincing he was as whenever I have seen him, I have always thought I was watching David Bowie.

Both Johnny Cash and Willie Nelson made several film appearances and again, they worked best when they are more or less themselves and we tune in to their natural charisma. Johnny Cash and Kirk Douglas played aging gunfighters drawn into a showdown in *A Gunfight* (1971), but the film was ruined, in my view, by having a fake ending. Willie Nelson was fine as Robert Redford's manager in *An Electric Horseman* (1979) but, more importantly, he contributed mightily to the soundtrack.

After Simon and Garfunkel made a fortune from the soundtrack of *The Graduate* (1967), the director Mike Nichols unwittingly brought about the end of the duo by inviting them to appear in the film of Joseph Heller's novel, *Catch-22* (1970). The script was too long and Paul Simon's character was dropped. Garfunkel made the film without him which overran at a time when Simon wanted to complete the *Bridge over Troubled Water* album. Hence the song 'The Only Living Boy in New York'. The film gave Garfunkel a taste for making films and he starred along Jack Nicholson as the disillusioned friend in *Carnal Knowledge* (1971). In 1980, he had his best role, playing a detective in Nicolas Roeg's *Bad Timing*. Both Paul Simon and Lou Reed had cameos in Woody Allen's *Annie Hall* (1977) but Simon was not resilient enough for his own film, *One-Trick Pony* (1980), which was only saved by the brilliance of his songwriting.

For many years, Kris Kristofferson put his musical career on hold as he was making movies. Virtually all his key songs are on his first two albums and then because of his astonishing good looks (especially with a beard) and his agility, he accepted action roles. He started slowly with roles in the hippie movies *The Last Movie* (1971) and *Cisco Pike* with Doug Sahm (1972) and then he played the outlaw role in *Pat Garrett and Billy the Kid* (1973). His major breakthrough was in *A Star Is Born* (1976) alongside Barbra Streisand. You can see that Bradley Cooper copied his mumbled speech and mannerisms in the 2018 remake and it is hilarious when Cooper's older brother accuses him of copying him. Just how many Kristoffersons was the remake going to have? Kristofferson's diction could be clearer but he has worked well as a Poundland Clint Eastwood. He was at his best in *Heaven's Gate* (1980) and its much-trumpeted failure wasn't his fault.

Turning in the other direction, there have been many actors who have made records, sometimes with extraordinary success. In 1969 Lee Marvin asked Nelson Riddle, the MD for *Paint Your Wagon*, who was going to do his vocals and was surprised to be told 'You are'. Riddle amused himself by working out how Marvin's lived-in voice could be used to best effect and 'Wand'rin' Star' was so striking that it became a Number 1 record. In the same film, Clint Eastwood just about got through 'I Talk to the Trees' but they don't listen to me and who could blame them.

Both Rex Harrison and Richard Harris won through in *My Fair Lady* (1964) and *Camelot* (1967) by half-singing, half-speaking their lines. Richard Harris was coaxed to a remarkable performance by Jimmy Webb for 'MacArthur Park' (1968) and his version outclasses that of any trained singer because he brought an actor's interpretive skills to the song.

Telly Savalas scored a Number 1 by reciting David Gates' 'If' (1975) but he couldn't succeed with that same trick twice. Another TV detective, David Soul, had a decent singing voice and he scored four Top 10 hits as well as starring in the highly controversial stage musical, *Jerry Springer: The Opera*.

Not much could save Peter Fonda in *Outlaw Blues* (1977) but Keith Carradine won an Oscar for his own song, 'I'm easy', from the country music satire, *Nashville* (1975).

There has been no straightforward biopic of Bob Dylan and, as we shall see, *I'm Not There* (2007), lived up to its title. His career is too long and labyrinthine for a standard biopic, but there are segments of his career that could be used for films – Bob Dylan in London, Bob Dylan and the Judas Tour and Bob Dylan and the making of *Pat Garrett and Billy the Kid*, to name but three.

It is a shame that the more compelling and fascinating music performers have been largely overlooked by the film-makers. Even Billy Bob Thornton couldn't interest the money men in a film on his hero, Captain Beefheart and I'd have paid good money to have seen Billy Bob in that role. The recent successes of biopics on Freddie Mercury and Elton John could lead to several more. I would expect Frank Zappa, Patti Smith and Leonard Cohen to make good subjects.

Writing this book has been like painting the Forth Bridge: you are never really finished, although they now use more durable paint. In January 2020, it was announced that Timothée Chalamet would be playing Dylan in *Going Electric,* directed by James Mangold and based on Dylan in the mid-60s. Chalamet, who is in *Little Women* looks like good casting. *The Times* reported that Dylan was an advisor on the project, which is novel and will be highly significant if it happens. Possibly Dylan, approaching 80, wants to set the record straight but it would be out of character for him to do so.

II. So Much Older Then: 1972–1973

One constant factor about Bob Dylan is that he enjoys seeing other performers. He doesn't generally give endorsements but he is very supportive, none more so than in 1972. Maybe he was just contemplating his own future, but he spent much of the year watching others at work. He was a man about town, mostly in New York. He saw Link Wray and Loudon Wainwright at Max's Kansas City and Jackson Browne at the Bitter End.

He heard the Russian poet Andrei Voznesensky at Town Hall and afterwards he and Allen Ginsberg took him to Greenwich Village. His old friend Mike Porco had moved Gerde's to 130 West 3rd Street and was promoting rock and jazz as well as folk.

When Dylan was a guest at Mick Jagger's birthday party in New York, Peter Grant said to Dylan, 'Hello, I'm Peter Grant. I manage Led Zeppelin' and Dylan replied, 'Hey, I don't come to you with my problems.'

There was plenty for Bob to see and hear even if he wasn't performing himself. Although Bob Dylan often made his own records hurriedly, he did enjoy attending other people's sessions including Joe Cocker, Bette Midler and Roger McGuinn.

Dylan was irritated by Neil Young's 'Heart of Gold'. He said, 'I used to hate it when it came on the radio. I'd say, "Shit, that's me!" If it sounds like me, it might as well be me.' Bob Dylan cited George Jones' 'Small Time Labouring Man' as one of his favourite records and he enjoyed seeing Waylon Jennings in a small club. Dylan signed a public letter in support of John Lennon's plea for a green card to stay in the US.

In June 1972 Bob saw Elvis at Madison Square Garden, then the Grateful Dead and the Allman Brothers at Roosevelt Stadium, Jersey City. In July he attended the Mariposa Folk Festival on Centre Island, Toronto. He and Sara socialised with Gordon Lightfoot, Dave Bromberg and Bukka White. He took a boat with Leon Redbone and sailed around the island. The organisers requested a guest appearance but he wasn't biting. Elsewhere he played a short set on a riverboat on a whim and he got up with John Prine and Dave Bromberg at the Bitter End. He played harmonica and joined Prine on vocals for 'Donald and Lydia', an indication that he had been listening to what Prine was doing.

He played piano and sang harmony on Steve Goodman's 'Election Year Rag' and 'Somebody Else's Troubles' using the splendid alias of Robert Milkwood Thomas. The producer Arif Martin had to contend with the unlikely mix of Bob Dylan on piano, Dave Bromberg on gut-string guitar and Steve Goodman on kazoo.

Dylan was friendly with Doug Sahm, who combined Cajun, country and rock and had had a massive hit with the Sir Douglas Quintet, 'She's about a Mover'. He agreed to play on *Doug Sahm and Band* which was being produced by Jerry Wexler for Atlantic in New York. 'Wallflower' was a fine old-time country song written by Dylan about girls who hadn't been asked to dance. Dylan was shown on the front cover cartoon as a smiling, dancing hillbilly in a purple shirt. Jerry Wexler wrote in his autobiography that Doug Sahm was 'very singular with his own sound on guitar, his own voice, his own songs…the album didn't sell.' Maybe not but it's great fun with Dylan, Dr. John, David 'Fathead' Newman, Dave Bromberg and Augie Meyer – what's not to like?

Bob Dylan was enjoying himself, not pressurising himself and having a good time, perhaps getting ready for the Next Big Thing, whatever that might be. As we all know, Dylan is unpredictable, but his next move took even himself by surprise…*Pat Garrett and Billy the Kid*.

Dylan was offered a small role in a western being made by one of his favourite directors, Sam Peckinpah, but it got spectacularly out of hand, although it was a remarkable experience. Commenting on Peckinpah, Dylan said, 'He was an outlaw. A real hombre. Somebody from the old school. Men like they don't make anymore.'

Kris Kristofferson: 'One of Sam Peckinpah's regular stunt men put it very well. He said, "Sam likes to be surrounded by chaos." Peckinpah was surrounded by turmoil the whole time: usually it was fighting with the studio and in *Pat Garrett* he was arguing with them all the time. He was fighting the good fight as he was trying to make a good piece of art.'

Sam Peckinpah was born in Fresno, California in 1925. He obtained a degree in theatre and worked on the TV series, *Gunsmoke* and *The Rifleman*. He wrote and directed the feature films, *Ride the High Country* (1962) and *Major Dundee* (1965) and became famous for a western bloodbath, *The Wild Bunch* (1969). Sam had been a marine who had been horrified by war and he ended up examining violence in slow motion.

Peckinpah continued to be controversial with the brutal *Straw Dogs* (1971) starring Dustin Hoffman as the mild-mannered academic who takes revenge on the locals who raped his wife. The next two films, *Junior Bonner* and *The Getaway*, both with Steve McQueen in 1972, were more mainstream and he was returning to his favourite theme, the western, for *Pat Garrett and Billy the Kid*. McQueen could have played Garrett but he was fed up with a director who was generating more publicity than his actors.

The story of Billy the Kid had been told often, notably in *The Left Handed Gun* (1958), even though Billy was right handed. Billy was a cold-hearted killer but Peckinpah saw his nemesis, Sheriff Pat Garrett, as little better: he just had the law on his side. Garrett was obsessed by capturing or killing Billy and in the film, when he does finally shoot him, he sees his own reflection in a mirror and shoots that too.

The idea was to film on location around Durango, Mexico, or to be more precise, the desert, in November 1972 and with a bit of luck, they would be home for Christmas. Additional scenes could be shot on a Hollywood sound stage.

Peckinpah's casting was exemplary. Brando was proposed for Garrett but in the end, he was played by one of Hollywood's leading men, James Coburn. He had made his name in the ensemble action films, *The Magnificent Seven* (1960) and *The Great Escape* (1963). He had worked for Peckinpah in *Major Dundee* (1965), although Dundee was played by Charlton Heston, and a year later he starred in a James Bond pastiche *Our Man Flint*. He had just finished a spaghetti western, *Duck You Sucker*, for Sergio Leone with music by Ennio Morricone.

For the role of Billy the Kid, Peckinpah signed the up-and-coming country songwriter, Kris Kristofferson. He had excelled in the title role of the low-budget *Cisco Pike* (1972) where he had to act alongside Gene Hackman and Harry Dean Stanton. He was prone to mumble but the camera loved him. Pat Garrett shot Billy the Kid when he was 21: Kris was 36 but what the heck, this is the movies.

Peckinpah thought that the two protagonists could be linked by a nameless character, Alias, who would comment on the action. In Lee Marvin's *Cat Ballou* (1965), you have the linking device of a song performed by Nat 'King' Cole and Stubby Kaye. If that's too light-hearted, then consider the Fool in *King Lear* who also comments on what is happening. Much of it was to be improvised and as Dylan said to Kristofferson once the filming started, 'Well, at least you're in the script.'

Originally, Peckinpah had thought of John Stewart, formerly of the Kingston Trio, for Billy the Kid. That made sense as his western narration 'Mother Country' showed how commanding he could be. His widow Buffy Ford told me, 'John was so excited that he was up for it and he wanted it so much. He was a natural actor. He thought he had the role and he was very disappointed. It was the Billy the Kid part and then they thought of the Alias part but Dylan got that.'

Nevertheless, John Stewart would have been happy as Alias. 'I had Dylan's role. I had it, my bags were packed. I met the producer, he liked me and he said, 'You're going to Mexico.' I talked to Kristofferson and he said, 'It'll be great, John. We'll go down there and have a lot of fun.' I was ready to go, then I got a call from the producer who said, "John, I'm sorry, but Dylan has agreed to go." I said, "Ah well, he'll be terrific." In retrospect, talking to Kris afterwards, it turned out to be miserable. Peckinpah wouldn't leave his trailer for five days; the wind was blowing; and they all got colds, but it sure would have been fun to work with Coburn and Peckinpah and Kris. But Dylan was terrific. I thought he did a great job.' Stewart recorded 'Durango' about his lost role.

Possibly Dylan too thought that he could play the Kid. Al Aronowitz recalled Bob looking into a mirror in 1968 and asking him, 'Do I look like Billy the Kid?' In terms of physical appearance, Dylan looked more like Billy the Kid than Kris Kristofferson did. Bert Block, who had managed Janis Joplin with Albert Grossman, was managing Kris Kristofferson and secured him the role.

Bob Dylan talked to scriptwriter Rudy Wurlitzer and saw *The Wild Bunch (1970)* at a private screening. He went to see Peckinpah as he realised, as with Pennebaker, that this was a good way to learn about film-making.

There is some historical basis for Alias. In Pat Garrett's autobiography, he describes Billy arriving at Camp Bowie, Arizona with his partner who was so given to changing his name that it was difficult to call him by the right one. Billy called him 'Alias'. Alias was shot in the back on 29 Feb 1908. Billy the Kid himself used an alias from time to time: he wasn't born William Bonney but Henry McCarty. Alias was a perfect identity for Dylan himself.

'Who are you?' asks Pat Garrett (James Coburn) 'That's a good question,' responds Alias, just the answer Bob Dylan would give. Some dialogue owes as much to Dylan's legend as Alias. 'How does it feel?' asks the Kid, and Garrett replies, 'It feels like times have changed.' The Kid comes back, 'Times maybe, but not me.'

This film was being shot outside Durango, really in the desert, and it was ridiculous that Dylan brought his wife and family. They arrived on 23 November 1972. The filming started with the turkey scene the next day. They were living in an impoverished area with no irrigation and plenty of dust, creating lung infections. Sara was unhappy to be there, both for herself and more specifically for the children. When they started coughing, she took them to Los Angeles.

Bobby Neuwirth came as Dylan's roadie. Neuwirth had played 'Me and Bobby McGee' to Janis Joplin and was to introduce her to Kristofferson. Kristofferson was not to hear her version of the song until after her death in October 1970. It became a posthumous US Number 1.

Kris had some of his musicians to hand and Donnie Fritts was given a role in the film. Donnie Fritts recalled, 'Kris did get his friends into the movies and obviously I would never have met Sam Peckinpah without him but nobody could have convinced Sam Peckinpah that he should use somebody that he didn't want to. I said to Sam, "I've never acted before." He said, "Hell, that doesn't matter. You do what I tell you to do and you'll be all right".'

For much of the time, Peckinpah was drunk and argumentative. Kris Kristofferson, 'Sam Peckinpah was not a man who could have done a daytime job; he wanted to make great pieces of art. He thrived on conflict and was always arguing with the studio and with the producers. Sam was trying to make a good film but it got harder for him, especially as the drinking got out of hand.' Dylan put it more succinctly: 'I was trapped deep in the heart of Mexico with some madman.'

Willie Nelson and wife Connie came to see them in Durango. Willie said, 'Dylan was a little shy of horses, scared to death. They had him jumping and running on them horses and he ain't no cowboy.' Kristofferson added, 'Bob stuck it out without knowing what he was really supposed to be doing.'

Donnie Fritts: 'Bob Dylan was there the whole time we were there. I loved Bob and for a while we were filming about 30 miles out of Durango, Mexico. It was one of the poorest states in Mexico and it was very rough. He would pick me up every morning to go to the set as our scenes were together, He was fine with it.'

There was a scene where Coburn rides off into the sunrise after killing Billy and they had about five minutes to get it right but they were shooting it as sunset-for-sunrise. Billy and Harry Dean Stanton, who weren't on call decided to go for a jog, only part of it was through the line of action. Sam was furious: 'You have cost me thousands of dollars'. Harry Dean Stanton responded, 'Hell, Sam, I was trying to catch up with him and stop him.' Sam threw a knife at Harry. Dylan said, 'Okay, let's do a concert and pay him back.'

Sam Peckinpah's film did have blind spots and one of them was the score. He thought Dylan had been imposed on him. He had made a western with orchestral music, *Ride the High Country* (1962) which Dylan admired, but Dylan's score would be nothing like that.

On the first day of shooting, Dylan had already written 'Billy'. Sam liked that and had Bob sing it over and over. It was different from the music on his other films. Dylan's lines could come from real life. When the technicians sent Sam a print of a scene, he said, 'It's dark, too dark to see' and then pissed on the screen. Dylan put that incident into 'Knockin' on Heaven's Door'.

'Knockin' on Heaven's Door' was meant for Slim Pickens dying in the arms of Katy Jurado. The opening lines of 'Knockin' on Heaven's Door' echo Dylan's own frustration.

On 20 January 1973 Bob Dylan went to Mexico City to record the soundtrack with Kristofferson's band. He took with him Kristofferson, James Coburn and the screenwriter Rudy Wurlitzer. They were all glad to be free of Peckinpah for a while. At one point Dylan said, 'Hey, we need Sam here to tell us what to do', and Rudy said, 'Sam is here, man. I feel him.' The results were okay but Dylan later redid them in Los Angeles with Roger McGuinn and Bruce Langhorne on guitars.

The producer Gordon Carroll brought in the classic screen composer, Jerry Fielding. Fielding said of Dylan, 'Just because you can play a guitar and can sing doesn't qualify you for scoring a picture. I give Dylan credit for writing several great pieces of music and a lot of nonsense which is strictly for teenyboppers. His repetitive chords offend me as a musician.'

No love lost there then. Fielding didn't like 'Knockin' on Heaven's Door' but thought 'Billy' was okay – he could use verses throughout the film. He said, 'You don't need "Knock-knock-knockin' on heaven's door" when the guy is dying as the emotion speaks for itself. When Dylan looked at me, he saw the Establishment and so he didn't listen to me at all.' Kristofferson's own song plus two more about the film are a DVD extra.

It is a good album and it sits finely alongside *John Wesley Harding*. Gordon Lightfoot: 'I love the *Pat Garrett and Billy The Kid* soundtrack album. That's fantastic with Bruce Langhorne on guitar.'

Following the film, there have been several western themes in Dylan's work. He wrote 'Romance in Durango', which is not related to the film, and there is much Mexican imagery and sound on *Desire*. Dylan dedicated 'Romance in Durango' to Sam on stage and he dedicated the soundtrack album to him.

MGM was building the Grand in Las Vegas and they needed the film out as soon as possible to bring in some profit. They hoped for another *Wild Bunch* but Sam had made, by his standards, something more lyrical. The film had a hard time, partly because it had been cut badly without Peckinpah's approval. The director's cut has now been issued and the film is regarded as an epic western, though the story of it being made beats anything on the screen.

Donnie Fritts: 'I love the film for so many different reasons. I love that it got its recognition when they restored Sam's cut. It was the movie that Sam wanted to make and it was Jim Coburn's best movie.'

Roger McGuinn: 'It was a very violent movie but that is what Sam Peckinpah was known for. I always liked the music a lot. Bob Dylan did a really great job on the score and I had a great time on the sessions. I was on 'Knockin' on Heaven's Door' and I played banjo on 'Turkey Chase'. I was on 'Billy 7' and the final theme too. When you score a movie, you see it in the studio. It is running as you are playing so you can get the timing right. I saw the scene where Slim Pickens was shot and holding his stomach. His wife was comforting him and the song started playing, it really was a moving experience. I thought it was a great song. I was in the Rolling Thunder Revue with Dylan shortly after that and we closed the show with it every night. We could get the audience to sing along. It is a short song because he was writing it for a film score and there is only so little time in the scene.'

Kris Kristofferson: 'I loved Dylan's music. 'Knockin' on Heaven's Door' was in that scene where Slim Pickens was dying and it was the strongest use of music that I had ever seen in a film. Unfortunately Sam didn't include it in his Director's Cut as he had a blind spot. He thought that the producer had forced Bob on him to make the film commercial and he didn't appreciate who Bob was. I thought Dylan was great in the film, he looked great and you couldn't take your eyes off him, and his music was fantastic.'

Kristofferson worked with Peckinpah again on the highly successful trucking movie, *Convoy* (1978). Because of his drinking, Peckinpah was taken off *Convoy* and was being replaced and Kristofferson, now a star, pleaded for him to be reinstated. Sam returned to the set and said through clenched teeth. 'Son of a bitch, I was out of this movie.' Kristofferson said, 'Sam, you got me into this movie.'

At a Hollywood event honouring James Cagney, Kristofferson told Peckinpah not to get drunk as 'You get confused and you can take out your anger on anyone.' Sam was thrown out as he grabbed Jack Lemmon by the throat.

At the time, Dylan was free of contractual obligations but Columbia won the bid for the soundtrack, probably because they didn't like Dylan to be elsewhere.

As a teenager, Keith Secor heard an unissued snippet 'Rock Me Mama' from the *Pat Garrett* soundtrack on a bootleg and built on it to create the hitchhiking song, 'Wagon Wheel'. In 2004 he recorded it with his band the Old Crow Medicine Show and then ten years later, it was a US country hit for Darius Rucker and a Number 1 in Ireland for the Country and Irish star from Liverpool, Nathan Carter. Dylan must have been delighted: quite by chance he had written, or rather co-written, a major country song. The phrase, 'Rock me mama, like a wagon wheel', goes back to Big Bill Broonzy if not earlier.

Following the film-making, Bob Dylan enjoyed himself in Los Angeles. He went to see Willie Nelson and Waylon Jennings; he played harmonica on Roger McGuinn's 'I'm So Restless'; and he and Harry Dean Stanton saw David Blue at the Troubadour. Dylan agreed to co-produce an album with Jerry Wexler for Barry Goldberg on Atlantic: he added some back-up vocals and percussion.

In 1971 Dylan had a mansion in Woodstock, a townhouse in Greenwich Village, a beach house on Long Island and a ranch house in north Phoenix, Arizona. Enough for anyone you might think, and just consider the upkeep. They decided to sell their Woodstock property but kept some undeveloped land on Ohayo Mountain. In December 1971, the Dylans bought a house from LA sports writer Jim Murray at Point Dume, a rugged peninsula ten miles north of Malibu and close to Zuma Beach. Dylan acquired neighbouring land – 12 acres in all – and built a mansion with 20 rooms and an onion dome. The main room was 'big enough 'to ride a horse through' – Dylan's words not mine. So much building work was needed that a kiln was constructed on site to manufacture tiles. Supervised by Sara, it would take the architect David Towbin, two years to build with many elaborate hand-carvings and a dome on the roof.

Dylan had some interesting neighbours. Martin Sheen lived next door and was a keen fan: 'I give each character I play a theme and he was the basis for every single character since I first heard him in 1964.' The actress Dyan Cannon lived close by and was into Primal Screaming. Her partner Cary Grant took LSD and they had a daughter: they lived apart but close together.

David Geffen lived in Malibu and saw this as his opportunity to sign Dylan for his label, Asylum. David Geffen had founded Asylum in 1970 when he was 27 and sold it two years later for $7m. Then he returned to it and was making a fortune with the Eagles. He suggested a tour with The Band to his friend Robbie Robertson when they were in Paris, and Joni Mitchell wrote 'Free Man in Paris' about Geffen. Dylan agreed and Geffen suggested a new album. He wanted to arrange the tour and cut a deal for one studio album and one live album. Led Zeppelin and the Rolling Stones were playing the biggest venues around and Geffen wanted some of that. The tours would change rock music forever.

In July 1973 *Writings & Drawings* was published by Knopf and considering the brilliance of Dylan's lyrics, it is surprising that the reviews were mixed. Clive James called him 'a talent who can't tell good from bad'. He cites the 'cannonballs' line in 'Blowin' in the

Wind' as a bad line as well as 'the mystery tramp' in 'Like a Rolling Stone'. He was praised for bringing extended stanzas into popular music. Robert Nye compared him to the Great McGonagall.

In September 1973 Bryan Ferry's 'A Hard Rain's A-Gonna Fall' turned a caustic folk song into a pop record with full orchestration, accompanying voices, violin phrases and a highly mannered vocal. To many, he improved on Bob Dylan's original. Bryan Ferry said, 'I think it's a beautiful song although I can't be bothered with all that Cuban crisis stuff. I like the images.'

On 10 September 1973 Muhammad Ali fought Ken Norton at the LA Forum. There was a luxury coach for the music industry with Bob Dylan, Neil Diamond and James Taylor. Phil Spector came with his bodyguard. Afterwards, they went to Trader Vic's and saw Frank Sinatra. He said to the industry executive Joe Smith, 'What are you doing with these creeps?' Smith said, 'Frank, they sell more than you, so come over and say hello' and he did.

At the time, Dylan wasn't selling many copies of *Pat Garrett and Billy the Kid*, but 'Knockin' on Heaven's Door' was a Top 20 single in both Britain and America. The album was nominated in the Grammys for Best Original Score Written for a Motion Picture or a Television Special (Composer's Award). It lost to Neil Diamond's *Jonathan Livingston Seagull*.

Dylan's biggest contribution to a hit single in 1973 was unknown at the time, maybe until now. Dr. John told me that he was talking to Bob Dylan who said, 'I've been on the right trip, but in the wrong car' and that prompted him to write 'Right Place, Wrong Time', a US Top 10 single in 1973.

For most of October, Dylan was writing new songs for *Planet Waves*. He recorded them with The Band over three days in November. *Planet Waves* was recorded at the Village Recorder in West LA, close to Malibu. It was owned by George Hormel – heir to Hormel food who formulated Spam. It was a good album to be sure but The Band was not as distinctive nor as original as they could have been. I don't think that they were holding back: it was just the way that the album was made and for some daft reason, they didn't sing. How their backing vocals would have enhanced 'Forever Young', 'On a Night like this' and 'You Angel You'. Maybe it was contractual but it was crazy. The Band were obviously five believers but they don't connect here.

To quote David Crosby of Crosby, Stills and Nash, 'If Bob Dylan had stayed with The Band, they could have been the most powerful music entity that ever happened. Nobody ever put a better beat to him than Levon Helm. Nobody laid down a better bass line than Rick Danko or better guitar licks than Robbie Robertson.'

Garth Hudson recalls, 'On the whole, Bob liked to sing a song once. The songs on *Planet Waves* had three takes at the most and very often by the second take, he was done with the song. He had everything ready before he went in the studio and he didn't make mistakes or forget words. He would perform the song and what he did for that first take was probably fine. The next take was for the rest of the group, getting an acceptable performance and maybe we did the third take to get it right, and then he would move on.'

The opening track and first single, 'On a Night like this' sounded like musicians having fun and it had the spirit of 1966, but the instruments did not coalesce as they should have done. Dylan, however, never really connected with his song saying, 'It is like a drunk man who's temporarily sober. This is not my type of song. I just did it to do it.' The intention was to give David Geffen something cheerful and commercial that he could sell.

'You Angel You' is the same category: 'I might have written this at one of the sessions, you know, on the spot. It sounds to me like dummy lyrics.' So why hadn't he tidied up the lyric? Dylan knew he could do better. His voice was sounding good, possibly because he had stopped smoking.

The best songs had come from his own experiences rather than being songwriting exercises. 'Wedding Song', which was recorded a week later, was about his relationship with Sara: 'I love you more than life itself, you mean that much to me.' He talks about their children 'one, two, three': it should have been 'one two three, four' but a lyric does have to scan. He returns to the theme of 'My Back Pages' with 'It's never been my duty to remake the world at large'.

To quote Dylan talking to Anthony Scaduto in 1972, 'I'm just a songwriter, man. Not a culture hero or any crap like that.' Scaduto added, 'He is a songwriter who happens to believe that his songs are the best around today.'

The fourth child, omitted from the song, was Jakob, but not to worry as he had his own song, 'Forever Young', easily and deservedly the best song from the album. It is a song from father to son and by Dylan's standards, sentimental. He had written it in Tucson while just thinking about one of his boys and he said, 'I certainly didn't intend to write it.'

In 1988 Rod Stewart recorded his own song, 'Forever Young' and the similarity to Dylan's song was obvious. He agreed an out of court settlement. However, in February 1973, the Glaswegian singer / songwriter John Martyn released his album, *Solid Air*, which included the poignant 'May You Never' in which he passes on his wisdom and good wishes to his son, hoping he would avoid barroom fights. 'Forever Young' and 'May You Never' are distinctly different but it is easy to believe that Dylan heard 'May You Never' and decided to write his own version. Dylan included two versions (fast or slow, take your pick).

Dylan plays piano on 'Dirge', which is not a dirge at all – did Dylan think that it was? It is about the destructive nature of fame: David Bowie was following the same line in his 'Ziggy Stardust' songs, which ended with the death of Stardust. It is a very strong performance by Dylan and contains some very strong lyrics, 'You were just a painted face on a trip down Suicide Row'. It might be a song of self-loathing.

Rory Gallagher recommended 'Tough Mama' to me, saying it was one of Dylan's most neglected songs. It is a blues song about two travelling people with colourful pasts getting together. 'Jack the Cowboy' could be Ramblin' Jack Elliott, could be Kerouac, who knows? This track has the best ensemble playing on the album from The Band.

The album included 'Going, Going, Gone' (Robbie Robertson and his whammy bar), 'Hazel', 'Something There Is about You' and 'Never Say Goodbye', which was recorded before Levon arrived and had the feel of *The Basement Tapes*. At the same time Dylan recorded 'Nobody 'Cept You', a fine love song that Dylan passed to the country singer Johnny Rodriguez. Rodriguez never did it and Dylan should have put it on the album.

The album was called *Planet Waves*, and had a curious drawing of Dylan with the musicians on the cover. He included a CND motif and described the contents as 'Cast-Iron songs and Torch Ballads'. The title *Planet Waves* could be a nod to Allen Ginsberg's collection, *Planet News* (1968).

It could have been spite, most probably was, but on 16 November 1973, Columbia Records rush-released a spoiler to Dylan's new album, an unattractive looking LP called *Dylan* with a strange silhouette on the front which lost Dylan's nose. It was like a poor attempt at one of those multi-coloured posters from the mid-60s. If Columbia hoped that fans would buy this, thinking it was the new Dylan album, it was unlikely to work. However, his cover of 'A Fool such as I' was released as a single and even made the US charts, albeit to Number 25. The album itself made the US Top 20.

The tracks had been recorded by Dylan around the same time as *Self-Portrait* and *New Morning*. It is possible that he had been thinking of a second *Self-Portrait*. Some performances were poor and it is possible that they were to warm up the band. Al Kooper remarked, 'They were the wrong tapes and the mixing was diabolical. I have this great version of 'Mr. Bojangles' which is not the take used on that album.' Was Columbia trying to humiliate Dylan for switching to Asylum? It had the opposite fault to *Planet Waves*: that had no backing vocals whereas here they were often too prominent.

Dylan must have known that his take on 'The Ballad of Ira Hayes' was way below Johnny Cash's. I suspect that he had seen the lyric in a folk song magazine and thought it would be fun to try it. Similarly he can only be having fun with Joni Mitchell's 'Big Yellow Taxi': does he go for the big note and laugh at the end? Of course not.

His versions of the Elvis hits – 'A Fool Such As I' and 'Can't Help Fallin' in Love' – sound like a night out at the British Legion and Dylan loses the melody during the second song. Al Kooper's views notwithstanding, his version of Jerry Jeff Walker's 'Mr. Bojangles' is fine and you can tell that he relishes the lyric.

'Spanish is the Loving Tongue' is a beautiful song written in 1925 and Bob merges it with the melody of Ben E. King's 'Spanish Harlem'. It is disjointed and they could have been combined for a superb track. Butch Hancock wrote a continuation of this song, 'She Never Spoke Spanish to Me'.

There are three traditional songs – the cowboy song 'Lily of the West', an old song Dylan had been singing for years 'Mary Ann' and the playful 'Sarah Jane'. They were okay but there wasn't much point to releasing them.

In December 1973 Dylan visited Joni Mitchell at her home in Laurel Canyon and she played him her new album, *Court and Spark*, which had also been recorded for Asylum. It included 'Free Man in Paris' and 'Help Me' and showed strong jazz influences. Joni's 'Down to You' prompted Dylan to write 'Up to Me'.

Bob Dylan still saw members of The Band from time to time. When he told Levon Helm that he was thinking of touring with the Grateful Dead, Levon said, 'Keep us in mind.'

CHAPTER 10

And the New Bob Dylan is...

I. With Bob on Our Side

Nowadays if some singer or entertainer becomes famous, a host of tribute acts spring up in every city, copying the songs, the looks and the demeanour. I saw a very good Queen tribute from Brazil and as Freddie Mercury's shoelaces had come undone at *Live Aid*, the lead singer's shoelaces were similarly undone: such attention to detail. I'm sorry that I've never seen anyone try and replicate Bob Dylan's *Live Aid* performance. Wouldn't it be great to attend a recreation of Bob's 1966 performance where the audience is given cards on the way in to tell them whether they were to be pro-the electric Bob or against?

Tribute acts can make good money and if the artists in question can only be seen at huge stadium gigs with high-priced tickets, the cut-price alternatives can seem attractive. In some instances, the performers themselves have sanctioned the imitators in exchange for a percentage of the take.

The first tribute act surely belongs to Sonny Boy Williamson. The blues singer was born in 1914 and became a noted harmonica player in St. Louis and Chicago. Rice Miller, who was older than Sonny Boy, appears to have borrowed his name around 1941 and was working on radio shows and in clubs in Arkansas. After the original Sonny Boy was killed in a mugging in 1948, he took over the name and recorded for several labels, ending up with Chess Records in Chicago. They must have known that this wasn't the real Sonny Boy, but they didn't let on.

In recent years, a veteran blues man Lil Jimmy Reed has been touring the UK. He knew Jimmy Reed's repertoire and would sometimes stand in for him when he was too drunk to perform. This was highly unusual at the time and there was very little of it until the 1980s.

Until then there were no Bootleg Beatles, no Simply Dylan, no Strange Doors, no Australian Pink Floyd. The Beatles spawned hundreds of beat groups, usually with the same three guitars and drums line-up but those groups would write their own songs or perform R&B covers. They often wore similar suits to the Beatles but no one pretended to be them.

Bob Dylan had started as a son of Woody and once his records were successful, many others wanted to be on the road as singing troubadours. Just as the beat groups rivalling the Beatles were signed up by the London-based record companies, so too were the other performances around Greenwich Village. They were in the same bag as Dylan and yet distinctive in their own right: Phil Ochs was more political, Tom Paxton more compassionate, Peter La Farge more indigenous and David Blue more laboured. They weren't the new Dylans so much as Dylans with a difference. You paid your money and you took your choice. And in a way there was a Dylan for everyone. Okay, you don't like his spikey voice, here's Eric Andersen. Okay, you want sharper wit, here's John Prine. Okay, you want more country, here's Guy Clark.

One great thing that Dylan had done, perhaps inadvertently, was to open up the subject matter and you could now write a song about anything.

The friendship and rivalry between Bob Dylan and Phil Ochs is an underlying theme of this book. In 1966 Phil Ochs, riding in Dylan's limousine, expressed doubts about his forthcoming single, 'One of Us Must Know'. It is possible that Dylan himself had some doubts about its viability but he didn't want Ochs telling him that. He stopped the car and threw him out saying 'You're not a folk singer, Ochs: you're a journalist.'

Biographer Michael Gray: "It wasn't just Phil Ochs. Almost everybody turned on Dylan when he went electric and wrote more personal songs. They were wrong and the history of Bob Dylan is littered with people wrongly telling him that he should have been singing 'Masters of War' for the rest of his life. On one level, this is the same as telling Elvis that he shouldn't wiggle his hips on television.'

Singer / songwriter Tom Russell: 'The bottom line is that Bob Dylan came in a neophyte, a kid from Minnesota, and became their friend and cohort. Two years later he has shot through the scene. That must have devastated Phil Ochs.'

How it must have rankled Phil Ochs in Greenwich Village to see Bob Dylan receive so much acclaim. I don't think for one moment that Ochs thought that Dylan was a better writer: he just wondered why it hadn't happened to him. The jealousy ate away at him and destroyed their friendship. Phil's end is very sad but could it have been any other way?

When Dylan went electric, the singer / songwriters had to decide whether to follow him or not. Phil Ochs criticised Dylan at first but when he eventually widened his own horizons, he had left it too late. *Pleasures of the Harbour*, released in 1967, was still a fine record. 'Outside of a Small Circle of Friends' was the only direct social comment on the album, but on his second A&M album, *Tape from California*, he blends the poetry with protest. Ramblin' Jack Elliott joins him for 'Joe Hill', while 'The War is over' has Ochs saying, "Words have turned to water, and the women turn to wine".

It's uncomfortable to play Phil Ochs' records knowing of his suicide in 1976 and realising how often he referred to his own death. This occurs throughout his work and 'When I'm Gone' and 'My Death' ('My life is now a death to me') deal with nothing else. Quite evidently, he was a troubled man. His marriage had broken up and he was drinking hard and he had the wild elation and severe depression of the manic-depressive. This combined with the assassinations and racial violence of 1968 led to the agonising *Rehearsals for Retirement*. His own tombstone graces the cover of the album and he feared assassination. 'The soul of America is dying,' said Ochs, 'The flag, loyalty, patriotism and the lifestyle are losing meaning.'

It's a frightening, sombre record with such lines as 'I am a masculine American man / I kill therefore I am.' The dark mood is set by the paranoid 'Pretty Smart on My Part' in which Ochs sees all the hatred directed at him personally. The choppy Bo Diddley beat reinforced the instability of the lyric and despite Ochs' problems, he reached a creative peak with this album. At the same time, he sounded close to suicide and the very title implied this was his final album.

Happy Traum: 'One of the reasons Phil's songs didn't last the way that Bob's did was because they were more specifically about things that were happening at the time. Some like 'There But for Fortune' are universal but he never got the huge recognition that Bob got. He had psychological problems, which caused him to take his life and it was a tragic end for a guy like that.'

Clive Selwood was promoting Elektra's catalogue in the UK: 'We had a reception for Phil Ochs at the Elektra office, which was attended by left-wing intellectual folkies, mostly with beards and duffle coats. Phil made some comment and one of the ladies responded with a quote from Karl Marx which caused Phil to borrow some lipstick and write it in large letters on the office wall. It was still there when we left the building.'

Johnny Rogan: 'The comparison between Bob Dylan and Phil Ochs was valid for its time but Dylan went on to do things that were beyond Ochs' imagination. But at the time a lot of people said that Ochs was better and he possibly was.'

Patrick Humphries: 'Ochs was a lot more political and a lot more vehement than Dylan but I'm not sure that created the tension between them. Ochs was intelligent and I think he could see that Dylan had a genius that he didn't possess. Instead he was deeply troubled and he didn't have that balance that you need to be a survivor. His 'Flower Lady' was lovely but most of the time he was raving against the establishment.'

Billy Bragg told Daniel Rachel, 'Dylan isn't really a political songwriter. If you want to talk about political songwriters, you've got to look at people like Phil Ochs. 'Blowin' in the Wind' sounds really nice but it doesn't actually say shit, does it?'

Dylan never wanted to lead a revolution but Phil Ochs did. John Stewart from the Kingston Trio: 'I knew Phil Ochs very well. That was very tragic. One of the great blows for him was this apparent revolution that Huey Newton and Abbie Hoffman were leading. That is what Phil wanted to do. He wanted to be the leader of a new revolution. The revolution never did pan out and everybody was back selling stock, cutting their hair and working day jobs, but it looked like there was going to be a revolution and that tore at Phil. He wasn't at the front of it and yet he was one of the first to think that America should be shaken up.'

Then Phil Ochs found new clothes, Elvis' in fact. He bought a replica of Elvis Presley's gold lamé suit and copied the sleeve of an Elvis album for *Phil Ochs' Greatest Hits*, a collection of new songs with country-rock arrangements played by Ry Cooder and James Burton. Although the music is snappy and melodic, you only have to scratch the surface to discover Ochs' bleakness. "I would be in exile now but everywhere's the same", he sings in 'One-way Ticket Home'. There are some brilliant lines:

'I thought Johnson was the devil, I thought we couldn't do no worse,
Now the White House stands in Disneyland, this country must be under a curse.'

Another track, 'Chords of Fame' was about being true to yourself: 'God help the troubadour who tries to be a star.'

In 1973 Ochs visited Africa where a robbery and attack damaged his vocal cords. On 9 April 1976, Phil Ochs, who was severely depressed, hanged himself, his body being found by his sister. Dylan found this news hard to take and left his rehearsals for the Rolling Thunder tour for two days but when Ochs' sister invited him to appear on a memorial concert, she didn't get a reply.

Ochs had been among the first in the western world to enthuse over Bruce Lee and in *Requiem for a Dragon Departed*, he speculated on his death: 'Maybe he did die of an aneurism. There were rumours in Hollywood of cocaine. Maybe he was killed by some crazy person or rival business faction. Maybe he wasn't meant to be cast as a James Bond figure. Maybe he lived more intensely than any human being can live. Or maybe he died for the same reason James Dean died. He had taken too much of their fire, and the Gods were jealous.'

Paul Simon embraced the change to electricity better than anyone, perhaps because he had never really been a folkie in the first place. Clinton Heylin says, 'Paul Simon is much more old school. He is a Tin Pan Alley songwriter who was born at the wrong time.'

Chris Hockenhull: 'Robert Shelton took Dylan to a Simon and Garfunkel concert in Greenwich Village but apparently Dylan was yattering throughout, so there were tensions from the start. Much later on when they did a joint tour, they only did four songs together and you could tell from the body language that it wasn't right.'

Tom Paxton felt that going electric was not for him and anyway he preferred touring on his own or with one other acoustic musician. Paxton's career took a fascinating sideways turn in 1968 when his *Morning Again* album included 'Now That I've Taken My Life', which was inspired by Jacques Brel. For about three years, his work showed Brel's influence and, to my mind, produced some fine songs which have been ignored outside his fan base.

Donovan had been promoted as the Scottish Bob Dylan and he found his own individuality when he went electric with 'Sunshine Superman' and 'Wear Your Love like Heaven'. He embraced flower power in a way that Dylan never did. Donovan says, 'I was inspired rather than influenced by Bob Dylan.'

Born in 1936, Freddie Neil had come up with Bob Dylan in Greenwich Village but also wrote for the Brill Building publishers: Buddy Holly recorded 'Come Back Baby' and Roy Orbison 'Candy Man'. His first solo album, *Bleecker and MacDougal* (1965) paid tribute to the Greenwich Village folk clubs. His first Capitol album, *Fred Neil* (1967), contained two stunning compositions, 'The Dolphins' and 'Everybody's Talkin'', which Nilsson sang in *Midnight Cowboy*. Neil was obsessed by saving dolphins. He stopped public performances around 1977 and he died from cancer in Florida in 2001, surrounded by his beloved dolphins.

Peter La Farge was a man with a mission. Born in 1931, he was older than his contemporaries and he had served in Korea and been a rodeo rider. He was of American Indian heritage and was strongly influenced by his father, Oliver, who had won a Pulitzer Prize for his novel about Indian life, *Laughing Boy*.

Tom Russell: 'La Farge was a fascinating guy, he was a bronc rider, he was from Fountain, Colorado and he was sent to Korea to fight. On his way back they made him spy on his fellow soldiers who may have been bringing heroin back to the States. The job broke his heart and he was never right again. He had a lot of drug and alcohol problems and that ended up killing him.' Peter La Farge died in 1965, probably from an overdose of a sleeping drug.

La Farge's first album, *Ira Hayes and Other Ballads*, contained 'Ballad of Ira Hayes', which was based on the true life humiliation of a war hero. Tom Russell: 'Johnny Cash recorded an album of Peter La Farge songs *Bitter Tears* which was very influential to me. A lot of radio stations wouldn't play his single of 'Ira Hayes' and Cash took out a full page ad in *Billboard* saying "Disc jockeys and radio planners, where are your guts?" It was about a Pima Indian who went to war and battled at Iwo Jima and he was in that famous scene where they are raising the flag and it became a sculpture. He went back to the States and died drunk and unknown. He was even in the movie, *The Battle of Iwo Jima*, as an extra. It is so ironic that this guy who fought for America goes back home to Arizona and he raised the flag and lowered it "like you throw a dog a bone". There is so much in that song: there is the flag raising and the water thing – "the white man stole his water rights" and as he dies drunk in a ditch with two inches of water, that reappears. It is a very complex, well written protest song.'

Buffy Sainte-Marie: "About every 30 years it is hip to be seen as Indian or to study them, and then it goes back to sleep again. Peter was part Narraganset and he had mixed blood. He had very strong feelings about the injustice that had been done to native people in the western hemisphere. The colonial robber barons formed a society and ripped everybody off, not only the Indians."

Of Irish and American Indian extraction, Patrick Sky had a sound knowledge of folk traditions and knew several different versions of some traditional songs. Buffy Sainte-Marie recorded his best-known song, 'Many a Mile', the opening track on his first album, *Patrick Sky*, in 1965. Paul Brady recalls, 'Patrick never reached the dizzy heights but nonetheless had a faithful following. Around the mid-70s he got disillusioned in the music business, and he opted out. Apart from his own songs, he was very interested in acoustic blues singers like Mississippi John Hurt and Blind Willie McTell. He was a cantankerous curmudgeon and he always looked for the underbelly of society or the darker side of the room. He made an album of entirely gross songs, *Songs That Made America Famous*, songs that you would never hear on the radio. He was gross and he wasn't afraid to be gross, and I admire him for that.'

As Eric Andersen had a tuneful, distinctive voice and wrote good songs, I reckon that he was just unlucky. His first album, *Today Is the Highway* (1965) was a good start with his first wife, Debbie Green on second guitar. His second release, *'Bout Changes 'n' Things* (1966) contained 'Violets of Dawn' and 'Thirsty Boots'. He saw how the scene was changing and within months, he issued new versions of the same songs with electric accompaniment. *'Bout Changes 'n' Things, Take 2*, was a bold but confusing move, and his career never got back on track. His work though is immensely rewarding: there is the 26 minute 'Beat Avenue', set in November 1963, and the ultra-moody 'Trouble in Paris'.

As an example of goodwill in the folk environment, consider how 'Thirsty Boots' got to Judy Collins. Eric Andersen: 'Phil Ochs knew she was recording an album and he said, "Get down here right away, Judy should record that song." I was living on 95th Street and she lived on 72nd Street. I got out on the street, it was very cold outside, and I wrote the third verse then and there.'

Judy Collins' account is different in every detail and yet the story is essentially the same. 'Al Kooper called Eric Andersen and said that I was looking for songs for my third album, so he said, "Get over there with your guitar." Eric lived on 86th Street and I lived on 79th and coming down on the subway, he had written the song on a matchbook for me. (Sings chorus of 'Thirsty Boots') I said, "That's mine, finish it and I'll record it. "Thirsty Boots" was a beautiful expression.'

Judy Collins was very good at championing little-known writers: 'Tom Rush is extraordinary. I have become a huge Tom Rush fan. I didn't know his music very much when I was younger – I didn't have time to check everything out! I have now been able to work with him and travel with him and he is amazing. "No Regrets' is a beautiful song and it would suit me fine.'

Tom Rush came out of Boston coffeehouses and his first album, *Tom Rush at the Unicorn*, was released in 1962. He was blues-based in the early years and he made *The Circle Game* in 1968 which included 'No Regrets' (a hit for the Walker Brothers) as well as songs from Jackson Browne, James Taylor and Joni Mitchell.

In the late 1960s when Dylan was secluded in Woodstock, the press was constantly championing new performers as the New Dylan, Tom Rush being an example. They were a very eclectic bunch having little in common with Dylan or indeed each other. John Prine added, 'The new Dylan? Well, none of us figured there was anything much wrong with the old one.'

Unexpectedly perhaps, in many instances the first album was the best. Blues singer Chris Smither recalls, 'I met Tim Hardin but I didn't know him, just the briefest of acquaintances. I was a tremendous admirer of his songwriting. His first album was in my opinion hit after hit after hit. The first album is a distillation, the cream of the crop of what you have been doing and then all of a sudden you have to come up with a bunch more within a year. It's a hard bridge to cross. The music business encourages that sort of self-destructive behaviour.'

Maybe Hardin was too fragile for stardom but his first album, *Tim Hardin 1* (1966), contained 'Reason to Believe, 'Hang on to a Dream' and 'Misty Roses'. I remember feeling cheated that the playing-time (27 minutes) was so short. His second album, would you believe *Tim Hardin 2* (1967) contained his most famous song, 'If I Were a Carpenter', although the rhyme of 'onlyness' and 'loneliness' grates on me. Hardin died of a heroin overdose in 1980 and you can feel his circumstances on *The Homecoming Concert*, recorded in Oregon shortly before he died.

Tim Rose: 'Tim Hardin and I worked together in Holland and most nights he forgot his guitar and had to use mine. I was petrified that he was so bombed that he would fall and break it. His demons were eating him up and he couldn't get out of bed in the morning. The beautiful songs had been written ten years earlier and he couldn't recapture that. He did a song at an electric piano in Worcester and he didn't realise that the piano wasn't on. The tour was unsuccessful and it was exhausting as I couldn't spend my time apologising for him. I told the agency that I couldn't carry the guy. God love him, but a couple of years later he died. Tim always wanted to be in another age, another period, he was never comfortable with who he was and it killed him. He was very world-weary and it got to be a worn record, but I loved his songs and for two or three moments a night, he would be magic.'

Harvey Andrews saw him in the UK: 'I saw Tim Hardin in Portsmouth and he was out of it. He had all these gorgeous songs and he did them in a completely different way. He was doing them in a blues style and re-interpreting them. It was like watching jazz musicians where you had to know the body of the work. They played a few bars of 'Blue Moon' and then would improvise upon it. It was a staggering performance of virtuosity but the audience was leaving. I wanted to say, "What are you doing, sit down and listen – you're walking out on a genius", but there you go.'

I did see one of Hardin's last performances when he was touring the UK, a sorrowful wreck of a man. He appeared at a folk club in Liverpool and when the audience was restless, he said, 'I knew you'd leave' but someone said, 'Oh no, Tim, it's not you. It's late and they don't want to miss the last bus.' Hardin said, 'Man, they do this at matinees.'

Tom Russell: 'I saw Tim Hardin once after he had gotten back from England and he was in bad shape and not performing well. He did a great concert in Eugene, Oregon, his last concert and his grandmother was in the audience. He was on his last legs, but it was a real emotional performance.'

Bob Lind: 'There is a deep core of sadness in me and I can sound like "Send Donations to Orphan Bob". The difference is that Tim Hardin could never come to terms with it. Neither could Tim Buckley or Janis Joplin. I am very fortunate in that I am able to absorb that pain and make it a part of me, and of course a lot of my best songs come out of that.'

Probably the first person to be called the New Dylan was David Blue whose self-titled album was released by Elektra in 1966. He copied the sound of *Highway 61 Revisited* but his voice lacked character and the songs were nothing special. David Blue hated the second album with the group, American Patrol, and he signed to Reprise on the condition that they bought the tapes and didn't release them. They kept their word and the title track of *These 23 Days in September* is a poignant song of a fading relationship, worthy of Leonard Cohen, but Blue's voice is dull. There is a better, more atmospheric cover from Eric Andersen.

Blue's best-known song, indeed his only well-known song, is 'Outlaw Man', which was recorded by the Eagles. Play it now and hear what Dylan borrowed for 'Gotta Serve Somebody'. Mr. Blue died jogging in Washington Square Park in 1982.

Townes Van Zandt found his expressionless, downbeat voice was ideal for his material and his first album, *For the Sake of a Song* (1968) included 'Tecumsah Valley', 'Waitin' Around to Die' and 'I'll Be There in the Morning'. Steve Earle said in 1987, 'Townes Van Zandt is the best songwriter in the whole world, and I'll stand on Bob Dylan's coffee table in my cowboy boots and say that.'

When I quoted that back to Steve Earle, he said, 'Well, I don't think that he's the best. I just think that he was the best in my immediate circle. Bob Dylan doesn't have trouble promoting himself. I didn't really believe that Townes was a better songwriter than Bob Dylan but Bob was doing okay and Townes needed the help.'

Tom Russell: 'It's the same for Phil Ochs, Peter La Farge and Townes Van Zandt. They were so deeply caring about certain things that they just can't handle real life. It's tough.'

Ramblin' Jack Elliott: 'There have been lots of very talented people who have died or committed suicide or just didn't make it for one reason or another, but really because they didn't have that drive. Dylan had that drive: he always had it.'

Steve Earle adds, 'Nearly all Townes' songs are about Townes. That first verse of "Pancho and Lefty" is about Townes and he is talking to himself: he is not really singing the first verse, that's my theory anyway. More than any other songwriter, Townes was writing about himself.'

You may have seen *Heartworn Highways* (1981) in which Townes falls into a ditch, the story of his life. In 1989 we presented a concert by Townes at BBC Radio Merseyside and he arrived so sleepy and wasted that I wondered if he would live through the day, let alone play the gig. My colleague Kenny Johnson, who was far more experienced than me, went out and bought a bottle of whiskey. He gave it to Townes and the concert was fine, could hardly have been better.

Combining Dylan's drive with an element of self-destruction is Kris Kristofferson. *Kristofferson* (1970) is a contender for the best-debut album of all-time with 'Me and Bobby McGee', 'Help Me Make It through the Night', 'For the Good Times and 'Sunday Mornin' Comin' Down'. Although they have their moments, his subsequent albums have often been disappointing as he is prone to re-cutting his best-known tunes or rewriting them with new lyrics.

Kristofferson produced the first album by Steve Goodman called *Steve Goodman* in 1971 and it included a glorious saga of American life, 'City of New Orleans', a Top 10 hit for Arlo Guthrie. Goodman was a witty and confident stage performer, often performing standards and favourites from other performers He promised much but he died from leukaemia in 1984.

When it comes to quirkiness, Loudon Wainwright III lived up to his extraordinary name and could never have been a New Dylan except in the sense that he did his own thing. His shtick was to write about himself, his friends and his family. He started this with *Loudon Wainwright III* (1970) and is still doing it today. He is best known for his novelty 'Dead Skunk', although that could be a political allegory for America; you never know with Loudon Wainwright.

Loudon Wainwright: 'I have to say it was helpful to be billed as the New Dylan. It was helpful because everybody was looking for a new Bob Dylan. It drew attention to me and people came to see me. It was bad because I was not the new anybody else but me, but you know how media people like to call somebody a new somebody or other. It's the only way they can describe you and they can go so far as to say. "Well, he even looks like Bob Dylan!" I knew that certainly didn't apply to me.'

Similarly introspective was James Taylor who began his career with the heavily-orchestrated *James Taylor* for the Beatles' Apple label in 1968 and George Harrison was listening closely as one song began 'Something in the way she moves me'. His songs are essentially folk and with his producer Peter Asher, he created a California soft rock, which at different times has embraced Joni Mitchell, Jackson Browne and the Eagles. Especially in performance, Taylor came across as a mellow Bob Dylan; Colonel Parker recognised his talent right away but didn't think he had charisma.

Very early on, James Taylor said, 'Dylan is in a class of his own. Everybody's got to find their own voice. I'm just trying to be me. I don't think it's fair at this point in my career to compare me to any of the greats. I'm just starting out and I have a lot of work to do.'

Mary Chapin Carpenter: 'I remember the *James Taylor* record on Apple so well. I loved opening it up. There was this gatefold picture of him reclining, a beautiful man with long hair, and he was such a tall guy. I've never forgotten that album and it is hard to describe how thrilled and grateful I am to have a song where he sings with me all these years later. He called me before he recorded his part to talk to me about the song and when I heard his voice on the phone, I almost dropped it. I couldn't get over that I was talking to James Taylor as he was just so special. He never went out of fashion in my house and he has always been iconic to me. He has gone to many different places artistically and that is the kind of career you want Not every career can sustain these high, top-of-the-mountain existences.'

Leonard Cohen was also too idiosyncratic to be anything other than the first Leonard Cohen. He had come from an academic world and had written poetry books and novels before songwriting. Despite his lack of confidence about the transition, *Songs of Leonard Cohen* (1967) was an outstanding debut including 'Suzanne', 'Sisters of Mercy' and 'So Long, Marianne'.

Gretchen Peters: 'There is a hall of songwriting genius that contains Bob Dylan and Leonard Cohen. They have this constant search for something new, and so they are never really done. Both of them seemed to enjoy being on the road and although the songs are often 40 years old, they were finding new things in them.'

Starting with his 1973 album *Closing Time*, Tom Waits has had an extraordinary persona as a down-and-out night club pianist. Unlike Bowie, he has never shed that skin and his albums are variations of being Tom Waits. His biographer Patrick Humphries says, 'Before Dylan and the Beatles, popular music was safe and unthreatening and hearing Dylan in the very early 60s, it wasn't just the lyrics that were different but it was that voice. He sounded like someone in his sixties and a lot of people felt that about Tom Waits too. It was a routine of too much drink, too many cigarettes and too many late nights that hammered the voice and by the time of *Small Change*, the great Tom Waits album, it was really lived in. That husk and bark is like a reaction to that smooth production line pop of the early 60s. The New Dylan thing started in the early 70s and Waits was seen as part of. It didn't matter whether you could sing or not as long as you could write your own songs. Look at Kris Kristofferson and John Prine but Tom Waits is the most extreme example. He had had about ten years on the road and he wasn't eating his five portions of fruit and veg a day. That endless rock'n'roll lifestyle did it for him.' On *Theme Time Radio Hour*, Dylan praised Waits' 'The Piano Has Been Drinking': 'Tom Waits has played a lot of lousy gigs in his life and here he puts all of them to music.' In it, the singer gives all manner of excuses for his lousy performance, ending with ''he piano has been drinking, not me.'

Dylan quoted from a critic who said that Tom Waits sounded how you'd sound if you drank a quart of bourbon, smoked a pack of cigarettes and swallowed razor blades after not sleeping for three days. Bob commented, 'Or, as I liked to put it, beautiful.'

From 1968, Jackson Browne was writing for Nico and the Nitty Gritty Dirt Band, but he didn't release his first solo album, *Jackson Browne*, until 1972. It opened with a brilliant love song, 'Jamaica, Say You Will' and included 'Song for Adam' and 'Doctor My Eyes'. It had that soft rock sound from the west coast including harmonies from David Crosby. A few months later, he wrote a major hit, 'Take It Easy' for the Eagles. He was at his best on *The Pretender* (1976) and he recorded new songs live for *Running on Empty* (1977).

Although only 19 when he made his first album, Tim Buckley, the Washington DC singer and guitarist created sophisticated rhythms that owed as much to jazz as rock and folk and he often worked with the poet Larry Beckett. The albums were not radio-friendly as Buckley and his writing partner Larry Beckett were not tied to conventional structures. On later albums, Buckley embraced avant-garde rock and funk. Like Bob Dylan, he was considered for Woody Guthrie in a biopic, which would have been interesting casting, but he died of a heroin overdose in 1975.

Larry Beckett: 'Dylan knew who Tim Buckley was but what he thought of Tim and me, I have no idea. There was a lot of originality but if you listen to 'Once I Was', there is a strong connection between that and 'Dolphins' by Fred Neil. We loved the songs of Tim Hardin and he was an influence. The wonderful people at Elektra gave us full creative control. We had a brilliant producer in Jerry Yester who was very sympathetic. Tim and I worked out the instrumentation for each piece. If there is an oboe on something, then that is because we decided that there should be an oboe.'

Like Tim Buckley, David Ackles was very much a one-off, in his case writing thoughtful songs with grandiose arrangements. Ackles came from Illinois but had studied English literature at Edinburgh University. He wanted to be a songwriter but Elektra persuaded him that he could do his own songs better than anyone. The first album *David Ackles* (1968) contained his much-covered 'Road to Cairo' and the emotional, avant-garde 'His Name Is Andrew'. *Subway to the Country* (1969) was equally strong but *American Gothic* (1972) was a *tour de force*, a brilliant collection of songs about American life. 'Waiting for the Moving Man' is about the end of a relationship and rather like Sinatra in his *Watertown* phase. The pen pictures in the title track are as defining as the famous picture it credits. Possibly the album had too many influences from musical theatre but the mix of Gershwin, Brecht and Dylan was edifying. I'm not alone in praising this – he was a major influence on Bernie Taupin.

The Chicago postman, John Prine, began brilliantly with a self-titled album in 1971 which included 'Hello in There' (a study of Alzheimer's as well as the distance between generations), 'Angel from Montgomery' (picked up by Bonnie Raitt) and 'Donald and Lydia' (a favourite of Dylan's in which the two lovers are miles apart). Prine was too unhurried a songwriter to make a major impact and once he settled in Nashville, he became more involved in country music. More than any other writer, John Prine goes in unexpected directions. When his girlfriend loses interest in him, he sings, 'Oh my stars, Linda's gone to Mars, Wonder if she'll bring me something home.'

In 2009, Dylan told the *Huffington Post* that John Prine was one of his favourite writers, stating 'Prine's stuff is pure Proustian existentialism. Mid-western mind-trips to the nth degree and he writes beautiful songs. All that stuff about 'Sam Stone', the soldier junkie daddy, and 'Donald and Lydia' where people make love from ten miles away. Nobody but Prine could write like that.'

John Prine: 'Having a writing block is just something you have to accept because you are always going to run into it. It seems so simple when you are not blocked and I don't know what causes it. It may not just be a block as you've always got to have the desire, that is, if you're writing for artistic reasons. If you get your heart broken, that's a good one – you want to explain to the world why your heart was broken. I'd rather not go through divorces but it's a good way to go through writers' block. I have been through two divorces and I have written an album's worth of material after each one because I had time on my hands and I was trying to explain to myself why the marriage failed.'

On a par with John Prine but country from the word go was Guy Clark. His first two albums for RCA, *Old Number 1* (1975) and *Texas Cookin'* (1976) inspired a generation of songwriters. Jerry Jeff Walker had a country hit with 'LA Freeway' and Clark's relationship with an old man, 'Desperados Waitin' for a Train' is a telling study of old age. He likened songwriting to slow, careful craftsmanship in his evocative 'Boats to Build' (1992).

Steve Earle has recorded Clark's great song about a gunfighter who has survived into the modern world and gets run down by a car. "The Last Gunfighter Ballad' is a great story and it influenced a lot of songs that I wrote. Guy is fascinated by anachronisms, perhaps because he was one himself. My theory is he is like Merlin in the Arthurian Legends, he was born backwards in time. He was born an old fart and maybe he was getting younger.'

Guy Clark: 'I like Townes Van Zandt and Jesse Winchester best of all but Bob Dylan is no slouch, a pretty good songwriter. I like his early stuff but I have never seen him live. I don't go to many concerts. (laughs)'

Steve Earle: 'Me, Townes, Guy, that whole group of songwriters, none of us thought of it in terms of country music. It was called country music because it was around Nashville and that was the place for singer /songwriters to go. We're all songwriters because of Bob Dylan, not because of Hank Cochran or anyone else – and I admire Hank Cochran by the way – and we all learned by trying to get songs cut in Nashville. We thought we could make a living that way, but we are all post-Bob Dylan singer / songwriters.'

I've no idea why but John Stewart was ignored by almost everybody. He had been with the Kingston Trio and his first solo album, *California Bloodlines* (1969), doesn't put a foot wrong. If you want to hear somebody professing his love for his country you can do no better than 'Mother Country', while 'July You're A Woman' is a touching road song about an unobtainable girlfriend. Stewart followed his album with 'Armstrong', a fine single about the moon landing which for some daft reason was classed by US radio stations as unpatriotic.

Gordon Lightfoot had an unusual career trajectory. The Canadian artist cut his first records in 1962 and his single, 'Negotiations', likened his girlfriend's iciness to the Cold War. *Lightfoot* (1966) included 'For Lovin' Me' and *The Way I Feel* (1967) both 'Song for A Winter's Night' and 'Canadian Railroad Trilogy' but he moved away from folk for the crumbling relationship in 'Sundown' (1974). In 1976, he scored a big US hit with a tale of a shipping disaster, 'The Wreck of The Edmund Fitzgerald'.

Steve Forbert from Meridian, Mississippi made an impact with his first album, *Alive on Arrival*, in 1978 and his second album, *Jackrabbit Slim* (1979), contained a US hit single, 'Romeo's Tune'. He's an engaging but nervy live performer. 'I suppose it was the Byrds with 'Mr. Tambourine Man' that really kicked it off for me. I liked the idea of folk-rock as there was something in my bones that appealed to the folk element. I went to Greenwich Village in 1976 as it seemed the best option at the time. Because of CBGB's there were new things happening but there was also the so-called folk scene. Even some new folk clubs were opening so it was good timing for me.'

The New Dylans could even be referenced by Dylan in his 1974 song 'Idiot Wind' as he sings about 'imitators who steal me blind'. Many of the New Dylans found their own place in the music world, leading Bob Dylan to remark in 1984, 'I never hear anybody sounding like myself anymore.'

Of course there were tribute acts a-plenty in folk clubs and Eric Bogle had audiences laughing with his song, 'Do You Know Any Bob Dylan': 'When Bob was God, there were an incredible number of Bob Dylan imitators without an original chord or note in their bodies. It used to annoy me immensely. They say imitation is the sincerest form of flattery but in Bob Dylan's case I didn't think so. I got heartily sick because none of them were as good as the original. My song was a dig at them. People were asking me to sing Bob Dylan songs all the time when I was struggling to get my own songs known. It probably seems like arrogance that I would sing my songs instead of Bob Dylan's. No insult to Bob, but I was trying to get my own songs known. They would see the label singer / songwriter and for them there was only one singer / songwriter in the world and that was Bob Dylan. In desperation I wrote that song, just a little dig at those who asked me.'

Some musicians were wasted, perhaps as a result of trying to match Bob Dylan. I saw it myself on Merseyside with Mike Hart, who had previously fronted an R&B band, the Roadrunners. He brought out a collection of his own songs, *Mike Hart Bleeds*, in 1969. He was our own, the Liverpool Dylan. His close friend Mike Evans from the Liverpool Scene says, 'There was a picture of a girl on the cover, I think it was a girl who lived in Belgium, and the blood dripping on the photograph was his own blood. He dripped it on the photograph of this girl and burned her eyes with cigarettes, and so there are the cigarette holes in it too. He got the whole thing photographed and that was the cover of the album.'

Roger McGough: '*Mike Hart Bleeds* is a brilliant title and 'Please Bring Back the Birch for the Milkman' has a music hall, vaudeville quality about it which sounds quite different with his heart-wrenching voice. He was raw and emotional and he was complicated too. He lacked confidence and he would back away from opportunities. He couldn't believe that people admired him. He didn't trust that and maybe that is where the pain and the soul came from.'

John Cornelius: 'I place Mike Hart on the same pedestal as Bob Dylan and John Lennon, I thought he was that good. He let himself down in the way that he conducted his affairs but he was the genuine article, a Woody Guthrie with a rolling stone lifestyle. He was a very gifted songwriter, great singer and a great performer, very charismatic. He was happiest playing to a handful of people. Some of the most stupendous performances I have seen from anybody have been from him performing to five or six people in Jesse's club in Hope Street or in O'Connor's on an off night. On a bigger, more organised show, he might fail to turn up or give a very desultory, perfunctory performance, but I would definitely say he was a genius.'

Mike Evans: 'Mike Hart was idealistic. He was concerned about selling out but of course some of the most radical musical statements ever, whether it is Bob Dylan or the Velvet Underground have been made on very established record labels. They haven't been released on avant-garde underground labels. To get the message across, I am sure it is more important that Dylan was on Columbia than ESP.'

His songs had a local feel about them. 'Almost Liverpool 8' starts with the words, 'Friday, got a Ribble bus'. Mike Evans: 'They caught on immediately locally. They had this poetic quality as well being so personal. I remember him singing 'Shelter Song' at a gig at Liverpool Cathedral and in the song he suggests that it becomes a hostel for the homeless.'

His then girlfriend, Jude Kelly says, "Shelter Song' was very moving as Mike himself was very near the edge of being somebody who was dispossessed. He had a real empathy for sadness and neglect and for the outsider. He had a wonderful voice as well, a Tom Waits voice, not a folk voice at all. He wasn't fanatical about Dylan, but then he didn't believe in heroes.'

Mark Kelly, then a Liverpool poet, now a writer for Jo Brand: 'I was first struck by the honesty of his songs but I now think of it as a very double-edged thing. Antonin Artaud was a very influential figure, the inspiration for the Theatre of Cruelty movement, and that was in the air. There was a lot of confessional art. You can admire the integrity and honesty but it can tip into being cruel and there are songs of his that are very specific indeed. In 'Bitchin' on a Train', his girlfriend has gone off with the lighting man from Principal Edwards' Magic Theatre, which is very specific and clearly true.'

His relationships were doomed to failure. Jude Kelly: 'I was only 17 and he was quite a lot older than me. He had a very dysfunctional life style and there was me doing my A-levels. There was no way I could have brought him home to meet my parents, for example. The age difference was too big and his lifestyle too chaotic. It was a wonderful time as I really admired him and we got on marvellously. We loved each other but we were like Mia Farrow and Frank Sinatra, it was a bit of a stretch. I didn't know what to do with somebody who drank so much.'

There is perhaps one artist who has run with the New Dylan and turned it to his advantage – Bruce Springsteen, who was also signed by John Hammond to Columbia. His first album, *Greetings from Astbury Park, N.J.* (1972) sounds a mess today as he packed so many lyrics into his songs but it did contain 'Blinded by the Light' and 'Growin' Up' and certainly got him started. Springsteen was touted as 'the future of rock and roll' and now he is The Boss. Rock writer Jon Savage: 'I can't abide Bruce Springsteen – he is just as highly constructed as any other rock star but it is a construction of a particular kind of authenticity. I don't buy it.'

Clinton Heylin adds, 'I had access to Paul Nelson's interview with Springsteen from 1972 which had never previously emerged, the first known interview, and even Paul is saying, "What is this thing about Dylan? I don't get it. You sound more like Van Morrison to me." I don't see it either, apart from the opening lines of "Blinded by the Light" which are quite funny and Dylanesque, but then a love of rhyme is not unique to Dylan.' Loudon Wainwright has said of the New Dylans: "Well, we all meet once a year at Bruce's house because he has the biggest house."

II. So Much Older Then: 1974–September 1975

In January 1974 Bob Dylan played his first North American tour since 1966. In the eight years since his last tour, the world had changed dramatically for the big acts. Large, impersonal arenas were the order of the day: everything was streamlined and much more efficient. Artists were playing to over 10,000 fans every night and that's a lot of tickets to sell: they were expected to undertake PR duties such as press, radio and TV interviews to promote the tour. It was big business: Bob Dylan and The Band would be touring on a jet called Starship One, and it was all uncomfortable for a sensitive soul like Bob Dylan. He told the *New York Times*, 'Being on tour is like being in limbo. It's like going from nowhere to nowhere.' Not admittedly a line that PR people want to hear, but Bob was doing his best. He wore silk shirts and smart suits, the neatest he has ever been on tour. He talked to *Newsweek*, emphasising that he was not part of the nostalgia market. He mightn't have thought he was but the public thought differently. Maybe the term contained some sentimentality that Dylan didn't like.

Nevertheless, Dylan appreciated that his concerts had become social occasions and that audiences wanted the big hits. He succumbed to a singalong 'Blowin' in the Wind' as a closer. This was before the large screens and he commented, 'We're like a puppet show in the distance and the music is an excuse for something else.'

There would be nearly 40 dates in six weeks, sometimes two in a day, and over 660,000 people would see Bob Dylan and The Band live, roughly at $10 a time, but the demand was so enormous that five million people had their applications rejected. David Geffen wanted more dates but Dylan had had enough. When it was over, Dylan commented, 'I was playing a role on that tour. I was playing Bob Dylan. It was all sort of mindless.'

By then, The Band had forged a very successful career of their own with the albums, *Music from Big Pink* (1968), *The Band* (1969), *Stage Fright* (1970) and *Cahoots* (1971), along with the live *Rock of Ages* (1972). The new one, *Moondog Matinee*, harked back to their time with Ronnie Hawkins as it was a collection of covers.

Once again, The Band was on stage with a cantankerous, idiosyncratic front man, but they had cut their teeth on Ronnie Hawkins so they knew how to handle him. As three of their albums had gone Top 10, they were able to negotiate their own spot, culminating in 20 minutes acoustic Dylan, 40 minutes The Band, and an hour of Dylan with The Band.

Dylan's last tour, which was, roughly speaking, with The Band, had been controversial but times had changed. He had been well received at the Isle of Wight, the Woody Guthrie tribute concert and as a guest on the *Rock of Ages* tour. So long as he performed well and didn't deliberately alienate audiences, he would do fine, but his behaviour could never be guaranteed. If all went well, there would be a knock-on effect for sales of back catalogue and new product. The tour itself would be financially rewarding.

At the first gig at a hockey stadium in Chicago, the audience was in semi-darkness waiting for the show to begin. Somebody flicked his lighter and then somebody else and soon there were little lights all over the arena. Dylan had not seen this before and wondered humorously if the place was about to be burned down: that would have been more extreme than the 'Judas!' tour.

Dylan opened with a rewritten 'Hero's Blues' from 1963 but his regular opener was 'Most Likely You Go Your Way and I'll Go Mine', probably because he was amused by opening with "You say you love me and you're thinking of me, But you know you could be wrong." A live single of this would make the US Hot 100.

The double-album *Before the Flood*, which was released in July 1974, made Number 3 on the US album charts. Surprisingly perhaps, this was Bob Dylan's first official live album. It had 21 tracks – 13 by Dylan, 8 by The Band: no introductions and rapturous applause throughout.

This was the time of Watergate but Dylan didn't need a new song. He had said it all in 'It's Alright, Ma (I'm Only Bleeding)'. When he got to the line, 'Even the President of the United States sometimes must have to stand naked', the whole audience cheered. That has continued through to this day irrespective of the incumbent. When *Newsweek* asked him about President Nixon, he said, 'I'm not really into presidents, I prefer kings and queens.'

Bob Dylan and the Band's tense arrangement of 'All Along the Watchtower' was inspired by the Jimi Hendrix Experience's version. He said, 'I liked Jimi Hendrix's record and ever since he died, I've been doing it that way. When I sing it, I feel like it's a tribute to him.' He reworked 'Masters of War' in a way Hendrix might have done it.

There was a lively 'Rainy Day Women, Numbers 12 and 35', which was a real crowd-pleaser. 'Highway 61 Revisited' suited a blues arrangement and Levon Helm's drumming propelled 'It Ain't Me Babe', which ended with Dylan's harmonica. Garth Hudson's organ lifted 'Ballad of a Thin Man'.

The Band scored well with 'The Weight' and a cover of Bobby Bland's 'Share Your Love with Me' from *Moondog Matinee*. Dylan let Richard Manuel take the lead for 'I Shall Be Released'.

Dylan occasionally included something unexpected such as 'As I Went out One Morning' in Toronto. He had a new verse for 'Knockin' on Heaven's Door': "Mama, wipe the blood from my face, I'm sick and tired of this war, I need a new hiding place, Feel like I'm knockin' on heaven's door."

Rolling Stone said that Dylan was 'singing the lyrics as though they either mean nothing at all or something very different from we've always understood them to signify.' This is unfair but 'Lay Lady Lay' was no longer a romantic love song: he was emphasising key words like a Dylan parodist. His unruly vocal on an acoustic 'Just like a Woman' could have been improved but the audience loved it.

Unlike other artists, Dylan did not do fund-raising performances for politicians but after his show in Atlanta, Georgia, he attended a reception at Governor Jimmy Carter's mansion at the invitation of his son, Chip. When running for President, Jimmy Carter asked Bob Dylan to lunch. From then on, he said Bob was his friend and quoted his songs. Dylan was quoted in his inauguration speech.

Bob thanked everyone on the tour on stage for the last gig but didn't thank David Geffen. It was probably an oversight as Dylan did attend his birthday party and sang 'All I Really Want to Do' with Cher.

Considering his organisational skills, it is odd that Geffen did not release *Planet Waves* until the tour was underway. Still, his promise to Dylan was fulfilled as it did make Number 1, pushing aside Jim Croce, but its initial sales of 600,000 were regarded as disappointing. Geffen was hoping to top a million, but he did get another big seller with *Before the Flood*.

'Forever Young' notwithstanding, *Planet Waves* is not one of the best albums in Bob Dylan's catalogue, but it does have its champions. Leonard Cohen defended its critical reception by saying, 'Most critics can't comprehend songs about the complexities of lasting relationships.' Dylan's chum, Larry 'Ratso' Sloman, who will soon play a significant part in the story said, 'It is a tremendous statement about the balancing of domesticity with the concerns of a mystical artist.'

'Forever Young' was the obvious single, but it wasn't released as such. Dylan had a minor US success with 'On A Night like This' while 'Something There Is about You' hardly sold at all.

After the tour, Dylan was restless in Point Dume and he moved to New York, attending some painting classes by Norman Raeben, who became Dylan's Maharishi. Norman Raeben had been born in Russia in 1901. His father Sholem Aleichem was a leading Yiddish writer, creating Tvye, whose story was adapted for the musical *Fiddler on the Roof*. Norman told Dylan to draw a vase and, pleased with the result, he took him on. Dylan attended his classes most weekdays and found it was also helping him write lyrics. He had been taking him time to do what he had done unconsciously and he wanted to get back.

Raeben saw the link between painting and poetry and told him that 'Love minus Zero / No Limit' was a painting in maroon and silver. Raeben said that a part of the painting could be looked at individually or as part of the whole, and Dylan saw that he could play with time and perhaps have past, present and future in the same song. This arises on his next album, *Blood on the Tracks*, and is particularly noticeable on 'Tangled Up in Blue'. He switches from first to third person and back, but that can also be heard in an earlier song, 'Lay Lady Lay'.

Blood on the Tracks was about the strain on his marriage, which wasn't helped by his philandering. While in New York, he renewed his friendship with Ellen Bernstein, who worked for Columbia Records. For someone who had wanted to keep his private life away from public gaze, *Blood on the Tracks* was a cryptic look at his relationships. He wrote about Ellen in 'You're Gonna Make Me Lonesome When You Go', which mentions her birthplace, Ashtabula. It's an infectious song which notes his interest in Paul Verlaine and Arthur Rimbaud: Verlaine shot Rimbaud in the wrist and spent 18 months in prison.

There were press reports that Bob and Sara were splitting up, but they were linking Bob to Lorey Sebastian, John Sebastian's wife, who denied it. It's ironic, telling perhaps, that one of Dylan's new songs was 'You're a Big Girl Now' when one of John Sebastian's successes was 'You're a Big Boy Now'.

In May 1974 Bob Dylan met Phil Ochs over drinks at the Chelsea Hotel and Dylan agreed to guest on the Friends of Chile concert at the Felt Forum in New York three days later. When he arrived, Ochs locked him in his dressing room as he feared that Dylan might leave without performing. Surely that would make him less likely to perform. In the event, they plied Dylan with Chilean wine and the concert was a shambles with drunken performances from Dylan, Ochs and Dave Van Ronk.

The concert paid tribute to Victor Jara, the songwriter who had been critical of the Pinochet regime. In 1973, he had been brought into a stadium and had his hands smashed in public before facing a firing squad. The day after the concert Bob Dylan took Jara's widow, Joan to the New York Museum of Modern Art, but he did not appear to take his interest in Chile any further.

Dylan had now separated from Sara and he spent the summer on his farm in Minnesota with his children and with his brother living down the road. He was fired up about writing songs and these formed the basis of *Blood on the Tracks*.

On 1 August 1974 Dylan was resigned to re-signing with Columbia and possibly Ellen had been persuading him to do this. He spent time in San Francisco with her. They visited his friend, songwriter and cartoonist Shel Silverstein, on his houseboat. Dylan, Silverstein and Peter Rowan played each other their new songs and came away feeling good. Bob played some new songs to the guitarist Mike Bloomfield but Mike thought that they weren't right for him: they were too long and had too few key changes.

Bob knew the guitarist Eric Weissberg, who had been a member of the Tarriers. He had been featured on the soundtrack for the Jon Voight film, *Deliverance* (1973) and, as a result, had had a US Number 2 with 'Duelling Banjos', playing with Steve Mandell. Eric's new band was called Deliverance and Bob Dylan invited them to some sessions. They started on 16 September at Columbia's studio in New York. Other musicians included Paul Griffin, who had played organ for Bob in 1965. This time the producer, or at least the engineer, would be Phil Ramone. The album *Blood on the Tracks* is missing a producer's credit. Maybe it should be Dylan himself. Weissberg had doubts about Dylan's musicality, saying of one of his suggestions, 'If it had been anyone else, I'd have walked out.'

The album, *Blood on the Tracks*, is known as the Divorce Album, although Dylan has never acknowledged this. He has never spoken publicly about the background to the songs. However, he did say this on a TV show with Mary Travers which indicates how personal the album was: 'A lot of people told me that they enjoyed that album. It's hard for me to relate to that – I mean, people enjoying that type of pain.' In recent times, Dylan has said that the songs are not autobiographical but can we believe him? There is a parallel with Woody Allen who clearly wrote films about his own predicaments but always denied it. In 2018, an album of outtakes, *More Blood, More Tracks*, was released and we can hear how Dylan changes, drops and adds lines and verses.

The sessions began with 'Up to Me', a song that Dylan was to revise before recording it again.

'Tangled Up in Blue' was brought on by his split with Sara ; it is about their meeting and their relationship over the years but the tenses and persons keep changing so you are never sure what is going on.

'Call Letter Blues' was a song that Dylan rewrote as 'Meet Me in the Morning', completing the new version a week later. Bob wanted a steel guitar and Ellen suggested Buddy Cage from the New Riders of the Purple Sage. Dylan told him to play only on the last verse. He was insulted by this and did it rather angrily – which was exactly what Dylan wanted.

With just Tony Brown on bass, Dylan performed 'Simple Twist of Fate', a song of lovers parting but the singer keeps his distance through the use of third person. He does acknowledge, 'I still believe she was my twin.'

With its theme of carrying a message, 'If You See Her, Say Hello' has similarities to 'Girl from the North Country' and Gordon Lightfoot's 'Did She Mention My Name'. Unlike the other songs, it is more relaxed and not crammed with words. It was about being casual in the midst of emotional turmoil and it works equally well with just voice and guitar.

'Idiot Wind' was as venomous as 'Like a Rolling Stone' and 'Positively Fourth Street'. The opening line refers to gossip columnists drawing wrong conclusions. He examines his marriage but 'Peace and quiet's been avoiding me so long it seems like hell.'

John Bauldie: 'The line "People see me all the time and they can't remember how to act" has to be about how people react when they see him. It is his comment on shouldering the burden. People don't react normally to him and usually respond in one of two ways. They may deliberately and very obviously ignore him, or they stare at him and perhaps run up for an autograph.'

'Lily, Rosemary and the Jack of Hearts' is a tall tale of frontier life that could be made into a film. It takes place in a mining town so how much goes back to his memories of Minnesota? Is Dylan the Jack of Hearts? Michael Gray has suggested that the song was inspired by W.H. Auden's *Victor*. The melody is similar to his own 'Buckets of Rain' and Tom Paxton's 'Bottle of Wine'.

Tom Russell: 'People have been trying to figure out the complexities of what Dylan is talking about. Even Ian Tyson said, "What the hell is Dylan saying? Who's killing who in this song?" It is like a Shakespearean play and I'd like to record it with different people playing the parts. Joe Ely has a great voice for Big Jim and Eliza Gilkyson could be Lily and I could be the Jack of Hearts. But who killed Big Jim? Is it Lily or Rosemary? I don't think Dylan has to answer anything and you can interpret it any way you want.'

Raul Malo: 'I did 'You're Gonna Make Me Lonesome' and the songs on that album are difficult to record. Bob delivers the lyrics so quickly and his phrasing is uniquely his. I remember singing that song in the studio and it took a while. Usually I pick up a song quickly and can do it straight away. His influence as a writer is undeniable, his lyrics, his subject matter, his prose, the way he phrases his words is sometimes beautiful and sometimes very difficult. He is hit or miss. Sometimes it is not so good but it is still brave. That's what makes him brilliant.'

In late September, when the album was being mixed and sequenced in New York, Dylan realised that he was unhappy with it. He talked it over with his brother David who recommended some musicians in Minneapolis who might breathe new life into the songs.

In late December Dylan spent two days in the Sound 80 Studios in Minneapolis, where Prince was to record. He cut new versions of 'Idiot Wind', 'You're a Big Girl Now', 'Tangled Up in Blue', 'Lily, Rosemary and the Jack of Hearts' and 'If You See Her, Say Hello'.

'Tangled Up in Blue' was redone with Kevin Odegard on guitar. Dylan later added 'born again' references and the version on *Real Live* (1984) is different again. He said, 'On *Real Live* it is more like it should have been. I was never really happy with it. On *Real Live*, the imagery is better and more the way I would have liked it on the original recording.'

The revised words for 'Idiot Wind' are less autobiographical and have some sorrow about them. The song is more vitriolic on his live *Hard Rain* (1976) although there is some regret.

When *Blood on the Tracks* was released in January 1975, it was half New York, half Minneapolis. Dylan asked Pete Hamill to write a sleeve note, which won a Grammy but was then replaced by an illustration. The album topped the US charts and sold over a million copies. Strangely, when 'Tangled Up in Blue' was released as a single, it only made Number 31.

The album has endured well. The novelist Rick Moody spoke about it for Dylan's 60th birthday. 'No filler, no topicalities, no gimmicks – the best album ever made.'

Former England cricket captain Bob Willis: 'I think my favourite Dylan album is *Blood on the Tracks* from when I was on tour in Australia. We were getting a terrible hiding on that tour from Jeff Thomson and Dennis Lillee, and it gave me great comfort, especially the first track on side one, 'Tangled Up in Blue', and it's been a favourite ever since.'

In 1995 when I first heard Hootie and the Blowfish's 'Only Wanna Be with You', I thought the second verse was a great joke. The singer is with his girlfriend and he plays 'a little Dylan' and wonders what the line about 'shooting a man named Gray' in 'Idiot Wind' is all about. The lead singer, Darius Rucker, adds, 'Ain't Bobby so cool?' Not so cool as to let Hootie and the Blowfish get away with it. Dylan's publisher sued and received an out of court settlement. Darius Rucker didn't hold it against Dylan as he had a Number 1 country hit with 'Wagon Wheel' (2013). Dylan was unhappy when National Lampoon used 'Idiot Wind' for a spoof about him.

Sara moved out of Point Dume in the summer of 1974. Ironically, by the time the album was released, Bob and Sara were back together, largely for the sake of the children and she was fed up with his infidelities. In March 1975, they were seen at a charity show with Neil Young in San Francisco and at Paul McCartney's party on the Queen Mary, permanently moored in Long Beach, California. Bob soon had a new girlfriend, the actress Ruth Tyrangiel, who later considered suing him for palimony.

Joan Baez was never a prolific writer and she wrote her best song at the end of 1974, 'Diamonds and Rust', an affectionate look at her relationship with Bob Dylan and it has never left her repertoire. Joan Baez: 'I was writing a song about Vietnam veterans and I was struggling with that. It transformed itself in the middle and my feeling is that songs come from somewhere down among your toes and you don't have much control over what is coming out. It seemed to be a love song with enough tweak to the heart that most people relate to it.'

There is a wonderful image where she says his eyes were bluer than robins' eggs: 'When I got that line, I thought "Is that too awful?" and I tried it out on a few people and they thought it was okay. I just feel that songwriting is a secondary talent for me.'

Her sister Mimi continued to promote Richard's legacy, saying, 'I'll always love Dick. He's an impossible act to follow.' His novel, *Been Down So Long, It Looks Like Up To Me*, was filmed in 1971 with Barry Primus as the protagonist but it had no publicity and is forgotten. Somebody should try again as the novel is now a Penguin Twentieth-Century Classic with an introduction from his friend and fellow writer, Thomas Pynchon. In the same year, there was an off-Broadway show about Richard himself, *Long Time Coming and Long Time Gone*, written by Nancy Greenwald and starring an unknown Richard Gere and Vicki Sue Robinson. In 1974 Mimi founded the charity Bread and Roses, which was to bring music into prisons, hospitals and rest homes; it was funded through some all-star charity concerts. Mimi died in 2001, another lung cancer victim and yet she had never smoked.

Bob Dylan spent the early part of 1975 socialising in New York. Dylan performed on David Letterman's show and after the recording, he went to a basketball game and met Kevin McHale of the Boston Celtics who came from Hibbing. When McHale saw him, he exclaimed 'Dylan!' and Bob responded with 'Hibbing!'

The thought of Bob Dylan playing Woody Guthrie was probably never taken seriously by Bob Dylan nor the film producers. *Bound for Glory* was shot in 1975 (and released in 1976) with David Carradine as Woody Guthrie and directed by Hal Ashby. It captured Woody's spirit very well.

Dylan met Dana Gillespie again, who was in New York with David Bowie. Bowie's 'Somebody up There Likes Me' on his 1975 album, *Young Americans* is liked a slowed-down 'Subterranean Homesick Blues'. Elvis Costello's 'Pump It Up' is also in that ballpark, but it all goes back to 'Too Much Monkey Business'. Dylan met Bette Midler with Bowie and he agreed to join her for 'Buckets of Rain'.

In May 1975 Dylan spent six weeks on holiday in Corsica and in Marseilles with David Oppenheim who painted the back sleeve for *Blood on the Tracks*. On 24 May, they attended a gypsy festival for his birthday. They were worshipping the black Madonna, St. Sara. Dylan rapped about this on his 1978 tour. It prompted him to write 'One More Cup of Coffee' and Allen Ginsburg has said that 'the valley' in that song is death.

Robbie Robertson had been working through *The Basement Tapes* with a view to a double-album. Being a perfectionist, he doctored some performances by sweetening the sound. As they were working tapes not intended for public consumption, why shouldn't he do that? Many Dylan fans felt that he should have left well alone. They felt too that Robertson was favouring himself. When the double-album was released in the summer of 1975, there were 24 relatively short songs – 16 by Dylan and eight by The Band alone. Some of The Band's tracks had not even been recorded at Big Pink, thus losing the authenticity. The album could have had better reviews but this was because the reviewers knew the tracks all too well through bootlegs, whereas the majority of the general public hardly knew them at all.

The cover was shot in the boiler room of the Los Angeles YMCA and had nothing to do with Big Pink. It featured an assortment of circus characters as well as Bob Dylan, The Band, Neil Young (dark hat, dark glasses, whiskers), Ringo Starr and David Blue. Why with the jokey reference to Quinn the Eskimo on the cover was 'The Mighty Quinn' not included? The liner notes were written by Greil Marcus.

Much less well known (in fact, completely unknown!), Robbie produced an album *Hirth from Earth* in 1975 for the singer and songwriter Hirth Martinez, who sometimes sang with Maude, Garth Hudson's girlfriend. He wrote songs of loneliness with eccentric chord changes and Robbie found he had 300 to choose from. An unusual bossa nova, 'Altogether Alone', is really good. Bob was a big fan of Hirth's but then Bob liked Tiny Tim.

Around this time, Dylan was living in a loft in Greenwich Village and getting involved in New York life. He was impressed by Patti Smith and saw the Rolling Stones at Madison Square Garden.

In July 1975 Dylan spent five consecutive nights at the Other End. He joined Ramblin' Jack Elliott on stage and sang a new song, 'Abandoned Love'. Dylan was amused at the way Ramblin' Jack would improvise a song and say, 'I must write that down', but never did. He joined Bobby Neuwirth and Patti Smith together on stage.

More importantly, Dylan met two new friends in the Village who would shape his next album. Firstly, Jacques Levy, the bearded man next to Bob Dylan at the microphone on the back of the next album, *Desire*.

Jacques Levy was born in New York in 1935. He had trained as a psychologist and gone into the theatre in 1965. He knew Kenneth Tynan and they worked on the highly successful nude revue, *Oh! Calcutta*. He and Roger McGuinn intended to write a country-rock musical based on *Peer Gynt*, which would be called *Gene Tryp* (very funny!). They needed to raise $1m but stalled at $300,000. They lost interest but McGuinn cut some of the songs with the Byrds – the outstanding 'Chestnut Mare', 'Lover of the Bayou' and 'All the Things'.

Dylan had met Jacques Levy before and he lived by the Other End, close to Bleecker Street. When they met again, Dylan suggested a collaboration. This surprised Levy as he thought they were both lyricists. 'What's up?' said Bob, 'Don't you like my tunes?'

Levy said, 'Bob loves rhyme and the complications of it. He had never used a rhyming dictionary before. Bob had a keen sense of opening lines and how they meant so much. The first thing that hits the listener is very important. I like songs with strong narratives and you want to know what happens next. Dylan sometimes did that but usually he prefers sets of images.'

Dylan had a song he was working on, 'Isis' and they finished it together at Dylan's beach house in East Hampton, Long Island. Said Levy, "Isis' is about two guys going on an adventure and not sure what they will find. Nothing to do with Egypt just as Fanny had nothing to do with Nazareth.' That worked, so Dylan invited him to his home in East Hampton where they completed 14 songs in a week.

You can sense that love of a rhyming dictionary with 'Mozambique' where they were finding fun rhymes for '-ique'. Maybe it was the wrong subject for such an exercise as the song sounds like a tourist brochure, whilst, in reality, a civil war was tearing apart the country.

'Romance in Durango' has a dramatic tempo and was to feature Eric Clapton on dobro. Dylan had a Mexican melody and Levy had a postcard of a Mexican shack with chilli peppers on the roof, hence the opening line.

When Dylan had been in Spain, he had the phrase 'From the mountain high above' but hadn't found a way to develop it. He and Levy constructed 'Black Diamond Bay' which was set in a hotel on an island with a volcano. The guests are about to experience an earthquake and the whole town flees. Levy said that instead of sympathy for the devil, most people had apathy for the devil. In the final verse, the listeners realise that they are hearing the story through someone watching the development on the TV news in Los Angeles who couldn't care less as he never planned to go there anyway.

Dylan may have known Joseph Conrad's novel *Victory* from 1914, which has a Black Diamond Bay. Coal is known as the black diamond. There is a homosexual called Mr. Jones in the book (first name not given). Both are set on a remote island; both involve gambling rooms and volcanos.

Dylan and Levy had dinner with Jerry and Marta Orbach, who were planning a biography of their friend, the New York mobster, Joey Gallo. The Orbachs told them that Gallo had thrown a Byrds' album away as he was offended by 'Chestnut Mare'. That amused them and it led to 'Joey', a somewhat affectionate song for a psychopath.

Gallo thought his wife had been flirting with someone else. The next night he told her, 'Say, remember that guy in the club you were fooling with. He had a terrible accident on the bridge. His car went out of control.'

In October 1957 Joey Gallo killed Albert Anastasia, head of Murder, Inc., when he was in a barber's chair, which enabled Carlo Gambino to become the boss of bosses. Gallo didn't find any favour with Gambino and was jailed in 1962. He was released in 1970 and two years later, he was gunned down as he celebrated his birthday at Umberto's Clam House in

Little Italy. 'Joey' was included on *Desire* in place of 'Abandoned Love' at the last minute; note the informal start – the musicians had never heard it before.

'Golden Loom' was written by Dylan alone but the scientific references reflect the time spent with Jacques Levy.

By far the best-known song from the Dylan and Levy partnership is 'Hurricane'. Rubin 'Hurricane' Carter was a professional boxer with a mission. In April 1964 he complained to the *Saturday Evening Post* about white policemen harassing blacks in New York. The FBI had a file on him and he was arrested for no good reason from time to time. He did not join the civil rights march in Selma because he had received a death threat.

In 1966 Hurricane Carter was arrested for killing three white people in a barroom robbery. In June 1967, Rubin Carter and his friend John Artis were convicted by an all-white jury and he felt that he had been set up because he was a provocative figure.

In 1975 Dylan read his autobiography, *The Sixteenth Round*, and went to visit him in prison. Dylan felt that he had been wrongly convicted: so too did Muhammad Ali and Jesse Jackson, but Dylan had the ultimate means at his disposal as he could write a song about it. He and Jacques Levy intended to highlight the injustice in a way that would parallel 'The Lonesome Death of Hatti Carroll'. In that song, someone got six months for murder: in this song, someone got life and was, in their eyes, innocent.

It was a breathless, eight-minute song, opening like a film script and vividly describing the robbery and its aftermath. Howard Wyeth's drumming bangs out like pistol shots and Bob Dylan's performance adds to the urgency.

The trial had its faults and the evidence centred on Patty Valentine who saw a car leaving the scene which was allegedly Carter's. She was horrified by the song, claiming that it destroyed her anonymity and implied she had lied. She claimed royalties based on the sales figures for *Desire*.

Dylan and Levy had never talked to Valentine and said that their song had been based on press stories sent to them by Carter's defence committee. Dylan said that she became part of the song because she discovered the bodies 'and she's got a beautiful name', which is hardly the best way to defend your actions.

Hurricane Carter and John Artis had been found guilty of murder and in 1976, they were bailed for mistakes made by the prosecution and retried. Later in the year, they were reconvicted but in 1985, the convictions were overturned.

Also, Bob met Scarlet Rivera. He saw her holding a violin case at a bus stop. He flagged her down and said, 'Do you play that thing?' She had played with the jazz musician Ornette Coleman and with a Cuban band in Havana. He invited her to try out some songs and that night they saw Muddy Waters at the Bottom Line. The management asked Muddy to introduce Bob, which he did as 'John Dillon', presumably confusing him with John Dillinger. Bob went up with his harmonica and with Scarlet. The pianist, Willie 'The Lion' Smith, recalled, 'Muddy's singing one thing and he's blowing something else. Muddy said to me, "Do you know who he is?" I said, "I don't give a damn who he is. Get him off the stage." Muddy should have known who he was as he had just made the *Woodstock Album* with Levon and Garth.

Dylan was impressed with Scarlet and invited her to join the sessions for *Desire*. Scarlet gave the record a very distinctive sound, especially on 'Hurricane'. Incidentally, the story of Dylan finding Scarlet is identical to Kevin Rowland finding their fiddler for Dexys Midnight Runners, but Rowland may have known this story and been romanticising.

Bob Dylan: Outlaw Blues

Early in July 1975 Dylan had recorded two songs with Dave Mason's band, 'Rita Mae' and 'Joey'. 'Rita Mae' was a rocker rather like Johnny Burnette's 'Bertha Lou'.

By the end of the month, Dylan knew what he wanted. With the help of his producer, Don Devito, he handpicked an excellent band that included Eric Clapton, Yvonne Elliman, Emmylou Harris and Howard Wyeth. He also invited the British band Kokomo. Dylan had the songs, and once they had grasped the structure off they went. As usual, he was going for feel rather than polish.

Emmylou and Bob had microphones side by side and he might nudge her when she was to sing. Emmylou felt under pressure as she didn't want to blow a Dylan session. The mood was soft and sexy on 'One More Cup of Coffee'.

Eric Clapton: 'He wasn't sure what he wanted and it was very hard to keep up with him. I had to get out in the fresh air as it was just madness in there.'

The second night was just Dylan, Harris, Rivera, Stoner and Wyeth. They completed four takes for *Desire* that night. There are no drums in the first verse of 'Mozambique' as Dylan hadn't counted the drummer in.

'Catfish' is a hero song about a baseball pitcher, Catfish Hunter. Catfish had a dispute with his boss at Oakland and went to the Yankees. Joe Cocker recorded the song on *Stingray*.

On 31 July 1975, after doing 'Abandoned Love', Dylan was listening to the playbacks when Sara walked in. He was acting coldly towards her and Don Devito said, 'Let's go, Bob, that's everything.' Bob said, 'No, no, I have one more. Let's record this.' Don said, 'What's it called, Bob?' He looked at her through the glass and said 'Sara, Part One'. Everybody was blown away by its power and by Bob's nerve. When he finished, a girl in the studio said, 'I don't know who this Sara chick is but she'd better hurry up before she's six feet under.'

The next day the Dylans left for the wedding of his cousin, Linda Goldfine, in Minneapolis. Dylan performed with local musicians at the reception and sang 'Forever Young' and Kenny Loggins' 'A Love Song'. While he was there, Dylan asked his childhood friend Lou Kemp to organise a tour. This became the Rolling Thunder Revue.

In September 1975, Bob Dylan agreed to appear on *The World of John Hammond* for CBS-TV. Hammond had suffered some strokes but was looking okay and the performers included John Hammond Jr, George Benson, Marion Williams and Sonny Terry. Dylan performed 'Hurricane', 'Oh Sister' and 'Simple Twist of Fate'. Hammond continued working, bringing Stevie Ray Vaughan to Columbia in 1983. He died in 1987, aged 76.

Late in September 1975 Dylan and Sara attended the wedding of The Band's road manager Jonathan Taplin and Rosanna DeSoto in California. Taplin wanted to produce a film of *Lily, Rosemary and the Jack of Hearts* but it never materialised.

The new album was called *Desire*. It was possibly a reference to *A Streetcar Named Desire*. Tennessee Williams took his title from a bus in New Orleans which had Desire Street as its destination. The sleeve copied the photograph of John Phillips of the Mamas and the Papas on *The Wolfking of LA* (1970). The liner notes for *Desire* are as frank as anything Dylan has written about himself and he talks of the appeal of Joseph Conrad. It was his biggest album to date in the US, topping the charts for five weeks, although the singles, 'Hurricane' and 'Mozambique', didn't crack the Top 40.

Al Stewart: 'I gave up on Dylan after *Blood on the Tracks*. He released a number of records that just didn't move me in any shape or form and I stopped buying them. I moved onto other writers whom I thought were doing it better.'

Dylan said on the Rolling Thunder tour that 'Isis' was 'a song about marriage'. It's also a song about grave-robbing. In the 1990s Richard Dickinson killed his mother because he thought she was the evil goddess Isis from a Bob Dylan song. Dylan puts the songs out there but really he can't predict how they may be interpreted.

CHAPTER 11
The Thunder Rolls

'My marriage was a failure. Husband and wife was a failure but father and mother wasn't a failure.'
Bob Dylan

I. Pulled into Nazareth

Working with Bob Dylan was very constructive for The Band. They had played big shows and travelled the world; they had experienced hostility instead of standing ovations; and then in Woodstock, Bob Dylan had opened the American songbook for them.

Albert Grossman secured a $50,000 advance for their first LP with Capitol. They had enjoyed the informal way that they had been recording with Bob in Woodstock and so they didn't want the more rigid structures of a studio. They didn't want to use baffle boards as they wanted to see each other. The instruments might bleed through onto other microphones but that could add a warmth and a live feel. They wanted to sound like a band: The Band, in fact. They asked John Simon to produce them in Los Angeles: he had worked with Simon and Garfunkel, the Cyrcle and Leonard Cohen as well as on Peter Yarrow's film, *You Are What You Eat*.

Their songs were strongly influenced by working with Bob Dylan, although, on the whole, they didn't follow his approach of keeping them mysterious. Bob would never have revealed the origins of 'The Weight'. The listener assumes it has biblical connections as the opening words are 'I pulled into Nazareth.'

Robbie Robertson had a Martin guitar with the label, Nazareth, Pennsylvania, which had prompted the song. He admired the Spanish film *Viridiana* (1961), which had been denounced by the Vatican and banned by Franco for blasphemy. It is a brilliant film about how a novice nun recreated the Last Supper with the homeless of the city and the theme is that good deeds are not rewarded but punished. The protagonist in 'The Weight' pulls into Nazareth: he only wants to say hello but everyone wants him to do something for them.

Levon Helm sings the first three verses and then Rick Danko tells a shaggy dog story about Crazy Chester. Levon with Richard Manuel returns for the final verse. When Dylan first heard 'The Weight': he said, 'That is fantastic. Which of you wrote the song?'

'The Weight' has been recorded by Aretha Franklin, the Staple Singers and Jackie DeShannon. Peter Fonda and Dennis Hopper thought the song would be perfect for *Easy Rider*, but Levon was unhappy about a film that had such hostility towards the South. The film makers used a cover version from the group, Smith. Then Michelangelo Antonioni wanted to use it for his 1970 film, *Zabriskie Point*.

Robbie Robertson's only lead vocal on *Music from Big Pink* is the high pitched 'To Kingdom Come', another song with religious overtones. He wrote 'Caledonia Mission' (using Levon's memories of Arkansas) and 'Chest Fever' (which became an 'in concert' *tour de force* for Garth Hudson).

Dylan gave The Band the stunning 'I Shall Be Released' as well as writing 'Tears of Rage' with Richard Manuel and 'This Wheel's on Fire' with Rick Danko. 'Tears of Rage' features a brilliant vocal from Richard, Levon on tom-toms and Robbie playing Curtis Mayfield-style licks. It was the first time that Bob Dylan was sharing credits with his contemporaries.

Richard Manuel opened up his heart on 'In a Station', a song about disillusionment and another of love going sour, 'We Can Talk'. When The Band realised that they might have too many slow songs, they considered speeding up Richard's 'Lonesome Suzie' but changed their mind.

The Band performed a fine version of the ghostly country song, 'The Long Black Veil', recorded by country singer Lefty Frizzell in 1959. Other covers left off the album included Big Bill Broonzy's 'Key to the Highway' and the Stanley Brothers' 'If I Lose'.

Sounding very like Mose Allison, Jimmy Drew recorded a single, 'Baby Lou', for US Decca in 1961. Richard loved the song and they gave it a fine R&B arrangement with a tortured vocal and Garth on organ.

On 1 July 1968 *Music from Big Pink* from The Band was released. It was highly original, quite country with a religious feel. Some acts listened to contemporary music to see how they would fit in (Simon and Garfunkel, for example), but The Band and Dylan went back to pre-war sources: country and Delta blues. Despite Dylan's privacy, the publicity surrounding the album said where they all lived.

The cover painting for *Music from Big Pink* showed the five musicians and an elephant. Was there an elephant in the room? Depends on your view of the artist, Bob Dylan. The US issue came in a gatefold which included a photograph of The Band and their families, taken by Elliott Landy. Unlike Dylan, such publicity didn't bother them and the message was clear: this band is really bonding together. Landy also took the *Rolling Stone* cover of the five members of the band squeezing onto a small bench.

It was a popular album on FM radio and soon The Band had covered their advance and were earning royalties. George Harrison, Eric Clapton and Keith Richards praised the album. Eric Clapton left Cream when he heard *Big Pink* as he wanted to get into something like that. George Harrison went to a Beatles' session and told George Martin, 'We ought to sound like this.' When the Beatles sang 'Hey Jude' on *The Smothers Brothers Comedy Show*, Paul added, 'Take a load off Fanny', a line from 'The Weight'.

Happy Traum: 'Robbie Robertson is a genius songwriter and he had to have been influenced by Bob as they weren't writing like that before. They were playing rock'n'roll but Bob had combined it with poetry and it changed the world. It was abstract thoughts being put to rock music. I was such good friends with them and I heard the Band play so many times and I never got tired of them. They are the great American rock band. They are perfect for my taste because of their links to American roots music – Levon had heavily southern blues roots and he loved the blues from Memphis and Mississippi and he came from Arkansas, right on the confluence of those states. The other guys were Canadian and embodied that music too. They combined their fantastic songs with great vocal and instrumental arrangements. It was so beautifully done, and if I listen to any rock band, and I don't listen to a lot of them, I would choose The Band. They were fantastic.'

In 1965 Jonathan Taplin had been a weekend road manager for Albert Grossman while at college. At different times, he worked with Bob Dylan, Peter, Paul and Mary, Odetta and the Jim Kweskin Jug Band. Indeed, he was working with Kweskin when Dylan was at Newport in 1965. Albert Grossman made him full-time tour manager for The Band in spring 1969.

A key promoter, Bill Graham, wanted The Band in concert but there were difficulties as the group was accident prone. Rick Danko crashed a car and was on the critical list. He suffered a broken neck and skull injuries and was out of action for two months. Levon wrecked a Corvette after nodding off at the wheel. In the mid-70s, Richard broke his neck in a boating accident so there are plenty of fractured necks in this story.

Considering his reservations about Woodstock, it is odd that Levon then bought a house and a barn there and he was the only Band member to remain in the area.

The first album sold well but they told Capitol that they did not want to make the next one in the company's studio. They had enjoyed home recording in Woodstock and they wanted something similar in Los Angeles. Jonathan Taplin learnt that the pool house of Sammy Davis' former home in the hills above Sunset Plaza could become a makeshift studio. It was ideal.

The Band were calling their output 'mountain music', which today would be called Americana. Indeed, you can mount a strong argument for The Band starting Americana. The evidence would be their second album, starkly called *The Band*, which is a social history of America with tales of migration and life in the backwoods. There were stories of the American South like 'The Night They Drove Old Dixie Down'. At their best, their lyrics were as brilliant as Bob Dylan's.

The Band looked like frontiersmen on the cover with their felt hats, dark suits and facial hair. The sepia photography from Elliott Landy added to their appearance as nineteenth-century backwoodsmen, although this was the way they normally dressed. As a result, the album is sometimes called *The Brown Album*, which puts it alongside the Beatles and *The White Album*.

The songs are about people hemmed in by their history. The protagonists are people with experience and not youths. Steve Hackett from Genesis: 'You get a real sense of the American South from them, a bit like men from another century. Like Crosby, Stills and Nash who copied them with their sepia cover for Déjà Vu, they looked like guys from the backwoods. There are heartfelt songs about the South and I loved all that. It goes further back than rock'n'roll. They were brilliant and Levon Helm was absolutely great.'

The album opens brilliantly with Richard Manuel singing "Standing by your window in pain, a pistol in your hand." It's about a southern guy who has been cheating and is about to be shot by his girlfriend. He is pleading his case and right away we are in Band territory.

A roustabout is remembering his good times with Bessie in 'Up on Cripple Creek', on which Garth uses a clavinet and wah-wah pedal for a sound like a Jew's harp. The details like Bessie putting a doughnut in his tea add to the fun, particularly as it ends with yodelling. The Band chose to perform this song on *The Ed Sullivan Show*.

There is a colourful mix of tuba and accordion for a surprisingly cheerful song about being homeless, 'Rag Mama Rag', sung by Levon Helm, here playing mandolin. Richard Manuel plays drums, Garth Hudson piano, Rick Danko fiddle with John Simon on tuba substituting for the bass. Ragtime Willie could have been a character in 'Rag Mama Rag', but he has a song to himself, 'Rockin' Chair', a melancholic study of old age.

The Band's second album, simply called *The Band*, was released in October 1969. The album sounded modern and yet had an old-time feel. Garth Hudson; 'Yes, and that's thanks to Levon's mandolin playing when Richard would play the drums. Richard had a style that would fit in fine with more traditional straight-ahead music and Levon said that Richard was his favourite drummer. The stories were put together from Levon's tales of the Deep South with lines from the songs that his dad had taught him. A lot of the poetry of those songs came from Levon's storytelling ability.' That was to create friction as Robbie Robertson was shown as composer of all tracks, sharing the credits with Levon Helm once and Richard Manuel three times.

The promotion of the album was held back because of Rick and Levon's accidents but it didn't harm sales. Garth Hudson: 'We knew the album would be special but we didn't know how exceptional it would be. It is certainly a different sounding and unique album. I tried with my instrumentation to find a different sound for every song. I wanted something that would help the mood and the flavour of the words and the vision.'

Robbie Robertson said that no one at the time would have wanted songs about his Indian heritage, although look at the work of Johnny Cash, Buffy Sainte-Marie and Peter La Farge. Instead, Robbie locked into Levon's memories and historical stories, backed up with library research. The masterpiece was 'The Night They Drove Old Dixie Down'. Levon told Robbie to drop a verse about the President, 'Don't mention Abraham Lincoln – that won't go down well in the South.'

Jonathan Taplin commented, 'James Agee and Walker Evans had collaborated on *Let Us Now Praise Famous Men* and it had opened a window into the life of a sharecropper. 'The Night They Drove Old Dixie Down' was like a musical version of that book.' Landy's work seemed a continuation of Walker Evans' photographs.

The Band had a hit single with the playful 'Rag Mama Rag' but the big song was 'The Night They Drove Old Dixie Down', an international hit for Joan Baez in 1971. Donnie Fritts: 'Me and Billy Swan and a whole bunch of people were in the studio when Norbert Putnam cut 'The Night They Drove Old Dixie Down' on her. That was us singing in the background. She is a great singer, wonderful singer, and it was a wonderful record.'

When Dominque Robertson commented that Joan Baez had ruined 'Dixie' on her cover version, their friend, Bobby Charles remarked, 'Yeah, she fucked it up all the way to Number 1.' She did make a mistake, however, mishearing 'Stoneman's cavalry' as the senseless 'so much cavalry'. Still, considering the song's sympathy for the South, it is perhaps surprising that she recorded it at all. Then Donovan had recorded 'The Alamo' which seemed at odds with his pacifist leanings: it's a strange old world.

Steve Young's version has deliberate lyrical changes but they work as well as the original. I wouldn't have argued with Steve Young who told me he was the reincarnation of a civil war general so what do I know?

Rick Danko's sorrowful vocal on 'The Unfaithful Servant' is another highlight. 'Jawbone' features several time signatures and is about underworld characters from their Ronnie Hawkins days. 'Whispering Pines' is a quiet song with beautiful vocals from Richard and Levon.

Richard Manuel sings lead on 'King Harvest (has surely come)' where he plays a farmer praising his new union. Robertson's guitar solo sounds like Steve Cropper at Stax. Robbie was putting his guitar solos at the end of songs, another distinctive feature.

'Get up Jake', a fun song about a lazy worker, was dropped from the album. It was in the same vein as 'Up on Cripple Creek' and could have been a follow-up single.

Quite deliberately, Robbie Robertson didn't sing lead vocals on the album. He had written the songs and didn't want to dominate the group. There were four co-writes: three with Richard and one with Levon. However, the Band was unhappy with these credits. Levon Helm: 'When the second album came out I was credited with writing half of 'Jemima Surrender' and that was it. Rick and Garth were uncredited.'

The avant-garde jazz trumpeter Miles Davis opened for The Band at the Hollywood Bowl. Miles was a brilliant musician but very advanced and not for everyone. Rather Dylan-like, the audience started hissing. When he came off, he told The Band, 'Kind of tough crowd, but okay.'

The Band played Festival Express, a railway-sponsored tour across Canada with Janis Joplin and the Grateful Dead. It was a great bill but everyone was smashed. Also, Rick Danko and Robbie Robertson were so stoned before a concert at Madison Square Garden that the concert was almost cancelled.

When Elton John and Bernie Taupin visited The Band in New York, they told them that they had influenced *Tumbleweed Connection*. 'Nothing to worry about,' said Robbie. On the other hand, Levon wasn't happy with their song about him. He said, 'Englishmen shouldn't fuck with Americanisms', which greatly amused Bob Dylan.

Levon wanted to take his black girlfriend down South, but Robbie persuaded him against it. He said, 'Why submit her to that?' The relationship didn't last and Levon hooked up with the singer Libby Titus.

The American singer / songwriter Jesse Winchester had moved to Canada to avoid the draft. Robbie met him when he was living in a monastery in Ottawa. He recommended him for Albert Grossman's Bearsville label: Robbie produced *Jesse Winchester* (1970) with Todd Rundgren engineering and Levon on drums and mandolin. It included 'The Brand New Tennessee Waltz', which like The Band's second album, resonated with the Civil War, and a marvellous song about a relationship with an older woman, 'Yankee Lady'.

Robbie and Todd got on well and he was invited to engineer The Band's third album, *Stage Fright*. The first two albums were dominated by low notes and Rundgren wanted a brighter sound, more in line with British groups. The group wanted to recapture the good-time feel of *Music from Big Pink*.

In January 1970 The Band were on the front cover of *Time* but the Woodstock community was wary of them. It was an artistic community but mostly painters and writers.

The Band wanted to record their third album in concert at the Woodstock Playhouse, which could seat 600. The Playhouse was patronised by tourists in the summer months, but The Band planned a concert of new songs for the residents. The town council vetoed their plan: they remembered the Woodstock festival and feared an invasion from New York seeking tickets. The Band could use the Playhouse stage for recording but not with an audience. The idea of largely upbeat, positive songs with an audience faded away and the songs were more about paranoia and indeed, the disintegration of a band. Robbie Robertson was still storytelling but this time it was largely about themselves and the songs told of madness and self-destruction.

Rick Danko had had a cheque for $100,000 for co-writing 'This Wheel's on Fire' and he hadn't realised such money existed. Rick as well as Richard and Levon were taking heroin, which could make them unreasonable and unpredictable. Jonathan Taplin argued with them: he was the responsible adult who had to get them to their next gig and who tried to stop their wild parties. When Todd Rundgren was hurrying them in the studio, Levon threatened to 'kick his ass'.

For all that, the album was packaged in a colourful sleeve and opened with a happy song about addiction, 'Strawberry Wine', with Levon's great, strained vocals. Levon gets a songwriting credit with Robbie, his only one on the album. Robbie and Richard wrote 'Sleeping' and 'Just another Whistle Stop', but otherwise it is Robbie all the way.

'The W.S. Walcott Medicine Show' could have come from the second album and Robbie did say at the time, 'Levon told me the story and I wrote the song', an admission he might have regretted. It is about a genuine medicine show, presented by Walcott, and a comparison can be made with the Beatles' 'Being For The Benefit of Mr. Kite'. There are references which indicate that all is not normal, or at least shouldn't be, with the Klondike Klu Klux Steamboat Band.

When Robbie was writing with Richard, Richard fell asleep which led to the song, 'Sleeping'. This is a fine song with a strong performance from Richard but it sounds more like Jimmy Webb writing for Glen Campbell than The Band, though there's nothing wrong with that. The other song they co-wrote is 'Just another Whistle Stop', a twist on gospel trains taking us to heaven.

Robbie refers to their time off work and to the Catskill Mountains in 'Time to Kill', ostensibly about enjoying life but with a subtext that time to kill can be destructive, the vocal shared by Rick and Richard who both knew that.

'All la Glory' is a beautiful song about fatherhood with Levon's vocal and Garth's accordion. Robbie and Dominique had homes in both Woodstock and Montreal: their daughter had been born in Canada and the 'la' in the title shows her French connection, although Levon sings 'All the glory'.

The most commercial song was 'The Shape I'm in' with a powerful lead from Richard, strong back-up vocals and Garth shining on keyboards. Levon plays a homeless man back on the street after 60 days in jail but with nowhere to go. One classic section is 'Out of nine lives, I've spent seven, How in the world do you get to heaven, Oh, you don't know the shape I'm in.'

Richard takes the lead vocal for a variation of *Faust*, 'Daniel and the Sacred Harp', in which the singer realises that a musical gift isn't much in exchange for his soul. It is the Robert Johnson story too and can be found in 'The Devil Went Down to Georgia' from the Charlie Daniels Band in 1979.

Glenn Tilbrook of Squeeze says, 'I was very inspired by the way Bob Dylan and The Band sounded in the mid-60s, and if you were to listen to 'Up the Junction' without the melody line over the top, it is a very rambling track which was my interpretation as to how The Band sounded. The Band was astonishing. *Stage Fright* is a fantastic record.'

The best song on the album is the paranoid 'Stage Fright', performed by Rick Danko. Like 'Daniel and the Sacred Heart', it is about somebody with a gift who suffers for it. 'The Rumour' tells how gossip can destroy a community but it can be about the paranoia of a band.

The tracks were mixed by Todd Rundgren but they were sent to Glyn Johns in the UK for an alternative mix, perhaps because Johns had been working with the Beatles. The finished album has seven of Rundgren's mixes and three of Johns'. Despite all the trauma, *Stage Fright* is an excellent album, not up there with the first two but not far behind.

The Band included rock'n'roll oldies in concert, thereby going back to their time in the Hawks. There was a fine workout of Little Richard's 'Slippin' and Slidin'' where they are singing in unison together (all except Garth, who was creating magic on his keyboards).

They often sang 'Workin' in a Coalmine" and Levon Helm said, 'We figured we could play Lee Dorsey better than anyone other than Lee Dorsey.' They loved his 1970 album, *Yes We Can*. The horns were arranged by Allen Toussaint and they asked him to add horns to the opening track of their next album, *Cahoots*, the song being 'Life Is a Carnival'. It was an excellent song enhanced by the New Orleans horns, although they were added in New York.

The album, *Cahoots*, was recorded in the new Bearsville studio. The title came from a line in 'Smoke Signals', the first song to acknowledge Robbie's Indian heritage, "Young brothers join in cahoots" and it would have been a better album if The Band had been in cahoots. Still, there are some gems there.

The best song was given to them by Bob Dylan, 'When I Paint My Masterpiece', which was released before Dylan's own version. 'It was a brilliant song based on a great idea,' said Robbie. The Band gave it a sensitive arrangement with Levon singing and playing mandolin and Garth on accordion.

When Van Morrison visited The Band in Woodstock, Robbie was working out something on piano. Van joined in and they wrote a song that they recorded that very afternoon. The vocal interplay between Van and Richard was marvellous and the song was called '4% Pantomime', the percentage being the difference between Johnnie Walker Black and Johnnie Walker White and the pantomime being Van's movements as he sang. There was even more of a pantomime after the session as Richard was giving Van a lift. Van fell over in the snow behind the car and Richard almost ran him over.

The Band had fun with 'Endless Highway' which opened with a quote from Perry Como's 'Catch a Falling Star', but the take featuring Richard's vocal was not used on the album. They did it in concert with Rick singing lead but both arrangements are fine. A song, 'Bessie Smith', which appears to have nothing to do with the blues singer, was dropped. Another lost song was their funky arrangement of Marvin Gaye's 'Baby, Don't You Do It', retitled 'Don't Do It' and sometimes performed in concert.

Robbie's interest in foreign films came through as 'The Moon Struck One' came out of watching Truffaut's *Jules et Jim*. It is a mysterious song sung by Richard with Garth excelling on electric organ. It's good but you wonder why The Band are telling you this story. The Canadian jazz pianist Gil Evans was asked to write a horn arrangement but he didn't get round to it. In 1988 he recorded his own version with the Gil Evans Orchestra. There is a half-hour version on the internet by Robbie, Daniel Lanois and the Gil Evans Orchestra recorded for the Canadian Music Hall of Fame.

Richard was in fine voice on 'The Last of the Blacksmiths', which is helped by Garth's horns. Rick took the lead on 'Thinkin' Out Loud' and is double-tracked on 'Volcano'. Rick and Richard were together on another story song, 'Shoot Out in Chinatown'. Levon, joined by Libby Titus, sounded fine on 'The River Hymn' which Garth gives a 19th century feel on his organ.

After recording *Cahoots*, the Band did some European dates. They were given a real life private sex show by their Danish promoter. Jack Nicholson came to both Royal Albert Hall concerts and remarked how tight their harmonies were. It was not so tight backstage though as Levon Helm threw Jonathan Taplin against the wall and threatened him. It was the drugs, as Levon often thought everyone was out to get him. Taplin had had enough, saying working with The Band was like rounding up a bunch of cats.

The *Cahoots* album was released in October 1971 and they toured to promote it. Despite the fact that they were not always as one in the studio, The Band were usually okay on the road. They recorded four nights at the Academy of Music in New York City, now known as the *Rock of Ages* concerts. The horns would be arranged by Allen Toussaint. He lost the briefcase containing his horn parts at the airport and had to restart from scratch. He was staying in a cabin in the woods and he had never witnessed four feet of snow before. He got an ear infection but he was okay for the rehearsal on Boxing Day. Fortunately, he had hired top players and all was well. Howard Alk and Murray Lerner were going to film a complete concert but union issues had not been resolved and they could only shoot a few songs. Mostly The Band sang material they had previously recorded and they were splendid performances. Garth was on brilliant form with improvisations that amazed everybody. Garth Hudson concluded The Band's set with a wild 'Chest Fever'. They encored with Chuck Willis' 'Hang up My Rock and Roll Shoes' and the Four Tops' 'Loving You Is Sweeter than ever'.

On New Year's Eve Bob Dylan joined The Band for 'Down in the Flood', 'When I Paint My Masterpiece', and a bluesy 'Don't Ya Tell Henry', which had such strong group singing that it couldn't be anyone else but them. Dylan said, 'We haven't played this one in six years' to which Robbie responded 'More like 16', before launching into 'Like a Rolling Stone'.

The double-album was called *Rock of Ages* after the hymn and there was a tiny, ancient gold statue on the cover. Ralph J. Gleason in *Rolling Stone* said it was one of the best live albums, up there with *Charles Mingus at Monterey*, *Ray Charles in Person*, *Duke Ellington's Seattle Concert* and *Miles Davis in Person, Friday and Saturday nights at the Blackhawk, San Francisco*.

The coming of 1972 was no delight for The Band. The group was falling apart or rather Richard Manuel was. Alcohol and drugs had affected his liver and he wasn't taking care of himself. He didn't even clear dog excrement from his house. Rick and Levon could be bad enough but Richard was told that the group was planning to replace him. The solution: Richard decided to get off heroin by switching to cocaine.

Bobby Charles was a Louisiana songwriter and one of the pioneers of swamp pop. His songs included 'See You Later Alligator' (Bill Haley and his Comets: note the swamp touch in the title!), 'Walkin' to New Orleans' (Fats Domino), and 'But I Do' (Clarence 'Frogman' Henry). He spent time in Woodstock with the Band and Rick Danko produced *Bobby Charles* for Bearsville. Levon, Richard and Garth were among the musicians. Rick and Bobby wrote a brilliant song about the problems of gossip, 'Small Town Talk'. Levon and Garth worked on an album by Peter Yarrow and Levon spent four months at the Berklee College of Music in Boston.

The Band were standing still in 1972 and Robbie was trying to break into film projects. He worked for the Canadian National Film Board and he discussed with Marlon Brando the possibility of a film based on the book, *Bury My Heart at Wounded Knee*. He wanted to write some expanded themes and was toying with a potential album, *Works*.

In 1973 the Band played to 600,000 at Watkins Glen Raceway. The concert was opened by the Grateful Dead who announced they would play for three hours or until the drugs wore off. The Dead were followed by the Allman Brothers Band and then The Band. The festival had tragic consequences as a skydiver was killed. The Band album, *Live At Watkins Glen,* was released with studio cuts of Chuck Berry's 'Going back to Memphis' and Robbie Robertson's 'Endless Highway', this time with Rick's lead vocal, and both had overdubbed applause. The Band were unhappy about this release.

Bob Dylan: Outlaw Blues

The Band had a contract to make a new album for Capitol. Robbie suggested an album of covers. This ticked the boxes: The Band would acknowledge their influences and have fun at the same time. They would not be under pressure and they would be fulfilling the contract – what's not to like. The very title, *Moondog Matinee*, was a nod to the rock'n'roll DJ, Alan Freed, although only Garth Hudson had listened to him at the time.

Reviving oldies had suddenly become popular. Sha Na had stormed Woodstock and the soundtrack of *American Graffiti* would make the Top 10. The Band were too hip to make an easy listening album of 1950s covers. Although they wanted to do a Buddy Holly song, they had been done too many times already. They avoided more comical songs like 'Bony Moronie' or at least they chose a lesser-known one, Clarence 'Frogman' Henry's 'Ain't Got No Home'. They gave it a New Orleans treatment with Levon Helm singing through a hose to get the froglike sounds and being backed by Garth's saxophones.

Garth proved to be a *tour de force* on piano and sax when Levon sang another New Orleans song, Fats Domino's 'I'm Ready'. When Levon ran through Chuck Berry's 'Promised Land', Billy Mundi from the Mothers of Invention played drums and Ben Keith steel guitar.

Rick Danko was in his element with 'Holy Cow', which had a horn arrangement from Allen Toussaint, who had done the same for Lee Dorsey's original. Rick sang falsetto for Sam Cooke's song about civil rights, 'A Change Is Gonna Come' with very sensitive saxophone playing from Garth Hudson.

Moondog Matinee was the ideal music for The Band's jukebox and all but one of the tracks originated with black artists. The outsider was the film theme, 'The Third Man', dating from 1949 and written and performed on zither by the Austrian, Anton Karas. The revival worked in the context of the album and was also issued as a single. It inspired Robbie Robertson to write a theme for their concert, *The Last Waltz*.

It is rare for a cover version to improve on the original but Richard Manuel's heart-breaking vocal on Bobby Bland's 'Share Your Love with Me' is an example of song and singer being perfectly matched. It is the only song from *Moondog Matinee* that the Band regularly performed, both before and after the album. Richard is fine on LaVern Baker's 'Saved' and on a song from his days in the Rockin' Revols, the Platters' 'The Great Pretender'.

'Mystery Train' was originally written and recorded by Junior Parker for Sun Records and then revived for the same label by Elvis Presley. Robbie added a new verse and the song is propelled by both Richard and Levon playing drums.

They recorded *Moondog Matinee* at Bearsville and at Capitol in Hollywood. The advertising said, 'The Band Remembers the Hawks', implying it was their own tribute album. This was spot on and yet it wasn't. This was no mere run-through of oldies as they had worked out how to bring something new to them. They wanted to complement rather than compliment the original records.

Robbie met John Lennon at Capitol when *Moondog Matinee* was to be released. Lennon said he was doing an album of rock'n'roll tunes, *Rock'n'Roll*. *Moondog Matinee* sold respectably but The Band didn't promote it and didn't play any gigs. John Lennon's album was a bigger seller but didn't deserve to be.

Capitol executives gave The Band cocaine to thank them. The album came with a poster by Edward Kasper, putting The Band into a 50s setting. They are shown at the Cabbagetown café in Toronto. They used to travel in a pink and black van and note the Hawk logo. An EMI executive Rupert Perry brought the *Moondog Matinee* painting to England and kept it.

The album only had ten tracks and could have had more as further tracks had been completed. There is the gospel song, 'Didn't It Rain', sung by Levon and based around Mahalia Jackson's recording from 1953. Rick Danko sang Johnnie and Jack's country song, 'Crying Heart Blues' and although they recorded several takes, The Band didn't use Rick singing 'Bring It on Home to Me': maybe one Sam Cooke song was thought enough. Levon sang a song from Sam Cooke's *Shake* LP, 'It's Got the Whole World Shakin''. Chuck Willis' 'What Am I Living for' was recorded as well as Faye Adams' 'Shake a Hand'.

Next came the *Before the Flood* tour with Bob Dylan. They each had their own sets, but it was the magic of them together which worked best. Possibly because it was an arena tour, they increased their energy and Dylan is singing urgently and more highly pitched than usual. It was fine but he wasn't using The Band to the best of their capabilities.

The Band didn't record again until 1975 when they worked in the Shangri-la Studio, which was a converted ranch house – well, actually it had been a brothel for cowboys. The layout meant that they had accommodation so artists could stay there whilst they made their albums.

Rick Danko visited Neil Young when he was working there. Neil Young and Bob Dylan were swapping songs and they asked Bobby Charles to sing one. He sang 'The Jealous Kind' and they both said, 'We can't top that.'

The studio either lived up to its name, or was the opposite as there was a plentiful supply of drugs. Ronnie Hawkins who was there around the time of *The Last Waltz* said, 'You went in young and you came out old.' The studio is now owned by Rick Rubin.

In February 1975 Garth joined Levon in Woodstock and they worked with Muddy Waters on *The Muddy Waters Woodstock Album*, the best of his later works. Paul Butterfield was in the line-up and they worked on Butterfield's album for Bearsville, *Put It in Your Ear*.

Robbie Robertson realised that this was the time to record new songs as The Band or they would drift apart. The album, *Northern Lights – Southern Cross*, was criticised for sounding too much like The Band, but heck, we were thinking that we would never hear them again. They confessed to their problems in 'Forbidden Fruit' – "There's a stranger inside of me."

There were only eight songs but long ones, all written by Robbie. They are all good but there was no obvious single, although 'Ring My Bell' was an attempt to go back to old times with Levon, Rick and Richard swapping lines in a goodtime song about being busted by the Mounties. Rick sang a superlative soul ballad, 'It Makes No Difference', but the title was too similar to 'It Makes No Difference Now', recorded by Ray Charles.

Robbie Robertson had discovered that the country comedian Minnie Pearl had been born Ophelia. He wrote a song around that name, evoking the travelling shows in the South. It perfectly suited Levon's voice. Richard sang 'Rag and Bone' about growing up in Toronto during the Depression and it is filled with the characters of the day. 'Jupiter Hollow' had come from reading a book on Greek mythology. With several layers of sound, it sounded fine.

The best track is 'Acadian Driftwood', which came out of Robbie seeing a show *Acadie, Acadie* in Montreal. It tells of the British forcing the French farmers from their homes in Nova Scotia around 1760: "Nothing to declare, all we had was gone". A number of farmers had moved to Louisiana and the word 'Cajun' comes from the southern country slurring of the word, Acadian.

The 1976 compilation *The Best of The Band* had an unreleased track, the ballad 'Twilight', recorded for *Northern Lights* but not used. The reviewer in *Crawdaddy* said that they were 'unerring in their dark vision' and had songs 'any lonely soul could tailor to his own predicament'.

The Band recorded a seasonal single, 'Christmas Must be Tonight', which Robbie wrote for the birth of his son Sebastian, but Capitol did not think it was worth promoting. It was used on the next album, *Islands*. It was a good song but its melody owed something to Joe South's *'Games People Play'*.

All The Band apart from Richard backed Ringo Starr on 'Sunshine Life for Me' for his big-selling album, *Ringo*. It's enjoyable but disjointed.

Robbie played guitar on Joni Mitchell's 'Raised on Robbery'. He suggested the laid-back arrangement for 'Mockingbird' by Carly Simon and James Taylor, which was a US Top 10 single. He produced a hit album for Neil Diamond with songs about the Brill Building, *Beautiful Noise*. When Robbie's immune system had shut down, a hypnotist got him through concerts at Fillmore East and the Toronto Pop Festival.

Throughout all the chaos, Garth never bothered anyone, even when his house burned down.

The Band came to the UK for a huge Wembley concert with Crosby, Stills and Nash and Joni Mitchell.

On *Saturday Night Live,* The Band performed 'Georgia on My Mind' with Richard singing lead. They had chosen the song because Jimmy Carter, a Georgia boy, was standing for President.

By 1976 The Band was no longer a viable entity but the promoter Bill Graham had the idea of a Thanksgiving meal and a concert at Winterland. Winterland was a former skating rink in the poorer part of San Francisco and it was the first place they had played as The Band. This time five thousand could attend at $25 a ticket with food.

Garth Hudson: 'I wasn't involved in the planning, logistics and the priorities. I just had to make sure that my own equipment worked. The rehearsals in the basement of the hotel were great and I wish we had recorded the one with Muddy Waters. Everybody was relaxed and playing well. A friend of mine came from London, Ontario and I told him not to record it. We were very particular about non-legit recordings and I wish I had told him "Go ahead, yeah. Let it run".'

There were numerous good moments, none better than Ronnie Hawkins fanning Robbie's guitar as he took the solo in Bo Diddley's 'Who Do You Love'. Bobby Charles had new words for 'Down South in New Orleans'. Dr. John, looking great in French beret, bow-tie and shades, sang 'Such a Night'. Ever eccentric, Van Morrison dressed like an acrobat so he could do high kicks. As well as his famed 'Caravan', he and Richard did a tremendous version of an Irish lullaby, 'Tara Lura Lura', although no baby could sleep through it. Lawrence Ferlinghetti and Michael McClure read poetry in the interval, which was odd thing to do when people are moving around. Ferlinghetti offered his take on 'The Lord's Prayer.'

Although only connected with Robbie, Neil Diamond was a guest artist. He told the press, 'I'm only going to sing one song but I'm gonna sing it good.' It was 'Dry Your Eyes', his reaction to the assassination of Martin Luther King. As he came off stage, he said to Bob Dylan, 'You'll have to be pretty good to follow me' and Dylan responded, 'What do I have to do, go onstage and fall asleep?' On another occasion Dylan ran into Diamond at an airport. He gave him a hug and said, 'Keep on doing what you're doing. You're an inspiration to us all.'

Dylan sang 'Baby, Let Me Follow You Down' with passion and also strong versions of 'Hazel', 'Forever Young' and 'I Don't Believe You'. Dylan had not been happy with the show being filmed, but Bill Graham insisted that his performance be shot: the worst that could happen would be Dylan destroying it.

The whole ensemble sang 'I Shall Be Released' with verses sung by Bob Dylan and Richard Manuel. Ringo Starr and Ron Wood were in the audience and Bill Graham invited them up for that last song. The final words from The Band were 'Goodnight, goodbye'. The Sex Pistols played their final show at Winterland, albeit without all the paraphernalia of the Band.

Although The Band had been happy about the event, Levon had not wanted it to be filmed. Even though it would be directed by Martin Scorsese, he felt it added problems. He was overruled and later said, 'I was in shock over how bad the movie was', which is just being awkward.

Scorsese had mapped out a shooting script to go with the lyrics and switches in lead instruments, so he always got the right shot. Neil Young came on stage with cocaine on his nose, which had to be removed frame by frame. There had been some ragged performances and some parts were redone. In 1978, *The Last Waltz* was released as a film and a three-LP set. Emmylou Harris and the Staple Singers, who couldn't make the concert, were recorded on a sound stage. There were some great one-liners from The Band. The reviews were very good but some thought that The Band had become too slick.

Levon felt that Robbie was pushing for the movie as he saw his future in Hollywood. The irony is that Levon himself became a movie star with *Coal Miner's Daughter* (1980). The film did well, feeding into the popularity of the music films, *American Graffiti* and *Grease*. It was overlooked at the Oscars and yet it was the year of *The Buddy Holly Story* and *American Hot Wax*.

Amazingly, the Band had thought the best way to rehearse for *The Last Waltz* was to work on new songs. In 1977, the album *Islands* was released, the final album by all five members. They were all new songs with the exception of the Stax classic by Homer Banks, 'Ain't That a Lot of Love'. The title track was an instrumental written by Rick, Robbie and Garth and maybe the title was saying 'No man is an island' but the Band had become five islands.

Robbie even sang one of the songs, 'Knockin' Lost John', which is a fun song set in the Depression, if there can be such a thing. It sounded like something from *The Basement Tapes*. The songs lacked imagination and Rick Danko's 'Street Walker' was banal. Richard sound fine on 'Right as Rain', a song about Paris. The final song on the record was about living in a dream and it ended with Levon whistling, a fitting end to The Band's career.

When Robbie Robertson went to Ireland to record with U2, he found them recording in a living room. Bono asked, 'Where do you think we got the idea from?'

In 1969, a songwriter's royalty had been two cents per track, so a songwriter might get 24 cents off an album, while the performers could share $2.50. In the 1980s the introduction of the CD brought The Band a lot of money through reissues. Then the American Federation of Musicians (AFM) was caught napping by the Napster website because by not monitoring and controlling a changing situation, the provision of music was completely changing.

As a result, the Band's performance income dropped from $100,000 a year each to almost nothing. Eventually, the courts determined that there was a breach of copyright and Napster was closed in 2001. However, the situation had changed for good as the entire online community wanted free music.

The big companies could have stopped what was happening in the way, for example, that the Chinese government has blocked many things. Similarly there have been programmes to stop terrorist-related content, but this didn't happen with copyrighted music. I'm not saying that they should have done this but they certainly didn't act in their clients' interests until it was too late.

Some musicians were more relaxed about it than others. Bob Dylan said to Jonathan Lethem in *Rolling Stone* in 2006, 'I remember when the Napster guys came up. It was like everybody's getting music for free. I was like, well why not? It ain't worth nothing anyway.'

The AFM didn't appreciate what was happening until it happened. However, the songwriters had a better deal through their organisations, ASCAP and BMI. It ended up that the fees for playing music on the radio only went to the songwriters. Hence, the members of The Band were only getting income from songs they wrote, obviously creating friction.

Any money that was being made out of their catalogue came from use in films and advertising. Robbie Robertson had the bulk of those songwriting royalties and he wouldn't split them with the rest of the Band, but why should he? He had written the songs, although he had taken Levon Helm's experiences. Levon was furious, especially when he had throat cancer and medical bills to pay, but Robbie had written the songs, no doubt about that, while Levon was partying.

'I liked Levon a lot,' says the guitarist Mark Clarke from Colosseum. 'He was very similar to Bob and the same size too. Both were five foot six and slightly built, but Levon was even more sparrow-like. When I knew him, he was drinking Jack Daniel's and would occasionally eat. He knew Keith Richards and they would never say, "Let's go out for dinner." It was just food for fuel. Levon was a great singer and he was very complimentary to me and very helpful and very nice. The last time I saw him was in his motorhome after we'd done a gig and he said, "Mr. Mark, we're going to see Uncle Jack" and we polished off a bottle of Jack Daniel's between us. It was great to sing with him. I have always been a good listener so if I am backing somebody, I will hear how they are ending their notes and I came up with stuff to match him and he would look over and wink.'

In October 2012 the internet investor Alexis Ohanian suggested a benefit for The Band. Their former manager Jonathan Taplin wrote, 'It wasn't the music industry that created Levon's plight. It was the bloodsuckers who made millions off the hard work of musicians and filmmakers. Levon just wanted to earn an honest living. Just let us get paid for our work and stop deciding that you can unilaterally make it free.'

Levon's anger at Robbie for not sharing his songwriting income remained unabated, but he, Rick and Garth did play concerts and record as The Band. In 1999 Levon contracted throat cancer and had to stop performing for some time. He did manage to perform again, and even sing, and he put on *Midnight Rambles* with guest musicians in his barn at Woodstock to help pay for treatment. Levon died in 2012 and a benefit was held for his wife Sandy so she could retain their house.

On 4 March 1986, Richard Manuel hanged himself in a motel room in Winter Park, Florida. Among the tribute songs to him are 'Too Soon Gone' (The Band). 'Fallen Angel' (Robbie Robertson) and 'August' (Eric Clapton).

II. So Much Older Then: October 1975–1978

Although Bob Dylan had been happy with the reception and the company, he hadn't enjoyed the stadium tour with The Band. The venues were too big and he hardly knew where he was. His next tour would be down to earth and 'kinda like a circus'. The inspiration could have been Delaney and Bonnie and Friends.

During the 1970s, Bob Dylan had seen many performers and he had the concept of a touring revue. He'd headline and the supporting musicians would be friends and like-minded musicians, mostly from around the Village. In October 1975, he moved into the Gramercy Park Hotel in New York which he used both as an office and a home while he was planning what he first called the Montezuma Revue but the Aztec name was replaced by Rolling Thunder. For Native Americans, Rolling Thunder was originally an Indian term meaning 'Speaking the truth', but the American military had also used it in Vietnam.

Once he had the concept, he didn't hang around. Ideally, somebody has an idea for a tour and it is a year in planning, not least because busy artists have commitments and many potential venues are already booked. That was not Dylan's way and he was particularly lucky that Joan Baez was available. She, more than anyone, knew how unpredictable and unreasonable he could be. On the other hand, Bob was ten years older now and she'd be in the company of other artists and musicians that she knew and liked.

On 23 October 1975 the concept for Rolling Thunder was previewed in a late night show at Gerde's Folk City, ostensibly to celebrate the owner Mike Porco's sixty-first birthday. There was a cake although it fell on the floor when it was presented. Bob and Joan started off the jam session with 'One Too Many Mornings'. Bob had invited Patti Smith to Gerde's, but she wasn't sure whether this approach would suit her. She anticipated that she would end up singing country-styled harmonies and she didn't want that.

Journalist Larry Sloman, who was Kinky Friedman's sidekick, recalls, 'Roger McGuinn was an old friend of mine and he was in town and I said to Roger, "Hey, I hear Bob is hanging out in the Village. Let's go check it out." We went to The Other End and we saw a big table at the back and there was Bob. He yelled out, "Roger, Roger, we're going to do this tour like a carnival and we are going to hit little towns. You gotta come, man!" Then he saw me and he said, "Hey, Larry, you should cover this tour!" It was a dream come true to see these great performers night after night, especially Dylan who was at the height of his powers.'

Dylan invited Emmylou Harris to join Rolling Thunder but she was making *Luxury Liner*. Not to worry. When Bob saw David Blue at The Other End, he heard Ronee Blakley harmonising from the back of the room. Ronee was in the controversial Robert Altman film, *Nashville* (1975). She would be nominated for Best Supporting Actress and the soundtrack album was doing well. When The Other End closed, Dylan at the piano sang with Ronee. He invited her along but she was committed to a promotional tour for her new album *Welcome*. When she said she couldn't join Rolling Thunder, Bobby Neuwirth exploded, 'What do you mean, No? The Beatles want to be on this tour.'

Ronee flew to Alabama and told the musicians and her producer, Jerry Wexler about the revue. They thought that she should join Dylan and cancel the promotional dates. Joe Smith at Warner wasn't happy but could appreciate how this could raise her profile. She returned to New York and told Bob and they recorded his rewritten 'Hurricane' that very night as Bob was working on his next album, *Desire*. More for fun than commercial release, Dylan sang Kinky Friedman's 'Ride 'em Jewboy' and the Browns' 'Jimmy Brown the Newsboy'.

Ronee started with a decent spot on the tour performing 'Dues' (from *Nashville*) and 'Need a New Sun Rising' (from *Welcome*). Her spot was cut to make way for Joni Mitchell, but she always sang 'Just like a Woman' with Bob. Patti Smith had anticipated this.

Ian Hunter from Mott the Hoople: 'I was living in New York and Mick Ronson went to The Other End one night. We were sitting in the café area and in walks Dylan with Bobby Neuwirth and he started playing songs from the *Desire* album. There was me and Mick a table away and that was the start of *Rolling Thunder*. The way he was singing was hilarious: he was really exaggerating that 'five to ten' line and it was an amazing evening. A couple of days later Mick rang to say that he was playing with Bob Dylan. I said, "What's it like?" He said, "C, F and G". Nobody got invited, people just turned up and did things. Mick asked me to join but I'd have been embarrassed in case they said, "What are you doing here?"'

Mick Ronson: 'Ian Hunter was the big Dylan fan in the group. I thought he'd be okay about it, but I think he was jealous.'

Phil Ochs was too much of a drinker and a loose cannon to work in a multi-artist package. It was just as well that he wasn't included as he usually brought out the worst in Dylan. Neither Arlo Guthrie nor Pete Seeger could make the tour as they were touring together with a very successful joint concert, but Arlo was to make a guest appearance.

By October 27, Dylan was holding rehearsals at the Seacrest Hotel in North Falmouth, Massachusetts. There was Joan Baez, Ronee Blakley, Ramblin' Jack Elliott, Bobby Neuwirth, Mick Ronson, Scarlet Rivera and Allen Ginsberg. The run-through started with Ginsberg reading from his epic poem about his mother, *Kaddish*. The following day they were joined by Joni Mitchell and Roger McGuinn.

Howard Alk had made a film *Snapshots* about living in the US in 1972. Dylan had been thinking of making a *faux* documentary about himself and America in 1975. Being Dylan, he thought he might as well make it at the same time as Rolling Thunder.

Dylan was friendly with Sam Shepard who had been in the Holy Modal Rounders as well as being an experimental and talented playwright. Shepard was asked to go on the road with them and write the dialogue for *Renaldo and Clara*, which would be filmed as they went along. The main characters, who weren't actors anyway, would never remember their lines so most of it would be improvised.

Kinky Friedman's friend Larry Sloman (Ratso) was the chronicler for the tour. He would report on it for *Rolling Stone* and possibly complete a book. 'Bob invited me to join the tour. I had written a preview piece about *Blood on the Tracks*, his great album, and I told him that my roommate at the time was Phil Ochs. I inherited my apartment in SoHo from Phil Ochs and Jerry Rubin. It was the end of the anti-war movement and Jerry Rubin was moving out to California and going to get into meditation and health food. Phil stayed in New York, he had nowhere to go and was depressed and would crash on the couch. When Bob found out that Phil was living with me, he was interested. The two of them may have had friendly competition but they really loved each other. That took away some of the suspicion that Bob might have had about me, you know, that I was just a media guy.'

Within a week, Dylan had a touring party, tour dates, a film cast and crew, a scriptwriter and a chronicler. Even if the tour had been led by the most supremely organised performer, it would have been chaotic. And this tour was led by Bob Dylan.

Bob Dylan said, 'That tour was always intended to be a movie. It always existed on more than one level. That's why we had the costumes, the make-up, something to make it a little more different, to put it in a time setting, of which the movie would revolve around.'

The tickets for the venues were on sale only a few days before the shows but this was no handicap as the very name 'Dylan' would ensure sell-outs and they were not playing large venues.

The first gig was at the home of the Pilgrim Fathers, namely Plymouth, Massachusetts. With the town's population of 60,000, it was hardly a regular touring venue. Two dates were booked at the War Memorial Auditorium on 30 and 31 October 1975. The shows were enthusiastically received and reviewed. Dylan wore a Richard Nixon mask as he sang 'When I Paint My Masterpiece;' with Bobby Neuwirth.

Ramblin' Jack Elliott: 'We shot some scenes on board the Mayflower in Plymouth, Massachusetts. I had lost interest in the film because I was back on board the Mayflower as I had worked on the rigging in Devonshire in 1957. She had sailed from Plymouth, England to Plymouth, USA and there she was. They were filming some dumb scene but I couldn't get interested. I went off the poop deck where they were filming and went up the foc'sle head to be alone. I was climbing the rigging and I was looking over the yard and inspecting the masts. They filmed me doing that, but I didn't know that at the time.'

Scarlet Rivera was dating Gene Simmons from KISS. Dylan asked her why they always wore make-up and it was because they could be seen from the back. This led to him painting his own face for the Rolling Thunder shows, and Joan Baez sometimes did the same. Dylan had a hat with feathers. In Burlington, a fan tried to grab it and was stopped by a security guard, whose arm was then bitten.

But there may be more to the white make-up than that. Larry Sloman: 'I asked him that and of course you can't get a straight answer out of him. He said he put it on so that people could see his face at the back. (laughs) I think it was an homage to the film, *Children of Paradise*, which was a film that he loved. The lead character in that had that clown makeup. *Ronaldo and Clara* is very much influenced by that movie.' (Dylan could have called his tour LP, *The White Album*.)

On 1 November 1975 the revue was in North Dartmouth, Massachusetts and the following day in Lowell in the same state, Bob and Allen Ginsberg visited Jack Kerouac's grave.

Author Mike Evans: 'Allen and Jack were great chums from Greenwich Village, and the poetry scene and the folk scene were connected there. They played the same coffee houses and bars, it was part of the same bohemian scene. Dylan used to sing at the White Horse and Kerouac would get thrown out of the White Horse for being drunk. It was like the Liverpool scene in the 60s, all one nice bohemia.'

On 4 November 1975, it was a long day for Dylan in Providence, Rhode Island. He participated in a sunrise ceremony with a Cherokee medicine man and played two shows in a large venue. They took $158,000 in ticket money which helped to subsidise the smaller venues.

How did Larry Sloman come to be called Ratso? 'I was called Ratso by Joan Baez during the Rolling Thunder Tour. I had my own car and I was following the tour. Most of the performers were travelling in two buses and Bob had a camper and was the lead driver. I was following them in my rental car. You're driving on the road and you are staying in cheap motels and you don't shave and you may skip a shower and I drove up to where they were one day. It was in Vermont and everybody was playing volleyball, it was a beautiful Indian summer day, and Joan Baez came over to my car and grabbed my greasy hair and shouted, "Hey, it's Ratso!" I said, "Do I remind you of Dustin Hoffman?" He played Ratso Rizzo in that great movie, *Midnight Cowboy*. Anyway, it stuck. My book *On The Road With Bob Dylan* was written in the first person until she called me Ratso. Then it goes into third person and Ratso becomes a character in the book of this crazy tour. I embrace my Ratso-ness and it has given me a good alter ego. I can do outlandish things as Ratso that Larry Sloman would never do.'

In Waterbury, Connecticut, Dylan discarded his white make-up, though it soon returned. Then in New Haven, Bob and Joan sang the mining song, 'Dark as a Dungeon'. At Niagara Falls on November 15, Dylan performed 'Like a Rolling Stone' for the only time on the tour.

The next day Dylan was filming with the Tuscarora Indians and several more dates followed. When they were filming in Quebec, Joan and Sara discussed an imaginary affair; Allen Ginsberg took a boy to a brothel; and Bobby Neuwirth and Harry Dean Stanton pulled a rope in different directions. How these scenes would connect in a film was anybody's guess.

It was a cluttered stage but it worked and Dylan was singing well, working up unlikely arrangements for 'It Ain't Me Babe' and 'The Lonesome Death of Hattie Carroll'. Mick Ronson and Howard Wyeth kept the band up to scratch but Dylan hardly spoke to Ronson. There is a scene in *Renaldo and Clara*:

Ronee Blakley to Mick Ronson, 'I like Bob a lot, don't you?'

Mick Ronson: 'I don't know, he's never spoken to me.'

That is typical of Dylan as he liked to keep musicians in the dark. However, there is no need to make much of this as there were 60 people on the road with performers, partners, road crew and management. A fortune was being spent before even a note was played.

Larry Sloman: 'I had a fight with *Rolling Stone* who were screaming at me, "Why is he playing bigger venues now and how come the ticket prices are up?" and I said, "What is this? *Forbes* Magazine? Nobody cares about that. It is an incredible cultural event with all these people. Joni Mitchell comes one night and she stays on the tour. This is history." They didn't agree. I left *Rolling Stone* but I wanted to stay on and write my book and Bob was fine with that.'

The Rolling Thunder reviews were favourable with Bobby Neuwirth being the only performer who was not rising above average. I loved the title of one of his songs though, 'Where Did Vincent Van Gogh?'

Pete Frame: 'I was in America in 1975 and I did get to see the Rolling Thunder Revue and that was phenomenal. It was one of the greatest shows I have seen. They had the safety curtain at the front of the stage with *Rolling Thunder* written on it. Suddenly the lights went dark and you could hear two acoustic guitars strumming and Bob Dylan and Joan Baez were singing 'Blowin' in the Wind'. During the second verse, the screen rolled away and revealed them and it was an absolutely brilliant moment.'

Bob Spitz: 'Bob did 'Mama, You Been on My Mind' on the Rolling Thunder revue and he looked at Joan every night and winked. She could never follow where he was going but Bob knew she was a good sport. When he found someone who would tolerate his monkey business, he played with them for as long as he could. Bob loved to torment her. He knew that she was emotionally fragile and that has been a characteristic of the people who have come into Bob Dylan's life. When he finds someone who idolises him, someone he can kick a little, he has his day with them.'

A chase sequence was filmed when they played the Maple Leaf Gardens in Toronto with a guest appearance from Gordon Lightfoot. Dylan's mother, Beatty, joined the entourage for the encore. A clueless news reporter interviewed Larry Sloman and then Ronnie Hawkins under the impression they were Bob Dylan. In *Renaldo and Clara*, Joan and Sara are obviously discussing Bob when they agree that Renaldo never gave straight answers.

Bobby Neuwirth put his fake leather jacket in Gordon Lightfoot's fireplace and smoked out his house. Nevertheless, Lightfoot was pleased to have a fantastic endorsement from Dylan: 'Every time I hear a Gordon Lightfoot song I wish it would last forever.'

They went to Montreal on December 4. Leonard Cohen was in the audience but he didn't want to perform, saying, 'It's too obvious.' What's wrong with being obvious? Possibly it was too disorganised for him. Dylan dedicated 'Isis' as 'a song about marriage to Leonard if he is still here.' Great performance too.

Larry Sloman: 'Both Leonard and Bob are two guys with some of the greatest senses of humour that I have ever experienced. Bob is very droll and very dry but he is very funny too. People look at the surface of some of Leonard's songs but if you dig deep, you will find a tremendous sense of humour running through them.'

At one stage, Ronnie Hawkins plays Bob Dylan in the film: 'I got a knock at 4am as Bob was in the mood to film. He said, "You're talking her into running off with you." That's all the clue I had. She was an Israeli actress with the Rolling Thunder revue. The film is really the story of him and his wife and Joan Baez – he would live with one for a while and then with the other. Who else has made a film about his wife and his mistress?'

Ronee Blakley is cast as Mrs. Dylan in *Renaldo and Clara*. Baez is dressed as Dylan, and Sara and Ronee put their hands on Joan's shoulder. Ronee says that she never had a sexual relationship with Bob Dylan, but she saw all of four of them as looking similar. Some exchanges could be telling. Talking about their relationship, Clara (Baez) says of Renaldo (Dylan), 'It wouldn't have worked as I was too political and he lied too much.'

When Joni Mitchell hosted a party, Bob Dylan and Paul McCartney started a jam session but Rod Stewart didn't join in as he was seducing Britt Ekland: you've got to get your priorities right.

When someone in the audience shouted 'Sing a protest song', Dylan obliged with 'Oh Sister'. Ratso told him that 'Oh Sister' started like something else, probably 'Girl from the North Country', and that is why the audience immediately applauded it. Dylan said, 'Oh, I influence myself.'

Dylan amended many songs including a thoroughly revised 'Tonight I'll Be Staying Here with You'. He had a new verse for an elegiac 'Knockin' on Heaven's Door', and sang revised lyrics for 'Tangled Up in Blue' and 'It Ain't Me Babe', and put 'Don't Think Twice, It's All Right' into reggae. There are numerous albums where Dylan is reworking his songs but *The Bootleg Series Volume 5* on the Rolling Thunder Revue is the most entertaining as so many arrangements are surprising.

On December 7, the revue performed a free show at the Clinton Correctional Institution for Women in New Jersey. There was a press conference with Hurricane Carter who thanked Dylan for taking up his cause.

The following night was the benefit, *The Night of the Hurricane* at Madison Square Garden. It was to help with legal bills and was introduced by Muhammad Ali. Roberta

Flack was a guest artist. The second half opened with two Dylans as Baez came on dressed just like him. Joan was enjoying herself and Robbie Robertson joined them for 'It Takes a Lot to Laugh, It Takes a Train to Cry'. Dylan dedicated a song to Albert Grossman 'who is not running for President' as Muhammad Ali was turning the event into a political rally. The first leg of the Rolling Thunder tour ended at Madison Square Garden but it would continue in 1976. Dylan also had thoughts about appearing in Russia though that wasn't to happen for many years.

Dylan had a house in Zuma Beach, Malibu and kept moving the chimney in the kitchen until the builders gave up. Sara took the children to stay with Ron and Chrissie Wood for a while.

On 6 January 1976 Nicky Horne of Capital Radio in London announced that he was having a UK exclusive on *Desire* the next day. John Peel at BBC Radio 1 rang CBS to ask about an advance copy. They had a white label and they would send it round. Peel didn't dare ask for recording details to complete the logging sheets in case CBS realised their error. The album was 55 minutes long. Peel started his Radio 1 programme by saying how fed up he was that another station had a *Desire* exclusive the following night. 'Now that is really annoying,' said Peel and put on Side 1. The whole of it. He played a reggae record 'Dreadlocks Coming for Dinner' by Michael Rose while he turned it over, which was the only other record in the programme. After playing the whole of Side 2, John Peel passed the album to Johnnie Walker, who was following him in order to inflict more damage.

Desire was released in the US on January 16. It had a sleeve note from Allen Ginsberg headed *Songs of Redemption*. More, *Songs of Desire and Passion* to me. Bob Dylan gave Ginsberg a gift of a piano. In its third week of release, *Desire* topped the US album chart.

For the second leg of Rolling Thunder, Dylan considered tightrope walking and he had a slack wire outside his motorhome, though he never took it on stage. He did, however, have an affair with the woman hired to teach him the tightrope.

In Tucson, he introduced his backing singers as 'My ex-wife, my next wife, my girlfriend and my fiancé.' A very funny line, not far from the truth. Dylan recorded 'Buckets of Rain' with Bette Midler. It is said that he gave her a lift and she tried to seduce him. Odd that he didn't respond.

The second benefit for Hurricane Carter at the Houston Astrodome had a disappointing attendance, a quarter full, possibly because the venue had been switched from the Louisiana Superbowl. Stevie Wonder was the opening act and this was the only Rolling Thunder event not to feature Joan Baez. Dylan's guitar was out of tune throughout: apparently, his tech had wrongly calibrated the strobe-tuner. He was replaced by Joel Bernstein the following night. Nobody thought of replacing Bob Dylan. Joel Bernstein said, 'Bob is not a perfectionist like Prince. When he says he wants things done right, he just wants to be able to do his own thing without worrying about whether his guitar's in tune or the amps are going to work.'

The proceeds were disappointing but Rubin Carter was released pending an appeal. In February 1977 Rubin Carter was found guilty for a second time.

A TV play could be written around 30 March 1976, Eric Clapton's thirty-first birthday at the Shangri-La Studios in Malibu. Eric Clapton was making his *No Reason to Cry* album and he celebrated his birthday with a bleary-eyed jam session with Bob and Ronnie Wood. Eric sang Bob's 'Sign Language' but didn't want 'Seven Days'. Ronnie Wood asked if he could do it instead.

Dylan was more concerned about where he slept. He took the sheets from Ronnie's bed and created a makeshift tent in the grounds. He was with a girl who had her arm and leg in plaster. Ronnie said, 'It was like *Invasion of the Zombies* to see her in the garden.'

In April 1976, Dylan assembled the new Rolling Thunder Revue for rehearsals at the Belleview-Biltmore Hotel in Clearwater, Florida, as it happens the oldest working wooden structure in America. The songs included 'Weary Blues from Waitin'' and 'Ridin' down the Highway'. The rehearsals ended with a show for the hotel staff.

The first night of the second leg was on April 18 at Lakeland, Florida. Dylan was well received, ending with an ensemble 'Gotta Travel On', the way Buddy Holly's final tour had ended. Dylan was playing a white National guitar with 'Rimbaud' on it.

No show could be mediocre with Kinky Friedman on board, a Marmite performer if there ever was one. He wore a 'Jesus' jacket that Nudie's had made for Johnny Dollar, who was with Jesus before he could wear it. Kinky sang his parody of 'Okie from Muskogee', 'Asshole from El Paso', which Dylan followed with 'Visions of Johanna' – a ridiculous but fantastic segue. Bob said to Kinky, 'You'll never make it as an entertainer but you're a born politician', which started Kinky thinking that he should run for Governor of Texas.

The Rolling Thunder Revue continued through Florida with dates in St. Petersburg, Tampa (with Steve Martin as opening act), Orlando, Gainesville, Tallahassee, Pensacola and Mobile (where Dylan sang 'Stuck Inside of Mobile'). They returned to the Bellevue-Biltmore Hotel to film an NBC special with Joan Baez singing 'Diamonds and Rust' and Bobby Neuwirth 'Mercedes-Benz'. Dylan was unhappy with the results, choosing to film a later show at Fort Collins.

Sara was around on occasion and on May 1 she was in the reserved area in Hattiesburg. Somebody else wanted to sit there and protested. Security tried to move him and Dylan joined in. Fortunately for them, the guy was on his own.

When they moved to Louisiana, they played New Orleans (where Dylan did the only live version of 'Rita Mae') and Baton Rouge, but Lake Charles was cancelled due to poor sales. Not to worry: Bob went to see Bobby Charles who lived in the swamps.

On May 8, Dylan played the Hofheinz Pavilion in Houston which was two-thirds full although there were still 8,000 customers. Willie Nelson was a guest artist and they ended in true Willie fashion with 'Will the Circle Be Unbroken'. A second show in Houston was cancelled.

They moved to Corpus Christi, where Bob gave the first live performance of 'One of Us Must Know', but due to poor sales, the San Antonio show was moved to a smaller venue. There Bob and Joan sang Woody Guthrie's 'Deportee'.

The Rolling Thunder tour had started as a milestone and now it was a millstone. An afternoon show in Austin was cancelled and there was chaos in the evening when the reserved seats became general admission. When a show in Dallas was cancelled, they gave a free concert at the Gatesville State School for Boys.

From May 20 to 22, the revue was rehearsing for the NBC-TV special at Hughes Stadium, Colorado State University, Fort Collins. It was constantly raining and Sara unexpectedly turned up with his mother Beatty and her children. Bob was perturbed as his current girlfriend was around.

The concert on May 23 was in an open-air stadium in pouring rain. The performers all wore Arab headdresses. The crowd was enthusiastic and sang 'Happy Birthday' to Bob before the second encore. Dylan had had too much to drink but who could blame him?

The final Rolling Thunder concert was on 25 May 1976 at Salt Palace, Salt Lake City, Utah. There were 8,000 people in a half-filled arena. They performed for four hours with Bob and Joan working through 'Lily, Rosemary and the Jack of Hearts' and Allen Ginsberg reading *Holy Ghost on the Nod over the Body of Bliss,* which baffled as many listeners as it satisfied.

In September came the *Hard Rain* LP, taken from second leg shows in Fort Worth and Fort Collins. Despite the title, 'A Hard Rain's A-Gonna Fall' was not among the tracks. 'Lay Lady Lay' had been given a Stax-like arrangement and Dylan sings, 'Forget this dance, let's go upstairs, Let's take a chance, Who really cares?' 'Shelter from the Storm' had a heavy metal ending and Mick Ronson was at his best on 'Maggie's Farm'. The NBC-TV special from Fort Collins was broadcast in October. The *TV Guide* interviewer asked Dylan, 'How do you imagine God?' and he replied, 'How come nobody asks Kris Kristofferson that?'

On 5 December 1976 *Bound for Glory* with David Carradine as Woody Guthrie was released in the US, but it didn't do much business. It had taken several years to come to the screen. *Renaldo and Clara* was heading that way.

On 13 February 1977, Sara came down for breakfast at their Malibu home and found Bob Dylan with Malka and their children. According to the lawyer's statement, Dylan struck Sara on the face and asked her to leave. She filed for divorce, mentioning his violent outbursts and temper tantrums.

In April, Dylan wrote some songs about divorce and the fight for custody including 'I'm Cold', but enough was enough as he wasn't going to record another *Blood on the Tracks*. The songs were written as therapy and played to T Bone Burnett.

Later that month, Leonard Cohen had gone to the Troubadour to hear Allen Ginsberg. The next evening Allen Ginsberg and Bob Dylan were eating with Ronee Blakley and Ginsberg said that Cohen and his producer Phil Spector were at the Gold Star Recording Studio. They dropped by and Spector said, 'There are so many Jews in the room, we could have a bar mitzvah.' They joined in 'You Can't Go Home with your Hard-On' and there is an outtake, 'Caper Sin Motel'.

Asked by the *Times Literary Supplement* to name the most overrated and underrated books of the century, Dylan opted for the Bible in both categories.

In May 1977 Dylan signed a management deal with Jerry Weintraub, his first manager in ten years. Weintraub was managing Neil Diamond and was keen to get Dylan back into arenas. Okay, the Rolling Thunder had had some poor attendances but that didn't matter: it was all down to publicity and Weintraub was perfect for that. Furthermore, many fans preferred shows that were 100% Dylan.

Throughout 1977, Howard Alk edited *Renaldo and Clara*, having 80 hours of film at his disposal. The footage was indexed according to themes, characters and performances. He persuaded Dylan to let him cut it into a four-hour film.

Dylan liked Emily Dickinson's poem, *Success in Circuit Lies*. He had the poem on his wall and he called his film company, Circuit Films. Its opening line, 'Tell all the truth but tell it slant'.

Allen Ginsberg convinced him that *Renaldo and Clara* could make sense and was worth releasing. He taped interviews in which Dylan opened up about his film. Ginsberg even interviewed Dylan when he was at the chiropodist: too many years of wearing cowboy boots? The Woman in White is apparently a ghost and so Renaldo rids himself of death when she leaves. Dylan, the man with the white face, has no name because he is like the Greek chorus.

Dylan even asked, 'Is this too intellectual, Allen?' Dylan compared his film to the French film *Les Enfants du Paradis* (1945), which lasted over three hours. Length wasn't a problem for Marcel Carné and it wouldn't be for Dylan. The interview was not published at the time as Dylan told Ginsberg that he had revealed too much – no, more likely that he knew he was talking bollocks.

Dylan must have been fairly happy about the film as on Halloween in 1977, Dylan, Ginsberg and Alk donned Halloween masks and sang and played on the streets of Malibu.

In December 1977, Dylan and his chums rounded up an audience from local restaurants and showed them the film. They got mixed reviews but imagine finishing off your meal at 9pm and you have an invitation from Bob Dylan. How would you feel if the film was then four hours long? Ronee Blakley said, 'Some of the laughter is nervous because people don't know what they're seeing.'

Ramblin' Jack Elliott: 'I've saw the four hour version a few times. I don't know how it ever got out like that but I suppose there are people interested in that sort of thing. There were other scenes that were better than the ones you saw. There were some scenes in the Pilgrim Mayflower Wax Museum. They have a model of the small boat as she's rowing ashore with seven or eight pilgrims standing up. It is coming into Plymouth Rock which is made out of papier-mâché and fake trees and stuff. An electric motor rocks the boat, so these pilgrims are going back and forth in the boat. They had me sitting, squatting on the rock there, and told me to make up some stuff to say to the pilgrims, welcoming them to the New World. I told them some hocus pocus based on my own life, told them to be careful because there's strange people around and to be careful if they were hitchhiking. It was a great comedy show and I can't understand why they didn't include it in the film.'

Better to read Ratso's book. Ratso was a funny, entertaining writer: he described Bobby Neuwirth as looking like 'a 1930s Cuban porn star'. Ratso reported that Ronee Blakley often irritated the other performers, but Ratso himself could be outrageous and annoying, so who was annoying who? *Rolling Stone* gave Ratso a hard time, particularly over his photographs, and he remarked, 'I don't intentionally send bad pictures.'

It was like inviting Bill Bryson to cover your tour: you were going to get the story but it would be gently mocked along the way. His book has surreal passages along the lines of Hunter S. Thompson.

Howard Alk loved Ratso's draft manuscript for his book and he passed it to Bob Dylan who said, 'That is how we should have made *Renaldo and Clara*.'

Even more revealing though was Joan Baez, who put Dylan without naming him at the centre of her *Gulf Winds* album. 'Sweeter for Me' is when she thought she was pregnant by Dylan and 'O Brother!' is a comical song about his appalling behaviour. Reflecting on their off-on relationship in 'Time Is Passing Us By', she admits she is 'good for one more try'.

Dylan had partly financed the film so he wanted at least his money back. In January 1978, Dylan realised that the easiest and the cheapest way to publicise *Renaldo and Clara* was to give interviews so off he went. He told the *New York Times*, 'I've learned as much from Cézanne as I have from Woody Guthrie.' Joel Kotkin had a sour interview with Dylan by suggesting he was doing this for free publicity. Dylan defended himself but not well, as it was true. He was interviewed by *Rolling Stone* and he even invited Japanese journalists to his new studio in Santa Monica for a press conference. He had converted a rehearsal space into Rundown Studios on a five year lease.

On 25 January 1978, *Renaldo and Clara* opened in New York and then a week later in Los Angeles. It took a critical battering and Dylan did more interviews to defend it. Commenting on the bad reviews, he told Robert Hilburn of *Los Angeles Times*, 'The reviews weren't about the movie. They were just an excuse to get at me' without explaining why anyone would want to get at him (apart of course from past lovers and Phil Ochs). He issued a four-track promotional EP: 'People Get Ready', 'Never Let Me Go', 'Isis' and 'It Ain't Me Babe'. On the other hand, Nigel Andrews of the *Financial Times* called *Renaldo and Clara* his film of the year, which makes you wonder what else he saw that year. The music is fine but the acting and the storyline, such as it is, is ridiculous.

In May 1978, possibly at the Last Chance Saloon, Dylan went to Cannes to promote *Renaldo and Clara*. It partially worked as the European reviews were generally okay.

At the end of June 1977, Faridi McFree was looking after Sara's house in LA while Sara was in Hawaii. She was a New Age art therapist who helped children cope with divorce through painting. She asked Bob if he was okay after the trauma of divorce. You know what happened next: Dylan invited her over and she stayed the night. They were to go to a party at Linda Ronstadt's but ended up at Sara's house looking at his children's art. When Sara returned home, McFree had moved in with Dylan.

In July, Dylan took Faridi and his children to his farm in Minnesota. Dylan was back on his feet again and he wrote *Street-Legal* there. Dylan said that this album was his best example of using Norman Raeben's techniques.

When Elvis Presley died on August 16, Bob was morose for a couple of days. He said, 'If it wasn't for Elvis, I couldn't be doing what I do today.'

In August 1977 the Dylan's divorce was granted by Santa Monica court. Sara charged Bob with 'violent outbursts and temper tantrums and bringing another woman into their Malibu mansion'.

Sara wanted the children to move to Hawaii with her and sought court approval. Dylan wanted sole custody as Sara had already taken the children to Hawaii without permission. Sara was awarded $13.5m. and 50% rights to songs written during their 12 years of marriage. They settled later for $36m.

On November 3, Bob Dylan was instructed to return the children to Sara. Notice was served at Point Dume but the guards were refused entry. Sara accused Faridi McFree of brainwashing the children. Sara went with three private detectives to the school and demanded them. She punched a teacher who asked to see the court order and she was fined. Jakob Dylan has called it the worst day of his life.

In November 1977 Ron Rosenbaum interviewed Bob for *Playboy*, published in March 1978. In the preamble to the interview, Dylan's psychic adviser Tamara Rand is mentioned. She takes him into his previous existences and Dylan apparently sent his girlfriends to her for approval.

Whilst all this was going on, Jerry Weintraub had been preparing a world tour starting early in 1978 and he had come up with some spectacular dates including the Budokan in Tokyo. Dylan himself would make over $1m from the tour, not to mention all the ancillary benefits from album sales, posters and T-shirts.

During December, Dylan invited some musicians to Rundown Studios in Santa Monica to prepare for the tour. He had a large band in mind. In the end, he went for an eight-piece band with three female vocalists, which turned out to be similar to his later gospel records. He had the idea from seeing Bob Marley and the Wailers. The drummer

Denny Seiwell was invited but because he had been with Wings at the time Paul McCartney was busted, he was refused a visa.

Bob did rehearsals with Mickey Jones on drums but Mickey would be losing work in Hollywood if he was off for six weeks and he wanted $10,000 a week. Dylan found Ian Wallace from King Crimson came cheaper. A performer in his own right, Jesse 'Ed' Davis was on guitar. It was the first job for Helena Springs, one of the backing singers, since leaving school. Dylan reworked 'Blowin' in the Wind' in a reggae arrangement and he had new songs such as 'First to Say Goodbye'.

Around the time I suggested to Tom Paxton that Dylan, that great champion of the underprivileged, was doing the tour for money. 'What's wrong with that?' said Tom, 'Balzac wrote for money. Dumas wrote for money. Dostoevsky was up to his arse in debt and desperate to write for money. Do you think I have come to Liverpool to sing tonight because I felt like it? Would you be talking to me if someone wasn't going to pay you for it? It is totally ridiculous to say that someone's art is holy and that he shouldn't be thinking of money. Of course Bob Dylan did that tour for money and there's nothing wrong with that.'

The intention was for Dylan to play a fortnight in Japan – seven nights at the Budokan, Japan and three at the Matsushita Denki Taiikukan, Osaka. On February 17, Dylan gave a press conference at the airport in Tokyo. There was chaos as fans wanted to get to him and with a full head of hair, Dylan looked more like a rock star than he had since 1966. Dylan went to the Budokan to see ELO, which was fronted by Jeff Lynne, who would become a close friend and fellow Wilbury.

In his own perverse way, Dylan opened his first show with a vintage blues, 'Lonesome Bedroom Blues', but his set, all played with the band, on February 20 covered his entire career. He had new lines for 'Simple Twist of Fate', 'All I Really Want to Do', 'The Man in Me' and 'Going, Going Gone.' There were fine harmonies on 'Shelter from the Storm', not to mention a storming sax from Steve Douglas, noted for his work with Duane Eddy. 'Knockin' on Heaven's Door' was given a reggae treatment, but 'All I Really Want to Do' could have come from Blackpool. 'Forever Young' sounded forever cabaret but Dylan was in terrific voice here. A mournful 'Blowin' in the Wind' was very good but his closer, 'The Times They Are a-Changin'', was too show-biz: however, singing such songs in Japan was a brave move anyway. He had performed 28 songs and at three hours, it was his longest-ever solo show.

The set didn't vary much in Japan but in Osaka, he performed Tampa Red's 'Love Her with a Feeling' and in the later shows at Budokan, he gave the first performance of 'Is Your Love In Vain'.

Sony in Japan had insisted on a live album from Budokan and a double-album, *Bob Dylan at Budokan*, with 22 tracks was released. It became so popular on import that it was officially released in the US and UK. Both Bob Dylan and Cheap Trick have recorded live albums there. One reviewer said it was 'like a nightmare cabaret act', which was cruel but certainly it didn't have the bite of Bob Dylan in 1965/6. The arrangements on the Rolling Thunder had been more imaginative but with too many guitars, and this was certainly slicker.

On the album sleeve, Bob Dylan wrote, 'The more I think about it, the more I realise what I left behind in Japan – my soul, my music and that sweet girl in the geisha house – I wonder does she remember me?'

After Japan, the entourage played a month of arena shows in Australia and New

Zealand. By now he was the hooded man often going out around the cities anonymously. On 8 March 1978, Dylan was jogging in Albert Park, Auckland at 5am (as you do or rather as Dylan does). He met a Maori princess Ra Aranga in the hotel lobby and he asked her to join him for a run the next day. Then he invited her to his concert at Western Springs Stadium.

Dylan played four days at the Festival Hall in Brisbane. He was interviewed by Craig McGregor for two hours: he had met him in 1966. He mentioned a new song, 'Her Version of Jealousy' and said *Renaldo and Clara* would be around when the critics are dead and gone. Outside the stadium, it said 'Bob Dylan George Benson Wrestling', which would have been an interesting event. A photograph of them was included on the LP sleeve for his next album, *Street-Legal*.

Dylan played dates in Adelaide, Melbourne, Perth and Sydney and he was opening with Robert Johnson's 'I'm a Steady Rollin' Man'. He had some private time in Christchurch with Ra Aranga.

England fast bowler, Bob Willis: 'I drove the guys mad on tour. I have always been an early riser and the cassette would go on and it would be Bob Dylan beaming out. I managed to convert some of the lads but not all. I went with several of the guys to the concert in Auckland in 1978 and several more came to London and Ian Botham and Alan Lamb went with me to Newcastle in 1984. Our captain Mike Brearley was a great psychologist. He knew that I would bowl better if I had my fix of Bob Dylan.'

Bob started writing with Helena Springs in Brisbane. He asked her to sing something and he'd take it from there. They wrote 'Coming from the Heart', 'Stepchild', 'If I'm Not There in the Morning' and several more.

Back in America in April 1978, the bass player Rob Stoner left the band and Jerry Scheff, who had been playing with Elvis, was recruited. Jerry Scheff: 'There was a saxophone player called Steve Douglas who was a member of the Wrecking Crew and he had played on hundreds of hit records. I was putting together a band for Tanya Tucker at the time called the TNT band, and it was supposed to be a crossover band. Steve told me that they had just got back from the first leg of a world tour and their bass player was leaving.'

Jerry Scheff expected that they would be rehearsing for the next leg of the tour but this is Dylanworld and he decided to make a new album instead. Jerry Scheff: 'The first time I played with him on stage, I had never played half the songs before: We had been at the rehearsal studio and Dylan said that he was going to record an album and we did *Street-Legal*. That took up the rehearsal time and when we did the first show in Los Angeles, I hadn't played half the songs. I had little notes on the drum riser. First show, I nailed it and did it really good. The second show I blew it because I thought I didn't need to think about it. I don't know if anybody else noticed because nobody mentioned it, but I knew.'

Dylan spent a week cutting *Street-Legal*. The side door of Rundown Studios was on the cover of *Street-Legal* and Dylan's accountant was on the back sleeve, which is one way of saying 'thank you', I suppose. Elvis had recently died and Bob Dylan's garb on the back photo shows him dressed rather like Elvis on stage. *Street-Legal* is a bikers' phrase for roadworthiness and the tax and insurance of their vehicles.

The critic Paul Williams said, 'Bob Dylan is at his best when mixing reality with fantasy and he didn't do this in the late 1970s.' I can appreciate the point he is making but the songs are stimulating, although there were some truly terrible lines on the album as though he has been listening to a Barry White album and decided to parody him. 'Can you cook and sew, make flowers grow' from 'Is Your Love in Vain?' is an obvious example. But, and this is a big But, he could be setting up a bad line deliberately to lead into a new one or he could be playing a character who would say that. You can make all sorts of excuses for Bob Dylan.

In 'Señor', Dylan rhymes 'headin'' with 'Armageddon', and one advantage of his truly unique voice is that he can make it work. As Sinatra's lyricist Sammy Cahn told me, 'I'd never rhyme heading and Armageddon because they don't rhyme, but when Dylan says "headin'" and "Armageddin'", I buy it.'

Greil Marcus has called 'Señor' a pastiche of 'Hotel California', but I think it is more a nod to Ennio Morricone's music for the Clint Eastwood westerns. It sounds like something he could have given to Sam Peckinpah for *Pat Garrett and Billy the Kid*: indeed, it would have brilliant on the credits. You can detect other influences in it – Richard and Linda Thompson's 'The Calvary Cross' from 1974 and even straying into Neil Diamond territory in the middle eight. Dylan has said the song is about 'two people who are leaning on each other and then breaking apart.', but has offered no further explanation.

'Is Your Love In Vain' is possibly a reference to Robert Johnson's 'Love In Vain', but is Dylan the man in the song or is he playing a character? Considering Dylan is showing compassion on 'Baby Stop Crying', he sounds cold here. 'New Pony' is about a new girlfriend and celebrating her flanks.

'Where Are You Tonight?' looks back on a marriage (his own?) with regret, but he ends up being born again, which leans forward to what happens next. It's a good song and you keep thinking Dylan is about to go into a great chorus as in 'Like a Rolling Stone', but the song doesn't deliver.

The album was criticised for its horns and female chorus. It sounded corny for Bob Dylan but most of all, it lacked warmth. In December 1978, he told a journalist, 'What they were doing in the mobile truck wasn't what was happening in the room.' The album was remastered in 2003 and sounded much better. It is often messing with sacred territory to remix an album but it can work as in this case and as with the Grateful Dead's *Anthem of the Sun*, and the catalogue of the Who and the Beatles.

It is a pity that 'Stepchild' (which he did in concert several times) and 'Coming from the Heart' were not included as they were excellent songs.

Dylan had a new backing vocalist in Carolyn Dennis on *Street-Legal* and the 'Thanks to Queen Bee' relate to Mary Alice Artes, who also comes into the story and is the subject of 'Precious Angel'.

Ramblin' Jack Elliott: 'I may not have liked Dylan's new songs at first, I may have been befuddled, but then I found out that whatever he did was always just right. *Street-Legal* was the first album that I hadn't taken to.'

In June 1978 Bob Dylan resumed his world tour with a week at the Universal Amphitheatre in Los Angeles. He had eight musicians and three back-up singers. He was performing 'Is Your Love In Vain' from the forthcoming album and had turned 'Tangled Up in Blue' into a torch ballad.

After recording another new song, 'Stop Now', at Rundown, the touring party flew to London. Dylan was playing five dates at Earls Court but he had time for socialising. He saw the reggae band Merger at the 100 Club and asked them to open for him at Blackbushe Aerodrome in July. He saw George Thorogood and the Destroyers at Dingwall's in Camden and a film about art forgery, *The American Friend* which starred Dennis Hopper. He met up with George Harrison and saw the Clash and Graham Parker.

He saw Robert Gordon and Link Wray at the Music Machine in Camden with Rob Stoner on bass. Dylan commented, 'Link's never done a bad show.' Sid Vicious and his girlfriend Nancy were there and Sid Vicious said, to him, 'Aren't you Bob Dildo?' Sid may have been punk but he never got as vicious as 'Like a Rolling Stone'.

The CBS press office gave him a welcome pack of recent albums including *New Boots and Panties* from Ian Dury and the Blockheads. When he met Ian Dury on the set of *Hearts of Fire* in 1986, he said 'Hi, sweet Gene Vincent!'

C.P. Lee of Alberto y Lost Trios Paranoias says, 'There was a huge boardroom table in the Blackhill office of Stiff Records and we would sleep under it and one night someone else was under it, a little Irishman, B.P. Fallon. He had picked the name at random from the phone book. He fell in with Dylan's crew and he took Dylan around London and presented him with a box of Stiff Records. Allen Ginsberg thought that we were funny and he told Dylan that he had to see us, and so they trooped off to a club in Camden where we were playing. I was at the side of the stage and B.P. said, "Dylan's here. He's at the back waiting to see you." What do you do when confronted with a god? I said to the audience, "We were going to play a number by Bob Dylan but he never plays any of ours, so stuff him." Dylan walked out, outraged apparently, but I thought he would like that.'

The British promoter Harvey Goldsmith put Dylan on at Earls Court, his first London concerts for 12 years. At a press conference: he was asked 'Why have you been away so long?' and he replied, 'The weather.'

The tickets had gone on sale at midnight in January with hundreds in the queue and sold out in eight hours. The future Radio 1 DJ, Andy Kershaw had his Economics A-level on the same day: he scribbled some answers and rushed away. He got to London and realised, 'I had to confront a terrible reality – Bob was bloody awful. The band was a revue orchestra and there were dozens of the buggers. I wanted The Band of 1966 and Dylan was quite wilfully disregarding the tunes of his own songs.' It was difficult for anyone to make out the first song as he was opening with Tampa Red's 'Love Her with a Feeling'. Still, he was collecting £350,000 for six nights' work.

He did look rather showbiz with a metallic strip down his flares, still in evidence in 2019. The audience was holding up lighters when he sang 'Forever Young'. The guy next to Andy Kershaw set his *Evening Standard* alight. Oh, and Andy got a Grade A in Economics.

Andy Kershaw notwithstanding, the reviews for Earls Court were mostly excellent and the TV and press coverage was extensive. Robert Shelton asked him about *Renaldo and Clara* and he said, 'I've talked too much about that film already.' Time to move on: the film was a dodo.

A fan from Liverpool, George Orr wrote a letter to *Sounds* criticising their reviewer who had missed half the show – and he had free tickets and lived in London! George added, 'I was there for the whole show and I had come from Liverpool. I didn't mind a bad review but I hated that glibness. I know that Dylan can be bad – it's a bit like following Everton. A lot of people would like him doing a set from 1963 to 1965 but he won't do that. No one told Picasso how to paint and it is the same with him.'

Chris Hockenhull: 'On the last night of the triumphant Earls Court concerts in 1978, someone shouted, "When are you coming back?", and he said, "I'm thinking of moving up to Liverpool." I've not seen him around. I do think he had a fondness for Liverpool: he knew the Beatles and I'm sure he liked their humour.'

Merseyside journalist Michael Gray: 'The record company press officer rang me one Saturday morning and said, "Would you like to come backstage tonight and say hello?" She said that Bob had liked a piece I had written in *Melody Maker* the previous week. It was a very weird and difficult situation. He was standing in the backstage area behind the curtains at Earls Court and the people with the right hospitality passes were in the white room behind. People were being called to meet him in groups of two and three. I was with my son who was nine years old. When we were brought out, the people standing with him included Jack Nicholson and Bianca Jagger. He was talking to somebody else and ignoring them. Jack was fine about this, just standing there and smiling, while Bianca was fuming. Nobody was uncool enough to ask Bob Dylan for his autograph but my son didn't know that. He wanted an important autograph and he hadn't got a pen. He turned to Bianca Jagger and said, "Excuse me, have you got a pen please?" She looked her in her bag and gave him a plebeian biro rather grumpily. He pushed in and said to Bob Dylan, "Excuse me, can you sign this please?" Dylan got down on one knee so that he was on the same level as Gabriel, and he asked him how he spelt his name as he didn't want to make a mistake. Gabe thought he was talking to a complete idiot and went "G-A-B-R-I-E-L." (laughs) Bob went "Okay" and wrote, "To Gabriel, Be safe always, Best wishes, Bob Dylan", a curiously unDylanish thing to write, certainly not his motto in life.'

When Dylan played to 55,000 in Rotterdam, he also used the time to see Anne Frank's house and a late night show by Elvis Costello and the Attractions. Dylan commented, 'Hey, he's a pretty normal guy.' Well, he had just met Sid Vicious.

On July 1 Dylan performed for 80,000 fans at the site of the Nuremburg rallies, standing where Hitler stood, which added resonance to some of his material. Eric Clapton joined him on guitar. Some neo-Nazis threw things on stage.

Bob gave Eric a cassette of some songs he had written with Helena Springs. Two were included on his album, *Backless,* released in November 1978. The opening cut 'Walk Out in the Rain' is typical of Clapton's AOR rock at the time. After a gruff vocal, Clapton delivers a guitar solo and it is a fine track. The vocals are indistinct on 'If I Don't Be There by Morning', almost as though Clapton was performing in the house next door, so it was not only Dylan that had recording problems. It deserved a better performance as it is a good song.

Dylan had a week of dates in Paris in front of enthusiastic audiences (and reviewers). He had an extra verse for 'New Pony' and working his way through the Tampa Red catalogue, he alighted on 'But I Forgive You'. In an interview, Dylan said that he only listened to old blues and country singers, but he was keeping abreast of what was happening.

Hugues Aufray saw all the French shows and Bob was travelling with his paralysed friend Larry Kegan. Hugues invited the entourage to his house for a party which went well. Harry Dean Stanton, Dylan and Aufray sang Mexican drinking songs together.

On 15 July 1978 Dylan was back in the UK, performing at his biggest concert since the Isle of Wight and earning £300,000 for entertaining 200,000 fans at a new music venue, Blackbushe Aerodrome, near Camberley. There had been much publicity for the event: even barrage balloons with 'Bob Dylan' on them. The organisers did allow fans with forged tickets in as there was so much space. Dylan was on fine form but although the show was recorded, it has never been released. It would be perfect for *The Bootleg Series*. Blackbushe was a huge success but it turned out to be the first and last event to be staged there.

As Dylan's bass player Jerry Scheff had played with Elvis , I asked him if Elvis would have liked such a large audience. '(Laughs) Of course Elvis would have loved to have done a show like that but that sort of thing was never in the Colonel's plans. It was a good show. Eric Clapton was opening and Joan Armatrading was on. There was a sea of people but you couldn't really see anybody, but Bob didn't lack confidence.'

Eric Clapton joined him for 'Changing of the Guards'. He saw Dylan being asked for his autograph, but as the fan hadn't got a pen, Dylan dropped the paper on the floor. 'Cold but poetic,' said Clapton, 'his sense of humour is the greatest thing about him. He does not trust his voice. He does not trust his guitar playing. He doesn't think he is good at anything but songwriting, and even there he has doubts.'

Liz Thomson: 'Blackbushe was like our Woodstock and in an old airfield. Dylan wore a top hat he had borrowed from the doorman of the Royal Garden Hotel. It was a beautiful evening. The stars came out and the moon rose and Dylan performed this incredible set. 'Forever Young' was near the end of it. It is a hymn really and a beautiful song.'

From September to December, Dylan was performing shows throughout America. He said that he had wanted a regular band for some time. The US critics branded it *The Vegas Tour*. He opened, strangely, with 'A Hard Rain's A-Gonna Fall' as an instrumental. During 'Ballad of a Thin Man', Dylan took the microphone from the stand and shook hands with the audience. He played 64 three-hour shows in 92 days. At Madison Square Garden, he found that 'Baby Stop Crying' sounded good and it became a regular item.

He was also trying 'Watching the River Flow', 'Coming from the Heart' and Willie Dixon's 'I'm Ready'. At soundchecks, he did a new song, 'Legionnaire's Disease' as well as Dr. Hook's 'Carry Me Carrie' (written by his friend Shel Silverstein), 'St Louis Blues' and 'Daddy's Little Girl'.

He tried a new song, 'I Love You Too Much' and dropped it as he wasn't happy with it. In 1981 Dylan gave Greg Lake of Emerson, Lake and Palmer this 'half-completed song'. Greg completed it and recorded it as 'Love You Too Much'. Greg Lake said, 'I wanted to do something by Bob Dylan and our tour manager was on Bob's tour and knew him. Bob had this song he had been working on but hadn't finished. He had two verses and I wrote some more. It was a strange thing to do. It wasn't a particularly great song, just a 12-bar really.'

The world tour ended on December 16 at the Hollywood Sportatorium, in Miami. The 29-song set included the new 'Do Right to Me Baby', but he was to change the lyric. It ended with his second encore, 'I'll Be Your Baby Tonight'. Dylan had played 115 live shows in ten months and by the end of the year, the excessive singing was affecting his voice. The band was getting a little restless and doing the songs too fast in the end. A month before the end of the tour, Dylan had also grown a Fu Manchu moustache, so Bob Dylan started Movember.

Dylan was having a boat built in St. Vincent in the Caribbean. The boat, the *Water Pearl*, was launched in 1979, though Dylan wasn't there for the launch. In February 1983 Dylan sailed to Barbados on his boat.

CHAPTER 12

The Missionary Times

I. Religion and Rock

Here's your starter for ten: which song has been recorded by Bob Dylan, Frank Sinatra, Elvis Presley, Johnny Cash, Dolly Parton, Nat 'King' Cole and Aaron Neville? There are two correct answers: 'Silent Night' and 'O Little Town of Bethlehem'.

The singing of Christian songs, especially carols by popular entertainers from the western world is nothing new. The majority of songs are about romantic love but it is surprising to find how many hit songs have been about faith. As society has become more diverse and less believing, there are fewer religious songs today but at the time Bob Dylan was making his Christian albums, which is around 1980, it was not totally unusual. It was unusual in that Bob Dylan was known to be Jewish and that he was very much his own man, but many artists had made religious albums and in the States, both Word and Myrrh were big-selling labels and Jesus Rock was even a genre.

Nearly every year there had been new and impressive inspirational songs. There was 'Over The Rainbow' (written as World War II was about to start), 'You'll Never Walk Alone' (written at the end of the war), 'I Believe', 'Climb Ev'ry Mountain', 'The Impossible Dream', 'Bridge over Troubled Water' and 'Let It Be'. They don't always mention God or Jesus but their intention is clear: you overcome your troubles by appreciating that there is a greater plan. You saw me crying in the chapel, but the tears I shed were tears of joy.

Even if you are a sinner, you can be saved, although in LaVern Baker's record of that name, her only misdeeds are to smoke, drink and dance. In 1748 John Newton was the captain of a slave ship and when a severe storm abated, he thanked the Lord and devoted his life to God, writing amongst things 'Amazing Grace': 'Amazing grace, how sweet the sound that saved a wretch like me.' That same theme is in Kris Kristofferson's 'Why Me, Lord': 'Why me, Lord, what have I ever done, To deserve even one of the blessings I've known.' The conversion doesn't have to be immediate – in another song, 'One Day at a Time', Kris Kristofferson likened it to recovering from alcoholism and taking one day at a time.

The reward when it came would be enormous: Pat Boone had a multi-million selling hit in 1958 with 'A Wonderful Time up There', which was based on a spiritual, 'Gospel Boogie'. I thought it was fantastic when I first heard it. I was 13 years old and I had never heard anything this vibrant in church. In the charts at the same time was a 14-year-old boy, Laurie London, with a spiritual associated with Mahalia Jackson, 'He's Got the Whole World in His Hands': I'd never even heard of Mahalia and I thought Laurie was great.

It is fascinating to see how the broadcasting authorities related to these songs, especially the BBC. Any mention of religion in a song was shunted off to the Head of Religious Broadcasting for approval. Although the identity of 'HRB' changed with the years, the views did not shift substantially. In essence, HRB did not like popular singers recording religious songs as he felt that they were doing them for commercial ends.

Take for example 'It Is No Secret (what God can do)', which had been recorded by the Ink Spots, Jo Stafford and Elvis Presley. HRB considered it 'a sincere, if misguided, presentation of a very personal aspect of the Christian gospel.' He suggested that 'it should only be used in request programmes in which the responsibility for the choice does not rest directly on the Corporation.' In other words, the BBC could shift the blame to the audience, which is hardly a Christian philosophy.

These days 'It Is No Secret', written by the country singer Stuart Hamblen in 1951, is regarded as a hymn. HRB thought 'Crying in the Chapel' even worse, being 'nauseating but theologically unexceptional'.

One of the greatest records ever made, 'God Bless the Child' by Billie Holiday from 1942, was considered unsuitable for broadcasting as prayers in popular songs were not allowed. In 1952, the lyricist pleaded his case to the BBC: 'It is merely another way of saying "God helps those who help themselves" and in no sense could it be considered sacrilegious.' I'd have considered that a perfectly reasonable explanation but HRB was not persuaded and the ban remained.

What riled HRB were songs which used religious words like angels, chapel, heaven and paradise, not to mention God, Jesus and the Devil. Frankie Laine's 'Answer Me' was about somebody asking God to help him get his girlfriend back, which HRB saw as 'a sentimental mockery of Christian prayer', but 'it is conceivable that a disappointed lover might sincerely utter such a prayer, if he was totally ignorant of the real nature of prayer.' Bunny Lewis, the quick-witted manager of David Whitfield, called such songs 'God-botherers', and with minor adjustments, the song became 'Answer Me, My Love' for David Whitfield and went to Number 1 with BBC airplay.

In a similar manner, HRB didn't like the explanation of the Lord's good works in Jimmie Rodgers' 'Honeycomb'. Johnny Franz at Philips amended the lyric for Marty Wilde's first single and his version had airplay. Tom Lehrer was almost in a special category and his cynical view of the end of the world, 'We Will All Go Together When We Go' was banned but mistakenly played on *Housewives' Choice*.

There were relatively few records about atheism, one being 'The Unbeliever' by Guy Mitchell in 1957. It is typical Guy Mitchell – bright and breezy with French horns. According to the song, the unbeliever has a hard time in life, so it's better to be on the sunny side of the street with the Christians. HRB may have applauded its sentiments but it was too gaudy for broadcasting.

HRB was kept busy as he had to pass judgment on such songs as 'Stranger in Paradise', 'Earth Angel', 'My Special Angel', 'I Saw the Light', 'The Village of St. Bernadette', 'Three Stars' (about the Buddy Holly plane crash), 'Little Drummer Boy' and 'It Wasn't God Who Made Honky Tonk Angels', a definitive no-no for Kitty Wells. Actually, if you believe God made the world and all that is in it, then, yes, God did make honky tonk angels.

Even 'Deck of Cards' was suspicious as someone is playing cards in church but that record should have been banned for poor arithmetic: the number of spots on a deck of cards cannot be equal to the number of days in a year as it has to be a multiple of four.

HRB was super-busy in December and an artist's chance of a Christmas hit depended on his judgement: Harry Belafonte's 'Mary Boy's Child' was close to rejection but HRB passed it and it made Number 1. HRB would listen to religious albums by Johnny Cash, Pat Boone and Tennessee Ernie Ford and assess each track.

In 10 August 1962 our friend HRB determined 'Baby, Let Me Follow You Down' by Bob Dylan was 'not to be broadcast (religious grounds)'. It'll be the phrase, 'god-almighty world'.

However, by then, times were changing and soon, with a few notable exceptions, individual producers were allowed to determine what could be played on their shows. Religious songs were still being released – 'Go Tell It on the Mountain', 'Spirit in the Sky', 'Oh Happy Day', 'Loves Me like a Rock', even the score of *Jesus Christ Superstar* – but very few of them were banned. A few years earlier, Bob's 'Highway 61 Revisited' with its light-hearted 'God said to Abraham, Kill me a son' would never have been passed.

Right from the start of his songwriting, Bob Dylan has borrowed or played with biblical images. Many commentators have related this to his upbringing but staying in hotel rooms played its part. Back in the 1960s nearly every hotel room contained a Gideon's Bible. If you are writing a song, you might open the Bible for an idea or two as the images and the language are so powerful. Paul Simon admitted that the Gideons were 'very useful if you were stuck for a few words'. Talking of 'The Boxer', he told Robert Hilburn that phrases such as 'workman's wages' and 'seeking out the poorer quarters' could have easily have come from there. In his collected works, Hunter S. Thompson acknowledges the Book of Revelation. The Beatles refer to Gideon's Bible in 'Rocky Raccoon' and the Swinging Blue Jeans tell me that Brian Jones of the Rolling Stones like to sign Gideon's Bibles, 'Best wishes, God'.

Newsweek had called 1976 the year of the evangelical. *Born Again* by Chuck Colson was a best seller. Hal Lindsey's *The Last Great Planet Earth*, published a few years earlier, was about Christ's return and another bestseller. Even the future President, Jimmy Carter said he was saved, but Dylan said that this was not a fad. 'It's the future. We are laying the foundation.'

There was a big 'born again' record market and Pat Boone's daughter, Debbie, topped the US charts for ten weeks in 1977 with 'You Light up My Life', another inspirational song.

The Jesus Rock brigade was unhip and often aligned to Billy Graham's crusades. Graham featured plenty of music saying, 'He who sings prays twice.' His crusades were mocked by cynics such as Mort Sahl who said, 'If he really wanted a challenge, why didn't he go to Vegas?' The music was often provided by Pat Boone and his daughters in the US and Cliff Richard in the UK.

Oddly, Cliff Richard's 'Devil Woman' would have been a solid bet for rejection by HRB. Similarly, the Charlie Daniels Band wouldn't have got far with 'The Devil Went Down to Georgia'.

The Osmonds came from a staunch Mormon family and so there was no rock style living for them, although 'Crazy Horses' was worthy of any band.

Others who had paraded their faith were the Beatles (Maharishi), Peter Green (for the Children of God sect), Pete Townshend (Meher Baba), Richie Furay, Robert Fripp, Bruce Cockburn and Donna Summer. Arlo Guthrie's *Outlasting the Blues* was about his conversion to Catholicism.

Sinéad O'Connor wanted to be a professional singer who was both religious and sensual. There is much Old Testament imagery in her first album, *The Lion and the Cobra*.

At the time Dylan found Christianity, he was approaching 40, which would be the age of his core followers and certainly an age when people are wondering about the afterlife (or lack of it).

In one way or another, Dylan was always being born again and he didn't like the term, telling Robert Hilburn: 'Born again is a media term that throws people into a corner and leaves them there. When I get involved in something, I get totally involved. I don't just play around on the fringes.'

Randy Newman called himself a 'born again atheist' and his songs were similarly witty. He imagined himself as God to deliver 'God's Song', designed to show how stupid we were. In 'Jesus – the Missing Years', John Prine delivered a quirky song about why we learnt nothing of Jesus' childhood from the Gospels.

As late as 2008 Hayes Carll did 'She Left Me for Jesus', he was an alt. country artist as opposed to a more traditional one but even so, he was chancing his luck in the Bible belt.

So we come now to Bob Dylan and the storm of controversy when he moved from 'Judas!' to Jesus. If HRB had been around, he would had difficulty with the albums, especially the first, *Slow Train Coming*, because Bob Dylan was promoting a fundamentalist brand of Christianity which would predict the imminent end of the world and the prospect of hell for non-believers. These songs would not have found favour with the BBC.

At least we can be thankful that Dylan didn't adopt Scientology, the highly suspect faith that has found so many followers in Hollywood.

The world has moved on again and is very different now from 1980. A remarkable number of people have abandoned their faith, me included. The percentage of non-believers in the UK is now over 50%.

II. So Much Older Then: 1979–1984

When writing about Bob Dylan in 1978, I left out one significant detail which has a bearing on 1979 and what follows. On 17 November 1978, somebody threw a small silver cross onto a stage in San Diego where Bob Dylan was performing. He picked it up and he was to say it transformed his life. A year later when he returned to San Diego, he thanked the unknown person who had thrown the cross.

Two nights after the cross had been thrown, Dylan was in Tucson, Arizona and he remarked after the show, 'There was a presence in the room that couldn't have been anybody but Jesus. Jesus put his hand on me. I felt my whole body tremble. I truly had a born-again experience.'

Dylan took to wearing the cross and writing Christian songs, the first being 'Slow Train Coming' (based on a common gospel theme, the train to heaven), 'Do Right to Me Baby' and 'This Way, That Way'. He amended old ones – in Houston, the woman in the topless bar in 'Tangled Up in Blue' had discarded the Italian poet and was quoting Matthew's gospel. He said, 'She opened up the Bible, Started quoting it to me, Gospel according to Matthew, Verse 3 chapter 33.' There's no such verse and he must have known that: another time, he had her quoting Jeremiah.

In January 1979 Mary Alice Artes told Bob Dylan about the Bible classes run by the Vineyard Fellowship in Reseda, Southern California. Dylan was interested, even obsessed, as he and Mary then attended Bible classes four mornings a week for three months. The fellowship did not have a permanent church but used different locations, even having services on the beach. Dylan loved going to black churches with Mary on Sundays. He said, 'Jesus put his hand on me. It was a physical thing. I felt my whole body tremble. The glory of the Lord knocked me down and picked me up.' Bob Dylan was baptised in Pat Boone's swimming pool.

Bob often played new songs to the pastor Larry Myers for his comments and he had thought of producing an album sung by Carolyn Dennis. *Slow Train Coming* would be her album. He established his own record label, Accomplice, though nothing came of it.

By the end of March, he had decided to record the songs himself and he was impressed by Dire Straits whom he saw at the Roxy in Los Angeles. Their own sound had been developed from Dylan, so to a certain extent, Dylan was looking in a mirror. Dylan said, 'Mark Knopfler does me better than anybody.'

Charlie Gillett, the London broadcaster who discovered Dire Straits, told me: 'I loved Mark Knopfler's songs. If I were a songwriter, they were songs that I would like to have written. I loved 'Down to the Waterline'. There is an influence of Lou Reed and Bob Dylan in there. That was no limitation. Lou Reed was only occasionally as good a songwriter as Mark was all the time."

The soul producer Jerry Wexler had been recording *Communiqué* with Barry Beckett and it would be a major success for Dire Straits. Dylan invited Mark Knopfler and their drummer Pick Withers to Rundown Studios to hear his new songs and talk about arrangements, and Dylan asked Knopfler if he could play like Albert King.

Jerry Wexler was keen to produce Bob Dylan but wasn't struck on the subject matter. He told Bob, 'I'm a 62-year-old, confirmed Jewish atheist. Let's just make an album.' Wexler told me, 'I had known Bob Dylan for a few years. When he called me and asked me to do the next album, I was thrilled to death. I was knocked out. It was "How high shall I jump and where do you want me to land?" My co-producer, Barry Beckett and I went to California where Dylan was living to select the material. It turned out to be wall-to-wall Jesus. I didn't care, it could have been the telephone directory. It was Bob Dylan and so we brought him to Muscle Shoals with Mark Knopfler as the lead guitarist.'

Pick Withers: 'There was one impromptu session at Dylan's office in Santa Monica and I only played tambourine. Mark and I flew to Muscle Shoals with Jerry Wexler. Barry Beckett was already there: it was partly his studio. We had a large space and some instruments had been set up. Dylan played the outline of a song and you went to your instrument which was all miked up and you did it. If we didn't get it in three takes, it was time to move on. Those were the master vocals. I am very grateful that some people choose to work like that. The drummer usually works with virgin tape and often with Dire Straits that was the performance which survived right through to the record. You could change all the other instruments, but I had to make my play for the record there and then. Mark sometimes said, "Second verse same as the first" and he was half playing guitar and just listening to the feel and the tempo. He was putting his parts on later. It was stepping out onto the highway for me – "I'm going this way, lads!" Tim Drummond was the bass player for *Slow Train Coming* and he had played with Neil Young. His playing was understated and yet it grew on me and helped me set down a better groove. I could relax a little.'

Jerry Wexler: 'There are not enough encomia in the language to do justice to that great Muscle Shoals rhythm section. After Dylan had decided the songs he was going to do, he laid them out for us. They didn't have much problem in getting the tracks together. In the first week we had finished the rhythm tracks and Dylan's vocals and at the end of the week, Dylan went home. Even the vocal backgrounds had been done because Dylan had brought a gospel group with him. Then we did the sweetening. It was all done quickly and on the cheap.'

Pick Withers: 'People take pot-shots at Dylan's voice but he phrases fantastically. There is instant identity too which is worth so much more than what we have these days. Music today is a bottle of milk; everywhere you go, it is the same. It has the same filters as pasteurisation. They all use Auto-Tune and even Michael Bublé had it on a live television show. It is killing individuality. Obviously, you must do your best to sing in tune but there are blue notes – that curious modulation in between the black and the white notes – and Auto-Tune doesn't tolerate any of it. That is awful really.'

Bob Dylan had accepted Christ as his saviour, but he had become an advocate of fundamentalist Christianity. He wrote uncompromising Bible-based lyrics even though his music itself had been rejuvenated. Dylan sounded like a Christian who is being unchristian, but musically he was performing well and singing excellently. Dylan did retain his humour. In 'Gonna Change My Way of Living', he tells us that he has 'A God-fearing woman, one I can easily afford'. What's more, she can do the Georgia crawl, a sensuous black dance from the 1920s.

The lyric of the opening track, 'Gotta Serve Somebody' went through various occupations and situations and said that, no matter what, you had to serve somebody. He included, 'You can call me Zimmy', a line he never sang on stage. Did it relate to some childhood taunt? When Natalie Cole wanted to do 'Gotta Serve Somebody', she was uncomfortable with the lines about guns and tanks, not to mention the Zimmy line. Her producer Phil Ramone contacted Bob and he wrote new lines for her including this fabulous couplet: 'You might be going nowhere or you might have been there before, Maybe all of a sudden you don't know yourself no more.'

The second track 'I Believe in You' is one of Dylan's greatest performances. The song is very good but is it a love song or a song about Jesus? It can be taken either way.

Bob had written 'Precious Angel' as a thank you to Mary Alice Artes, although the lyric is cryptic: why should she be 'suffering under the law'? The song contains the chilling image that 'Men will beg God to kill them and they won't be able to die': a grotesque line but not original – see Revelation Chapter 9 Verse 6. The track features Mark Knopfler at his most distinctive and some fine drumming in double-time from Pick Withers.

Pick Withers: 'Bob had Ron Tutt as his standby drummer on a retainer. He paid him a flat wage for the first call on his services. He told me when he was comfortable with the whole process – "I like the way you play the drums, Pick" – I had been playing reggae at the time, and he said, "I got this drummer and he can't play like that." So why did he have him on a retainer? Why not get in somebody else? It was an odd rationale. It's like a football manager putting someone who can't score at centre forward.'

The songs have lengthy lyrics, largely because Dylan is writing 'list songs', made famous by Cole Porter: that is, you get the idea for the first verse and then create numerous variations. 'Do Right to Me, Baby (Do unto Others)' is a good example: Dylan tells us one minute that he doesn't want to wink at anybody and the next that he doesn't want to shoot anybody: there's a big difference.

A reggae tune 'Man Gave Name to the Animals' was written to amuse the three-year-old son of a backing singer, Regina Havis. She was the daughter of Rev. Sam McCrary from the Fairfield Four.

Pick Withers: '*Slow Train Coming* was a good album and was one of his better sellers in that period, but I would have preferred to have played on *Blood on the Tracks* or *Desire*. I was deflated by all these Christian songs but 'God Gave Names to all the Animals' was beautiful.

It is like a lullaby but there is a scorpion's tail when he sings about the serpent: there is no couplet at the end and he just leaves it hanging there. It is Dylanesque.'

The album title and title song was later used in a Billy Ocean song, 'When The Going Gets Tough, The Tough Get Going', the line being 'Your love is like a slow train coming.'

At times, it seemed like Dylan wanted to return to the political arena. In 'When You Gonna Wake up', he railed against 'counterfeit philosophies' whether they came from Karl Marx or Henry Kissinger.

'When He Returns' had the same theme as 'The Mighty Quinn', though this is more serious. Dylan had originally written it for Carolyn Dennis but it suited his voice and had some fine gospel piano from Barry Beckett.

The album had nine tracks but with 46 minutes playing time, they were long ones. 'Gotta Serve Somebody' was a US Top 30 single and the B-side 'Trouble in Mind' had been left off the album. It is a conversation with Satan about women. Is it revealing or does it show he had been listening to Howlin' Wolf?

An outtake 'Ye Shall Be Changed' was sometimes performed live. Using the Old Testament terminology was deliberate, but it's hard to see what point he was making. Two years later, he wrote a different song with a similar theme and title, 'You Changed My Life'.

The irony, though, is that Bob Dylan of all people was telling people not to think for themselves. He said, 'If my followers are following me, indirectly they're going to be following God because I don't sing any song which hasn't been given to me by the Lord.' That sounded ominous.

Slow Train Coming had a cover in which a railway worker's axe had been turned into a cross. It was a Number 3 US album, his only Top 10 entry from 1976 to 1996. It was highly praised in *Rolling Stone* by Jann Wenner. It was not a compassionate album: non-believers would burn in hell. The answer, my friend, was coming from within.

George Melly said, 'People look for an answer but it seems to me that with as subtle a mind as Bob Dylan displayed in his early work, to embrace the certainties and simplicities of being a born-again Christian indicated a kind of panic. I didn't like that period. I found it cloying and irritating.'

Richard Thompson: 'There is always a tendency for songwriters to tell people about their own experiences and sometimes it's a good thing and sometimes it's not. I think you have to be gentle with people because whatever you feel, whatever you want for people, you can drive them away, no doubt of that.'

Possibly the biggest critic was John Lennon who was at home in the Dakota, parodying what he heard: 'Serve Yourself', 'Mama, Take this Make-Off Offa Me' and 'Stuck Inside of Lexicon with the Thesaurus Blues Again'.

Johnny Rogan: '*Slow Train Coming* was an extraordinarily good LP and in terms of his writing it was consistent. When I hear 'Gotta Serve Somebody' and 'When You Gonna Wake Up', it reminds me of the feelings I had when I first heard 'Positively Fourth Street' or 'It Ain't Me Babe'. It has the same viciousness. When Dylan converts to religion, he doesn't do it in the normal way. People say it is evangelical and it certainly is but if you note the way Dylan treated women in his songs, you will find that he is treating non-believers in the same way.'

Dylan biographer Paul Williams: 'Howard Alk lived next door to Dylan in Malibu and looked after his property when he was away. He liked my book *Dylan – What Happened* but said I had missed Dylan's awareness and fear of death, which led to his conversion. Elvis had died and that had affected Dylan. The book had concentrated on loneliness and guilt and the emptiness following the collapse of his marriage. Nevertheless, Dylan bought 100 copies to circulate amongst his friends.'

There is little about Dylan in *The Billboard Guide to Contemporary Christian Music*. Although *Slow Train Coming* was marketed as a Christian rock album, it was being bought by his fans, rather than those who followed Jesus Rock. One chain of stores wouldn't take his records. His mother, on the other hand, was trying to get him to listen to the rabbis.

On 22 May 1979 Bob Dylan was back in court defending himself regarding the defamation of Patty Valentine in 'Hurricane'. Dylan was asked about his wealth and he replied, 'You mean my treasure here on earth?' She claimed that Dylan implied that she had conspired to convict Hurricane Carter. In 1983, a federal court threw it out.

Bob Dylan knew Dave Kelly through the Vineyard Fellowship. He wanted to tour with the new songs and he asked Dave to be his PA as he had been through a similar experience and had made his own records. Bob knew that if he were to play only his gospel songs, he couldn't command arena audiences, though that would have been an enthralling experience – maybe it would have been a replay of 1966. After the euphoria of the world tour, Jerry Weintraub can't have been happy to promote a low-key affair, but on the other hand, he couldn't predict where this was going to end up.

In October 1979, Dylan rehearsed with both horns and female singers and decided it would be too expensive. He said to Dave Kelly, 'What do you think, the horns or the girls? We can't have both. It's financially ridiculous', but he had already decided that the horns had to go.

On 20 October 1979 Bob Dylan and his band performed three Christian songs on *Saturday Night Live* in New York where the guest host was Eric Idle. Dylan did it for Jerry Weintraub to promote the tour, but unlike Paul Simon., he hated doing the show and was grumbling throughout. After the show he was photographed with a fan, actually Mark Chapman, who would assassinate John Lennon the following year. It is possible that Chapman was thinking of other victims but we don't know.

For the first two weeks in November, Bob Dylan was playing the Fox Warfield Theatre in downtown San Francisco, seating 2,200. There were communal prayers for the musicians before the shows began. The show opened with the black girl singers (Regina Havis, Mona Lisa Young and Helena Springs) singing traditional gospel songs and ending with 'This Train Is Bound for Glory'. Dylan was on stage for 90 minutes, opening with 'Gotta Serve Somebody' and with Spooner Oldham on organ. There was no talking on the first night until the end: 'That's the show for tonight. I hope you've been uplifted.'

Dylan performed the same set each night as he was only doing his new material. Because of the content, Dylan wanted his vocals to be clear and he took care with his pronunciation. He commented afterwards, 'It was a whole different show and I don't know any other artist who has done that. It was a lot to remember.' Maybe, but actors do it all the time.

Joel Selvin's poor review for *San Francisco Chronicle* was widely syndicated. It was headlined, *Bob Dylan's God-Awful Gospel* and said that audience members were booing and walking out. Selvin wanted to make it another 1966. Dylan rang him at home to withdraw his rights to review further concerts: well, he could hardly stop him going, but no free tickets. It would have been pleasingly ironic if someone had shouted 'Jesus!' From a UK perspective, Dylan was coming across as a nutter. When Dylan saw the reviews, he wondered if the critics had been at the same show. Some of the audience had walked out but not many. A group of atheists picketed his shows.

The band improved night by night and Dylan's confidence grew. The final show at the Warfield was very good and he now ended the first half with a *Slow Train Comin'* outtake, 'No Man Righteous (No, Not One)'. During the fortnight, he performed the whole of *Slow Train Coming*, the first time he had done a complete album on stage, and seven unreleased ones. There was a banner at one show, 'Jesus loves old songs too!', but Dylan took no notice.

Some stage raps were printed in *Wanted Man*, but on the whole Dylan said little between songs. Dylan was preaching on the final show at the Warfield. He had become dogmatic and self-righteous: 'There's only two kinds of people. There's saved people and there's lost people.'

After the concerts, the band would go downstairs and Dylan would be playing again, but doing old rock'n'roll songs. On stage Dylan didn't sing any songs that hadn't been given to him by the Lord.

The Warfield was followed by four shows for World Vision International in Santa Monica. He was well received and Mona Lisa Young sang a new Dylan song, 'God Uses Ordinary People'.

Dylan was confrontational when he reached the Gammage Centre, Tempe, Arizona. He said to the hecklers, 'Don't you walk out before you hear the message. We know there's gonna be a new kingdom set up in Jerusalem. That's where Christ will set up his kingdom.' The next night he told them to repent their evil ways: 'Jesus is Lord and every race shall bow to him.'

Dylan was talkative when he got to Albuquerque, New Mexico: 'I told you the times they are a-changin' and they did. I saw the answer was blowin' in the wind and it was. I'm telling you now that Jesus is coming back and he is.' Even so, he was to say, 'I didn't care for the born again Christian audience – it was too much of a cult and too intense for me.' Really? He said that he wasn't pushing religion: 'Christ is no religion. Religion is another form of bondage which man invents to get himself to God.'

Dylan was full of choice quotes, and it was as though he was trying to get himself in a Dictionary of Quotations: 'Being noticed can be a burden. Jesus got himself crucified because he got himself noticed.' And 'Walking with Jesus is no easy trip, but it's the only trip.' Dylan told one audience, 'They used to say I was a prophet. Now I say Jesus is the answer and they say, "Bob Dylan, he's no prophet".'

In 2018 BBC-TV broadcast an *Arena* special, *Trouble in Mind*. There was film of Dylan performing and an actor Michael Shannon spoke some of his rants including an attack on lazy housewives who feed their children junk food. Around the same time, Shannon was playing Elvis in *Elvis & Nixon*.

The 2CD package to go with the documentary included previously unissued songs notably 'Blessed Is the Name', a gospel rave-up that would have been brilliant for Wilson Pickett but Dylan's voice was not up to it. Judging by the strapline referring to the 'legendary 1979-81 tours', this was an attempt to rewrite history and put the songs into Dylan's main cannon.

Dylan toured in January and February 1980 with Carolyn Dennis replacing Helena Springs in the backing group. When they were in Seattle, Dylan purchased a $30,000 engagement ring but the paper didn't know the intended recipient. He was dating Dennis at the time and would marry her in 1986.

Dylan returned to Muscle Shoals to make a second gospel album, to be called *Saved* and with Jerry Wexler and Barry Beckett producing. There was one cover, the country standard, 'A Satisfied Mind', which had good interplay with the backing voices but sounded like a warm-up at the beginning of a session. The title song 'Saved' was not the great Leiber and Stoller song recorded by LaVern Baker, but a rather nondescript one of his own.

The best song, 'In the Garden' was written on the piano and Dylan called it his 'classical piece'. Dylan had imagined a symphony orchestra behind him but he made do with Allen Ginsberg on harmonium. When Ginsberg said, 'The Christian God is one of forgiveness', Dylan responded with 'God also comes to judge.' Dylan provided a quote for *Allen Ginsberg Collected Poems 1947-1980*. He called him 'probably the single greatest influence on the American poetical voice since Walt Whitman.'

'Pressing On' rammed its point home, but again it would have sounded better with a gospel singer. Similarly, 'Solid Rock' was disappointing: a rave-up which didn't go anywhere.

'Covenant Woman' is an intriguing song about a girlfriend who has a contract with the Lord and knows plenty of unknown things about him.

There is some classic Dylan harmonica on 'What Can I Do for You' and the album was completed by 'Saving Grace' and 'Are You Ready'. It was nowhere near as good as *Slow Train Coming* and lacked the soulful groove which propelled the first one.

Straight after cutting the album, Bob Dylan and his band went to the Grammys at the Shrine Auditorium in Los Angeles where they performed 'Gotta Serve Somebody'. His track was up for Best Rock Vocal Performance and he sang it well with a few lyrical changes. He won his first Grammy beating Joe Jackson, Robert Palmer, Rod Stewart and Frank Zappa. He said, 'I didn't expect this and I want to thank the Lord for it.' He also thanked Jerry Wexler and Barry Beckett 'who believed'. Oddly, the record wasn't nominated for Best Inspirational Performance, which was won by B.J. Thomas with 'You Gave Me Love (When Nobody Gave Me a Prayer)'.

In March, Dylan played harmonica for his friend Keith Green on 'Pledge My Head to Heaven'. Keith was killed in a plane crash in July 1982.

Ronnie Hawkins met Dylan at Massey Hall, Toronto: 'Dylan had this black chick following him everywhere, carrying a Bible and praising the Lord every two seconds. Dylan told me that he had sold 12 million records since he became a Christian. I told him to become a Muslim and he might sell 60 million.'

He told the audience at Massey Hall: 'You just watch your newspapers. You're gonna see – maybe two years, maybe three years, maybe five years from now – but Jesus is coming back.'

Dylan was losing his sense of humour. When the *Montreal Gazette* ran a cartoon of Dylan, he returned it with a note: 'The law was given to Moses, but grace and truth comes through Jesus Christ (Book of John). Love, Bob Dylan.'

When Dylan was in Syracuse, New York, he said on stage, 'You know Bruce, he was born to run…but you can't run and you can't hide.' In Providence, Rhode Island, he said of his former glories, 'My old stuff's not gonna save anyone.' A couple of days later in Akron, Ohio, he told the audience, 'What a friendly crowd! I'm not used to friendly crowds. We're used to the Devil working all kinds of mischief in the crowds we've faced.'

Dylan had regarded colleges as his core audience but now hell could break loose at his gospel shows. He said, 'This really surprised me, that these kids didn't know any better, all from good homes and liberal minded to boot. It was a tough challenge but I was happier with the pimps and the hookers.' (Fox Warfield was in the midst of porno theatres.)

Saved was released in June 1980. Dylan had met Tony Wright who was designing the sleeve. He liked Wright's idea of a hand coming down and other hands stretching to reach it. Columbia didn't like it as the gospel intentions were too prevalent and this could affect sales. After a while, it was replaced with a photograph of Dylan on stage, the only Dylan cover to be replaced.

There was talk of Dylan doing Wembley Arena with Billy Graham and Billy Preston, but it seemed unlikely. His extremism wasn't what Billy Graham preached, who was more forgiving and regarded his job as winning everybody over to Christ.

Dylan was nominated in the Grammys for *Saved* as the Best Inspirational Performance, but Debby Boone was clearly more inspired with her album, *With My Song I Will Praise Him*.

By now many fans had given up on automatically buying the new Dylan album. It was not a hit album in the States. 'This turgid and featureless work was by some margin, the lowest point in the great man's career. But I was wrong: a year later *Shot of Love* had appeared which was even worse,' said Mark Ellen. Facing declining sales, Dylan probably realised that he needed to soften his approach, although he never said as much.

In October 1980, Bob was preparing for his next tour but backing down from his wholly Christian perspective. There would now be three categories: Christian, covers and chart successes. The covers included 'A Couple More Years' (Shel Silverstein for Dr. Hook), 'We Just Disagree' (Dave Mason), 'Fever' (Little Willie John, Peggy Lee) and 'Abraham, Martin and John' (Dion, Marvin Gaye). Audiences might have had a glimpse of recognition when he sang, 'Has anybody here seen our old friend Bobby?' A new version of 'Mr. Tambourine Man' was used in radio ads to promote the shows.

In November 1980, Dylan played 12 shows at the Fox Warfield. The audiences were thrilled when he went into 'Like a Rolling Stone'. There were new songs: 'City of Gold', 'Caribbean Wind' and 'The Groom's Still Waitin' at the Altar' (which sounded like vintage Dylan and was another biblical title). Oddly, he rarely did 'Knockin' on Heaven's Door' on his gospel shows. There were still several gospel songs in the shows and the *San Francisco Chronicle* called it 'a bore'.

Dylan talked about Leadbelly doing children's songs 'but he didn't change, he was the same man.' He referred to staying with Joan Baez in Carmel and nearly drowning in an underwater cave with the tide coming in.

His guests over the residency included Carlos Santana, Jerry Garcia and Maria Muldaur. He did 'Mr. Tambourine Man' with Roger McGuinn, while Michael Bloomfield was made for 'The Groom's Still Waiting at the Altar'. It was Bloomfield's last live performance before dying from a heroin overdose. He died, an addict and alcoholic in February 1981, after an erratic career, and yet Electric Flag had the potential to be a great band.

Dylan, who was smiling rather than scowling, said, 'This is a stage show we're doing. It's not a salvation ceremony.' So there's a change. He got more and more into the concerts as he was doing 17 songs at first and 25 by the end. Although not played in the shows, the band had worked on 'Over the Rainbow' (Judy Garland), 'Sad Songs and Waltzes' (Willie Nelson) and 'Sweet Caroline' (Neil Diamond).

Dylan said he first heard 'Fever' by Little Willie John in a bingo parlour in Detroit when he was 12 and then he did a fine version. He dedicated 'Señor' to 'Victoria whom I met in Mexico in 1972'. On his final show, he performed 'To Ramona' with David Grisman on mandolin.

For Christmas, Dylan gave Tim Drummond a gift-wrapped, bulletproof vest. Tim had been playing with Bob and had written 'Saved' with him. Now he would be the only white musician in James Brown's band.

In March 1981 Dylan was working on new songs at Rundown and then went to LA with Jimmy Iovine producing. When a song was not going well, Dylan said, 'Okay. Let's do 'White Christmas'.' 'Caribbean Wind' was on its fourth set of lyrics, and Dylan said, 'The inspiration had gone and I couldn't remember why I had started it in the first place.' He had started it in St. Vincent when he saw women working in a tobacco field and smoking pipes. It was about living with somebody for the wrong reasons.

In April he was back at Rundown and doing the title song of his next album, 'Shot of Love' with Bumps Blackwell, who was associated with Little Richard, as a guest producer. Otherwise the new album would be with Chuck Plotkin.

'Shot of Love' had a similar structure to 'Gotta Serve Somebody', and Dylan said, 'The song 'Shot of Love' is where I am spiritually, musically and romantically. It is my most perfect song.' Some lines were decidedly odd, 'Why would I want to take your life, You've only murdered my father, raped his wife.' Things were also suspect on 'Property of Jesus': you may be mocked but it doesn't matter because you're the property of Jesus. The song had been prompted by some snide remarks by Mick Jagger. With its rhythm and its message, it would have suited the Staple Singers.

He recorded 'Heart of Mine' with Ronnie Wood, Ringo Starr (on toms) and Clydie King at Rundown. Ronnie Wood commented on Bob and Clydie, 'They were chalk and cheese – she is outrageous and hamburger-eating while Bob nibbled. A fiery talent.' Howard Alk directed videos for 'Shot of Love' and 'Heart of Mine'.

'Heart of Mine' and 'Dead Man, Dead Man', despite its reggae groove, both sounded similar to 'Shot of Love', which gave the album a mind-numbing feel. It would have been better to include 'The Groom's Still Waiting at the Altar', which has been added to the reissue and lifts the whole product. It had been the B-side to 'Heart of Mine' and it was the first time that Dylan had changed the contents of a released album: Dylan's performance was too hurried, but that urgency was part of its strength.

Dylan wrote his best Christian song for this album, 'Every Grain of Sand'. It was about his conversion and was much more positive than usual, although it had an undercurrent of isolation and despair: 'The hour of my deepest need'. Some of its imagery was taken from William Blake who saw the world 'in a grain of sand'. The song itself is close to 'I Believe' in spirit.

There is a very good publisher's demo with Jennifer Warnes but with a dog barking in the background. For the recording, Dylan went to the piano and started singing. Dylan said, 'Clydie sings this with me. She is one of the greatest singers ever.' Bob sent 'Every Grain of Sand' to Nana Mouskouri who recorded it and it was also sung by Emmylou Harris. Bob rang Emmylou and said, 'I've heard 'Every Grain of Sand' and I'm blown away. That's as soulful as anything Aretha Franklin ever did.'

In the midst of his Christian songs, Bob recorded a tribute to the most contentious of all comedians, Lenny Bruce, and simply called that. He sings about sharing a taxi with Bruce and it has the bizarre line, 'He never robbed any churches, Nor cut off any baby's head.' That's presumably a reference to Herod but what is Dylan on about, or perhaps more to the point, what is Dylan on? Lenny Bruce would have been damned by the Born Again, very moral Christians, so this is another sign of Dylan's complexity. 'Watered-Down Love' had a great soul riff but it was too close to Betty Wright's 'Clean up Woman' for comfort. Writing in *Melody Maker*, David Fricke said, 'The tune is a dirge and the lyrics tenth-rate drivel.' Why though was *Shot of Love* so often reviewed as a trilogy? What did the reviewers know that we didn't?

Bob used a remake of the Everly Brothers' 'Let It Be Me' for a B-side. He discarded an excellent new song, 'Angelina'. It had a strong lyric with great rhymes, a fine tune and Dylan in great voice, a major work in fact: 'His eyes were two slits, make any snake proud'. It's surreal and mysterious and wholly engaging. Why is a black Mercedes driving in the combat zone? Who knows but it sounds good.

Dylan allowed Ry Cooder to rewrite 'I Need a Woman' before he recorded it for *The Slide Area* (1982). There are not many differences but in *Bob Dylan Lyrics 1962-1985*, Dylan reproduces Cooder's variations rather than his original.

Amazingly, that book doesn't even mention 'Angelina', a brilliant, brilliant outtake from *Shot of Love*. A staggeringly good lyric with a border sound and a moving vocal.

In May 1981 Bob and his musicians were planning a European tour at Rundown. A large number of songs were rehearsed although the tour itself was rigid. He planned to perform duets with Clydie King. In a try-out, the audiences heard him rocking up 'Masters of War'. Dylan came to Europe, but he was following a triumphant tour from Bruce Springsteen. The critics preferred Springsteen, although Philip Norman called Springsteen 'limp' in *The Sunday Times*.

In Colombes, France, police clashed with youths throwing bottles outside the stadium. Inside, *The Times*' reporter said that Dylan had 'reached rare heights of power and authority'.

The BBC broadcast a new play, *Bobby Wants to Meet Me* by Janey Preger and starring Philip Sayer and Michael Angelis. Alan Bleasdale: 'I would never want to write a play about Dylan partly out of respect and partly because he's a much better writer than me. If I did one it would be a play about Dylan's effect on people like *Bobby Wants to Meet Me*.'

A divorce was going through the Scottish High Court. Apparently, the husband used to disappear and once he went to London to see Bob Dylan. 'And this Mr. Dylan,' said his judge, 'is he a friend of the family?'

In another court, Albert Grossman sued Dylan for over $1m, claiming that Dylan overpaid royalties to himself and withheld other payments, but surely all earnings had been going through Grossman as his manager? Dylan had 30 days to respond. Dylan's lawyer maintained, 'Grossman owed Dylan a duty of undivided loyalty and honesty and had no right to take advantage of him.'

This was dragging on in September 1984. After the submissions, Grossman said, 'Dylan has claimed a lack of understanding of certain agreements, but the words which he does not understand are simple English words like partnership, purchase and simple numerical concepts like 10 years and 25%. This man is a master of the English language.' Justice Martin Evans told Bob to rewrite his submission in paragraphs containing concise, factual statements.

Bob Dylan played Earls Court from six nights from 26 June. *New Musical Express* said he was 'bored again'; *Melody Maker* 'bringing it all back wrong'. *The Guardian* 'He sells out and yet isn't a prisoner of his audience's expectations.' Bob and Clydie sang Jimmy Webb's 'Let's Begin'. Dylan played organ on 'Heart of Mine'. There was a half-hearted 'Here Comes the Sun' which ran out of steam when Dylan forgot the words. Dylan was slow hand-clapped during 'Abraham, Martin and John'.

Fred Dellar: 'I saw him at Earls Court. I found that a Dylan audience was not prepared to listen to anybody else. When Dylan brought on a gospel group to give himself a break, the audience started chatting amongst themselves and you could hardly hear them. It was only when Dylan came back that they would listen. They weren't interested in the new songs. I don't know why they went really. They might as well have sat at home with his old recordings.'

Dylan commented from the stage, 'A whole lot of people like to live in the past. I know I do myself sometimes – here's a song I used to do before I wrote songs.' He then performed 'Barbara Allen'.

The shows at Earls Court were followed by ones at Birmingham NEC. Dylan was in poor voice on the second night and some songs were cut short. Over in Stockholm, Dylan said he had heard Michael Wicke singing 'It's All Over Now Baby Blue' in Swedish and he hoped he could perform it as well. When they played Basel, Brigitte Bardot was in the audience. The band played one of her film themes as an instrumental.

The tour ended with a fatal accident in Avignon. A member of the crowd fell onto some electrical cables and in the confusion a girl fell from a wall, with both of them being killed. Oblivious to this, Dylan and band played acoustically until power was restored and his electric set could continue, but surely the concert should have been cut short.

Columbia had been against the third Christian album, *Shot of Love*, and they didn't like Pearl Beach's cover based on the op-art cartoons of Roy Lichtenstein. They changed the back cover: the original idea was to have a Cadillac in the sky with the number plate M1125 666. That is St. Matthew's Gospel, Chapter 11 Verse 25. Instead, there was a photograph of Dylan sniffing a rose. More to the point, Columbia should have asked why 'Caribbean Wind', 'Angelina' and 'The Groom's Still Waiting at the Altar' were not on the album.

Bob was back in the running at the Grammys. *Shot of Love* was up for Best Inspirational Performance, but the category was won by B. J. Thomas for *Amazing Grace*.

In early October, Dylan was preparing for a North American tour. He had brought Al Kooper into the band, but Carolyn Dennis had left. When Bob was playing 'Like a Rolling Stone' really slow, Al suggested he sped it up. Dylan said, 'I'll drink some coffee before I go on tomorrow night.'

Al Kooper wryly said, 'By the end of the tour, it was hardly Christian songs at all and so I helped to bring Bob back to the real world. This is what I should be remembered for, if nothing else.'

Larry Kegan joined them in Milwaukee and they played Chuck Berry's 'No Money Down' with Larry on saxophone. On the same show, Bob and Clydie did a duet of 'It's all in the Game'. Bob gave an interview to *Milwaukee Journal* and there wouldn't be any more for two years.

The *New York Times* said it was a 'fascinating performance by a magnetic renegade'. Howard Alk filmed the concert in New Orleans and there was talk of a live album, but only two performances have been officially released. On one concert, Dylan and the band sang 'Happy Birthday to You' to Howard: would anybody else have known what was going on?

The tour finished in Lakeland, Florida on 21 November 1981 as a further date in Tallahassee had been cancelled due to poor sales. Dylan performed 28 songs including a six-song encore. Apart from guest appearances, this would be his last concert for three years and his voice was drained.

On 1 January 1982 Howard Alk died at Rundown, possibly an accident, possibly suicide. As a result, Dylan was to close the studio. One of the final sessions was with Allen Ginsberg and they were writing lyrics together.

In March 1982 Bob Dylan was inducted into the *Songwriters Hall of Fame*. Dylan said, 'I think this is pretty amazing because I can't read or write a note of music. Thank you. It's thrilling, kinda like the Baseball Hall of Fame.' Bob wanted to be photographed with Dinah Shore.

Sammy Cahn told me, 'I knew Bob Dylan because I had inducted him into the Songwriters Hall Of Fame. He said to me, "I've done one of your songs." I said, "YOU have done one of MY songs?" I expected him to say something like 'Teach Me Tonight', but it was 'All My Tomorrows'. That song was in the same film as 'High Hopes' and was sung by Sinatra but it is not as well-known.'

Despite the award, Dylan was feeling blocked. He left a message on Doc Pomus' answerphone and asked if he could meet him. Doc wasn't busy and had his friend Joel Dorn ring him every 15 minutes to maintain a pretence that he was wanted for film scores. Dylan said that when he was young he felt like a transmitter; now he was self-conscious and his mind wandered. Doc told him that to believe in himself. Dylan asked if they could work together, but nothing came of this.

On 6 June 1982, dubbed Peace Sunday, Bob played at the anti-nuke rally at Rose Bowl, Pasadena in front of 85,000. He sang 'Blowin' in the Wind' (with Joan Baez, forgetting words and being wilfully idiosyncratic), 'With God on Our Side' and Jimmy Buffett's 'A Pirate Looks at 40', a rare occasion where he had the lyric to hand. Dan Fogelberg, Jackson Browne and Stevie Wonder were on the bill, and Dylan left straight after his set.

He recorded with Clydie King in Los Angeles, probably for an album of duets. Again, nothing was released. Dylan: 'It's great but it doesn't fall into any category that a record company knows how to deal with.'

In August 1982 Dylan appointed Elliot Roberts as his manager – good luck.

Dylan was no longer passionate about writing Christian songs and he commented cryptically, 'Jesus only preached for three years.' He was back with Judaism as if nothing had happened. Bob Spitz: 'Bob Dylan is an Orthodox Jew these days, but he has never renounced Christianity. He has a capacity for spirituality, certainly more than most people. He embraced Christianity and now he had turned a corner and gone on.'

Dylan arranged the bar mitzvah of his son Samuel. The following year he was at the Western Wall in Jerusalem, wearing a prayer shawl, for the bar mitzvah of his eldest son, Jesse. A photo on the hills above Jerusalem was on the inner sleeve of his next album, *Infidels*. (You could argue that Dylan was turning his back on Jerusalem.) In June 1983 Dylan spent time with a Jewish sect the Lubavitches in Brooklyn.

Dylan was always keen on family events. In June 1983 he was at Mari's graduation in St. Paul with Sara.

He wanted a producer for his next album. He talked to Elvis Costello and Frank Zappa but went with Mark Knopfler. Knopfler heard the new songs and in particular liked 'Prison Guard' although it was not recorded.

On 16 February 1983 Dylan saw Bonnie Koloc at The Other End and then headed to Lone Star Café to join Rick Danko and Levon Helm. Dylan joined them for 'Willie and the Hand Jive' and a few more oldies.

There was a new wave of UK political songwriting emerging from punk and the divisive premiership of Margaret Thatcher. Morrissey and Marr were seen as the new Lennon and McCartney and Billy Bragg the new Dylan. Said Peter Jenner, who managed Bragg, 'I thought that someone going round being a bit Dylanish, doing social-realism would go down well.' He was right or rather, left.

During April and May 1983, Dylan booked a month of sessions in the Power Station in New York. The musicians included Sly Dunbar (drums), Robbie Shakespeare (bass), Mick Taylor (guitar) and Mark Knopfler, who was producing. They recorded 16 original songs as well as 14 covers and instrumentals.

Dylan had written very good, if rather wordy, songs, some up there with his best work. The result was the album, *Infidels*, a title that might imply another religious selection. Dylan was moving away from religion (and its Vegas trimmings) and rather surprisingly, returning to the political arena: you could see the songs as his State of the Union address. *Infidels* is an album where Bob is hating everything and it was recorded shortly after he had been in the Middle East: the world is on the brink and about to explode.

The song that resonates best is 'Licence to Kill', a brilliant take on James Bond's authorisation as well as American gun control and suicide bombers ('His brain has been mismanaged with great skill.') Dylan appears to be saying that this is a male problem as the woman is just sitting there 'as the night grows still', and she could represent the assassin's mother.

In the opening verse of 'Licence to Kill', Dylan sings, 'Man has invented his doom, first step was touching the moon'. Dylan has commented on wasting money in space exploration but what does this mean? It's only a song and doesn't have to mean anything but it is still perplexing. Sometimes I wish Dylan's songs came with footnotes. This incidentally is one marked difference with Neil Young who is infatuated with space travel in several of his songs.

In 1986 he sang 'Licence to Kill' in Sydney dedicating it to the space programme. Seven astronauts had been killed in a space shuttle accident on the Challenger. Dylan told the audience, 'They had no business being up there in the first place, as if we haven't got enough problems down here on earth.'

'Neighbourhood Bully' has to be about Israel: 'He's made a garden of paradise in the desert sand' though it contains an element of sarcasm.

'Union Sundown' is about the twilight years for the unions as everything is manufactured abroad. He is encouraging listeners to buy goods made in America. This is muddled thinking, rather like Donald Trump, as well as a muddled arrangement. There is a Rastafarian reference in the very title 'I and I', a complex song which relates to 'Union Sundown' as 'I've made shoes for everyone, even you, while I still go barefoot'.

We return to religion for 'Man of Peace', a strong song about how Satan can come into the world disguised as a man of peace. But who was meant to be the man of peace? Dylan was being mysterious again.

There are two love songs on the album. Dylan has described 'Sweetheart like You' as 'a Byronesque ballad'. This was Dylan's first video since 'Subterranean Homesick Blues', made with Clydie King and Carla Olsen of the Textones and directed by Mark Robinson. He was performing to a cleaner in a deserted club and miming well.

'Don't Fall Apart on Me Tonight' could have been a power ballad as a big-voiced singer could have made this a pop anthem. It's not too late either. It's not Dylan's greatest song but it is a hit that has been missed.

The 'Jokerman' in Dylan's song is probably Dylan himself, a Mr. Tambourine Man singing while the world explodes, but it could be Jesus or even Satan. Whatever, it is an excellent track with a reggae rhythm.

There was a clever video for 'Jokerman' showing a lot of art works and the director George Lois was having no nonsense. Dylan would lip-sync correctly. He said, 'If it doesn't match up, you'll look like a schmuck.' Dylan later said, 'All I saw was a shot of me from my mouth to my forehead and I figure "Isn't that something? I'm paying for that".' The cutting in the video implies that the jokerman is Dylan himself.

Ian Hunter: 'If you are going to be influenced by somebody you might as well be influenced by the best. 'Jokerman' immediately comes to mind with its great chords. Dylan is not really a rocker, he is more of a novelist, up there with E.L. Doctorow, he's funny too, he makes me laugh, and now he's a lead guitar player, that makes me laugh too.'

Dylan and Knopfler fell out over the choice of songs for the album and the way they were mixed. Knopfler didn't think 'Union Sundown' was strong enough. Most of all, Knopfler liked clean, crisp music and Bob preferred something dirtier. Bob said, 'This sounds like the Eagles; it's predictable, you know what's coming.' They would have resolved their differences but Knopfler had commitments with Dire Straits. The tracks were mixed by someone else and Bob had final approval.

Infidels, which only had eight tracks, was released in October 1983. It was a competitive time to have an album released as he was vying with Paul McCartney, the Rolling Stones and the Who as well as newer acts. Dylan said, 'The purpose of music is elevate the spirit and inspire, not to push some product down your throat.'

Another track, a cover of a little known country song by Troy Seals, 'Angels Flying Too Close to the Ground', was used as a B-side, erroneously credited to Dylan at first. It's an excellent performance but the song needed a better-placed title line. Other covers recorded included 'Sultans of Swing' (Dylan singing Dire Straits – I'd love to have heard that!) and 'Green Green Grass of Home'.

The Dylan authority Ian Woodward says, "'Blind Willie McTell' was in the original track listing for *Infidels*. The album was going to be in two parts: Part 1, a criticism of society and Part 2, redemption, which would include 'Blind Willie McTell'. The art work was prepared but Dylan changed his mind, altered the track selection and did some new vocals."

Even though *Infidels* was a strong LP and better than we would have hoped after the Christian era, they could have done better and Dylan ignored two major songs – 'Blind Willie McTell' and 'Foot of Pride' as well as 'Death Is Not the End' and a song about McCarthyism, 'Julius and Ethel'. 'Someone's Got a Hold of My Heart' was reworked as 'Tight Connection to My Heart' for the *Empire Burlesque* album in 1985.

Tom Russell: 'Anyone who thought Bob Dylan's powers were waning in the 1980s was completely wrong. 'Series of Dreams' from 1989 is way beyond what anyone else is capable of writing and 'Blind Willie McTell' is outstanding. It is Faulknerian with mysterious flashes of the south. You couldn't say what it was about except some bluesman looking through a hotel window.' Or perhaps Dylan out on tour.

Patrick Humphries: 'I love the atmosphere of that song. You really feel that you are in this bleak hotel room. It is dark and the windswept plains of Texas are curling away in the night.'

Michael Gray: 'Blind Willie McTell was born in Georgia at the beginning of the twentieth century and he died when he was about 60 at the end of the 1950s. If he had lived a couple more years, he would have seen himself rediscovered in the Blues Revival. His great song 'Statesboro Blues' was revived by the Allman Brothers and it was released on the record that accompanied Sam Charters' book *The Country Blues*, which was published just after McTell had died. The song makes play of one of Dylan's early pseudonyms which was Blind Boy Grunt. Grunt suggests inarticulacy and McTell suggests articulacy. Dylan loved pre-war blues and Blind Willie McTell was an important figure in it.'

Is the song a generic song about the blues or is Dylan saying that there is nobody as good as Blind Willie McTell, or possibly both? I would say that he was paying tribute to the entire heritage of the blues. The lyric is packed with southern images, seeing things as they were. He is ruminating on corruption in the south but he is more sorrowful than angry.

Dylan knows that nobody sings the blues like Blind Willie McTell and that is almost a parody of the Columbia strapline of the 60s, 'Nobody Sings Dylan like Dylan', which pointed out that he didn't just write pretty songs for the likes of Peter, Paul and Mary.

Dylan recorded 'Blind Willie McTell' both acoustically and electrically. Michael Gray: 'Dylan never thought he sang it right and yet it is one of his most beautiful performances. Artists aren't always the best judges of their work. He was writing a lot of varied material around the time of *Infidels*. He could have made a great album out of *Infidels* and it is not just by adding 'Blind Willie McTell'. There were other things that were left off that record that should never have been left off. In my opinion of course, not in Bob's.'

Alan Bleasdale: 'The *Bootleg* series reveals what astonishing stuff he left out of his 1980s albums. 'Blind Willie McTell' is a throwback to 1962 but with more vision and awareness. He is not the best judge of his work: 'Blind Willie McTell' is left out and yet he releases 'Wiggle Wiggle'. Sometimes the writer is the last person to appreciate what he has written and that could be an argument for having critics. I am sure though that if I had written 'Blind Willie McTell', I'd have noticed it was good and put it out.'

In 1993 the reconstituted Band (Levon Helm, Rick Danko, Garth Hudson) recorded a superb version with Champion Jack Dupree on piano for their album, *Jericho*. Bob Dylan: 'I started playing 'Blind Willie McTell' because I heard The Band doing it. It had never been developed fully. Sometimes I hear a cover of one of my songs and figure I can do it just as well.'

Another excellent song was his lengthy 'Foot of Pride', which was about the perils of vanity and how you shouldn't trust anyone. Don't be manipulated, be yourself because, once again, the eternal judgment is coming. It didn't have a memorable tune but it had a stunning, cryptic lyric. If anything it is about hypocrisy and how benefactors sing 'Amazing Grace' all the way to the Swiss banks.

Other outtakes included 'Tell Me', a title he had purloined from the Rolling Stones, which was a pleasant pop song with a Spanish tinge with backing from the Full Force vocal group. 'Lord Protect My Child' is a prayer from a father to his God and hoping for protection should he die early: 'My only prayer is if I can't be there, Lord, protect my child'.

In January 1984 Bob Dylan gave some unissued songs to Dave Edmunds for the Everly Brothers' reunion album, but they went with 'Lay Lady Lay' at last.

In February Stevie Wonder announced the Song of the Year at the Grammys. It went to Sting for 'Every Breath You Take', but as Sting was in Australia, Bob accepted the award on his behalf. While in New York, Dylan attended gigs by Al Kooper and Peter Wolf and hung out with Keith Richards and Ronnie Wood.

Dylan appeared on *The Late Show with David Letterman*, backed by an LA band formed by Charlie Quintana of the Plugs. They had not worked together before and rehearsed the previous evening. Bizarrely, it worked, especially when the opener Sonny Boy Williamson's 'Don't Start Me to Talkin'' was a song they had not played. They also performed 'Licence to Kill' and 'Jokerman'. After recording the set, Dylan watched the New York Knicks playing basketball at Madison Square Garden.

Dylan agreed to a lengthy European tour as a double header with Santana, with a few dates as a triple-header with Joan Baez. There would be 29 shows over six weeks. Dylan and his musicians – Mick Taylor, Ian McLagan, Colin Allen, all Brits with Greg Sutton of Lone Justice – rehearsed in Los Angeles. They included three new songs – 'Dirty Lie', 'Enough Is Enough', 'Angel of Rain' – but they weren't used as this was a heritage tour with huge audiences. Dylan was asked at a press conference if he had any messages for the audience. He said, 'Nothing, I'm here to play a show.'

Formerly from the Small Faces and the Faces, Ian McLagen lived in Point Dume and he had heard a guitarist on a hill every day. It could have been Dylan. Ian said to Bob, 'It's a pleasure and an honour to work with you,' and Bob replied, 'I hope you feel the same when the tour is over.' Bob admired Ian McLagen's shirt so he gave it to him. Dylan wore it in Verona, where the tour opened. Bob is wearing the shirt on the cover of his 1985 album, *Empire Burlesque*: he has his sleeves rolled up as though he were Rod Stewart.

The band was under-rehearsed with ragged openings and endings, but blame Dylan for that. Mick Taylor sounded like he did on *Exile on Main Street* for 'Man of Peace'. Carlos Santana joined Dylan for 'Blowin' in the Wind' and 'Tombstone Blues'.

Dylan nearly cancelled a concert in Hamburg as his back was hurting him. Joan Baez felt they could have done more together but 'Bob is allergic to the word, rehearse.' She knew that anyway. She had been booked for eight well-paid concerts and would smile and do it. On June 3 in Munich, Dylan, Baez and Carlos Santana were all together for 'Blowin' in the Wind' and 'I Shall Be Released'.

In Rotterdam Dylan sang new verses for 'Tangled Up in Blue' and 'Simple Twist of Fate', though he struggled to remember them. In true show-biz fashion, he split the audience in two and had them singing different parts. The *Daily Express* reviewer said that this was 'the least inspired rock concert it has been my misfortune to attend.'

Reviewing Bob Dylan in Vienna in the *Sunday Times,* Simon Frith said it was 'Bob Dylan with a limited British pub rock band'. He complained of discomfort, poor visibility and drunks, but is that Dylan's fault? Dylan sang Mickey and Sylvia's 'Love Will Make You Fail at School', an odd choice for a 43-year-old man.

When Dylan was in Nice, he spoke to Antoine De Caunes, his first TV interview for nearly 20 years. Watch Dylan's face and notice how bored he is. He said that he wrote because he needed something to sing and that he had studied French poets, but the drift from the Beat poets to the French poets to his own surrealistic writing had happened naturally. Asked about the beautiful blonde he was seen with, he said, 'That was Mick Taylor.'

In Rome, Dylan appeared in a black velvet frock coat with a white ruffle-fronted shirt and waistcoat. Ian McLagen said, 'You're looking very Byronic.' Bob didn't speak to him for three days as he thought Ian had said, 'You're looking very moronic.'

There was an audience of 100,000 at Parc de Sceaux in Paris. Bob sang 'The Times They Are A-Changin'' with Hugues Aufray and 'It's All Over Now, Baby Blue' with Van Morrison.

On 5 July 1984, after a month of European concerts, Bob had an English speaking audience in Newcastle, doing a very good 'Knockin' on Heaven's Door' with his harmonica and Carlos Santana's guitar inspiring each other. He played with the melody of 'Masters of War' and the song had lost its bite. Maybe the singer has to be angry to make it work, especially the last line.

On July 7, the hottest day of the year, Bob Dylan and Santana were joined by Eric Clapton, Chrissie Hynde and Van Morrison with UB40 in support in front of 70,000 fans at Wembley Stadium. He did an excellent 'It Ain't Me Babe' with the audience joining in. Dylan took his final bow early and did a one-hour encore which featured ten songs.

Critics remarked that this concert didn't have the party atmosphere of Elton John a few days earlier, but Dylan didn't have giant screens and he changed 'A Hard Rain's A-Gonna Fall' so that the audience couldn't sing along, let alone himself. 'Highway 61 Revisited' was revisited as a guitar showcase. 'Maggie's Farm' had become the unofficial Labour party anthem and its reception might have taken Dylan by surprise.

Susie Pullen was in charge of Dylan's on-stage clothes. She obviously has a good sense of humour: indeed, I never knew until I rehearsed this book that he had any professional help and it's taken me by surprise. Here she had dressed him as a Victorian undertaker.

Dylan took the same approach with 40,000 fans at Slane Castle, County Meath by having another ten-song encore. Van Morrison sang 'It's All Over Now, Baby Blue' and 'Tupelo Honey' with him while Bono wrote and performed a new verse for 'Blowin' in the Wind'.

The estate was owned by Lord Henry Mountcharles. One fan, Kevin Leonard, 19, was drowned when he tried to swim the River Boyne to get in free. There was violence when some fans were refused drinks at a pub. The police station was under siege and it was described as the worst disturbance since the Battle of the Boyne in 1690, which is pushing it a bit. The Stones had played there in 1982 and everything had been fine.

Reporter to Bob Dylan: 'Where do you go from here?'
Bob Dylan: 'I'm going home.'
And he was. It was the end of the European tour.

Bono interviewed Dylan for *Hot Press*: Dylan said, 'You go into a studio now and they got rugs on the floor, settees and pinball machines and videos and sandwiches coming at you every ten minutes. Once you'd make an album in three or four days: now it takes four days to get a drum sound.'

Bootleg tapes were mounting and Dylan fans were eager to get the recordings of the latest performances, no matter how bad the recordings (and indeed the performances themselves). You could get good live recordings if Dylan happened to be switched on that night, but he never pandered to audiences, except ironically, and he relished being perverse.

The third official 'in concert' album, *Real Live*, was released in December 1984. It featured six performances from Wembley, two from Slane Castle and two from Newcastle. The most enjoyable track was 'It Ain't Me Babe' from Wembley and Carlos Santana joined him on 'Tombstone Blues' in Newcastle. This album included the revised lyric for 'Tangled Up in Blue': the girl is now married to someone four times her age and 'He had one too many lovers, And none of them were too refined.'

It was a ragged collection. Glyn Johns sent Dylan the rough mixes and asked him to pick what he wanted: 'He picked every performance that was absolutely fucked – wrong chords, bum notes, feedback, anything that would make it totally unacceptable.'

In mid-July, Bob and Ronnie Wood joined Al Green and his band for a few oldies including 'Mountain of Love' at the Intergalactic Studio in New York. In a separate session,

Ronnie joined him for a new song, 'Driftin' Too Far from Shore' and said, 'It should have been a brilliant, vibrant rock'n'roll track but when I heard it on the record, I said, "Bob, what happened. Where's your piano, where's the drums?" He said he didn't know the producer well and sometimes he didn't like to interfere.' This is a brilliant reply as Dylan produced the track himself.

Dylan's girlfriend Carole Childs suggested that he gave 'Go Way Little Boy' to the LA band, Lone Justice. Dylan and Ronnie Wood saw them in New York. Bob wasn't sure that they were doing the song right so Maria McKee sang it more like him and he was happy.

Van Morrison and Bob Dylan shared an accountant who invited them to dinner on the same night. Not a word was said by Van or Bob and when Bob left, Van said, 'I think Bob was on form tonight, don't you?'

George Harrison recorded a new Dylan song, 'I Don't Want to Do It,' which he performed on the *Porky's Revenge* soundtrack in 1984. The franchise had run its course and the crass teen movie flopped, The soundtrack album was lost and yet it contained a fine Dylan song from one of the Beatles.

In October, Bob Dylan played with Cruzados in Los Angeles – they had backed him on the *Letterman* show, led by Charlie Quintana. Their 'House of the Rising Sun' was not released. In November he recorded new songs: 'In the Summertime', 'Freedom for the Stallion' and several instrumentals. In December he recorded 'Something's Burning Baby' and the 12-minute 'New Danville Girl', which had 17 verses.

Dylan dedicated his 1985 *Lyrics* to his new-born daughter, Nanette. Who was she? Happy families!

CHAPTER 13

What Was It You Wanted?

I. Saving the World

It all began with Michael Buerk. In the autumn of 1984, the BBC news reporter told of the famine in Ethiopia and Bob Geldof of the Boomtown Rats was watching. He determined to do something about it as soon as possible. 'I'm not interested in the bloody system,' he said. 'Why has he no food? Why is he starving to death?' He rang his wife, Paula Yates, who was hosting *The Tube* in Newcastle and asked her to put him through to their guest, Midge Ure of Ultravox. Bob and Midge agreed that the only thing they knew about was making records and as 50% of the monies generated on a single went to the songwriters, it should be a new song. It was coming up for Christmas and Midge said, 'We knew if we made it a Christmas song, we would pull at the purse strings as well as the heartstrings.'

All-star charity singles date back to the 1950s, but Bob Geldof organised this one on an unprecedented scale. He secured a major studio for a day and requested one chart act after another to take part. Bob asked the stars 'to leave their egos outside the studio' and they recorded the song without any hassles. The single featured David Bowie, Boy George, Marilyn, George Michael, Paul Weller, Paul Young and members of Bananarama, the Boomtown Rats, Duran Duran, Frankie Goes To Hollywood, Heaven 17, Kool & The Gang, Shalamar, Spandau Ballet, Status Quo, Sting, U2 and Ultravox.

The singers were adding their voices to a track laid down by Midge Ure with Phil Collins on drums. Midge recalls, 'I sang my guide vocal in middling keys with no extremes, which meant that nobody would be given anything that they couldn't sing. I was standing next to Bono when he got the line, 'Tonight, thank God, it's them instead of me', a controversial line that Bob insisted should be included. They ran the track and Bono took that line up an octave and belted it out like you wouldn't believe. It was like standing next to a wonderful opera singer, and it was absolute magic.'

The picture sleeve was designed by Peter Blake, who was famous for his artwork on *Sgt. Pepper's Lonely Hearts Club Band*. The Band Aid single sold 3.5m copies, easily making the biggest-selling single in the UK to date: it topped the UK charts for five weeks, going into January 1985. The artists, the musicians, the record companies and the distributors had agreed to waive their profits, but Bob Geldof was less successful with the Government, who insisted on the payment of VAT, although this unpopular decision was revised for some subsequent charity singles. They hoped to raise £100,000, but it turned out to be several million and kept on growing as it is included on subsequent Christmas compilations and downloads. It was however only a moderate hit in the US, stalling at Number 13.

Harry Belafonte wanted to put together a benefit concert featuring black artists to raise money for Africa. The rock manager Ken Kragen thought a US version of Band Aid would be better and he handled Lionel Richie. Hence, America responded to Band Aid with USA for Africa (United Support of Artists for Africa), the prime movers being Belafonte, Michael Jackson and Lionel Richie. After three days of individual preparation, Michael Jackson and Lionel Richie wrote 'We Are the World' in a few hours – 'I'd throw out a line and Michael would come back with a greater one,' said Lionel. Unlike the sorrow of the British song, 'We Are the World' could be regarded as jingoistic. The record would be arranged and produced by Quincy Jones.

'We Are the World' was recorded after the Grammys ceremony on 28 January 1985. That was a brilliant move as most of the country's key performers were in Los Angeles for the event. Bob Dylan had chosen not to attend the Grammys but he was recording nearby at Cherokee Studios and he could leave early.

It was touch and go as he was not sure that such events were for him. He was to say: 'It's a worthwhile idea but I wasn't so convinced about the message of the song. I don't think people can save themselves.' Stevie Wonder encouraged him to take part.

The singers went to the A&M studios in Hollywood where the backing tape was waiting. They had to share six microphones. The soloists were Lionel Richie, Stevie Wonder, Paul Simon, Kenny Rogers, James Ingram, Tina Turner, Billy Joel, Michael Jackson, Diana Ross, Dionne Warwick, Willie Nelson, Al Jarreau, Bruce Springsteen, Kenny Loggins, Steve Perry, Daryl Hall, Huey Lewis, Cyndi Lauper, Kim Carnes, Bob Dylan and Ray Charles. Not to mention Bette Midler, Smokey Robinson, Waylon Jennings and several others singing in the background. Bob Geldof, although not American, was invited to join the recording. The comedian Dan Aykroyd was an unusual choice but he was one of the Blues Brothers.

The video is a remarkable piece of pop history and as Ben Elton remarked, 'You must know who Bob Dylan is. He's the one who can't sing in the 'We Are the World' video.'

Dylan heard Ray Charles and Willie Nelson talking about doing something separately for the impoverished farmers in the American south. This thought was to stay with Dylan and would manifest itself unexpectedly.

'We Are the World' was released in March 1985 with 800,000 copies shipped to record stores, which were all sold in the first week. It topped the US chart for four weeks and the UK equivalent for two. It won Grammys for the Song of the Year and the Record of the Year.

Because it was not a seasonal song like 'Do They Know It's Christmas?', 'We Are the World' has not been revived in the same way. The Canadian Band Aid single, 'Tears Are Not Enough' by Northern Lights (Bryan Adams, Gordon Lightfoot, Joni Mitchell, Neil Young and many more) was not released as a single in the UK, although it is, to my ears, the best of the three songs.

Bob Geldof wanted to continue his fund-raising and thought of a live concert for famine relief in Ethiopia. The broadcasters came on board and two concerts were arranged for 13 July 1985: one at Wembley Stadium in London and the other at JFK Stadium in Philadelphia. With the power of Concorde and a couple of helicopters, Phil Collins played at both events. As well as solo songs, he played with Sting in London and Eric Clapton in Philadelphia.

Pete Seeger: 'I think events like Live Aid and Farm Aid are worth doing but I wish they had kept that original name, Band Aid, because that is what they are. We're putting on a Band Aid and there is a basic problem that has to be solved. Just as doctors realise that there is only so much they can do to cure people who get sick, the big job is to prevent the sickness. Preventative medicine. We've got to look at the whole way our economic systems work in different parts of the world and stop these screwy situations where people are told not to produce food because if they do, they'll go broke, but there's hungry people in this world who need to be fed. We should be producing all the food we possibly can.'

Live Aid would be the biggest concert in rock history and through television rights would have the biggest audience ever. There were no problems in finding artists to appear and a few choices were controversial; why have Queen when they had played Sun City and why had Geldof included his own group, the Boomtown Rats, but fair do's, Live Aid was his idea.

Quite rightly in view of their songs for just causes, both Bob Dylan and Joan Baez were invited to appear. In retrospect, they should have been together: the two artists most associated with 60s protest could have made a stunning contribution.

They would have had to bury their differences, but Joan was always prepared to do that. Joan Baez says, 'We had been on bad terms since the Dylan / Santana / What's-her-name tour but he greeted me and was smiling like a nervous kid. I went over and hugged him.'

Joan Baez opened the Philadelphia show and 'There But for Fortune' and a rewritten 'We Shall Overcome' would have been ideal. Instead, she performed a cappella for six minutes with the crowd joining in, a bold move especially when most people didn't know the words of 'Amazing Grace'. She said each line before she sang it so it didn't sound musical at all. You could hear the sigh of relief in the stadium when she switched to an a cappella 'We Are the World', but the audience only knew the chorus. She did okay but she could easily have made a bigger impact. At Wembley, Elvis Costello, restricted to just one song, chose 'All You Need Is Love', perfect for a singalong.

Joan Baez had made a wrong judgment but compared to Bob Dylan, her set was one of genius. The promoter Bill Graham said he would create a band for him but Dylan wasn't too struck on that and thought of playing solo, which could have been fine. In the days before the concert, he was with Ronnie Wood. The Rolling Stones, surprisingly perhaps, were not on the bill, but Mick Jagger was performing with Tina Turner and had cut a charity single of 'Dancing in the Street' with David Bowie.

Ronnie Wood suggested to Bob that he called Keith Richards and they would accompany him. Bob thought back to *Concert for Bangla Desh* which had worked well with George Harrison and Leon Russell. So far so good but their rehearsal time was spent chatting and drinking and they cut it short to see Lonnie Mack at the Lone Star Café. Ronnie told Bob, 'Start them any way you like and we'll be with you.' Even then, it could have worked out fine as the musicians were talented and experienced.

Michael Des Barres: 'I was with Power Station because they had replaced Robert Palmer with me as he didn't want to tour. I did the tour and there I was at Live Aid. It was an amazing day. We all stayed in the same hotel. I loved performing with two billion people watching. There was Tina Turner writing words on her arm and Madonna throwing up. The key to these days is 'Don't think, just get up there and do it.' It was raising money for a wonderful cause but it was rock stars doing it so there was a duality to that day. Dylan was in the trailer billowing marijuana smoke and although I was fascinated to see Dylan and Keith and Woody, they were playing different songs at the same time.'

Dylan's biographer Howard Sounes: 'It was a very hot day and I spoke to his girlfriend Carole Childs who was with him and she said, "It was unbelievably hot so everyone was drinking." There was a lot of time waiting to go on stage and they were in his trailer drinking rum and Coke all afternoon.'

In an extraordinary over-the-top performance, even by her standards, Patti LaBelle let rip with a five-minute 'Forever Young', packed with grace notes and leaving the tune and the meaning of its lyric well behind. Patti went screeching into the audience while the backing girls repeated, 'Why don't you stay, stay that way?' Top marks for effort but none for sensitivity. Did Bob see it and what he did think?

There had been problems at Live Aid, notably with the last act on the Wembley stage, Paul McCartney. He was there for one song, 'Let It Be' and his microphone wasn't switched on. Fortunately the technicians resolved it after a minute and a huge cheer burst out in the stadium.

Because of his eminence, Bob Dylan was to be the final act, which would be followed by everybody singing 'We Are the World'. As they were waiting to go on stage, Ron and Keith weren't sure what the songs would be: 'Maybe we should do "All I Really Want to Do"', said Bob. Bob was introduced by Jack Nicholson who described him as 'transcendent', which is one way of putting it. His exact words were 'Some artists' work speaks for itself. Some artists' work speaks for its generation. It's a deep personal pleasure to present to you one of America's great voices of freedom. It could only be one man – the transcendent Bob Dylan.' Could anyone live up to that introduction?

Let's be fair: there were extenuating circumstances. The stage monitors were behind the curtains, out of earshot. Ronnie Wood was to say, 'Considering we couldn't hear what we were doing, it was all right.' Plus they had to contend with the artists assembling backstage, rather nosily and unprofessionally, for the finale.

Furthermore, Bob Dylan broke a string and took Ron's guitar. Ron had to get another from a roadie. This was why Dylan wondered where he was: 'Let me introduce some people who just came along tonight, Keith Richards and Ron Wood – I don't know where they are.' The whole planet was watching and they were on a different planet.

All that was bad luck, but they didn't look right. They had been drinking and they looked like they'd been thrown out of a bar. But let's face it: if it hadn't been for a good cause, Dylan would never have done it. He hates gloss and glamour and *Live Aid* was very unDylan. What is more, some performers were probably doing it for the wrong reasons. They weren't being paid but they could see the huge PR opportunities. Even so it is possible to mess it up and still come out on top; John Sebastian's way out performance at Woodstock testifies to that.

Bob Geldof said in his autobiography, *Is that It?* 'Bob Dylan singing his classics ought to have been one of the greatest moments of the concert but he was out of time and treated his songs with disdain. He displayed a complete lack of understanding of the issues raised by *Live Aid* by saying, unforgivably, that it would be nice if some of the money went to the American farmers. Live Aid was about people losing their lives, not their livelihoods so it was a crass and stupid thing to say.'

That's it. Bob Dylan who often seems to have taken a vow of silence had decided to open on stage. He should have taken note of Roy Orbison who only ever said, 'Thank you' on stage and so never got into trouble.

BBC commentator Mark Ellen: 'I have a tape of the rehearsal at Live Aid and I know how little they rehearsed. They were mostly drinking rum and Coke. They were going to travel to Philadelphia together and rehearse on the way down but they drank rum and Coke instead. Bob started 'Ballad of Hollis Brown' and Ronnie didn't know the song, there was a cough mixture called Collis Browne and Ronnie wondered why Bob Dylan was singing about cough mixture. This was chaos on an epic level.'

'Ballad of Hollis Brown' was a very good song that had been largely ignored, and maybe that was a reason Dylan was performing it at Live Aid. It was set in an American farming community in South Dakota, so its location was relevant to what Bob Dylan said next. Bob Dylan said, 'I hope some of the money that's raised for people in Africa…maybe they could just take a little bit of it…and use it, say, to pay the mortgages on some of the farms that the farmers here owe to the banks.' That would not have been possible: indeed, it would have been illegal to take money raised for one cause and give it to another. Bob hadn't thought it through. By all means, say something, but not that.

Howard Sounes: 'Bob Dylan is from a small town in the mid-west and a semi-rural area; Hibbing is in an expanse of nothingness really. There are farms all around, and he would have known farmers and the children of farmers. He spent time mid-west in the summer and he would have felt for the plight of the American farmers in the 80s with their crippling mortgages and the decline of the industry, and he would have seen this as a very big problem. As a whole, Americans are notoriously short-sighted and are more concerned with the problems of their own country. Bob Geldof was horrified by what he said and I think Dylan had rehearsed that speech as he wanted to get his point across and many people in America would thank him for it. Here we think, "Ridiculous, how could the Americans be so concerned about their farms when people are dying in Africa?" Well, from that, Willie Nelson launched Farm Aid and many people thought he was saying the right thing.' To support Howard's theory, the audience did cheer when Dylan said that, but that was the American audience.

Dylan's remarks were not frivolous and were said seriously, but he should have said, 'Live Aid is a wonderful thing and let's start something else for the farmers.' The comment was on a par with his address when he received the Tom Paine award. Dylan certainly has form when it comes to big events.

After his remarks, Dylan sang 'When the Ship Comes In', which contained the line – 'The whole wide world is watching' – but it was shambolically performed. They closed with 'Blowin' in the Wind' with Keith thinking he is playing a Chuck Berry song. When Bob asked Keith for a solo, Ronnie looked upwards.

Fourteen minutes and Dylan had hit his all-time low in front of two billion people. The plan was for Lionel Richie to come through the curtain, put his arms around Bob and say, 'Some of your friends are here tonight.' Then the curtain would open on 'We Are the World'. Bob hated that idea and exited stage right.

Live Aid had ended on a sour note, although it had raised £50m in pledged donations. After the event, most performers were experiencing big album sales from *Greatest Hits* collections. Many artists used Live Aid as a once-in-a-lifetime stepping stone and Queen and U2, in particular, enhanced their following. David Bowie, Madonna, and Neil Young all did well. Bob Dylan must be the only performer who has played to two billion people and lost fans.

Singer / songwriter Steve Young: 'I appreciate what he did. The other stars who came out with their artistic egos were much flashier. I still appreciate Dylan's approach, his unusual personality and his mannerisms and his dryness. I admired his courage and his willingness to say something that he thought was true.'

As a result of Dylan's comments, the first Farm Aid concert took place on 22 September 1985. Loudon Wainwright: 'I think he had a bad night at Live Aid. Everybody has a bad night. He played later at Farm Aid and did a cracking show. It wasn't a good show but everybody goes out from time to time and does a bad show. If you're Duran Duran, you go out and do a bad show every night. (laughs) I can forgive Dylan for a lot of things. Some nights I stink too.'

Tom Petty: 'He had a date to do Farm Aid and he'd had a bad experience at Live Aid where he'd tried to play acoustically but it didn't go well and he needed a band so he asked us.'

Tom Petty and the Heartbreakers were too dedicated for this to go wrong. As Dylan went on, Neil Young said, 'I got 'em all warmed up for you'. Dylan looked healthier and more comfortable as he sang 'Clean Cut Kid', a new song 'Shake' to the tune of 'Treat Her Right', 'I'll Remember You', 'Trust Yourself' (with Willie Nelson), 'That Lucky Ol' Sun' and ended with 'Maggie's Farm' (again with Willie), although that song criticised farmers.

The performance was exceptionally good and after the show, Dylan said, 'Man, it's a shame we worked out all this material. I'd like to take it on the road.' They were soon all playing dates in Australia.

The Farm Aid benefit raised $10m. Neil Young, who wrote a song about Farm Aid, 'Last of his Kind', said 'Farm Aid is now an American tradition, but it is like Band Aid. We ought to be able to get rid of them.'

In January 1986, a charcoal drawing by Bob Dylan was sold by auction for the Live Aid Foundation, which indicates the start of another phase of Bob Dylan's career. He also drew a Christmas card for the Save the Children charity. He was starting to think that there might be a market for his artwork.

II. So Much Older Then: 1985–1989

In February 1985, Bob Dylan had sessions at the Power Station in New York with Steve Van Zandt and Roy Bittan (both from Bruce Springsteen's E Street Band), Mick Taylor and Jim Keltner as well as Sly and Robbie. He was working on the songs that would form his next album, *Empire Burlesque*. Dylan returned the favour to Sly and Robbie by adding harmonica to their song, 'No Name on the Bullet'.

Calling in to say hello, Al Kooper found himself playing guitar on 'When the Night Comes Falling from the Sky'. Kooper said, 'It was a powerful song that has not been recognised. It is like 'All around the Watchtower: Part 2'.'

As well as the album tracks, there were a couple of oddities. Dylan had written a new song around Johnny Cash's Sun record, 'Straight A's in Love'. A high school prom song was an unsuitable theme for a man in his forties and it was given to the young Williams Brothers (Andy and David, sons of Andy), for their album, *Two Stories* (1987). They were part of T Bone Burnett's touring band. Dylan sang 'The Very Thought of You', but it was not the well-known standard but a new song written around his own 'You Angel You'.

Although he never said it publicly, Dylan wanted to match the sales of Bruce Springsteen, Madonna and Prince. Eric Clapton thought that Bob had nothing to prove as he commented, 'Springsteen's the rock and roll Donovan'. Dylan considered Arthur Baker was the right man to give him a contemporary sound. He asked him to overdub his new tracks as he thought fit.

Arthur Baker had worked with Afrika Bambaataa. He would give Dylan a radio friendly AOR sound, almost disco, replacing Jim Keltner with a beatbox on 'Trust Yourself'. 'Dylan said that he wanted to make a record like Madonna or Prince. I was mixing his record and he was in front of the board playing the guitar. I turned the sound down and I heard him singing 'Like a Virgin'.' He soon realised that he had to work around Dylan's dislike of the studio. Baker added three background singers, jokingly called the Dylanettes.

At the same time, Dylan gave an interview saying, 'Disregard the current stuff. Forget it. You're better off if you read John Keats and Herman Melville and listen to Robert Johnson and Woody Guthrie.' He said that he would like to be ordained as a rabbi, so his Christian days were over. He said, possibly reflecting on Christian concerts, 'People talk about Sylvester Stallone and Al Pacino and they talk about last year's floods and they talk about *Miami Vice* but God doesn't interest people for some reason.'

Whether Arthur Baker had done the right things to Dylan's tapes or not is arguable, but Dylan seemed happy, taking the revised tracks round to Allen Ginsberg's apartment. Ginsberg had Harry Smith as a house guest. Although Dylan wanted to meet him, Harry wouldn't get out of bed. When Harry died in November 1991, still at the Chelsea Hotel, mourners mixed his ashes with wine and drank them.

When Dylan asked Ginsberg for his opinion of the lyrics on *Empire Burlesque*, Ginsberg was very positive. Maybe Dylan had been thinking of Ginsberg for a sleeve note but if he had, he changed his mind and for the first time he had his lyrics printed on the inner sleeve. Dylan made a video in Tokyo for 'Tight Connection to My Heart', directed by Paul Schrader, but the idea of Dennis Hopper directing another video never materialised.

Empire Burlesque was a fascinating if flawed album. Like *Infidels,* there were several songs about the contemporary world. 'Clean-Cut Kid' was about an American youth who had been sent to Vietnam and come back a killer.

Dylan was writing his lyrics with the TV in the background. Maybe he was watching a box-set of Humphrey Bogart films as he often included phrases from them. The biographer Michael Gray studied this. In *The Maltese Falcon*, there is the exchange, 'We want to talk to you, Spade' to which he replies, 'Well, go ahead and talk.' In 'Tight Connection to My Heart', Dylan sings, 'You want to talk to me, Go ahead and talk.' The opening line in that song, 'Well, I had to move fast, And I couldn't with you around my neck' is what Bogie says in *Sirocco*. Whether this matters is debatable. John Lennon also wrote lyrics with the TV on and co-opted phrases. Dylan said of 'Tight Connection to My Heart', 'It's very visual and I wanted to make a movie out of it.' Maybe there had already been one.

The sound is mid-80s rock, which is what Dylan wanted but it stifles the songs. The final track, the folky 'Dark Eyes' is just Dylan, his guitar and harmonica and comes as a welcome relief. It has been suggested that the song is about Christ on the cross but if it is, what's a French girl doing in there? I've a bootleg of the album, made up of alternative takes and songs which had been dropped. It is called *Tempest Storm* and I prefer it because it has not got the over-production of the finished product.

Dylan and his band filmed a video for 'When the Night Comes Falling from the Sky' with Dave Stewart. Dylan wanted it in black and white to resemble an old Japanese movie. Dave then did a video for the love song, 'Emotionally Yours' with Dylan alone with a photograph of Elizabeth Taylor. The cover for *Down in the Groove* comes from this video.

Film-maker Jon Roseman: 'I was in LA doing something else and Dave Stewart asked me if I would like to produce and direct a video. Whilst I appreciated Bob's iconic stature,

I wasn't a big fan, but he was fantastic and cooperative and we had great fun. Dave Stewart, Bob Dylan and I had been out for dinner and we passed an old coach park with a 1950s coach and Dylan said, 'Jon, let's have the coach. We can go to a gig in a hall like a Prom gig and you can film it.' I said, 'Okay' but his manager and lawyer to me, 'You're not going to do that with these famous musicians.' The band included Clem Burke from Blondie and someone from Talking Heads, and we hired a very dodgy hall in west LA. I said, 'It's not my call. Speak to your client. He wants to do it.' So we all got into the coach and we were driving around west LA when it broke down. So these mega-names had to walk through the streets to the hall. Nobody recognised them. No one asked for an autograph. Halfway through the shoot, Bob said, 'I would like an audience here', so I rang up the local radio station and asked them to say that the first 100 people could come in. They had to be here at 5pm. There was not a single person around at 5pm. I rang up the station and they hadn't given it out as they thought I was joking. Anyway, we got them and we got a great video and Bob was great.'

In May 1985, Leonard Cohen played his first New York concert in ten years at Carnegie Hall. Joni Mitchell, Bob Dylan and Al Kooper were in the audience, praising his performance and Dylan said his songs were now like prayers. It was always thus.

In July 1985 Dylan sang three songs to a 6,000 strong invited audience at Lenin Stadium, Moscow for an event hosted by the Soviet Writers Union. He had been invited by Yevgeny Yevtushenko and his appearance had not been heralded in advance. While in the area, he went to the Ukraine to see Odessa, the homeland of his ancestors.

In September Dylan recorded the 'Sun City' song, produced by Arthur Baker. He sang the whole song and Baker picked out what he wanted. He didn't sound like Dylan, he wasn't in time and he wasn't in tune. So you could say, he did sound like Dylan and what's new? An insert of Dylan was included in the video, but blink and you miss it. The single was credited to Artists United against Apartheid and made the US Top 40.

On 13 November 1985, Columba Records held an event in his honour at the Whitney Museum, New York. Dylan had sold 35 million records and he was given an original Woody Guthrie drawing and songbook. He told the *Los Angeles Herald-Examiner*, 'I know I've done a lot of things, but if I'm proud of anything, it's maybe that I've helped to give Woody a little more attention.'

Both Bob Dylan and Lou Reed looked uncomfortable outside the museum and inside there was David Bowie, Robert De Niro and Billy Joel. Said Billy Joel, 'There's no way you can be a pop artist today without being influenced by Bob Dylan.'

At first glance, a photograph looks as though Bob met Princess Diana there but the lookalike was 33-year-old Susan Ross. Her father was a vice president at Revlon. She had been a road manager for the Moody Blues and ELO and had come off drugs. Three days later Bob was at her low-rent hotel, and the manager lent her his room to entertain Bob. She became Bob's road manager and they had a relationship. She asked him, 'Why don't we live together?' and he replied, 'Because I can barely live with myself.' After five years, he invited her to Malibu but he was uncomfortable when she was there. In 1992, she asked him not to call again and he sent a postcard back – 'If there's a change, let me know.' When 46, she wrote her memoir about her 12 year, on-off relationship. Susan Ross said of the book, 'It's my way of becoming visible instead of being another secret in your life.'

A compilation based around unissued tracks, *Biograph*, was issued in in October 1985: it had been proposed in 1983 and delayed because of *Real Live*. The delay worked in its favour as the CD revolution had come along. It was on five vinyl albums or two CDs, although two tracks had to be dropped for the CD version. It had an expansive booklet written by Cameron Crowe. Dylan said, 'I had a chance to clarify a lot of wrong things said about me.'

The title looked like a typo but referred to an old blues label. Dylan was not promoting it how CBS would like. 'All it really is is repackaging. It's repackaging and it costs a lot of money.' The set was partly to combat bootleggers: 'Those bootleg records are outrageous: they have stuff you do in a phone booth.' *Biograp*h became the second box set to receive a gold disc, following one by Elvis. Then came Eric Clapton's *Crossroads*. There was a burst of Dylan compilations in *The Bootleg Series* starting in 1991 and still continuing.

Many record companies had kept outtakes and unused songs and with the advent of the CD there was so much more space to hand. They wanted customers to buy their favourite records again so why not entice them with alternative takes and songs they had never heard? It was a windfall for Dylan.

In November 1985 Bob Dylan was going to record with Dave Stewart at his Church Studios in Crouch End, London. He went on his own and he got the right number but the wrong street. He asked if Dave was in and Dave's mum said he wouldn't be long. She made him a cup of tea. This Dave was a plumber who returned to find Bob in his sitting room and he was pointed in the right direction. There is an excellent episode in *Urban Myths* (Sky Arts) about this with Eddie Marsan as Dylan. Dylan recorded several tracks with Dave Stewart but only 'Under Your Spell' was released. He attempted 'We Will Not Be Lovers', written by Mike Scott of the Waterboys, but his vocal would be redone in New York.

The BBC DJ, Andy Kershaw was living in a dilapidated house in Crouch End. He had been in Boston for *Whistle Test* and on the plane, he read that Bob was recording with Dave Stewart in London. He realised that Bob was only a mile from where he lived and he knew Dave and his Church Studios. Dave answered the door and said Dylan was here and playing a Telecaster. Dylan agreed to a *Whistle Test* interview. The director Mike Appleton got a BBC news crew to Crouch End in double-quick time. Dylan had been chatty and now he dropped into monosyllables and grunts. It was a terrible interview. Andy Kershaw: 'So Bob are you gonna have your hair cut just like Dave's?' One step at a time, Andy: Bob had only just got a stud in his ear.

Dylan rehearsed with Tom Petty and the Heartbreakers for a Far East tour. He spent Christmas with his family on his farm in Minnesota.

On 20 January 1986, Bob Dylan joined in a televised celebration for Martin Luther King's birthday from the Kennedy Centre in Washington. Dylan had new words for 'I Shall Be Released'. He sang with Stevie Wonder on 'Let the Bells of Freedom Ring' and joined Peter, Paul and Mary for 'Blowin' in the Wind'. The finale was 'Happy Birthday', Wonder's song naturally. Dylan was standing with Elizabeth Taylor, once his dream girl and now his dinner date. A few months later, when Elizabeth Taylor was having dental surgery, Dylan sent her a get well greeting with a ten foot square poster of himself that she had admired. Bob Dylan sang with Michael Jackson at Elizabeth Taylor's birthday party at Burt Bacharach's house in February 1987.

On 25 January 1986 Albert Grossman died of a heart attack in London. He was on his way to MIDEM, the music industry festival with, more importantly for him, French cuisine. Grossman died intestate and his wife Sally had to go through the courts to obtain his assets. Dylan attended neither the funeral nor his memorial service.

Carolyn Dennis was born in Missouri in 1954 and her mother Madelyn Quebec had sung with the Raelets. In 1986 she also joined Bob Dylan on tour. By then, Bob was in a relationship with Carolyn and they had a daughter Desirée Gabrielle Dennis-Dylan on 31 January 1986. Was Dylan disowning or protecting her by never being seen with her? In 1989 Carolyn and her daughter moved to a bungalow in Tarzana.

Bob was to marry Carolyn in Los Angeles on 4 June 1986. This wasn't known until Howard Sounes researched his biography of Dylan: 'Dylan had been secretly married and there was a child by that marriage, and that is remarkable because if you're as famous as Bob Dylan, every writer in the world would happily write about your relationships if they knew about them. It is usually fairly easy to find out this stuff and yet Dylan had kept this secret for 15 years. The marriage didn't last. It was secret and furtive and ended in divorce and cost him a lot of money.' They were divorced in 1990.

The press would speculate about Bob's relationships and some thought that he may have married Clydie King or Carol Woods, who were both his backing singers. He had a fling with Brita Lee, the girlfriend of his road manager Gary Shafner.

How had Howard Sounes found this out? 'Bob Dylan is an active lover of the opposite sex and it seemed likely that he had been married again and had more kids along the way. There were no shortage of candidates and his friends gave me contradictory answers. Anyway I found that he had a child called Desirée and if you have children, you have to have a birth certificate and if you are married, you have to have a marriage certificate so I went through the courthouse database in Los Angeles, checking for Dylan and Zimmerman and every woman in his life I could think of and eventually found the paperwork. When I had the proof, I went back to my sources and indeed to Bob's family. They had known about it all along. My intentions for writing the book were entirely positive, I admire Bob Dylan, but I was digging for the truth. This doesn't reflect badly upon him in any way as he has been a good father.'

On 4 February 1986 Bob Dylan and the Heartbreakers were playing so loudly at the soundcheck at Athletic Park in Wellington, New Zealand that many neighbours wanted the event to be cancelled. The following night was the opening of the *True Confessions* tour. They opened with 'Like a Rolling Stone' and included 'Across the Borderline', 'I Forgot More Than You'll Ever Know' (a duet between Bob and Tom), 'Lenny Bruce' and Rick Nelson's 'Lonesome Town'. One reviewer said, 'Dylan has become too much of nothing' and another, 'All hail St. Dylan'. The guitarist Mike Campbell liked the 'looseness and, uh, chaos'.

While in Australia, Bob and the band recorded 'Hell Time Man' for the credits of an apocalyptic gangland film, *Band of the Hand*. It was ideal for large cinema speakers and for the film itself. Petty said the image of one-take Dylan was 'not as true as the myth. I've seen him work very hard on things.'

Dylan played four dates at the Entertainment Centre in Sydney. He had Mark Knopfler and Stevie Nicks on stage with him, the latter being in trouble as she didn't have a work permit. Dylan sang 'Cross on over and Rock 'Em Dead' and he prefaced 'In the Garden' with the words, 'I have my own hero. I'm going to sing about him right now.' Dylan went to a matinée of *Sweet Bird of Youth* starring Lauren Bacall and met her socially. Did he tell her that he had been using Bogie lines in *Empire Burlesque*?

When Dylan was in Sydney, he was eating in a classy restaurant. The BBC talk show host, Michael Parkinson went over to him. Dylan had previously turned down *Parkinson* and Parky hoped to persuade him. He said, 'Mr Dylan, I....' and Bob said, 'He ain't here.' The meeting was over. I'm not here.

On February 19 Dylan joined Dire Straits on stage at Melbourne for 'All Along the Watchtower', 'Knockin' on Heaven's Door', 'Licence to Kill' and 'Leopard-Skin Pillbox Hat'.

Amelia Caruana known as Gypsy Fire had an affair with Dylan in Melbourne but said publicly that she was never his sex slave. That's nice to know.

It seems patronising but Dylan was doing 'Sukiyaki' as an instrumental throughout his Japanese tour, where he played 25 songs a night. He played Budokan again and on March 8 in Nagoya, he introduced 'Ballad of a Thin Man' by saying it was 'written in response to people who ask me questions.' He introduced 'Lenny Bruce' with a quote from Tennessee Williams, 'I don't ask for your pity, just your understanding. Not even that, but your recognition of me in you, and the enemy, time, in us all.'

At the end of March, Dylan accepted the founder's award from ASCAP. In his acceptance speech, he quoted from 'Without a Song'. Elvis had done the same when he was named as one of the outstanding young men in America in 1971.

In the recording studio, Dylan rapped on Kurtis Blow's 'Street Rock'n'roll'. I think it was meant to be serious but it's hard not to laugh.

Bob Dylan and Tom Petty had thought of making an album together. Nothing came of it but they did have recording sessions before their *True Confessions* tour. They recorded a joint composition, 'Got My Mind Made Up', which is a good rocker but not distinctive. The song was also recorded by Petty without Dylan: again it's not bad but there isn't much he can do with the song.

Another joint song 'Jammin' Me' is on Tom Petty and the Heartbreakers' *Let Me Up* album. 'Jammin' Me' was written by Petty, Dylan and Mike Campbell from the Heartbreakers. The song was about media overload and had been prompted by Eddie Murphy saying there were too many TV channels. Bob and Tom wrote the song and then Tom and Mike changed the melody. There is a witty video for this song, which would have suited the Wilburys.

Working with various musicians including César Rosas of Los Lobos, Dylan recorded new songs and covers including Kris Kristofferson's 'They Killed Him' and the gospel favourite, 'Precious Memories', with a steel drum and too many voices.

Dylan created a new album from past sessions, which became *Knocked out Loaded*, released in August 1986. Dylan said, 'It's all sorts of stuff. It doesn't have a theme or a purpose.' That is, it's a mess: when you consider the wonderful tracks missed off albums, you wonder what Dylan was playing at. By all means, release sub-standard tracks for collectors at a budget price, but don't release an album like this where it has to stand alongside *Highway 61 Revisited* or *Blood on the Tracks*. Nick Kent in *Melody Maker* said it was 'shockingly bad, barely coherent.' I wouldn't go that far but it is a disgrace. It should have acted as a wake-up call but no, there was worse to come.

There are over 120 thanks on *Knocked out Loaded*. Martin Sheen and Ronnie Wood were neighbours but how about Richie Havens, Marty Feldman and Randy Newman? The implication is, 'This may be a bad record but I'm not the only one to blame'. Well, yes you are as the production credits are Bob Dylan and Tom Petty. Interestingly, he slipped his new daughter's name into the credits. There were only eight songs and 35 minutes playing time which was hardly right for the new CD age.

Many think that the worst song that Bob Dylan ever recorded was 'They Killed Him', a song about martyrs written by Kris Kristofferson. Michael Gray: 'When you are a very weary professional musician in the midst of a long period of writers' block, you get together with musicians and you try a number of things. You bore yourselves rigid most of the time and then you listen to playbacks and go, "That's not so bad", and it's a very different matter from going into a studio with an urgency to communicate as was the case in an earlier era.'

The album title is a phrase in the blues song, 'Junco Partner', which is not on the album. 'Under Your Spell' was written by Bob and Carole Bayer Sager and includes the phrase 'knocked down and loaded'. As might be expected with Sager on board, this is AOR, decent enough but not going anywhere.

There is a revival of 'I Wanna Ramble', an excellent 1955 Sun single from Junior Parker. Who knows why Dylan wanted to add new lyrics and change the title to 'You Wanna Ramble'. It would have been better without the girls.

Dylan's voice is high-pitched at times, almost like one of the Chipmunks, which is especially noticeable on 'Maybe Someday'. It's a decent song saying that the girl will eventually realise that he has been good for her.

For all that, *Knocked out Loaded* did contain one amazing track, the 11-minute 'Brownsville Girl'. Dylan said to Sam Shepard, 'One day I was standing in line for this Gregory Peck film' and Shepard said, 'Let's make a song out of that.' The result was the half sung, half spoken 'New Danville Girl' which became 'Brownsville Girl'. Woody Guthrie had written 'Danville Girl' but then Bob said there were too many Danvilles and it became 'Brownsville Girl'. It was a 17-verse song, mostly about the old west and based around the 1950 film, *The Gunfighter*. Shepard said that some of the lines were too long. 'Don't worry,' said Dylan, 'it'll work.' Sam Shepard later remarked, 'The way he squashes phrasing and stretches it out is remarkable.'

'Brownsville Girl' tells the story of a gunfighter who is shot by a young Turk. The crowd want to string him up but Peck says, 'Let him live' for the simple reason that he would have to watch his back as there would always be someone who wanted to kill the man who killed the gunfighter; it would be a fate worse than death. Quite a sophisticated thought for a western gunfighter.

The song rambles onto other themes and one of the great lines is, 'If there's an original thought out there, I could really use it right now.' There is not too much difference between 'New Danville Girl' and 'Brownsville Girl' besides the 2,000 miles between the places. I prefer the earlier version as Dylan's voice is more to the fore, although the backing singers add a force to 'Brownsville Girl'.

In 'New Danville Girl', Dylan says, 'Even the swap meets around here are getting corrupt' which puzzled me for some time. Had I heard it correctly? Swap meets is a US term for flea markets.

The odd thing is that even if Bob Dylan didn't know Lou Reed's 1984 track, 'Doin' the Things that We Want to', Sam Shepard definitely did. In the song, Lou Reed has just seen Shepard's play *Fool for Love* and he draws a flattering comparison with *Raging Bull*.

From June to August, Bob Dylan was touring with Tom Petty and the Heartbreakers, with Petty performing two four-song sets. In all, he was to play over 100 concerts with them, though he said, 'I'm not going to give it my all. I'm not Judy Garland who's going to die onstage in front of a thousand clowns.' When one interviewer quizzed Petty for opening for someone who had sold less records than himself, Petty said, 'How could it be any other way?'

Bob Dylan: Outlaw Blues

The tour opened with an Amnesty International benefit *Caravan of Hope* with the Heartbreakers in which they performed 'Band of the Hand', 'Licence to Kill' and 'Shake a Hand'. Later, they did an anti-drugs telethon in which Dylan sang the Hank Williams song, 'Thank You'.

Every night they enjoyed performing three or four covers. Rick Nelson's 'Lonesome Town' had become a favourite and Dylan told audiences, 'Ricky Nelson did a lot of my songs. I'd like to do one of his.' He played Wilbert Harrison's 'Kansas City' in Kansas City, remarking 'That's the first time I played that song. Anyway, I know where I am.'

His other covers included 'Bye Bye Johnny' (Chuck Berry), 'I Still Miss Someone' (Johnny Cash) and, quite adventurously, 'Unchain My Heart' (Ray Charles). He sang John Hiatt's poignant song about the Mexican border, 'Across the Borderline' and the standard, 'That Lucky Ol' Sun'. When he invited his dresser Susie Pullen on stage, the crowd sang 'Happy Birthday'.

In New Jersey, Bob said, 'This is the land of the Boss' and played 'Like a Rolling Stone' with Al Kooper and a Springsteen stop-start ending. Dylan with his leather vests and bare arms was getting into Springsteen mode himself.

Despite the fiasco of Live Aid, Bob had Ronnie Wood as a guest and also John Lee Hooker, who sang B.B. King's 'Rock Me Baby', evidence that Bob was aware of the 'wagon wheel' line. He performed 'One Too Many Mornings' in San Diego because 'somebody bet me $1 that I couldn't remember it all.' He had new lyrics for 'Gotta Serve Somebody' and had rewritten 'Union Sundown' but it is doubtful if anyone in Houston could make out the new words. David Hepworth interviewed Dylan for *Q* magazine and Dylan commented afterwards, 'That guy kept me asking me questions.'

At the Greek Theatre in Berkeley, he spoke to Jerry Garcia from the Grateful Dead. They shared an interest in vintage folk and blues, and the Dead performed several Dylan songs. Dylan liked the way they varied their set from night to night. With Petty, he had a core set and only made a couple of changes here and there. A few nights later he joined the Dead in Akron for 'Little Red Rooster', 'Don't Think Twice, It's All Right' and 'It's All Over Now, Baby Blue', which worked fine, but when he joined them again a couple of nights later, they did 'Desolation Row' together – badly.

Rock writer Ellis Amburn saw Dylan at a fairground in a town close to where James Dean had died. Ellis Amburn: 'The worst show I ever saw was Bob Dylan at the mid-state county fair in Paso Robles, California in 1986. Tom Petty was wonderful but Bob Dylan was not recognisable as Bob Dylan. I guess he was so tired of singing those classics that he had changed them. 'A Hard Rain's A-Gonna Fall' was hardly recognisable and so I was terribly disappointed.'

That comment notwithstanding, the Tom Petty tour was seen as too slick and Dylan fans were disappointed that there were not changes from night to night. It was a Greatest Hits tour but Dylan did do songs from *Empire Burlesque*.

In May 1986 it was announced that Dylan would star in *Hearts of Fire*, a film with a budget of $13m, which would be shot in the UK over seven weeks and the US for four.

The director Richard Marquand had been born in Cardiff in 1937 and gone to King's College, Cambridge. He had made a BBC-TV documentary on Brendan Behan and done well with a low-budget film, *The Birth of the Beatles*, in 1979. Four years later he entered the big league by making the *Stars Wars* film, *Return of the Jedi*. His latest film was the thriller, *Jagged* Edge with Jeff Bridges and Glenn Close.

Marquand knew Dylan's agent and Dylan read the script and said yes. Marquand went to Point Dume and they drank Cabernet Sauvignon. He filmed a couple of scenes with Dylan and Fiona which went okay. Marquand thought that he had great presence. Dylan couldn't change the plot but he could alter lines to make them realistic. Most of the time he would play his usual disinterested, sarcastic self.

Rupert Everett thought the script was terrible 'but with all those American films you just can't tell. It could easily have turned out to be a hit movie. It turned out bad and doing the film was a big mistake. It took me years to get over it.' Everett got on well with Dylan who listened to music late in the night and could get by with four hours sleep. The producer Iain Smith became chummy with him, introducing him to the Scottish Malt Whisky Society.

They started with a press conference at the National Film Theatre with Dylan taking part. Richard Marquand called this film 'a red-hot love triangle'. In *Hearts of Fire*, Fiona is rock singer Molly Maguire (oh dear) playing covers like 'Proud Mary' in a dying town in Pennsylvania. Dylan plays Billy Parker, an American rock star who retired ten years earlier and is a chicken farmer. Both Parker and the synth star James Colt (Rupert Everett) spot her potential and she becomes a star. She has affairs with both of them and when she returns to her hometown, they join her on stage. Parker trashes a hotel room and throws a TV out of the window. Yeah, I know: *A Star Is Born*.

Dylan was struggling to write new songs and yet he was meant to provide six for the film. He managed two – 'Night After Night' and 'Had a Dream about You, Baby'. Dylan had to have a song which would have been a creditable hit single in the 60s. Instead of writing one, he asked John Hiatt who gave him 'The Usual', a really good song with Eric Clapton on guitar. Dylan had been doing Hiatt's 'Across the Borderline' in concert.

In one scene Dylan sings Shel Silverstein's 'A Couple More Years', which had been recorded by Dr. Hook. Dennis Locorriere: 'In *Hearts on Fire*, Bob Dylan sings 'A Couple More Years' to a girl who is younger than himself and it creates the right mood. He is saying, 'All I have on you is experience but you'll get there'. A love scene with Dylan was dropped and Fiona Flanagan said, 'He likes buxom blondes and I'm certainly not that.' The incidental music came from John Barry. Rupert Everett performed Soft Cell's 'Tainted Love'. There is a scene where Molly watches Billy Parker in 1971 which is a clip from *Concert for Bangla Desh*.

A live concert with Billy Parker was filmed at Colston Hall, Bristol. There were scenes in the London disco, Heaven, the Electric Ballroom in Camden Town and supposedly in the Cavern, which looked nothing like the Cavern. Whilst in Camden, Dylan visited the Rock On shop and bought records, praising the Milkshakes, a Goth band from the East End. Ian Dury, Ronnie Wood, Richie Havens and Mark Rylance (as Fizz!) have cameo roles. They lost a day's filming as Zodiac Mindwarp had a court appearance for exposing himself in public to a policeman. His defence: 'It is society that is to blame': he was only a pawn in the game.

The premiere of *Hearts of Fire* in London took place in October 1987. Rupert Everett and Fiona attended (bravely) but not Dylan although he was around playing Wembley Stadium. The audience was bored and many sniggered. The film played for a week and was never shown again. It was Dylan's worst film and one of the worst rock movies. According to Sean Egan's book on Dylan, the soundtrack LP of *Hearts of Fire* is now selling for £50 and I have one!

Dylan said he took the role because it was 'the right time, the right place and the right words'. No, no, no. It was the end of Dylan's film career. A pity as Kinky Friedman was pushing for a film of his novel *A Case of Lone Star* and he had a role for Dylan. He never got it made and if Dylan had said yes, it might have fallen into place.

How could everyone have been so bad? Scriptwriter Joe Eszterhas and Richard Marquand should have known better: they had worked together on *Jagged Edge*. We will never know what Marquand thought as he died before it was released on 4 September 1986. The poster, incidentally, was even worse than the film. No, maybe not, Dylan stopping a bus with his harmonica masquerading as a gun was worse.

While he was in the UK, Dylan was interviewed by Christopher Sykes for BBC's *Omnibus*. Dylan talked to him while sketching him in his trailer. Dylan comments, 'If you're looking for revelations, it's not going to happen.' But maybe it does. Dylan sniffs away and says that he is going out of the room to reenergise himself.

John Bauldie: 'He treated that guy fairly typically. He doesn't suffer fools gladly and he can't stand people who don't know what they are talking about and ask irrelevant questions. If someone is serious, he will respond perfectly well.' Bob Dylan said, 'Listen, I've come through some good times and some bad times. Right now, we're making a movie, playing some big tours, but I've seen the bottom too, so if you can work, that's all you can ask for.'

In November Bob Dylan inducted Gordon Lightfoot into the Juno Hall of Fame in Toronto, Canada's Grammys. He called Lightfoot 'a rare talent'. While in Toronto, he was not admitted to Tanya Tucker's concert at the Royal York Hotel in Toronto because of his appearance.

In January 1987 Roy Orbison was inducted into the Rock and Roll Hall of Fame by Bruce Springsteen. Talking of 'Born to Run', he said, 'I wanted to make a record with words like Bob Dylan, that sounded like Phil Spector but most all I wanted to sing like Roy Orbison.' Was Springsteen trying to induct himself?

Later in the month Dylan had a couple of sessions with the Grateful Dead where they tried various things. It was Bob's Beatles period as they included 'She Loves You', 'Nowhere Man' and 'Come Together'. He played harmonica on 'The Factory' for Warren Zevon who was aiming at the blue collar Springsteen market. It is about the boredom of his job and there's a passing reference to asbestos.

On 19 February 1987, the so-called Graffiti Band with Jesse 'Ed' Davis and Taj Mahal played the Palomino in North Hollywood. George Harrison, John Fogerty and Bob Dylan joined them on stage for 90 minutes with Dylan mostly in the background. The songs included 'Lucille', 'Peggy Sue', 'Twist and Shout', 'Knock on Wood' and 'Watching the River Flow' with George leading on 'Willie and the Hand Jive' and 'Bo Diddley'. It was filmed and later bootlegged as *Live! The Silver Wilburys*.

Nils Lofgren got a call to say Bob Dylan wanted to speak to him. Dylan was about to appear in a George Gershwin tribute concert and Nils thought, 'Great, he wants me with him.' Bob said, 'Nils, you know that acoustic guitar on the 'Fire' video? That sounded great. Where can I get a guitar like that?' Someone collected it and returned it the next week. Dylan with just Nils' guitar and harmonica sang 'Soon' at the Gershwin gala, a song recorded by Ella Fitzgerald. It wasn't what the audience was expecting but it was a beautiful performance and Dylan had a wonderful head of hair, his best since 1966.

In April 1987 Dylan was in Los Angeles recording the tracks for his next album, *Down in the Groove*. As with *Knocked out Loaded*, he wasn't giving his best and he almost certainly knew that.

Eight of the ten tracks for the next album were recorded here and the album was completed with 'Had a Dream about You, Baby' from *Hearts of Fire* and the sober and intense 'Death Is Not the End', an outtake from *Infidels*. It wouldn't have stood out on *Infidels* but it did here.

There are only two other songs that are Dylan's compositions, both written with the Grateful Dead's lyricist, Robert Hunter, and backed by the Dead. It's hard to tell whether 'The Ugliest Girl in the World' is serious or comic but it's tasteless either way. 'Silvio' is about an 'old boll weevil looking for a home' and possibly is Hunter writing about Dylan himself. It has a 50s rhythm like Bill Haley, which works fine. This infectious track deserves more attention.

The blues guitarist Dave Alvin said that Dylan had been thinking of *Self Portrait, Volume 2* and was even considering 'You'll Never Walk Alone'. The songs here were mostly covers and Dylan simply said, 'I like the songs.' Robert Christgau said it represented 'his patented and by now meaningless one-take sound.' Trouble is, most of the covers are not well done. Wilbert Harrison's 'Let's Stick Together' has a dreary vocal. Maybe when he heard Bryan Ferry's take in 1988, he realised what he should have done. 'Shenandoah' deserved much better. Just contrast this with Roy Orbison's version.

Lou Reed said he would have loved to have written '90 Miles an Hour (Down a Dead End Street)'. It is a superb country song about a dangerous love affair and is performed with passion by Dylan alongside Willie Green and Bobby King, similar to the way they did country songs with Ry Cooder. They are around too on 'Sally Sue Brown', which had been written and recorded by Arthur Alexander. There is a decent vocal of 'Rank Strangers to Me', a strange bluegrass song about death recorded by the Stanley Brothers.

Tony Martin was the first to record 'When Did You Leave Heaven' and it was not a standard that had aged well; 'Have they missed you, can you get back in?' It was too saccharine for 1987, let alone today. An odd choice from Dylan who normally avoided sentimental nonsense.

Although not on the album, Bob recorded a good doo-wop styled arrangement of Gene Vincent's underrated 'Important Words' and had a fairly standard workout of Slim Harpo's 'Got Love If You Want It'.

With U2 at Wembley, Bono attacked Mrs. Thatcher with new words to 'Maggie's Farm', urging listeners not to vote for her. Dylan was friendly with U2, appearing at their gig in LA and performing 'I Shall Be Released' and 'Knockin' on Heaven's Door' with them, Bono having new lyrics for the latter. The big difference between Bono and Dylan was that Bono really did want to save the world. Perish the thought but could Bono have found himself in the Wilburys.

Bono had started 'Love Rescue Me' and Bob helped him finish it. In February 1988, Bob played Hammond organ on 'Hawkmoon 269' and sang backing vocals on 'Love Rescue Me', which was on the best-selling album, *Rattle and Hum*. Dylan and Bono wrote 'Prisoner of Love' but Dylan was reluctant for it to be on *Rattle and Hum*. Bono recommended Daniel Lanois, which was sound advice.

Dylan played harmonica for Ringo Starr in Memphis but Ringo was against releasing the tracks as the former Beatle was 'under the influence'. While he was there, Bob toured Graceland but unlike Paul Simon, he didn't write a song about it. Bob Dylan and the Grateful Dead decided to perform concerts together. The Dead referred to him as the Oracle. There is a three-hour rehearsal tape but I doubt if they were serious about some of the songs – 'Oh Boy!', 'The Boy in the Bubble', 'The French Girl' (Ian and Sylvia) and 'Rollin' in My Sweet Baby's Arms'. Using a cheap ghetto blaster, Dylan worked through his albums, picking suitable songs. He was going to perform 'Chimes of Freedom' for the first time since the 60s. Almost every Dylan show has been recorded illegally but the Grateful Dead went further. They had a special area for bootleggers. These were big shows with audiences coming as much to see the Dead as Dylan. At their first gig in Foxborough, Massachusetts, they came out with surprises, performing 'John Brown', 'Queen Jane Approximately' and 'Joey'.

On 10 July 1987, they were at the JFK Stadium in Philadelphia, the site for Live Aid. Whatever bad memories Dylan had of the event were banished as the show went very well. It was, however, a sad time as Bob Dylan's first record producer, John Hammond, had died at the age of 76. He appeared to have enjoyed every minute of his life. Dylan didn't attend his memorial service but Bruce Springsteen sang a Dylan song, 'Forever Young'.

It was a short tour by Dylan standards and he only performed 13 or 14 songs a show. They are considered substandard, but why? Dylan fans blame the Dead and vice versa. Dylan said, 'I'd had a hard time grasping the meaning of my songs. I'd reached the end of the line and was going to pack it in.'

Not too sure about that. When he performs 'Queen Jane Approximately' on the *Dylan & the Dead* LP, he sings 'And you wish your situation be more drastic' – and the final verse, the 'bandits' one is nonsense, but he does sing it twice. Never mind, it is a surrealistic song so you can argue that anything goes.

With the Dead, Dylan performed four songs that he had never performed live, 'Queen Jane Approximately', 'Frankie Lee and Judas Priest', 'The Wicked Messenger' and 'Joey'. Both 'Tomorrow Is a Long Time' and 'Mr. Tambourine Man' failed to impress, bearing in mind Steve Sutherland's criticism, 'The Dead still manage to sound as though they only met yesterday.' Dylan played with them on 'Touch of Grey'. They did 'Gotta Serve Somebody' together and on the *Dylan and the Dead* LP, it's a really strong version, better than the original.

In all, they played to 250,000 fans, probably as many Deadheads as Bobcats, but the fans had much in common. Their heroes ignored public approval and ploughed their own courses.

Well, they weren't called Bobcats yet. John Bauldie, editor of *The Telegraph*, said in 1992, 'The term Bobcats was originally a joke when I first mentioned it. I was in the States a few years back and everywhere Bob Dylan was playing, the Grateful Dead were playing the following night. As we were leaving the venues, the Deadheads would be arriving in their old psychedelic buses. We were travelling in a very nice car and we were thinking that Dylan fans were a little bit older and a little more affluent and I said we could be the Bobheads, and then somebody in the car changed it to Bobcats.'

The album was released February 1989. Dylan in his own perverse way selected the tracks, even ones where he can't remember the words. Jerry Garcia takes three guitar solos in 'All Along the Watchtower', but then he did produce the album. Robert Christgau commented, 'What Dylan makes of his catalogue here is exactly what he's been making of it for years – money.'

Although they didn't schedule any more concerts, they did join each other on stage from time to time and Bob played electric guitar with them in 1989 for Jesse Fuller's 'The Monkey and the Engineer'.

After the Dead, it was time to return to the Heartbreakers, this time for overseas dates. Dylan chose the opening act, Roger McGuinn. The tour was named *Alone and Together*. Bob would be playing his first dates in Israel, and he took his sons, Jesse and Samuel. The press took this as a sign of support for Israel but things are rarely that clear with Dylan and he did refuse to meet Shimon Peres, the foreign minister. Israel was milking the tour for all it was worth, similar to the red carpet for Barbra Streisand.

Because he was sightseeing, Dylan missed his first soundcheck, which was at Hayarkon Park in Tel Aviv on 5 September 1987. The show started with Roger McGuinn delivering his club act, talking too much, commenting on President Reagan and singing 'My Back Pages' and 'Mr. Tambourine Man'. There was some booing and some rubbish was thrown on stage. McGuinn had misread the audience.

In a 17-song set, Dylan opened with 'Maggie's Farm' and included 'Senor' (forgetting the words), 'Joey' and the original lyric for 'Simple Twist of Fate'. He ended with 'Go down Moses' but he hadn't included 'Neighbourhood Bully' which depicted Israel as a misunderstood hero. He did well but not great.

Two nights later Dylan was at Sultans Pool, Jerusalem, Israel with no songs duplicated from the previous venue. The show ended with a power cut. Still no 'Neighbourhood Bully' but three gospel songs – 'Shot of Love', 'Slow Train' and 'Gotta Serve Somebody'.

Dylan was less than a week in Israel and then it was business as usual in Switzerland and Italy. In Modena he joined a singalong in the hotel lounge which included 'Sittin' on the Dock of the Bay'. He performed for 100,000 in East Berlin, where he included 'I Dreamed I saw St. Augustine'. This show was in response to his Berlin concert in 1986 where East Berlin fans were pushed back as they tried to see it.

Four fans were killed on their way home from the concert by two drunken Russian soldiers driving a lorry. Friends put a notice in the paper headlined *Forever Young*. The soldiers were arrested and executed by a firing squad on the orders of President Gorbachev.

In Rotterdam, McGuinn and Dylan were backed by the Heartbreakers for 'Chimes of Freedom'. The next night in Copenhagen Dylan and the Heartbreakers performed an effective 'Desolation Row'. But maybe Dylan's popularity was suffering from too much touring or no recent hit records. It could just be poor promotion but Rome was less than half full and in Milan he only had 4,000 in an arena which held 80,000.

In Locarno on October 5, Dylan suddenly had an epiphany and realised his worth. 'All of a sudden everything just exploded. I noticed that all the people out there – I was used to them looking at the girl singers, they were good-looking girls, you know? But when that happened, nobody was looking at the girls anymore. They were looking at the main mike. After that, I knew I had to go out and play these songs.'

'Man Gave Names to the Animals' had been issued as a single in France under the title of 'Animals' and it had made their Top 10. This amused and surprised Dylan, who performed it with great success in Paris and Brussels.

Dylan played three nights at the National Exhibition Centre in Birmingham. Dylan was feeling below par but Tom Petty met both Jeff Lynne and George Harrison and they hit it off. Then came four nights at Wembley. Bob was given a platinum disc by CBS to celebrate 5m UK record sales. One reviewer said that he wore biker gear and had a dead 'rodent on his head'. He went to see the film *Rita, Sue and Bob Too* at the Empire, Leicester Square.

On October 16 there was a hurricane in the south of England, one of the most severe storms that the UK has known. There was £2bn damage and the loss of thousands of trees, but still they came to see Bob. Lee Simmonds: 'I went to one of his Wembley shows and it was the night of the hurricane. Dylan seemed to treat the audience with contempt and I don't think he was enjoying himself. He had written brilliant songs but he was destroying their melodies and you could hardly recognise them. It was a waste of money and a tragedy as he could have been the greatest entertainer in the world. He was so amusing and good in *Dont Look Back* and I was sure he could still do it if he wanted to.'

After the final concert, Bob was staying with George Harrison in Henley. Joe Brown: 'I met Bob Dylan at George Harrison's house one day. I had gone round to see George about something and Bob Dylan was eating toast in the kitchen. I said, "Hello, Bob" and he grunted at me, and that was the end of our conversation.' Jools Holland described how he went to George's house and found Bob watching George Formby on a large screen, so George Harrison was working on him. Mark Markin restored guitars in Nottingham. George Harrison saw that he had two National Resonators from the 1930s for sale and said he would take both. He said, 'I'm giving one to Bob.'

Around this time, I did an interview with Pete Seeger who asked me in return for some George Formby records so Bob may have been getting George Formby from all sides.

On November 14, Dylan did a corporate event for Applied Materials with his son Jakob's group the Wallflowers as the opening act. Both went down well.

Dylan wrote a note for a Jimi Hendrix exhibition saying it is more difficult to cover his songs than with the Beatles or Chuck Berry as you have to get 'somewhat inside and behind them'.

During the year there were stage productions of *Tarantula* by Darrell Larson in Santa Monica and a new show *Words and Music* in San Francisco with Bob Miles as Dylan. The show was written and directed by Peter Landecker with Bob Johnston as MD. Whoever did it was going to find *Tarantula* a hard sell but a show based on his best songs had potential, although it would be many years before someone saw how to get it right.

In March 1988 Bob Dylan and the Beatles were inducted at the third Rock and Roll Hall of Fame dinner at the Waldorf-Astoria, Manhattan, so how respectable is that? They'd been going 25 years (by the museum's reckoning) and so were eligible for inclusion. Also inducted were the Beach Boys, the Rolling Stones and the Supremes. No Lennon (obviously) and no McCartney (some Beatle feud) and Diana Ross didn't want to meet the other Supremes.

Over the years this annual event has become a platform for sounding off, Mike Love being the first. He said, 'We do 180 performances a year and I'd like to see the Mop Tops do that. I'd like to see Mick Jagger get on stage and do 'I Get Around' instead of 'Jumping Jackflash'. I dare the Boss to climb stage with the Beach Boys and jam. I want to see if Billy Joel can tickle the ivories.' George Harrison said to Al Jardine, 'I guess Mike Love didn't listen to Maharishi.'

Mick Jagger inducted the Beatles and Elton John, the Beach Boys. Bob Dylan was inducted by Bruce Springsteen. Springsteen said that Dylan's recent work was 'unjustly under-appreciated' because his early work cast such a long shadow. Bruce Springsteen said of Bob Dylan: 'You were the brother I never had.' A cliché to be sure but isn't that also from an early Dylan lyric? When Dylan spoke, he said, 'I play a lot of dates every year too. I'd like to thank Mike Love for not mentioning me. Peace, love and harmony are all important but so is forgiveness.' The evening ended with a very ragged all-star jam but Les Paul, George Harrison and Bob Dylan were trading licks on 'All Along the Watchtower'. Watch this 40-minute jam through and you'll wonder how any of them got into the Hall of Fame.

Over at the Grammys, there was an outlandish Little Richard performance: he was there to present the Best New Artist to Jody Watley and he said, 'You never gave me no Grammys and I've been singing for years.' When he opened the envelope, he said, 'And the winner is me!' The audience gave him a standing ovation.

Bob was there with Jerry Wexler and the film director Wim Wenders who was married to Ronee Blakley. When U2 got the Album of the Year for *The Joshua Tree* beating Michael Jackson and Prince, Bono thanked everyone including Dylan. He couldn't finish his speech as the audience was laughing so much, hardly the reaction he had been expecting.

Dylan attended a radical chic exhibition from Giorgio Armani at Los Angeles Museum of Contemporary Art. Dylan wore an Angora knitted hat, although it was a black tie event. He shared a table with Martin Scorsese and Steven Spielberg. Martin Scorsese, Robert De Niro and Robbie Robertson had worked together on several projects.

In March 1987 Bob returned to films with a cameo role in *Catchfire*, a Dennis Hopper film with Jodie Foster and Vincent Price. It was a Mob film in which Dylan, an installation artist with a chainsaw says, 'I used to work in concrete' and Dennis Hopper responds, 'I used to work in concrete too.' He is killed by Hopper although you can still see him breathing. Hopper was unhappy with the film and he changed the name of the director to Alan Smithee, a name sometimes used by directors when they don't want their name attached to it. The film was released in 1990 as *Backtrack* but no one paid it any attention, least of all Dennis Hopper.

In April 1988 George Harrison asked Bob Dylan if he could use his Point Dume garage studio to record a bonus track for a 12-inch single with Jeff Lynne producing. As it happened, George and Jeff went to dinner with Roy Orbison and George invited Roy to sing on the track. George had to collect his guitar from Tom Petty's house. George told Tom that he was going to Bob Dylan's studio and Tom said, 'Oh I was wondering what to do tomorrow.'

When they got to Bob's studio, they had no specific idea of what to record but George saw a crate with a label 'Handle with Care' and felt a song coming on. Dylan said, 'That's good' and off they went. They had a great time writing the song and George worked out who should sing what as it was his record. The end result was not far from ELO, but then the production was down to Jeff Lynne. They got excited when Roy sang his part in 'Handle with Care'. Bob told him, 'You could have been an opera star'. It was way too good for a bonus track and they wanted this to continue. Why not write and record an album together? Bob was on the road in May and so any album had to be made quickly. This was a great incentive: act now rather than think about it.

In early May, they were recording at Dave Stewart's studio in Los Angeles, but Dave was away. Roughly speaking they had to write a song a day for the album. They enjoyed writing together and kidding each other. Roy Orbison said, 'We used to tease Tom and Jeff about when they were going to get in the Rock and Roll Hall of Fame.'

When George Harrison and Jeff Lynne had performed together at the Prince's Trust in 1987, Prince Charles had suggested that they form their own band. When asked for a name, he said 'The Traveling Wilburys': a wonderful story but was it one of George Harrison's jokes?

They would have pseudonyms and Bob's was Lucky Wilbury, taken from 'I can't help it if I'm lucky' in 'Idiot Wind'. Roy Orbison's Lefty Wilbury was a tribute to the country singer, Lefty Frizzell. Tom Petty was Charlie T. Wilbury Jr, George Harrison was Nelson Wilbury and Jeff Lynne Otis Wilbury. There was talk of the guitarist Duane Eddy becoming a sixth Wilbury but they decided to leave it with the five vocalists.

'Tweeter and the Monkey Man' came out of Tom Petty and Bob Dylan discussing American TV while George and Jeff were laughing at their American references. The end result is a nod to Bruce Springsteen with references to 'Thunder Road', 'Jersey Girl' and 'Mansion On The Hill'.

Inspired by 'Dirty Mind' and 'Little Red Corvette', 'Dirty World' is mostly Bob Dylan parodying Prince. When Roy added the trembling Wilbury line, everybody laughed. The end result wasn't like Prince; indeed, there are elements of Benny Hill in there. Note the nod to 'Shenandoah' towards the end.

Dylan took lead vocals on 'Dirty World', 'Tweeter and the Monkey Man' and 'Congratulations'. He sang a verse of 'Margarita' and sang harmony, in his own way, throughout the album. Roy Orbison was at his magnificent best on 'Not Alone Anymore'. George had the chorus for 'End of the Line' and Bob and Tom worked on the verses.

'Congratulations' was Bob's idea and the others added comic lines. Roy Orbison said, 'It was all in fun. We were serious about the music but we weren't trying to write the greatest songs ever.' He's right: it worked superbly and it was a tremendous album, certainly Dylan had his mojo back. George Harrison said that the album helped Bob to get enthusiastic again.

Sid Griffin: 'Dylan was very unhappy in the 80s. His fans were like people in the desert looking for a cool drink of water. He woke up with the Traveling Wilburys. He regained his pride and craftsmanship.'

Jim Horn played saxophone, Ray Cooper percussion and Jim Keltner drums. Because Dave Stewart's studio was small, they were using the kitchen for recording as the five Wilburys could sit there with their guitars. On the rockabilly song, 'Rattled', Jim Keltner ran his sticks across the fridge. He played on everything and called himself Buster Sidebury.

The Wilburys hadn't told their record companies that they were doing this: far better to present it as a *fait accompli*. (Mo Ostin at Warners says he was told from the start as he was waiting for that B-side from George.) One record executive said, 'Well, I'm not going to stand in the way of history.' Warners released the album. *Traveling Wilburys, Vol. 1* went triple-platinum and was on the US charts for a year. It was Dylan's biggest selling album since his *Greatest Hits* and sold several million. *Highway 61 Revisited* did not top a million until 1999. I wouldn't argue that this album was anything like as good but it was a terrific, 'feel good' product and enhanced with a bogus history of the Wilburys from Michael Palin.

The album was so successful that there was talk of a Wilburys tour but George and Jeff hadn't played live in years and knew nothing about the new touring world. It was discussed but never brought to fruition. It would be too much of a circus, but George was keen on doing one show and filming it. It was a supergroup – much more than any other so-called supergroup. There was talk of a short film featuring Eric Idle and Michael Palin, but it didn't happen. There is home footage of Wilburys on the CD/DVD retrospective issued in 2007 and they made a video for 'Handle with Care'.

Two tracks weren't used, the folky story-song 'Maxine' and 'Like a Ship', which has rather croaky vocals (stand up, Mr. Dylan). Either of them could have been polished up for the album.

Jeff Lynne and Tom Petty did 'Handle with Care' at the Concert for George and at the Rock and Roll Hall of Fame in 2004, and occasionally Bob Dylan has sung 'Congratulations' on stage. In 2019 Jeff Lynne was including 'Handle With Care' in his stage performances and saying it came from his 'other group'.

In May 88 Bob Dylan visited the Lone Star Cafe in New York and joined Levon Helm on stage for 'The Weight' and 'Nadine'.

Two days later, Dylan's new album *Down in the Groove* was released to lukewarm reviews. Dylan was defensive: 'There's no rule that says everyone must write their own songs. I liked the songs and every so often you've got to sing the songs that are out there.'

In late May Bob Dylan was getting ready to tour with G.E. Smith (lead guitar), Marshall Crenshaw (bass) and Chris Parker (drums). It didn't quite coalesce and Dylan brought in Kenny Aaronson for Crenshaw. It was a stripped-down sound and this started the so-called Never Ending Tour. Dylan has performed around 100 gigs a year ever since, mostly in theatres rather than arenas.

Dylan said, 'I can't stand to play arenas but I do play them, but I know it's not meant to be heard in football stadiums. The best sound is in an intimate club room where you've got four walls and the sound just bounces.' Unlike Bruce Springsteen and other rock gods, he didn't accept the protocol: 'I don't say "How are you doing tonight in Cleveland?" Nobody gives a shit about how you're doing tonight in Cleveland.' Sometimes he didn't speak at all: Surely the money we place in Bob's pocket entitles us to a friendly word or two.

In 2000, Andrew Muir wrote a book *Razor's Edge* about the tour, which had reached 1,200 shows by then. The set lists were analysed, and every show unofficially recorded: many were officially recorded too. The set lists featured unexpected items and could change from night to night.

The tour started on 7 June 1988 at the Concord Pavilion, Concord, California, and 'Subterranean Homesick Blues' with G.E. Smith on guitar began the show with excitement. Dylan included the folky 'Lakes of Pontchartrain' and gave 'Gates of Eden' its first electric setting. There was a tough, punchy sound that the audiences liked. There were 13 songs in 70 minutes that first night and the highlight was Neil Young joining him for 'Gotta Serve Somebody'.

Next stop, Sacramento. Dylan was in a foul mood, possibly because only half the 12,000 seats had been sold. He only retained two songs from the first show and performed 12 songs in an hour. He included 'The Man in Me' and the Spanish-American war song, 'The Two Soldiers'. The promoter Bill Graham told Dylan that such a short set wouldn't do and Dylan gave a 17 song, 90-minute performance at the Greek Theatre in Berkeley the following night. He did a local favourite, 'San Francisco Bay Blues'. He performed 'She Belongs to Me' for the first time in seven years and the smoky ballad, 'I'm in the Mood for Love'. Bob met Mimi Fariña at the concert and said, 'Hey, that was a drag about Dick. Made me think.'

Dylan was reading his reviews out at the next gig, criticising a journalist for calling 'I'll Remember You' from *Empire Burlesque* an obscure song. Dylan told the audience, 'I don't think that's an obscure song. Do you think that's an obscure song? I don't think so.'

Among the songs that Dylan performed over the next few days were 'Barbara Allen', 'One More Cup of Coffee', 'Nadine' (sung in Chuck Berry's hometown), 'Silvio', 'Across the Borderline', 'Trail of the Buffalo', 'Tomorrow Is a Long Time', 'Give My Love to Rose', 'Pretty Peggy-O' and Leonard Cohen's 'Hallelujah'.

When Dylan met the boxer Donny Lalonde, Lalonde told him that he played his music while training. Dylan said he shadow boxed to keep fit. In November, Dylan flew to Las Vegas as he had a ringside seat for Lalonde's fight but he was soon knocked out. Dylan left immediately afterwards – an expensive trip!

After a show at the State Fairgrounds, Indianapolis, Dylan travelled to Fairmount, James Dean's hometown. He arrived at midnight and stayed for three hours visiting his grave and the Historical Museum opened for him to see James Dean relics. He left at 3am. A couple of days later he visited the Country Music Hall of Fame in Nashville.

Dylan performed an excellent 'Pretty Boy Floyd' (voice, guitar, harmonica) for *Folkways: A Vision Shared*, a star-packed tribute to Woody Guthrie and Leadbelly with Bruce Springsteen, U2 and Brian Wilson. *Folkways: A Vision Shared*, was to win a Grammy for Best Traditional Folk Recording. Oddly, Dylan's performance of 'Pretty Boy Floyd' was in the same category

When he was in a studio, Bob wanted to do 'Come Rain or Come Shine' but he was discouraged by the chords. He simplified it and eventually in 2016, he recorded it for *Fallen Angels*.

As for the MOR singers themselves, Bob later demonstrated his affection for Frank Sinatra by recording several of his songs, but in his youth he was drawn to the more flamboyant of those singers, notably Johnnie Ray. On the Never Ending Tour, Bob was exploring the early rockabilly and country hits.

The Welsh band, the Alarm was formed in 1978. They moved to London at the start of the 1980s, found a manager, Ian Wilson, and got a record deal with IRS. Bono offered them a support slot in the States in 1983, which led to a small tour of their own. They had hits, opened on the Pretenders' world tour, had more hits, met Elliot Roberts – sometime Bob Dylan manager, dumped Ian Wilson, made friends with Neil Young, went on another huge tour and in June 1988 were the first support act of the Never-Ending Tour, playing 40 shows with Dylan. On August 4 in Hollywood, Dylan brought them on to augment his own band for 'Knockin' on Heaven's Door'. The same thing happened again on August 7 in Santa Barbara, the Alarm's last night with Dylan.

Tracy Chapman took over as support and she too joined him for 'Knockin' on Heaven's Door'. In Edmonton, Doug Sahm sang with him on 'She's About a Mover'. Perhaps realising that *Down in the Groove* wasn't making any headway, Dylan started performing some of the songs; 'Rank Strangers to Me', 'Silvio' and 'Had a Dream about You, Baby'.

On September 25, Dylan was at the Audubon Zoo, New Orleans. His voice was in terrible shape and he was virtually shouting – what did the animals think?

While in New Orleans, Dylan met the Neville Brothers and Daniel Lanois who had been recording 'Ballad of Hollis Brown' and 'With God on Our Side' for their album, *Yellow Moon*. The Neville Brothers added a verse about Vietnam to 'With God on Our Side'. Not only did Bob approve but he added it to his own version, performing it a week later – he didn't do that with Bono.

On October 5, Dylan was at a post-tour party for George Michael with Carole Childs. He and Carole were to spend time on his farm in Minnesota. He and his brother David owned the Orpheum Theatre in Minneapolis but it was put on sale for $1.4m.

The Scottish folk performer Jackie Leven met Dylan on a train. He showed him his lyric, 'As We Sailed into Skibbereen' and Dylan suggested he set it to the tune of 'One Too Many Mornings'. He didn't do that but there is a touch of 'One Too Many Mornings' about it.

In mid-October, Dylan was back on the road doing a band version of 'Bob Dylan's 115th Dream', which lost its humour, and 'The Wagoner's Lad'. He sang that with great empathy, so he does understand women after all.

On October 18 there was the much heralded release of *Traveling Wilburys Volume 1*. (Had the title come from Dylan as a few years later he wrote *Chronicles Volume 1*.)

On December 4 in Oakland CA, there was an all-acoustic Bridge School Benefit, organised by Neil and Pegi Young for disabled children. Dylan did six songs including 'San Francisco Bay Blues' and 'Pretty Boy Floyd'.

On December 7 Roy Orbison (Lefty Wilbury) had a fatal heart attack. The video for the second Wilburys' single, 'End of the Line', was filmed the day after his funeral but that was what Roy would have wanted. If Roy and Bob had continued their friendship, who can say what would happened? They had both grown up in dying towns – in Orbison's case, Wink, Texas, which lost its oil revenues. They might have come together on a song about that.

Orbison had completed an album for Virgin, *Mystery Girl*. It was partly produced by Jeff Lynne and the musicians included Tom Petty and the Heartbreakers. The hit single, 'You Got It', was written by Lynne, Orbison and Petty and produced in George Harrison's studio, so a high Wilbury content even though Bob wasn't involved.

In March 1989, Bob Dylan started a new album, *Oh Mercy*, with Daniel Lanois and his engineer Malcolm Burn in New Orleans. Bob was given a package price by Lanois, $150,000 for everything. Lanois said, 'Bob now knows how to record with modern facilities. That was lacking in the past.' The mural on the control room was of a swamp and there were stuffed animals including an alligator to hand. The sound of crickets added atmosphere. Bob took a house in Audubon Avenue and rode his Harley-Davidson around New Orleans.

Lanois didn't want Dylan to lose his spontaneity but he wanted the details to be right. Sometimes Bob nailed it in one: 'Man in the Long Black Coat' is one take without a rehearsal. He didn't want Dylan to be lazy and accept something that was sub-standard. Lanois was intrigued by the way Dylan would take couplets from one song and put them in another. 'Broken Days' became 'Everything Is Broken'.

Bob knew the actress Kim Basinger. The title of his album, *Oh Mercy*, probably relates to her 1986 film *No Mercy* in which she plays a person from New Orleans alongside Richard Gere who never appears without a long black cloak. She is illiterate, 'there was nothing she wrote' and there is a background of crickets. Hence, 'Man in the Long Black Coat'. It is about a girl who has gone with somebody in a long black coat. Is it death? Dylan isn't saying.

Everything fits in *Oh Mercy*. Dylan had written songs that are compatible with Lanois and at the same time, Lanois hasn't tried to bend Dylan's songs to fit his project. The atmospheric, swampy sound is perfect for the material. The musicians included the soul drummer Willie Green, the Cajun accordionist Rockin' Dopsie and the percussionist, Cyril Neville from the Neville Brothers.

The album opens with the quickest and most urgent of the songs, 'Political World'. Dylan said, 'Just because it's called 'Political World' doesn't necessarily mean it is a political song.' True, but that's a red herring as Dylan is complaining about the world today. People are confused and depressed; peace is not welcomed and there is tension between the sexes. You may shout out God's name but what's the point as you don't know what it is, do you,

Mr. Jones? The promotional video was directed by John Mellencamp but it was so disjointed that I doubt that anyone wanted to see it for a second time.

Daniel Lanois' lap steel and Rockin' Dopsie's accordion are to the fore in 'Where Teardrops Fall'. You could say that the character in 'Political World' has gone away to cry, which ends effectively with John Hart's saxophone. Lanois wanted to use Rockin' Dopsie more but his button accordion could only be played in D or G and so was of limited use.

In 2019 'Political World' was used to highlight the tension in the series, *The Loudest Voice* (2019), the story of Roger Ailes (Russell Crowe), the founder of Fox News. The series also used 'Gimme Some Truth' (John Lennon).

It sounds like Bob is going into the Batman theme on 'Everything Is Broken' but it's a funky riff for a list song: 'Broken hands on broken ploughs, Broken treaties, broken vows'. The line about 'broken strings' wasn't on an early take, so possibly Dylan added it because someone had broken a string.

'Ring Them Bells' is mostly Dylan and his piano with some guitar and keyboard. Dylan is returning to the Day of Judgement: 'Ring them bells for the chosen few, Who will judge the many when the game is through?' Good point. There are not many covers of this song but one is by Gordon Lightfoot: 'I like the song and we do it well, me and my little band. I think we are about the only ones who do that one. Bob was here and I told him that we were doing it and he said, "Play it for me", and I had to sit right there and play it for him. Right in his face. I got quite nervous about it. (Laughs) He was okay about it.'

The musicians were jamming on 'Most of the Time' when Dylan came into the studio. He said, 'That's not how it goes, this is how it goes' and off they went in a different direction. There are distorted guitars in the background, which add to the feel. An early vocal, guitar and harmonica demo exists on *Bootleg 8,* which sounds like an update of *Another Side of Bob Dylan.* The album track was released as a single and was on the soundtrack of *High Fidelity.*

'What Good Am I' is a confession. The singer has not shown empathy with someone, especially when death was near. It is followed appropriately by 'Disease of Conceit' and then 'What Was It You Wanted'. Blues singer Chris Smither: 'I think Dylan has written some things that are as good as 'Visions of Johanna'. 'What Was It You Wanted' is equally unclear but it is still very rich in the potential for the listener to build his own construct.'

On 'Shooting Star', Lanois features the omnichord, which he had used on *The Joshua Tree*. It had originally been a children's instrument but it has been used by several performers including Elvis Costello and the Manic Street Preachers.

It wasn't all plain sailing. Dylan did have a row with Lanois and turned up at 3am with a portrait of an olive branch. In my book, that would lead to a further row. Lanois mixed *Oh Mercy* in New York and had more than enough for an album. Lanois said, "Series of Dreams' was a fantastic, turbulent track that should have been on the record but he had the last word.' It's a series of images, probably with no literal sense, about someone trying to make sense of his dreams. It would have a better fit for his 1997 album, *Time Out Of Mind*.

'Born in Time', which had an Oriental feel, could easily have been used but Bob was to revisit the song for *Under the Red Sky*. Similarly, he recorded 'Dignity' rather slowly on piano with an early verse that he dropped. It was a superb song but Dylan being Dylan was throwing it away for the moment.

When Dylan was cycling in Hell's Kitchen in New York on his way to the studio, he saw a mural by street artist Trotsky on the wall of a Chinese restaurant. He asked if he could use it for *Oh Mercy* and it led to Trotsky having exhibitions. The mural had been used on Tom Kimmel's *Tryin' to Dance* (1987). When a Dylan fan wore an *Oh Mercy* T-shirt, Trotsky said he hadn't negotiated the rights.

Lanois saw *Yellow Moon*, *Oh Mercy* and his own album *Acadie* as a trilogy. *Oh Mercy* sold 130,000 worldwide, so it was not a hit, but was the biggest seller of the three.

Columbia wanted a promotional film for 'Most of the Time' and Dylan made two, one directed by his son Jesse Dylan, the other by Tony Curtis (not the actor).

In May, Dylan was ready for the road and during rehearsals in Montana Studios, New York, he taped several familiar tunes: 'I Can See for Miles', 'You Keep Me Hangin' on', 'Where or When', 'Mystery Train', 'Sweet Dreams', 'Walkin' after Midnight', 'Little Queen of Spades', 'Poison Ivy' and 'High School Confidential'.

Dylan's European tour began on 27 May 1989 at a castle 30 miles from Malmo, namely Christinehof Slott, Andarum, Sweden. For the first week, Dylan wore a hooded anorak with a cap beneath it. At the National Stadium at Patras in Greece, he asked for the lights to be turned off for 'Silvio' and they remained that way for the rest of the show. Dylan played harmonica on this tour: indeed, it was hard to get him to stop.

Bono joined Dylan on stage in Dublin: they sang the three famous verses of 'Blowin' in the Wind' and then Dylan said, 'You carry on', which was taking the mick. Moving to Scotland, he became the first Wilbury to perform one of the songs live, 'Congratulations'.

On June 8, Kenny Aaronson had to leave the band for an operation and Tony Garnier took over on bass for a month. He had been with Asleep at the Wheel and was an excellent chef who liked to make gumbo. Among the covers Dylan was doing in Europe were Hank Williams' 'House of Gold', Townes Van Zandt's 'Pancho and Lefty', 'Peace in the Valley' and the country standard, 'Making Believe'.

He was filmed overlooking the Acropolis with Van Morrison and they recorded 'Crazy Love', 'One Irish Rover' and 'Foreign Window' for a BBC documentary. Back in the States, two Morrison songs, 'One Irish Rover' and also 'And It Stoned Me' were in his set. He did Leadbelly's 'Black Girl', one of the few instances where he had a lyric sheet. He was performing Steve Earle's rocker 'Nothing but You', Jimmy Cliff's 'The Harder They Fall' and that Orbison classic, 'Legend in My Time', written by Don Gibson.

When Dylan was interviewed by Edna Gundersen of *USA Today*, he said he hadn't been talking to audiences because 'it just don't seem relevant anymore. It's not stand-up comedy or a stage play. Also it breaks my concentration to have to think of things to say or to respond to the crowd. The songs themselves do the talking.' He referred to it being a never-ending tour and this was picked up by the Bobcats.

With the release of *Oh Mercy*, Elliot Roberts bowed out as Dylan's manager. In came Jeff Kramer, but chiefly as a tour manager.

Dylan appeared on the Chabad telethon *L'Chai – To Life* produced by his son-in law-Peter Himmelman, who was married to Maria. He and Harry Dean Stanton called their band Chopped Liver and played 'Hava Nagila'. Dylan played flute and recorder and was blessed by a dancing rabbi.

While at the Beacon Theatre in New York, Dylan played knee-bending harmonica on 'Leopard-Skin Pillbox Hat' and jumped into the audience, departing from the fire exit. Nothing is ever predictable in a Bob Dylan show. A couple of nights later, a woman jumped on stage and stripped to her G string. Dylan, clearly amused, kept playing. The next night Roger McGuinn joined him for 'Knockin' on Heavens' Door' and kept his clothes on. For the final show of the year, Dylan was performing the traditional 'When First Unto this Country' and the mining song, 'Dark as a Dungeon'.

In November 1989 Dylan recorded the Curtis Mayfield song, 'People Get Ready' for the soundtrack of *Flashback,* another Dennis Hopper film. It was recorded at John Mellencamp's studio in Brown County, Indiana.

Steve Earle and the Dukes were the support act to Dylan and told that they would have no contact with him. Steve got a message that Bob disapproved of his language on stage. Steve said, 'Fuck him!' That got back to him and he started speaking after that.

CHAPTER 14

Gruff and Ready

I. Tombstone Blues

Since the mid-1960s, songwriters have written about their own lives, often with uncommon frankness, the definitive example being Joni Mitchell. As the songwriters and performers age, a new and exclusive genre is developing: those who have life-threatening illnesses and record goodbye albums. George Harrison, Johnny Cash, Warren Zevon, Robin Gibb, Jesse Winchester, Glen Campbell, Bobby Vee and Leonard Cohen have all done this, perhaps adding Wilko Johnson who made a valedictory album, *Going Back Home,* and then recovered. By far the most striking example has to be from David Bowie. Looking very ill on a hospital bed, he sang his new song, 'Lazarus' and yet the public was still surprised by his death in January 2016.

These artists know they are not going to be around much longer but, on the whole, they look at life not despairingly but with a warmth in which they acknowledge how they have been blessed. On his album, *Popular Problems,* Leonard Cohen, in good health but 80 years old, mocked the atheist philosopher Richard Dawkins and indeed, there is nothing negative or even particularly morbid about the recordings. It is the songwriter adapting his talents to new subject matter. Here we look at how death has been treated in popular songs and how this new strain offers a fresh perspective. Zimmertime and the living ain't easy.

From operas with their rivers of blood to battle-scarred computer games, death has been an important factor in entertainment. The poverty and discrimination experienced by black musicians in the southern states came out in their songs and they hoped to be in a better place when they died. The blues songs told of troubles on earth and the gospel songs told of delights in heaven. In 1933 Josh White recorded 'In My Time of Dyin'' as the Singing Christian and the blues songs have included 'See that My Grave Is Kept Clean' (Blind Lemon Jefferson), 'Death Cell Blues' (Blind Willie McTell) and 'Death Letter Blues' (Son House). Feel sorry for Lightnin' Hopkins who returned home to find that everybody had gone in 'Death in the Family'. The emotional 'Don't Put No Headstone on my Grave' has been recorded by Esther Phillips, Charlie Rich and Jerry Lee Lewis; its second line is 'All my life I've been a slave'.

Go to any folk club and you will realise that the folk repertoire is littered with corpses – Barbara Allen, Matty Groves, the sailors on the Golden Vanity. The Kingston Trio told of the fate of Tom Dooley (in real life, Tom Dula) and sang a most thoughtful anti-war song, Pete Seeger's 'Where Have All the Flowers Gone'. It is even more poignant when sung in German by Marlene Dietrich. Its 30 words are perfectly chosen. The flowers have been picked by young girls who have married and their husbands have become soldiers. They are killed but are buried in graveyards where once again young girls are picking flowers.

There is the touching song of the life and death of Jimmy Brown, 'The Three Bells (Les Trios Cloches)', actually a Swiss song, recorded by Edith Piaf and Les Companions de la Chanson and then a country hit for the Browns. The French had many songs about death and Charles Aznavour was writing about old men from a young age, most famously in 'Yesterday When I Was Young (Hier Encore)'. His song about losing your mother, 'La Mamma', kept 'She Loves You' off the top of the French charts and it became a UK hit as 'For Mama' for Matt Monro.

A famous Belgian, Jacques Brel wrote 'My Death (La Mort)' and 'Seasons in the Sun (Le Moribond)', which is about a dying man who knows of his wife's infidelity. In 'Funeral Tango (Le Tango Funèbre)', Brel views the mourners at his funeral, an idea picked up by Tom Paxton for 'Now That I've Taken My Life'.

Country music is full of death songs. The Carter Family and nearly everybody else has sung about the death of their mother in 'Will the Circle Be Unbroken'. Hank Williams asked whether you were ready to meet the Angel of Death and recorded emotional narrations about fatalities as Luke the Drifter. Kitty Wells outlined the consequences of liquor in 'Death at the Bar'. One of the oddest but most successful country songs has been the frontier epic from 1949 about a herd of ghostly cattle, 'Ghost Riders in the Sky'.

There are gunfighter songs like Tex Ritter's 'High Noon', Marty Robbins' 'El Paso' and Patti Page's 'One of Us (Will Weep Tonight)'. Gene Pitney recorded Burt Bacharach and Hal David's 'The Man Who Shot Liberty Valance' and all three of them at different times have expressed surprise that John Ford didn't use it in his film. The reason is simple: there was no need to see the film after hearing the song as it gave away the plot. Western songs have persisted over the years including Bob Dylan's 'Knockin' on Heaven's Door' for *Pat Garrett and Billy the Kid* and Bob Marley's 'I Shot the Sheriff'.

On his début album in 1975, Guy Clark wrote 'Let Him Roll' about the funeral of a wino which is attended by an old flame who had been a whore in Dallas. Guy concludes 'I bet he's gone to Dallas, rest his soul.' On the same album is a wonderful story of a young boy visiting an 80 year old man, 'Desperados Waiting for the Train', the title being an analogy for death. When the old man dies, he says to the singer, 'Come on, Jack, that son of a bitch is coming'. David Allan Coe changes it to 'Don't cry, Jack, it's only sweet Jesus coming.' Less dramatic but no less poignant is the death of a war hero in 'He Went to Paris' by Jimmy Buffett.

Bobbie Gentry sang the mysterious 'Ode to Billie Joe', which left much to the imagination. What did Billie Joe and his girlfriend throw off the Tallahatchie Bridge and why did Billie Joe go back the next day and drown himself? As Bobbie said, 'The song is a study in unconscious cruelty' as the family is talking about the suicide whilst enjoying a family meal.

In 1959 Lefty Frizzell recorded the first version of 'The Long Black Veil', later a favourite with Johnny Cash and The Band. A condemned man is facing death for a murder he didn't commit but he can't tell the truth because 'I'd been in the arms of my best friend's wife.' The song has a spooky ending:

'She walks these hills in a long black veil
She visits my grave when the night winds wail
Nobody knows, nobody sees
Nobody knows but me.'

A condemned man in his cell is contemplating his fate in 'Green Green Grass of Home', an unlikely subject for a No. 1 record but Tom Jones took it there in 1966. Two years later the Bee Gees were at the top with another prison visit in 'I've Gotta Get a Message to You'. We don't know the crime in 'Green Green Grass of Home', but in the Bee Gees, he has killed his rival. Tom Jones stuck to the drama for 'Delilah' (also 1968) with a brilliantly concise lyric from Barry Mason, 'I felt the knife in my hand and she laughed no more.' The stabbing arrangement from Les Reed was reminiscent of the shower scene in *Psycho*.

Curly Putnam Jr (who happens to be the Junior of 'Junior's Farm') wrote 'Green Green Grass Of Home' and, in 1980, he wrote the equally bleak 'He Stopped Loving Her Today' with Bobby Braddock. George Jones plays a man who has only stopped loving his cheating woman because he has died. As in 'Let Him Roll', the woman goes to his funeral. George Jones had reservations about the song and told the producer Billy Sherrill, 'Nobody will buy that morbid SOB'. It was a No. 1 country single in 1980 and it is near the top of any list of favourite country songs.

The country singer Leon Payne wrote a song about a serial killer 'Psycho' which was covered by Eddie Noack in 1968. It received little airplay but the song has become a cult classic largely because it was recorded by Elvis Costello, who drew attention to Eddie's version. Bob Dylan has praised the song. The killer has gone to see his mother for a meal after killing his ex and her lover. During the song, we learn that he has also killed his son, a little girl and a dog and it ends,

'You think I'm psycho, don't you, mama,
I didn't mean to break your cup,
You think I'm psycho, don't you, mama
Mama, why don't you get up?'

In 1934, Cole Porter, wanting to parody country music, wrote 'Miss Otis Regrets'. The lady in the song can't accept a lunch invitation as she is about to be hanged. Although a very American theme, this song was premiered in the West End show, *Hi Diddle Diddle*. The most famous recording is by Ella Fitzgerald, and Ella with Louis Jordan recorded an entertaining duet, 'Stone Cold Dead in de Market'.

In the early 1960s there was the cult of death discs in both Britain and America, many of which were banned by the BBC on grounds of taste. They included 'Tell Laura I Love Her' (death in a stock-car race, a UK No. 1 for Ricky Valance), 'Teen Angel' (Mark Dinning), 'Endless Sleep' (death by drowning, Marty Wilde), 'Ebony Eyes' (death in an air disaster, Everly Brothers), 'Leader of the Pack' (death on a motorbike, Shangri-las) and 'Terry' (death on a motorbike, Twinkle).

Kenny Everett nominated Jimmy Cross' 'I Want My Baby Back' as the world's worst record and it's hard to argue with his choice. In the song, Jimmy takes his girlfriend to a Beatles concert but she dies in a crash with the 'leader of the pack' on the way home. With sound effects galore, Jimmy digs up her grave and climbs into the coffin where his muted voice can be heard proclaiming, 'I've got my baby back.'

Bob Luman had success with the positive message, 'Let's Think about Living'. And how eerie is this? In 1964, Jan and Dean sang about a fatality in a road race in 'Dead Man's Curve' and two years later, Jan was seriously injured in a car accident close to the song's location.

Bob Dylan: Outlaw Blues

In 1966 Mel Tillis wrote, and Johnny Darrell recorded, 'Ruby, Don't Take your Love to Town' about a crippled veteran from the Korean war who watched his partner getting ready for a new man: 'If I could move, I'd get my gun and put her in the ground.' In order to get airplay, Mel Tillis referred to that 'crazy Asian war' and said that the song was about Korea, but everyone related it to Vietnam on its revival by Kenny Rogers and the First Edition in 1969. By then there had been many songs about Vietnam and there would be many more: 'Jimmy Newman' who dies on the verge of going home by Tom Paxton and the rehabilitation and death of 'Sam Stone' by John Prine.

The surf music songwriter P.F. Sloan took home a Bob Dylan album, which prompted his view of world events, 'Eve of Destruction', a million-seller for Barry McGuire. The record was banned by the BBC but the pirate stations programmed it heavily. Even today it is a record unlike any other, the musical equivalent of someone standing on a corner with the sign, 'The End Is Nigh'.

Curtis Mayfield wrote the score for a Blaxploitation film about drug dealing, *Superfly* (1972), although his song, 'Freddie's Dead', was not used in the film itself. It became a US million seller but a BBC ban prevented UK airplay.

In 1939 Billie Holiday recorded a bitter song about lynchings in the South, 'Strange Fruit', the strange fruit hanging from the trees being the victims. It became a Civil Rights anthem and in the 1960s, there were many songs about the cause including 'He Was My Brother' (Simon and Garfunkel), 'The Lonesome Death of Hattie Carroll' (Bob Dylan) and 'Abraham, Martin and John' (Dion, Marvin Gaye) for the assassinations of Abraham Lincoln, Martin Luther King and the Kennedy brothers. Wilson Pickett was affected when he heard Moms Mabley perform this song but he changed it to his musical influences, 'Cole, Cooke and Redding'.

There are tribute songs by the thousand. Many are sincere and made for the right motives: others are intended to boost the performers' careers by touching on public sympathy. Some incorporate snatches of the subjects' songs, especially with Elvis tributes where the singers hope familiarity will increase sales. Elton John and Bernie Taupin's tribute to Marilyn Monroe, 'Candle in the Wind', was made with the best of intentions, but was it a good idea to amend it for Diana's death in 1997? In terms of the sum raised for charity, then yes, but surely Diana merited a song of her own rather than a quick rehash of Marilyn's lyric.

Among the better and more heartfelt tributes are 'Al Bowlly's in Heaven' (Richard Thompson), 'A Young Man Is Gone' (about James Dean by the Beach Boys), 'The Late Great Johnny Ace' (Paul Simon), 'Three Stars' (about Buddy Holly, Ritchie Valens and the Big Bopper by Eddie Cochran, himself the subject of a tribute by Heinz), 'First You Lose the Rhyming' (for Phil Ochs by Harvey Andrews), 'Memphis Skyline' (for Jeff Buckley by Rufus Wainwright), 'Boulder to Birmingham' (for Gram Parsons by Emmylou Harris), 'Elvis and Marilyn' (Leon Russell), 'From Graceland to the Promised Land' (Merle Haggard), 'Hound Dog Man' (for Elvis by Roy Orbison) and 'Rough on the Living' (about Lester Flatt, not Elvis, and recorded by Bobby Bare). Frank Sinatra's life was celebrated in 'Two Shots of Happy, One Shot of Sad' by U2 and as Nancy Sinatra recorded it, she must have thought it was okay. When Mrs. Thatcher died, it wasn't a tribute single (perish the thought) but 'Ding, Dong! The Witch Is Dead' from the soundtrack of *The Wizard of Oz* that found itself at No. 2.

In 1988 Lou Reed and John Cale wrote a suite of songs for the late Andy Warhol, *Songs for Drella* and this was followed by Reed's eloquent tribute to the songwriter Doc Pomus, *Magic and Loss*. Death is rarely far from Reed's songs and the same can be said of Nick Cave, whose album titles include *Murder Ballads* (1996), *No More Shall We Part* (2001) and *Abattoir Blues* (2004). Is there a more unnerving video than Nick Cave and P.J. Harvey performing the murder ballad, 'Henry Lee'?

The worst tribute song is surely Neil Diamond's 'Done Too Soon' (1971) in which he lists those who have died early: a strange bunch to be sure – Jesus Christ, Humphrey Bogart, Chico Marx, murderer Caryl Chessman and Alan Freed. This concept is continued to this day by Marty Wilde who slows down his act to perform 'Are You Lonesome Tonight' and for the narration, he reads a list of fellow travellers who have passed on. I have seen him do this ten years ago and I have seen him do it now and the list is getting longer. Once you start this kind of thing, it is very hard to stop and you can't really omit anyone for fear of causing offence.

In 2009 Bruce Springsteen dedicated his album *Working on a Dream* to a departed member of the E Street Band, Dan Federici and the final track 'The Last Carnival' was about touring without him. Jackson Browne wrote the intensely moving 'For a Dancer' after an ice-skater he knew had died in a fire: death is one dance that he will do alone, and indeed, this metaphor has meant that the song is played at funerals. In 1991 Eric Clapton celebrated the life of his four-year-old son, Conor, in 'Tears in Heaven', a song of comfort which, nevertheless, he still finds agonising to perform. Clapton never met his own father and his reflections on that and on his own relationship with Conor are in 'My Father's Eyes', written in 1998.

John Lennon wrote 'A Day in the Life' after a friend and an heir to the Guinness fortune, Tara Browne, had been killed in a car accident. In the same year, the Pretty Things recorded 'Death of a Socialite'. Cat Stevens wrote 'Lady D'Arbanville' after his girlfriend Patti D'Arbanville had gone to New York to work as a model. From the lyric, you might assume that she had died, but she is still around.

When Neil Young purchased his Broken Arrow Ranch in 1970, he compared his life to the caretaker's in 'Old Man', a track on his *Harvest* album. He is trying to show, not too successfully, what they have in common.

David Gates wrote a beautiful song to remember his father, 'Everything I Own', first charting for his group Bread in 1972 but going to No. 1 for reggae artist Ken Boothe. A more complex tribute to a father has been paid by Randy Newman, again called 'Old Man' and dating from 1972. Newman confronts his father's atheism and the fact that he did not want a funeral service. He sings, 'Won't be no God to comfort you, You taught me not to believe that lie.'

Up to that time, the songs largely conformed to the Jewish / Christian way of death, and indeed, in 1970, a Jewish songwriter, Norman Greenbaum, had a transatlantic smash with Jesus taking us to the Spirit in the Sky. He is going to heaven because he has 'never sinned' but possibly Jesus will mark him down for arrogance. In 1966 Laura Nyro offered a novel twist in 'And When I Die': she thinks there is no heaven but there may be a hell. In 1970 George Harrison reflected on death in 'Art of Dying'. In his original handwritten lyric, he said that when he died there was nothing 'Mr. Epstein can do' but he then changed it to 'Sister Mary', probably a reference to the consolation in Paul McCartney's 'Let It Be'. The song states his belief in reincarnation but if 'most of us return here', how does he know who will be chosen?

Tom Waits' musings in 'After You Die' in 2011 are disappointing. He asks what it will be like after death but his analogies – 'Like a necktie flapping, like a rich guy clapping' – mean that he hasn't a clue, but then neither has anybody else. If by any chance some scientist does discover what happens when we die, the entire world will change overnight: it would be a great subject for a novel.

The inevitability of dying didn't bother McGuinness Flint in 'When I'm Dead and Gone', a goodtime single that rose to No. 2 in 1970. It was handled more soberly in Pink Floyd's 'The Great Gig in the Sky' (1973). Roughly 40,000 people die a day in the USA and this statistic found itself in Blue Öyster Cult's 'Don't Fear the Reaper' – the lead guitarist Buck Dharma was thinking about dying and said that there was no need for anxiety.

The band denied that 'Don't Fear the Reaper' was about suicide. However, there have been many songs about suicide, starting with the final verse of Leadbelly's 'Goodnight Irene' where he is going to the river to drown. Buddy Knox sounds surprisingly upbeat in 'I Think I'm Gonna Kill Myself' (1959). The same title was used by Elton John for teenage thoughts on suicide in 1972 and three years later, he recorded 'Someone Saved My Life Tonight', which is about Long John Baldry doing exactly that. Leonard Cohen is contemplating the end in the bleak 'Dress Rehearsal Rag'.

In 1972 Gilbert O'Sullivan had his most enduring success with 'Alone Again (Naturally)'. In the song, his parents had died and he had been stood up and was contemplating suicide. Again there was a questioning of religion: 'If God exists, why did he desert me?'

The final track on David Bowie's *Ziggy Stardust* album was 'Rock and Roll Suicide', which Bowie said was inspired by French chanson. Around this time, Bowie was performing Jacques Brel's 'My Death'.

In 1974 Hot Chocolate had a UK Top 10 hit with Errol Brown's song, 'Emma' about his love for Emmaline from the age of five. They married but she wanted to be a movie star and when she didn't make it, she committed suicide. On the face of it, fiction but Errol Brown based his feelings on fact. "Emma' is a very personal song to me and it is to do with the death of my mother when I was 19 years old. That scream was very real.' A fictional character who couldn't live up to her dreams was depicted in Shel Silverstein's 'The Ballad of Lucy Jordan', recorded by both Dr. Hook and Marianne Faithfull.

Simon and Garfunkel described the death of a lonely man that nobody knew in 'A Most Peculiar Man', while the suicide of a friend troubled James Taylor in 'Fire and Rain', a song which has brought comfort to thousands.

In 'Yer Blues', John Lennon sings, 'Feel so suicidal, even hate my rock and roll.' Cat Stevens wonders about the point of working at all in 'But I Might Die Tonight' but Marvin Gaye is simply using the thought of 'If I Should Die Tonight' to get his end away, although surely the girl doesn't want his corpse in her bed. Albert Hammond is afraid of flying in 'I Don't Want to Die in an Air Disaster'.

The American way of death was succinctly parodied by Tom Paxton in 'Forest Lawn'. This complements Evelyn Waugh's novel, *The Loved One*, in which the mortician brings a smile to the dead, no matter how they died. Contrast with the R&B song, 'Brother Bill (The Last Clean Shirt)', recorded by the Animals where that clean shirt is wanted for his funeral.

Both Screamin' Jay Hawkins and Screaming Lord Sutch used coffins in their stage acts. Sutch sang about the undead in 'Til the Following Night' and was banned for making light of true crime in 'Jack the Ripper'. That was produced by Joe Meek who specialised in ghoulish sounds and made the Moontrekkers' 'Night of the Vampire'. There was horror rock with the US TV presenter John Zacherle's 'Dinner with Drac'. Sticking in a comic vein, the Beatles recorded 'Maxwell's Silver Hammer' which in view of all the school shootings would never have been made today. The Bee Gees sang of a 'New York Mining Disaster 1941' and yet there are no mines in New York.

You can see how the more preposterous discs spawned Goth. Black Sabbath and Uriah Heep were rock bands with gothic overtones and soon there was a macabre sub-genre of dark and foreboding songs incorporating medieval myths, devil worship, blood sacrifice and the undead. It was too ridiculous for some but there are classic records like Bauhaus' 'Bela Lugosi's Dead' (or rather 'Bela Lugosi's Undead' as he played Dracula), but this record isn't sinister or unnerving in the way that Talking Heads' 'Psycho Killer' still is.

Prior to the mid-1980s, criminals like Leadbelly didn't accentuate their time in prison when they performed, but then gangsta rap developed, a hardcore music full of braggadocio and, in many cases, the real thing. The Notorious B.I.G's first album was called *Ready to Die* and released on Puff Daddy's Bad Boy label. Undeterred by Biggie Smalls' reputation for beating up promoters and his arrests for drug and gun possession, a rival rapper Tupac Shakur recorded 'Hit 'Em Up' which included a boast regarding Biggie's wife, Faith Evans, saying 'I fucked her, Biggie'. A short while later, Tupac was shot dead and no one knows if Biggie was responsible. Biggie's next album was *Life after Death* and included 'You're Nobody ('til Somebody Kills You)'. In March 1997 Biggie was murdered and it prompted Puff Daddy and Faith Evans to rework Police's No 1 'Every Breath You Take' as 'I'll Be Missing You'. Bizarrely this was included in the tribute album to Princess Diana. The murders of both Tupac Shakur and Biggie Smalls remain unsolved.

Freddie Mercury was hardly seen in 1990 and the following year he announced that he had AIDS. He wrote a song in the style of Charles Aznavour about his predicament, 'The Show Must Go on', in which he announced, 'I'll soon be going round the corner.' He had a play on words with 'I'll top the bill, I'll overkill.' The show couldn't go on and the promotional video was made without new footage of him. The song entered the charts early in November and he died later that month.

George Harrison had been a smoker all his life and he succumbed to lung cancer in 1997, dying in 2001. He had the time to write and record a final album, *Brainwashed*, although it was not released until after his death. In 'Stuck inside a Cloud', he says, 'Talking to myself, crying as we part, Knowing as you leave me, I also lose my heart.'

Maybe Paul McCartney is practising for his valedictory album. In 2007 he released the reflective *Memory Almost Full*. He discussed childhood memories and then he sang 'The End of the End', calling it 'the start of a journey to a much better place.' He says how he would like his life to be celebrated when he dies. I have heard this song played at a funeral as the lyric has a general application. His biographer Peter Ames Carlin says, 'McCartney knows how to take a sad song and make it better: it's God's gift to that guy. There is a lot of autobiography and looking within on that album and some songs are about growing up. 'The End of the End' is very unsentimental. He wants songs to be sung on the day he dies. He knows his contribution to the world.'

By the early 1990s and after an unsatisfactory time with Mercury Records, Johnny Cash had lost interest in creating new music. His career was tailing off as he played Butlin's in Bognor Regis. Enter Rick Rubin, producer of Run DMC and the Beastie Boys. He told the 61-year-old Cash that he would record him away from Nashville conventions with just voice and guitar. Though Rubin was to add instrumentation on some tracks, he kept the sound sparse and because he had his own studio, he recorded song after song with Cash. The result was a stunning series of albums in stark contrast to the rest of his career and equally valid. Cash was singing about getting old and as he aged and suffered diabetic complications, the material became more poignant. His former producer, Jack Clement, said, 'It's not the kind of stuff I'd record myself.'

The contract permitted Cash to record elsewhere on special projects, notably with his mates, Waylon Jennings, Willie Nelson and Kris Kristofferson as the Highwaymen. On *The Road Goes on forever* (1995), they perform Waylon's questioning song, 'I Do Believe', a brave composition from someone who relied on support from the Bible Belt. On the same album, we get Johnny Cash's ruminations on 'Death and Hell' ('Death and hell are never full, And neither are the eyes of men') and 'Live Forever', a song from hell-raiser Billy Joe Shaver, who was always wondering if he was doing the right thing and had lost his wayward son, Eddy, through a drugs overdose.

The album which really highlights Cash's age is *American Recordings IV: The Man Comes Around*, from 2002. The title song was Cash's ruminations on the Book of Revelation. 'Hurt' was not a low-key version of Timi Yuro's big-voiced ballad but a poignant song by Trent Reznor which had originally been recorded by Nine Inch Nails. Following flood damage, his museum in Nashville, the House of Cash, had been closed to the public and Rubin had the idea of recording the video there. The aged, white-haired Cash was shown next to his younger self. His final recording was 'September When It Comes', a song about memories written by his daughter Rosanne and recorded with her. He admitted his frailty and when September came, in 2003, Johnny Cash died.

Warren Zevon often discussed his problems in public. In 1976, he wrote and recorded 'I'll Sleep When I'm Dead'. In 2000 he wrote an album, *Life'll Kill Ya*, exploring sickness and death. In one song he visits his doctor with the complaint, 'My Shit's Fucked Up'. On many of his albums including that one, there is a picture of a skull wearing his glasses and smoking a cigarette. When he suffered through being exposed to asbestos in his youth, he wrote his final album, *The Wind*, recording it with famous friends. He said, 'There's nothing like an experience like this to really make you start living from day to day.' The album included a song for his wife, 'Keep Me in Your Heart', without his trademark irony, which is about taking comfort in memories. ('Shadows are falling and I'm running out of breath, Keep me in your heart for a while.')

Robin Gibb was working hard when he learnt in 2010 that he had an inoperable cancer. With great resolution, he completed his *Titanic Requiem* and a solo album, *50 St Catherine's Drive*. He sang of the importance of making every day count in both 'Days of Wine and Roses' and 'All We Have Is Now'.

The first song to refer to Alzheimer's disease was 'Hello in There' written by John Prine for his debut album in 1971. It was a confident and sensitive composition about an aged couple who have little contact with their children and with each other. The man is longing for friendship, waiting for someone to say 'Hello in there', the same words he uses for his wife as he struggles to understand her illness.

Although Glen Campbell was in the early stages of Alzheimer's disease, he undertook a farewell tour with three of his children in 2011 which passed without any embarrassments. He appeared on the Grammys in 2012 and gave his final show in November 2012.

Glen released what was seen as his final album, *Ghost on the Canvas*, to coincide with the tour. It contained several instrumentals which showed he was still a fluid guitar player. His producer Julian Raymond had noted his conversation and used that to write new songs like 'A Better Place'.

Then there was a second album from the sessions, *See You There*, and a feature-length documentary about his illness, *I'll Be Me*. A song, written for the documentary, 'I'm Not Gonna Miss You', and attributed to Campbell and Julian Raymond, is a marvellously poignant composition that owes much to Jimmy Webb's style. From its title, it's easy to imagine 'I'm Not Gonna Miss You' being a song of lost love, but knowing his illness, the title has a completely different connotation. His wife's face will be the last one he will recognise and when the disease has set in, he won't know who she is so 'I'm not gonna miss you'. It's brilliantly original and was a Grammy nominee for best country song.

When Bobby Vee's family announced that he was suffering from Alzheimer's disease, it was thought we would not hear from him again. Bobby used to tour with his children, Jeff, Robby and Tommy aka the Vees, and as therapy they recorded his favourite songs at their home studio. Originally there was no intention to release them but they were so content with the results that they have put them out as *The Abode Sessions*. It has to be viewed as a farewell to his fans rather than definitive performances of well-known songs. It's uncomfortable to hear his frail voice struggling with familiar songs. Despite the presence of Daniel Lanois' poignant 'The Maker', I don't think that this CD has the depth of Johnny Cash's final recordings where Cash was publicly coming to terms with his Maker.

Although Willie Nelson does not suffer from Alzheimer's, he writes about the disease on his *December Day* album in 2014 with 'I Don't Know Where I Am Today' and 'Amnesia'. In 2013 he took Irving Berlin's look at hard times, 'Let's Face the Music and Dance', and it became a song about old age with no change in the lyric. In concert, he performs 'Roll Me Up (and Smoke Me when I Die)' and it's said in Austin that when you die, you go to Willie's house.

When 57, the singer / songwriter Gretchen Peters confronted mortality on her album, *Blackbirds*, which strangely considering its bleak subject matter found favour with Terry Wogan and led to a sell-out UK tour in 2015. Writing about cancer in 'The Cure for the Pain', she sings, 'There ain't no shelter from this hard rain.'

Gretchen Peters: 'Dylan and Cohen and definitely Rodney Crowell and Nick Lowe have been able to write about this, but they are mainly men and that is because women talking about ageing and mortality is taboo. But we should be able to deal with anything in our songs. It was risky but what have I got to lose? I didn't have one huge hit or a career precipice that I could have fallen off.'

Legend has it that Beth Nielsen Chapman wrote about the death of her husband Ernest Chapman on *Sand and Water* (1997), but much of it was written before he was known to be ill. 'When I wrote 'No One Knows But', I thought it could have been because my parents are getting older. 'Seven Shades of Blue' was just two verses and he said, "I love that song, it is like a Bob Dylan song." It is about being in a sorrowful place and not knowing where it is going. Six months, later, we were in the middle of dealing with his diagnosis which was very abrupt. He was given a couple of months to live and his cancer was very advanced and I had the startling feeling that this is what the song was about. I remember writing the last verse just weeks before he passed away and I played it for him. He wanted to have his ashes scattered in the Gulf of Mexico and I wrote this verse, "The whales will steal my laughter and the birds will sing my song, And I'll be happy ever after, And the world will get along." I thought it was perfect but he said, "You have got to change that song. I don't know whether I will be happy ever after. I am not too happy about this, I would rather stay here." I changed it to "I'll be OK forever after", and when I sing that song, I get a smile on my face as he was very opinionated right out to when he was stepping out upon the shore.'

Back in 1967 the jazz composer Billy Strayhorn wrote 'Blood Count' for Duke Ellington and his Orchestra, but it was released after his death from oesophageal cancer.

Steve Earle wrote and recorded 'Remember Me': 'I have a little boy and dying before he is old is one thing that could happen and I wanted to write it just in case. I am hoping that I will live long enough to see him through high school. I could do that. I am only 58. I quit smoking a long time ago and I take pretty good care of myself now, but you can't control that. There were four guys that I came out of high school with – we were the four smart guys who dropped out of high school – and it is a peer group of exactly four and I am the only one left, the others of died of cancer and heart attacks. I felt I would write it just in case.'

Jesse Winchester cut an album in 2013 as he was hoping that his bladder cancer had been cured. Having had a near death experience he had been musing on his mortality but he knew it was likely to return. He died in April 2014 and the album, *A Reasonable Amount of Trouble*, was released posthumously.

The album opens beautifully with 'All We Have Is now', about the joy of living for the moment: how nice to feel the sunshine in the park. A little sadder, Winchester considers his diagnosis in *'Every Day I Get the Blues'*: 'I know the sun is shining but it feels like rain' but even a song with that title can be uplifting. With such albums, you expect the final song of the final album to be the ultimate triumph and Jesse Winchester excels himself with 'Just So Much'. He sings,

'Where do I find him, it's never quite clear,
I'm dying to find him but dying's my fear,
Is there perfection, Will there be pain,
Will I see Mama and Dad again?'

Philip Larkin said that if you should write the perfect poem about death, you would never want to write anything again. That could be true. This is a faultless goodbye to the world and I am sure that as the years go by, we will find artists putting final albums on their bucket lists.

In his heyday, David Bowie was a master of timing. He planned everything meticulously and little was left to chance. Even when he was suffering from cancer, his farewell to the world was equally perfect, both with his album, *Blackstar* and the accompanying videos. The meanings of those songs and visuals will be discussed for years and clearly he planned his typically enigmatic farewell.

In 2016 Leonard Cohen spent his final weeks completing his album, *You Want It Darker*, which had the feeling of a Jewish funeral. He didn't know that the end was so near but he had severe back pain: 'If you are the dealer, I'm out of the game, If you are the healer, I'm broken and lame.'

Of course your plans can go wrong. In 2005 the jazz guitarist Derek Bailey thought he would chronicle the deterioration in his playing ability by way of albums, *Carpal Tunnel* being the first with each title citing how long he had been suffering. Unfortunately for him, the diagnosis was wrong, he had not got carpal tunnel syndrome but motor neurone disease and he did not live to see the next year.

It is surprising that so few songs have been written around famous last words. The dying curses of Sam Hall on the gallows in 1707 became an English folk song and was recorded, quite defiantly, by Johnny Cash on *American Recordings IV* in 2002.

In 1973 Paul McCartney was in Lagos recording *Band on the Run*. He was having an evening meal with Dustin Hoffman who wanted to see him write a song. McCartney, showing off but who cares, picked up a newspaper and wrote 'Picasso's Last Words' which happened to be, 'Drink to me, drink to my health, you know I can't drink anymore.' Until a few weeks ago, I hadn't come across another song like this and then I heard 'Oh Wow Wow' by D.C. Bloom, written around the last words of Steve Jobs. You might have thought that the CEO of Apple could have done better, but even if you plan your final words, how do you know that they will be your final words? You might be carrying the *bon mots* around for a fortnight, and then, after repeating them at ten-minute intervals, you suddenly die asking for the bedpan.

Of course you don't really have any say as to when or where your final goodbye will be. Tom Russell wrote and recorded 'You Will Never Hear Me Say Goodbye' but don't count on it? 'If I die on stage, that'll be fine by me. I played in Reno as part of a charity thing and we played in a couple of old folks' homes and I thought, "I'm not going to end up in a place like this." I will die on stage or like Edward Abbey, please drop me in the middle of the desert and let the coyotes eat me.'

II. So Much Older Now: 1990–1999

Bob Dylan was busy in the early weeks of 1990 as he was making a new solo album, *Under the Red Sky*, another with the Traveling Wilburys and preparing for a world tour. The Wilburys were continuing without Roy Orbison and although there was speculation that they would invite Del Shannon, they remained a quartet. Del was on their minds as they recorded his biggest hit, 'Runaway', although it was not included on the album, which in true Dylan fashion, was called *Traveling Wilburys, Volume 3*.

The *Under the Red Sky* album included the lyrics and added that the artist's notes on the songs were only available in a collectors' item from an address in New York. As far as I know, nobody ever saw the notes and so it looks like an abandoned project. Dylan has hardly commented on this album and so we are no further forward.

Critically, the album had a torrid time. In the *New Musical Express*, Charles Shaar Murray said, 'It only sounds like a great Dylan album from the next room.' Most critics missed the point that Dylan was, like Woody Guthrie and Leadbelly before him, making a children's album and the clue is surely in the dedication, to his daughter, 'For Gabby Goo Goo'. Dylan was writing simple, minimalist lyrics and after all, that great wordsmith Woody Guthrie wrote 'Car Car'. Why though does Bob Dylan give special thanks to his girlfriend, Carole Childs, rather than his wife?

Dylan had addressed parenting famously in 'Forever Young', but it was not one of his regular subjects. The album could have explored many interesting issues such as how to raise children when you have been a rebel yourself. Perhaps this was not the place as Dylan wanted to write songs *for* children rather than *about* them. Some of them sound like nursery rhymes. 'Cat's in the Well' is Dylan playing around with 'Ding Dong Dell, Pussy's in the Well'; and 'Under the Red Sky' is his take on 'There was a little boy and there was a little girl'. His producer Don Was said, "Wiggle Wiggle' is like him writing 'Tutti Frutti', and what is 'Tutti Frutti' but an adult nursery rhyme? The album is called *Under the Red Sky*, UTRS – say that fast and you have Uterus, another indication that this is a children's album. There are exceptions as 'Born in Time' is about a crumbling relationship.

Under the Red Sky was started in January 1990 but couldn't be completed until March because Dylan was on tour. When he was in London in February, Dylan walked around and encountered Speakers' Corner in Hyde Park on the day of the Poll Tax riots and he wrote about it in 'TV Talkin' Song'. The speaker is not denouncing the proposed tax but bemoaning that we show young children TV rather than singing them lullabies. The irony is that the TV cameras were shooting in Speakers' Corner and Dylan ends up watching it on TV.

The starting point for 'Handy Dandy' has to be the nursery rhyme, 'Handy Dandy, Jack-a-Dandy', although Dylan veers off and most of the song is about himself: how many other people have been around the world and back again? The track starts with Al Kooper playing the riff for 'Like a Rolling Stone' and what new song is going to match that?

Daniel Lanois told *The Telegraph*, 'I share your fascination with Bob Dylan. The longer you get to know him, the less you really know him. Dylan hated the fact that everybody wrote about how great *Oh Mercy* was. Whenever he gets praise for something, he wants to do something different. We couldn't do *Under the Red Sky* because I wasn't free and Dylan is impatient.'

The duo David and Don Was of Was (Not Was) had met Bob Dylan on tour in 1989 and he was impressed by their arrangement of 'Maggie's Farm' for the film, *The Freshman* (1990), starring Marlon Brando and Matthew Broderick. Six months later Dylan asked them if they would work on a new song, 'God Knows'. He liked the way they worked at Oceanway Studios in Los Angeles and also their admiration for old Sun Records. David Was recalled, 'He had the sort of primitive naivety of a so-called blues artist. I was surprised to find that core beneath the sophisticated exterior; this is a blues man.'

Never before, or since, has a Bob Dylan album been so star-studded. The guests included George Harrison, Elton John, Slash, David Crosby, Bruce Hornsby, Jimmie and Stevie Ray Vaughan and Al Kooper, and was even marketed as such.

The Hawaiian-styled instrumental break with George Harrison on 'Under the Red Sky' is magical. Dylan told Don Was that 'Under the Red Sky' was about the people who lived in Hibbing and never left. Possibly, as the song ends, 'The man in the moon went home and the river went dry.'

The urgency of 'Unbelievable' is conveyed by Kenny Aronoff's drumming but the lyric is all over the place. Is Dylan boasting when he sings, 'It's unbelievable you can get rich this quick'?

When Slash got to the studio, he found Kim Basinger there with a mysterious man in an anorak with a hooded sweatshirt and fingerless gloves. It was Bob Dylan. Dylan asked him to play 'Wiggle Wiggle' exactly like Django Reinhardt. Slash gave him three choices but Dylan thought that two of them were too much like Guns N' Roses and used his acoustic playing.

Dylan was playing accordion for the first time on record on 'Born in Time'. The Was team said that this song would be improved if it had a pause in it like 'The Weight'. Dylan agreed and it worked.

David Crosby sang backing vocals on 'Born in Time' and '2 x 2'. Dylan played the first song and said, 'Okay, let's record it'. Crosby asked to hear it again and this time Dylan sang it differently. Crosby knew there was no point in asking to hear it again as Dylan wanted spontaneity: 'He does it on purpose. His songs are the found art of the moment.'

Bob was pleased to have the guitarists Jimmie and Stevie Ray Vaughan on board who played on three tracks: '10,000 Men', 'God Knows' and 'Cat's in the Well'. In 'Handy Dandy' Jimmie doesn't come in until the second verse as he was out of the room. However, Bob decided that Stevie's playing was too intense for 'Handy Dandy' and reworked the take with Waddy Wachtel on lead guitar.

Under the Red Sky contains good songs and is a perfectly acceptable album. It isn't among his best work, but it doesn't deserve to have been ignored. It would have been better if Dylan had stuck to the idea of a children's album. A few months down the line, he recorded a delightful 'This Old Man' at his home studio for a Disney charity album for children with AIDS, *For Our Children*. Dylan could have combined the children's songs from this album with old favourites like 'This Old Man' and 'Ol' McDonald' for his album, and used the other songs in a different project, but then I am saying that Dylan should act as other performers would – and this is Bob Dylan.

A video for 'Unbelievable' was made in the Mojave Desert with Bob Dylan, Sally Kirkland, Molly Ringwald and a pig. Was this prompted by the line 'Feed that swine' in the song? Bob is laughing at one point but it doesn't last.

On 12 January 1990, Dylan had a warm-up concert for his world tour at Toad's Place, New Haven, a rare appearance. He performed 50 songs in four hours to an audience of 700. The 18 wide-ranging covers included 'Walk a Mile in My Shoes', 'Everybody's Movin'' (Glen Glenn, 1958), 'Help Me Make It through the Night', 'Dancing in the Dark', 'Black Girl in the Pines' and 'Precious Memories'. He sang the old folk song, 'Hang Me, O Hang Me' (which was sung by the Dylan character in the film, *Inside Llewyn Davis*) and his most recent composition was 'Tight Connection to My Heart'. Dylan was chatty and in a good mood, saying that 'Man of Peace' was from his religious period and 'Lay Lady Lay' was a song 'from the days when romance was important to me': beat that for an introduction.

On January 14, he tried out 'Wiggle Wiggle' and did 'You Angel You' in response to an audience request, his first live performance of the song, but he didn't know the words.

Four days later he was appearing to over 100,000 festivalgoers in San Paulo, Brazil with Bon Jovi, Eurythmics and Tears for Fears also on the bill. He talked to Dave Stewart about making a film together. There was another huge festival in Rio de Janeiro and Dylan appeared on Brazilian TV but the published interview with Eduardo Bueno was faked.

At the end of January, Dylan was at the Grand Rex Theatre, Paris and singing 'Man Gave Names to All the Animals'. One night, Dylan played a gold guitar, wearing a gold suit with white cowboy boots. The following day he received France's highest cultural honour at Palais Royal, Paris, Dylan was Commandeur dans l'Order des Arts et des Lettres.

Bob Dylan and Leonard Cohen met in a café in Paris and talked about songwriting. Dylan asked how long it had taken him to write 'Hallelujah' and Cohen said, 'Two years, and how long did it take you to write 'Jokerman'?' Dylan said it had taken 20 minutes. Neither was telling the truth.

Although Dylan was back in an English speaking country, he decided not to talk to the audiences at Hammersmith Odeon. He took the band by surprise with 'Tonight I'll Be Staying Here with You'. Dylan had learnt 'You Angel You' and was performing an electric

'Hang Me, O Hang Me'. He played a superb version of 'Disease of Conceit' on the piano at the final show with flourishes like Jerry Lee Lewis.

Liz Thomson: 'There were times in the 90s when he forgot his lyrics. I saw him at Hammersmith where he forgot the lyrics to 'Desolation Row' and blew harmonica in the wrong key for his guitar.'

On February 24 Bob was at a tribute concert for Roy Orbison at Universal Amphitheatre, Universal City, Los Angeles and sang 'Mr. Tambourine Man' with the Byrds, but they each performed their own arrangement at the same time! He played guitar on 'He Was a Friend of Mine' and joined in an ensemble 'Only the Lonely' with Bruce Hornsby, Bonnie Raitt and B.B. King.

John Jorgenson explains what went wrong: 'I was playing with the Byrds who at the time were Roger McGuinn, Chris Hillman, David Crosby and Steve Duncan. We had recorded tracks for their boxed-set and done a few live shows around Southern California and there was a big tribute to Roy Orbison. The showstopper was going to be the Byrds playing 'Mr. Tambourine Man' with Bob Dylan. I had an extra electric guitar ready and Roger McGuinn liked to tune up higher than standard pitch; the note A is 440 cycles, and he liked to tune to 444 as it gets a brighter sound. I took one of my guitars and tuned it to that pitch, put a strap on it and put it down for Bob to play. Roger was going to sing the first verse and then Bob was coming out. We finished the first verse and Roger was moving his head as if to say, 'Come on out, man.' He came out but holding a guitar that wasn't mine, I thought, 'Oh no', because he didn't know that we were tuned to that pitch. He plugged into an amp and turned every knob as loud as it could be. He hit this chord so loudly that it sounded like a vacuum cleaner and Chris looked at his bass to make sure he was on the right fret. It wasn't musically satisfying but the audience didn't care as they were so ecstatic that they probably didn't hear the music anyway. It's always a good idea to at least talk through the song before you're doing it before thousands of people for a live recording, but you can't tell Bob Dylan that.'

Bob did turn up for a soundcheck when he was joining Tom Petty and the Heartbreakers at Great Western Forum, Inglewood, California. They did 'Come Together' but not on the show. Bob, Tom and Bruce Springsteen performed 'Travellin' Band' (Creedence Clearwater Revival) and 'I'm Crying' (Animals) with Bruce dominant. Dylan and Petty sang the rockabilly song, 'Everybody's Movin'.

In late March, Dylan was back making *Under the Red Sky* in Hollywood. He cut some tracks with NRBQ (New Rhythm and Blues Quintet), although they didn't make the album. One was 'Some Enchanted Evening', which he returned to in 2015.

Bob Dylan with Don and David Was wrote a song for Paula Abdul called 'Shirley Don't Live Here Anymore', which she never recorded. Some years later, Was (Not Was) recorded it as 'Mr. Alice Don't Live Here Anymore'. The funky song is another 'Everything Is Broken' with an odd reference to Judy and Phil Collins. Okay though.

Dylan would work with the Wilburys during the day and then see Was (Not Was) each evening. *Under the Red Sky* was being made in a cellar in Hollywood where he would also sleep.

The Traveling Wilburys had rented a ranch house from the 1920s in the hills of LA and set up a mobile studio in the library, hiring equipment from Herb Alpert. They named it the Wilbury Mountain Studio and flew a flag. Surely Bob, now known as Boo Wilbury, should have been sleeping there.

Derek Taylor wrote a fake biography of the Wilburys: their father was Charles Truscott Wilbury and they all had different mothers. The new album was dedicated to Lefty Wilbury. Roy Orbison was the selling feature of the first album as his voice soared above the others. This time the songs were far more in the middle ground and lacked the playfulness of 'Tweeter and the Monkey Man'. This time round, Dylan was the most prominent Wilbury and although the album sold two million, it was only 40% of what the first album achieved. The same could be said of the contents. Joe Brown disagrees, 'I thought both the Traveling Wilburys albums were fantastic, and I loved all the tracks too. I particularly loved 'Where Were You Last Night' and I did it on an album.'

'She's My Baby' had been cut completely by Bob Dylan and then the other voices were segued in to make it a group recording. It's a decent song but the sort of list Dylan could write in his sleep and possibly did. '7 Deadly Sins' is also songwriting by rote; it lists the girl's seven deadly sins, which sound more like inconveniences to me.

'Inside Out', which starts with Dylan, is a neat song about things not being quite what they seem, while 'You Belonged to Me' has similarities to 'End of the Line'. There is an excellent line about an uncaring girl who likes to see cowboys fall off their horses at the rodeo. Similarly the title line, 'You Took My Breath Away' is followed by the humorous 'I want it back again.'

'Cool Dry Place' sounds like Bob Dylan in his comfort zone circa 1975 and works well. The album ends by copying the torrid drumming on Eddie Cochran's 'Somethin' Else' for 'Wilbury Twist'. Videos were made for 'She's My Baby', 'Inside Out' and 'Wilbury Twist'.

They recorded Hank Snow's 'Nobody's Child' at the instigation of George Harrison's wife, Olivia, and it was released for the Romanian Angel Appeal.

At the end of May, Dylan started his summer tour in Montreal. He featured his harmonica and included 'Desolation Row' and Joel Sonnier's 'No More One More Time'. *Ottawa Citizen* criticised his harmonica playing on the first night and he came out apologetically on the second night and said, 'Would you mind if I played harmonica?' The crowd roared its approval. Before he started 'It Ain't Me Babe', he asked if a stolen guitar could be returned to him.

In Toronto, someone shouted for 'Tomorrow Is a Long Time' to which he responded, 'It sure is'. He obliged and sang the song. He did 'John Brown' in a very mannered fashion, again as a request. 'Early Mornin' Rain' was a nod to Gordon Lightfoot, and Bob and Ronnie Hawkins sang 'One More Night'.

On 27 June 1990, Bob played his first gig in Iceland. He rapped about the Vikings settling in Minnesota but he was referring to a football team.

In Germany Bob sang 'Old Rock and Roller' as 'an autobiographical song' and Jack Scott's 'Let's Learn to Live and Love Again'. At the Montreux Jazz Festival, he performed 'Across the Borderline' with Flaco Jiménez.

Returning to the US, Dylan and Michael Bolton wrote 'Steel Bars' at Dylan's home in Malibu. Bolton was amazed to be writing with him. The song was nominated for an award from the songwriting organisation, BMI.

When John De Staley joined the tour as second guitarist, he was given a list of 160 songs. (That's your starter!) The band was rehearsing for US summer dates. They worked on Neil Young's 'Southern Man' and Willie Nelson's 'Family Bible' but neither were performed live. Dylan performed 'Sittin' on The Dock of the Bay' with a harmonica instead of whistling, and he sang 'Nowhere Man' and 'The Water Is Wide'. When he played the Zoo,

Oklahoma City, they played 'Old McDonald' as an instrumental.

On August 26 Stevie Ray Vaughan was killed in a helicopter crash. The next night in Merrillville, Indiana, Dylan dedicated 'Moon River' to him and covered 'Friend of the Devil'.

When the tour ended, *Under the Red Sky* was released with the Wilburys' album following in October.

On September 2 Brian Wilson played a new track to fans, 'The Spirit of Rock'n'Roll' at a Beach Boys convention, with Dylan singing along out of tune. This was intended for *Sweet Insanity*, which was rejected by Sire. Still, it was a commercial song on a familiar theme and should have been released.

Dylan was back on the road in October in Greenvale, New York with G.E. Smith leading the band and César Díaz on rhythm. César Díaz came from Puerto Rico and came to the US in 1969 with Johnny Nash. He had first worked for Dylan as a guitar and amp tech and was to replace G.E. when he left, staying with Dylan until 1993.

Dylan performed for 4,000 cadets in the Dwight D. Eisenhower Hall at the US Military Academy, West Point, New York. The cadets joined in 'Blowin' in the Wind' – and Dylan included 'Masters of War'. How times had changed.

Even shimmying on stage, Dylan had a lively week's residency at the Beacon Theatre in New York. Lenny Kravitz on saxophonist joined him for 'Masters of War'. It marked G.E. Smith's last show. Smith sang the final verse of 'Highway 61 Revisited' and Lenny Kravitz and his band were on stage for 'Maggie's Farm'.

When at the Tad Smith Coliseum, University of Mississippi, Dylan opened with Z.Z. Top's 'My Head's In Mississippi'. He had written 'Oxford Town' about events at the university and he received a standing ovation for it (as he should).

In January 1991 Bob Dylan was putting together a new band for a European tour in New York. The musicians were Tony Garnier, César Díaz, John Jackson (lead guitarist for Jo-El Sonnier's band) and Ian Wallace. The tour started in Zurich but the band was under-rehearsed and didn't know 'Most Likely You Go Your Way and I'll Go Mine'. There were live performances, the first, for 'Bob Dylan's Dream' and 'God Knows'.

Dylan performed in Belgium and the Netherlands before concerts in Glasgow, Dublin and Belfast. In Belfast, Van Morrison joined him for 'Tupelo Honey'. In Dublin, Dylan threw his arms around Carole King after 'Real Real Gone' and then she fell into the stage pit and broke her arm. He did eight nights at the Hammersmith Odeon but the band was not on top of the music and the lighting was poor (though that might have been Dylan's wishes). When Ronnie Wood joined him on stage, they had difficulty finding their microphones.

Bob Dylan received a Lifetime Achievement award at the Grammys. The award was presented by Jack Nicholson. Dylan accepted it without thanking anyone and by not giving a perfunctory upbeat message. Instead, Dylan said that his father had told him, 'It's possible to be so defiled in this world that even your mother and father won't know you. But God will always believe in your own ability to mend your own ways.' What is Dylan saying? 'You may become a mass murderer but God will still have faith in you'?

As if by way of example, Dylan sang 'Masters of War', described by the *New York Times* as 'an unfamiliar song'. I sympathise as the performance was unintelligible. This event was in the midst of the Gulf War and on national TV, so Dylan had picked his most anti-war song to perform to a patriotic nation attacking Saddam. Was Dylan intending it to be a comment on Iraq? Why did he sing the lyric as though it were one long word? Maybe he doesn't know why he does things sometimes.

Michael Gray: 'There is a self-destructive streak in him but there is a much stronger, creative streak that says, "Well, we have had that version, what else can we do with it?" Sometimes you get a thrashing of the material and sometimes you get a brilliant reinvention. Nothing could have surprised me more than he could have bettered the 1967 version of 'Tears of Rage' and yet he managed it in the 1990s in France.'

Columbia would have preferred Dylan to have embraced this celebration and used it for stocktaking. He could have publicised the 3CD retrospective, *The Bootleg Series, Volumes 1-3*, over three hours of material which had not been officially released. Put together by Jeff Rosen, it included lost tracks like 'She's Your Lover Now' and the first take of 'Like a Rolling Stone' as a waltz. There were nearly sixty tracks in chronological order, fully annotated and weighted towards the 1960s. When Elliot Mintz interviewed him about the set, he had little idea as to what was on it. To be fair to Dylan, there could be a valid reason for this: Sony had bought Columbia and that could have been the reason for his indifference.

Columbia made a brilliant video for 'Series of Dreams' to promote the package. It took Dylan footage over 30 years and merged it with the lyric and recent scenes of Dylan in New York. A reporter for *New York Daily News* asked why Dylan was dressed as a homeless man and got the reply, 'No, he's dressed as Bob Dylan.'

Back on the road, Dylan performed 'Mr. Tambourine Man' in Macon, Georgia as 'one of my anti-drug songs'. Elsewhere he said, 'A lot of people came down on me for writing this next song, but the truth just had to come out' before singing 'Man in the Long Black Coat'. What's that all about?

When he performed 'Wiggle Wiggle', he suggested that the audience stood in one spot and wiggled, showing he knew Jerry Lee Lewis' 'Mean Woman Blues'. He sometimes sang 'These visions of Madonna' in 'Visions of Johanna'.

Bob Dylan turned 50 on 24 May 1991. Senator Joseph Lieberman tabled a birthday greeting: 'Back in 1963, it is hardly likely any member of Congress would have been talking about Bob Dylan, at least not in favourable terms. It was he who said of them, "Come senators, Congressmen, please heed the call, Don't stand in the doorway, don't block up the hall." Times have changed though Dylan's sentiment still holds true when we consider how many problems we still have to heed. I am sure he sings those words with the same spirit and intensity as he did 28 years ago. There is a mystery to Bob Dylan, which is surprising, given how freely he has expressed himself through his music. But the mystery results, I think, from Dylan's refusal to play roles society might seek to assign him – roles like superstar, rock idol, prophet. 'I tried my best to be just like I am, But everybody wants you to be just like them.' How true.

Among the birthday tributes was Loudon Wainwright's 'Talking New Bob Dylan', a funny but touching track stating that his 'old stuff still sounds new'.

Dylan began a European tour in Rome on June 6. He started appropriately with 'When I Paint My Masterpiece'. He included Paul Simon's 'Homeward Bound' and John Prine's 'People Putting People Down'. Van Morrison was the double-header for his three Italian dates –Rome, Bologna and Milan. Dylan added harmonica to Van's 'Whenever God Shines His Light' and 'Enlightenment'. Moving to Austria, he did an electric 'Homeward Bound'. In Offenbach, he introduced 'Two Soldiers' by saying, 'This is a song from another place, another time.'

We could list perplexing introductions. In Munich, Dylan described seeing somebody run over 'and there wasn't anything for me to do but go back and write this song', the song being 'Don't Think Twice, It's All Right'. In Denmark, 'Positively 4th Street' had become 'one of my songs about friendship'. He called 'Simple Twist of Fate' 'my invasion of privacy song'.

At Yale University, New Haven, he introduced 'Gotta Serve Somebody' by saying, 'You know the saying "Thou shalt not murder". It doesn't say, "Thou shalt not kill".'

Back in the US in July, he sang 'Pancho and Lefty' in Cleveland, saying it was 'the only song in my repertoire that mentions the city of Cleveland'.

On September 15, Dylan made his third appearance on a Chabad telethon, this time accompanying Kinky Friedman on 'Sold American', Kinky's attempt at writing a 'Streets of London'. Privately, Dylan asked Kinky Friedman to sing 'Ride 'Em Jewboy' for Larry Kegan. Kinky said, 'Dylan is vacillating between being an orthodox and a reformed Jew.'

In October, Dylan went to Seville, Spain for the Guitar Greats Festival. He had a soundcheck with Keith Richards' band, but then asked Richard Thompson to accompany him acoustically. Thompson was not told what they would be doing. They did 'Boots of Spanish Leather', 'Across the Borderline' and 'Answer Me'. He performed 'All Along the Watchtower' with Jack Bruce and his band, and 'Shake Rattle and Roll' with Keith Richards' band.

Dylan told Robert Hilburn for the *LA Times*: 'A lot of people were coming to see the legend and I was just trying to get on the stage and play music.' And on songwriting, 'There was a time when the songs would come three or four at the same time, but those days are long gone.'

On November 6 at South Bend, Indiana, Dylan introduced 'All Along the Watchtower': 'Anybody heard of U2? They recorded this song but they did it with all the wrong words. These are the correct words. All about businessmen. All about people getting on with the business of their lives.'

Dylan met Barry Manilow at a Hollywood party. He liked the way Manilow had made the concept album, *Paradise Café* (1984): Manilow was flattered that he even knew it.

Dylan told the journalist Paul Zollo said that he didn't write lies and he couldn't have written 'Feelings' or 'People'. He paused. 'Maybe people who need people are the luckiest people in the world.'

In January 1992, Dylan added harmonica to Nanci Griffith's 'Boots of Spanish Leather' for her album of covers.

For its tenth anniversary, the producer of *Late Night with David Letterman* asked Dylan to perform 'Like a Rolling Stone'. Backed by a large band and a backing chorus of Mavis Staples, Michelle Shocked, Rosanne Cash, Emmylou Harris and Nanci Griffith, Dylan could have performed a definitive version but he sang it devoid of meaning. As Clinton Heylin says, 'Nobody sings Dylan like Dylan and even he on occasion doesn't even sing Dylan like Dylan.'

In March and April 1992 Dylan was touring in Australia, New Zealand, Hawaii and America. He had borrowed Bucky Baxter, the steel guitarist from Steve Earle's band, who proved highly effective for 'Most of the Time' and a country-styled 'Drifter's Escape'. Dylan was performing 'Idiot Wind', albeit remorsefully, and his covers included 'Dolly Dagger' (Hendrix), 'West LA Fadeaway' and 'Black Muddy River' (both Grateful Dead). He had not sung 'The Bold Lieutenant' in public since 1961.

In Hobart, Richard Dickinson had killed his mother while listening to Dylan's 'One More Cup of Coffee'. Dickinson believed himself to be the Son of God. He was put in a correction centre but allowed to see Dylan as part of his treatment for schizophrenia. He was deemed to have been cured. (Sounds like I am making this up but I'm not.)

On June 30, Dylan performed at a festival in Dunkirk. John Bauldie: 'We were in a little café on the sea front. Bob stared straight at us, looked like he was going to have a glass of wine, but then he went on down the promenade. The fantasy of fans is that their hero will like them and employ them in some way. I am happy as a critic and commentator.' While in France, Dylan performed 'Pretty Peggy-O', 'I Dreamed I Saw St. Augustine' and 'Hey Joe'.

When Dylan appeared at Bally's Goldwyn Events Centre, Las Vegas, what better choice could there be than 'Joey'?

In June 1992, Bob Dylan recorded at Acme Studios in Chicago with David Bromberg. They recorded 'Miss the Mississippi and You', 'Polly Vaughan' (a traditional ballad – someone who mistakes his wife for a swan and shoots her), 'Sloppy Drunk' (from blues man Jimmy Rogers), 'Kaatskill Serenade' (written by Bromberg and based on 'Rip Van Winkle'), 'Lady Came From Baltimore', 'World of Fools', 'Casey Jones', 'Rise Again' and 'Duncan and Brady'.

The intention was to release an album of folk covers but Dylan had a better idea, so nothing was released. In his garage studio, he recorded 13 songs for the jokingly-titled *Good As I Been to You*, with just a producer and an engineer. An outtake 'You Belong to Me' is on the soundtrack of *Natural Born Killers*. When someone asked why he wasn't writing, he said, 'There are already enough songs. These old songs are my lexicon and prayer book.' Sounded like he was quoting 'Deck of Cards'.

The album mostly consisted of pre-war blues and old ballads, emphasising betrayal and loss. Some have criticised it for closing with a children's song 'Froggie Went A-Courtin'', but that song ends in a massacre.

He did Stephen Foster's 'Hard Times' and the wonderful 'Tomorrow Night', which was recorded by Lonnie Johnson in 1948. He learnt 'Arthur McBride' from Paul Brady, who had recorded it in 1976.

Bob thought that the Australian song, 'Jim Jones', was traditional. Mick Slocum had written a new tune for the Bushwackers' version in 1977 and Dylan followed this. Columbia acknowledged the mistake.

'Diamond Joe' had been recorded by Tom Rush and James Taylor but Dylan would have heard it way back from Ramblin' Jack Elliott, who said, 'I learnt 'Diamond Joe' from a cowboy in Brussels. I'd gone over to see Derroll Adams and we decided to ride our scooters looking for work. We wanted to sing at the rodeo. The producer had run off with the money and there were over 60 angry cowboys and Indians in Brussels who hadn't been paid. It was raining too. The rodeo was under a bridge and it was hard to find. They still put on a show for a small audience. One of the cowboys George Williams picked up a guitar and sang 'Diamond Joe' for me. Later in Japan I was singing the song and there was a yell and it was George. He'd brought back some horses.'

All this is positive but with just a voice and guitar, it was clear that Dylan's vocal range was diminished. If he wanted to pay tribute to Harry Smith's anthology, he should have done it ten years earlier. Dylan was largely playing the melody on bass strings, which he hadn't done since 'Blowin' in the Wind' in Verona in 1984.

Bob Dylan: Outlaw Blues

From August to November, Dylan spent most of the time touring the USA and Canada. Although he could have included acoustic songs from *Good as I Been to You*, Dylan didn't do this but he did have an acoustic spot. It's endearing that he broke with all the normal marketing conventions. In Little Rock, the 50s rockabilly performer Billy Lee Riley joined him for his own 'Red Hot'.

It was coming up for 30 years since Bob Dylan had signed with Columbia Records and there was to be a 30th Anniversary Concert Celebration at Madison Square Garden. *Columbia Records Celebrates the Music of Bob Dylan* required enormous planning and the production team included Jeff Kramer, Harvey Goldsmith and Jeff Rosen. They would collect $1m in ticket sales and merchandising as it was bound to sell out and they negotiated $10m for TV rights on pay per view channels. It would be available in 68 countries with the public paying $20 or the equivalent to watch it. Neil Young called it Bobfest and that nickname stuck.

The producers knew they would have no difficulty in securing the performers: they could easily sell 18,000 tickets and the pay per view rights; but they would have difficulty in getting Bob's cooperation. As usual, he was predictable in his unpredictability: Bob probably doesn't think he is a stereotype but sometimes he is. He hated to be feted and he hated showbiz events and he left his options open as to whether to appear until the last moment. If Dylan was impressed, it didn't show: he echoed Alfred Hitchcock who said a lifetime award means 'Surprised you're still around'.

For different reasons it mirrored the problem in 1983 as to whether Berry Gordy Jr was going to turn up at *Motown – The Concert* which was to celebrate the 25th anniversary of him founding the Tamla-Motown organisation. In his view, there were too many artists on the bill who had left his company. He did turn up and that has become the basis for the stage show, *Motown – The Musical*.

G.E. Smith was recruited as musical director and the house band was pretty much Booker T. and the MGs. Nobody could argue with that. Unfortunately, Columbia were to invite too many artists and in most cases, they would be limited to four minutes. If you only have four minutes to make an immediate impression, then you may decide to crank everything up to 10.

John Mellencamp with Al Kooper on organ opened with 'Like a Rolling Stone', which was loud and insensitive but unquestionably Grade A stadium rock. The female vocalists took it over the top. Perhaps because he had accepted the opening slot, he was allowed a second song, an equally raucous 'Leopard-Skin Pillbox Hat', which lost the song's humour.

After being introduced by Kris Kristofferson, Stevie Wonder put some of Sam Cooke's inflections into 'Blowin' in the Wind'. He said the song was about civil rights and still applicable.

Ah, Lou Reed. Publicly, Lou Reed said he was a great Dylan fan but privately he wondered why Bob Dylan got these honours and he didn't. (There's always one.) Dylan's 'Foot of Pride' sounded like he had been influenced by Lou Reed and now we had Reed backed by Booker T. and the MGs doing the song – well, reading the lyric from a music stand. The audience roared when he eventually reached the chorus, even more when he got to the end.

Reed was a poor performer: I saw him in Liverpool where he seemed mesmerised by the autocue and yet surely he knew his own lyrics. Still what do I know? Donald Trump was backstage at Bobfest and he congratulated Lou Reed and Tom Petty on their jamming.

In a glorious backstage moment, Stuttering John from Howard Stern's shock jock programme asked Lou Reed a question: 'Do you still masturbate?' Lou turned away and then turned back and grabbed him by the throat for several seconds before putting him down.

When you've only got one song, make the best of it –hence Eddie Vedder and Mike McCready of Pearl Jam with an excellent 'Masters of War'. They were followed by Tracy Chapman who often opened for Bob with 'The Times They Are A-Changin'', again okay. According to Bill Flanagan in the DVD booklet, 'These young artists took on what might have seemed to be the most dated songs – 'The Times They Are A-Changin'' and 'Masters of War'.'

Johnny Cash would have been fine singing 'It Ain't Me, Babe' on his own but June Carter ruined it with childish antics and weak harmonies. I suspect that she knew her voice wasn't up to it and was trying to compensate. The country section continued with Willie Nelson's stately 'What Was It You Wanted' and Kris Kristofferson's good-humoured 'I'll Be Your Baby Tonight'.

John Hammond Jr had originally requested 'I'll Be Your Baby Tonight' but when Kristofferson wanted it, he was asked to perform something else and he took 'See that My Grave Is Kept Clean', the only performer not scheduled to sing a Dylan song at Bobfest. George Thorogood performed the little-known 'Wanted Man' and Sophie B. Hawkins 'I Want You'. The President of Sony Music was booed for saying how kind and wonderful his company was.

Sinéad O'Connor had been a guest on *Saturday Night Live* where she sang Bob Marley's 'War' as a protest against the abuse of children by the Catholic Church. She had a picture of Pope John Paul and cut it up, saying 'Fight the real enemy'. We now know that she had a real point but her contribution was not well received. She was going to sing 'I Believe in You', which is about clinging to faith in the face of opposition. It was her first live appearance since the telecast and she was both cheered and jeered. Kris Kristofferson went to up to her and said, 'Don't let the bastards get you down'. She then sang Bob Marley's 'War'. After her performance, Lou Reed commented, 'You'd think that if any audience would be responsive to protest music it would be Bob Dylan's.'

It was just possible to determine that Johnny Winter was performing 'Highway 61 Revisited' but impossible to make sense of what he was singing. It was a rave-up that had little to do with Bob Dylan. Ronnie Wood was sounding like Dylan on 'Seven Days', which was okay but Joe Cocker would have been better: Ronnie was on stage as a mate of Bob's rather than as a great singer. Richie Havens did a fine 'Just like a Woman', although it was a bit wayward. It was good that the Clancy Brothers and Tommy Makem had been invited and they did a good version of 'When the Ship Comes in'.

Carolyn Hester: 'Nanci Griffith and I did 'Boots of Spanish Leather' and we were knocked off our seats because the audience was responding so well to us, and we were just the folkies. The high point was seeing Eric Clapton, that was wonderful, and I got to have a conversation with George Harrison. He talked about Ravi Shankar who was still playing. So we were saying, "We're still young." (laughs)' Then Mary Chapin Carpenter, Rosanne Cash and Shawn Colin did 'You Ain't Goin' Nowhere', which didn't deliver as much as it promised.

Neil Young was allowed two songs and at the rehearsal, he said to Booker T. 'Play whatever the hell you want', which sounded like Bob talking. Neil sang the verses of 'Just like Tom Thumb's Blues' in the wrong order, but it was a superlative version. You can tell he is enjoying himself. Equally powerful was his terrific 'All Along the Watchtower', not quite up to Hendrix but not far away.

Chrissie Hynde did a fine 'I Shall Be Released' and then Eric Clapton with a new haircut was featuring his voice more than his guitar on 'Don't Think Twice, It's All Right', although he did let rip at the end. At the afternoon rehearsal, he and Dylan had worked up 'It Takes a Lot to Laugh, It Takes a Train to Cry'. They were told not to add it to the list as there were so many guest artists.

The O'Jays performed with a back-up gospel choir on their recent hit, 'Emotionally Yours', the only hit song from *Empire Burlesque*. Levon Helm, Rick Danko and Garth Hudson represented The Band on 'When I Paint My Masterpiece'.

Bob Dylan rehearsed 'If Not for You' for the Bobfest but it was down for George Harrison. George wanted G.E. Smith to take the slide guitar solo. He did so and Bob came over to him at the end. He thought he was going to be praised but Bob said, 'Nice suit'.

George Harrison with only an acoustic guitar joined the house band for 'Absolutely Sweet Marie'. It was a fine version with George emphasising words à la Dylan.

Tom Petty and the Heartbreakers' very intense 'Licence to Kill' was a highlight with its neat dramatic flourishes such as when Petty stops the music. His rollicking 'Rainy Day Women Nos. 12 & 35' was excellent: this could have, indeed should have, opened the show. Tom Petty loved the evening: 'I really admired everyone on the show and it was so much fun.'

Perhaps the most surprising thing about the Bobfest is that Bob turned up. Before he went on, he said to Chrissie Hynde, 'I've been left with the dregs' – and whose fault is that? He could have had first choice.

Bob Dylan began with 'Song to Woody', modestly taking everything back to where it started but being Bob, he plugged in wrong. He then delivered a croaky 'It's All Right Ma (I'm Only Bleeding)'. McGuinn, Petty, Young, Clapton and Harrison then joined him for 'My Back Pages', swapping lines and vocals. Dylan's vocal was so wayward that he re-did it for the live album. It must have been bad for him to agree to that.

Actor Warwick Evans: 'You never get any better and if you're on a big show, you might be thinking, "What am I doing in front of all these people? Am I any good?" It is a heavy burden to carry.'

Everyone came on stage for 'Knockin' on Heaven's Door' and then Dylan sang a tender 'Girl of the North Country' to conclude the night as the credits rolled for the broadcast. Hence, many viewers would be switching off during his best vocal.

Elvis Costello had to be dropped from the show. He could not perform 'Positively Fourth Street' as his visa was not in order. But why wasn't Jerry Garcia included?

After the four hour show, several of the performers went to Tommy Makem's Irish Pavilion on 57th Street where Dylan sang Irish ballads with Liam Clancy. Ian McLagen was drunk and asked Dylan for $1m in cash, a regular joke but this time it misfired.

Carolyn Hester: 'That concert was very controlled with a lot of bodyguards. They kept changing the security. "If you don't have this card, you can't go in there", this kind of thing. Bob, Willie Nelson and I collided in a hallway and we had a chat early on. The great thing was the party later where we got to meet him. Bob would request, "Send so and so" – King Bob had us coming up. They only let Nanci and I go, not the musicians with us. It was very nice. He said, "They say my son is a better songwriter than I am." He was just a proud parent. He wasn't remote or non-committal.'

Here comes the son, no, that's Dhani Harrison's potential album title. Jakob's band, the Wallflowers, was doing okay. The first Wallflowers album sold 40,000 which sounded promising. Jakob had been listening to Hank Williams and Charley Patton, but he wanted to be Joe Strummer.

The day after the concert Dylan recorded 'Heartland' with Willie Nelson, produced by Don Was in the Power Station in New York. Bob had sent Willie a melody which he had hummed and sang the word 'Heartland'. Willie thought it could be a farm song, obviously prompted by Farm Aid. Willie wrote the lyric and Dylan only saw the lyric the day he recorded it.

Dylan was then back on the road, his set including 'I Can't Be Satisfied', 'Dear Landlord', 'Mama, You've Been On My Mind' and 'Farewell to the Gold', probably because he knew Nic Jones' *Penguin Eggs*.

In November, a new version of 'This Wheel's on Fire' was recorded by Julie Driscoll for the TV comedy series, *Absolutely Fabulous*. In one episode the song is screeched by Patsy and Edina, their version of the *Basement Tapes*. Julie Driscoll: 'The *Absolutely Fabulous* team phoned me up and said that they wanted to use 'This Wheel's on Fire' for the signature tune. They said, "Will you do it or shall we get a session singer in?" I didn't mind doing it but I never perform the song on stage. Why would I want to perform something that I recorded years ago? If you keep performing things you did when you were young, how can you move on? The only way to do that would be by interpreting them in a different way. That would be a musical development. If people want to play those things, fine, but there's no way I am going to perform them. I have to develop as a musician. We have to discover something new with the wonderful gift we have been given. Explore it. Find something in yourself. It can make you feel so much better.'

Bob rounded off a busy year on November 15 at West Palm Beach, Florida, signing off with some wild harmonica riffs. He had played 93 shows during the year.

Bob Dylan was a performer at an inaugural event for President Clinton, *A Call for Reunion: A Musical Celebration*. It was staged outdoors at the Lincoln Memorial in January 1993, which might have accounted for Bob's perma-scowl. Bill and Hillary, well wrapped-up, were sitting and laughing happily, even though Bob was singing 'Chimes of Freedom', a serious song about human rights. Their 12-year-old daughter, Chelsea, was next to them and she was mystified: she knew nothing of his history but was hearing something tuneless, cheerless and probably hopeless. There was no way you could enjoy Bob Dylan that day unless you knew the back story.

Michael Gray: 'At the Clinton inauguration, he was just awful but he was being deliberately defensive. I regret that stance in his work – you know, you people are not going to understand this, so I am not going to do it properly. There is no value in that as far I can see.'

In the evening he joined The Band with special guests at the National Building Museum in an event for campaign workers, an unofficial event known as the Bluejeans Bash. Dylan did 'To Be Alone with You', 'Key to the Highway' and 'I Don't Want To Hang up My Rock'n'Roll Shoes'. Stephen Stills joined them all for 'I Shall Be Released'.

Dylan then set off on tour, suffering from a bad back and moaning that air conditioning was bad for his voice. On February 5, Dylan was at The Point in Dublin including 'Tomorrow Night' and 'Jim Jones' from the previous album in his act. He hung around for Van Morrison the next night and joined him for 'It's All Over Now, Baby Blue'.

Dylan had his third residency at Hammersmith Odeon. 'Don't Think Twice' wasn't all right as the band hadn't agreed on the chords, causing Dylan to self-righteously remark, 'This has been rehearsed 100 times'. Dave Stewart joined them for 'Highway 61 Revisited'. Before returning to America, Bob had a break at Ronnie Wood's home in County Kildare.

During April, Dylan gave an excellent show at the New Orleans Jazz and Heritage Festival, performing on the highly appropriate Ray-Bans Stage. Dickie Betts from the Allman Brothers Band played guitar on 'Cat's in the Well'.

Dylan attended but did not perform at a tribute to Townes Van Zandt in Austin, but while there, he wrote 'Howlin' at Your Window' with Jude Johnston. It was well performed by the rough-voiced Tim Hockenberry from *America's Got Talent*.

Dylan took part in a TV special for Willie Nelson, *The Big Six-O*, commenting that he thought Willie was 160. Dylan did 'Hard Times' solo and 'Pancho and Lefty' with Willie, the latter a rehearsal slipped into the broadcast by the producer, Don Was.

Dylan recorded 'The Ballad of Hollis Brown' with Mike Seeger on banjo for Mike's LP *Third Annual Farewell Reunion*. Look at the title of that album: there's a performer who was ahead of the pack. Mike was a half-brother to Pete Seeger.

In May 1993 Bob Dylan recorded more vintage blues and folk at his home studio in Malibu. It wasn't what Columbia wanted, especially after the success of Madison Square concert, but that's Bob Dylan for you. He said, 'The songs are personal but very universal' but they weren't new. He had made the album 'without a single change of strings', which indicated his spontaneity but was hardly an endorsement.e had been taken with an old 78rpm by the Mississippi Sheiks and recorded both titles, 'Blood in My Eyes' and 'World Gone Wrong'. The record had been made in 1931 and because of the Depression, only 250 copies were pressed. Dylan saw how 'World Gone Wrong' was applicable to modern times while 'Blood in My Eyes' was a sexual song with a great title: just what did it mean? Are the eyes bloodshot or has there been an accident? Dylan's broke-down voice is highly suited to 'Blood in My Eyes' and it is the most powerful of his blues covers on this or the previous album.

Dylan wrote his own sleeve note and acknowledged that he had taken two songs from Tom Paley's repertoire for the New Lost City Ramblers. Tom Paley was flattered: 'I'm very pleased that Bob learnt some things from my recordings. 'Love Henry' is an old ballad and I can't remember where I first heard it. I think it was in a book of American folk songs. Very often I knew the tune and some words and I have to look up the rest of the text. He also mentioned me in connection with 'Jack-A-Roe'.'

Dylan took 'Broke down Engine' from Blind Willie McTell's repertoire. There are marvellous analogies in the lyric and you can imagine Chuck Berry doing justice to this song.

Bob Dylan had been performing 'Two Soldiers' on stage and he had taken the song from Jerry Garcia's repertoire. He sang a variant on 'Stagger Lee', 'Stack a Lee' and again, the Grateful Dead had been singing about this gambling quarrel. 'Delia' is a variant of 'Delia's Gone', which had been a minor hit for Pat Boone in 1960.

The Delta blues guitarist, Willie Brown, had recorded 'Ragged and Dirty' in 1942 – a one-take recording as Brown coughed towards the end – and Bob had taken 'Lone Pilgrim' from a Doc Watson record.

Dylan wrote the sleeve notes for the album, stressing how the aura of these songs had endured and they were very readable by his standards. The cover had been shot in Fluke's Cradle, a café in Camden High Street. The album only made No. 70 in the US but it won a Grammy for Best Traditional Folk Album. The outtakes included '21 Years' (which he referred to in a letter to Dave Glover in 1963), '32.20 Blues' (Robert Johnson), 'Goodnight My Love' (Jesse Belvin) and 'Hello Stranger' (Carter Family).

In June Dylan took a holiday in Ireland before playing the Fleadh Festival at Finsbury Park. He did 'One Irish Rover' with Van Morrison, and then moved onto a European tour. He missed a show in Lyon because of his back problem, his first cancellation for health reasons since 1966 and he was on stage the next night.

In Athens, he sang 'Shooting Star' just after a shooting star had occurred. He had silver studs down his seams but they were too long and rolled up rather than shortened: where was that wardrobe mistress?

Returning to Dave Stewart's studio in Camden, Dylan wore a top hat, gloves, frock coat and tails, looking like an undertaker. Dave was filming a video of 'Blood in My Eyes'. Dave took him to Camden Market and he walked around, talking to residents and singing with a busker. He was accompanied by his bodyguard Jim Callaghan but he was approachable. Dylan thought of buying a five-bedroomed house in Crouch End, but the story was leaked and he forgot about it. Still, the result was a striking monochrome video with Dylan miming decently.

In August, Bob had two months of gigs, double-billed with Santana. He said that playing brought meaning to his life and it was no hardship, though with his bad back, it surely was. Still he was on good behaviour, even attending sound checks. Because of the O'Jays' success with 'Emotionally Yours', Dylan was performing the song, sometimes stretching it to nine minutes. After he started the intro of 'Boots of Spanish Leather' instead of 'It Ain't Me Babe', he realised his mistake and said, 'Well, it's the same chords.'

On the final gig in Mountain View, California, Neil Young joined him for 'Leopard-Skin Pillbox Hat'. He went to Stevie Nicks' recording session and played guitar on her mechanical cover of 'Just like a Woman'.

MTV had introduced a very successful *Unplugged* TV series. The intention was to present major stars in acoustic sessions, though some didn't seem to appreciate what 'unplugged' meant. Bob Dylan was an obvious choice, but Dylan decided to film his own version, presumably for sale to a rival channel. Free tickets were given out by Tower Records for two nights at the Supper Club in New York. He sang 'Queen Jane Approximately', 'My Back Pages', 'Ring Them Bells', 'Jim Jones' and 'One More Cup of Coffee'. We have the first known performance of Dylan singing Blind Boy Fuller's 'Weeping Willow'. The performances were not particularly country but a steel guitar was featured. He asked the audience for the first line of 'I Shall Be Released', which he performed. When Dylan viewed the footage, he wasn't happy, and nothing came of it until the *Highway 61 Interactive* CD-ROM.

On New Year's Day 1994, the first advertisement to feature a Bob Dylan song was shown at the Orange Bowl Stadium in Miami. Dylan had previously refused such requests. After all, Johnny Cash's 'Ring of Fire' was used to sell haemorrhoid cream. Here it was Richie Havens singing 'The Times They a-Changin'' for Coopers and Lybrand. The song was also used by the Bank of Montreal in 1996.

'I was in Canada and saw 'The Times They Are A-Changin'' being used for an advert for a bank,' says Billy Bragg, 'and I was furious. I was doing a union rally in Toronto and I whacked the shit out of it with all the venom I got from the Clash. I don't think you should be gentle with it.'

On film, Bob recorded a tribute to Van Morrison for his special award at the Brits. Set to the rhythm of 'Gloria', he said, 'Congratulations on this prestigious award. No one's more deserving of it than you for writing all those fine songs and giving us all that inspiration over the years. God bless you, Van. Blah blah blah blah blah blah.'

When Dylan went to Japan, he played Koseinenkin Hall, Hiroshima, which surprised me as I had assumed the whole area would have been uninhabitable. Dylan had the right song for the right occasion – a tense and acoustic 'Masters of War' and he received a standing ovation.

Michael Gray: 'That version of 'Masters of War' at the Grammys was absolutely hopeless, yet then he did a concert in Hiroshima and he performed the most beautiful, delicate, really heartfelt version. It takes a very brave person to sing 'Masters of War' and not make it cheap, inappropriate or tasteless. It was completely worthy of the occasion, let alone the 1963 phase of his work.'

Back in the US, Dylan sang 'Tomorrow Night' with Trisha Yearwood for an all-star show for *Rhythm Country and Blues*. They both knew the song but only Dylan knew how he was going to sing it.

In May 1994, Dylan makes his first studio recordings with the Never Ending Tour band. At Ardent Studio in Memphis, Dylan recorded Gordon Lightfoot's 'I'm Not Supposed to Care', 'Boogie Woogie Country Girl' (for a Doc Pomus tribute CD), 'My Blue-Eyed Jane' (for a Jimmie Rodgers' tribute album), 'One Night of Sin' and 'Easy Rider (don't deny my name)'.

Later in May, Bob was back in Japan for The Great Music Experience in Nara City. The event was to build cultural bridges and from the west there was Ry Cooder, Bob Dylan and Joni Mitchell. They were accompanied by the Tokyo Philharmonic Orchestra, conducted by Michael Kamen. Dylan did 'A Hard Rain's A-Gonna Fall' (with Joni Mitchell), 'I Shall Be Released' and 'Ring Them Bells', followed by an ensemble 'I Shall Be Released'. The concert was performed three times so it was unusual for Dylan to be doing the same thing every night. It was televised and shown on the BBC.

On August 14, Dylan played to 300,000 (plus a pay-per-view audience) at Woodstock II, Winston Farm, Saugarties, NY. For once, he was coherent and energetic, following the Red Hot Chilli Peppers and going down well. He performed a 75-minute set including a ten-minute 'It's All Over Now, Baby Blue' with Tony Garnier on stand-up bass. Johnny Cash's manager turned down Woodstock II as Cash would not be on the main stage.

On September 30 Dylan recorded three songs for an Elvis Presley tribute album: 'Lawdy Miss Clawdy', 'Money Honey' and, on top form for these days, 'Anyway You Want Me (that's how I will be)', which is hardly his credo. The tracks were never released.

'Two Soldiers' opens with the line, 'He was just a blue-eyed Boston boy', so he used it to good effect at the Orpheum Theatre in Boston. A few days later, he joined the Grateful Dead for 'Rainy Day Women Nos. 12 and 35' when they played Madison Square Garden. He played three nights at the Roseland Ballroom, New York and on the final show was joined by Neil Young and Bruce Springsteen for 'Rainy Day Women Nos. 12 and 35' and 'Highway 61 Revisited'.

In November 1994, Ruth Tyrangiel initiated a $5m palimony lawsuit in LA alleging that she co-wrote songs and managed his career in a 20-year relationship from 1973 to 1993 after which he broke it off. She had played one of his girlfriends in *Renaldo and Clara*. She did receive an out of court settlement.

Over two nights in November 1994, Bob Dylan relented and recorded MTV shows for *Unplugged* in the Sony studios in New York. As per their norm, there were beautiful models in the front row. Bob kept on his shades and with his polka-dot shirt, it was like 1966 revisited. It was unusual for him to play sitting down. He had a strong band with him: John Jackson (lead guitar), Tony Garnier (bass), Brendan O'Brien (Pearl Jam's producer, keyboards), Bucky Baxter (pedal steel, dobro) and Winston Watson (drums). The second show was more in keeping with what MTV wanted as he did his greatest hits.

Dylan included a very good and slow 'I Want You' (which may have given the Old Vic a few ideas), 'Hazel' and 'Dignity'. He started 'Like a Rolling Stone' very slowly and sped it up. There was a great groove for 'Knockin' on Heaven's Door' but Dylan sang 'Mama, wipe my guns into the ground.' MTV said, 'Dylan has been the spiritual godfather of the whole *Unplugged* concept, and every person here felt we wouldn't have done our job if we hadn't gotten him on the show.'

While he was in New York, Dylan went to see the Liverpool musical *Blood Brothers* on Broadway with Carole King. She had been offered the main role and decided to take it.

John Peel read that Ismael Lô was known as the Bob Dylan of Senegal and commented, 'What Ismael has done to deserve this sort of abuse, I do not know. Perhaps it means he hasn't made a decent record in 20 years and makes a virtue out of not communicating with his audience.'

Dylan was going in other directions. In January 1995, he gave an interviews to promote the exhibitions for his touring sketchbook, the *Drawn Blank* series, at which customers could buy signed prints. He told *Newsweek:* 'These drawings go with my primitive style of music.' Maybe, but most people would rather have more of his primitive style of music.

Then in February the CD-ROM *Highway 61 Interactive* was released. It was produced by Graphix Zone from California with Dylan's office cooperating. They had undertaken a similar project for Prince. The CD-ROM included ten takes of 'Like a Rolling Stone' and a rock version of 'House of the Rising Sun'. I did pick one up cheaply a few years later but I soon got it rid of it as it was annoying and slow to operate and once you'd seen the goodies, there wasn't much purpose to it.

In March, Dylan flew to Prague for three concerts, but as he had picked up a virus, the first night had to be postponed. Fortunately he had a rest day scheduled after the third show and he could perform the missing show that day.

His first concert in Prague was unusual in that he only played guitar for 'Watching the River Flow' but played plenty of harmonica. He performed a ten-minute 'It's All Over Now Baby Blue'. He did ask a girl in the audience if she could play guitar so who knows what was going on? The second and third nights were more standard fare.

At the Brighton Centre, Dylan sang the 'ragged clown' verse in 'Mr. Tambourine Man', the first time he had sung it since the 60s. A friend of Ralph McTell's shouted out to him, 'Bob, have you heard of Ralph McTell?' Bob replied, 'No, but I've heard of Guy Mitchell.'

Elvis Costello joined Dylan at Brixton Academy for a good-natured 'I Shall Be Released' with Carole King and Chrissie Hynde on backing vocals. The song's meaning was rather lost but it was a strong performance. Dylan may have seen the burial of Reggie Kray on the news, prompting him to include 'Joey'.

John Cornelius: 'I saw Bob Dylan at Brixton Academy and Elvis Costello came on stage for the last number. It was like Dylan was bringing on his dad as he had a bulging stomach, was balding and wore horn-rimmed glasses.'

The *Unplugged* CD was released in April 1995. It was a good album but why have a tape loop of applause under 'Knockin' on Heaven's Door'? It was his first UK Top 10 album since *Oh Mercy*. Interviewed for *USA Today*, he said, 'I delivered something that was preconceived for me.' *Woodstock II* was 'just another show' and he had some new songs with no plans to record them.

Dylan sang 'Dignity' at the Apollo in Manchester, but he suffered indignity at the hotel. He had booked the Presidential Suite but Michael Barrymore wouldn't budge. He was driven to Preston to another hotel but returned to stay in Manchester.

His European tour ended at the Point, Dublin. It was a very good show with Carole King on keyboards for his second set. Dylan did 'Real, Real Gone' with Van Morrison and 'I Shall Be Released' and 'Rainy Day Women Nos. 12 and 35' with Elvis Costello. In France, Dylan opened for the Rolling Stones and joined them for 'Like a Rolling Stone'.

In June, Dylan was touring the US, sometimes joined by the Grateful Dead and playing to a packed house in the Giants Stadium in New Jersey. In August, Jerry Garcia died at a rehab clinic. Elliot Mintz issued this statement from Dylan, 'He really had no equal. He was like a big brother who taught and showed me more than he'll ever know. There's a lot of spaces and advances between the Carter Family and Ornette Coleman, a lot of universes, but he filled them all without being a member of any school.'

Dylan normally avoided funerals and the fact that he attended Garcia's showed his affection for him. Dylan added, 'There's no way to measure his greatness or magnitude. I don't think eulogising him will do him justice. There's no way to convey the loss. It just digs down really deep.'

Country Joe McDonald was similarly moved. 'I quit when Jerry Garcia died, I didn't want to play any music at all, and slowly I began to listen to music again, which I hadn't had time to do before, and I became a housewife. I have five kids altogether, and I asked my wife who is a registered nurse to work a little bit more, and I stayed home. After a year of that, I started playing guitar again. I decided that I would never play anywhere that I did not want to. I have to like the place, the situation, the people, the cause and the money has to be right. It doesn't have to be a lot of money, it just has to be the right amount. In some cases, it is free, I was sick of playing around tobacco smoke and alcohol. Jerry Garcia fell over dead and he had had a lousy, miserable time for the past two years, working, working, working, working, and that was no way to live and no way to die.'

In September, Dylan took part in a pay-per-view concert at Cleveland Stadium to honour the Rock and Roll Hall of Fame. Dylan performed four songs and was then joined by Bruce Springsteen for 'Forever Young'.

Dylan had been rehearsing in Florida and he suddenly decided to do a free gig. He and his band went to The Edge in Fort Lauderdale and performed for an audience of 200. They did many covers including Van Morrison's 'Real, Real Gone', Chuck Willis' 'It's Too Late' (also recorded by Buddy Holly) and Big Bill Broonzy's 'Key to the Highway' as well as Grateful Dead songs.

During his autumn dates, he had guest appearances from Alison Krauss, Dickie Betts, Doug Sahm and Stevie Nicks. He performed at the Hard Rock Hotel in Las Vegas, his third Vegas show in six months.

Dylan was asked to take part in a celebration for Frank Sinatra's 80th birthday in the Shrine Auditorium, Los Angeles. Two days before he had an impromptu singalong with Sinatra, Springsteen, Steve Lawrence and Eydie Gormé. At the concert, Dylan performed

'Restless Farewell' backed by a string quartet, a good choice for an older man. Sinatra seemed to like it.

Dylan did dates on the east coast with Patti Smith in support. Patti had not toured in 16 years and had lost her husband and her brother: Dylan said coming on tour would help her. She joined him for 'Dark Eyes' and Clinton Heylin was impressed, 'They're almost singing the same song!' At the Electric Factory they got together for 'Knockin' on Heaven's Door' but Dylan was going off piste. He had done 118 shows in a year, his most ever.

Q: Who would top the bill on a concert featuring Bob Dylan and Suede?

A: Dylan was on the top of the poster, but Suede was on the right.

At the start of 1996, a new website bobdylan.com was sponsored by Columbia Records. It is still going and is an invaluable source of all things Dylan. They do try and sell you product including special whiskeys known as Heaven's Door and books which have influenced Bob.

During January, Dylan was snowed in on his farm in Minnesota and found himself writing again. He said he was inspired by the phrase, 'Work while the day lasts because the night of death cometh when no man can work.' His new songs had common themes – heartbreak, mortality and solitude – nothing very joyous then. Playing the album *Time out of Mind* now, it sounds unlikely that it was written before he fell ill. However, that was the case and so the album seems full of premonitions of his illness, which we will come to. When the album was released in September 1997, it seemed perfect timing as his illness had been widely reported.

On February 2, Dylan played a private gig for the bankers Nomura Securities and their clients at the Arizona Biltmore resort in Phoenix. Dylan and his band were paid $250,000 and the contract stated that Dylan was not required to speak to the audience, presumably added at Dylan's request but maybe the bankers didn't want one of his rants. Crosby, Stills and Nash played the previous night and Rod Stewart the next.

In April, Dylan was back with his Never Ending Tour. The many guests included Roger McGuinn and Van Morrison.

A new album by Carole King's former husband, Gerry Goffin, was called *Backroom Blood* and included two songs co-written with Dylan, 'Tragedy of the Trade' and 'Time to End This Masquerade'.

Al Kooper rejoined Dylan in June for UK dates. There were two shows in Liverpool and one at Hyde Park for The Prince's Trust. At Hyde Park, Gary Glitter sang with the Who. Dylan ended his set with 'Seven Days'.

The first time Dylan came to Liverpool, Liverpool won the FA Cup. Second time, Everton. Third time, it was the day of England v Germany, the biggest game in the UK for thirty years and Germany were to win on penalties. There were empty seats in Liverpool Empire, presumably bought by fans who chose the game instead.

I didn't go that first night and I remember that my boss in Royal Insurance didn't like me having time off. He said, 'The report you're working on is your top priority and by that I mean your top priority. It has to take priority over your day-to-day work and your home life.' Nice guy: didn't like to tell him I had tickets for Bob Dylan.

I went to Dylan's second night at the Liverpool Empire, and he had spent some of the day at the dockside exhibition, *The Beatles Story*. Dylan came on stage at 8.15, looking very showbiz in silver pants, black t-shirt and white waistcoat. For the first number, he was holding a mic and singing 'Leopard-Skin Pillbox Hat'. The songs included 'Silvio', 'Under the Red Sky', 'Just Like Tom Thumb's Blues', the much underrated 'Man In The Long Black Coat', and Grateful Dead's 'Alabama Getaway'. Dylan's unplugged set with mandolin and double-bass featured 'John Brown' and 'It Ain't Me Babe' with an excessively long harmonica solo. We didn't know when to applaud in 'Mr. Tambourine Man' as every time the song seemed to wind down, Dylan would lift it up. Dylan even introduced the band, but Al Kooper's organ was low in the mix. The younger generation had weak bladders – I had never seen such an exodus to the toilets. Or such a smell of pot.

From time to time, I wondered if Dylan was being criticised unfairly. Sitting in a stadium is never comfortable: there can always be tall or noisy people in front of you or an annoying audience. Plenty of things can spoil a Bob Dylan performance besides Bob Dylan.

On his return to the US, Dylan recorded a slow-paced 'Ring of Fire' for the *Feeling Minnesota* film starring Cameron Diaz. An alternate take of 'Shelter from the Storm' was used in *Jerry McGuire*, directed by Cameron Crowe and starring Tom Cruise.

After Ziggy Bowie, Julian Lennon, Louise Goffin, Wilson-Phillips, Jason Bonham and Jeff Buckley, we now had Jakob Dylan of the Wallflowers. His dad had taken him to the Clash when he was 12 and it had made him want to play guitar. He was glad to see though that he had been kept out of the limelight by his parents: 'I think I'm pretty well put together mentally and the credit for that goes to them.'

He formed the Wallflowers in 1990. Their first album *Wallflowers*, released on Virgin, did moderately well and the group left for Interscope. Their album, *Bringing Down the Horse* (1996) was produced by T Bone Burnett, and two of the tracks, 'One Headlight' and '6th Avenue Heartache' were hit singles. *Bringing down the Horse* outsold any of his father's albums.

Having said that, Dylan was responsible for the UK No. 1 that Christmas.

Dunblane was a sleepy Scottish village, a few miles north of Stirling and with a population under 10,000. In March 1996, a gunman had opened fire in a school gym and killed 16 pupils and their teacher, before turning the gun on himself. Within hours, Dunblane was associated across the world with mindless slaughter.

The local music shop owner Ted Christopher adapted 'Knockin' on Heaven's Door', adding a verse about the 'bairns of Dunblane'. Dylan gave permission for the new version to be recorded for a charity single and Mark Knopfler agreed to play alongside children from the school. The single topped the charts. Unlike the US where endless killings seem to make no difference, UK legislation was passed, making it illegal to own, buy or sell any handgun of .22 calibre and above without a licence.

Dylan was ready to make a new album and he felt confident about the songs. A potential title was *Stormy Season* but they settled on *Time out of Mind*, which had a ring of *Blonde on Blonde* about it. 'Time' is a key Dylan word: it's in many song titles and lyrics, but there's nothing unusual in that.

Dylan wanted to work again with Daniel Lanois who recommended an abandoned theatre in Oxnard, California. The eerie venue was decorated with Mexican movie posters, which Lanois believed would add atmosphere. They were also to use Criteria Studios in Miami: it had an orchestra room and Lanois wanted a depth rather like Dr. John records where he could imagine the performers scattered around the room. The engineer Mark Howard often worked with Lanois and all three were keen on motorcycles and early rock'n'roll. They would relax by riding motorbikes late at night.

The guitarist Bob Britt said, 'We went through 140 reels of tape in three weeks – there was no rolling back to go over something. We used a few mics and stayed away from headphones as much as possible. They set me up between two drummers so I didn't need headphones to hear the groove.'

The musicians included Augie Meyers from the Sir Douglas Quintet on Vox organ and never sounding starker than on 'Million Miles'. Having the blues guitarist, Duke Robillard of the Fabulous Thunderbirds was a major coup although Lanois wasn't after flash picking. There was Tony Garnier, Jim Dickenson, Jim Keltner and others who drifted in and out. Drifting in and out is about right: Lanois was treating the instruments like characters in a landscape. It gives the record a ghostly feel rather like that film, *Paris, Texas*.

While writing this book, I have replayed Dylan's records in chronological order and been surprised at how differently I hear some of them. When I first heard *Time Out of Mind* in 1997, I thought it was fine: now I'd put it up there with his best work. Every track contributes something to the whole and there are no weak ones.

In 1995 Daniel Lanois had made an unnerving album with Emmylou Harris, *Wrecking Ball*, unlike anything she had done before. It worked well although when I saw her in concert, the audience wanted the old Emmy. *Time Out of Mind* is like a continuation of *Wrecking Ball*.

Dylan's songs share an overall sound. The album sounds like one continuous song as Dylan sings of facing death, uncertainty, isolation, lost love, ageing, mental illness and the futility of life. A desolate island disc all right, although you can't assume that the narrator is always Dylan himself. The narrator is constantly on the move and walking endlessly.

Gretchen Peters: 'I've never understood that exploring that territory, that going into the dark corners of your soul, is somehow depressing. To me it is cathartic and the most uplifting thing that you can do. You are saying to another human being, 'I've been there. We all go there and you are not alone.'

After all, in 1828 Franz Schubert and Wilhelm Müller had published a song cycle, *Winterreise*. The songs are about facing death. Schubert was ill at the time and died later that year.

Had Dylan got the crabby habit and made his grumpiest album yet? Would the listeners feel sorry for him after hearing the album? He said, 'I can't help those feelings. I'm not even going to try to make a fake Pollyanna world view. Why would I even want to? I'm not going to deny my feelings just because they might be a little dismal.'

Dylan's phlegm-drenched vocals are not far from Captain Beefheart, who in turn followed Howlin' Wolf. This is especially noticeable on 'Can't Wait'. Although gloomy and claustrophobic, 'Can't Wait' could be a hit song with a different arrangement. It is a song of lost love, possibly from someone contemplating suicide.

Tim Rice: '*Time Out of Mind* was a great album. It didn't make you want to go out and have a party afterwards, but it was a great album and it was one of the first by a rock act to deal with death. People think of rock as a young man's music but it is for anyone who was born in the 1940s onwards.'

Ian McNabb from The Icicle Works: 'I think *Time Out of Mind* is fantastic, it is his best album. He deals with the breakdown of relationships and the uncertainty of his faith. It doesn't leave you down, it is very uplifting. The songs are witty too.'

The opening track, 'Love Sick', sets the tone for the album. Dylan with his half-singing, half-speaking rasp sounds like someone who is totally fatigued. Dylan has said, "Love Sick' is a spooky record because I felt spooky.' Unexpectedly in 2002, Dylan's track was used in a

TV ad for lingerie in Victoria's Secret and although it's hard to see the logic, it did mean the song reached many who had never heard it – and maybe it sold lingerie too, who knows?

'Standing in the Doorway' opens with an Elvis quote, 'Wise men say' and you can pick up musical references throughout the album. Lanois loved the waltz sound of 'Sad Eyed Lady of the Lowlands', which led to 'Doorway' being a waltz.

What could be more despondent than 'Tryin' to Get to Heaven', and what does it all mean? Why should God limit the people going to heaven – 'I'm tryin' to get to heaven before they close the door'. All around him is misery: even if you lose everything 'you could always lose a little more', hence, you could reach heaven and find that it was full.

In 'Tryin' to Get to Heaven', Bob Dylan acknowledged his youth with 'I've been to Sugar Town, I've shook the sugar down', possibly a reference to a 60s hit by Nancy Sinatra, written and produced by Lee Hazlewood. Lee said, 'It's possible and it is a drugs song. I was in a folk club in LA which had two levels. I could see these kids lining up sugar cubes and they had an eye-dropper and were putting something on them. I wasn't a doper so I didn't know what it was but I asked them. It was LSD and one of the kids said, "You know, it's kinda Sugar Town." I went home and started writing 'Sugar Town'. Nancy knew what the song was about because I told her, but luckily Reprise didn't. The kids loved it and oh boy, was Nancy cool!'

In a similar way, 'Not Dark Yet' is a poignant picture about getting old; it's like a tired old blues man in Mississippi saying, 'It's not dark yet, but it's getting there'. Emmylou Harris said, "Not Dark Yet' is the greatest song ever written about growing old. Bob Dylan puts poetry into this experience.' There could be a parallel with John Keats' 'Ode to a Nightingale' and it's easy to imagine that poem in a Dylan voice.

Tom Russell: 'I kissed Dylan off back in the late 70s when he was religious and writing about America and I thought he had lost his mind. I go back and listen to those records now and I realise that he was making very brave comments about America. He didn't really care whether people were buying his records or not. It is never been about the money with him. "It's not dark yet but it's getting there" is a very profound observation. I was with this woman for 20 years, and the moment we were breaking up, she was playing that song. It must have been a coincidence but it was certainly a warning of what was coming. (Laughs)'

Suzie Ungerleider (Oh Susanna): 'I love Bob Dylan but I came to his music after I started writing. His lyrics are incredible but there is something about his singing that I adore. Everyone laughs at his singing but I love it. I also David Bowie and Kate Bush. With the sound of his voice, you can feel a character so vividly even if you don't always know what he is talking about. The depth is always there. I love 'Not Dark Yet'. You get a feel of where the narrator is coming from, the emotional landscape as it were.'

The electronic sounds made by Duke Robillard and Augie Myers create a very effective sound on 'Cold Irons Bound'. The song is about someone on the road, bound for Cold Irons, and the opening line, 'I'm beginning to hear voices and there's no one around', suggests this is about schizophrenia.

It should have been clear from the git-go that 'Make You Feel My Love' had enormous potential, but many early reviews called the song insipid. The song was a welcome respite on the album, although it didn't deny the problems of the world. No matter how bad your life was, the singer would be there for you. It was one of Dylan's best love songs. It was recorded by Garth Brooks for the film, *Hope Floats*, and added by Billy Joel as a new track on a greatest hits compilation. Then it was a hit after Adele sang it on the soundtrack of

When in Rome. It has been used on *The X Factor* and *Britain's Got Talent* and been a Top 10 single for Gamu Nhengu. It works!

In terms of structure, *Time Out of Mind* was like *Blonde on Blonde* as it ended with a lengthy song, in this case the 16-minute narration, 'Highlands'. The tempo and the melody never changes and Bob is telling you a tale as you are walking along. The inspiration was Charley Patton's 'Dry Well Blues' (1930) but the overall effect is not far from J.J. Cale. Biographer Howard Sounes says, 'There's a lot of humour in his songs. 'Highlands' is a shaggy dog story about talking to a waitress in a Boston café and trying to order eggs and it goes wrong because she is star-struck and wants an autograph. It's very funny. When he sings it live, people laugh and he laughs.' All the concert versions are different as he doesn't stick to the same lyric but everyone applauds the line, 'I'm listening to Neil Young'. The final line of 'Highlands' and also of the album is 'That's good enough for now', so who says Dylan hasn't got a sense of humour?

Neil Young loved the album saying it was 'like getting a telegram from the last man on earth'. Greil Marcus said, 'The album was a western, made up of ghost towns and bad earth.' Sean Egan said it was an album of 'fatalism, self-loathing and the fear of death.'

There are also outtakes which are really good. 'Dreamin' of You' was a six-minute song with a funky drum pattern that should have been on the album. He sings about being locked in a cage and thrown on the stage and 'Some things just last longer than you thought they would.' 'Mississippi' only exists as an excellent demo with Dylan and Lanois but the song was to resurface in a different setting on *Love and Theft*.

'Marchin' to the City' sounds fine but Dylan reworked and rewrote it for ''Til I Fell in Love with You', the most overlooked song on *Time out of Mind*.

It seems absurd that they left 'Red River Shore' behind. This was a traditional song that Dylan had reworked for the album. The Kingston Trio had recorded an excellent version in 1965: I presume that Dylan had heard this version and decided to expand the story. In the final verse, Dylan refers to Jesus resurrecting the dead and he wonders if they do 'that kind of thing anymore'.

On 5 April 1997 Allen Ginsberg died of a heart attack, aged 70. On stage, Dylan dedicated an excellent 'Desolation Row' to him, saying 'That was one of his favourite songs.' His final words were 'I'm tired and I have to go to sleep' and he did.

Then in May came Dylan's mystery illness – he went out to observe a flock of locusts but they turned out to be birds and they infected the membrane around his heart and created severe chest pains. Dylan commented, 'I really thought I'd be seeing Elvis.' At first it was thought that Dylan had suffered a heart attack but it was a viral condition, histoplasmosis. The treatment was not severe: he was told to rest for two months. Tour dates were cancelled including UK bookings with Van Morrison.

Dylan was back on tour by August but he was ordered not to play harmonica. He included J.J. Cale's 'Cocaine', 'Tough Mama', 'Roving Gambler' and 'Blind Willie McTell', which would become a concert favourite. The damage that had been done to his voice with the years and then the illness was apparent.

For once, he was including songs from his new album in his stage repertoire. There is a bootleg CD which gathers together live performances of nine different songs from *Time out of Mind*. For all the gloominess of the songs, Bob was in good humour. Introducing the pedal steel player, Bucky Baxter, he said, 'When I first met Bucky Baxter he didn't have a penny to his name. I told him to get another name.'

Paul Morley: 'What I love about Dylan is that people are waiting for him to play 'Like a Rolling Stone' and finding out that he played it four songs earlier. He has turned his songs into Cubist versions of themselves. For him it would be a death in life just to repeat note for note what are ultimately other people's memories. He is still trying to find the perfect version of these songs. Some people think that he had already recorded the perfect version but it is never that way for Dylan: he has always been reworking them.'

On 30 September 1997, *Time out of Mind* was released and sold over 100,000 in the first week in the US. There had been no videos although he later shot ones for 'Love Sick' and 'Not Dark Yet' in Memphis.

Dylan, the Rolling Stones and the Buena Vista Social Club were showing that age was no barrier to success. The Rolling Stones' *Bridges to Babylon* was released at the same time with the 'Lock up your grandmothers!' reviews. There wasn't much different in their approach: electric blues mostly based around a 12-bar structure.

Chris Hockenhull: 'I think getting near to death changed the public's view on him and swung it for the old man. It became very trendy to be into Bob again. Of course it helped that there were good songs in *Time Out of Mind*, but then there were good songs in *Under the Red Sky*.'

The reviews for *Time out of Mind* were Dylan's best for years. Michael Gray: 'Dylan's popularity has been cyclical – there have been periods of great popularity and periods of great unpopularity. For many years, the mainstream media did little but sneer at him. It changed after 1997. Even *The Sunday Times* accepted him as a great artist. 'For so many phases of post-60s culture, Bob Dylan has been dismissed as a 60s man. There is nothing more embarrassing than the recent past and Bob Dylan, having shaped the 60s so tremendously, was naturally the one who got thumped on the head for its evils.'

The *Sunday Times* called him 'a twentieth century genius'. Bryan Appleyard went into overdrive in the same newspaper. He has said that Dylan has made the greatest rock albums ever made: nobody else could rank about No. 42 as Dylan's complete *oeuvre* came first.

James Delingpole took an opposite view: 'Whenever you try to preach his merits to unconverted friends, all they see is a miserable old codger who can barely play, let alone sing; who can't perform his old songs without mangling them or his new ones without sending everyone to sleep. No wonder then, that whenever he manages to turn out an even halfway listenable new album, his acolytes treat it like the Second Coming. It's the sort of bog-standard blues and R&B you'd ignore completely if weren't being done by someone who was once jolly famous.'

The multi-artist production *Songs of Jimmie Rodgers* was released in September. Dylan sang one of the best tracks 'My Blue-Eyed Jane', and it was really enjoyable with a classic country sound. It was a strong album with Van Morrison giving 'Mule Skinner Blues' a New Orleans feel, although it was recorded in England. Steve Earle, rather appropriately, was given 'In the Jailhouse Now'.

In September 1997, there was the oddest of all photo-ops: Bob Dylan with the Pope. Dylan was a guest at the World Eucharist Congress in Bologna, Italy. The Pope delivered a short sermon, saying, 'How many roads must a man walk down? One. There is only one road for man and that it is the road of Jesus Christ.' Bob played 'Knockin' on Heaven's Door'. Daniel Lanois commented, 'I think he's got a few more albums in him but I did get a bit concerned when he went to see the Pope.'

When Bob Dylan was given a medal at the twentieth Kennedy Centre Awards in December 1997, he grinned. His mother was there with tears in her eyes. Gregory Peck compared him to Walt Whitman and Mark Twain and said he was flattered to be in 'Brownsville Girl'. Bruce Springsteen sang 'The Times They Are A-Changin''. David Ball did 'Don't Think Twice, It's All Right' and Shirley Caesar 'Gotta Serve Somebody'. There was a White House lunch for the five new recipients the following day. President Clinton said, 'He probably had more impact on people of my generation than any other artist. His voice and lyrics haven't always been easy on the ears but throughout his career Bob Dylan has never aimed to please.' (Bit harsh!)

The next day Dylan was performing in New York City with Joan Osborne as his opening act. He said very amusingly, 'Joan and I are going to sing a song together but not tonight.'

Joan Osborne: 'Dylan's manager got me on the bill and maybe he wasn't in the mood. Later on we did something for an American TV show and we were singing on the same microphone which was pretty cool for me. I had to remind myself that it was for real. He does have unique phrasing but it is familiar as I have heard him so often. In the studio, he had a restless imagination and he was coming up with ideas and steering us in different directions. He wasn't interested in the technology or guitar sounds, but he did want to try the song in different ways.'

Dylan was often singing 'The White Dove' written by Carter Stanley of the Stanley Brothers and he recorded a duet of 'The Lonesome River' with Dr. Ralph Stanley on his *Clinch Mountain Country* set. You need a high voice to do bluegrass well but he was doing his best.

Dylan did contribute to a video for Wyclef Jean of the Fugees. The video for 'Gone 'Til November', was set in LAX and when the singer referred to 'Knockin' on Heaven's Door', who should be sitting next to him but Bob Dylan.

For the first time Dylan won a Grammy for the Album of the Year and also for Best Contemporary Folk Album of the Year. His son Jakob won a Grammy for his song, 'One Headlight'. Dylan sang 'Love Sick' at the plush ceremony. A performance artist Michael Portnoy, shirtless and with 'Soy bomb' painted on his chest, stood alongside doing a robotic dance. At first no one was sure if it was part of the show and Dylan never acknowledged his presence. Portnoy was removed by security and put out in the cold, his coat and his wallet still being inside.

Dylan was back to a full touring schedule in 1998. He toured South America with the Rolling Stones and sang 'Like a Rolling Stone' with them every night. He toured the US at various times with Joni Mitchell, Van Morrison and Lucinda Williams and Australia with Patti Smith. He played Glastonbury for the first time and his *Live 1966* album was released to great acclaim.

In 1999 Dylan did 48 shows with Paul Simon and they sang several songs together. Paul Simon said, 'I was always angry at being compared to him.' The film, *The Hurricane* with Denzel Washington and directed by Milos Forman used several Dylan songs on the soundtrack.

In October 1999 Bob and his band made a guest appearance on *Dharma and Gant* on ABC. It is a rubbishy sit-com and Dylan's appearance is out of character. He is auditioning a female drummer and he is laughing along with her wayward drumming. 'I guess that's too funky for you,' she says. 'Not at all,' says Bob.

Andy Fairweather Low: 'There was a big concert in New York for Eric Clapton's *Crossroads* charity. Bob was one of the guests and we had heard that he was tricky and hard to work with. There were others on that bill who were hard to work with but not Bob Dylan. He turned up on time and he never stopped talking. He reminded me of Parker in *Thunderbirds*, he has this wobble on him, 'M'lady', but he loved the blues and talked about Robert Johnson. He was gracious enough to do whatever was required of him.'

A 9CD bootleg set *Never Ending Covers* with 130 live covers appeared including 'Nowhere Man' and Charles Aznavour's 'The Times We've Known'. There could still be surprises every night as Bob was singing the hymns, 'Rock of Ages' (1776) and 'Pass Me Not, O Gentle Saviour' (1868). For some it was the moment when you went for a beer but he did them well, more in a country way than a gospel one. When he was in Normal, Illinois, he said, 'I can't believe I'm here. People always say I'm a long way from normal.'

As we came up for the turn of the century, there were many opinion pieces about the highlights. The poet laureate Andrew Motion said in *The Observer* that Dylan was 'one of the greatest poets of the century': others disagreed.

Despite all the accolades for *Time out of Mind*, many critics sensed that this was Bob Dylan saying goodbye. Bob didn't feel that way at all, musing in 1998, 'I didn't feel the album was an ending, more like a beginning.'

CHAPTER 15

'Me, I'm Still on the Road'

I. Don't Start Me Talkin'

What I love most about Bob Dylan is his unpredictability. If a reader is coming to Bob Dylan for the first time with this book, then I don't think he or she could predict what would be on the next page. Not only that: Bob Dylan himself, as he was living his life, often didn't know his next move. Many artists have five year plans but not Dylan: he found out what worked and what didn't almost on a whim. He had seen Elvis Presley become a hamster on a wheel, first with Hollywood films and then with stage performances in Vegas and elsewhere, and he didn't want that.

In public, Bob hadn't been one for small talk. He avoided talk shows with other guests and in interviews, he countered questions with questions. He enjoyed being a celebrity but on his own terms and he had little to do with the general trappings of celebrity.

But you know all this.

In 2005 I would have said that Bob Dylan would have been a most unlikely choice for a radio DJ as he never could have handled the small talk or faked bonhomie. On the other hand, he was a perfect choice as he had such a wide appreciation of music.

Enter XM Satellite Radio which broadcast to subscribers in North America. It cost a listener $13 a month for a range of services covering news, weather, sports, music, drama and comedy. In 2006 there were six million subscribers. XM was trying to find its niche with some special programmes. When the programme director Lee Abrams talked to Bob Dylan, he found he was already listening and loved their country and blues shows.

Bob Dylan agreed to present a weekly *Theme Time Radio Hour* for XM Satellite, which was rebroadcast in the UK on BBC Radio 2. One of the celebrity stings said, 'Hello, this is John C. Reilly and you are listening to Bob Dylan with *Theme Time Radio Hour* – imagine that.'

When the first series was announced, it made the front page of the *New York Times* and the *Washington Post*. The shows have been repeated from time to time and in 2015 Radio Eins in Germany broadcast a previously unheard episode with songs about Kissing where Dylan, in a nod to a Frank Sinatra films, calls himself the Kissing Bandit. He comments, 'The average person spends 336 hours of his life kissing. Doesn't seem like enough.'

Theme Time Radio Hour is an opportunity to hear Bob Dylan in his own words and I am glad that there is a website with all 100 programmes. I love them although Dylan does speak in a monotone but I don't think he is monotonous. He does mumble and so the shows are not background listening and you have to concentrate. His speech is as much an acquired taste as his singing.

Although there were exceptions, each programme was based around a theme (the weather, US presidents, around the world, Christmas) and created initially from Dylan's own record collection including his 78s: Dylan commented, 'I file everything alphabetically. I don't do it by genre so Thelonious Monk is next to the Monkees.' He claimed that everything came from his own collection but I doubt that – nobody has got such a vast collection and there must have been records that he needed for certain themes but didn't own.

Each programme lasted at least an hour and would feature around 15 tracks. The one on Time lasted 80 minutes while Presidents stretched to two hours. There were no ads, causing Bob Dylan to remark, 'We don't have advertising. These Kellogg's Corn Flakes are delicious.'

On his Christmas show, Dylan said that his mission was to 'expand the musical tastes of listeners'. He certainly did that with his wild-ranging choices as the shows were treasure chests of popular music.

Dylan fan Steve Hardstaff says, 'My wife is very good and very tolerant. She loves Bob Dylan and she realises that a lot of the stuff I listen to is actually the roots of Dylan. Dylan's radio shows are terrific as he has a great skill in juxtaposing music that you wouldn't normally hear together back to back.'

There were researchers who came up with potential choices; in fact, what puzzled me most was the long list of credits on each show. I would have thought you needed no more than Dylan, a producer, an editor, a secretary and a couple of researchers – and even that's pushing it. Taking a *Theme Time Radio Hour* at random, I counted 27 people in the credits. His producer was Eddie Gorodetsky, a highly experienced backroom figure and comedy scriptwriter noted for his work with David Letterman and *Saturday Night Live*.

The format was ideal for Dylan as you can sense his love of lists in *Chronicles, Volume 1*. His lists created odd bedfellows but they worked extremely well. Dylan put 'Mule Train' into his programme on Trains, but you could argue that's his humour. There were both dreadlocks and Alicia Keys in his *Locks and Keys* programme.

Each week there was an introduction from the actress Ellen Barkin, which began 'It's night-time in the big city' and then had appropriate images for the subject. There were celebrity guests like Tom Waits, Steve Earle and Elvis Costello making short, pithy comments. George Clooney asked Bob to play a record by his Aunt Rosemary, which I enjoyed as he had missed her out of his *Desert Island Discs*.

Bob didn't play his own discs but he did perform occasionally, notably an a cappella 'Take Me Out to the Ballgame'. He hardly referred to his own career, but there were some humorous asides: 'In 2002, *Time* magazine called Lucinda Williams America's best songwriter. I guess I was out of town.' On playing Rockin' Sidney's 'You Ain't Nothin' But Fine', he says, 'That sounded like me playing harmonica.' His life on the road prompted, 'Lowell Fulson was born in Tulsa, Oklahoma where you can still get the best steak sandwich in the country.'

There were plenty of odd facts and number games: 'Bookkeeper is the only word in the English language with three sets of double letters' and 'It's called a tip because it stands for To Insure Promptness.'

Some of his best one-liners are in his take on divorce: 'It takes two to make a divorce' and 'It is better to have a separation before a divorce as that gives you time to hide your money.' Bob returns to divorce in the Nothing show saying 'If you do get divorced, you can start writing country songs'.

Dylan played tracks by his associates like Phil Ochs, Stephen Stills and the Clancy Brothers and Tommy Makem. He quoted from the Beat writers and he mused on Jack

Kerouac's line, 'I'd rather be thin than famous.' He repeated Charles Bukowski's one liner: 'I don't like jail; they have the wrong kind of bars there.'

Dylan shows his love for Raymond Chandler and Harold Hart Crane and praises a book by George Jacobs, Frank Sinatra's valet *Mr. S.* and he tells us how well read Peter Wolf from the J. Geils Band is. There's gossip in *Theme Time Radio Hour* which seems out of character for Dylan, especially when talking about Connie Francis who was still alive. On the whole though, it was great fun and he enjoyed describing the feud between Warren Smith and Jerry Lee Lewis.

Sid Griffin: '*Theme Time Radio Hour* is scripted as I have talked to a guy who has worked on it. He is a reading a lot of it as you can tell but he has some input and he does pick the records. Younger people wouldn't be able to pull these old songs together. They wouldn't have the cultural reference. The jokes are his. He is having a great time and doesn't come over as the dour, unhappy guy you might think he is. He has a sense of humour and I am a big fan of the show. He has played the White Stripes and Nick Cave and some contemporary records and maybe his kids have introduced him to some of it. It is great that he is working so enthusiastically and this is much better than the somnambulistic Dylan that was putting out *Knocked out Loaded* and *Down in the Groove*. He didn't have the fire burning then.'

Sid Griffin is right – Dylan is full of knowledge and jokes. When he announces the Presidents show he refers to Watergate by saying there won't be an 18-minute gap in his tape. He even cracks mother-in-law jokes: 'What do you do if you miss your mother-in-law? Reload and try again.'

There are neat asides: Dylan considers the opening of 'The Train Kept A-Rollin" by Tiny Bradshaw (1951). 'Listen to the call and response on boodow and booday, but one guy still says boodow. Nowadays you can use Pro-Tools and take that guy out or re-record it but back then it was more important to be great than to be perfect.'

And how about this on the Monkees' 'Last Train to Clarksville'? 'The first rule of being subversive is not to let anyone know you are being subversive. The train is taking him to an army base, "I don't know if I'm ever coming home".' It had never occurred to me that this was a Vietnam song, but he's right.

There are few mistakes, although Dylan did think that Little Eva's 'The Locomotion' was a hit in 1959 when it was 1962. Dylan admonishes Michael Martin Murphey for writing 'Geronimo's Cadillac' as the Indian chief isn't in a Cadillac in the famous photograph; okay, but what's wrong with using artistic licence? I don't think that Dylan is immune from that.

Dylan loves to quote song lyrics. He comments on how blues and country singers like to borrow lines and images from existing songs, certainly one of his own practices.

Best of all are his comments on other performers and songs:

'Why isn't Charlie Feathers a bigger star?'

'Johnnie Ray had some kind of strange incantation in his voice, like he'd been voodoo'd.'

'Slim Harpo wrote a bunch of songs with his wife. Boy, I wish I had a wife like that, helping me write songs.'

'Jimmy Reed was once on *Beat the Clock*. I'd pay good money to see that.'

On one of the Carlisle Brothers: 'He had a comic alter ego. I'm going to get me one of those.'

On Clyde McPhatter: 'Nobody sings like that anymore. He just makes it sound effortless.'

Vince Taylor's 'Brand New Cadillac' is 'the best rockabilly record to come out of England'.

'The Everly Brothers always had a strong sense of family even when they're not speaking to each other.'

'Mark Knopfler is one of the few guys I know who fingerpicks an electric guitar and he does it awful pretty.'

'Emmylou's not a slave to traditional music. She likes to stretch the boundaries and you can hear that in her album from a couple of years back called *Wrecking Ball*.'

'If you drop a guitar down the stairs, it will play 'Gloria' as it gets to the bottom.'

'If you haven't heard Beethoven before, it's new.'

There are many obscure records in the programmes. Songwriter Donnie Fritts: 'The first song of mine that Charlie Rich cut was 'Tears a go-go', which was a hit in a few different places. Bob Dylan had a radio show and on the first season, he picked that song. I don't know where he had heard it, but that was pretty cool.'

Theme Time Radio Hour is the clearest indication yet that Dylan loves the Great American Songbook and this was to manifest itself in the 2010s.

The series finished with the 100th edition on 15 April 2009. In introducing his final show, *The Long Goodbye*, Dylan said, 'The show might be a little long this week but what are they going to do – fire me?' He offered a genre-hopping panorama about saying goodbye. He signed off with the words, 'Every goodbye is the birth of a memory' and surely he could have got a song out of that. His final record was 'So Long, It's Been Good to Know You' by Woody Guthrie.

II. So Much Older Now: 2000–2012

Bob Dylan's mother Beatty had remarried and was to outlive her second husband. She died from cancer on 25 January 2000 at the age of 84. She was buried next to her first husband and so Bob's parents are together in Duluth.

The film director Curtis Hanson was shooting a story on an American campus *Wonder Boys* about a literature professor Grady Tripp (Michael Douglas) and his relationships with those around him at Wordfest, notably James Leer (Tobey McGuire). One academic has his own library consisting of overdue library books. Grady has written over 2,000 single spaced pages – and has only one copy (major plot point!). The professor loses his novel, of course, but the final scene shows him working on a novel and this time pressing 'Save' on a computer.

Hanson was sure that Tripp would have grown up with the singer / songwriters of the 1960s and their subsequent work and would have admired their well-turned phrases. Quite unusually, he got the rights for the records he wanted: Tom Rush's 'No Regrets', John Lennon's 'Watching the Wheels', Neil Young's 'Old Man' and Bob Dylan's 'Buckets of Rain', which also tied in with the weather in Pittsburgh. 'Not Dark Yet' represented Grady's mood and 'Shooting Star' reflected the two wonder boys (Grady and James). Now that is a film score…

Usually, Bob Dylan didn't say yes. In 2000 there was a cameo in *High Fidelity* by Bruce Springsteen after Bob Dylan had turned it down.

What's more, Dylan saw some rough cuts of *The Wonder Boys* and agreed to write a new song, his first film song since *Pat Garrett and Billy the Kid*. He called it 'Times Have

Changed' and like many Dylan songs, it worked on several levels. First of all, it was a nod to 'The Times They Are A-Changin'' and secondly, we can see it as a song of impending doom, of Dylan thinking that his illness might recur. It was a song about somebody out of step with the times (Bob Dylan and Grady Tripp) and finally, it was very catchy and Dylan was in good voice, much better than on *Time Out of Mind*.

Michael Gray: 'The line, "I used to care but things have changed" is from the same Dylan who wrote on *Time Out of Mind*, "My sense of humanity has gone down the drain." It is an appalling thing to say but it is a brave thing to say. I think that the whole of 'Things Have Changed' is about his own decay. It is about someone who used to be central and relevant in a profoundly constructive way, feeling side-lined but not in a 'poor me' way. He is bravely confronting the comparative irrelevance of old age. It is a response to 'The Times They Are A-Changin'' where the know-all young Turk who has never known much disappointment or personal struggle can write a declamatory anthem about changing the world. He is looking back and saying, "Things haven't changed in the way they were supposed to; what has changed is that I used to be that and now I feel more like this." He has looked back in that way before. In 1981 he changed the pace and a couple of chords on 'The Times They Are A-Changin'' and by doing so he changed the whole way that the song felt. He was saying that the times hadn't changed. It was a paean of regret rather than a swaggering anthem.'

Dylan's video for 'Things Have Changed' is hilarious with Dylan mostly miming the song with a straw hat and cane. He is placed into scenes from the film and at one point Michael Douglas starts miming the song, which emphasises that the lyric was meant to echo his character's thoughts.

Curtis Stigers cut 'Things Have Changed' in 2006: 'I'd had a tumultuous couple of years. I was married for a long time and it has been heartbreaking and difficult since then. That came out in this album of covers. It is as personal as anything that I have written. I love 'Things Have Changed'. It's cynical, it's dark, it's romantic and I like to think it is about me. Dylan is so poetic and so sly and able to say things in an oblique and backhanded way. It took me a while to get into that song as there is so much there but once I started singing it I thought "Oh yeah, this is me." I am the guy who used to care but things have changed. I've been through that.'

In the lyrics there are references to 'Worried Life Blues' (The Carter Family), 'Forty Miles of Bad Road' (Duane Eddy) and the Book of Revelation: "If the Bible is right, the world will explode."

Michael Gray: 'The line about the wheelbarrow comes from a nursery rhyme and Dylan likes its playfulness. It sounds a bit Chris Rea on the surface, a bit adult-oriented rock, but there are many things that make it more complex than you would necessarily think at first hearing. He is singing about this dead place that he is in and saying he should be in Hollywood. Then he sings "but I'm looking up into the sapphire-tinted skies". That is from a Shelley poem, 'Lines Written among the Euganean Hills'. If you get the reference, it deepens the resonance of the song. Shelley is looking down on the glittering citadel of Venice, the apex of European civilisation, and he is contemplating its decay. Dylan is looking on himself as a now decayed cultural icon, so it couldn't be more pertinent. It doesn't matter if you don't get it but if you do it is an inspired use of somebody else's work to deepen your own.'

'Things Have Changed' won an Oscar for Best Original Song. Dylan said, 'I'd like to thank the Academy for being bold enough to vote for this song, a song which doesn't pussyfoot around nor turn a blind eye to human nature. God bless you all with peace, tranquillity and good will.' It's one of the few times we know that Dylan was delighted to win something.

Tony Palmer: 'When he won an Oscar, he seemed embarrassed, he kept saying, "Thank you." He was proud about it, no doubt about that.' As indeed he was. Eric Clapton, 'I like awards. They are confidence boosters and remind you that people do care. We all like a pat on the back.'

When I saw Dylan in Liverpool, he had his Oscar on a table at the back of the stage and at one point he grabbed it and held it aloft. Howard Sounes: 'That is just his sense of humour, he is a funny guy. I am sure that he does not take it that seriously.'

Michael Gray; 'Dylan doesn't usually do anything that is cheap, and that was cheap. He had the Oscar with him at a lot of concerts but he didn't always pick it up and wave it. I prefer the Bob Dylan that we see in *Dont Look Back* where someone tries to give him a silver disc and he says, "No, you keep it, I don't even want to see it".'

Sid Griffin: 'Well, who would dream that Dylan would do a lingerie commercial or a Cadillac ad? He likes to do what people don't expect him to do. He was out of protest music when he did the 'George Jackson' single and then 'Hurricane'. Being a Jesus fanatic was unexpected too. He did two acoustic records in the early 1990s and he revels in the unexpected. He does it time and time again.'

You could say that too about the version of 'Blowin' in the Wind' on *Best of Bob Dylan, Volume 2*. Greil Marcus said that the 'verses were crooned, whispered and overstated'. The performance was more about it being an iconic song than about its meaning.

In 2001, Dylan recorded a reflective version of Dean Martin's 'Return to Me' with accordion for *The Sopranos*, singing in both English and Italian and sounding very docile by his standards. He was followed on the soundtrack CD by Keith Richards, so nobody could say anymore that Bob Dylan can't sing.

A new generation of musicians and producers wanted to be associated with the heroes from the previous generation. In particular, Junkie XL from the Netherlands had done wonders for Elvis Presley's sales figures. A Danish house producer Funkstar De Luxe had an international hit by recasting Bob Marley's 'Sun Is Shining' with modern technology. After imposing his style on Barry White and Grace Jones, he got permission to create a new environment for Bob Dylan's original vocal on 'All Along the Watchtower', making both four minute and eight minute versions. Total bollocks of course but if it drew some new people to Bob Dylan, then fair enough.

Further indignity came in 2007 when Amy Winehouse's producer Mark Ronson created a 're-version' of 'Most Likely You Go Your Way and I'll Go Mine' with totally unnecessary brass and even worse neighing, so I'm a neigh-sayer.

In May 2000, Bob was recording and self-producing his next album, *Love and Theft*. The title came from a book on blackface minstrels published in 1995. Its two themes are the love and life of an outlaw – that is, love and theft. The fact that Bob refers to the Darktown Strut in 'Sugar Baby' is surely a reference to the well-known blackface song, 'Darktown Strutters Ball', recorded by Al Jolson in 1917.

But that is not the main influence on the record. That is the book *Confessions of a Yakuza: a Life in Japan's Underworld*, written by a 62-year-old doctor Junichi Saga. It was published in 1991 and featured his conversations with a dying gangster.

Bob Dylan. 'My approach is to just let the songwriting happen and then reject the things that don't work.' He was more light-hearted than on *Time out of Mind*. The lines included 'I'm no pig without a wig' and 'Freddie or not, here I come.' Because Dylan was producing himself there were none of Lanois' embellishments and so the sound is clearer than on *Time out of Mind*, although that album is far more atmospheric. I don't think *Love and Theft* is as strong as *Time out of Mind* but it is still an exceptional album with 12 songs and 57 minutes playing-time.

Dylan made the album with his road band and his old friend, Augie Meyers from the Sir Douglas Quintet. There is a photo inside the CD booklet of them all listening to what Augie is playing. Bob is displaying his new Vincent Price moustache, although on the back cover, he resembles Kinky Friedman.

Although it is by no means the best track, 'Cry a while' is the most revealing in showing how Bob Dylan writes. Revenge is a familiar Dylan theme and one we have seen in 'Like a Rolling Stone' and 'Positively Fourth Street'. Here Dylan has tossed us into the middle of a story: we don't know why he feels trapped, who Mr. Goldsmith is or why he wants the girl to know he is a union man. Why does he talk about the problems of travelling in Pennsylvania and Denver when they are 1,500 miles apart? The sound is an edgy mix of Delta blues and swing and there are references in the song to 'Your Funeral, My Trial' (Sonny Boy Williamson), 'I Cried for You' (Billie Holiday), 'Stop and Listen Blues' (Mississippi Sheiks), the comic opera *Don Pasquale* and 'My Generation' (The Who). 'I'll die before I turn senile' sounds like a take on 'Hope I die before I get old'. It is a good example of how much confusion Bob Dylan can cause with just one song.

Maybe it's the same girl that he is addressing in 'Sugar Baby' which is set in the Prohibition era. Dylan is hiding out with his Aunt Sally and he thinks the girl should repent before 'Gabriel blows his horn', which confirms his starting point was Gene Austin's 'Lonesome Road' (1927). There is a Dock Boggs record called 'Sugar Baby' (1927) and the repeated line 'Might as well keep going now' could have come from Samuel Beckett.

Leon Redbone has shown a fondness for pre-war tea-room jazz and he could have prompted Bob's 'Bye and Bye' and 'Floater'. You could imagine Sinatra recording these songs, but there are quirky lines that suggest all is not as it seems. 'I'm going to establish my rule through civil war' in 'Bye and Bye' and 'My grandfather was a duck trapper' in 'Floater'. The second song has a fine example of Dylan taking a banal line to set up an unexpected one, 'Honey bees are buzzing, I'm in love with my second cousin'.

Although Leon Redbone may be an influence, I am more confident about Tom Waits for 'Po' Boy'. This is a relaxing, lolloping blues very much in Waits' style. There is an indication that Bob is not taking things too seriously with 'Call down to room service, said send up a room.' Indeed, 'Bye and Bye' has the comic line, 'I'm sitting on my watch so I can be on time.'

It sounds like Dylan was trying to write a song for the long gone Mills Brothers with 'Moonlight'. His voice is stretched but the song works well and for once the lyric doesn't contain oblique references.

Maria Muldaur: 'I still have an amazing love and respect for him. He has never disappointed me. I recorded an album of his love songs called *Heart of Mine* and it was inspired by hearing his gorgeous song 'Moonlight'. His poetry and his imagery never fail to get to me.'

His slide guitar blues 'Honest with Me' is really good but again, what are the Siamese twins doing there? There is the rockabilly of 'Summer Days', which follows the tune of

'Matchbox' for most of the way. It has a witty verse about a politician and the neat line, 'What looks good in the day, by night is another thing.'

The opening track, 'Tweedle Dee and Tweedle Dum', could have been on *Under the Red Sky*. The song doesn't appear to have anything to do with Lewis Carroll's creations. It is possible that Dylan's frivolity is misleading and he is commenting on the relationship between Israel and Palestine.

'Lonesome Day Blues' is the most forceful track on the album, featuring guitar riffing from Dylan and Charlie Sexton but the song itself is confusing. At first I thought it was about a disgruntled soldier talking about the American Civil War, but then Dylan refers to listening to a car radio. At the start of the song, Dylan says he is sitting, thinking with his mind 'a million miles away'. Maybe we should take Dylan at his word and treat this as random thoughts. There seems to be a personal note as he says, 'I wish my mother was still alive'. If there is a theme, it is that you can lose but still pull through.

Dylan dedicates 'High Water' from Charley Patton, possibly because he has taken the title from one of Poole's songs about the southern floods, the two-part 'High Water Everywhere' released in 1930. He doesn't refer to Patton in the song, but he does credit Big Joe Turner. It seems misogynistic: 'Throw your panties overboard' and it quotes from 'The Cuckoo' and 'Dust My Broom'. It's a fine track but Dylan has been there before and surely 'Down in the Flood' is better.

The New Orleans floods were not until 2005 so the song is not about that though it could be prescient. However, when the flood came Joe Bonamassa revived Charley Patton's original song: 'I thought it was very relevant and that was a good way of doing it without doing a corny 'Tribute to Katrina'. It was a fitting political commentary. I combined the two parts of the song to make three verses and it told the story of today even though Charley Patton wrote it 70 years earlier.'

Dylan often did his own 'High Water' after the New Orleans flood and it became more intense and ferocious but as so often with Dylan, a new listener wouldn't have known what he was singing so the point was lost.

Dylan had decided against using 'Mississippi' on *Time Out of Mind*. He had given it to Sheryl Crow who was to release it on *The Globe Sessions* (1998). The Dixie Chicks performed it on stage and put it on a live album. In 2001, we at last heard Bob Dylan's version, newly recorded for *Love and Theft*. It lacked the energy of the Dixie Chicks but its resignation was moving. Possibly it has too many verses as the title line, 'Only one thing I did wrong, Stayed in Mississippi a day too long', is rather lost. Still, it has an excellent arrangement, a strong melody and a fine, allegorical lyric.

The CD was available in a special limited edition with a bonus CD, which included just two tracks – 'I Was Young When I Left Home' (1961), his best performance before he was signed to Columbia and it was really the folk song '500 Miles', and an alternative take of 'The Times They Are A-Changin'' (1963), which is sung very properly and distinctly with little of the passion of the hit single.

Mark Ellen was a keen supporter of the new songs: 'Bob gets a lot of stick. I don't like hearing him play those early songs as I grew up with those albums. They mean a great deal to me but evidently they don't mean a great deal to him anymore. He is disrespectful in the way he sings them and the emphasis he puts on the wrong notes. All I want to hear is him playing his more recent material. He has made several albums of American roots music: jazz, swing, blues, folk, jump jive, and lovely ballads like 'Po' Boy' and 'Floater' on *Love and*

Theft. It is an evocation of a lost America and the big riverboats. He has grown older with his music and it is better than a rock star trying to recruit a new generation.'

Dennis Locorriere: 'I've never met Bob Dylan. He's like McCartney. I feel they don't owe us anything else. If they're still recording and touring, then we're the lucky ones. When they put out albums, there will be some brilliant stuff on there, maybe four or five songs that make us glad that they are on the planet. The baby boomers are a lucky generation. Back in the day, everybody expected Elvis Presley to have a few hits and then grow up, put on a tux and go to Vegas. There was no rock'n'roll life after 26. The Beatles and the Stones said, "No, no, we can get old and we can change and we can still be the same people".'

When Jack Dee was on *Celebrity Big Brother*, he took his guitar into the house and sang Dylan to the other contestants including 'Memphis Blues Again'. Whether Jack Dee's renditions secured Dylan new fans is debatable but unquestionably the public interest in Eva Cassidy and her covers some five years after her death brought him a new following. Katie Melua says, 'I was so moved by Eva Cassidy and by the style and presentation of her records. That was the first time I had heard soulful acoustic music and that is where my heart lies. She led the way for me to discover Joni Mitchell, Bob Dylan and Paul Simon.'

Carolyn Dennis issued a statement that the reports that she and Dylan had tried to hide their relationship were malicious and ridiculous. Their marriage was a private matter and they made a joint decision to shield their daughter from publicity in order to give her a normal upbringing. Dylan, she said, was a wonderful and active father.

When Bob Dylan came to the UK on tour, he got some unexpected publicity from an old lover or perhaps an existing one. The actress Sarah Miles told *Scotland on Sunday* that she had had an off and on affair with Bob Dylan for 26 years: 'I beat him at chess and you have a bad sex life if you win chess games against guys.' (Amazing what you can learn from this book.)

On Thursday 12 July 2001, I found myself on the breakfast show on BBC Radio Merseyside to talk about Bob Dylan who was appearing at the Summer Pops festival in Liverpool. It took place in a huge tent and I said, 'I heard the weather report and the tent might be blowing in the wind' – how embarrassing. Later in the morning, I was invited to see the stage for Bob Dylan with an offer of canapés, but not of course Bob Dylan. BBC-TV had been hoping for a chat with Bob Dylan but nothing was possible and so Alan Urry asked me if I would be his stunt double, as it were, for the north-west news programme. I rather suspect I repeated my corny joke. The promoter Chas Cole said that having Bob Dylan at the Summer Pops meant that he could attract bigger names next year. He would like to get Sting. Imagine living in a world where Sting was regarded as more important than Bob Dylan, but maybe in box office terms, he was.

It was another unusual time for Bob to be in Liverpool as there was a huge parade for Orangemen's Day. I was offered £50 for my £30 ticket when I walked into the arena but I held onto it. The show was scheduled to start at 8pm, but it was late. Whilst waiting, I took a sample of the audience and counted 100 men and 29 women.

The show didn't start until 8.45pm, but with no explanation or apology. Indeed, there were no spoken words during the evening as Dylan didn't even say 'Thank you'. He did seem to be enjoying himself. I was in C block and both the view and the sound was very good with a strong smell of marijuana in the air.

On the evidence of recent releases, Dylan's voice was shot to pieces, so I wasn't expecting too much, but he has a fine four piece band with him (lead, rhythm, bass, drums – with the lead guitarist playing steel on occasion) and they were very well rehearsed. Dylan, wearing a black shirt and black trousers with white piping, often played lead guitar and picked up harmonicas from a table towards the back of the stage. 'To Ramona' was as much a harmonica solo as a vocal.

Dylan opened with a rockabilly song, 'Mighty Fine', and then 'To Ramona'. I'd have been happy with this sound for the rest of the show but during the third song, 'Desolation Row', things went rockier. Dylan sang several verses and his old phrasing could be heard when singing about the jealous monk. The arrangement of 'Maggie's Farm' resembled Newport but with more percussion. 'Just like a Woman' was a stately waltz and there was fine harmony singing for 'This Wheel's on Fire'. The seventh song was 'Visions of Johanna' and Dylan was having no trouble with the long lyric.

'Fourth Time Around' was a minor song on *Blonde on Blonde* ('minor', what am I talking about, the whole album is wonderful), and so effectively Bob was playing 'Norwegian Wood' in Liverpool. Even though the audience applauded 'Boots of Spanish Leather' at the outset, Dylan garnered more applause when he got to the title line. There was a blackout after each song and Dylan came quickly back with the next, a device which meant he didn't have to say anything and so this was akin to a classical concert in that respect. 'Memphis Blues Again' was okay but the lyrics would be meaningless to anyone hearing it for the first time and then came the vituperative 'Positively Fourth Street'. He went to the 90s for a song from *Time out of Mind*, but I wasn't sure which – it was a clanging arrangement and Dylan's diction was poor. It was back to *Blonde on Blonde* for 'Leopard-Skin Pillbox Hat'. And that appeared to be it. Dylan took his bow and left the stage.

The band returned after a couple of minutes and I wondered what Dylan would do for an encore. Probably 'Like a Rolling Stone', I guessed, and I would have been well pleased with that. We had had 90 minutes, but now he continued for another 40. The first song was 'Things Have Changed' and then he went to the back of the stage and came back with his Oscar. Why had he brought his Oscar on tour? Maybe he was saying, 'I may be 60 but I can still cut it.'

Then we had 'Like a Rolling Stone' (a huge cheer for this one), 'Knockin' on Heaven's Door' (with an additional line, 'like I've done so many times before' – a reference to his illness?), 'Highway 61 Revisited' and 'I Shall Be Released'. He was halfway through 'All Along the Watchtower' before I realised what it was: the heavy metal arrangement didn't work. He ended with 'Blowin' in the Wind', the only protest song of the night and the chorus sounding like a folk-club singalong.

A couple of hundred fans who couldn't get into the concert heard it from outside and someone told me that it had sounded fine, but not as good as the Bootleg Beatles on the Monday.

Dylan was preparing for the release of *Love and Theft* on 11 September 2001, saying, 'I think of it as a greatest hits album. Without the hits. Not yet anyway.' There's confidence for you. Other things happened on 9/11, but Dylan's album did sell 134,000 in its first week and made No. 5 on the albums chart. One of Dylan's finest concerts was in New York right after 9/11.

Love and Theft was a US No. 2 album and it won a Grammy as the Best Contemporary Folk Album. In 2009, *Newsweek* listed it as one of the best albums of the decade.

Earlier in 2001 Bob Dylan had talked to some writers about doing some TV comedy shows – yes, really. Dylan had a box of jottings which he passed to Larry Charles, who had made his name on *Seinfield*. These notes developed into the film script, *Masked and Anonymous* (2003), which Larry Charles and Bob Dylan wrote under pseudonyms – masked and anonymous; Dylan was Sergei Petrov, so make what you will of that. The film was costed at a modest $7m and was partly funded by the BBC. It was to be directed by Larry Charles, his first job as a director, and he would be directing Bob Dylan, whose acting ability was, shall we say, unproven. Although it contained black humour and even a reference to Laurel and Hardy, *Masked and Anonymous* was not a comedy.

Larry Charles, doing his best for his new partner, said, 'I respect Paul McCartney and the Stones but they have essentially become nostalgia acts and Bob is not a nostalgia act, he is still a vital artist, recreating and creating new work all the time.'

In order to get the financial backing, the film was said to star Val Kilmer, Jessica Lange, John Goodman, Jeff Bridges, Penélope Cruz and Mickey Rourke, all of whom were to appear to a greater or lesser extent. Unquestionably, Dylan and Charles were relying on goodwill. Jeff Bridges said that he wanted to get to know his hero Bob Dylan and wasn't bothered about the money. Jeff helped Bob with his acting, though you'd never know it, but he didn't get his dream which was to jam with Bob.

When we first see Jeff Bridges he is in a black hooded jacket with sunglasses, Bob's usual casual wear. He looked like he hadn't had a good night's sleep for a long time, but maybe that's good acting.

Filmed over three weeks in a rundown section of Los Angeles, America has become a banana republic and progress is hampered by civil war. Bob Dylan plays Jack Fate who looks, speaks and sings surprisingly like Bob Dylan. His father had ordered his arrest but the new regime has released him to perform a tribute concert to help victims, which has been organised by the unscrupulous Uncle Sweetheart (John Goodman). Jack Fate performs 'Simple Twist of Fate' (the title now a pun) with his road band in the combat zone. He sings the Civil War song, 'Dixie', like a pub singalong and he has an argument with a journalist which is reminiscent of *Dont Look Back*. The reporter invades his privacy and wants to expose him. His editor says that if he can't find a story, make one up.

Jack Fate hates anyone giving him their theory on what he does. He adopts a stone face until they've finished and gives nothing away. Remind you of anyone? Jack Fate's final line in the film is 'I stopped trying to figure everything out a long time ago.'

Dylan wanted to cry in the scene where his father died. A menthol concoction was sprayed into his eyes which temporarily blinded him and he needed medical attention. It was washed out and instead the production team put glycerine tears on his cheek.

Masked and Anonymous was shown at the Sundance Film Festival in 2003 and Dylan was cheered on entering the cinema. By the end of the film, half the audience had left. Any further showing involved a walkout. Roger Ebert called it, 'A vanity production beyond all reason' and Michael Gray said that it was 'really just an Elvis movie'. It was released on DVD in 2003 through BBC Worldwide, and I shouldn't think that the investors got a return on their money. There is a very good Director's Commentary on the DVD and Larry Charles, still trying to do his best, says that the viewer has to be involved with the film: he says that if you see it ten years later, you might see it differently. I doubt that.

The soundtrack album is better than the film. The Grateful Dead's long 'It's All Over Now, Baby Blue' is tremendous and, though not in the film, the Dixie Hummingbirds perform an excellent version of Dylan's 'City of Gold'.

Dylan wore a Tom Petty wig in the first scenes of *Masked and Anonymous* and liked it so much he wore it at the Sundance showing and then at the Newport Folk Festival in August

2002, his first return since 1965. He wanted the Newport banner behind him removed before he performed in his wig and, I suspect, fake beard. He sang 'Not Fade Away' in the Grateful Dead's arrangement.

In 2002 Dylan wrote and performed 'Waiting for You' for the soundtrack of *Divine Secrets of the Ya-Ya Sisterhood* which starred Sandra Bullock and Ellen Burstyn and had a soundtrack produced by T Bone Burnett. Dylan's song was a cheerful, affirmative country ballad, somewhat like the ones Shel Silverstein wrote for Dr. Hook.

Joe Henry was gathering songs and recording them for a new Solomon Burke album, *Don't Give Up on Me*. Bob Dylan gave him 'Stepchild' which Solomon recorded with Daniel Lanois playing electric guitar. It's fair to say that Bob didn't write the line, 'Anything you ask me, then I'm willin', But I sure can't be Bob Dylan'. There's a second reference too. Good song though and an excellent bluesy performance from Solomon Burke.

Around this time, Dylan was performing Don Henley's 'The End of Innocence', Neil Young's 'Old Man' and three Warren Zevon songs – 'Boom Boom Mancini', 'Mutineer' and 'Accidentally like a Martyr'. He had a shot at the Rolling Stones' 'Brown Sugar', appearing with both the Stones and Warren Zevon at the Tehama County Fairgrounds, Red Bluff in October 2002.

In 2002, George Harrison's final album, *Brainwashed*, was released. The title song contained the line, 'They brainwashed my great uncle, Brainwashed my cousin Bob'.

When he died, both Dylan and Paul McCartney did 'something' in their concerts and Dylan said, "He was the sun, he was the moon." When an actor had asked George Harrison how he should play Bob Dylan, Harrison said, 'Whatever the director tells you to do, don't do it.'

In November 2002 Dylan sang 'Masters of War' at Madison Square Garden, possibly because the second Iraq war had started. The main attack on President Bush came from an unlikely source, the country band, the Dixie Chicks. It harmed their career as if you criticise George Bush, you could be seen as unpatriotic. Eric Andersen: 'You'd think there'd be more than Steve Earle and a few others criticising Bush, but we were so deluged and beleaguered with information that nobody knew how to analyse it. Your BBC is great because it does step back and let somebody say what it all means. CNN is like somebody throwing ping pong balls at you: you don't know whether one thing is more important than another and there are few explanations. To make it worse, there are strap lines underneath the picture for you to read. It is like the whole nation has Attention Deficit Disorder. Bush had a smirk on his face, and his mantra is 'Don't apologise, don't explain, just do it.' It's not a blank cheque, you can't give someone that much power. There is a patriot law now – they can go into your bank account, they can go to the library and see what books you read, they can go to the stores and see what you've bought. This is non-specific surveillance and it is weirder than McCarthyism.'

I wondered if the hoo-ha over the Dixie Chicks had something to do with their youth: the former Sixties folkies might say the same things but their remarks could never achieve notoriety. After all, I had heard Art Garfunkel in Liverpool go even further than the Dixie Chicks by telling the audience, 'I would like to apologise for being an American', and ending his concert by intoning Marvin Gaye's 'War is not the answer' from *What's Going On?* over and over. 'Yes,' said Joan Baez, 'I've been mouthing off at concerts all my conscious lifetime – I was born in 1941 – I was told the Germans were the bad guys, and now they've been replaced by the Americans.'

Dylan made his point in other ways. In 2003 he wrote an eight-minute song, 'Cross the Green Mountain' for the soundtrack of a US-TV series about the general Stonewall Jackson and the Civil War, *Gods and Generals*. It is Dylan at his best and the song could have been written at the time. Dylan shot a video in long hair and straggly beard and riding a horse.

Dylan was experiencing arthritis in his fingers and he found it easier to play piano than guitar on stage. He often wore a pink jacket (shades of Elvis?) and he cancelled a show at Brixton Academy because of laryngitis, though how could he tell?

On 23 June 2004, he received an honorary doctorate in music from St. Andrew's University in Scotland, fortunately not a repeat of 'Day of the Locusts'. He knelt before the Chancellor who greeted him in Latin as a doctor. The university choir sang 'Blowin' in the Wind' in English.

In 2004 Dylan and Willie Nelson played a tour of baseball parks and he took part in *A Hot Night in Harlem*, which celebrated the 70th anniversary of the Apollo Theatre. His voice still had character when he sang 'The Lonesome Death of Hattie Carroll' and Sam Cooke's civil rights song, 'A Change Is Gonna Come'. Dylan sang the 'movie' verse, thereby showing that he knew the album version and not just the single. It seemed odd for a white singer to be performing a black man's song about civil rights in the country's foremost black theatre but perhaps because of this, it worked perfectly.

In 2004, *Rolling Stone* put his pay packet for the year at $10m which included $1.25m for the use of his music in ads for Victoria's Secret. He made money in a partnership with an Italian wine company, Planet Waves.

Bob Dylan's autobiography had been on the cards for some years but this can be state normal in the rock world. Mick Jagger had been promising his book for years and then he changed his mind and returned the advance. It was said that Mick couldn't remember enough for a book but I don't believe that – any major star could get by with a batch of press cuttings. Dylan did at one stage request memories via the internet for things that he might have forgotten.

Being Dylan, he didn't want to write a straight timeline biography: he didn't want to describe how he had been raised or discuss his mistakes. Eventually, in October 2004, Simon and Schuster published *Chronicles, Volume 1*. It consisted of memoirs – mostly relating to New York in the early 1960s but taking in *New Morning* and *Oh Mercy*. We'd have liked more but the title suggested further volumes (which haven't appeared). Maybe Dylan had no intention of writing anymore and the title was simply to soften criticism. The book sold well, clearing 180,000 hardback copies in the UK.

The book was easy to read, which in itself was surprising considering *Tarantula*. It was an opportunity to see the world through Dylan's eyes. He decided not to read it for a talking book and Sean Penn took his place.

Both CBS and Simon and Schuster were owned by Viacom, hence Bob publicised the book on CBS' *60 Minutes* with an interview with Ed Bradley. Dylan thought that 'It's All Right, Ma' was 'almost magically written' but he couldn't write like that anymore. He said that he had made a pact with the Chief Commander for this talent, so is this alluding to Robert Johnson at the crossroads? Ed Bradley said, 'You said in your book that you couldn't write those songs anymore' and Dylan said, 'Could you?' He meant, of course, 'Could anybody?' By and large, he had on his poker face and gave nothing away. This prompted a spoof interview on *The Simpsons*.

The most surprising feature about the book was Bob's generosity. He is kind to a fault to his fellow travellers and there is none of the spite of 'Like a Rolling Stone' and 'Ballad in Plain D'. As a result, it really stands out when he does complain: he didn't like Jon Pankake, who wasn't a musician, criticising him and he hated Joan Baez's 'To Bobby': what right did she have to tell him what he should be singing? Bob says that he can't explain his earlier songs as he's a different person now and they mystify him too. It's a good excuse certainly but I don't know if I buy it.

Judy Collins: 'Any memoir, even if it is in emotional terms, can never tell the whole truth because no one knows the whole truth. One knows the truth of the moment, that's true, and maybe tomorrow when you are writing about the same situation, the truth will look a little different.'

It's never been really appreciated but since Dylan's Oscar win for 'Things Have Changed', he has been willing to write songs for film and TV soundtracks and has become very good at it. In 2005 he contributed to *North Country* which starred Charlize Theron and Frances McDormand and was set in a mining town in Minnesota about the first successful claim for sexual harassment in the US.

Dylan's 'Tell Ol' Bill' sounds like a folk song from the 1920s and indeed it has its origins in the Carter Family's 'I Never Loved but One'. It is sung chirpily but it is about nearing death and wanting to get something off your chest.

The next year he wrote 'Huck's Tune' for *Lucky You*. Eric Bana played Huck Cheever, a professional poker club player who had personal problems including his relationship with Drew Barrymore. Dylan's song sounds like an old Scottish ballad and mirrors Huck's frustration: 'The game's gotten old, the deck's gone cold'.

Since 2000 Dylan's company, Grey Water Park had been filming interviews with people associated with Bob Dylan for a TV biography. Dylan himself was interviewed for nine hours by Jeff Rosen, seemingly talking with honesty and openness. Grey Water Park brought in six other companies to the production including the WNET Network and the BBC. Martin Scorsese agreed to direct the film and he had access to all Pennebaker's films of Bob Dylan in concert. The material was so rich that Scorsese announced a three hour film in two parts which would end with the motorcycle crash in 1966. The film *No Direction Home* was shown on 26 September 2005 on both BBC and PBS. It has since been issued on DVD with additional footage.

Michael Gray: 'I was as surprised as most people that his memoir was as detailed as it was. He wrote about what he felt like writing about and he missed out almost every major event in his life. He related with marvellous vividness the Greenwich Village of the 1960s. That book is in 3D and then Martin Scorsese has put him in a time and place and made him a part of that as well as showing what made him special.'

The film was accompanied by an excellent 2CD set of 1960s material including home recordings and alternative takes from *Bringing It All Back Home, Highway 61 Revisited* and *Blonde on Blonde*. The CD notes were written by Andrew Loog Oldham, Eddie Gorodetsky and Al Kooper and included several unseen photographs. Following a deal with the coffee chain, in August 2005 Starbucks issued a CD of Bob Dylan, *Live at the Gaslight*.

Dylan was one of the friends on the televised concert, *Willie Nelson and Friends*. Nils Lofgren: 'I did the *Willie Nelson and Friends* TV show. Willie is very mellow but everything is chaotic in TV. They are very precise in their timings and the TV company was working with Jerry Lee Lewis, Keith Richards, Merle Haggard and Bob Dylan – in the same programme! It was hilarious to watch TV producers telling these people where to be and one morning, they wanted Keith Richards there at 8.15 and I didn't think that was ever going to happen. But the show was great. It was a beautiful night recorded live at Wiltern Theatre in Los Angeles. I got to sit back and play mostly rhythm guitar and watch this beautiful cast of characters come out and sit with Willie.'

When Dylan was at Nottingham on 16 November 2005, he did 'Masters of War' which was based on 'Nottamun Town'. He was also performing several songs from *Love and Theft*.

There was a *Talking Bob Dylan Blues* tribute concert at the Barbican with Odetta, Martin Carthy, Liam Clancy, Loudon Wainwright, Billy Bragg and Robyn Hitchcock. Rather surprisingly, this emerged as a DVD with the package for what there was of *Madhouse on Castle Street*.

Around this time Bob was having trouble with a portaloo at Point Dume. It had been put there for use by the security guards who then refused permission for the local authority to inspect it.

By now it was clear that touring and other projects were more important than making records. From 1988 to 2005 he performed 1,856 concerts. The most performed songs were 'All Along the Watchtower' (878), 'Highway 61 Revisited' (745) and 'Tangled Up in Blue' (733), so no song reached 50%. You couldn't predict what you were going to hear at a Bob Dylan concert. Even his biggest crowd-pleaser 'Like a Rolling Stone' was only played 653 times, just over one-third of the time. This assumes that the Dylan fans who put together these statistics could recognise all the songs.

In March 2006 Dylan and Patti Smith were asked to save a dilapidated house at 8 Royal College Street in Camden which had been used by Rimbaud and Verlaine, who had been lovers in the 1870s. It was also associated with Graham Greene. A film had been made about Rimbaud and Verlaine, *Total Eclipse*, in 1995. Rimbaud is mentioned in Patti Smith's 'Piss Factory'. The building has been saved and there is a plaque to mark their relationship.

In 2006 there was a more recent affair, that between Dylan and Edie Sedgwick in *Factory Girl*. The film does not mention Dylan by name as his office threatened to sue but there is an actor called The Musician.

A Dylan ballet from Twyla Tharp *The Times They Are A Changin'* opened in San Diego and was set in a travelling circus. It got to Broadway but was killed by bad reviews.

In 2006 Bob Dylan released *Modern Times*, the title a nod to Charlie Chaplin's 1936 comedy as well as a reference to Dylan still being relevant. Dylan had been compared to Chaplin in his first reviews. On the cover was a picture of a 1947 New York cab that was nothing special. The press was keen to say that this formed a trilogy with *Time out of Mind* and *Love and Theft*. 'It's not a trilogy,' said Bob. '*Time out of Mind* was getting back in and fighting my way out of the corner after illness. For *Love and Theft* I was out of the corner. *Modern Times*, I'm way gone. Maybe this one can be the start of a trilogy.'

The songs are as doom-ridden as *Time Out of Mind*, but some are about having a good time, albeit with consequences. Dylan knew the players he wanted and how he wanted the songs to sound so he produced it himself as Jack Frost, saying 'I didn't want to be over-produced anymore.'

Michael Gray: '*Modern Times* was the last Chaplin film in which he played a homeless tramp and it is about the small person's haplessness in the face of an inhumane and speeded-up technological world. Bob Dylan has placed himself as that figure for some time now. It sounds like *Love and Theft, Part 2*. Dylan doesn't usually do a new album the same as the last, no matter how popular the previous one was. His voice was largely shot but what he did with it was very nuanced and full of attention to detail. It was well recorded and that had gone missing in the 1980s. Back then his voice was better but the productions were on the other side of the ocean.'

In an interview Dylan said that modern recordings are atrocious and that no one in the past 20 years had released a record that sounded any good. 'Even these songs sounded ten times better in the studio,' Dylan told *Rolling Stone*. He was an analogue man, thinking it had more character and less uniformity. Possibly, he had been talking to Neil Young who bangs on endlessly about this.

It is an astonishingly wordy album. It lasts 63 minutes and apart from title phrases, Dylan is rarely repeating lines. Indeed, there are hit songs here if they were recorded by singers with editing pencils.

This time Dylan had taken some lines and images from the Civil War authority Henry Timrod and he commented on it in *Rolling Stone*, perhaps a little irked that he had been rumbled. 'In folk and jazz, quotation is a rich and enriching condition. That certainly is true, but there are different rules for me, and as far as Henry Timrod is concerned, have you even heard of him? Who's been reading him lately? Ask his descendants what they think of the hoopla. It's called songwriting. It has to do with melody and rhythm and then after that, anything goes. You make everything your own. We all do it.' Quite possibly he had been reading Timrod when he was researching his song for *Gods and Generals*.

The album started positively with the rockabilly 'Thunder on the Mountain', although rockabilly songs were never so literate. The song received much press attention as Dylan said he was searching for Alicia Keys. He clarified it by saying, 'I saw Alicia Keys on the Grammys and I said to myself, "There's nothing about that girl that I don't like".' Keys said that she was 'excited and honoured to be on his mind'. The song has nothing to do with her except that Dylan liked her name: in a similar way, Chuck Berry wrote a song called 'Brenda Lee'. The song has several good lines but it isn't clear whom Bob Dylan is addressing and how it hangs together. At one stage, he wants to build an army from those in orphanages. It's like somebody going to sleep with thoughts wandering in and out of his mind.

'Spirit on the Water' finds Bob making his play for a woman who's already got the key to his brain. She has been putting herself around as Bob has heard stories about her 'sugar'. Even if they do stay together, they won't meet in Paradise as Bob has killed someone. The song ends with jazz guitar and Bob hoping that they have 'a whopping good time'.

Although Dylan claims authorship for 'Rollin' and Tumblin'', that is not wholly correct. The first recorded version of 'Rollin' and Tumblin'' was by Hambone Willie Newbern in 1929 and the most influential was by Muddy Waters in 1950. The Rolling Stones, the Yardbirds, Captain Beefheart and many others have played around with this song. Dylan has written new verses about women trouble, but really it's a familiar blues that still sounds good.

Dylan is offering support to someone in 'When the Deal Goes Down', but again we don't know what is going on – something major is happening but what sort of deal and who is he addressing? It is a touching country waltz and the melody is close to Bing Crosby's 'When the Blue of the Night'.

Similarly, the melody of 'Beyond the Horizon' is not far from Bing Crosby's 1935 hit, 'Red Sails in the Sunset' and he refers to Bing's 1945 film, *The Bells of St. Mary*. In both songs, something better is coming: Dylan could be talking about life after death, but there are too many clichés here.

The title 'Nettie Moore' goes back to a 19th-century folk song, 'Gentle Nettie Moore' and the opening line, 'Lost John sittin' on a railroad track' is from a skiffle favourite. It's about a singer in a 'cowboy band' but something dramatic has happened, 'The world has gone black': just who are Albert and Frankie –Einstein and Sinatra?

After the Great Mississippi Flood of 1927, Kansas Joe McCoy and Memphis Minnie recorded 'When the Levee Breaks'. It was reworked by Led Zeppelin in 1971. In the aftermath of Hurricane Katrina, it would have been good if Dylan had written a new song with a telling commentary, but he chose to rewrite 'When the Levee Breaks' about somebody escaping from the flood. Indeed, the line about 'plenty of cheap stuff out there' suggests that he is looting. There is a passing reference to Carl Perkins' 'Put Your Cat Clothes on'.

As for 'Someday Baby', I prefer the quieter, more resigned take as a country blues on *Tell Tale Signs*. One line says, 'I'll wring your neck', so it's not as gentle as it seems.

Bob knew Merle Haggard well and they had toured together. He liked Haggard's praise for blue collar workers in 'Working Man's Blues' (1969) and he wrote his own take on it in 'Workingman's Blues Number 2'. Bruce Springsteen had also written several blue collar songs. This song would have been perfect for Bob in his Farm Aid days. Towards the end, Dylan on piano is playing something akin to 'Like a Rolling Stone'.

The album closes with another apocalyptic song, 'Ain't Talkin''. The singer has been mistreated and is plotting revenge, but where is he going and what has happened? It's mysterious but no more so than the rest of the album.

Modern Times was a strong album, given much publicity. I live in a village and there was even a poster at the bus stop. The album was helped by an Apple iTunes commercial which featured 'Someday Baby'.

Mike Smith of Columbia Records said, 'We see Dylan as a front line artist, not a heritage act, so the same people who work on Kasabian and The View were working on Dylan and they did a great job backed by the iTunes commercial which placed him in a very contemporary context.'

Modern Times entered the US albums chart at Number 1, selling 192,000 copies in the first week. It made No. 3 in the UK. It won a Grammy for the best Folk / Americana album and Dylan won the best solo rock performance for his gravelly 'Someday Baby', which was an odd choice but fair enough. *Modern Times* was to lead to other older artists having similar success. Neil Diamond topped the album charts in both the UK and US with *Home before Dark* in 2008.

At the same time, Columbia issued *Bob Dylan – The Collection* on iTunes, released the same time as *Modern Times*. You could download 763 tracks by Bob Dylan for $200 and receive a PDF book as well.

The film director Todd Haynes had made a controversial film about the Carpenters with a cast as Barbie dolls, *Superstar: the Karen Carpenter Story* (1989), and its distribution was blocked by her estate. Then he had a hit film with the Glam Rock film, *Velvet Goldmine* (1998) starring Ewan McGregor and Eddie Izzard.

Haynes developed a unique film project, *I'm Not There*, which would tell Dylan's story but he would be portrayed by several actors: not just another side of Bob Dylan but seven sides of Bob Dylan. The title *I'm Not There* came from a little-known song from *The Basement Tapes* that Bob had recorded but not released at the time. It contained the line,

'Here I'm visible, even to myself.' The lyric ties in with Rimbaud's 'I is another' and this is how the film was pitched to Dylan.

Like his music, the film is full of allusions and in-jokes. It is about an artist's need to evolve in order to survive. Haynes said that Dylan's responses in press conferences were performance art, up there with Warhol. According to the press release of *I'm Not There*, the film was 'inspired by false stories'.

The film is often humorous, providing you get the jokes. It assumes prior knowledge and plays fast and loose with facts, starting with Dylan dying in a car crash in 1966. At times it is as funny as the Johnny Cash film, *Walk Tall*. There are pastiches of *A Hard Day's Night* and *Dont Look Back*. There are mock ads and news conferences and Dylan guns down the audience at Newport. It's a pity that the various actors playing Dylan don't meet each other. The film is confusing, kaleidoscopic and experimental but not as much as *Renaldo and Clara*, and it works much better than Jean-Luc Godard's film with the Rolling Stones, *Sympathy for the Devil*.

The narrator is Kris Kristofferson and the youngest Bob Dylan is 11-year-old Marcus Carl Franklin, who dreams of being a hobo during the Depression. He goes to see Woody Guthrie in hospital with 'Blind Willie McTell' on the soundtrack. Richie Havens performs an intense 'Tombstone Blues' with the young boy.

The protest period has Ben Whishaw playing Dylan as Arthur Rimbaud. The controversy at the Tom Paine award is amusingly recreated and shows how bad a public speaker Dylan was – why was he so bad when his thoughts were so coherent? His girlfriend, Joan / Alice, says, 'He gave voice to the ideas I wanted to express but didn't know how', which is surely spot on.

Bob Dylan in 1966 did have a feminine look and so Cate Blanchett as Jude (Judas?) Quinn works superbly and gives the most Dylanesque performance. There is a very good recreation of 'Ballad of a Thin Man'. Todd Haynes said, 'It's an incredibly sadomasochistic, homoerotic song with all of these images of high heels and going down on his knees, the Freudian slippages for fellatio and all that stuff. It is curious if you are starting with this idea of Dylan as a white male heterosexual master of the popular song. This song arguably shows another side of Dylan's imagination.' You could have made a whole film around this character. Haynes' film is dedicated to his partner and editor Jim Lyons who died of AIDS.

Richard Gere as Billy is a western loner. This was a pastoral look at Dylan's love of American folklore. Harvey Weinstein was the American distributor and he wanted the scenes out, but Haynes won the day. 'I don't understand it,' said Weinstein.

For the *Blood on the Tracks* period, Dylan is played by Heath Ledger as the selfish, misogynist Robbie divorcing a French painter Charlotte Gainsbourg. On the soundtrack, Charlotte offers a breathy 'Just like a Woman'. Then there is the born-again, hellfire preaching of Christian Bale as Jack Rollins. It is a brilliant impersonation and his album in the film is called *Time Will Come*.

The record producer and Madonna's brother-in-law, Joe Henry produced the music. The 2CD album package is really good: sometimes the songs are so radically changed that you forget it is a Dylan album; 'Dark Eyes' by Iron and Wine and Calexico took me by surprise. The Hold Steady, who were signed to Jakob Dylan's Vagrant label, offer 'Can You Please Crawl out Your Window'.

In 2008 *The Bootleg Series Volume 8* was called *Tell Tale Signs* and featured outtakes and alternative takes from 1989 to 2006. The main thrust was for a single CD for £10, but then there was also a double-CD for £20. There was a good photo of Dylan on the back of the single CD, his best look in years. Furthermore, there was a 3CD version with a vinyl single and a booklet of album sleeves for £100, one sure way to annoy diehard fans. 'Dreamin' of You', a *Time Out of Mind* outtake, was a single.

Dylan won a Pulitzer Prize in 2008 'for his profound impact on popular music and American culture, marked by lyrical compositions of extraordinary poetic power.' He did not attend the ceremony and Jesse Dylan received the award in his place. Peter Ames Carlin comments, 'Dylan has just won a Pulitzer and you think of him as an incredibly important artistic figure but he wanted to be Little Richard. He wanted to play rock'n'roll in a gold lamé suit and he wanted to get laid, which is a major force for everything that goes on in the world.'

Bob and Sara's children were doing well: Jakob a musician, Jesse a video director, Samuel a photographer, Anna an artist, Maria a lawyer. Dylan welcomed his grandchildren.

Jakob Dylan released a solo album on Columbia, *Seeing Things*. He said, 'Do people think I have the nerve trying to prove I can write something as good as *Blonde on Blonde*?' I'm sure Bob must have enjoyed his wordplay on 'This End of the Telescope' and cracked a wry smile at the line, 'There's no need to bring God into this.' Jakob saw himself more as a team player with the Wallflowers and the solo project was a one-off. He ran Vagrant records with Eels and the Hold Steady among his artists and had four boys.

What must have been unnerving for Dylan were the things that were done in his name. In Hobart, a Dylan fan beat his mother to death. He sprinkled instant coffee over her body while playing Dylan's 'One More Cup of Coffee'. (There seems to something about killers in Australia and Bob Dylan – note the earlier story.)

The French film director Oliver Dahan (*La Vie en Rose*) asked Dylan to write songs for his next film, *My Own Love Song*, one that would capture Renée Zellweger's thoughts, indeed, her own love song. She is a musician in a wheelchair who goes on a road trip from Kansas to New Orleans with her best friend, Forest Whitaker.

Dylan came up with 'Life Is Hard', a ballad with Bob starting in a high register, or at least, trying to. It's a good song about her life, the melody being reminiscent of 'Autumn Leaves'. Several more Dylan songs were included in the film, but there was no soundtrack album.

After writing these songs, Dylan was motivated to complete his next album, *Together through Life*, with 'Life Is Hard' being a key track, although Bob didn't perform that one in concert. Bob wrote all the melodies but most of the lyrics were written by Robert Hunter with Dylan acting as editor.

When the album was released, the press realised they had been hasty in calling his last three albums a trilogy. Still, I didn't read anyone who now called it a tetralogy.

Dylan was working with familiar musicians including David Hildago on accordion and guitar and Mike Campbell from the Heartbreakers on guitar and mandolin. Donny Herron on trumpet added a New Orleans flavour. 'It's percussive and orchestrative at the same time,' said Dylan, creating a new word.

Were the songs about Dylan himself? 'It's me who is singing the songs, plain and simple. We shouldn't confuse singers and performers with actors.' That implies that the songs do come from his own life, but we know that Robert Hunter started some of these songs and that he was working on a film score, and so maybe they are not personal at all. Trust the song: not the artist.

The cover photograph, taken by Bruce Davidson in 1959, was of a Brooklyn Gang, the Jokers. A montage of his photographs was used in the video for the opening track, 'Beyond Here Lies Nothin''. There are photographs of them getting tattoos, taking their shirts off and going to Coney Island. There is a dead ringer for Amy Winehouse: she has the experience that the boys don't have.

'Beyond Here Lies Nothin'' is about a passionate relationship. There was an explicit video of a man keeping his girlfriend prisoner and she runs him over and goes back to him, showing that there is nothing stronger than love. It's a fine song, a little like J.J. Cale or Tom Waits.

The witty 'My Wife's Home Town' sounds like a George Jones title, but in Dylan's case, 'Hell is my wife's home town'. She is a manipulative person who gets him to do bad things but he chuckles at the end and he did say in an interview, 'The song is meant as a compliment anyhow.' The melody isn't far from Etta James' 'I just Wanna Make Love to You'.

You could describe 'I Feel a Change Comin' On' as a nice, romantic song if you think 'You're as whorish as ever' is a compliment. There's a neat touch where Dylan is listening to Billy Joe Shaver and reading James Joyce.

'Shake, Shake Mama' sounds like an old rockabilly record from *Theme Time Radio Hour*. Who are Richard Lee and Judge Simpson? Dylan provides no clues: it could be part of a larger work or Dylan could simply be throwing them in to confuse the experts. Of course, some listeners will not know who Billy Joe Shaver is.

Probably an outtake from his film work, 'If You ever Go to Houston' is about somebody losing his way after the war of Texas Independence in 1835. Dylan is walking the streets and the barrooms looking for his girl. The theme is continued in the ballad, 'Forgetful Heart', which starts with the same chords as 'Yesterday'. It's a decent ballad that would have suited *Oh Mercy*.

When you consider the vast number of girls' names, it's odd that Dylan should have chosen 'Jolene': maybe he was hoping that some of Dolly's royalties would get to him by accident. It's a good song but would have been better served with a different name.

'This Dream of You' is like a Drifters' 45 being played at 33, but it works okay. When Dylan was asked by Bill Flanagan if the Drifters were an influence, he said, 'Doc Pomus was a soulful cat. If you said that there was a little bit of him in 'This Dream of You', I would take it as a compliment.' Doc Pomus wrote songs for the Drifters.

Some people say 'No worries' or 'It's all good' when something bad has happened, and Dylan liked the irony for his final song, 'It's All Good'. Everything is getting progressively worse (lying politicians, poor restaurant hygiene, marriages breaking down) and yet the singer keeps repeating 'It's all good'. There's little to the tune, a Cajun riff repeated again and again but the song works.

Together through Life was Bob Dylan's fifth US No.1 album, selling 125,000 copies in the first week, but the competition was hotter in earlier decades. The album took over from Rick Ross' *Deeper than Rap* and the Number 2 album was *Hannah Montana: The Movie*. The album topped the UK charts, not bad for someone well past his pension age.

Roger McGuinn: 'Dylan knows what he sounds like and so he is gearing his songs to that. He does a lot of bluesy things that are like the old blues singers: they have more emotion than melody. He is not writing a lot of melodic lines now but he is still a wonderful, brilliant songwriter. I have always loved his work.'

Dylan's UK tour coincided with the release of *Together through Life*. On 1 May 2009, Dylan was in Liverpool and during the day he visited John Lennon's childhood home, Mendips, now a National Trust property. Its custodian Colin Hall says, 'I had no idea what was going to happen that day and I hadn't got a ticket for the concert. I knew he was in town but I was working and oblivious to it. The last tour of the day arrives at 3.30pm and the driver Neil brings the visitors on a National Trust bus. He remarks occasionally that I don't keep to schedule but the visitors can ask loads of questions. I got a phone call and I thought it would be Neil telling me that I was running late and I should get the people out to do the swap over. He said, "Be quick. Bob Dylan is not going to wait much longer". I thought it was a joke as he has a good sense of humour but I ushered everybody out and there standing before me at the gate was Bob Dylan. He had come on the National Trust tour and had bought a ticket! My mind went blank and I brought him into the house. I said my regular piece and that helped to calm my nerves. They are turning up for John and I want them to enjoy themselves. Bob was a guest who asked questions and I'm sure he enjoyed himself because at the end, he very graciously invited me to his concert that night. I had my own room in the house and he let me get a CD and he signed it.'

So Colin went to see Bob at the Liverpool Echo Arena. 'He opened with 'Watching the River Flow' and I think that was acknowledging that he was in Liverpool. He sang 'Something' so that was noting the legacy of the Beatles and his connection with them. He only spoke to introduce his band, which is probably unique to Dylan these days as everybody else interacts with the audience. He did an encore or two though.'

The security was not good as someone was able to get on stage. Colin Hall: 'I had very good tickets and I saw this figure on the stage. The bass guitarist had put himself between Bob and this feller and I think he would have got the bass guitar around his head if he had tried anything. It was alarming and shouldn't be happening at a venue like that. It must have been a scary moment for Bob as the world is not a benign place. He was vulnerable. Even if someone just wanted to hug him, it was not the right thing to do.'

Howard Sounes: 'His primary motivation in touring is that he loves it. There is something genuine there that is wonderful. It is a big deal when he comes to London or Liverpool, but when he is playing in small town America, it is not a big deal and there are not big audiences and not a lot of money in it. I saw him play to 2,000 people in a sports hall. So why is he doing this? He is extremely wealthy, he has done everything he wants to do, he has achieved all that, so why is he doing it? He simply loves it. It is his job and he takes a workaday attitude to it. This is his craft, like a carpenter. He is not a man who wants to drive around in Ferraris like Rod Stewart and go to parties. He lives on the stage and I think he would do it for nothing. The fact that he can still make 'Blowin' in the Wind' sound interesting is remarkable. If you see the Rolling Stones they are sucking up the dollars and there is a great deal of cynicism involved. Their aim is to make as much money as possible, but Bob Dylan is having fun. You can't ask for anything more than that.'

Still in August 2009, Bob himself was picked up by police as a pensioner who was loitering outside an empty house in New Jersey. He had wanted to see Bruce Springsteen's childhood home. Bob was on his summer tour with Willie Nelson and John Mellencamp. Merle Haggard, who was recovering from cancer, was hanging out with Willie and as a result, he and Bob wrote a song called 'The Ballad of Martha Stewart' about the TV star who had been jailed: the song has not appeared anywhere.

George Wein returned to Newport and did the 50th anniversary Folk Festival with

Pete Seeger, Joan Baez, Judy Collins and Ramblin' Jack Elliott but not Dylan. Seeger revived the old Newport workshops, calling them *For Pete's Sake*.

Mary Travers from Peter, Paul and Mary died in September 2009 and over 2,000 mourners attended her funeral. Pete Seeger, Theodore Bikel and Judy Collins spoke fondly of her, and Harry Belafonte and President Clinton taped messages but there was nothing from Dylan.

You can always expect the unexpected with Dylan but a seasonal album was right off the scale. In 2009, Bob released *Christmas in the Heart* and if Christmas is meant to make you smile, then Bob Dylan succeeded. With his producer Jack Frost nipping at his nose (actually, Dylan himself), Dylan recorded standard Christmas fare – six carols, five songs anticipating Christmas, two songs about Santa, one about winter and one about having the Christmas blues. The musicians include David Hidalgo of Los Lobos on guitar and mandolin and Phil Upchurch on guitar. The Mexican backing for the frantic 'Must Be Santa' features Hidalgo on accordion and there is a Hawaiian feel for 'Christmas Island'. Sammy Cahn had written 'The Christmas Blues' for Sinatra and it was recast as a blues. The overall result is like a Christmas *Theme Time Radio Hour*.

When this album was released, I happened to be in a studio at BBC Radio Merseyside with a local minister. I said, 'I won't tell you who this is, but would you give this singer a place in your choir?' I played 'Hark the Herald Angels Sing' and he said, 'We're fairly tolerant about the singers in our choir but that would be stretching it a bit.'

Said the *Daily Telegraph*, 'Is his voice only tolerable because of the legend behind it?' One reviewer compared Dylan's voice to Louis Armstrong's, but surely Armstrong's was always musical. Dylan was struggling but was he worse than Shane MacGowan's 'Fairytale of New York'? Well, yes he was with 'I'll Be Home for Christmas', the worst vocal of his career.

Bob did no interviews for the album and his photograph wasn't in the CD booklet. The front cover was a conventional choc-box cover plus a photograph of a 1950s pin-up, Bettie Page on the back of the insert. She had died the previous Christmas at the age of 85. Did Bob pick her because she had been born again and worked for Billy Graham? Indeed, why was Bob singing carols: was it a return to Christianity or just a goodwill offering? I suspect that he simply liked the songs and wanted to do them. He was being altruistic as the royalties were to benefit the homeless in different territories.

A couple of surprises: Dylan sings the first verse of 'O Come All Ye Faithful' in Latin and in 'Must Be Santa' he renames the reindeer with those of US Presidents – Vixen is close enough to Nixon so off we go. Dylan in a Santa hat and Tom Petty wig made a video at a wild Christmas party where somebody is causing as much trouble as possible. Oh, some titles that didn't make the album: 'A Hard Reindeer's A-gonna Fall', 'Like a Rolling Snowman'. 'Sleigh Lady Sleigh' and 'Sad Eyed Lady of the Snowlands'. (There's getting to be an end of term feel to this book.)

In 2010 Bob Dylan played 'The Times They Are A-Changin'' for President Obama and his First Lady, Michelle, and Joan Baez also performed. He shook the President's hand, gave a little grin and left. That's Bob Dylan for you: you want him to be a little sceptical about the whole exercise. His son Jesse directed a video for Obama's campaign. There is a photograph of Barack and Michelle Obama walking down Pennsylvania Avenue which is reminiscent of the *Freewheelin'* cover.

Why did Dylan call his next album, *Tempest*? When it was pointed out that Shakespeare's final play was *The Tempest*, many wondered if this was a sign that Dylan was about to finish.

'No', he said, pointing out that Shakespeare's play was *The Tempest* and his album was just plain *Tempest*. It could have been called *The Winter of Our Discontent* as this album contains some of the most miserable songs of all time. The corpses mount up: excessively if you include the loss of life on the Titanic. In terms of style and presentation, it falls in with his last few albums and Nick Cave's 1996 album, *Murder Ballads*. If Sam Peckinpah had made an album, it would be this one. *Tempest* was a No. 3 album in both the UK and US but it was a chart-topper in several other countries.

Tempest was recorded at Jackson Browne's studio in Los Angeles and made with Dylan's road band and extra musicians. Dylan said, 'I was planning to make something more religious. I just did not have enough songs.' So what do we have instead? As per usual, there are lengthy songs with long lyrics that appear full of unconnected images even if they are not. If Dylan comes across a good rhyme, he may put it in just because he likes it.

Duquesne is a city in Pennsylvania and hearing the train on 'Duquesne Whistle' brings to mind Leadbelly in his cell waiting for the 'Midnight Special'. Dylan appears to be a gambler and a pimp who has a lot of sexual relationships. He has had a misspent life and when the gospel train comes, can he get on board? This song was written with Robert Hunter but the rest were Dylan's.

There is an official video which tells of a stalker trying to win a girl with a single red rose. When he is chased by the police, he knocks a ladder over, injuring the man on it. The victim's friends beat him up and Dylan and his chums are walking down the road and at one stage walk over his body. I don't think the video is connected to the song.

Paul Morley: 'For me the late work of any artist or painter or writer has to be folded into the context of everything they have done. It didn't come out of nowhere: it came out of the entire history of who Bob Dylan is. There was a video for one of the tracks where he had a hip hop entourage walking through the dark streets on his way to somewhere mysterious. There he is in his seventies with a hip hop entourage.'

At first hearing, 'Soon after Midnight' sounds a perfect doo-wop song and it could be cast into that setting very effectively. The singer is talking about his girlfriends but something has happened to them all. Is the singer a serial killer and now talking to his next victim? One victim is Charlotte the Harlot, herself the subject of a bawdy folk song.

The seven-minute 'Narrow Way' takes its tune and the final line of each verse from the Mississippi Sheiks' 'You'll Work Down to Me Someday' (1934). It is a neat idea: if I can't work up to you, then one day you'll work down to me. Dylan explores the idea in 11 verses with some intriguing lines: 'I saw you buried and I saw you dug up' and a reference to the British burning the White House down in 1812.

More of a narration than a song, Dylan is discussing a relationship in 'Long and Wasted Years', which started well but he's bitter and resentful. Maybe he has left his family for her and he wonders where they are, twenty years later. There is a reference to the Isley Brothers and the Beatles with the line, 'Shake it up, baby, twist and shout'.

'Pay in Blood' is a song of vengeance: Dylan has been cruelly wronged and is seeking retribution with the title line being, 'I pay in blood but not my own'. The ways that he is going to get his revenge are spelt out.

In the folk song 'Barbara Allen', Sweet William was on his deathbed and the story is continued in 'Scarlet Town'. Dylan's lyric draws on some verses by the nineteenth century Quaker poet and abolitionist John Greenleaf Whittier.

The most intriguing title on the album has to be 'Early Roman Kings'. The tune is similar to Muddy Waters' 'Mannish Boy'. There was a gang in the Bronx called the Roman Kings and the song is probably about them rather than ancient history. It would sound good in a Scorsese film. Although Dylan takes a title from Joni Mitchell, 'Tin Angel' is more like a variant on 'Black Jack Davy' or 'Matty Groves'. It is the same riff over and over for ten minutes but it does encompass adultery, murder and suicide.

The Carter Family sang 'The Titanic' which Dylan had been fooling with. He said, 'I liked that melody but where could I go with it?' Staying in waltz-time, he drew on fact and fiction for his tale of the sinking ship. The ship was hit by an iceberg, but Dylan has it running into a tempest. There's no evidence that the passengers turned on each other and surely Leonardo DiCaprio was only in the film! Post-modernism meets folk music. The 45-verse song lasts 14 minutes and the song fades out as the ship goes down. 'Yeah, Leo,' said Dylan 'I don't think the song would have been the same without him, or the movie. The songwriter doesn't care about what's truthful. What he cares about is what should've happened, what could've happened. It's like Shakespeare.' I don't think that's right: a songwriter for example would be heavily criticised if he wrote a song about the Hillsborough disaster of 1989 and changed the facts. If you visit Titanic Belfast, there is a final section on cultural references to the disaster. Dylan's record is not mentioned, nor Harry Chapin's 'Dance Band on the Titanic'.

In 1962 Bob Dylan had sung 'Roll on John', recorded by the Greenbriar Boys in 1946. Now he thought that he could pay tribute to John Lennon with a new song called 'Roll on John'. As usual he plays hard and loose with the facts: John Lennon wasn't shot in the back. The fact that he played for hours in the Cavern doesn't mean that he had been treated like a slave.

In 2012 Dylan was performing 'All Along the Watchtower' as his final song in a very slow arrangement. It sounded like *film noir*. 'Best performance of it I've heard,' declared Greil Marcus.

Ray Connolly: 'Bob Dylan sure as hell can't sing anymore. He was never very good but he is terrible now. I thought, "No one is this bad", and he doesn't address the audience either. He had his back to the audience, sideways on playing piano.'

In an attempt to combat Bob Dylan tracks going into public domain in certain countries including the UK, Sony released *Bob Dylan – The Copyright Extension Collection* in December 2012 but only 100 copies were available in each of the problem territories. They did something similar a year later. The overall legislation was if the tracks had laid dormant for 50 years, then somebody else could legitimately release them so this release was to combat 'use it or you lose it'. In the first instance, it was to stop the release of a concert on 2 July 1962 at the Finjan Club, Montreal with outtakes from outtakes from *The Freewheelin' Bob Dylan*: in all, a cheaply produced collection of 86 tracks.

In 2014 *Lyrics Since 1962* edited by Christopher Ricks was published and ran to 960 pages. Even on Kindle, it cost £96, although several of the lyrics were priceless.

In 2019 Alexis Petridis of *The Guardian* asked famous fans of Elton John what they would ask him. Amazingly, Bob Dylan responded and asked of 'Tiny Dancer', 'Did you work your way up to the cathartic chorus gradually, spontaneously, or did you have it thought out from the start?' Bear in mind, Dylan would never respond to a question like that and certainly not like this. Elton said, 'Writing a song like that is a bit like having a wank, really. You want the climax to be good, but you don't want it to be over too quickly – you want to work your way up to it.'

In March 2020 the world was in lockdown because of the Coronavirus. The public had been advised, indeed ordered, to stay at home and were preparing for weeks of box sets and Netflix. The musicians were no longer touring and indeed, Bob had cancelled his dates in Japan. As a result, they sent out messages to their fans – John Fogerty performed in his back garden, and Willie Nelson and his sons sang 'Turn Off The News (Build a Garden)' from Willie's ranch. Elton John announced a living room concert with some of his famous friends. There will be more of this as the weeks go by and I predict, here on 30 March 2020, that this is going to be one of the most productive years ever for singer/songwriters and I hope that is going to include Bob Dylan.

On March 27, Bob Dylan tweeted 'Greetings to my fans and followers with gratitude for all your support and loyalty across the years. This is an unreleased song we recorded a while back that you might find interesting. Stay safe, stay observant and may God be with you.'

That in itself is fascinating. It is unusual for Dylan to acknowledge his fan base and what does "Stay observant" mean? What does even "May God be with you" mean? In his song, he criticised nations who behaved abominably with God on their side. I love the understatement that we might find his new song 'interesting'. He must know that the meaning and the allusions and the references in 'Murder Most Foul' are going to be discussed for years.

At nearly 17 minutes, it is Dylan's longest ever composition and judging by his voice, I would think it was recorded at the same time as the *Tempest* album in 2012 or possibly for its follow-up. It is his first new composition to be issued since then and indeed, since he was awarded the Nobel prize.

The title, 'Murder Most Foul' is said by the ghost of Hamlet's father but it is also the title of a Miss Marple film starring Margaret Rutherford in 1964. The song itself is based around the assassination of President Kennedy. Dylan thinks it is a conspiracy and he turns Lee Harvey Oswald's statement, 'I'm just a patsy' into 'I'm just a patsy like Patsy Cline.' In the song, Kennedy knows something is going to happen to him as he is threatened by his killers.

Dylan runs through the 1960s referring to the Beatles, the Stones and even Gerry and the Pacemakers. Then we get into the Eagles and Fleetwood Mac. Some of the references are like cryptic crossword clues and to work out one section you would need to know that Warren Zevon was backed up by Carl Wilson when he sang a song about Gower Street in Los Angeles, 'Desperados Under the Eaves'.

It's world gone wrong, full of foreboding and dread, but what does 'It's 36 hours since Judgment Day' signify? There is a line about Kennedy's missing brain and possibly Dylan is alluding to his own soul being missing for 50 years. If so, it is a chilling thought. But does it all add up to anything – as Dylan sings, 'It is what it is and it's murder most foul.'

The song has been recorded with piano, violin and light drums. The melody is nothing special but it's really there to contain the lyric. It is a great lyric and it couldn't have been written by anybody else but Bob Dylan.

Nearly 80 years on and Bob Dylan can still surprise us. Let's hope he can do it again.

CHAPTER 16

Oh Mama, Can This Really be the End?

*'Bobby's all right, Bobby's all right,
He's a natural born poet, He's just out of sight.'*
'Telegram Sam', Marc Bolan for T. Rex, 1972

I. Nobel-minded

Throughout the twentieth century, there were endless discussions as to whether popular music could be poetry, and, from 1965 onwards, could rock music be poetry, and even more specifically, could Bob Dylan be a poet?

I've waxed hot and cold about this over the years but now I don't give a damn as to whether popular music is poetry or not and it doesn't affect whether I like or dislike what I'm hearing. The discussion implies that we can separate the words from the music, but why should anyone want to do that? It is the combination which rivets our attention. The spoken word recitations by Sebastian Cabot on *Bob Dylan, Poet* (1967) show the folly of doing this, although I am sure Cabot meant well by it.

Similarly Captain Kirk, William Shatner, released *The Transformed Man* LP in 1968 and he took it seriously, the only one who did, by saying, 'Poets are now writing pop songs whereas poets of yesteryear wrote literature.' To be fair to him, you can see the sense of that remark.

The combination of words with music is skewed in Dylan's case because of his emphasis on certain syllables and phrases. The lines may not look right when they are free-standing, but Dylan can make words sound like rhymes when they are miles apart, such as 'near' and 'mirror' in 'Visions of Johanna'. It may be that he doesn't think about it but it gives him more flexibility. Sometimes too his bad rhymes are just fun such as 'sandwich' and 'language' in 'Sign Language'. Similarly, 'January' is rhymed with 'Buenos Aires' in 'The Groom's Still Waiting at the Altar', and 'skull' and 'capital' in 'Idiot Wind', a bizarre rhyme which Allen Ginsberg has praised. It's unfair to cite these as examples of bad writing when it is more likely to be Bob Dylan having fun. You can argue, too, that this is a good thing as the precision of rhyming can force a lyricist or a poet into irrational lines.

Songwriter Roger Greenaway: 'His lyrics may not always scan on paper but he wrote them to be sung and for his own voice at that. The lyrics scan when he sings them and that's fine. He's a genius and really you can only move on if somebody is being innovative. Dylan found a new way of writing songs and making music.'

It is certainly true that the public at large cares little about getting rhymes right. When

Bob Dylan was talking about songwriting with Paul Zollo in 1991, he said, 'People have taken against rhyming now, it doesn't have to be exact anymore.'

No one, I think, would deny that Bob Dylan is a great lyricist but does that make him a poet? And if it does, can you be a great lyricist and a bad poet? Also, what does poetry mean? Do we take an academic view of poetry or a public perception? There is a pertinent line in Willy Russell's play, *Educating Rita*, where Rita tells the professor about Roger McGough. She says, 'You probably would think it wasn't any good. It's the sort of poetry you can understand.'

The public at large has different parameters from the academics. There is now a National Poetry Day every October. When the nation has been asked to vote on the UK's best poems, the song lyrics 'Imagine', 'Angels' and 'Bohemian Rhapsody' have come high in the listings.

There is clever wordplay and astute characterisations in the deft show tunes of Cole Porter, Noël Coward and Stephen Sondheim. Their rhymes are nearly always exact. Ogden Nash is seen as one of the wittiest poets of the twentieth century, although his funny poems made serious points. I could easily mix lines from Porter, Coward, Sondheim and Nash in a quiz and I think you would have difficulty spotting the ones that were Ogden Nash and therefore, the poetry.

This distinction holds less power in Europe. Bertolt Brecht is regarded as a great poet, playwright and author and therefore his lyrics for *The Threepenny Opera* which includes 'Mack the Knife' are seen as poetry. Jacques Prevert was a major French poet: is 'Les Feuilles Mortes' any less of a poem because Joseph Karma set it to music and Edith Piaf performed it? Indeed, Edith Piaf was always asking poets to write for her.

The leading *chanson* singers are often regarded as poets – Jacques Brel, Georges Brassens and Leo Ferré. Even when a young man, Charles Aznavour wrote very perceptive songs about growing old while Serge Gainsbourg played with French idioms so much that they are untranslatable. The French President Emmanuel Macron compared the late Charles Aznavour to Apollinaire and said, in a glorious tribute, 'In France, poets never die'.

David Horn from the Institute of Popular Music at Liverpool University: "You can use totally inappropriate tools to analyse things. Dylan being compared to Wordsworth and Blake is a very good example. One problem of looking at it from an academic perspective is that you could be using tools that have been used on Shakespeare and Blake and they may not be wholly appropriate. That is one of the challenges of looking at popular music within a university. It is to find the appropriate ways and not just the ones that have always existed and reapply them."

The link between Bob Dylan and poetry was there from the start. Why did he name himself after Dylan Thomas? His comments over his name have been contradictory but I am convinced that he knew his work and lifestyle. No one, not even Dylan, would name himself after somebody he disliked, so the change of name can be seen as a tribute.

Robert Shelton in 1963 called Dylan 'the young singing poet laureate of young America' and *Little Sandy Review* hailed him as 'a new Yevtushenko'. In 'I Shall Be Free No.10', Dylan says, 'Yippie, I'm a poet and I know it, Hope I don't blow it.'

On the sleeve of *Bringing It All Back Home*, Bob Dylan comments, 'Some people say I'm a poet.' He passes no opinion on this matter but it shows the idea was in circulation. Then Dylan told *Chicago Tribune*, 'I don't like the word. I'm a trapeze artist.' Yet he allowed Johnny Cash to call him a poet on the sleeve of his own album, *Nashville Skyline*.

Dylan did say to Robert Shelton, 'That's such a huge goddamn word for someone to call themselves. A poet. I think a poet is anyone who wouldn't call himself a poet.' That's a typically cryptic reply, implying that somebody stumbles into being a poet without realising it. Shelton was convinced he was a poet and made a strong case for his press receptions being literary performances.

Dylan commented in 1968, 'A great singer like Billie Holiday makes a great poet.' He called Smokey Robinson of the Miracles 'America's greatest living poet'. Certainly Robinson had some excellent wordplay on his Motown songs but was Dylan joking? Smokey told Jonathan Ross that he knew Bob Dylan and they had laughed over this.

Dylan read poetry and he loved Arthur Rimbaud and the Beat Generation writers. He called Allen Ginsberg's *Kaddish* 'the best thing yet'.

A big difference between Dylan and the poets is that most poets do not have a gigantic following. Even Allen Ginsberg as a performance poet couldn't command such attention. A poet writes poems for a select audience: Dylan knows that his best work appeals to millions. Sometimes he takes that into account and sometime he doesn't. Certainly very few poets have spoken for a generation.

In 1972 the literary critic Frank Kermode said of Bertolt Brecht and Bob Dylan: 'There's quite a lot of good poetry which started life in a similar way – Greek tragedy, medieval ballad.'

True. William Blake sometimes sang his words for the *Songs of Innocence and Experience*. Robbie Burns had a melody in mind for 'My Love is Like a Red, Red Rose' and who knows, maybe John Keats sang 'Ode to a Nightingale'?

Poets themselves often quote the literacy of Lennon and McCartney, especially 'Eleanor Rigby', and Bob Dylan. A former Poet Laureate Andrew Motion called Dylan one of the great artists of the century and cited 'Visions of Johanna' as the best song he had ever written.

The detractors include Dannie Abse who said, 'His writing is inferior poetry, and inferior poetry is not really poetry at all' and Norman Mailer who snorted, 'If Dylan's a poet, then I'm a basketball player.' The playwright David Hare in the early 1990s said that John Keats was better than Bob Dylan, which generated some debate.

Julie Felix: "I think Bob Dylan is very wise for not explaining his songs. If you do that, you cut off somebody else's interpretation and I know as a writer that you are not always aware of the complete meaning. I can look back on my own songs and learn something from them. They are like letters to myself and I am sure that is how it is with most poets. He would not want to deny someone's own adventure or exploration into his songs. He would be doing that if he had provided explanations.'

In 2008 Bob Dylan was awarded the Pulitzer Prize 'for his profound impact on popular music and American culture, marked by lyrical compositions of extraordinary poetic power.' That's a fascinating citation, emphatically stating that he is a poet.

The *New York Times* said in 2013, 'His lyricism is exquisite; his concerns and subjects are demonstrably timeless; and few poets of any era have seen their work bear more influence…it's time to take the idea seriously.'

Ironically, everybody calls John Cooper Clarke a poet but isn't he really a lyricist in search of a tune? He's good certainly but Dylan's work has more substance, more longevity and more, shall we say, poetry.

If you've read this far in the book, you will know Dylan borrows phrases and lines from elsewhere and is a literary shoplifter. Does this weaken the claim for him to be considered a good poet and take away from his originality? I don't think so and anyway, William Blake wrote, 'The good artist does copy a great deal.'

When it comes to poetry and rock, the most striking example, outside of Dylan, has to be Leonard Cohen who wrote much-admired volumes of poetry before he ever thought of writing songs. Cohen was Canadian, Dylan American, but they had much in common: both Jewish and aware of their history, with similar musical interests and vocal limitations that they turned into assets. Cohen was less gifted as a singer initially than Dylan but his voice became richer and more carnal with age.

Radio 2 DJ, Mark Radcliffe: 'Leonard Cohen is someone I came to moderately late and I got fixated on him. I knew his records but I had never seen him until Glastonbury. It was my 50th birthday and I was on the side of the stage and transfixed by the way he could slow down this massive event. He brought it all down to Leonard Cohen-time. It was relaxed and slow and really beautiful and everyone sang 'Hallelujah'. I do like seeing a dapper old man and you should dress more smartly as you get older. The scruffy, grunge looks only works if you're young and thin. Even Dylan is more dapper – he wears these intricately embroidered suits, very country and western. Leonard Cohen used very cheap synthetic keyboard sounds and he made a joke of that. When he played that ham-fisted little solo on 'Tower of Song', he said, 'If I leave this alone, it will play itself.' I saw about four or five dates on that tour, but I prefer Jeff Buckley's 'Hallelujah' as that takes you to another world. That really soars and it is an extraordinary song, like one of those eternal conundrums.'

And so to the Nobel Prize.

Every year the Swedish Academy in Stockholm awards Nobel Prizes, according to the provisions of Alfred Nobel's will, and he died in 1896. It established a fund in which interest 'shall be annually distributed in the form of prizes to those, who during the preceding year, shall have conferred the greatest benefit on mankind.' There are five fields of human activity: peace, literature, physics, medicine and chemistry. Having invented dynamite, it is unlikely that Nobel himself would have qualified for the Nobel Peace Prize, although he could have won one for Chemistry.

The short definition determines that the awards should go to the living. It is possible for somebody to be on the short list for several years and then to die before selection. There is also the contentious phrase 'during the preceding year'. Bob Dylan won the Nobel Prize in Literature in 2016 when he had done little of exceptional merit during the preceding year: there had been no album of new songs, just an album of standards *Fallen Angels* and regular touring appearances, which left all but his die-hard fans baffled. This implies that the definition is more a guideline than an instruction but it is not possible to say that for certain as the deliberations of the Academy are sealed until 50 years after the event and individual members are not permitted to discuss their decisions. As it is highly unlikely that I will live to be 120, I will never know how and why Bob Dylan came to be chosen.

The Academy has, however, been clear that the Nobel Prize in Literature (never 'for Literature') has never been picked on political grounds, although it is sometimes hard to believe that this hasn't been a factor. In terms of literary merit, George Orwell would surely have been a suitable candidate but his best-known works (*1984, Animal Farm*) can be seen as political and maybe this ruled him out. On the other hand, you could argue that his work is humanitarian rather than political.

The choosing of Russian writers has always been seen as political and there was worldwide debate over Boris Pasternak (1959) and Aleksandr Solzhenitsyn (1970). Pasternak had a long impressive career and in the late 1950s had worldwide success with *Dr. Zhivago*, which had been smuggled out of Russia and not published in his homeland. His writer's bloc was not of the standard variety. At first Pasternak was pleased to receive the award but a couple of days later he sent the Academy a telegram: 'Considering the meaning this reward has been given in the society to which I belong, I must reject this undeserved prize which has been presented to me. Please do not receive my voluntary rejection with displeasure.' The Cold War was on and he was being coerced into turning it down. He did not mention Russia by name but we can be sure that there was nothing 'voluntary' about it. The pressures may have affected his health as he died, aged 70 in 1960 and so he never saw the outstanding film made of *Dr. Zhivago* in 1965.

The citation for Solzhenitsyn praised him for pursuing the 'indispensable traditions of Russian literature', which was judiciously linking him to the great authors from the past. With such novels as *One Day in the Life of Ivan Denisovich*, he revealed life in Russian labour camps and his acceptance speech had to be smuggled out of Russia. Undeterred, Solzhenitsyn wrote his famed *Gulag Archipelago* (1973), which was about living in a police state and was based around his own experiences.

The classic refusal came in 1964 from the French writer Jean-Paul Sartre, who hated the grading of human beings and did not want to be part of a literary hierarchy. This was not a new idea from Sartre who had turned down other awards and if the Academy was really *au fait* with his work, this could have been predicted. The Academy responded, 'The fact that he has declined this distinction does not in the least modify the validity of the award.' In other words, Sartre won the Nobel Prize whether he liked it or not.

The dramatist Harold Pinter won the Nobel Prize in 2005. He had been politically active in recent years against Blair and Bush and although his Nobel lecture started by talking about his dramas, it soon went into a rant against the USA. Pinter said he would bypass President Bush's speechwriter to offer something more appropriate: 'My God is good. Bin Laden's God is bad. Saddam's God was bad, except he didn't have one. He was a barbarian. We are not barbarians. We don't chop people's heads off. We believe in freedom. We are a compassionate society. We give compassionate electrocution and compassionate lethal injection. We are a great nation. I am not a dictator. I possess moral authority. You see this fist? This is my moral authority. And don't you forget it.'

Other winners of the Nobel Prize in Literature include W.B. Yeats (1923), Eugene O'Neill (1936), T.S. Eliot (1948), William Faulkner (1949), Ernest Hemingway (1954), John Steinbeck (1962) and Samuel Beckett (1969). Strangely perhaps, James Joyce never received the Nobel Prize, but it has certainly had its fair share of mavericks.

Could Bob Dylan win this prize? The citation for Dylan by Bruce Springsteen at the Rock and Roll Hall of Fame in 1988 placed him much higher than a rock performer. 'The way that Elvis freed your body, Bob freed your mind and showed us that just because the music was innately physical did not mean that it was anti-intellect. He invented a new way that a pop singer could sound, broke through the limitations of what a recording artist could achieve, and he changed the face of rock'n'roll forever and ever.' Very impressive but maybe the Swedish professors thought that rock'n'roll didn't belong there, and who was this Bruce Springsteen anyway?

Professors of Literature and certain other respected individuals can nominate writers to the Academy. Back in 1996 Professor Gordon Ball, who specialised in the Beat writers, was the first to nominate Dylan and several other professors joined him. He said of Dylan's work, 'Its literary qualities are exceptional; its artful idealism has contributed to major social change, altering and enriching the lives of millions culturally, politically, and aesthetically; the voices acclaiming it are many and distinguished. The Nobel Prize for Literature, which in over a century of being awarded has covered a territory broad and diverse, is a deserved form of recognition for such extraordinary accomplishment.'

Dylan didn't win at first but Professor Ball kept pushing his name forward. The filmmaker Tony Palmer told me in 2007, 'Last week in *The Times* they were quoting Bob Dylan's lyrics and saying what extraordinary lyrics they were as poetry. I know that Bob Dylan has been proposed to the Nobel Literature Committee for over 15 years and I saw one of the proposals as I signed it. The letter pointed out that whether you liked his songs or not, whether you liked his voice or not, there is no other lyrical poet in the second half of the twentieth century who has had such a phenomenal influence and surely you should acknowledge that.'

The English poet Grevel Lindup said, 'Dylan deserves considerable credit for having almost single-handedly made symbolism and verbal complexity acceptable in popular music.'

John Peel: 'Bob Dylan made it possible for people who can't sing to make records. He opened the door for impenetrable lyrics and songs that didn't contain their titles. He was making songs that record companies did not appreciate. In a sense, he led the way for punk.'

Paul Morley: 'His songs are timeless as they could come from 500 years ago or they could come from 500 years into the future. It doesn't matter that they are rooted in country or blues or rock'n'roll as there is something about them that has an abstract quality that transcends whatever genre they are in. It becomes great writing about being alive and it is now about what is going to happen when he dies. He has this self-awareness of the abyss ahead of him and I find that intoxicating.'

In 1984 in Berlin, Bob Dylan had said to Robert Hilburn, *LA Times*: 'I don't think I'll be perceived properly until 100 years after I've gone. I really believe that.' It's an indication that, on that day at least, he was aware of his worth.

But contrast that with Dylan in 2006: 'They talk about music being an art form but I was never part of that. That was just documentation.'

By the turn of the century, the awards were coming thick and fast. Bob Dylan naturally ignored the symposiums for him turning 70 and kept on touring. In 2012 Bob Dylan received the Presidential Medal of Freedom, America's highest civilian award.

The law professor Alex Long found that Dylan was not only the most cited songwriter in American legal writing but that he was was way out in front.

In October 2016 Bob Dylan was awarded the Nobel Prize in Literature 'for having created new poetic expressions within the great American song tradition'. The last American to win was the novelist and academic Toni Morrison in 1993, but more importantly Dylan was the first modern songwriter to be so honoured. The Bengali author and songwriter Rabindranath Tagore won the same prize in 1913.

Although the citation referred to the great American song tradition, none of its creators had been honoured. Surely Cole Porter or Irving Berlin justified inclusion or, in more recent times, Stephen Sondheim. In the rock world, impressive claims could be made for Leonard Cohen and Paul Simon. Indeed, Paul Simon's Broadway musical, *The Capeman*, was co-written by Derek Walcott, who won the Nobel Prize in Literature in 1992.

When the prize was announced, nobody knew what Dylan thought for a couple of days and then he said, 'Thank you'. His default position is against authority figures and institutions but in this instance, he could have said how pleased he was that the Academy had recognised a lyricist.

He did not want to attend the banquet and he asked Patti Smith to go in his place. She sang 'A Hard Rain's A-Gonna Fall', a wordy song that is difficult to sing if you are not used to it. In the second verse, she got lost and stopped, saying rather endearingly, 'I'm sorry, I am so nervous.' She took a few seconds to regain her composure and the rest of it contrasting the bitter lyric with a beautiful pedal steel was very good.

Dylan was supposed to respond with an acceptance speech at the banquet. He wrote an eight-minute speech which was delivered, very well, by the American Ambassador to Sweden, Azita Raji. He, or rather Dylan, made the valid point that Shakespeare never considered he was writing literature as he was more concerned on who would be saying his words, what facilities were available, would the sponsors have good seats, and where was he going to find a human skull for *Hamlet*. Four hundred years later, Dylan said that he never once considered whether he was writing literature as he was more concerned as to where he would record his songs and who would play on them. He thanked the Academy for considering the question and for 'providing such a wonderful answer'.

Similarly, he was reluctant to give the Nobel Lecture. He recorded a 25-minute lecture which was played to the Academy and is now on YouTube and has been issued in book form. He talked of his love for Buddy Holly, Leadbelly, John Donne, *Moby Dick* and *All Quiet on the Western Front*. In a neat aside, he likened *The Odyssey* to 'Homeward Bound' and 'Home on the Range'. His conclusion: we all like telling stories and hearing them.

Many people have named their children after Dylan. Nils Lofgren's stepson is called Dylan and one of the promoter Sid Bernstein's children is also called Dylan. The meteorological office has even named a storm Dylan, which may not be a compliment as it was volatile and unpredictable. Oh wait, that's about right.

The artists appearing at the Blackpool Opera House are more wide-ranging than its name suggests and they have a roll of honour in the entrance. It goes back over a hundred years with a choice for each year. Back in 1918 it was Sir Thomas Beecham; in 1939, George Formby; in 2005, David Essex; in 2006, Roy 'Chubby' Brown; in 2010, Peter Andre; and in 2013, Bob Dylan.

In 2017 President Trump told the National Security Council that the soldiers on the ground in Afghanistan could run things better that the generals and their advisers. He said, 'How many more deaths will it take? How many more lost limbs? How much longer are we going to be there?' He could have concluded, 'The answer my friend is blowin' in the wind'. So even an ignoramus knows Bob Dylan.

II. So Much Older Now: 2013–2020

For many years, artists had been making albums based around the so-called Great American Songbook and Willie Nelson, Rod Stewart, Robbie Williams and Paul McCartney had fared well. Dylan wanted to do the same and maybe he thought that his wrecked voice could bring an experience to the songs.

Hence, his first album of standards, *Shadows in The Night,* in 2015. We shouldn't have been too surprised: he had previously made a Christmas album and his fondness for old-time pop songs was evident on his radio shows. The marketing was excellent and the newspapers and music magazines gave plenty of space to his change in style.

Dylan was working with his road band with the addition of pedal steel and muted brass. He chose languid songs that had world-weariness and darkness about them. Dylan referred to them as 'uncover versions' as he was rescuing the songs from the grave: that is untrue as songs like 'Autumn Leaves' and 'That Lucky Old Sun' will last forever.

It was clear that Dylan respected these songs as he treated them all straight and with none of the irreverence he often brought to his own work. He was recording songs that been recorded by Frank Sinatra. The results were in the same jazz and country combination as Willie Nelson's *Stardust*.

Dylan commented, 'I used to play the phenomenal 'Ebb Tide' by Frank Sinatra a lot and it never failed to fill me with awe. The lyrics were so mystifying and stupendous. When Frank sang that song, I could hear everything in his voice – death, God and the universe, everything. I had other things to do though and I couldn't be listening to that stuff much.'

The first song was a confessional song written by Frank Sinatra in which he admitted his love for Ava Gardner, 'I'm a Fool to Want You'. It worked very well.

'Stay with Me' is a religious ballad and is in line with his own work. The low-key approach doesn't work with 'Some Enchanted Evening' which was written as a big-voiced ballad.

In a way, it sounds more a Leon Redbone tribute album than a Sinatra one, and it's significant that Dylan said in the 1970s he would like to start a record label and sign Redbone.

Ricky Ross of Deacon Blue: 'I always think that there is Dylan and then there is the rest of us. He is in a category of his own in so many different ways. And now he's in the autumn of his life, he is going back to the 40s and 50s and loving great songwriters like Sammy Cahn. He knows that he is indebted to them.'

Dylan was the MusiCares Person of the Year at a fundraiser in Los Angeles, the 25th person to receive this award. Dylan was also dispensing advice: 'Everything worth doing takes time. You have to write 100 bad songs before you can write one good one. You have to sacrifice a lot of things that you might not be prepared for. Like it or not, you are in this alone and you have to follow your own star.'

In 2016 Dylan released another album of standards, *Fallen Angels*. He recorded it in the Capitol building in Hollywood where Frank Sinatra had often worked and indeed where Paul McCartney had made his album of standards, *Kisses on the Bottom* (2012). Only one song, 'Skylark', had not been recorded by Sinatra and unlike *Shadows in the Night*, he was getting away from the theme of ageing.

The wonderfully rhythmic 'That Old Black Magic' was beyond his grasp, but his version of 'All the Way' was good. I would have preferred Dylan to have ventured away from the Sinatra songs and found lesser-known gems to promote, *à la Theme Time Radio Hour*. The fragmentary 'On a Little Street in Singapore' is a little-known Sinatra song, but not very distinctive. My favourite track is 'Skylark', which features some neat jazz guitar and could have been made any time in the last 70 years.

Now 75, Bob Dylan decided to give up some of his secrets. The Helmerich Centre for American Research at the University of Tulsa bought 100,000 items from Bob Dylan for $15m, thanks to a generous banking and oil billionaire, George Kaiser. It will take time to catalogue them and then they will be filed alongside their Woody Guthrie collection.

It includes handwritten lyrics, a congratulatory note from George Harrison for *Nashville Skyline* and 30 hours of *Dont Look Back* outtakes. Kaiser believes that the archive will benefit tourism. However, admission to the archive is nigh on impossible – just look at the website. There is also an earlier, much smaller collection at New York's Morgan Library and Museum which includes his notebooks for *Blood on the Tracks*.

It is encouraging that Dylan kept so much of his songwriting material so that in time people can see how he wrote the songs. In a TV documentary, Paul Simon went to a filing cabinet where he had the early drafts of *Graceland* and presumably they will be given or sold to a university or library. Allen Ginsberg was someone who noted nearly every aspect of his life and his papers are now with Columbia University in New York.

In 2017 Dylan continued exploring the standards with a triple CD, *Triplicate*, the title surely implying all three albums were the same, and again recorded at Capitol. The total playing-time was 96 minutes and covered 30 songs, again many associated with Sinatra. The first album called *Til the Sun Goes Down* starts with the lightly swinging 'I Guess I'll Have To Change My Plans', which shows that Dylan was leaning more towards the original arrangements on this album. His voice sounds strained on 'My One and Only Love' but 'That Old Feeling' is really good. The second album, *Devil Dolls*, begins with a delightfully Dick Haymes song 'Braggin'', which has been overlooked. Dylan also sings 'There's a Flaw in My Flue', a ridiculous song which Sinatra had recorded to give the finger to Capitol. The third CD *Comin' Home Late* finds Bob Dylan singing 'Stardust' competently.

Had Sony given up on Bob Dylan making videos? There were three promo videos for 'I Could Have Told You', 'My One and Only Love' and 'Stardust' but they were all just a picture of vinyl record going round on a turntable.

In 2017 Dylan wrote a lyric 'Gone but Not Forgotten' that was recorded by Bear and a Banjo. There was also talk that Bob was developing his own Dylan Whiskey which came to the market in 2019.

For the past few years, I've been thinking that we will get little new from Bob Dylan but then, in April 2019, he had a splendid outburst at a concert in Vienna. The audience had their smartphones out and Dylan stopped performing and said, 'Take pictures or don't take pictures. We can either play or we can pose – okay?' He stood still for a few minutes and then went into 'It Takes a Lot to Laugh, It Takes a Train to Cry'. Of course any superstar could have made a similar request – Rod Stewart, Bono – but they didn't and Dylan with his wonderful use of the word 'pose' was saying something about stardom.

I am writing this in March 2020 on the day that Bob Dylan cancelled his Japanese dates. The Coronavirus had brought his Never Ending Tour to an end. We'll conclude with Bob Dylan on *Theme Time Radio Hour* discussing Ends. 'According to scientists we have a 50 per cent chance of making it to the next century – good luck, everybody.'

III. Drawing Blanks?

In the 1950s Andy Warhol designed jazz sleeves for the Blue Note label and, in my opinion, produced some of his best work. Although there were some superb sleeves during the rock'n'roll era, notably Elvis Presley's first album, it was the British beat boom that led to artistic covers which perfectly defined the contents – Angus McBean and Robert Freeman for the Beatles, David Bailey and Gered Mankowitz for the Rolling Stones. Two leading artists, Peter Blake and Richard Hamilton, did the sleeves and the packaging for *Sgt. Pepper's*

Lonely Hearts Club Band and *The Beatles* (aka *The White Album*) respectively. Andy Warhol created the zipper fly for the Rolling Stones' *Sticky Fingers* (1971).

Many leading rock musicians came from art colleges and so were disposed towards sleeves that had some artistic merit. Peter Blake said in 1999 that 'The LP cover has found recognition as a serious and valid art form', but unfortunately it was being replaced by the smaller CD packaging which gave artists and photographers less space to play with.

Dylan has always enjoyed painting and sketching and in another life, might have been a commercial artist. When he read Woody Guthrie's *Bound for Glory*, he was taken by Woody's pen and ink illustrations.

Dylan's first commercial artwork was on The Band's album, *Music from Big Pink* (1968) and then *Self-Portrait* (1970), although that self-portrait wasn't recognisably Bob Dylan. There was much talk about the novelty of a performer painting an LP sleeve, but they were considered primitive and not very good. Biographer Howard Sounes: 'The cover of *Self Portrait* is terrible and the painting on The Band's *Music from Big Pink* is very much like a Marc Chagall painting.'

The comparison was made with Joni Mitchell's covers and her portraits were regarded as much better. Dylan persevered and one of his drawings is on the cover of *Planet Waves* (1974). The drawing owes something to the style of Edvard Munch.

With training and experience, Dylan became a better artist and it became his way of relaxing on tour. He could work in ink and pencil. Watercolours too were easy to work with on the road, but the acrylics and oils were done in his studio or sometimes, other painters' studios.

Although there has been a long debate over the years as to whether or not Bob Dylan is a poet, there is no doubt that he is a painter. This word is used indiscriminately to describe the great masters and the Sunday painters. However, the word 'artist' is used more judiciously and the art world has mixed feelings over his talent.

In 1994 the term *Drawn Blank* was used for a book of 92 Bob Dylan drawings, dating from 1989 to 1992 and published by Random House.

Ingrid Mössinger, the curator at Kunstsammlungen Chemnitz, Germany saw the book in New York and asked Dylan if his work could be exhibited. Dylan made paintings from the drawings using watercolour and gouache. Dylan often painted several versions of the same image using different colours. He may have been following Andy Warhol's lead but it was also the way he approached performing familiar songs.

In 2007 the first public exhibition of Dylan's paintings, *The Drawn Blank Series,* opened at Kunstsammlungen Chemnitz. There were 200 exhibits and a book was published called *Bob Dylan: The Drawn Blank Series.*

By now Bob was riffing with colour on top of black and white images and he produced 320 different pictures in 2007. I wished he'd spent the time writing songs instead but he is entitled to do what he wants.

In 2008 *Drawn Blank* was exhibited at Halcyon Gallery in London and big business had swung into operation. Limited signed prints of 300 copies of each picture were available to the public at £1,200 a time. Dylan was now reluctant to sign autographs and it is easy to see why. It was in his interest that the only way to obtain his autograph was on a signed print. It's Ain't Free, Babe.

By the *Drawn Blank* series in 2012, each standard signed print was £1,500 (unframed!) with all eight available in a presentation box for £11,250. The accompanying book was £40.

Bob Dylan was once counterculture, now with all the merchandise he is another form of counter culture.

In 2010 the National Gallery of Denmark in Copenhagen exhibited *The Brazil Series*, which was 40 acrylic paintings on canvas and looked at the streets of the country rather than presenting a travelogue. There was a very good image of train tracks receding, which has since been revisited in several different colours. No one could deny that Dylan has a good sense of perspective.

Dylan's paintings were also seen in Turin and Tokyo and in the same year, *Bob Dylan on Canvas* was exhibited at the Halcyon Gallery on New Bond Street. The gallery had asked Bob to paint American landscapes and he liked to portray the back roads and the sense of America's past. He said, 'Your past begins the day you were born and to disregard it is cheating yourself of who you really are.' (Well, he has often done just that.) Judy Collins was a satisfied customer: 'I did buy six of his prints at the Halcyon Galley in London. They are quite wonderful.' Bruce Springsteen has some too.

Neil Young: 'I'm sure Bob has the master's touch, whether he is painting from a photograph or a memory of something he has seen. He chooses his images. His songs have known no bounds in their influences, and the folk process transfers well to painting. He may just be getting started. Like music, the world of art has its own rules to break.'

In 2011 the Gagosian Gallery in Madison Avenue exhibited *The Asia Series*, which reflected his time in China, Japan Vietnam and South Korea. It was described as a visual journey of his visit to Asia with 'first hand depictions of people, street scenes, architecture and landscape.'

Dylan said, 'I paint mostly from real life. It has to start with that', but the *New York Times* thought otherwise. It reported that 'some fans and Dylanologists have raised questions about whether some of these paintings are based on the singer's own experiences and observations, or on photographs that are widely available and were not taken by Mr. Dylan.' There were close links between Dylan's paintings and some historic photographs including some by Dmitri Kessel and Henri Cartier-Bresson. It sounded like Bob was up to his old tricks but the art critic Blake Gopnik defended him by saying, 'Ever since the birth of photography, painters have used it as the basis for their works: Edgar Degas and Edouard Vuillard and other favourite artists – even Edvard Munch –all took or used photographs as sources for their art, sometimes barely altering them.'

Dylan's second show at the Gagosian Gallery in New York, *Revisionist Art*, opened in November 2012. The show consisted of thirty paintings, transforming and satirizing popular magazines, including *Playboy* and *Babytalk*. They were fake covers and quite fun.

In February 2013 Dylan exhibited the *New Orleans Series* of paintings at the Museum of Art in New Orleans as well as the Palazzo Reale in Milan. This was the Royal Palace which had previously displayed work by Monet and Picasso.

In August 2013 the National Portrait Gallery hosted Dylan's first major UK exhibition, *Face Value*, which was unusual as the gallery concentrates on figures from the UK. The exhibition went to Kent State University Museum, Ohio and Kunstsammlungen Chemnitz.

In November 2013, the Halcyon Gallery in London mounted *Mood Swings*, a sculpture exhibition in which Dylan made exhibits out of spanners, wrenches and chains. Dylan displayed seven wrought iron gates he had made. This took him back in memory at least to Hibbing as Dylan said, 'I've been around iron all my life ever since I was a kid. I was born and raised in iron ore country, where you could breathe it and smell it every day. Gates appeal to me because of the negative space they allow. They can be closed but at the same time they allow the seasons and breezes to enter and flow. They can shut you out or shut you in. And in some ways there is no difference.' Make what you will of that. President Clinton was given one of Bob's gates for his 65th birthday. A 26-foot long archway by Bob Dylan is now permanently on display in Maryland.

In 2014 there was *Revisionist Art* and *Side Tracks*, a running series with 300 prints at the Halcyon Gallery. Dylan said, 'I just draw what is interesting to me. I can take a bowl of fruit and turn it into a life and death drama.' (Let's see it then.)

In November 2016, the Halcyon Gallery featured *The Beaten Path*, a collection of drawings, watercolours and acrylic works by Dylan. It depicted American landscapes and urban scenes, inspired by Dylan's travels. They were all fairly anonymous – a river, a horse and a bed. There were 14 pictures, somewhat larger than usual, and you could own the complete collection, all signed by Dylan, for £32,000. Dylan said that the soundtrack to the paintings could be Peetie Wheatstraw, Charlie Parker, Clifford Brown, Blind Lemon Jefferson or Guitar Slim, 'artists that make us a lot bigger when listening to them.'

In 2019 I think there was a clear example that Dylan's work was as much commerce as art. The Castle Fine Art Gallery in Liverpool displayed a large, colourful picture of railway tracks going into the distance and the signed prints were £15,000 in a worldwide edition of 200. An artist with a good negotiating team can probably pocket 40 per cent of the sales and Dylan would obviously fall into that category so that is £3m in sales if they all sold, with £1.2m of that in Bob's pocket. It was also possible to negotiate the purchase of the original painting, perhaps for £100,000.

By 2020, Bob Dylan hadn't released an album of new songs for eight years and even though that last album, *Tempest*, had sold well, it could easily be more lucrative to be drawing or painting.

Then with the lockdown came the surprise, Bob Dylan was releasing new songs with a view to a double-album in June, *Rough and Rowdy Ways*. The title tipped its hat to a country song, 'My Rough And Rowdy Ways' written and recorded by Jimmie Rodgers in 1929, although that song is not included.

At the time of writing, three songs have been issued in advance First, 'Murder Most Foul', which was discussed earlier, and then 'I Contain Multitudes' and after that, 'False Prophet'.

In his 1892 poem, *Song of Myself*, Walt Whitman wrote, 'Do I contradict myself? Very well, then, I contradict myself; I am large – I contain multitudes.' That thought and that conclusion surely appealed to Bob Dylan.

False Prophet was probably recorded before the publication of a science book of the same name by Ed Yong in 2016. Yong says that each of our bodies contains trillions of microbes and he draws the links between them. Dylan has taken a different but complementary route: what about all the things we see and hear that alter our attitudes and our behaviour?

In 'I Contain Multitudes', Dylan lists some of his influences (William Blake, Sun Records, Gene Vincent) and even includes Anne Frank, Indiana Jones and the Rolling Stones. The song follows on from 'Murder Most Foul' but the choices, on the whole, seem more personal. Does Dylan really play Beethoven sonatas and Chopin preludes and will we ever hear his versions? But then again, maybe he is just playing them on CD. Cryptic as ever, Dylan sums himself up beautifully: 'I'm a man of contrasts, I'm a man of many moods, I contain multitudes.'

The third track, 'False Prophet', is largely based around a Muddy Waters' blues riff and they all confirm what we have suspected, that Dylan has lost the ability to write strong melodies. Most of the time, he is half-singing, half-narrating his material and it doesn't bother me as Dylan's talking voice still sounds good.

Again, the song is mysterious with the verses being somehow connected but not quite. Dylan attests to the truthfulness of his work with 'I ain't no false prophet, I know what I know' and ends with the brilliant 'Can't remember when I was born, And I forgot when I died.'

Acknowledgements

I've been writing and broadcasting on popular music since the 1970s and I knew that I had asked interviewees about Bob Dylan from time to time, but I had no idea that I'd done it so much. Naturally there are many who have been directly involved with Bob Dylan but there are hundreds more where I have just sought an opinion. Rather like asking musicians about the Beatles, there are a vast range of views, probably even more so as there are plenty of folk who have little time for him. There is a whole range of views in *Bob Dylan: Outlaw Blues*. I never mind someone having an opposing view to mine so long as it is well argued – and this occurs over and over again. The book demonstrates what a divisive character Bob Dylan is – and a lot of it is of his own making.

My thanks to Andy and Caroline Peden Smith at McNidder and Grace for having faith in this book and to Paula Beaton who has been the copyeditor. My thanks to John Keane and David Charters for reading over the text so diligently and for pointing out discrepancies as well as typos. Thanks also go to Jeffrey Side, who shared his thoughts on poetry and rock, and it's always good to go to Mark Lewisohn for a second opinion on something.

Thanks also to Anne Leigh, who has put up with Bob as a partner in our marriage for 46 years, and my friends Tim Adams, Mike Brocken, Andrew Doble, Norman Killon and John Walsh as we have often talked Dylan.

Thanks to John Bohanna who gave me copies of all Dylan's programmes in the series, *Theme Time Radio Hour*. I heard many of them the first time round but it was great to play them one after another and I was sad when I'd finally heard them all.

What follows is a list of my interviewees and I am sorry that it does not include Robert Shelton. I did call him when he was working for the *Brighton Argus* about an interview on my BBC Radio Merseyside programme but he demanded payment (£30) and the show had no budget. Not to worry: when his Dylan biography was published, he did an interview with Bob Azurdia for the station and I have had access to that.

Ellis Amburn has written biographies of Roy Orbison (*Dark Star*) and Buddy Holly (*Buddy Holly – The Real Story*).

Based in Greenwich Village in the 60s, **Eric Andersen** wrote 'Thirsty Boots'.

Brian Auger ran Brian Auger and The Trinity and they teamed up with Julie Driscoll for 'This Wheel's on Fire' (1968).

A delight to meet, **Joan Baez** is by no means as serious as her image suggests. On the *Joe* episode of *Theme Time Radio Hour*, Dylan played her version of 'Joe Hill' and called her 'the very talented and ever-generous Joan Baez'.

Derek Barker founded the Dylan magazine, *Isis,* in 1985 and wrote a comprehensive 500 page book on the songs Bob performed but didn't write, *Bob Dylan – Under the Influence* (2008).

John Bauldie, a writer for *Q*, founded the Dylan magazine, *The Telegraph*, but was killed in a helicopter crash in 1996 having just seen his team, Bolton Wanderers defeat Chelsea. He started the phrase, Bobcats, and saw Dylan over 100 times, beginning with the Isle of Wight festival in 1969.

Poet and lyricist **Larry Beckett** wrote many songs with Tim Buckley.

Contemporary blues singer **Eric Bibb** knew the Greenwich Village scene through his father, Leon Bibb, a folk singer and actor in several Broadway productions.

Alf Bicknell was the Beatles' chauffeur from 1964–66. I told him to call his autobiography, *Chauffeur, So Good*, but he went with *Baby, You Can Drive My Car*.

Liverpool playwright **Alan Bleasdale** is best known for his TV drama, *Boys from the Blackstuff*.

Scottish singer / songwriter **Eric Bogle** wrote and recorded 'And the Band Played Waltzing Matilda'.

Blues guitarist **Joe Bonamassa** is so prolific that I am surprised he found time to talk to me. Many of his albums pay tribute to the blues greats and to the 1960s.

American record producer **Joe Boyd** made his mark in the UK by producing Nick Drake, Pink Floyd, Fairport Convention and Richard Thompson.

There was a new wave of protest songs with the rise of Margaret Thatcher and **Billy Bragg** was at the fore. He has made Grammy-nominated albums with Wilco featuring melodies for Woody Guthrie's lyrics.

Based in New York, **Oscar Brand**, folk singer and radio host, released albums of bawdy songs and Presidential campaign songs.

Singer / songwriter **Jonatha Brooke** had the opportunity to write melodies for some of Woody Guthrie's lyrics.

Bob Brozman, who died in 2013, often toured the UK with his exotic 1920s mix of blues and Hawaiian music.

Eric Burdon was the lead singer of the Animals.

Best known for her song about suburban life 'He Thinks He'll Keep Her', **Mary Chapin Carpenter** is a superb singer / songwriter, often pushing herself to exceptional limits. Based in Nashville, **Beth Nielsen Chapman** is one of America's best songwriters, writing a remarkable album *Sand and Water* (1997) following the death of her husband.

Chris Charlesworth was a key writer for *Melody Maker* and then a commissioning editor for Omnibus Press. He has an anecdote for almost every rock musician, all told in his wonderful lugubrious accent: he's a Yorkshire Jack Dee.

David Charters is a perceptive journalist associated with the *Liverpool Daily Post and Echo*. He wrote the poem for the Hillsborough memorial by the Museum of Liverpool.

Liam Clancy was a member of the Clancy Brothers and Tommy Makem.

Based in Nashville but always a maverick, **Guy Clark** was arguably the finest of the 1970s country writers and he made his own guitars and boats.

Liverpool guitarist **Mark Clarke** has been part of Colosseum, Uriah Heep and Mountain and wrote 'The Wizard'.

Melody Maker editor **Ray Coleman** interviewed Bob Dylan and wrote biographies of John Lennon and Brian Epstein.

Judy Collins possessed the purest, loveliest voice of the 1960s and she still sounds good today. A quirky interviewee though – she told me about Stephen Stills' bunions and said, 'What would you like to hear tonight? Anything special?' I requested 'Liverpool Lullaby' and got it.

Ray Connolly started as a journalist on the *Liverpool Daily Post* and wrote the film scripts for *That'll Be the Day* and *Stardust*.

John Cornelius was a poet, artist and songwriter on the Liverpool 8 scene of the late 60s. His memoir, *Liverpool 8*, is terrific.

Tony Crane has been a member of the Merseybeats since their inception in 1962,

A.J. Croce is the son of singer / songwriter Jim Croce and is an engaging performer in his own right.

Rodney Crowell is a Nashville writer, producer and performer, writing both commercial hits and intensely personal songs.

Karl Dallas wrote about folk music for *Melody Maker*. I met him once and I have no idea why he was so confrontational. He wrote 'The Family of Man' which was recorded by the Spinners.

Tony Davis was a member of the Liverpool folk group, the Spinners.

Michael Des Barres is a rock vocalist best known for taking over from Robert Palmer in Power Station.

Jackie DeShannon wrote 'When You Walk in the Room' and recorded the original version of 'Needles and Pins'.

Bruce Dickinson is a novelist and member of Iron Maiden.

Bonnie Dobson, folk singer best known for 'Morning Dew'.

Originally in Chris Barber's jazz band, **Lonnie Donegan** established skiffle music in the 1950s and had hits with 'Rock Island Line' and My Old Man's a Dustman'.

Seen as Scotland's Bob Dylan, **Donovan** developed his own style and had hits with 'Catch the Wind', 'Colours' and 'Sunshine Superman'.

Hugh Douglas saw Bob Dylan in Liverpool.

Julie Driscoll was dubbed the Face of 68 and had a hit with the Bob Dylan song, 'This Wheel's on Fire'. Usually works with her husband, the jazz pianist Keith Tippett.

Singer / songwriter **Steve Earle** brought left wing politics to country music.

Music journalist, **Mark Ellen** co-presented *The Old Grey Whistle Test* and wrote his memoir, *Rock Stars Stole My Life!* (2014).

Ramblin' Jack Elliott lives up to his name as a travelling folk singer.

Keyboard whiz **Keith Emerson** was part of Emerson, Lake and Palmer.

Mike Evans is a rock saxophonist with Liverpool Scene and chronicler of the Beats.

Warwick Evans, Welsh actor, particularly known for *Blood Brothers*.

One of the UK's top R&B vocalists, **Chris Farlowe** topped the charts in 1966 with *Out of Time*.

Singing in both English and Spanish, **José Feliciano** was possibly the most intense performer of the 1960s.

Born in Santa Barbara, **Julie Felix** came to the UK in the 60s and made her name on *The Frost Report*, particularly scoring with Tom Paxton's 'Goin' to the Zoo'.

The American record producer **Kim Fowley** was known as much for his eccentricity as his talent. Discovered the girl group, the Runaways and has an astonishingly varied CV.

Everyone must have seen **Pete Frame**'s meticulously drawn Rock Family Trees, the source of a highly-praised BBC-TV series.

Funky **Donnie Fritts** is a noted Muscle Shoals musician and songwriter.

Rory Gallagher, the Irish guitar hero, formed Taste and then formed his own band.

Singer, songwriter and actress **Dana Gillespie** fronts her own blues band.

Broadcaster **Charlie Gillett** wrote a definitive book about American record labels of the 50s and 60s, *The Sound of the City* as well as being a champion of world music.

A session pianist and songwriter known for his work with Linda Ronstadt, **Andrew Gold** had his own Top 10 hit with 'Never Let Her Get Away' in 1978.

Michael Gray is the author of several authoritative books on Bob Dylan, especially *Song & Dance Man*. He is known for his exhaustive research into Bob Dylan and the blues.

Roger Greenaway has been the chairman of the Performing Right Society and is known for his long songwriting partnership with Roger Cook, which includes 'You've Got Your Troubles' and 'I'd Like to Teach the World to Sing'.

Sid Griffin of the Long Ryders and the Coal Porters is an American music writer and musician based in the UK.

Mick Groves was a member of the Liverpool folk group, the Spinners.

The son of Woody Guthrie, **Arlo Guthrie** is best known for 'Alice's Restaurant', a song, an album and the only major film to be made about litter.

The daughter of Woody Guthrie, **Nora Guthrie** is the keeper of his archive.

The guitarist **Steve Hackett** is best known for his years with Genesis.

The biographer **David Hadju** wrote *Positively 4th Street: The Lives and Times of Joan Baez, Bob Dylan, Mimi Baez Fariña and Richard Fariña*. (2001)

Colin Hall is the custodian of John Lennon's childhood home in Liverpool.

Terry Hamblin is a New York music professor currently writing a book on the Beatles and the politics of the 60s.

Johnnie Hamp was the head of light entertainment at Granada TV and was the first producer to put the Beatles on TV.

Mike Harding is a folk singer and comedian.

Steve Harley is known for his solo hits and his time with Cockney Rebel.

Roy Harper has merged folk, rock and sometimes experimental music in a series of albums unlike any others. He wrote the perfect goodbye song in 'When an Old Cricketer Leaves the Crease' in 1975. Dylan's baseball references leave me cold but I love the nods to Geoffrey Boycott and John Snow.

When I interviewed **Ronnie Hawkins** in a London hotel, he went up to the classical harp player in the lounge and asked her to join his band, but that could have been coded language for something else.

Record producer **Joe Henry** has recorded with Billy Bragg and is Madonna's brother-in-law.

Folk singer **Carolyn Hester** worked with both Buddy Holly and Bob Dylan.

Author of many books, **Clinton Heylin** is a methodical and highly opinionated Dylan biographer.

Chris Hillman was a founder member of the Byrds.

Noddy Holder was the front man for Slade.

Garth Hudson was the organist and saxophonist with The Band.

Rock biographer **Patrick Humphries** has specialised in folk-rock: Lonnie Donegan, Bob Dylan, Fairport Convention, Paul Simon and Richard Thompson.

Ian Hunter was the front man of Mott The Hoople.

Burl Ives is best known for acting in *Cat on a Hot Tin Roof* and *The Big Country* and performing 'The Ballad of Davy Crockett' and 'A Little Bitty Tear'. He was a controversial figure as he cooperated with the McCarthy committee.

Hughie Jones was the Spinner most interested in songwriting. Still hosts a weekly folk club in Liverpool.

Paul Jones was the front man for Manfred Mann and today fronts both the Manfreds and the Blues Band.

John Jorgenson was a member of the Hellecasters and the Desert Rose Band and played in Elton John's band for six years and again in 2019. Check out his Django-styled arrangement of 'Man of Mystery'.

Martyn Joseph is a Welsh singer and songwriter, who often writes social commentary.

Howard Kaplan was a member of the Turtles.

Will Kaufman is a university lecturer who tours with his one-man show about Woody Guthrie.

Jude Kelly is a leading arts administrator and theatre director on the South Bank but used to be part of the poetry scene around Liverpool 8.

Mark Kelly is a poet and comedy writer working for Jo Brand and Ruby Wax.

Cajun fiddler **Doug Kershaw** is best known for his autobiographic song, 'Louisiana Man'.

Joe Klein wrote the definitive biography of *Woody Guthrie: A Life* (1981).

After studying at Oxford University and becoming a helicopter pilot, **Kris Kristofferson** became a country songwriter writing 'Help Me Make It through the Night' and 'For the Good Times'.

Jim Kweskin was a stalwart of the Boston folk scene who popularised jug band music.

Manchester musician, writer and academic **C.P. Lee** wrote his autobiography, *When We Were Thin* in 2007.

Gordon Lightfoot is a Canadian singer/ songwriter, best known for 'Sundown' and 'If You Could Read My Mind'.

Bob Lind is known for his hit song, 'Elusive Butterfly': still writing, recording and performing (bet you didn't know that).

Dennis Locorriere is the former lead singer of Dr. Hook.

Nils Lofgren is a singer / songwriter who spent many years in Bruce Springsteen's band.

Andy Fairweather Low has had hit records with Amen Corner and his own band as well as working as a sideman for Roger Waters and Eric Clapton.

Country Joe McDonald is famed for his Fish cheer at Woodstock.

As a poet and member of Scaffold, **Roger McGough** has shown both insight and a remarkable gift for language.

Roger McGuinn was the leader of the Byrds.

Tom McGuinness has been with Manfred Mann, McGuinness-Flint and the Blues Band.

Barry McGuire came to fame in the New Christy Minstrels and then had a solo hit with 'Eve of Destruction'.

Ian McLagen started with the Small Faces and played with Bob Dylan and Billy Bragg.

Ian McNabb is a compelling stage performer, both on his own and with The Icicle Works.

UK blues guitarist **Tony (T.S.) McPhee** founded the Groundhogs.

UK singer / songwriter **Ralph McTell** has written 'Streets of London', 'Zimmerman Blues' and many other poignant songs.

BBC broadcaster **Stuart Maconie** has also written several amusing books.

Raul Malo leads the Mavericks.

In the early 60s, **Barry Mann** was a Brill Building songwriter, his hits including 'You've Lost that Lovin' Feelin'' and 'We Gotta Get out of This Place'.

Keyboard player **Manfred Mann** ran the group of the same name.

Greil Marcus is among the most acclaimed of rock academics with studies of Elvis Presley, Bob Dylan and Van Morrison.

Bernd Matheja is the author of several books about the German beat scene.

Social commentator, jazz singer and proud Liverpudlian, **George Melly** wrote *Revolt into Style* (Penguin, 1970), one of the first books to analyse youth culture.

Georgia-born **Katie Melua** came to the UK as a child. She was discovered by Mike Batt, who produced her No.1 album, *Call Off The Search* in 2003.

Before he was in Badfinger, **Joey Molland** was part of the Masterminds, who recorded 'She Belongs to Me'.

I don't think it's possible to have a music documentary on the BBC without a comment from **Paul Morley**, a gifted and opinionated social historian. Applies to this book too.

With her mixture of traditional and new music, **Nana Mouskouri** became one of the world's biggest stars. Dylan sometimes played her songs before going on stage.

Blues guitarist and singer **Geoff Muldaur** is best known for his work with Jim Kweskin.

Maria Muldaur was part of the Jim Kweskin Blues Band and she had a million seller with 'Midnight at the Oasis'.

Graham Nash was in the Hollies and then Crosby, Stills and Nash.

One of the most enthusiastic people I have met, **Willie Nile** is a lively singer / songwriter who has often worked with Bruce Springsteen and lives in Greenwich Village.

British singer / songwriter **Hazel O'Connor** is known for the hit singles, 'Eighth Day', 'D-Days' and 'Will You', and the 1980 film *Breaking Glass*.

The folk singer and activist **Odetta** was one of the breakthrough artists for the folk revival in the late-1950s. In 1961 Martin Luther King called her 'The queen of American folk music'.

Joan Osborne is best known for her 1996 hit single, 'One of Us', and album, *Relish*.

Tom Paley worked with Woody Guthrie and was a member of the New Lost City Ramblers.

Tony Palmer is a prolific documentary film-maker known for the series *All You Need Is Love* and *Cream's Farewell Concert*.

After his army service, **Tom Paxton** gravitated to Greenwich Village and recorded several albums of his own songs, which included 'The Last Thing on My Mind' and 'Ramblin' Boy'.

Nashville songwriter **Gretchen Peters** has written many hit songs ('Independence Day', 'You Don't ever Know Who I Am') and also made several albums of her own.

As well as handling the UK publicity for Bob Dylan's 1960s UK tours, **Ken Pitt** managed Manfred Mann and the young David Bowie.

Alan Price used to be an Animal, but seems very civilised now.

When it comes to **John Prine**, you can often say you've never heard a song like that before – 'Sam Stone', 'Hello In There' and 'Linda's Gone to Mars'.

Maddy Prior fronts Steeleye Span.

Bolton-born **Mark Radcliffe** is well-known for his programmes on BBC Radios 2 and 6 and has played in various folk and rock bands.

Singer / songwriter **Dave Rave** is a popular Canadian artist, almost, it seems to me, their answer to Elvis Costello.

Tim Rice has been knighted for his contribution to musical theatre.

Jon Riseman is an agent and video producer whose memoir is called *From Here...to Obscurity* (2010).

Bruce Robinson is a film director, best known for *Withnail and I* (1987).

Biographer **Johnny Rogan** has written about John Lennon, the Byrds and Morrissey. His book on rock managers *Starmakers and Svengalis* (Queen Anne Press, 1988) is both witty and highly informative.

Tim Rose is an American singer / songwriter who spent his later years in London and touring the UK. Jimi Hendrix heard his version of 'Hey Joe' and he recorded an early version of 'Morning Dew'.

Ricky Ross is the lead singer and chief songwriter for Deacon Blue.

Singer, pianist, songwriter, arranger and producer **Leon Russell** has done the lot and worked alongside Joe Cocker, Bob Dylan, George Harrison and Elton John.

The prolific US singer / songwriter **Tom Russell** should be much better known. His song about the proposed border wall between Mexico and the US, 'Who's Gonna Build Your Wall', is classic protest songwriting.

Willy Russell is a Liverpool playwright, whose credits include *John, Paul, George, Ringo... and Bert*, *Educating Rita* and *Shirley Valentine*.

Buffy Sainte-Marie is best known for 'Universal Soldier', 'Until It's Time for You to Go' and many songs about her native American heritage.

Music writer **Robert Santelli** is an executive director of the Grammy Museum.

The highly perceptive music writer **Jon Savage** is best known for his study of punk, *England's Dreaming* (1992).

Mike Scott is the leader of the Waterboys.

John Sebastian led the Lovin' Spoonful. His stoned ramblings at Woodstock are an unexpected highlight of the film.

Peggy Seeger is the half-sister of Pete Seeger and the widow of Ewan MacColl and is highly acclaimed as a folk singer in her own right.

Pete Seeger is the father of folk singing, the man who created 'Where Have All the Flowers Gone?', 'Guantanamera', 'If I Had a Hammer' and 'Turn! Turn! Turn!'

Clive Selwood was the UK label manager for Elektra and managed John Peel.

Del Shannon scored with forceful beat-ballads ('Runaway', 'Little Town Flirt', 'Keep Searchin") between 1961 and 1965.

Lee Simmonds has worked in managing UK record labels for many years, notably the country catalogue for RCA.

Martin Simpson is a UK folk singer, songwriter and guitarist.

Larry Sloman, known as Ratso, was the official chronicler of the Rolling Thunder tour. Check out his fantastic book, *On the Road with Bob Dylan* (1978).

Blues guitarist and singer **Chris Smither** wrote amongst many other songs, 'Love Me like a Man', recorded by Bonnie Raitt.

David Soul is an actor associated with *Starsky and Hutch* and *Jerry Springer – The Musical* and with several hit singles of his own.

The biographer **Howard Sounes** has a mixed CV: biographies of major criminals like Fred and Rosemary West; biographies on Bob Dylan, Paul McCartney and Charles Bukowski.

Bob Spitz wrote *Dylan – A Biography* (Michael Joseph, 1988) and *The Beatles – A Biography* (Little, Brown, 2005).

Bob Stanley is part of Saint Etienne and a music critic for *The Times* and other prestigious publications.

John Steel is the drummer for the Animals.

The Glasgow-born songwriter **Al Stewart** knew Paul Simon when he came to the UK and made his own mark with *Year of the Cat* (1976).

John Stewart was a member of the Kingston Trio and wrote 'Daydream Believer' and 'Gold'.

Now mostly a jazz performer, **Curtis Stigers** had his biggest hits in 1992 with 'I Wonder Why' and 'You're All That Matters To Me'. He said to me, "Spencer Leigh is a really cool name, you sound like a blues singer" so thanks to my parents for that.

Allan Taylor, very stimulating UK singer / songwriter, folk-based but also influenced by French *chanson*.

Once a member of Fairport Convention, **Richard Thompson** is a superlative singer, guitarist and songwriter.

Elizabeth Thomson is the co-editor of *The Lennon Companion* (Macmillan, 1987) and *The Dylan Companion* (Macmillan, 1990), both with David Gutman. Co-edited the revised edition of Robert Shelton's biography of Bob Dylan.

Without doubt **Billy Bob Thornton** is the coolest person I've met, although you could argue that a really cool guy wouldn't be talking to someone from local radio.

Peter Tork was one of the Monkees.

Folk singer **Happy Traum** knew Bob Dylan in both Greenwich Village and Woodstock. He lives up to his name.

Canadian born singer and songwriter, **Ian Tyson**, came to prominence as part of Ian and Sylvia and has written and recorded many albums. His best-known song is 'Four Strong Winds'.

Canadian born singer and songwriter, **Sylvia Tyson**, came to prominence as part of Ian and Sylvia and has written and recorded many albums. Her best-known song is 'You Were on My Mind'.

Midge Ure is associated with Ultravox as well as his own solo career.

Hilton Valentine was a member of the Animals.

Plagued by addiction, **Townes Van Zandt** was a remarkable singer / songwriter, best known for 'Pancho and Lefty.

Bobby Vee was a 60s pop star born in Fargo, North Dakota, best known for 'Take Good Care of My Baby'.

Loudon Wainwright III is the centre of a remarkable family of singer / songwriters who invariably write about each other, and who else has a repertoire of songs about dead skunks, suicide, vampires, bees and doggy do?

Elijah Wald is an American blues musician who worked with Dave Van Ronk on his autobiography and wrote *Dylan Goes Electric!* (2015).

Julian Lloyd Webber has been one of the UK's top cellists and is dedicated to promoting music teaching in schools.

Cynthia Weil wrote many 60s hits with her partner, Barry Mann, including 'You've Lost that Lovin' Feelin''.

Jerry Wexler was a record producer for Atlantic and has worked with Aretha Franklin, Solomon Burke and Bob Dylan.

Josh White Jr is the son of the folk singer, Josh White, and a fine artist in his own right.

Paul Williams is an American rock journalist best known for his series on *Bob Dylan: Performing Artist.*

England fast bowler and test captain, **Bob Willis**, was motivated by listening to Bob Dylan.

Pick Withers was the drummer for Dire Straits.

Ian Woodward is a Dylan authority, noted for his detailed *Tracking Dylan* series in the ISIS magazine. He wrote at length about mistakes in the sleeve notes for *The Bootleg Series*.

Bob Wooler was the DJ at the Cavern.

John York was a member of the Byrds. I met him in Wigan when he was working with Barry McGuire on a gospel tour.

The Wicked Messenger – A Bob Dylan Bibliography

"Never trust the artist. Trust the tale. The proper function of a critic is save the tale from the artist who has created it."

(D.H. Lawrence)

"A lot of my songs are misinterpreted by people who don't know any better."

(Bob Dylan to Robert Hilburn, 2001)

Positively Main Street, Toby Thompson (New English Library, 1971: republished with interview with author, University of Minnesota Press, 2008)
The first Bob Dylan book and one concentrating on the Minnesota years. Thompson makes himself part of the story and indeed, has a romance with Echo Helstrom. When the book came out, Bob phoned up Echo and said, 'You come off pretty good in my book.' Thompson is a city dweller taking us into a mysterious land and I suppose it was the opposite effect for Bob Dylan: he lived in this strange land and it clouded how he looked at the world.

Bob Dylan, Anthony Scaduto (Grosset & Dunlap, 1971: several revised editions)
The first investigative study of Bob Dylan's career to date. Robert Shelton criticised the book because Scaduto had had little access to Dylan. That isn't necessarily a drawback. Scaduto seems to draw some valid conclusions when Shelton was sucked into the vortex.

Song And Dance Man, Michael Gray (Hart-Davis, 1972: two major updates and the so-called Song And Dance III was published by Continuum in 2002)
Michael Gray said in 2002, '*Song And Dance Man III* is four times the size of the previous edition; 75% of it is new and it is over 900 pages. It is my magnum opus and more magnum than ever before. Even if I thought at the time that it was pretty good, I had no idea what the reviewers would say. The first reviews could easily have said, "Who needs half a million words on this boring old fart?" If *Q* or *Uncut* or *Mojo* had said that, a lot of the other reviewers would have taken the same line. The first one was from *Uncut* and that was a fantastic review. Five stars and it said wonderful, amazing things. *Q* said it was an event. It was the first time in my life I had had particularly good reviews. Half of them were praising the first edition from back in the early 70s but I had had very little feedback back then.'

Dylan: A Biography, Bob Spitz (Michael Joseph, 1989)
The book is divided into sections and his Greenwich Village years are labelled *The Twerp*. He says, 'The distinction between fact and fiction has proved elusive to many of my predecessors.'
John Bauldie to Bob Spitz: 'What printed material do you have respect for?'
Bob Spitz: 'None whatsoever. None at all. I read Toby Thompson's book in 15 minutes and discounted it.'
Well, that shortens the reading list.

Dylan – Behind Closed Doors, Clinton Heylin (Penguin, 1996)
A first-rate list of Bob Dylan's recording sessions from 1960 to 1994, giving the number of takes, unissued tracks and personnel. Heylin is an opinionated writer, which is half the fun in reading his work and he starts by saying, 'This book is not dedicated to Jeff Rosen'. The introduction is a critique of Mark Lewisohn's work on the Beatles – and the connection is…

A Life in Stolen Moments, Clinton Heylin (Schirmer, 1996)
A comprehensive day by day guide to Bob Dylan from 1941 to 1995. Superbly researched and not as assertive as many of his books. Dylan is a major star and as the book goes on you realise how many people depend upon him for a living, which must have a bearing on his creativity.

Invisible Republic: Bob Dylan's Basement Tapes, Greil Marcus (Picador, 1997)
Oddly enough much more about Dock Boggs and Harry Smith than Bob Dylan. Clever stuff but a nomadic mind. Bought my copy in Poundland.

Razor's Edge: Bob Dylan and the Never Ending Tour, Andrew Muir (Helter Skelter, 2001: revised and expanded 2004)
This book contains some fine passages and observations but it is a chronological list of Dylan's 1,200 appearances and reads like a never-ending book. Lots of artists are on never-ending tours but Dylan is unique in that he rarely plays the same set twice.

On the Road with Bob Dylan, Larry 'Ratso' Sloman (Bantam 1978, new edition Helter Skelter, 2002)
Book slips from first to third person. Includes interviews with some key people including Dylan's mother. Eric Andersen is misspelt throughout! Everyone seems to be awake at all hours; Ratso: 'I need access to all the people on the tour.' Dylan: 'You need Ex-Lax. What have you been eating?'

Dylan's Visions of Sin, Christopher Ricks (Penguin, 2003)
A 500-page analysis of Bob Dylan's lyrics with copious footnotes and literary references. I liked it to begin with but I soon got bogged down. The university professor is too clever for his own good and ends up writing nonsense, largely because he has divided Dylan's lyrics into the seven deadly sins, the four cardinal virtues and three heavenly graces. 'Mr. Tambourine Man' comes under sloth. He likens the line about either making love or expecting rain in 'Desolation Row' to cows which, anticipating a downpour, sit down and create a dry patch.

Isis: a Bob Dylan Anthology, Edited by Derek Barker (Helter Skelter, 2001)
20 Years of Isis – Bob Dylan Anthology, Volume 2, Edited by Derek Barker (Chrome Dreams, 2005)
All manner of interviews and essays about Dylan. Tremendous, but some are ridiculous: Aidan Day studies Dylan's use of the word 'hill' for example. Both books are constantly engaging, even when you have Dylan fatigue like me.

Studio A – The Bob Dylan Reader, Edited by Benjamin Hedin (W.W. Norton & Co, 2004)
Around 40 well-chosen articles, poems and analysis about Bob Dylan with contributions from Allan Ginsberg, Clive James, Sam Shepard and Bruce Springsteen.

America over the Water, Shirley Collins (SAF, 2004)
In 1959 Shirley Collins went to America to help Alan Lomax with his field trip through America's heartland, recording many traditional songs and notable, if little-known, performers. This book is an invaluable account of how Lomax worked and is comparable to Peggy Seeger's memoir of living and working with Ewan MacColl.

Which Side Are You On? An Inside History of the Folk Music Revival in America, Dick Weissman (Continuum, 2005)
The banjo player with the Journeymen became an academic and this is a fine study of the 1960s, although there is the feeling that he is holding back.

Like a Rolling Stone: Bob Dylan At The Crossroads, Greil Marcus (Faber & Faber, 2005)
The story of an explosive year and a lot more besides.

Bob Dylan: Performing Artist, 1986–1990 & Beyond, Paul Williams (Omnibus, 2005)
A curious title but a detailed look at Dylan's albums and concerts from 1986 to 1990 and then essays on later albums. It's cobbled together from his other writings but overall it is highly impressive with some brilliant ideas of how Dylan manages his set list. It shows that you can never second guess Bob Dylan. Many first-hand accounts too as Williams, at the time of writing, had seen Dylan in concert 148 times.

The Rough Guide to Bob Dylan, Nigel Williamson (Rough Guides, Penguin, 2006)
Informative guide that is well laid out. The author is besotted by Howard Sounes' biography and I found myself thinking, 'Oh no, he's not quoting from that again!'

The Bob Dylan Encyclopedia, Michael Gray (Continuum, 2006)
£25 and 750,000 words, sewn binding and a PDF CD as an extra. It is a bargain.

Backstage Passes and Backstabbing Bastards, Al Kooper (Backbeat, updated edition 2008)
A Grade A memoir by a Grade A character. Funny, entertaining, score-settling and a fine read.

The Mammoth Book of Bob Dylan, Edited by Sean Egan (Robinson, 2011)
This is in the same series as Mammoth Books on casino games and tattoo art, but by and large this 520-page paperback works. There are many reprinted articles (Phil Sutcliffe and Blackbushe) interviews (Nat Hentoff, Craig McGregor) and analysis (Michael Gray, Mark Ellen), but a good half of the book is the editor's take on all of Bob Dylan's albums. It is wildly opinionated – 'Lily, Rosemary' is 'as dull as ditchwater' – and I don't think anyone else would say that Dylan was vain about the way he looked – but that adds to the fun: you want to respond and I suppose I have done so in this book.

Testimony, Robbie Robertson (William Heinemann, 2016)
One of the frankest rock biographies ever written and full of stories and insights into Ronnie Hawkins, Bob Dylan and the individual members of The Band. Robertson credits himself too much (he doesn't admit to many faults) but it's an utterly compelling read, bringing out the day to day side of Bob Dylan. You despair for The Band: how could a group with so much talent mess it all up with drug abuse? Surely the astonishing pile-up of crashed cars would have told them something was very wrong.

APPENDIX 1
Bob Dylan – US and UK discography

Discography

UK and US record numbers are shown until the time they switched to bar codes and who wants a list of barcodes and anyway, would I type them correctly? Also, from about 1995, CD releases often sold in different territories with the same number so UK releases are effectively European releases. Some people want to know if the vinyl is 150g or 180g, but I'm not getting out the kitchen scales.

Singles

Mixed-up Confusion / Corrina Corrina (US Columbia 42656, 1962, but soon withdrawn: released in Benelux CBS 2476; released in UK, CBS 202476, 1967) (France No. 21 in 1968)

Blowin' in the Wind / Don't Think Twice, It's All Right (US Columbia 42856, August 1963). Pressed also as a jukebox single, although it is an unlikely choice for amusement arcades.

The Times They Are A-Changin' / Honey, Just Allow Me One More Chance (UK CBS 201751, 1965) (UK No. 9)

Subterranean Homesick Blues / She Belongs to Me (US Columbia 43242; UK CBS 201753, 1965) (US No. 39; UK No. 9; France No. 23)

Maggie's Farm / On the Road Again (UK CBS 201781, 1965) (UK No. 22)

Like a Rolling Stone / Gates of Eden (US Columbia 43346; UK CBS 201811, 1965) (US No. 2; UK No. 4; France No. 5; Germany No. 13; Ireland No. 9). A 12-minute single: a special two-part Like a Rolling Stone was pressed for US jukeboxes. That way an operator can get 20 plays in an hour instead of ten.

Positively 4th Street / From a Buick 6 (US Columbia 43389; UK CBS 201824, 1965) (US No. 7; UK No. 8)

Can You Please Crawl out Your Window / Highway 61 Revisited (US Columbia 43477; UK CBS 201900, 1965) (US No. 56; UK No. 17). The underlined 'you' is clear evidence that Dylan wrote 'finger pointin' songs'.

One of Us Must Know / Queen Jane Approximately (US Columbia 43541; UK CBS 202053, 1966) (UK No. 33)

Rainy Day Women Nos. 12 & 35 / Pledging My Time (US Columbia 43592; UK CBS 202307, 1966) (US No. 2; UK No. 7)

I Want You / Just like Tom Thumb's Blues (Recorded Live in Liverpool) (US Columbia 43683; UK CBS 202258, 1966) (US No. 20; UK No. 16)

Just like a Woman / Obviously 5 Believers (US Columbia 43792, 1966) (US No. 33). Should have been a UK single.

Leopard-Skin Pillbox Hat / Most Likely You Go Your Way and I'll Go Mine (US Columbia 44069; UK CBS 2700, 1966) (US No. 81; B-side No. 66)

If You Gotta Go, Go Now / To Ramona (Benelux CBS 2921, 1967)

I Threw It All Away / Drifter's Escape (US Columbia 44826; UK CBS 4219, 1969) (US No. 85; UK No. 30; France No. 29)

Lay Lady Lay / Peggy Day (US Columbia 44926; UK CBS 4434, 1969) (US No. 7; UK No. 5; France No. 10; Ireland No. 13)

Tonight I'll Be Staying Here with You / Country Pie (UK CBS 4611, 1969)

Wigwam / Copper Kettle (US Columbia 45199; UK CBS 5122, 1970) (US No. 41; France No. 15 and on the chart for 5 months; Germany No. 33)

If Not for You / New Morning (UK CBS 7092, 1971)

Man Gave Name to All the Animals / When He Returns (UK CBS 7270, 1971) (France No. 9 in 1979 as Animals)

Watching the River Flow / Spanish Is the Loving Tongue (US Columbia 45409; UK CBS 7329, 1971) (US No. 41; UK No. 24). There are fake copies on the internet which are said to have Dylan's protest song, Friday, as the B-side – there is no such song, or at least he never wrote or recorded a song of that name.

George Jackson (acoustic and 'big band' versions) (US Columbia 45516; UK CBS 7688, 1971) (US No. 33). George Jackson had been shot to death in San Quentin in August. This was Bob Dylan's Christmas single.

Precious Angel / Trouble in Mind (UK CBS 7828, 1972). Not a US single.

Knockin' on Heaven's Door / Turkey Chase (US Columbia 45913; UK CBS 1762, 1973) (US No. 12; UK No. 14; Germany No. 50; Ireland No. 9)

Just Like a Woman / I Want You (UK CBS 1158, 1973)

A Fool Such as I / Lily of the West (US Columbia 45982; UK CBS 2006, 1974)

On a Night Like This / You Angel You (US Asylum 11033, 1974) (US No. 44)

On a Night Like This / Forever Young (UK Island WIP 6168, 1974)

It Ain't Me Babe / All Along the Watchtower (US Asylum E 45212; UK Island WIP 6215, 1974) Live recordings.

Tangled up in Blue / If You See Her, Say Hello (US Columbia 10106; UK CBS 3160, 1975) (US No. 31)

Million Dollar Bash / Tears of Rage (US Columbia 10217; UK CBS 3665, 1975)

Hurricane (Part 1) / (Full version) (US Columbia 10245; UK CBS 3878, 1975) (US No.33; UK No. 43; France No.13; Germany No. 37)

Lay Lady Lay / I Threw It All Away (UK reissue CBS 3945, 1976 and again CBS A 4595, 1984)

Mozambique / Oh Sister (US Columbia 10298; UK CBS 4113, 1976) (US No. 54; Germany No. 21)

Rita May / Stuck Inside of Mobile with the Memphis Blues again (US Columbia 10454; UK CBS 4859, 1976). Title of B-side varies on different releases.

Baby Stop Cryin' / New Pony (US Columbia 10805; UK CBS 6499, 1978) (UK No. 13; Ireland No. 5). Also available on 12-inch.

Is Your Love in Vain / We Better Talk This Over (US Columbia 6718; UK CBS 6718, 1978) (UK No. 56; Ireland No .20). Also available on 12-inch.

Changing of the Guard / Señor (US Columbia 10851; UK CBS 6935, 1978)

Forever Young / I Want You / All along the Watchtower (UK CBS 7473, 1979)

Precious Angel / Trouble in Mind (UK CBS 7828, 1979)

Man Gave Names to all the Animals / When He Returns (UK CBS 7970, 1979)

Gotta Serve Somebody / Trouble in Mind (US Columbia 11072, 1979) (US No. 24)

Gotta Serve Somebody / Gonna Change My Way of Thinking (UK CBS 8134, 1980)

Saved / Are You Ready (UK CBS 8743, 1980)

Heart of Mine / Let It Be Me (UK CBS A 1406, 1981)

Heart of Mine / The Groom's Still Waiting at the Altar (US Columbia 02510, 1981)

Lenny Bruce / Dead Man, Dead Man (UK CBS A 1460, 1981)

Union Sundown / Angels Flying Too Close to the Ground (UK CBS A 3916, 1983)

I and I / Angels Flying Too Close to the Ground (European CBS A 3904, 1983)

Jokerman / Licence to Kill (UK CBS A 4055, 1984)

Jokerman / Isis (live from *Renaldo and Clara*) (US Columbia 04425, 1984)

Highway 61 Revisited (live) / It Ain't Me Babe (live) (UK CBS A 5020, 1985)

Tight Connection to My Heart / We'd Better Talk This Over (US Columbia 38-04933; UK CBS A 6303, 1985)

When the Night Comes Falling / Dark Eyes (UK CBS A 6469, 1985). Also available on 12-inch.

Band of the Hand /B-side not Dylan (US MCA 52811; UK MCA 1076, 1986). Also available on 12-inch.

The Usual / Got My Mind Made Up (UK CBS 651148 6, 1987). Also available on 12-inch with They Killed Him. There are faulty pressings where the third track is either Drifting Too Far from Shore or Precious Memories.

Silvio / When Did You Leave Heaven (UK CBS 651 406-7, 1988). Also available on 12-inch.

Everything Is Broken / Death Is Not the End (UK CBS 655 358-7, 1989)

Everything Is Broken / Dead Man, Dead Man / I Want You (UK CBS 655 358-6, 1989). 12-inch single available with a free print.

Everything Is Broken / Where Teardrops Fall / Dead Man, Dead Man / Ugliest Girl in the World (UK CBS 655 358-2, 1989). CD single: CBS doing everything to make Everything Is Broken a hit. In the US, it only appears to have been issued as a cassette single.

Political World / Ring Them Bells (UK CBS 655 643-7, 1990)

Political World / Ring Them Bells / Silvio / All Along the Watchtower (live) (UK CBS 655 643-2, 1990). 12-inch single.

Political World / Caribbean Wind / You're a Big Girl Now / It's All Over Now, Baby Blue (live, 1965) (UK CBS 655 643-5, 1990). CD single.

It's Unbelievable / 10,000 Men (UK CBS 656 304-7, 1990). Vinyl single.

It's Unbelievable / 10,000 Men /In the Summertime / Jokerman (UK CBS 656 304-2, 1990). CD single.

Series of Dreams / Seven Curses (UK CBS 656 707-4, 1991). Vinyl.

Series of Dreams / Seven Curses / Tangled Up in Blue / Like a Rolling Stone (UK CBS 656 707-5, 1991). CD single.

Dignity (live and studio versions) / A Hard Rain's A-Gonna Fall (with Tokyo New Philharmonic Orchestra) (Europe Columbia 660 942, Europe, 1995) (UK No. 33)

Love Sick / Can't Wait (live) / Roving Gambler (live) / Blind Willie McTell (live) (Europe Columbia 665997 5, 1998) (UK No. 64)

Love Sick (Album version and Grammy Awards performance) (US Columbia XPCD 1015, 1998)

Million Miles (live) / Love Sick (Grammys) / Can't Wait (live) / Cold Irons Bound (Europe Columbia SAMPCM 7194, 1998)

Things Have Changed / Blind Willie McTell (UK Columbia 669 379 7, 2000). Wow! A vinyl single and two superlative tracks.

Things Have Changed (audio and video) / To Make You Feel My Love (live) / Hurricane (Europe Columbia 669 379 2, 2000) (UK No. 58)

Things Have Changed (live) / Cold Irons Bound (live) and four album tracks (Columbia SAMPCD 101942, 2001). Given away with *The Daily Telegraph*. A Bob Dylan record had never been in so many British households – at least until the binmen came.

Summer Days / Bye and Bye / Honest with Me / Floater (Too Much to Ask) (US Columbia, promotional CD, 2001)

All Along the Watchtower (Bob Dylan vs Funkstar De Luxe) (Club Tools 012 805 6, 2001). 'Versus' is the right term for it.

Million Miles (live) / Blowin' in the Wind (live) / Blind Willie McTell (live) (Columbia SAMPCM 11408 2, 2002). This was a CD single pressed for participating HMV stores but given away free to anyone who purchased a Bob Dylan album. Which were the non-participating HMV stores? A thoroughly daft idea.

Most Likely You Go Your Way ('Re-version' with Mark Ronson and original) / Down Along the Cove (live) (UK Columbia 88697 163192, 2007) (UK No. 51)

Dreamin' of You (Single and album version) (UK Columbia 886973 580226, 2008). More a promo than a single as Dylan gave the song away as a free download on his website.

Extended Plays

Mini-compilations from the early albums. The UK EP chart was short-lived.

Dylan (UK CBS EP 6051, 1965) (UK No. 3)

One Too Many Mornings (UK CBS EP 6070, 1966) (UK No. 8)

Mr. Tambourine Man (UK CBS EP 6078, 1966) (UK No. 4)

Albums

Bob Dylan (US Columbia 8579; UK CBS 62022, 1962) (UK No. 13, 1965)

You're No Good / Talkin' New York / In My Time of Dyin' / Man of Constant Sorrow / Fixin' to Die / Pretty Peggy-O / Highway 51 Blues / Gospel Plow / Baby, Let Me Follow You Down / The House of the Rising Sun / Freight Train Blues / Song to Woody / See that My Grave Is Kept Clean

The Freewheelin' Bob Dylan (US Columbia 8786; UK 62193, 1963) (US No. 22; UK No. 1)

Blowin' in the Wind / Girl from the North Country / Masters of War / Down the Highway / Bob Dylan's Blues / A Hard Rain's A-Gonna Fall / Don't Think Twice, It's All Right / Bob Dylan's Dream / Oxford Town / Talkin' World War III Blues / Corrina, Corrina / Honey, Just Allow Me One More Chance / I Shall Be Free

The Times They Are A-Changin' (US Columbia 8905; UK CBS 62251, 1963) (US No. 20; UK No. 4)

The Times They Are A-Changin' / Ballad of Hollis Brown / With God on Our Side / One Too Many Mornings / North Country Blues / Only a Pawn in the Game / Boots of Spanish Leather / When the Ship Comes in / The Lonesome Death of Hattie Carroll / Restless Farewell

Broadside Ballads, Vol.1 (US Broadside/Folkways BR 5301, 1963)

Dylan, listed as Blind Boy Grunt, performs John Brown, Only a Hobo and Talking Devil

Newport Broadside (US Vanguard VSD 79144, 1964)

Recorded at the Newport Folk Festival July 1963, Bob Dylan and Pete Seeger perform Ye Playboys and Playgirls and Bob Dylan and Joan Baez perform With God on Our Side.

Evening Concert at Newport, Vol.1 (US Vanguard VSD 79148, 1964)

Recorded at the Newport Folk Festival, July 1963, Bob Dylan performs Blowin' in the Wind.

We Shall Overcome (US Broadside/Folkways BR 5592, 1964)

Recorded at the Civil Rights March on Washington August 1963, Bob Dylan performs Only a Pawn in the Game.

Another Side of Bob Dylan (US Columbia 8993; UK CBS 62429, 1964) (UK No. 8)

All I Really Want To Do / Black Crow Blues / Spanish Harlem Incident / Chimes of Freedom / I Shall Be Free No.10 / To Ramona / Motorpsycho Nightmare / My Back Pages / I Don't Believe You / Ballad in Plain D / It Ain't Me Babe

Bringing It All Back Home (US Columbia 9128; UK CBS 62515, 1965) (US No. 6; UK No. 1)

Subterranean Homesick Blues / She Belongs to Me / Maggie's Farm / Love Minus Zero – No Limit / Outlaw Blues / On the Road Again / Bob Dylan's 115th Dream / Mr. Tambourine Man / Gates of Eden / It's Alright Ma (I'm Only Bleeding) / It's All Over Now, Baby Blue

Highway 61 Revisited (US Columbia 9189; UK CBS 62572, 1965) (US No. 3; UK No. 4)

Like a Rolling Stone / Tombstone Blues / It Takes a Lot to Laugh, It Takes a Train to Cry / From a Buick 6 / Ballad of a Thin Man / Queen Jane Approximately / Highway 61 Revisited / Just Like Tom Thumb's Blues / Desolation Row

Blonde on Blonde (US Columbia C2S 841; UK CBS 66012, 2LP, 1966) (US No. 9; UK No. 3)

Rainy Day Women Nos. 12 & 35 / Pledging My Time / Visions of Johanna / One of Us Must Know / I Want You / Memphis Blues Again / Leopard-Skin Pillbox Hat / Just like a Woman / Most Likely You Go Your Way and I'll Go Mine / Temporary like Achilles / Absolutely Sweet Marie / 4th Time Around / Obviously 5 Believers / Sad-eyed Lady of the Lowlands

Greatest Hits (US Columbia 9463; UK CBS 62847, 1967) (US No. 10; UK No. 6)

John Wesley Harding (US Columbia 9604; UK CBS 63252, 1968) (US No. 2; UK No. 1)

John Wesley Harding / As I Went Out One Morning / I Dreamed I Saw St Augustine / All Along the Watchtower / The Ballad of Frankie Lee and Judas Priest / Drifter's Escape / Dear Landlord / I Am a Lonesome Hobo / I Pity the Poor Immigrant / The Wicked Messenger / Down along the Cove / I'll Be Your Baby Tonight

Nashville Skyline (US Columbia 9825; UK CBS 63601, 1969) (US No. 3; UK No. 1). Also available in quadrophonic sound.

Girl from the North Country (with Johnny Cash) / Nashville Skyline Rag / To Be Alone with You / I Threw It All Away / Peggy Day / Lay Lady Lay / One More Night / Tell Me that It's Not True / Country Pie / Tonight I'll Be Staying here with You

Self Portrait (US Columbia C2X 30050; UK CBS 66250, 2LP, 1970) (US No. 4; UK No. 1)

All the Tired Horses / Alberta No.1 / I Forget More than You'll Ever Know / Days of 49 / Early Morning Rain / In Search of Little Sadie / Let It Be Me / Little Sadie / Woogie Boogie / Belle Isle / Living the Blues / Like a Rolling Stone / Copper Kettle / Gotta Travel on / Blue Moon / The Boxer / The Mighty Quinn / Take Me as I Am / Take a Message to Mary / It Hurts Me Too / Minstrel Boy / She Belongs to Me / Wigwam / Alberta No. 2

New Morning (US Columbia 30290; UK CBS 69001, 1970) (US No. 7; UK No. 1)

If Not for You / Day of the Locusts / Time Passes Slowly / Went to See the Gypsy / Winterlude / If Dogs Run Free / New Morning / Sign on the Window / One More Weekend / The Man in Me / Three Angels / Father of Night

Greatest Hits, Vol. 2 (US Columbia 31120; UK CBS 67238/9, 2LP, 1971) (US No. 14; UK No. 12)

Includes new tracks Watching the River Flow / Tomorrow is a Long Time / When I Paint My Masterpiece / I Shall Be Released / You Ain't Goin' Nowhere / Down in the Flood

Broadside Reunion (US Broadside/Folkways BR 5315, 1971)

Dylan, again credited as Blind Boy Grunt with Train A-Travellin', Dreadful Day, The Ballad of Emmett Till, The Ballad of Donald White.

The Concert for Bangla Desh (US Apple STCX 3385; UK Apple STCX 3385, 1971) (US No. 2)

Dylan performs A Hard Rain's A-Gonna Fall, It Takes a Lot to Laugh, It Takes a Train to Cry, Blowin' in the Wind, Mr. Tambourine Man, Just Like a Woman.

A Tribute to Woody Guthrie, Part 1 (US Columbia KC 31171, 1972)

Recorded at the Woody Guthrie Memorial Concert in New York, January 1968, Dylan performs I Ain't Got No Home, Dear Mrs Roosevelt and Grand Coulee Dam. The second volume from the second concert didn't feature Dylan and was issued in the US on Warner 2W 3007. Totally daft not to have the concerts as a double-album on one label: even crazier not to release them in the UK, though many shops had them on import.

Pat Garrett and Billy the Kid (US Columbia 32460; UK CBS 69042, 1973) (US No. 16; UK No. 29)

Main Title Theme / Cantina Theme / Billy 1 / Bunkhouse Theme / River Theme / Turkey Chase / Knockin' on Heaven's Door / Final Theme / Billy 4 / Billy 7

Dylan (US Columbia 32747; UK CBS 32286, 1973) (US No. 17)

Lily of the West / Can't Help Falling in Love / Sarah Jane / The Ballad of Ira Hayes / Mr. Bojangles / Mary Ann / Big Yellow Taxi / A Fool Such As I / Spanish Is the Loving Tongue

Planet Waves (US Asylum 7E 1003; UK Island ILPS 9261, 1974) (US No. 1 for 4 weeks; UK No. 7). Also issued in quadrophonic.

On A Night Like This / Going Going Gone / Tough Mama / Hazel / Something There Is About You / Forever Young (two versions) / Dirge / You Angel You / Never Say Goodbye / Wedding Song

Before the Flood (US Asylum AB 201; UK Asylum IDBD 1, 2LP, 1974) (US No. 3; UK No. 8). Live double-album with the Band.

Blood on the Tracks (US Columbia 33235; UK CBS 69097, 1975) (US No. 1 for one week; UK No. 4)

Tangled Up in Blue / Simple Twist of Fate / You're a Big Girl Now / Idiot Wind / You're Gonna Make Me Lonesome When You Go / Meet Me in the Morning / Lily, Rosemary and the Jack of Hearts / If You See Her, Say Hello / Shelter from the Storm, / Buckets of Rain.

The Basement Tapes (US Columbia C2 33682; UK CBS 88147, 2LP, 1975) (US No. 7; UK No. 8)

Odds and Ends / Orange Juice Blues / Million Dollar Bash / Yazoo Street Scandal / Goin' to Acapulco / Katie's Been Gone / Lo and Behold / Bessie Smith / Clothes Line Saga / Apple Suckling Tree / Please Mrs. Henry / Tears of Rage / Too Much of Nothing / Yea! Heavy and a Bottle of Bread / Ain't No More Cane / Crash on the Levee (Down in the Flood) / Ruben Remus / Tiny Montgomery / You Ain't Goin' Nowhere / Don't Ya Tell Henry / Nothing Was Delivered / Open the Door, Homer / Long Distance Operator / This Wheel's on Fire

Robbie Robertson chose material and arranged overdubs – why were they needed? Cover taken in YMCA in Los Angeles. Some tracks are not Dylan as referred to earlier.

Desire (US Columbia 33893; UK CBS 86003, 1975) (US No. 1 for five weeks; UK No. 3). Also available in quadrophonic.

Hurricane / Isis / Mozambique / One More Cup of Coffee / Oh, Sister / Joey / Romance in Durango / Black Diamond Bay / Sara

Hard Rain (US Columbia 34349; UK CBS 86016, 1976) (US No. 17; UK No. 3)

Live Dylan recordings from the Rolling Thunder Revue.

Masterpieces (Japan CBS/Sony 57 AP – 875/7, 3LP, 1978)

Special 39-track compilation for Japanese and Australian dates. Includes several lesser-known items like 'Mixed-up Confusion' and 'Rita May'.

Street-Legal (US Columbia 35453; UK CBS 86067, 1978) (US No. 11; UK No. 2)

Changing of the Guard / New Pony / No Time to Think / Baby Stop Cryin' / Is Your Love in Vain / Señor (Tales of Yankee Power) / True Love Tends to Forget / We Better Talk This Over / Where Are You Tonight (Journey through Dark Heat)

Bob Dylan at Budokan (US Columbia PC2 36067; UK CBS 96004, 2LP, 1978) (US No. 13; UK No. 4)

Intended as a souvenir of the Japanese concerts, it became so popular that it had worldwide release. Since then, several major acts have released Budokan albums including Bryan Adams, Cheap Trick, Eric Clapton, Duran Duran, Kiss, Ozzy Osbourne and Iggy Pop.

The Last Waltz (Warner, 3LP, 1978)

The Band's farewell concert in San Francisco has been issued in many forms – Dylan's set, issued in full on the 4CD box in 2002, was Baby Let Me Follow You Down, I Don't Believe You, Hazel, Forever Young and I Shall Be Released.

Slow Train Coming (US Columbia 36120; UK CBS 86095, 1979) (US No. 3; UK No. 2)

Gotta Serve Somebody / Precious Angel / I Believe in You / Slow Train / Gonna Change My Way of Thinking / Do Right to Me Baby / When You Gonna Wake Up / Man Gave Names to All the Animals / When He Returns

Saved (US Columbia 37496; UK CBS 86113, 1980) (US No. 24; UK No. 3)

A Satisfied Mind / Saved / Covenant Woman / What Can I Do for You / Solid Rock / Pressing on / In the Garden / Saving Grace / Are You Ready

Shot of Love (US Columbia 37496; UK CBS 85178, 1981) (US No. 33; UK No. 6)

Shot of Love / Heart of Mine / Property of Jesus / Lenny Bruce / Watered-down Love / Dead Man, Dead Man / In the Summertime / Trouble / Every Grain of Sand

Infidels (US Columbia 38819; UK CBS 25529, 1983) (US No. 20; UK No. 9)

Jokerman / Sweetheart like You / Neighbourhood Bully / Licence to Kill / Man of Peace / Union Sundown / I and I / Don't Fall Apart on Me Tonight

Real Live (US Columbia 39944; US CBS 26334, 1984) (UK No. 54)

Empire Burlesque (US Columbia 40110; UK CBS 86313, 1985) (US No. 33; UK No. 11)

Tight Connection to My Heart / Seeing the Real You at Last / I'll Remember You / Clean Cut Kid / Never Gonna Be the Same Again / Trust Yourself / Emotionally Yours / When the Night Comes Falling from the Sky / Something's Burning, Baby / Dark Eyes

Biograph (UK Columbia C5X 38830; UK CBS 66509, 5LP, 1985) (US No. 33)

Major retrospective issued with Dylan's cooperation. Previously unreleased tracks: I'll Keep It with Mine / Percy's Song / Jet Pilot / Lay Down Your Weary Tune / Abandoned Love / Caribbean Wind / Up to Me / Baby, I'm in the Mood for You / I Wanna Be Your Lover plus several alternative versions.

Knocked Out Loaded (US Columbia 40439; UK CBS 86326, 1986) (UK No. 35)

You Wanna Ramble / They Killed Him / Driftin' Too Far From Shore / Precious Memories / Maybe Someday / Brownsville Girl / Got My Mind Made Up / Under Your Spell

Hearts of Fire – Soundtrack (US Columbia SC 40870; UK CBS 460001 1, 1987)

Dylan performs The Usual, Night After Night and Had a Dream about You Baby.

Greatest Hits, Vol.3 (US Columbia CK 66783; UK CBS 4609071, 1988) (UK No. 47)

Down in the Groove (US Columbia 40957; UK CBS 4602671, 1988) (UK No. 32)

When Did You Leave Heaven / Sally Sue Brown / Death Is Not The End / Had a Dream about You Baby / Ugliest Girl in the World / Silvio / Ninety Miles an Hour / Shenandoah / Rank Strangers to Me

Dylan and the Dead (US Columbia 45056; UK CBS 4633811, 1989) (US No. 37; UK No. 38)

Hated in equal measure by Dylan and the Dead fans but generally okay and some unusual choices – Joey, Queen Jane Approximately.

Oh Mercy (US Columbia 45281; UK CBS 4658002, 1989) (US No. 30; UK No. 6)

Political World / Where Teardrops Fall / Everything Is Broken / Ring Them Bells / Man in the Long Black Coat / Most of the Time / What Good Am I / Disease of Conceit / What Was It You Wanted / Shooting Star

Under the Red Sky (US Columbia 46794; UK CBS 4671882, 1990) (US No. 38; UK No. 13)

Wiggle Wiggle / Under the Red Sky / Unbelievable / Born in Time / TV Talking Song / 10,000 Men / 2 x 2 / God Knows / Handy Dandy / Cat's in the Well

The Bootleg Series, Vol. 1-3 (Columbia 4680861, 3CD, 1991) (US No. 49; UK No. 32)

Superb 3CD set of unreleased material and alternative takes, 58 tracks in all and the CDs were not available separately. Dylan gave a very low-key interview about the set but I suspect Dylan was just being Dylan and he could appreciate that this was the way to go with his large catalogue of outtakes. Despite the low chart placing, the box-set went gold in the US.

Good as I Been To You (US Columbia C 53200; UK Columbia 4727102, 1992) (UK No. 18)

Frankie and Albert / Jim Jones / Blackjack Davy / Canadee-i-o / Sittin' on Top of the World / Little Maggie / Hard Times / Step it Up and Go / Tomorrow Night / Arthur McBride / You're Gonna Quit Me / Diamond Joe / Froggie Went A-Courtin'

World Gone Wrong (UK Columbia 4748572, 1993) (UK No. 35)

World Gone Wrong / Love Henry / Ragged and Dirty / Blood in My Eyes / Broke Down Engine / Delia / Stack A Lee / Two Soldiers / Jack-a-roe / Lone Pilgrim

The 30th Anniversary Concert Celebration (Columbia 474000 2, 2CD, 1993) (US No. 40) Dylan's only solo Girl of the North Country (sic).

Unplugged (UK Columbia 4783742, 1995) (US No. 23; UK No.10) Live album for MTV including John Brown and Dignity.

The Best of Bob Dylan (UK Columbia SONYTV 28CD, 1997) (UK No. 6)

Time Out of Mind (UK Columbia 4869362, 1997) (US No.10; UK No. 10)

Love Sick / Dirt Road Blues / Standing in the Doorway / Million Miles / Tryin' to Get to Heaven / 'Til I Fell in Love with You / Not Dark Yet / Cold Irons Bound / Make You Feel My Love / Can't Wait / Highlands

The Bootleg Series Vol. 4 Bob Dylan Live 1966 The 'Royal Albert Hall' Concert (UK Columbia Legacy 491485 2, 2 CD, 1998) (US No. 31; UK No. 19). The first box featured 3CDs and was labelled Vol. 1–3, so why wasn't this Vol. 4–5?

The Best of Bob Dylan, Vol.2 (UK Columbia Legacy 4983612, 2000) (UK No. 22). Entering the era of endless compilations from major acts.

The Essential Bob Dylan (UK Columbia STVCD 116, 2001) (UK No. 9)

Love and Theft (UK Columbia 504364 9, 2001) (US No.5; UK No. 3)

Tweedle Dee and Tweedle Dum / Mississippi / Summer Days / Bye and Bye / Lonesome Day Blues / Floater (Too much to ask) / High Water (for Charley Patton) / Moonlight / Honest with Me / Po' Boy / Cry a While / Sugar Baby

Initially issued with bonus CD of I Was Young When I Left Home (1961) and alternative version of The Times They Are A-Changin' (1963).

The Bootleg Series Vol. 5 Bob Dylan Live 1975 – The Rolling Thunder Revue (Columbia 5101403, 2CD, 2002) (US No. 56; UK No. 69) This edition of the bootleg series meant little but when the Rolling Thunder shows were issued in a 14 CD set in 2019 accompanied by a Netflix film, the interest in the tour increased dramatically.)

Kindred Spirits: A Tribute to the Songs of Johnny Cash (Lucky Day 509711 2, 2002) Dylan performs Train of Love.

The Classic Interviews 1965-6 (UK Chrome Dreams CIS 2004, 2003)

The Classic Interviews, Vol. 2 The Weberman Tapes (UK Chrome Dreams CIS 2005, 2004)

The Bootleg Series, Vol. 6 Live 1964 Concert at Philharmonic Hall (Columbia 5123582, 2CD, 2004) (UK No. 33)

Masked and Anonymous (Columbia COL 512556 2, 2003)

Bob Dylan performed Down in the Flood / Diamond Joe / Dixie / Cold Irons Bound. The CD came with a 7-track sampler for the Bob Dylan reissues. My copy say that it is CD-compatible for Super Audio CD Players. Well, that's one invention I never saw.

Gods and Generals soundtrack (Sony Classical, 2003)

Dylan performs Cross the Green Mountain. *The Bootleg Series Vol. 7 No Direction Home, The Soundtrack* (Columbia Legacy 520358 2, 2CD, 2005) (US No. 16; UK No. 21) Alternative takes and live versions to accompany the Martin Scorsese documentary.

Live at the Gaslight, 1962 (US Starbucks, 2005)

A Hard Rain's A-Gonna Fall / Rocks and Gravel / Don't Think Twice, It's All Right / The Cuckoo / Moonshiner / Handsome Molly / Cocaine / John Brown / Barbara Allen / West Texas

It's appropriate that a coffee chain should release something that relates back to the coffee houses in Greenwich Village. Some thought it represented corporate exploitation. Recorded between his first two albums. Early version of Don't Think Twice. Rocks and Gravel based on Brownie McGhee's Solid Road. Barbara Allen lasts eight minutes but West Texas is incomplete.

Omitted but around: Hezekiah Jones, No More Auction Block, Motherless Children, Ballad of Hollis Brown, Kind-hearted Woman Blues, See that My Grave Is Kept Clean and Ain't No More Cane.

Modern Times (Columbia 82876 883062, 2006) (US No. 1; UK No. 3)

Thunder on the Mountain / Spirit on the Water / Rollin' and Tumblin' / When the Deal Goes Down / Someday Baby / Workingman's Blues No. 2 / Beyond the Horizon / Nettie Moore / The Levee's Gonna Break / Ain't Talkin'

Initially issued with bonus DVD of Blood in My Eyes / Love Sick / Things Have Changed / Cold Irons Bound

Dylan (US compilation for Barnes and Noble only, 2006)

The Bootleg Series Vol.8 Tell Tale Signs Rare and Unreleased 1989-2006 (Columbia Legacy 88697 34747 2, single CD and 2CD versions, 2008) (US No. 6; UK No. 9)

Largely live versions of previously released songs. Ratso supplies liner notes.

Together Through Life (Columbia 88697 438932, 2009) (US No. 1; UK No. 1)

Beyond Here Lies Nothin' / Life Is Hard / My Wife's Home Town / If You Ever Go to Houston / Forgetful Heart / Jolene / This Dream of You / Shake Shake Mama / I Feel a Change Comin' On / It's All Good

Christmas in the Heart (Columbia 88697 573232, 2009) (US No. 23; UK No. 40)

Here Comes Santa Claus / Do You Hear What I Hear / Winter Wonderland / Hark, the Herald Angels Sing / I'll Be Home for Christmas / Little Drummer Boy / The Christmas Blues / O Come All Ye Faithful / Have Yourself a Merry Little Christmas / Must Be Santa / Silver Bells / The First Noel / Christmas Island / The Christmas Song / O Little Town of Bethlehem

The Bootleg Series Vol. 9 The Witmark Demos: 1962-4 (Columbia Legacy 88697 761792, 2CD, 2010) (US No. 12; UK No. 18)

Publisher's demos from Blowin' in the Wind in the summer of 1962 to Percy's Song in 1964. In all, 41 demos.

Tempest (Columbia 88725 457602, 2012) (US No. 3; UK No. 3)

Duquesne Whistle / Soon After Midnight / Narrow Way / Long and Wasted Years / Pay in Blood / Scarlet Town / Early Roman Kings / Tin Angel / Tempest / Roll on John

The Bootleg Series Vol. 10 Another Self Portrait, 1969-71 (Columbia Legacy 88883 73487 2, 2CD, 2013) (US No. 21; UK No. 5)

Shadows in the Night (Columbia 88875 057962, 2015) (US No. 7; UK No. 1)

I'm a Fool to Want You / The Night We Called It a Day / Stay with Me / Autumn Leaves / Why Try to Change Me now / Some Enchanted Evening / Full Moon and Empty Arms / Where Are You / What'll I Do / That Lucky Old Sun

The Bootleg Series Vol 11 Bob Dylan and the Band – The Basement Tapes Complete (Sony, 2CD and 6CD versions, 2014) (US No. 41; UK No. 17)

The Bootleg Series Vol 12 1965-6 The Best of The Cutting Edge (Columbia Legacy 88875124422, 2CD, 6CD & 18CD versions, 2015). Available in 2CD, 6CD and (get this) 18CD editions. (US No. 33; UK No. 12)

Dylan, Cash and the Nashville Cats: A New Music City (Country Music Hall of Fame, 2CD, 2015)

Despite the clumsy title, this is a tremendous 36-track compilation showing how country music was transformed by Bob Dylan and others. Dylan has four tracks including a previously unissued take of 'If Not For You'.

Fallen Angels (Columbia, 2016) (US No. 7: UK No. 5)

Young at Heart / Maybe You'll Be There / Polka Dots and Moonbeams / All the Way / Skylark / Nevertheless / All or Nothing at all / On a Little Street in Singapore / It Had to be You / Melancholy Mood / That Old Black Magic / Come Rain or Come Shine

The 1966 Live Recordings (Sony 36 CD, 2016) (36 CD set). Retailing around £80, Yes, you read that right.

The Real Royal Albert Hall 1966 Concert (Sony 2CD, 2016) (UK No. 60)

The Bootleg Series, Vol.13 1979-81 Trouble No More (Sony, 2CD, 9CD and 11 CD versions, 2017) (US No. 49; UK No. 21)

Triplicate (Columbia 3CD, Sony, 2017) (US No. 37; UK No. 17)

CD1 *'Til the Sun Goes Down* I Guess I'll Have to Change My Plans / The September of My Years / I Could Have Told You / Once Upon a Time / Stormy Weather / This Nearly Was Mine / That Old Feeling / It Gets Lonely Early / My One and Only Love / Trade Winds

CD2 *Devil Dolls* Braggin' / As Time Goes By / Imagination / How Deep is the Ocean / P.S. I Love You / The Best Is Yet to Come / But Beautiful / Here's That Rainy Day / Where Is the One / There's a Flaw in My Flue

CD3 *Comin' Home Late* Day in, Day Out / I Couldn't Sleep a Wink Last Night / Sentimental Journey / Somewhere Along the Way / When the World Was Young / These Foolish Things / You Go to My Head / Stardust / It's Funny to Everyone but Me / Why Was I Born

*The Bootleg Series, Vol. 14 More Blood, More Tracks (*Sony, 2018*)*. Single CD and 6CD versions, retailing at £104.

The Rolling Thunder Revue: The 1975 Live Recordings (Sony, 2019). 14CD set, also in vinyl. Only available in a 14CD edition: everybody's a collector now.

The Bootleg Series, Vol.15, 1967-1969, Travelin' Thru (Sony, 2019) 3CD set

CD1: Alternative takes from *John Wesley Harding* and *Nashville Skyline* songs. One previously unheard track, Western Shore.

CD2 and part of CD3: The informal Bob Dylan and Johnny Cash sessions from February 1969.

Rest of CD3: Bob Dylan on *The Johnny Cash Show*: Ring Of Fire and Folsom Prison Blues from *Self Portrait* sessions; Dylan with Earl Scruggs family band – East Virginia Blues / To Be Alone With You / Honey, Just Allow Me One More Chance / Nashville Skyline Rag

Rough and Rowdy Ways (Columbia, 2CD, 2020)
I Contain Multitudes / False Prophet / Murder Most Foul and seven others.

As part of the Traveling Wilburys
Singles

This is a magnificent example of marketing going mad. If Warner had just handled this conventionally, they would have had major hits. I doubt if Ann Summers catered for so many sizes. If they'd thought it through, we could have had customers going into an HMV and being told, 'Right, sir, 'Handle With Care': would you prefer it on vinyl or CD? If it's vinyl then you have a choice of 7 inch, 10 inch or 12 inch. We have postcards and stickers as bonuses if you're interested, but perhaps you would prefer the gatefold sleeve. If you want it on CD, we can give it you on 3 inch or 5 inch and if you say 3 inch, we can give you an adapter. What about the print, sir, do you like it silver or gold, and take your pick, should the title be Handle With Care or Handle Me With Care? You'll have the lot? Well, thank you, sir, that'll be £50.'

In the same way, the US was developing innumerable charts so almost any act could say that they had a US hit somewhere. 'Handle With Care' and 'End Of The Line' did well on the US Main (that is, mainstream rock) and the US AC (adult contemporary) charts.

Handle With Care / Margarita (US Wilbury 07599 277327; UK Wilbury W 7732, 1988) (US No. 45; UK No. 21) Marketing like Dylan had never had – a 7 inch single with a gatefold picture sleeve: some with stickers, a 10 inch, a 12 inch and believe it or not, a 3 inch CD but with a 5 inch adapter. They had a brilliant single so cut the razzamatazz, market it conventionally and bingo, No. 1.

End Of The Line / Congratulations (US Wilbury 07599 727637; UK Wilbury W 7637, 1989) (US No. 63; UK No. 52) This time a 7 inch single, a 12 inch single with stickers and a 3 inch CD without the adapter as presumably you already had one from buying the first single. Also, why are the UK catalogue numbers going backwards?)

Nobody's Child / (Dave Stewart) Lumière (UK Wilbury W 9773, 1990) (UK No. 44) (Only available as 12 inch and CD, and the CD had a bonus track of Ringo Starr singing With A Little Help From My Friends)

She's My Baby / New Blue Moon (instrumental) (UK Wilbury W 9523, 1990) (Available as 7 inch, 12 inch and CD) (UK No. 79)

Wilbury Twist / New Blue Moon (instrumental) (UK Wilbury W 0019, 1991) (Available as 7 inch, 7 inch with postcards, 12 inch and CD in either silver or black print)

Albums

The Traveling Wilburys (US Wilbury 25796; UK Wilbury WX 224W, 1988) (Available on vinyl and CD and cassette) (US No. 3; UK No. 16; Canada No. 1)

Handle With Care / Dirty World / Rattled / Last Night / Not Alone Any More / Congratulations / Heading For The Light / Margarita / Tweeter And The Monkey Man / End Of the Line

Dylan is Lucky Wilbury.

The Traveling Wilburys, Volume 3 (US Wilbury 26324; UK Wilbury WX 77992 324 2, 1990) (US No. 11; UK No. 14)

She's My Baby / Inside Out / If You Belonged To Me / The Devil's Been Busy / Seven Deadly Sins / Poor House / Where Were You Last Night / Cool Dry Place / New Blue Moon / You Took My Breath Away / Wilbury Twist

Dylan is now calling himself Boo Wilbury, the first name presumably relating to the recluse in Harper Lee's novel, To Kill A Mockingbird.

The Traveling Wilburys Collection (UK Rhino 8122 79982 4, 2CD & DVD, 2007) (US No. 9: UK No. 1, so the albums sold better on reissue). As well as the standard edition: there were boxed editions on CD and vinyl with a lavish book.

The two albums plus Maxine, Like A Ship, Nobody's Child & Runaway. Five videos plus 25-minute documentary, The True History of the Traveling Wilburys.

Oh, bootlegs! I've got the first album with nine extra tracks, either extended versions or the original run-throughs and I've also got *Unreleased Treasures* which includes 'Stormy Weather (with comments from Olivia about George's great guitar playing) and Fish And Chips.

Guest Appearances

A few surprises here, most notably that Dylan has a few guest appearances when he was starting out, then there's a break until the early 70s and then he starts and stops again. His work with The Band has been omitted here to avoid repetition.

Harry Belafonte – *Midnight Special* (US RCA LSP 2449, 1961)

Recorded Autumn 1961, Dylan plays harmonica.

Carolyn Hester (US Columbia CL 1796, 1962)

Recorded September 1961, Dylan plays harmonica on Come Back Baby, Swing and Turn Jubilee and I'll Fly Away.

Big Joe Williams, Roosevelt Sykes, Lonnie Johnson and Victoria Spivey – *Three Kings and the Queen* (US Spivey LP 1004, 1964). More from this session is on *Three Kings and the Queen, Vol. 2* (US Spivey LP 1014, 1972).

Recorded October 1961, Dylan sings backing vocals and plays harmonica behind Big Joe Williams on Sittin' on Top of the World and also plays harmonica on Wichita.

Dick Farina and Eric Von Schmidt (Folklore F-LEUT 7, 1967)

Recorded in London January 1963, Dylan sings backing vocals and plays harmonica on six tracks.

Dave Van Rock, John Koerner and others – *The Blues Project* (US Elektra EKS 7264, 1964)

Recorded 1963, Dylan as Bob Landy plays piano on Downtown Blues.

Jack Elliott (US Vanguard VSD 79151, 1964)

Recorded 1963, Dylan as Tedham Porterhouse plays harmonica on Will the Circle Be Unbroken.

Earl Scruggs: His Family and Friends (US Columbia KC 30584, 1971)

One of Earl Scruggs' friends, Bob Dylan plays acoustic guitar on his own Nashville Skyline Rag.

The Dial-a-Poem Poets – Disconnected (Giorno Poetry Systems GPS 003, 1974)

Recorded November 1971, Dylan plays guitar for Allen Ginsberg's Jimmy Berman (Gay Lib Rag). Two more tracks with Ginsberg, Vomit Express and Going to San Diego were issued on *First Blues*. (John Hammond Records W2X 37673, 1973)

Steve Goodman – Somebody Else's Troubles (US Buddah BDS 5121, 1972)

Dylan as Robert Milkwood Thomas sings backing vocals and plays guitar on the title track.

Steve Goodman – Election Year Rag (US single, Buddah BDS 326, 1972)

Dylan on piano.

Roger McGuinn (US Columbia KC 31946, 1972)

Dylan plays harmonica on I'm So Restless.

Doug Sahm & Band (US Atlantic SD 7254, 1972)

Dylan at his busiest receives credit for vocals, harmonies, guitar, Hammond organ and Vox organ. He shares vocals with Doug on Is Anybody Goin' to San Antone and Wallflower, takes a guitar solo on Blues Stay Away from Me and plays harmonica on Me and Paul.

Booker T Jones and Priscilla Coolidge – Chronicles (US A&M ST 4413, 1973)

Dylan plays harmonica on Crippled Crow.

Barry Goldberg (US Atco SD 7040, 1974)

Dylan sings backing vocals and also plays percussion on It's Not the Spotlight. Dylan co-produced the album.

David Blue – *Comin' Back for More* (US Asylum 7E 1043, 1975)

Dylan plays harmonica on Who Love.

Bette Midler – *Songs for the New Depression* (US Atlantic SD 18155, 1976) – great title!

Dylan and Midler sing Buckets of Rain together.

Eric Clapton – *No Reason to Cry* (US RSO RS 1 3004, 1976)

Dylan sings his own Sign Language with Clapton.

Leonard Cohen – *Death of a Ladies Man* (US Warner BS 3125, 1977)

Dylan part of the backing choir on Don't Go Home with Your Hard-On. Indeed!

Keith Green – *So You Wanna Go Back to Egypt* (US Pretty Good PGR 1, 1980)

Dylan plays harmonica on Pledge My Head to Heaven.

USA for Africa – *We Are the World* (Columbia, 1985)

Dylan is one of the vocalists. Bob Elton: 'You know who Bob Dylan is. He's the one who can't sing on the We Are the World video.'

Sly and Robbie – *Language Barrier* (Island, 1985)

Dylan plays harmonica on No Name on the Bullet.

Artists United Against Apartheid – Sun City (Manhattan, 1985)

Dylan sings on two versions of the song.

The Factory – Warren Zevon (1987)

Dylan plays harmonica, the only time they recorded together.

The Songs of Jimmie Rodgers – A Tribute (Columbia, 1997)

Dylan, produced by Daniel Lanois, performs 'My Blue Eyed Jane', perhaps the best of his one-off recordings. Bob Dylan wrote the introductory note in the CD booklet, saying that Jimmie Rodgers was "the man who started it all".

Good Rockin' Tonight – The Legacy of Sun Records (Sire, 1999)

Bob having fun with the rockabilly Red Cadillac And A Black Moustache, originally recorded by Bob Luman for Imperial and Warren Smith for Sun, both in 1957.

Gonna Change My Way of Thinking – Bob Dylan and Mavis Staples (2003)

Dylan took a 1979 song and rewrote it as a duet with Mavis Staples.

Enjoy Every Sandwich –The Songs of Warren Zevon (Artemis, 2004)

Badly recorded live version of Mutineer recorded in Australia. The song is fine for him but why didn't he go into a studio? Dylan sings, 'I was born to rock the boat, Some may sink but we might float'.

A New Music City – Dylan, Cash & The Nashville Cats (Country Music Hall of Fame, 2CD, 2015)

Four Dylan tracks including a beautiful outtake of If Not For You with pedal steel and violin.

Timeless – Alternative Versions of Classic Hank Williams Tracks (Lost Highway, 2011)

Country and western swing mix of I Can't Get You Off Of My Mind.

APPENDIX 2
The Band – US and UK discography

Curious fact: no Top 10 singles for The Band either in the US or the UK.

Singles

The Weight / I Shall Be Released (US Capitol 2269; UK Capitol CL 15559, 1968) (US No. 63; UK No. 21)

Up on Cripple Creek / The Night They Drove Old Dixie Down (US Capitol 2635; UK Capitol CL 15613, 1969) (US No. 25)

Rag Mama Rag / The Unfaithful Servant (US Capitol 2705; UK Capitol CL 15629, 1970) (US No. 57; UK No. 16)

Time to Kill / The Shape I'm In (US Capitol 2870, 1970) (US No. 77)

Time to Kill / Sleeping (UK Capitol CL 15659, 1970)

The Shape I'm In / The Rumour (UK Capitol CL 15675, 1970)

Interesting move here as clearly UK Capitol thought The Shape I'm In deserved to be an A-side but they couldn't get it into the charts.

Life Is a Carnival / The Moon Struck One (US Capitol 3199; UK Capitol CL 15700, 1971) (US No. 72)

When I Paint My Masterpiece / Where Do We Go from Here (US Capitol 3249, 1971)

Don't Do It / Rag Mama Rag (US Capitol 3433, UK Capitol 15737, 1972) (US No. 34)

Hang Up My Rock'n'Roll Shoes / Caledonia Mission (US Capitol 3500, 1972)

Ain't Got No Home / Get Up Jake (US Capitol 3758; UK Capitol CL 15767, 1973) (US No. 73)

Third Man Theme / The W.S. Walcott Medicine Show (US Capitol 3828, 1974)

Ophelia / Hobo Jungle (US Capitol 4230, 1976) (US No. 62)

Twilight / Acadian Driftwood (US Capitol 4316, 1976)

Ring Your Bell / Forbidden Fruit (UK Capitol CL 15861, 1976)

Twilight / The Weight (UK Capitol CL 15887, 1976)

Georgia on My Mind / The Night They Drove Old Dixie Down (US Capitol 4361, 1976)

Georgia on My Mind / Right as Rain (UK Capitol Cl 15921, 1977)

Out of the Blue / The Well (US Warner 8592, 1978)

Out of the Blue / The Last Waltz (UK Warner 17187, 1978)

Rag Mama Rag / The Weight (UK EMI Gold 4528, 1984)

Albums

Music from Big Pink (US Capitol 2955; UK Capitol ST 2955, 1968) (US No. 30)

Tears of Rage / To Kingdom Come / In a Station / Caledonia Mission / The Weight / We Can Talk / Long Black Veil / Chest Fever / Lonesome Suzie / This Wheel's on Fire / I Shall be Released

2000 reissue adds Yazoo Street Scandal / Katie's Been Gone / If I Lose / Long Distance Operator / Orange Juice Blues / Key to the Highway / Ferdinand the Imposter and two alternative takes.

The Band (US Capitol 132; UK Capitol EST 132, 1969) (US No. 9; UK No. 25)

Across the Great Divide / Rag Mama Rag / The Night They Drove Old Dixie Down / When You Awake / Up on Cripple Creek / Whispering Pines / Jemima Surrender / Rockin' Chair / Look Out Cleveland / Jawbone / The Unfaithful Servant / King Harvest (has surely come)

2000 reissue adds Get Up Jake and six alternative performances or mixes.

Stage Fright (US Capitol 425; UK Capitol EASW 425, 1970) (US No. 5; UK No. 15)

Strawberry Wine / Sleeping / Time to Kill / Just Another Whistle Stop / All La Glory / The Shape I'm In / The W.S. Walcott Medicine Show / Daniel and the Sacred Harp / Stage Fright / The Rumour

2000 reissue adds three alternate takes and mixes and a radio commercial.

Cahoots (US Capitol 651; UK Capitol EAST 651, 1971) (US No. 21; UK No. 41)

Life Is a Carnival / When I Paint My Masterpiece / Last of the Blacksmiths / Where Do We Go From Here / 4% Pantomime (with Van Morrison) / Shout Out in Chinatown / The Moon Struck One / Thinkin' Out Loud / Smoke Signal / Volcano / The River Hymn

2000 reissue adds Endless Highway / Bessie Smith, plus two alternative takes and a radio commercial.

Rock of Ages (US Capitol 11045; UK Capitol ESTS 111, 2LP, 1972) (US No. 6)

Live versions of album tracks plus Don't Do It, The Genetic Method and Hang Up My Rock'n'Roll Shoes. Subsequent reissues add Loving You Is Sweeter than Ever and songs with Bob Dylan. In 2013, expanded and reissued as *Live at the Academy of Music 1971*.

Moondog Matinee (US Capitol 11214; UK Capitol CZ 407, 1973) (US No. 28)

Ain't Got No Home / Holy Cow / Share Your Love with Me / Mystery Train / The Third Man Theme / Promised Land / The Great Pretender / I'm Ready / Saved / A Change Is Gonna Come

2001 reissue adds Didn't It Rain / Crying Heart Blues / Shakin' / What Am I Living For / Going Back to Memphis / Endless Highway

Planet Waves (US Asylum 1003; UK Island ILPS 9261, 1974) (US No. 1 for four weeks; UK No. 7) with Bob Dylan.

Before the Flood (US Asylum 201; UK Asylum IDBD 1, 2LP, 1974) (US No. 3; UK No. 8) with Bob Dylan.

The Basement Tapes (US Columbia 33682; UK CBS 88147, 2LP, 1975) (US No. 7; UK No. 8) with Bob Dylan.

Northern Lights – Southern Cross (US Capitol 11440; UK Capitol CZ 404, 1975) (US No. 26)

Forbidden Fruit / Hobo Jungle / Ophelia / Acadian Driftwood / Ring Your Bell / It Makes No Difference / Jupiter Hollow / Rags and Bones

2001 reissue adds Twilight and Christmas Must Be Tonight.

Islands (US Capitol SD 11602, 1977)

Right as Rain / Street Walker / Let the Night Fall / Ain't That a Lot of Love / Christmas Must Be Tonight / Islands / The Saga of Pepote Rouge / Georgia on My Mind / Knockin' Lost John / Livin' in a Dream

2001 reissue has an alternative Georgia on My Mind.

The Last Waltz (US Warner 3146; UK Warner K 66076, 3LP, 1978) (US No. 16)

Theme from The Last Waltz / Up on Cripple Creek / Stage Fright / It Makes No Difference / The Night They Drove Old Dixie Down / The Shape I'm In / Down South in New Orleans/ Ophelia / Life Is a Carnival /The Well / Evangeline / Out of the Blue / The Last Waltz Refrain

Guest performers: Who Do You Love (Ronnie Hawkins) / Helpless (Neil Young) / Coyote (Joni Mitchell) / Dry Your Eyes (Neil Diamond) / Mystery Train (Paul Butterfield) / Such a Night (Dr. John) / Mannish Boy (Muddy Waters) / Further on up the Road (Eric Clapton) / Tura Lura Lura and Caravan (Van Morrison) / The Weight (Staple Singers) / Baby Let Me Follow You Down / I Don't Believe You and Forever Young (Bob Dylan) / I Shall Be Released (Everyone above plus Ringo Starr and Ronnie Wood).

Jericho (US Pyramid, UK Essential ESSCD 199, 1993)

Remedy / Blind Willie McTell / The Caves of Jericho / Atlantic City / Too Soon Gone / Country Boy / Move to Japan / Amazon (River of Dreams) / Stuff You Gotta Watch / Same Thing / Shine a Light / Blues Stay Away from Me

Live At Watkins Glen (US Capitol COOP 31742, 1995)

High on the Hog (US Pyramid, UK Transatlantic TRACD 228, 1996)

Stand Up / Back to Memphis / Where I Should Always Be / Free Your Mind / Forever Young / The High Price of Love / Crazy Mama / I Must Love You Too Much / She Knows / Rumble Jungle

Jubilation (US River North 51416 1420 2, 1998)

Book Faded Brown / Don't Wait / Last Train to Memphis / High Cotton / Kentucky Downpour / Bound by Love / White Cadillac (Ode to Ronnie Hawkins) / If I Should Fall / Spirit of the Dance / You See Me / French Girls

The Very Best of The Band (UK Capitol 495 0512, 1998)

Garth Hudson Presents a Canadian Celebration of The Band (Canada Curve Music CURV 21, 2010)

Garth is featured on all 18 tracks and the performers include Bruce Cockburn, the Cowboy Junkies and Neil Young: an overlooked album that is most enjoyable.

APPENDIX 3

Take What You Need: Covering Bob Dylan

"My old songs have got something, I agree. If I was me, I'd cover my songs too."
(Bob Dylan, 2006)

Tribute Albums – Individual Artists

How Many Seas Must a White Dove Sail? – Linda Mason (1964)
A cheaply-made, privately pressed LP by a US folk singer – nothing exceptional but Linda was ahead of the pack. Includes both 'Who Killed Davy Moore?' and 'Tomorrow Is a Long Time' so she knew his catalogue.

Odetta Sings Dylan (1965)
Having the imprimatur of a legendary folk performer so early in his career was a great boost to his career.

Duane Eddy Does Bob Dylan (1965)
Dylan songs recast as twangy guitar instrumentals. Bob Dylan in *Chronicles* says that he was taken with this album as everybody was saying he could write lyrics and forgot about his melodies.

Aufray Chante Dylan – Hugues Aufray (France, 1965)
Helped to establish Dylan in France.

The Four Seasons Sing Big Hits by Bacharach, David and Dylan (1965)
Including the big hit, 'Don't Think Twice' as the Wonder Who, which is a bit like Shirley Temple singing Bob Dylan. I'm sure it was funny in the studio.

    Bob Spitz on cover versions: 'I think the funniest one that was ever done was by the Four Seasons as the Wonder Who. They held their noses and they sang the song and it was a big hit in the States.'

Any Day Now – Joan Baez (2LP) (US No. 30, 1968)

Hollies Sing Dylan (UK No. 3, 1969)
Graham Nash thought the arrangements were too cabaret, which is one reason he left the Hollies.

Dylan's Gospel – The Brothers and Sisters (1969)
The spiritual quality of Dylan's songs was recognised long before his 'born again' albums. The 28-strong choir from Los Angeles includes Merry Clayton, Gloria Jones, Clydie King and Edna Wright. It was arranged by Gene Page, who used a football whistle to draw attention and it was produced by Lou Adler.

Maura Kennedy of the Americana duo, the Kennedys: 'This album is now on CD and we have been taking it on tour with us. They are singing Bob Dylan songs but not his more religious songs, more ones like 'Mr. Tambourine Man' and 'Chimes of Freedom', all sung in a full-on gospel way. It's just great, great road music.' Oddly, not many gospel groups have recorded Dylan's Christian songs.

Lo and Behold – Coulson Dean McGuinness Flint (1972)
This album was prompted by *The Basement Tapes* and the result is not far behind The Band. The album was co-produced by Manfred Mann: 'Well, it was made in his Workhouse studio and he called in when he was passing,' says Tom McGuinness.

Richie Havens Sings Beatles and Dylan (1987)

Keene on Dylan – Steven Keene (1990)
25 tracks, both Dylan and Keene songs, including 'Talkin' Bob Dylan Imitators Contest Massacre Disaster Paranoid Blues

Don't Think Twice, It's All Right – Barbara Dickson (1992)

Judy Collins Sings Dylan Just Like a Woman (1993)
New recordings with personal reminiscences in the CD booklet.

Red on Blonde – Tim O'Brien (1996)

The Dylan Project – Steve Gibbons (1998)
This album made by Steve Gibbons with Simon Nicol, Dave Pegg and P.J. Wright led to tours and festival appearances as the Dylan Project. There was a *Live at Cropredy* (1999) and then a second volume, followed by reissues with bonus tracks.

Every Grain of Sand – Barb Jungr (2002)
Like Steve Gibbons, Barb Jungr is working her way through Bob's catalogue but here more Weimar cabaret than folk-rock. There is also *Man in the Long Black Coat* (2011) and *Hard Rain: The Songs of Bob Dylan and Leonard Cohen* (2014). Her two-hour touring show devoted to Dylan with just voice and piano is well worth catching.

Starry Eyed and Laughing – Julie Felix (2CD, 2002)

Positively 12th & K – Jackie Greene and Sal Valentino (2003)

Heart of Mine: Love Songs of Bob Dylan – Maria Muldaur (2006)

Dylanesque – Bryan Ferry (2007)

Gates of Eden – Ralph McTell (2007)
Songs of both Woody Guthrie and Bob Dylan.

Knockin' on Bob's Door – The Persuasions (2010)
Bob Dylan sung by a superlative doo-wop: great a cappella singing, great songs – I love it!

50 Years of Blonde on Blonde – Old Crow Medicine Show (2016)
The whole of the double-album reworked country-style. Very engaging.

Positively Bob – Willie Nile (2017)
Willie Nile: 'It's fun to go into his voice at times. Rock'n'roll is supposed to be fun but I do the songs because they are meaningful to me. He's a special cat. I was just going to make this album and sell it at gigs but it came out so good that I hired a publicist and radio people and I've had great reactions. Even his own Facebook page put a blast out about it and that doesn't always happen.'

A Tree with Roots – Fairport Convention (2018)
Bargain-priced collection that brings together their many covers through the years.

Official Bootleg – Dylancentric (2019)
Ashley Hutchings formed this band for the finale of the Isle of Wight festival to celebrate the earlier festival in 1969 when Dylan appeared.

Tribute Albums – Newly-made, Various Artists

Outlaw Blues, Vol.1 (Imaginary, 1992)

Outlaw Blues, Vol.2 (Imaginary, 1993)

Tangled Up in Blues (House of Blues, 1999) The cover states 'This ain't no tribute', but of course it is.

A Nod to Bob – Tribute on his 60th Birthday (Red House, 2001)

Forever Young – A British Folk Tribute to Bob Dylan (Delta, 2001)

Blowin' in the Wind – A Reggae Tribute to Bob Dylan (Madacy, 2002)

Gotta Serve Somebody: The Gospel Songs of Bob Dylan (Sony, 2003)

Is It Rolling, Bob? A Reggae Tribute to Bob Dylan, Vol. 1 (Sanctuary, CD & DVD, 2004) Don't think there was a second volume, but there is a dub version of most of this album issued as *Visions of Jamaica*.

Highway 61 Revisited Revisited (free with *Uncut*, 2005)

I'm Not There (film soundtrack, 2CD, 2007)

Younger than that Now (Circuit, 2CD, 2011)

Listen To Bob Dylan (Drive Thru, 2011)

Chimes of Freedom; The Songs of Bob Dylan (Amnesty International, 4CD, 2012)

The New Basement Tapes – Lost on the River (Harvest 025379 50140, 2014)
Down to the Bottom / Married to My Hack / Kansas City / Spanish Mary / Liberty Street / Nothing to It / Golden Tom – Silver Judas / When I Get My hands on You / Duncan and Jimmy / Florida Key / Hidee Hidee Ho (2 versions) / Lost on the River (2 versions) / Stranger / Card Shark / Quick like a Flash / Diamond Ring / The Whistle Is Blowing / Six Months in Kansas City
   Long-lost Dylan songs performed by Elvis Costello, Rhiannon Giddens, Taylor Goldsmith, Jim James and Marcus Mumford.

Blonde on Blonde Revisited (Free with *MOJO*, 2016)

Official Bootleg – Dylancentric (Talking Elephant, 2019)
Ashley Hutchings formed a band to close the Isle of Wight Festival in 2019.

Tribute Albums – Compilations

May Your Songs Always Be Sung – The Songs Of Bob Dylan (Three BMG compilations, 1987, 2001, 2003)

I Shall Be Unreleased (Sony, 1991)

The Songs of Bob Dylan (Sequel, 1993)
And the Times They Were A-Changin' (Débutante, 1998)
It Ain't Me Babe (Sequel, 2001)
Hard Rain, Vols.1 and 2 (Free with *Uncut*, 2002)
Tracks Inspired by Bob Dylan (Free with *Uncut*, 2005)
Dylan Covered (Free with *MOJO*, 2005)
How Many Roads: Black America Sings Bob Dylan (Ace, 2010)
Take What You Need: UK Covers of Bob Dylan Songs, 1964-1969 (Ace, 2017)

Cover Versions

Bob Dylan's most covered songs are 'Blowin' In the Wind' with around 400 versions on commercial labels, 'Don't Think Twice It's All Right' 230 and 'I Shall Be Released' 200. What follows is a list of the most significant covers whether by the reputation of the artist, chart success, quality of the performance or trying to be different.

John York, who joined the Byrds in 1968, says, 'Dylan's magic was transformed into another form by the Byrds, which worked for people who weren't listening to Bob Dylan. It was more pop but most of the songs were masterpieces and you can do them in any number of formats.'

Nana Mouskouri: 'The mystery of a great song is for it to belong to many people at the same time, although it was written for the person himself. In Bob Dylan, I find some of the special atmosphere that exists in Greek songs.'

Abandoned Love – Everly Brothers (with Liam O'Flynn of the Chieftains), George Harrison, Chuck Prophet, Paul Rodgers & Nils Lofgren, Willie Nile

Absolutely Sweet Marie – Dylan Project, Factotums, George Harrison, Jason and the Scorchers

Ain't No Man Righteous, No, Not One – Jah Malla

All Along the Watchtower – Alan Bown, Bryan Ferry, Funkstar De Luxe (worth hearing!), Richie Havens, Jimi Hendrix (US No. 20, 1968; UK No. 5, 1968; No. 52, 1990), Larry McCray, Dave Mason, Dave Matthews Band, Persuasions, Tim Rose, U2 (with extra words from Bono: 'All I got is a red guitar, three chords and the truth'), Eddie Vedder and the Million Dollar Bashers, Bobby Womack, Neil Young (superb version).

Tim Rose on his version: 'I always thought that I was a better singer than Jimi but I never came close to being the guitar player that he was. Hendrix hated his voice; Dylan hates his own voice too – he just sings because it makes him a lot of money as a songwriter.'

Bob Dylan on stage in South Bend, Indiana; 'Anybody heard of U2? They recorded this song but they did it with all the wrong words. These are the correct words. All about business men. All about people getting on with the business of their lives.'

All I Really Want To Do – Byrds (US No. 40, 1965; UK No. 4, 1965), Sebastian Cabot, Cher (US No. 15, 1965; UK No. 9, 1965), Bryan Ferry, Four Seasons, Hollies

Are You Ready – Fairfield Four

As I Went Out One Morning – Mira Billotte, Stan Ridgeway

Ballad of a Thin Man – James Solberg, Ben Weaver

Ballad of Hollis Brown – Julie Felix, Barb Jungr, Nazareth

Billy 1 – Los Lobos

Billy 4 – Gretchen Peters with Tom Russell

Blind Willie McTell – The Band, Dream Syndicate, Barb Jungr, Barrence Whitfield

Blowin' in the Wind – Laurel Aitken, Eddy Arnold, Bobby Bare, Marc Bolan (early demo), Sebastian Cabot, Glen Campbell (instrumental), Liam Clancy ('A song that changed the world'), Sam Cooke, Bobby Darin, Barbara Dickson, Marlene Dietrich (in German), Duke Ellington, Percy Faith, Marianne Faithfull, Steve Forbert, Four Seasons, Ted Hawkins, Hollies, Lena Horne, Spike Jones, Barb Jungr, Trini Lopez, Ziggy Marley, Chad Mitchell Trio, New World Singers, Willie Nile, Odetta and Liam Clancy, Dolly Parton, Persuasions, Peter, Paul & Mary (US No. 2, 1963; UK No. 13, 1963), Cliff Richard, Searchers (live), Settlers, Sonny and Cher, US Navy Steel Band, Dionne Warwick, Stevie Wonder (US No. 9, 1966; UK No. 36, 1966), O.V. Wright. Julie Felix performs the song with a new verse written by herself.

Bob Dylan's Dream – Judy Collins, Bryan Ferry, Silkie

Bob Dylan's 115th Dream – Taj Mahal

Boots of Spanish Leather – Joan Baez, Sebastian Cabot, Julie Felix, Richie Havens, Nanci Griffith, Martin Simpson

Born in Time – Barb Jungr

Buckets of Rain – Eric Bibb, Bette Midler, Edwina Hayes

Can You Please Crawl out Your Window – Jimi Hendrix (live), The Hold Steady, Sal Valentino

Catfish – When Joe Cocker asked Dylan for a song. He said, 'Tell you what. I got this blues I wrote about a baseball pitcher Catfish Hunter.' The perfect song for a guy from Sheffield, right? Also recorded by Kinky Friedman.

Changing of the Guard – Jez Lowe

Chimes of Freedom – Byrds, Dino, Desi and Billy, Julie Felix, Barb Jungr, Youssou N'Dour (as an anthem for Africa), Bruce Springsteen

Clothesline Saga – Roches

Cold Irons Bound – Tom Verlaine & the Million Dollar Bashers

Colours to the Mast – Dylan Project

Coming from the Heart (outtake from *Street-Legal*) – Searchers

Country Pie – The Nice (merged with Bach's Brandenburg Concerto, No. 6)

Dark Eyes – Judy Collins, Dylan Project, Patti Smith

Dear Landlord – Joan Baez, Joe Cocker, Fairport Convention

Death of Emmett Till – Coulson Dean McGuinness Flint

Delia – Spider John Koerner

Desolation Row – Grateful Dead, Chris Smither

Dignity – Steve Forbert Don't Fall Apart on Me Tonight – Aaron Neville

Dirty Lie – The Secret Sisters (Dylan had started this song in the 1980s and he gave the Secret Sisters a demo which they completed in 2014 and then recorded. Dylan's original demo is on YouTube.)

Don't Think Twice It's All Right – Hugues Aufray (as N'y pense plus, tout est bien, France No. 14, 1964), Joan Baez and the Indigo Girls, Brook Benton (who also recorded Think Twice), Sebastian Cabot, Eric Clapton, Bobby Darin (two versions), Barbara Dickson, Nick Drake (demo), Ramblin' Jack Elliott, Fairies, Bryan Ferry, Heinz, Ivy League, Barb Jungr, Johnny Marr, John Martyn, Persuasions, Peter Paul and Mary (US No. 9, 1963), Elvis Presley (Jam session: he doesn't know the words), Jerry Jeff Walker, Lawrence Welk, Wonder Who (aka Four Seasons, US No. 12, 1965), Steve Young.

Don't Ya Tell Henry – The Band, Coulson Dean McGuinness Flint

Down along the Cove – Cliff Aungier, Dylan Project, Georgie Fame (US single produced by Bob Johnston, 1969), Johnny Jenkins (with the Allman Brothers)

Down in the Flood – Sandy Denny, Flatt & Scruggs, John Pearson

Drifter's Escape – Joan Baez, Jimi Hendrix, Patti Smith

Dusty Old Fairgrounds – Blue Ash

Emotionally Yours – O'Jays

Eternal Circle – Coulson Dean McGuinness Flint

Every Grain of Sand – Julie Felix, Emmylou Harris (produced by Daniel Lanois), Barb Jungr, Nana Mouskouri (Dylan sent her a demo), Willie Nile

Everything is Broken – R.L. Burnside

Farewell – Lonnie Donegan, Ellen with the Wanderers, Pete Seeger

Farewell Angelina – Joan Baez (UK No. 35, 1966), Jeff Buckley, New Riders of the Purple Sage, Show of Hands

Father of Night – Manfred Mann

Foot of Pride – Lou Reed ('I chose 'Foot of Pride' because I just got back from an eight-month tour. Once a day I would listen to it and just fall down laughing.')

Forever Young – Harry Belafonte, Paul Brady, Christine Collister, Fairport Convention, Barb Jungr, Persuasions, Pete Seeger

Paul Brady on his live recording: 'The three girls on that night wanted to do something and Mary Black suggested 'Forever Young'. We all knew it. It is a song for his children and it is a lovely song. You can hear the effect it has on the audience. I am not above being populist.'

4th Time Around – Dylan Project, Terry Melcher, Yo La Tengo

From A Buick 6 – Gary US Bonds

Gates of Eden – Marc Carroll, Julie Felix, Bryan Ferry

Get Your Rocks Off – Coulson Dean McGuinness, Flint, Manfred Mann's Earth Band

Girl from the North Country – Hugues Aufray (as La Fille du Nord, France No. 11, 1966), Dave Burland, Joe Cocker, Roy Harper (variant as 'North Country Girl' – see text), Josh Macrae, Rod Stewart, Sting, Waterboys, M. West with Conor Oberst & Jim James

Going Going Gone – Gregg Allman (his final recording!), GP's (lead vocal, Richard Thompson)

Going to Acapulco – Jim James (used in *I'm Not There*)

Golden Loom – Roger McGuinn

Gotta Serve Somebody – Eric Burdon, Shirley Caesar, Natalie Cole (Bob wrote some new words), Judy Collins, Etta James, Barb Jungr, Mavis Staples

Hard Rain's A-Gonna Fall, A – Eric Andersen, Barbara Dickson, Julie Felix, Bryan Ferry (UK No. 10, 1973), Barb Jungr, Laura Marling (for *Peaky Blinders*), Willie Nile, Leon Russell

High Water – Barb Jungr

Highway 61 Revisited – Dave Alvin, Dr. Feelgood, Dylan Project, Mark Germino, P.J. Harvey, Johnny Winter (wayward vocal but great guitar)

Hurricane – Ani DiFranco

I Am a Lonesome Hobo – Dylan Project, John Pearson, Julie Driscoll with Brian Auger and the Trinity, Triffids

I Believe in You – Judy Collins

I Don't Want To Do It – George Harrison (1985 but originally demoed for *All Things Must Pass*)

I Dreamed I Saw St Augustine – Joan Baez, John Doe, Thea Gilmore

I Need a Woman – Ry Cooder

I Pity the Poor Immigrant – Joan Baez, Gene Clark, Judy Collins, Richie Havens

I Shall Be Released – Animals, Joan Baez, The Band, Box Tops (US No. 67, 1969), Beverley Sisters (what?), Boz, Julie Felix, Heptones, Hollies, Chrissie Hynde, Barb Jungr, Bette Midler, Beth Rowley, Telly Savalas (oh yes), Sting, Tremeloes (UK No. 29, 1968), Paul Weller. Great quiz question: which is the only act to have taken 'I Shall Be Released' into the UK Top 30? It might have gone higher too – there was a vinyl shortage and it lost its impetus. Still, it did sell 50,000.)

I Wanna Be Your Love – McGuinness-Flint

I Want You – James Blunt, Dylan Project, Sophie B Hawkins (UK No. 49, 1993), Hollies, Barb Jungr, Ralph McTell (taking it slowly), Willie Nile

Idiot Wind – Coal Porters

(If I Had to Do It All Over Again, I'd Do It) All Over You – Raiders

If Not For You – Bryan Ferry, George Harrison, Barb Jungr, Olivia Newton-John (US No. 5, 1971; UK No. 7, 1971),

If You Gotta Go, Go Now – Cowboy Junkies, Fairport Convention (as Si Tu Dois Partir) (UK No. 21, 1969), Flying Burrito Brothers (Chris Hillman: 'It was Jim Dickson's idea to do it fast. It was like punk rock and it made no sense'), Manfred Mann (UK No. 2, 1965), Mae West

I'll Be Your Baby Tonight – Graham Bonnet (shouted!), Brothers and Sisters (but hardly a gospel song), Cathryn Craig and Brian Willoughby, Adam Faith (like a conversation with himself), Marianne Faithfull, Georgie Fame (US single produced by Bob Johnston, 1969),

John Hammond, Hollies, Norah Jones (UK No. 67, 2003), Barb Jungr, Maria Muldaur, Kris Kristofferson, Robert Palmer and UB40 (UK No. 6, 1990), Linda Ronstadt, Harry Dean Stanton, Peter Sarstedt (adding a few chords of his own).

I'll Keep It With Mine – Judy Collins, Fairport Convention, Nico

I'll Remember You – Thea Gilmore, Nana Mouskouri

I'm Not There – Sonic Youth

Is Your Love in Vain – Barb Jungr, Liverpool Express, Show of Hands

It Ain't Me Babe – Hugues Aufray (French), Sebastian Cabot, Johnny Cash (with June Carter and mariachi brass. (US No. 58, 1964; UK No. 28, 1965), Bryan Ferry, Davy Jones, Barb Jungr, Lucy Kaplansky, Nancy Sinatra, Turtles (US No. 8, 1965)

It's All Over Now, Baby Blue – The Animals, Joan Baez (UK No. 22, 1965), Byrds, Chocolate Watch Band, Judy Collins, Cops 'n Robbers, Echo and the Bunnymen, Chris Farlowe, Bryan Ferry, Grateful Dead, Richie Havens, Barb Jungr, Barry McGuire, Milltown Brothers (UK No. 48, 1993), Them, 13th Floor Elevators

It's Alright Ma, I'm Only Bleeding – Byrds, Julie Felix, Barb Jungr, Roger McGuinn

It Takes a Lot to Laugh, It Takes a Train to Cry (original title, Phantom Engineer) – Black Crowes, David Bromberg, Dylan Project, Taj Mahal, Tracy Nelson, Stephen Stills with Al Kooper and Mike Bloomfield

Jack O'Diamonds – Ben Carruthers, Fairport Convention

John Brown – Eric Andersen, Heron, Staple Singers

Jokerman – Eliza Gilkyson

Just Like a Woman – Eric Bibb, Byrds (Jackson Browne on piano), Joe Cocker, Judy Collins, Roberta Flack, Formerly Brothers, Charlotte Gainsbourg & Calexico, Richie Havens, Hollies, Barb Jungr, Jonathan King, Manfred Mann (UK No. 10, 1966), Stevie Nicks, Hazel O'Connor, Persuasions, Carly Simon, Nina Simone, Rod Stewart

Just like Tom Thumb's Blues – Alex Campbell, Ramblin' Jack Elliott, Julie Felix, Bryan Ferry, Handsome Family, Bill Kirchen, Gordon Lightfoot, Tom Russell and Joe Ely, Nina Simone, Neil Young

Knockin' on Heaven's Door – Anthony and the Johnsons, Eric Clapton (UK No. 38, 1975), Dunblane (UK No. 1, 1996), Bryan Ferry, Guns n' Roses (UK No. 2, 1992), Antony Hegarty, Booker T. Jones, Arthur Louis (with Eric Clapton), Dolly Parton with Ladysmith Black Mombasa, Warren Zevon

Lay Down Your Weary Tune – Albion Band, Billy Bragg, Byrds, Coulson Dean McGuinness Flint

Tom McGuinness: 'By the time of Gallagher and Lyle, we were being published by the same publishers as Dylan in the UK and so we got all the Dylan tapes they had. I had a small library of them and 'Lay down Your Weary Tune' was one of my favourites. I'd never heard the song done by anyone else so I suggested that we did it. I'd never heard the Byrds' version.'

Lay Lady Lay – Acker Bilk, Byrds (with female choir: unadorned version has also been issued and it is better without), Cher, Everly Brothers, Ferrante and Teicher (US No. 99, 1970), Jose Feliciano, Richie Havens, Isaac Hayes, Isley Brothers (US No. 71, 1971), Barb

Jungr, Melanie, Mighty Diamonds, Paraffin Jack Flash Ltd, Persuasions, Harry Roche Constellation, Sandie Shaw, Stands

Leopard-Skin Pillbox Hat – Michael Chapman, John Mellencamp

Let Me Die In My Footsteps – Coulson Dean McGuinness Flint, Happy Traum

Licence to Kill – Elvis Costello, Richie Havens, Tom Petty

Like a Rolling Stone – Michael Bolton, Sebastian Cabot, Judy Collins (Judy sings one verse like Bob Dylan), Dino, Desi & Billy, Steve Forbert, Four Seasons, Jimi Hendrix (at Monterey), Barb Jungr, Lanne & the Leekings, James Last, Terry Melcher, John Mellencamp (with Al Kooper), Persuasions, Rolling Stones (UK No. 12, 1995), Seal & Jeff Beck, Spirit, Wailers (their 1966 Rolling Stone was based on Like a Rolling Stone). Around 2004 Rodney Crowell did Like A Rolling Stone in his stage show, 'It was just to show off to the band that I knew all the words.'

Lily, Rosemary and the Jack of Hearts – Joan Baez, Paul Jones (unreleased, mentioned in Tim Rice's autobiography).

Living the Blues – Leon Redbone

Lo And Behold – Coulson Dean McGuinness Flint

Lonesome Day Blues – Mick Martin

Lonesome Death of Hattie Carroll – Martin Carthy, Julie Felix, Mason Jennings, Christy Moore, Phranc

Love Is just a Four Letter Word – Joan Baez

Love Minus Zero / No Limit – Joan Baez, Jackson Browne, Eric Clapton, Judy Collins, Julie Felix, Eliza Gilkyson, Steve Harley, Willie Nile, Noel Harrison, Turley Richards (US No. 84, 1970), Steve Tilston

Love Sick – Blonde on Bob

Love You Too Much – Greg Lake

Maggie's Farm – Solomon Burke (not a chart hit in UK but very popular on Radio Caroline), Barbara Dickson, Richie Havens, Rage Against The Machine, Toots Hibbert, The Specials (UK No. 4, 1980: related to Thatcher), Tin Machine (UK No. 48, 1989). Bert Parks sings it in *The Freshman*.

Make You Feel My Love – Adele (UK No. 4, 2008), Mary Black, Garth Brooks, Bryan Ferry, Magna Carta, Julie Matthews, Kingdom Choir (BBC One World Together At Home, 2020)

Mama, You Been on My Mind – Lucien Alexander, Johnny Cash (first to release it), Dion and the Belmonts (as Baby, You Been on My Mind), Rod Stewart

The Man in Me – Joe Cocker, Persuasions

Man in the Long Black Coat – Emerson Lake and Palmer, Steve Gibbons, Barb Jungr, Mark Lanegan, Joan Osborne

Masters of War – Judy Collins (omits final indictment), Julie Felix, José Feliciano, Barb Jungr, Long Ryders, Leon Russell, Pete Seeger (with a Japanese translation of each line), Staple Singers, Eddie Vedder & Mike McCready

Memphis Blues Again – Hugh Cornwell, Dylan Project, Cat Power

The Mighty Quinn – Hollies, Kris Kristofferson, Ramsey Lewis (instrumentally), Lulu, Manfred Mann (US No. 10, 1968; UK No. 1, 1968), Persuasions, 1910 Fruitgum Company. Reggae treatment with new verses by Sheryl Lee Ralph for 1989 film, *The Mighty Quinn*, starring Denzel Washington.

Million Dollar Bash – Ashley Hutchings (with new words), Jonathan King, Mixed Bag, Stone Country

Million Miles – Alvin 'Youngblood' Hart

Mississippi – Sheryl Crow (released before Dylan's version), Chris & Kellie While

Mr. Tambourine Man – Byrds (US No. 1, 1965; UK No. 1, 1965), Chad and Jeremy, Chipmunks, Judy Collins, Julie Felix, Four Seasons, Gregory Isaacs, Marmalade, Melanie, Persuasions, William Shatner (preposterous but fun), Martin Simpson, Tweets

Moonlight – Maria Muldaur

Moonshiner – Bob Forrest

Most Likely You Go Your Way and I'll Go Mine – Patti LaBelle, Todd Rundgren

Most of the Time – Sal Valentino, Bettye Lavette

Motorpsycho Nightmare – Hugues Aufray (As Cauchemar Psychomoteur, France No. 11, 1965)

My Back Pages – Byrds (US No. 30, 1967), Marshall Crenshaw, Hollies, Nice. All-star version with Clapton, Dylan, Harrison, McGuinn, Petty, Young at 1992 Bobfest.

Nobody 'Cept You – Waterboys

North Country Blues – Joan Baez, Amy Goddard

Not Dark Yet – Julie Felix, Lew Fratis, Robyn Hitchcock, Barb Jungr, Shelby Lynne & Allison Moorer, Steve Phillips

Nothing Was Delivered – Byrds (Dylan's triplets changed to country shuffle).

Odds And Ends – Coulson Dean McGuinness Flint

Oh Sister – Andrew Bird & Nora O'Connor

One More Cup of Coffee – Julie Felix, Steve Earle & Lucia Micarelli, Roger McGuinn & Calexico

One of Us Must Know – Boo Radleys, Mick Hucknall, Chip Taylor

One Too Many Mornings – Association, Joan Baez, The Band, Beau Brummels (US No. 95, 1966), Johnny Cash and Waylon Jennings (very syrupy!), Julie Felix, Jerry Jeff Walker

On The Road Again – Try What's News, Pussycat by the Liverpool band, the Cryin' Shames: easy to spot what they've been listening to.

Only a Hobo – Rod Stewart

Only a Pawn in the Game – Morrissey

Open the Door, Homer – Coulson Dean McGuinnes Flint, The Floor

Outlaw Blues – Queens of the Stone Age, Thin White Rope

Oxford Town – Barbara Dickson, Richie Havens, Three City Four

Paths of Victory – Byrds, Odetta, Pete Seeger

Peggy Day – Dylan Project

Percy's Song – Fairport Convention, Arlo Guthrie

Please Mrs. Henry – Manfred Mann

Pledging My Time – Greg Brown, Luther Johnson, My Darling Clementine

Political World – Carolina Chocolate Drops

Positively 4th Street – Byrds, Bryan Ferry, Terry Melcher, Persuasions, Johnny Rivers (highly praised by Dylan! In *Chronicles*: 'Johnny Rivers "surpasses the feeling I put into it".'), Lucinda Williams

Pressing on – Anthony and the Johnsons, John Doe

Property of Jesus –Sinéad O'Connor

Queen Jane Approximately – Four Seasons

Quit Your Lowdown Ways – Sebastian Cabot, Hollies

Rainy Day Women Nos. 12 & 35 – Lenny Kravitz, Willie Nile, Tom Petty

Restless Farewell – Joan Baez, Liam Clancy, De Dannan, Mark Knopfler

Ring Them Bells – Joan Baez and Mary Black, Natasha Bedingfield, Barbara Dickson, Dylan Project, Barb Jungr, Gordon Lightfoot, Sufjan Stevens

Rita May – Jerry Lee Lewis

Romance in Durango – Julie Felix

Sad Eyed Lady of the Lowlands – Joan Baez, Julie Felix, Jim O'Rourke, Old Crow Medicine Show

Sara – Barb Jungr

Saved – Mighty Clouds of Joy, Third Day

Saving Grace – Aaron Neville

Señor – Dierks Bentley, Jerry Garcia, Willie Nelson & Calexico

Seven Curses – Albion Band, Joan Baez, Sebastian Cabot,

Seven Days – Joe Cocker, Ronnie Wood

She Belongs to Me – Neil Finn, Masterminds, Rick Nelson (US No. 33, 1970), Nice (Keith Emerson: 'It fitted in well with Lee Jackson's limited vocal range, bless him.')

Shelter from the Storm – Barb Jungr, Manfred Mann's Earth Band, Cassandra Wilson

She's Your Lover Now – Howard Devoto

Sign Language – Eric Clapton

Sign on the Cross– Coulson Dean McGuinness Flint

Sign on the Window – Melanie

Simple Twist of Fate – Judy Collins, Bryan Ferry, Michael Weston King, Diana Krall, Dylan Project, K T Tunstall, Jeff Tweedy

Song to Woody – Dave Van Ronk

Spanish Harlem Incident – Byrds, Chris Whitley

Steel Bars – Michael Bolton

Stepchild – Solomon Burke, Jerry Lee Lewis

Straight A's in Love – Williams Brothers

Subterranean Homesick Blues – Julie Felix, Jackie Greene, Willie Nile

Sugar Baby – Barb Jungr

Sweetheart like You – Eva Cassidy, Judy Collins, Guy Davis, Rod Stewart

Tangled Up in Blue – Robyn Hitchcock, Barb Jungr, K T Tunstall

Tears of Rage – Joan Baez, Band, Country Fever, Barbara Dickson

Things Have Changed – Barb Jungr, Persuasions, Curtis Stigers

This Wheel's On Fire – The Band, Billy Bragg & K T Tunstall, Byrds, Julie Driscoll with Brian Auger & the Trinity (UK No. 5, 1968: new version in *Absolutely Fabulous*), Siouxsie and the Banshees (UK No. 14, 1987), K T Tunstall & Billy Bragg

The Times They Are A-Changin' – Beach Boys, Blackmore's Night, Brothers & Sisters (Merry Clayton lead vocal), Byrds, Sebastian Cabot, Tracy Chapman, Barbara Dickson (harmony vocals, Gerry Rafferty), Bryan Ferry, Richie Havens, Hollies, Ian Campbell Folk Group (UK No. 42, 1965), Burl Ives, Mason Jennings, Barb Jungr, Bob Lind, Willie Nile, Peter Paul and Mary (UK No. 44, 1964), Silkie, Rag'n'Bone Man (BBC One World: Together At Home, 2020), Simon and Garfunkel

Tiny Montgomery – McGuinness-Flint,

Tombstone Blues – Richie Havens, Henry Kaiser

Tomorrow Is a Long Time – Harry Belafonte, Sebastian Cabot, Vikki Clayton, Nick Drake (demo), Clive Gregson, Ian & Sylvia, Barb Jungr, Kingston Trio, Magna Carta, Elvis Presley, Rod Stewart

Tomorrow Night – Etta James

Tonight I'll Be Staying Here with You – Jeff Beck, Charlatans, Rick Nelson, Esther Phillips

Too Much of Nothing – Peter, Paul and Mary, Spooky Tooth

To Ramona – Tony Capstick, Flying Burrito Brothers (Chris Hillman recorded vocal and guitar in dark and then band added), Humble Pie, Sinead Lohan, Alan Price Set, Texas Tornados

Tough Mama – Jerry Garcia

Trouble in Mind – Barb Jungr

Tryin' to Get to Heaven – Robyn Hitchcock, Lucinda Williams

Up to Me – Roger McGuinn

Visions of Johanna – Marianne Faithfull, Julie Felix, Robyn Hitchcock, Piccadilly Line, Chris Smither

Wagon Wheel – Nathan Carter, Old Crow Medicine Show, Darius Rucker

Walkin' Down the Line – Joan Baez, Baytown Singers, Byrds, Joe & Eddie, Rick Nelson, Odetta, Risin' Sons (Ry Cooder and Taj Mahal in 1965)

Walk Out in the Rain – Eric Clapton

Wallflower – Holmes Brothers, Buddy and Julie Miller, Doug Sahm

Walls of Red Wing – Joan Baez

Wanted Man – Johnny Cash

Watching the River Flow – Leon Russell

What Good Am I – Barb Jungr

What Was It You Wanted – Chris Smither, Willie Nelson

When He Returns – Rance Allen

When I Paint My Masterpiece – The Band, Barbara Dickson, Steve Harley, Persuasions

When the Night Comes Falling from the Sky – Black Crowes

When the Ship Comes in – Billy Bragg, Clancy Brothers, Barbara Dickson, Dylan Project, Marcus Carl Franklin, Golden State Boys (with Chris Hillman), Hollies, Peter, Paul and Mary (US No. 91, 1965)

Where Were You Last Night – Joe Brown

Who Killed Davey Moore – Sebastian Cabot, Donovan, Madison, Pete Seeger

Wicked Messenger – Black Keys, Faces, Patti Smith

Winterlude – Dylan Project, Five O'Clock Scholar

With God on Our Side – Judy Collins, Barbara Dickson, Barb Jungr, Manfred Mann, Buddy Miller, Gurf Morlix, Neville Brothers (UK No. 47, 1989), Wire Train

You Ain't Going Nowhere – Joan Baez, Byrds (US No. 74, 1968; UK No. 45, 1968), Barbara Dickson, The Floor (early Scandinavian cover), Barb Jungr, Willie Nile, Persuasions, Doc Watson

You Angel You – Manfred Mann's Earth Band (UK No. 54, 1979)

You Gotta Trust Yourself – Carlene Carter

You're a Big Girl Now – My Morning Jacket, Steve Gibbons

You're Gonna Make Me Lonesome When You Go – Christine Collister, Miley Cyrus, Raul Malo, Madeleine Peyroux

APPENDIX 4

Odds and Ends: Bob Dylan Lists

'I was so much older then...'

Older than Bob Dylan

1853 – John Wesley Hardin (26 May)
1903 – Big Joe Williams (16 Oct)
1910 – John Hammond (15 Dec)
1912 – Woody Guthrie (14 July)
1913 – Richard Nixon (9 Jan)
1914 – William Burroughs (5 Feb)
1915 – Frank Sinatra (12 Dec)
1917 – John F. Kennedy (29 May); John Lee Hooker (22 Aug)
1919 – Pete Seeger (3 May)
1920 – Oscar Brand (7 Feb)
1922 – Jack Kerouac (12 Mar)
1923 – Harry Smith (29 May), Hank Williams (17 Sep)
1924 – Marlon Brando (3 Apr); Jimmy Carter (1 Oct)
1925 – Sam Peckinpah (21 Feb); D.A. Pennebaker (15 Jul); Lenny Bruce (13 Oct)
1926 – Albert Grossman (21 May); Allen Ginsberg (3 Jun); Robert Shelton (28 Jun); Chuck Berry (18 Oct)
1928 – Andy Warhol (6 Aug); Bo Diddley (30 Dec)
1931 – Sam Cooke (22 Jan); James Dean (8 Feb); Ramblin' Jack Elliott (1 Aug)
1932 – Johnny Cash (26 Feb); Bob Johnston (14 May); Little Richard (5 Dec)
1933 – Willie Nelson (29 Apr)
1934 – Leonard Cohen (21 Sep)
1935 – Elvis Presley (8 Jan); Jerry Lee Lewis (29 Sep)
1936 – Ronnie Hawkins (10 Jan); Roy Orbison (23 Apr); Dave Van Ronk (30 Jun); Buddy Holly (7 Sep); Mary Travers (9 Nov)
1937 – Richard Fariña (8 Mar); Garth Hudson (2 Aug); Tom Paxton (31 Oct); Paul Stookey (30 Dec)
1938 – Happy Traum (9 May); Peter Yarrow (31 May); Gordon Lightfoot (17 Nov)
1939 – Judy Collins (1 May); Sara Dylan (25 Oct); Phil Spector (26 Dec)
1940 – Smokey Robinson (19 Feb); Levon Helm (26 May); John Lennon (8 Oct); Manfred Mann (21 Oct); Phil Ochs (19 Dec); Frank Zappa (21 Dec)
1941 – Joan Baez (9 Jan)

24 May 1941 – Birth of Bob Dylan

Younger than Bob Dylan:

1941 – David Blue (18 Feb); Paul Simon (13 Oct); Guy Clark (6 Nov); Tim Hardin (23 Dec)
1942 – Carole King (9 Feb); Leon Russell (2 Apr); Paul McCartney (18 Jun); Roger McGuinn (13 Jul); Jerry Garcia (1 Aug); John Hammond Jr (13 Nov); Jimi Hendrix (27 Nov): Paul Butterfield (17 Dec)
1943 – Eric Andersen (14 Feb); George Harrison (24 Feb); Richard Manuel (3 Apr); Bobby Vee (30 Apr); Robbie Robertson (5 July); Mike Bloomfield (28 Jul); Rick Danko (29 Dec)
1944 – Al Kooper (5 Feb); Townes Van Zandt (7 Mar); Kinky Friedman (1 Nov)
1945 – Mimi Fariña (30 Apr); Van Morrison (31 Aug)
1946 – Donovan (10 May); Loudon Wainwright (5 Sep); John Prine (10 Oct); Marianne Faithfull (29 Dec)
1947 – David Bowie (8 Jan); Emmylou Harris (2 April); Arlo Guthrie (10 Jul)
1949 – Dana Gillespie (30 March); Mark Knopfler (12 Aug); Bruce Springsteen (23 Sep)
1950 – Tom Petty (20 Oct)
1955 – Steve Earle (17 Jan)
1957 – Billy Bragg (20 Dec)
1961 – Barack Obama (4 Aug)

Songs about Bob Dylan

Bob Dylan Blues – Syd Barrett (1965) Written in 1965, recorded in 1970 and not released until 2001. Difficult to tell if it is serious or satirical or both. Neil Innes could have sung this.

A Simple Desultory Philippic – Paul Simon (1965) Paul Simon impersonates Bob Dylan.

The Hustler – Eric Andersen (1966) About Dylan selling out.

Morgan the Pirate – Richard Fariña (1968) Grumpy tribute.

My Front Pages – Arlo Guthrie (1969) 'Sing the songs you sang before'.

Behind that Locked Door – George Harrison (1970) 'Come out and play.'

Stage Fright – The Band (1970) 'They gave this poor boy his fortune and fame'.

Song for Bob Dylan – David Bowie (1971) A plea to write as he used to when he 'sat behind a million eyes and told them how they saw.'

To Bobby – Joan Baez (1972) Dylan objected to the arrogance of this song in *Chronicles*.

Looking into You – Jackson Browne (1972) 'The great song traveller passed through here, And he opened my eyes to the view'.

Zimmerman Blues – Ralph McTell (1972) Disillusioned with Dylan and knowing he can't match his talent.

Durango – John Stewart (1973) About making *Pat Garrett and Billy the Kid*.

I'm So Restless – Roger McGuinn (1973) 'Hey, Mr. D'.

Ragamuffin Minstrel Boy – Sammy Walker (1975) *Broadside* recording.

Diamonds and Rust – Joan Baez (1975) Written November 1974 about 'the unwashed phenomenon'.

Protest Song – Neil Innes (1976) First performed on *Rutland Weekend Television*.

O Brother – Joan Baez (1976) Joan can't keep away from him.

Take Me Away – Roger McGuinn (1976) Comments on the Rolling Thunder Revue.

At the Warfield – Greg Copeland (1982) On Geffen Records, produced by Jackson Browne, and about Dylan's gospel concerts – and what's more, Greg liked the Christian shows.

Castles in the Sand – David Allan Coe (1983) 'They said I could take your place': really?

A New Kind of Man – Van Morrison (1985) 'You're part of a plan for a new kind of man'.

The Man's Too Strong – Dire Straits (1985) Probably about Dylan – there is a 'Judas!' in the lyric but it has more of a military theme. Still the main character 'sulked like a child'.

Dylan for Dollars – Pinkard and Bowden (1985) Also on their album *PG-13* is 'Elvis Was a Narc'.

Self-Made Man – Tom Petty and the Heartbreakers (1987) 'If he don't wanna talk, leave him alone.'

King of the Hill – Roger McGuinn (1990) This is by two writers (McGuinn, Petty) who know Dylan well, but it seems more of a generic song.

Bastard Son – John Wesley Harding (1990) Harding claiming to be the son of Bob Dylan and Joan Baez with plenty of good lines.

Talking New Bob Dylan Blues – Loudon Wainwright (1991) Written for Bob's 50th birthday: 'Yeah, you were hipper than Mitch Miller and Johnny Mathis put together.'

Bob – Weird Al Yankovic (2003) Both song and video parody 'Subterranean Homesick Blues': not very funny but entertaining.

24/7 – Hugh Cornwell (2004) '24/7, it's got to be the greatest job – 24/7, just being Bob.'

Do You Know Any Dylan? – Eric Bogle (2005) Live recording with an amusing spoken intro about performing in folk clubs.

Dylan's Hard Rain – Ryan Bingham (2009) Give the man a packet of Zubes.

Over 10 Minutes Long

Admittedly not in the ELP (Karn Evil 9, 29.36) and Pink Floyd (Shine On You, Crazy Diamond, 26.01) league and miles away from the Allman Brothers Band (Mountain Jam, 33.41). Of Dylan's contemporaries, Eric Andersen reached 26.12 when recording 'Beat Avenue', the story of his day with the Beat poets when JFK was killed.

16.32 Highlands (*Time Out Of Mind*, 1997)

16.56 Murder Most Foul (2020)

13.54 Tempest (*Tempest*, 2012)

11.22 Sad Eyed Lady of the Lowlands (*Blonde on Blonde*, 1966)

11.18 Desolation Row (*Highway 61 Revisited*, 1965)

11.05 Joey (*Desire*, 1975)

11.01 Brownsville Girl (*Infidels*, 1986)

'Positively Wall Street' – Bob and advertising

On New Year's Day 1994, the first advertisement to feature a Bob Dylan song was shown at the Orange Bowl Stadium in Miami. Dylan had previously refused such requests. Now it was Richie Havens singing 'The Times They a-Changin'' for Coopers and Lybrand in a $10m advertising blitz. The song was also used by the Bank of Montreal in 1996.

'I was in Canada and saw "The Times They Are A-Changin" being used for an advert for a bank,' says Billy Bragg, 'and I was furious. I was doing a union rally in Toronto and I whacked the shit out of it with all the venom I got from the Clash. I don't think you should be gentle with it." Should this song have been used to promote banks? Stranger things have happened: Johnny Cash's 'Ring of Fire' was used to sell haemorrhoid cream.

2009 Ad for Victoria's Secret filmed in Venice to *Love Sick* with models looking glum, but they always do) While advert was being screened, several Bob Dylan CDs were sold in the store for $10 each.

2009 Co-op ad using 'Blowin' in the Wind'.

2010 Dylan doing ads for Cadillacs.

2014 Ads for Chrysler and Greek yoghurt. 'The Weight' was also used to sell Diet-Coke: appropriate title.

What's next? 'Gotta Serve Somebody' for McDonald's?

Theme Time Radio Hour
Bob Dylan's Best Observations

'Jerry Lee Lewis had such a strong left hand, he didn't need a bass player.'

'I got 70 George Jones albums. Look at them together and you get a great history of men's haircuts.'

'I've never understood any kind of border control when it comes to music.'

Bob Dylan's Best Jokes

'Put a beard on a Ford and it's a Lincoln.'

'The Flamingos or as I prefer to call them the Flaming O's.'

'He read about the evils of drinking, so he quit reading.'

That little bit extra…

Songs that have been given new non-Dylan verses. Bono has form here.

Blowin' in the Wind (Bono)

Knockin' on Heaven's Door (Bono, Dunblane)

Like A Rolling Stone (Wailers)

Maggie's Farm (Blues Band, Bono, The Specials)

The Times They Are A-Changin' (Billy Bragg)

With God on Our Side (Neville Brothers)

Ye Playboys and Playgirls (Carolyn Hester)

Billy Bragg wrote about English football hooligans in The Few, using the tune of Desolation Row.

Index

'Absolutely Sweet Marie' 202
Ackles, David 286–7
'Acne' 65
Acuff, Roy 65
Adams, Derroll 175
Adele 409
'Advice for Geraldine' (poem) 140
Alk, Howard 118, 166, 315, 336/7, 343/4
'All Along the Watchtower' 225, 237–8, 291, 356, 367, 395, 399, 419, 428, 437
'All I Really Want To Do' 136, 140, 168
'All Over You' 115
Allen, Steve 132, 156
Andersen, Eric 107–9, 129–30,162, 235, 282, 425
'Angelina' 341
Animals, The 69,73, 109, 137
Another Side of Bob Dylan (album) 132, 135–7, 167, 167, 191
Aranga, Ra 325
Aronowitz, Al 129, 139, 253, 271
Artes, Mary Alice 326, 333, 335
Asch, Moe 37, 49, 50, 62, 227
'As I Went Out One Morning' 129, 237
Aufray, Hugues 124, 135, 213, 228,328, 348

'Baby Blue' 165
'Baby, I'm in the Mood for You' 79
'Baby Let Me Follow You Down' 69, 234, 332
Baez, Joan
   Own career 32, 39, 40, 65, 67, 74, 78, 80, 82, 104, 133, 173, 241, 243
   With Fariñas 41, 74, 138, 169, 201, 206
   With Dylan 63, 85, 79, 91, 103, 113, 118, 123–5, 127, 132, 135, 136, 139, 140, 165, 295, 314, 317/8, 322, 348/9
   With Dylan in UK (1965) 170–9
   Songs about Dylan: 'To Bobby' 113, 427, 'Diamonds and Rust' 113, 295
Baker, Arthur 356–8
'Ballad in Plain D' 132, 187
'Ballad of a Friend' 74
'Ballad of a Thin Man' 109, 176, 187, 189, 193, 202, 329, 361, 431
'Ballad of Easy Rider' 247
'Ballad of Frankie Lee & Judas Priest' 238
'Ballad of Hollis Brown' 80, 98, 126, 355, 373, 401
'Ballad of Ira Hayes' 137

Band, The 26, 196, 199, 227–234, 252–5, 265, 275–6, 290–2, 301–13, 347, 399
   Danko, Rick 147–8, 214, 229, 308, 344
   Helm, Levon 145, 191/3, 198, 234, 277, 344, 371
   Hudson, Garth 11, 147, 204, 227–8, 233, 265
   Manuel, Richard 147, 226, 229, 231–2, 313
   Robertson, Robbie 146–8, 192, 196–7, 200–4, 213–4, 274, 296
   See also Ronnie Hawkins & the Hawks
Barrett, Syd 135
Basement Tapes, The (sessions) 227–234, (album) 228, 296, (*New Basement Tapes*) 233–4
Beach Boys, The 22, 211, 225, (Mike Love's outburst!) 369, (Brian Wilson) 393
Beatles, The 88, 102, 125, 130–1, 139, 158, 166, 188, 206, 214, 228, 254, 266
   Harrison, George 130, 139, 242–3, 260, 263–4, 350, 369, 384,398, 425
   Lennon, John 87, 110, 126, 151, 171–2, 177, 200, 257 (Lennon parodying Dylan) 336, (song, 'Roll On John') 437,
   McCartney, Paul 172, 227, 267, 295, 318, 354, 384, 388, 429
   Starr, Ringo 296, 311–2, 341, 366
Beckett, Barry 334
Beecher, Bonny Jean 36–7, 39–41, 64, 68
Before the Flood (tour album with The Band, 1974) 291
Behan, Dominic 118
Belafonte, Harry 67, 114
Bernstein, Ellen 292
Berry, Chuck 69, 105, 157, 163
Bibb, Eric 21–2, 129, 184
Bibb, Leon 33, 119
'Big Black Train' 13
Bikel, Theodore 123, 185
Biograph (box set) 41, 358–9
Blackbushe Aerodrome (venue) 326, 328–9
'Black Crow Blues' 136
'Black Diamond Bay' 297
Blackwell, Bumps 341
Blakley, Ronee 314–5, 318
Blanchett, Cate 431
Blonde on Blonde (album) 198–202, 211, 223, 234, 245
Blood on the Tracks (album) 188, 292–5
Bloomfield, Mike 118, 178, 180–1, 183, 187, 293, 340

'Blowin' in the Wind' 75–82, 110, 114, 122–3, 127–9, 169, 196, 263–4, 280, 317, 324, 344, 348, 355, 359, 376, 393
Blue, David 74, 162, 187, 222, 284, 296, 314
Bob Dylan (1962 album) 86, 113–4, 178
'Bob Dylan's Dream' 12, 102, 116–7
'Bob Dylan's 115th Dream' 164
Bogle, Eric 288
'Bonny, Why'd You Cut My Hair' 36
Bono 141, 312, 366, 370, 373, 376
Bootleg Series, The (albums) 7, 35, 221, 233, 318, 347
'Boots of Spanish Leather' 126
'Born in Time' 389–90
Boty, Pauline 98
Bowie, David 108, 267, 296
Boyd, Joe 113, 133, 183
Bragg, Billy 45, 55, 97
Brand, Oscar 22, 48, 58, 76
Brando, Marlon 11–3, 56, 195
Brel, Jacques 105, 135, 137
Bringing It All Back Home (album) 165–7, 178
Brooks, Harvey 187, 192, 262
Bromberg, David 269
Broonzy, Big Bill 19, 23, 96
Brown, Hugh 35, 39
Browne, Jackson 286
'Brownsville Girl' 9, 362
Bruce, Lenny 116, 135, (Dylan's song) 341, 361
'Buckets of Rain' 296, 319
Bucklen, John 12–4
Buckley, Tim 151, 286
Budokan (venue) 323/4, 361
Burke, Solomon 425
Burnett, T Bone 84, 233, 425
Burns, Tito 165, 172–3
Burroughs, William 25–30, 157, 166
Butterfield, Paul 148, 183–4
Buttrey, Kenny 200, 236, 243
Byrds, The 158, 167–8, 179–80, 197–8, 241, 252, 259, 391
   Crosby, David 179, 195, 261, 390
   Hillman, Chris 168, 179, 259, 391
   McGuinn, Roger 29, 31, 84, 139, 167–8, 179, 180, 198, 274, 365

Cage, Buddy 293
Cahn, Sammy 325, 344
Campbell, Alex 97
Campbell, Paul 70
'Can You Please Crawl out Your Window' 187, 196, 239, 431
Carawan, Guy 104, 169

Carnegie Hall (venue) 19, 23, 54, 57, 62, 64, 72, 74, 358, (Dylan appearances) 67, 80, 124, 128, 196, 240, (and non–appearance)195), (Ochs' disastrous appearance) 159
Carruthers, Ben 134, 136, 177
Carter, President Jimmy 235, 291, 311
Carter, Hurricane 318/9, 337
Carter, Sydney 134
Carthy, Martin 94–5, 98–9, 101, 117, 126
Cash, Johnny 12, 34, 82, 104, 119, 124, 137, 140, 199, 243–4, 246, 258, 267, 384/5
'Cast Iron Bounds' 409
Catchfire (film) 370
'Catch the Wind' 169, 171, 216, 229
'Catfish' 299
Chalamet, Timothée 269
'Change Is Gonna Come, A' 112, 138, 426
'Changing of the Guard' 329
Charles, Ray 156, 202
Chenier, Clifton 124
'Chestnut Mare' 297
'Chimes of Freedom' 132, 134, 251, 367–8, 400
Christmas in the Heart (album) 435
Chronicles, Volume 1 (memoir) 9, 36–7, 91, 113, 141, 415, 426
Clancy Brothers, The & Tommy Makem 23, 32, 56, 58–9, 62–3, 66, 72, 86, 130
Clapton, Eric 177, 233, 297, 319, 328–9, 382
Clark, Guy 287
Clarke, John Cooper 210
Clayton, Paul 15, 79, 132, 227
'Clothesline Saga' 230
Cohen, Leonard 28, 117, 189, 225, 227, 256, 285, 321, 387
'Cold Irons Bound' 409
Collins, Judy 32, 77–8, 88, 93, 108, 117, 127, 133, 135, 167, 169, 225, 257
'Come Back Baby' 65–6
'Congratulations' 370, 372. 376
'Coming from the Heart' 325
Conley, Walt 32–3
Cooder, Ry 54, 342
Cooke, Sam 112, 138
Concert for Bangla Desh, 263–4
'Corrina, Corrina' 40, 81–2, 120
Costello, Elvis 233–4, 328, 344, 353, 379, 399, 404–5, 415
'Couple More Years, A' 364
'Country Pie' 244
Croce, Jim 125
'Cross the Green Mountain' 426
'Cry a While' 420

Dallas, Karl 99
Daniels Charlie 243, 260, 306
Darin, Bobby 134, 138, 140, 167, 247, 267
'Dark Eyes' 357, 406, 431
Davenport, Bob 99
Davies, Hunter 88
Davis, Clive 226, 245, 251, 257
Davis, Rev Gary 24, 36
Davis, Spencer 207
'Day of the Locusts' 261
Dean, James 11, 17, 206, 222, 281, 373
'Dear Landlord' 172, 238
'Death of Emmett Till' 121
Dennis, Carolyn 338, 360, 422
Denver, Nigel 99, 101, 118
Desire (album) 299, 300, 319
'Desolation Row' 5, 9, 87, 190–1, 193, 195, 208, 368, 391, 410
'Dignity' 375, 404–5
'Dink's Song' 69
Dion 30, 67, 82
'Dirty World' 371
Dobell, Doug 101–2
Dobson, Bonnie 23, 82, 84, 128–9, 238, 257
Dogg, Tymon 211
Donegan, Lonnie 59, 60, 97, 102
Donovan 28–9, 54, 108, 112, 169–71, 174, 176, 183, 186, 227, 281
'Don't Fall Apart on Me Tonight' 345
Dont Look Back (documentary film) 31, 172–9, 189, 224, 369, 419, 424, 447
'Don't Start Me Talkin'' 348
'Don't Think Twice It's All Right' 79, 120, 123, 134, 137, 318
Doors, The 228–9
Dorfman, Bruce 224–5
'Down along the Cove' 236, 239
'Down in the Flood' 230, 264–5, 308
Down in the Groove (album) 372
'Down the Highway' 78
Drake, Pete 236, 243
'Drifter's Escape' 238, 395
Driscoll, Julie 233
'Duquesne Whistle' 474
Dury, Ian 327
Dylan, Bob (Zimmerman, Robert Allen)
  Family background 5–6
  Birth 7
  Childhood home in Duluth 8, 30
  Childhood home in Hibbing 9–13, 31–4, 86–7, 389
  Academic: Hibbing High 3, 13–4, 30–1, 248,

  Graduation 31: University of Minnesota 15, 32, 34, 68, 142
  Musical ability: piano 9, acoustic guitar 9, electric guitar 13, The Golden Chords 13–4, The Satin Tones 14, Elston Gunnn & the Rock Boppers 14, 30, 32, 35
  Health: asthma 11 (but a heavy smoker 173), accidents 13, 216, 222–4, virus 410, arthritis 426
  Race and religion: Judaism 5–8, 12, 34, 52, 101, 128, 263, 334, 441, Christianity 92, 332–4, 344, 435
  Changing name 35–6
  Personal relationships: Sara Lownds (first wife) – 133–4, 140–1, 177, 197 (wedding), 199, 223, 260, 292–5 (divorce), 321, 323
  Children: Maria Lownds–Dylan (adopted) 134, 140, 142, 248, 344, Jesse Byron Dylan 199, 432, Anna Lea Dylan 229, Samuel Isaac Abram Dylan 241, 344, Jakob Luke Dylan (Wallflowers) 257, 276, 400, 432
  Carolyn Dennis (second wife) 326, 334, 336, 338, 343, 360, 399, 422.
  Child: Desirée Gabrielle Dennis–Dylan 360
  Girlfriends: see entries for Ra Aranga, Joan Baez, Ellen Bernstein, Marianne Faithfull, Dana Gillespie, Echo Helstrom, Susan Ross, Suze Rotolo, Judy Rubin
  Interests: Baseball 9, 178, 295, 299, 343, Chess 64, 71, 118, 121, 228, 262, 422, Motorcycles, Painting 448–50, Tourism: haunted house 207, James Dean's grave 373, Kerouac's grave 29, 316, Lennon's childhood home 434, Bruce Springsteen's family home 434.
  Awards. Changing attitudes to; ASCAP 361, Tom Paine 113, 128, 355, 431, Grammys 339, 347, 352, 393, 402–3, 412, 423, 430, Songwriters Hall of Fame 344, Honorary degrees 261, 426, Pulitzer 432, 441, Nobel 442–5, Musicares 446
Dylan (1973 album) 276

Earle, Steve 284, 287, 376–7, 387
'Early Roman Kings' 436–7
Eat the Document (documentary film) 214, 224, 262
'Ebb Tide' 446
Edwardson, Monte 13, 32
Elliott, Ramblin' Jack 32, 43, 45, 51–2, 59, 62, 65, 69, 96–7, 125, 128, 135, 138, 175, 199, 216, 240, 316, 322

Ellis, Terry 176
Emerson, Keith 258
'Emotionally Yours' 357, 399, 402
Empire Burlesque (album) 346–7, 356–8, 360, 363, 372, 399
'End of the Line' 371, 374
Epstein Brian 130, 165, 235
'Eve of Destruction' 110, 217, 381
Everett, Rupert 364
Everly Brothers 14–5, 73, 81, 228, 244, 246, 264, 342, 347, 417
Evers, Medgar 121, 143
'Every Grain of Sand' 341

Factory Girl (film) 15, 199
Faithfull, Marianne 123, 141, 176
Fallen Angels (album) 446
'False Prophet' 450
'Farewell' 84
'Farewll Angelina' 165
Fariña, Richard & Mimi 32, 35, 41, 56, 60–1, 63, 65, 74, 78, 80, 100–2, 119–127, 132–3 138–9, 169, 184–5, 198, 201, 206, 229, 295, 372
Farm Aid 352, 355–6, 400, 430
Feinstein, Barry 131, 134, 206–7
Feliciano, José 137, 141–2
Felix. Julie 7–8, 89, 441
Ferlinghetti, Lawrence 19, 127, 198, 311
Ferry, Bryan 259, 260, 275, 366
Fiona 364
'Fixin' to Die' Blues' 73
'Foot of Pride' 347
Forbert, Steve 288
'Forever Young' 2, 16, 276, 292, 312, 327, 329, 334, 367, 405
'Fourth Time Around' 200, 208, 423
Free Trade Hall, Manchester 176, 211–3
Freewheelin' Bob Dylan, The (album) 15, 114, 116, 120, 130, 169
Friedman, Kinky314–5, 320, 365, 395
'Freight Train Blues' 68
Fritts, Donnie 272–3
'From A Buick 6' 188
Fuller, Jesse 32, 52, 72, 79

Garland, Judy 4, 57
'Gates of Eden' 164–5, 174, 176, 182, 372
Geffen, David 160, 259, 274–5, 290, 292
'George Jackson' 264
Gibson, Bob 31–2, 69, 76
Gillespie, Dana 141, 171–2, 176, 296

Ginsberg, Allen 25–30, 88, 156, 161, 176, 187, 198, 264, 315/6, 321–2, 344, 410
'Girl from the North Country' (song) 14, 100–1, 116–7, 244, 246, 294
Girl from the North Country (play) 15–6
Gleason, Ralph 59
Glover, Tony 37, 40, 68, 78
'Go Away You Bomb' (poem) 114
Going Electric (film) 269
'Going Going Gone' 231
'Going to Acapulco' 231
Goldberg, Barry 184, 274
Golding, William 262 (great story!)
Goldsmith Harvey 327, 397
Good as I Been to You (album) 396–7
Gooding, Cynthia 38, 72
Goodman, Steve 269
Goodwin, Harry 173
'Gospel Plow' 72
'Gotta Serve Somebody' 308, 339
'Gotta Travel On' 15, 79
'Grand Coulee Dam' 97
Grant, Peter 269 (Dylan's best one–liner)
Grateful Dead 220, 225, 251, 255, 269, 277, 305, 308, 363, 365–7, 395, 401, 403, 4,05, 424, 425,
  Garcia, Jerry 340, 401, 405, *Dylan and the Dead* (album) 367
Graves, Robert 100
Greatest Hits (album collections) (Vol 1) 226–7, (Vol 2) 264
Great White Wonder (bootleg) 220
Green, Keith 339
Greenbriar Boys 66, 74, 86, 223, 437
Greenfield, Manny 138, 165
Gregory, Dick 127
Gregg, Bobby 163, 180, 189, 198–9
Griffin, Paul 180–1
'Groom's Still Waiting at the Altar, The' 340
Grossman, Albert
  Early career 31, 39, 40, 64, 70
  Managing Bob Dylan 77–8, 87–8, 91, 97–8, 100, 116, 118, 120–1, 123–4, 128–9, 134, 138, 140, 147–8, 162, 171–2, 179, 184, 186, 193
  Falling out 222, 225, 228, 242, 253, 256–8, 352, 359
Grossman, Sally (previously Sally Buehler) 129, 134/5, 140, 198, 228, 256, 359, (*Bringing It All Back Home* cover) 165–6
Grunt, Blind Boy (Bob Dylan) 62, 101
Guthrie, Arlo 49, 51,–3, 58, 62, 97, 107, 124, 192, 254

Guthrie, Jack 49, 52
Guthrie, Woody
  Career 22–3, 42–55
  Influence on Dylan 37–9, 58–9, 62, 64, 71, 87–9, 97, 104, 115, 118–9, 125, 143, 162–3, 235, 240, 358, 373
  Bound for Glory (book) 37, 48, 54, 102
  Bound for Glory (film) 258, 295, 321
  Tribute to Woody Guthrie (1968) 54–5, 239

'Had a Dream about You, Baby' 364
Halee, Roy 182
Hallyday, Johnny 213
Hammond, John 19, 23, 39–40, 65–6, 68, 72, 74, 77, 83, 106, 116, 299, 367
Hammond Jr, John 83, 148–9, 184, 216, 239, 299, 398
'Handle with Care' 370
Hardin, Tim 283–4
Hard Rain (album) 294, 321
'Hard Rain's A–Gonna Fall, A' 80, 82–3, 102, 119
Hardy, Françoise 135
Hare, David 117
Harper, Roy 101
Harris, Emmylou 299, 314
Hart, Mike 288–9
Havens, Richie 80, 215, 225, 253–4, 361, 364, 398, 402, 431
Hawkins & the Hawks, Ronnie 144–9, 191 290, 304, 311, 318, 339 (The Hawks became The Band – see entry), Hawkins solo, 330, 318 (*Renaldo & Clara*), 339, 392
Haynes, Todd 193, 430–1
Hearts of Fire (film, album) 363/4
Helstrom, Echo 13–4, 35, 38, 87
Hendrix, Jimi 137, 196, 225, 238, 251–3, 255–5, 261, 291, 369
Henry, Joe 431
Hentoff, Nat 118, 135, 196, 202
'Hero Blues' 82
Hester, Carolyn 32, 39, 40, 60–1, 65–6, 68, 74, 78, 119, 125–6, 128, 164, 398
'He Was a Friend of Mine' 68–9
Hiatt, John 363–4
'Highlands' 123, 410
'High Water' 420
'Highway 51 Blues' 73, 115
Highway 61 (road) 5, 12, 18, 40, 188
Highway 61 Interactive (CD-Rom) 402, 404
'Highway 61 Revisited' 20, 157, 188, 200, 291, 332, 348, 393, 398, 403, 428

Highway 61 Revisited (album) 180–1, 186, 188, 190–1, 193, 199, 203, 371
Highwaymen, The 57, 65
Hoffenberg, Mason 135
Holiday, Billie 104
Hollies, The 110, 240
Holly, Buddy 14, 30–1, 65
Holzman, Jac 39, 87
'Honey, Just Allow Me One More Chance' 78
Hooker, John Lee 24–5, 62
Hootenanny (TV series) 119
'House Carpenter' 74
'House Of The Rising Sun' 63, 72, 137, 141
Houston, Cisco 32, 38, 48, 62
Howlin' Wolf 25, 74
Hunter, Robert 432
'Hurricane' 103, 298
Hurt, Mississippi John 25, 38

'I Am a Lonesome Hobo' 238
'I Contain Multitudes' 450
'I Dreamed I Saw St Augustine' 237
'I Need a Woman' 312
'I Pity the Poor Immigrant' 237
'I Shall Be Free' 83
'I Shall Be Free No.10' 136
'I Shall Be Released' 231, 264, 312, 359, 398, 402, 404
'I Threw It All Away' 243–4, 246, 255
'I Want You' 16, 201–3, 223, 398, 404
'I Was Young When I Left Home' 68, 421
Ian, Janis 88
'Idiot Wind' 294–5
'If I Had a Hammer' 50, 69–70, 114
'If I'm Not There by Morning' 325, 328
'If Not For You ' 260, 262, 399
'If You Gotta Go, Go Now' 115, 140, 174, 177–8, 194, 217, 248, 259
'If You See Her Say Hello' 294
'I'll Be Your Baby Tonight' 236, 239, 260, 329, 397
'I'll Keep It With Mine' 65, 195, 200, 211
'I'll Remember You' 356, 372
'I'm a Gambler' 39
'I'm Not There' (film) 15, 190, 268, 430–1
'Important Words' 365
Infidels (album) 345–6
'In My Time of Dyin'' 68
Inside Llewyn Davis (film) 83/4
'In the Garden' 339
Isle of Wight Festival 209, 249–56
'Is Your Love in Vain' 325

'It Ain't Me Babe' 136–7, 140
'It's All Over Now, Baby Blue' 165
'It's Alright Ma, I'm Only Bleeding' 165
'It's Good News Week' 110
'It Takes a Lot to Laugh, It Takes a Train to Cry' 181, 185, 187

'Jack O'Diamonds' 136
Jara, Victor 103, 293
Jefferson, Blind Lemon 20, 73, 141
Joel, Billy 191
'Joey' 297–8
'John Brown' 119, 367, 392, 407
John, Elton 258, 305, 369, 381, 389, 437–8
Johnson, Blind Willie 68
Johnson, Robert 18–9, 76, 325
Johnston, Bob 186–7, 200, 210, 235, 243–6, 260
'John Wesley Harding' 45, 237
John Wesley Harding (album) 231, 236–9, 242, 245, 273
'Jokerman' 345–6, 390
Jones, Max 99, 189
Jones, Mickey 119, 204, 324
Joplin, Janis 39, 257–8
'Just Like a Woman' 201, 204, 207–8, 223, 225, 264, 291, 314, 398, 402, 431
'Just like Tom Thumb's Blues' 187, 189, 210, 398

Kaufman, Murray (Murray the K) 193
Kegan, Larry 13–4, 35, 328, 343, 395
Kennedy, Jerry 200
Kennedy, President John F 70, 123, 128–9, 132, 142
Kennedy, Robert 139, 140, 241
Kerouac, Jack 25–30, 37, 56, 163, 316
Kershaw, Doug 246
Keys, Alicia 415, 429
King, Carole 257, 393, 403–6
King, Martin Luther 127, 133, 169, 241, 261, 359
Kingston Trio 32, 40, 57, 70, 82, 106–7, 114, 118
'Knockin' on Heaven's Door' 291, 318, 407, 411
Knocked Out Loaded (album) 361
Knopfler, Mark 334–5, 344–6, 360, 407, 417
Koerner, Spider John 34–5
Kokomo 299
Kooper, Al 162, 180–1, 184, 187–8, 192, 194–5, 199, 200–1, 260
Kramer, Daniel 166, 193, 227
Kristofferson, Kris 244–6, 255–6, 268–274, 284–5, 330, 361–2, 385, 398, 430
Kweskin, Jim 61, 64, 84, 118

La Farge, Peter 59, 137, 281
Lake, Greg 329
Landau, Jon 84
Landy, Elliott 242, 248
Langhorne, Bruce 66, 81, 130, 139, 163
Lanois, Daniel 307, 366, 373–5, 386, 389, 407–12, 411, 425
Larkin, Philip 190
'Last Thoughts on Woody Guthrie' (poem) 54, 115
Last Waltz, The (concert, album and film) 312–3
'Lay Down Your Weary Tune' 127–8
'Lay Lady Lay' 21, 219, 239, 243–6, 292, 321, 347, 390
Lay, Sam 184/5, 187
Leadbelly (Huddie Ledbetter) 21–3, 44, 97, 100, 102
Leiberson, Goddard 68, 124
'Leopard–skin Pill–box Hat' 199–200, 203
'Let It Be Me' 342
'Let Me Die In My Footsteps' 75–6
Lettermen, David 347
Levy, Jacques 296–7
Levy, Lou 56, 74
Levy, Morris 145–7
Lewis, Jerry Lee 33, 221, 244, 416, 427
Lewis, Sinclair 5
'Licence to Kill' 345, 347, 361, 399
Lightfoot, Gordon 97, 236, 242, 288, 318, 365
'Like a Rolling Stone' 15, 177–8, 181–2, 185–7, 193–4, 210–1, 214, 216, 226, 251, 308, 317, 394–5, 397, 404–5, 412, 428
'Lily, Rosemary and the Jack of Hearts' 294, 299, 321
Lind, Bob 284
Little Richard 12–3, 31, 144, 162, 252, 306, 370, 431
Live Aid 351–6
Live at the Gaslight, 1962 (album) 81
'Living the Blues' 245–6
Lloyd, Bert 95, 97, 99
'Lo And Behold' 228, 231
Lofgren, Nils 365, 427, 445
Lomax, Alan 22, 45, 57, 65, 69, 72, 96–7, 184
Lomax, John 21–2, 69
'London Waltz, The' 101
'Lonesome Death of Hattie Carroll, The' 126–7, 132, 174, 381
'Lonesome Town' 363
'Lord Franklin' 101, 102
'Lord Randall' 102
Love and Theft (album) 419–23

'Love Henry' 38
'Love Is just a Four Letter Word' 175, 243
'Love Minus Zero / No Limit' 136, 164
'Love Sick' 408–9
'Love You Too Much' 329
Lownds, Hans 133
Lynne, Jeff 324, 368, 370–2, 374

McCarthy, Senator Joe 25, 51, 56, 155
MacColl, Ewan 32, 38, 95–7, 99, 100, 102, 162
McCoy, Charlie 187, 190, 200–, 236, 243
McCurdy, Ed 32, 107
McDonald, Country Joe 54–5, 111, 127, 253, 405
McEwen, Alex & Rory 100
McFree, Faridi 323
McGhee, Brownie 23–4,32
McGough, Roger 175
McGuire, Barry 110, 119, 199, 214, 217, 381
McLagen, Ian 348
MacLeish, Alexander 261
McPherson, Conor 15–6
McTell, Blind Willie, 20–1, (song) 221, 346/7
McTell, Ralph 20–1, 44, 59, 109, 125, 136, 164–5, 201
Madhouse on Castle Street (BBC–TV play) 98–101
'Maggie's Farm' 164, 185, 349, 366
'Make You Feel My Love' 409–10
'Mama, You Been on My Mind' 136, 140, 313
Manfred Mann 178, 180
'Man Gave Names to All the Animals' 335, 369, 390
'Man in Me, The' 260, 324, 372
'Man in the Long Black Coat' 374, 394, 407
'Man of Constant Sorrow' 72
'Man of Peace' 25
'Man on the Street' 74
Marcus, Greil 15, 78, 126
'Margarita' 371
Markel, Bob 139, 215, 224, 242, 263
Martyn, John 276
Masked and Anonymous (film, album) 423–4
'Masters of War' 76, 101, 114–6, 124, 126, 137, 238, 257, 291, 348, 393, 397, 403, 425, 428
Masterminds, The 194
'Matchbox' 20, 421
Mayall, John 175, 177
Maymudes, Victor 91, 132, 134, 195, 205
'Memphis Blues Again' 201–2, 232, 422–3
Merman, Ethel 35
Meyers, Augie 420
Midler, Bette 319
'Mighty Quinn, The' 201, 231–2, 243, 296, 336

Miller, Henry 127
'Million Dollar Bash' 232, 236–7
'Million Miles' 408
'Mississippi' 410
'Mr. Tambourine Man' 5, 83, 117, 127, 129, 130, 134–5,139,164, 167–8, 171, 174–5, 179–80, 185, 206, 208, 287, 340, 391, 394, 404, 406
Mitchell, Chad 119
Mitchell, Joni 191, 257
'Mixed–up Confusion' 81–2
Modern Times (album) 428–30
Monkees, The 158
'Moonlight' 420
Morrison, Van 348, 393
Most, Mickie 69
Mothers of Invention 88, 186, 248,
 – Zappa, Frank 221, 339 344
Mouskouri, Nana 341
Moss, Wayne 200, 203
'Most Likely You Go Your Way and I'll Go Mine' 202, 291, 393, 419
'Most of the Time' 375–6, 395
'Mozambique' 297
Muldaur, Geoff 20, 22, 183, 185
Muldaur, Maria 72
Mumford, Marcus 234
'Murder Most Foul' 438
'My Back Pages' 135–6, 275
'My Life In A Stolen Moment' (poem) 5, 32, 36, 64
My Own Love Song (film) 432

Nash, Graham 128, 228, 240, 246
Nashville 243–6, 258
Nashville Skyline (album) 202, 219, 239, 242–7, 258, 440, 447
Neil, Fred 60, 281
'Nashville Skyline Rag' 243–4, 258, 262
'Neighbourhood Bully' 368
Nelson, Paul 37, 120, 227, 290
Nelson, Rick 125, 162, 363
Nelson, Willie 271, 320, 352, 355–6, 386, 398, 400–1, 426–7, 454
Neuwirth, Bobby 56, 64, 116, 141, 170,192, 272, 314, 317–8, 320, 322
Neville Brothers 373–4
New Lost City Ramblers 57, 97, 401
Newman, Randy 112
New Morning (album) 260, 262
Newport Folk Fesitval 248, 252
New World Singers 75, 81
Nico 135, 175

Nile, Willie 56, 80–1
Nobel Prize 5, 14, 81, 442–5
No Direction Home (documentary film) 427
'North Country Blues' 4, 126
'Norwegian Wood' 200
'Not Dark Yet' 15, 409, 411, 417'
'Nothing Was Delivered' 232, 235, 242
'Nottamun Town' 99, 126

Obama, President Barack 435
"Obviously Five Believers" 202
Ochs, Phil 11, 59. 64, 110–3, 127, 141–4, 159–60, 235, 279–81, 292–3, 315
O'Connor, Sinead 161, 398
'Odds And Ends' 235
Odetta 18, 39, 40, 65, 72, 78, 97, 100, 126, 162
Oh Mercy (album) 374–6, 389, 405, 426, 435
'Oh Sister' 299, 318
O'Jays, The 399, 402
Oldham, Spooner 337
Omnibus (BBC–TV arts programme) 365
'On A Night Like This' 2, 275
'One More Cup of Coffee' 296, 299
'One of Us Must Know' 199
'One Too Many Mornings' 75, 125, 204, 210, 244, 363, 373
'Only a Hobo' 125
'On The Road Again' 164
'Only a Pawn in the Game' 121, 123, 126–7, 129, 364
'Open the Door, Homer' 22
Orbison, Roy 79, 267, 354, 365,370–1, 374, 388, 391
Osborne, Joan 412
Oswald, Lee Harvey 129, 147
'Outlaw Blues' 164
'Oxford Town' 79, 82, 120

Pankake, Jon 37, 120, 427
Pat Garrett and Billy the Kid (film) 266–72, 275, 326, 379
Paxton, Tom 25, 64, 75, 79, 80, 84, 108, 111–2, 281
Peckinpah, Sam – See *Pat Garrett and Billy the Kid*
Pennebaker, D.A – See *Dont Look Back* and *Eat the Document*
'Percy's Song' 79, 131
Perkins, Carl 20, 146, 260, 430
Peter, Paul & Mary 24, 70–1, 77, 79, 92,106, 114, 121–2, 124
   Stookey, Noel (Paul) 56, 60, 63, 70, 198

   Travers, Mary 91, 131, 166, 177, 435
   Yarrow, Peter 120, 184–5, 228
Petty & the Heartbreakers, Tom 259, 356, 359, 361–3, 368, 370–2. 374, 391, 397, 399, 424
Pitt, Ken 134, 172
Planet Waves (album) 275–6, 292, 426, 448
'Please Mrs Henry' 243
'Pledging My Time' 202
'Political World' 374–5
Pomus, Doc 344
Porco, Mike 60–2, 71, 314
'Positively 4th Street' 38, 187–8, 198, 206, 217, 294, 395, 399
'Precious Angel' 326, 335
Presley, Elvis 12, 78, 115, 142, 156, 198, 254, 258, 265–6, 277
'Pretty Boy Floyd' 45, 323, 373
'Pretty Peggy–O' 72
'Pressing on' 339
Price, Alan 109, 171, 176
Prine, John 4, 111, 113, 287, 385
'Property of Jesus' 341

'Queen Jane Approximately' 189, 367
Quinn, Anthony 202
'Quit Your Lowdown Ways' 79

'Rainy Day Women Nos. 12 & 35' 179, 202–3, 205, 223, 227, 261, 398, 403, 405
Ramone, Phil 71, 293
Real Live (album) 349
Redding, Otis 204
'Red River Shore' 410
Reed, Lou 160, 397–8
Renaldo & Clara (film) 315, 317–8, 321–3, 325, 327, 403, 431
'Restless Farewell' 128, 406
'Return To Me' 419
Rimbaud, Arthur 178, 292, 320, 428
'Ring Them Bells' 374, 402–3
Rivera, Scarlet 298–9, 315–6
Roberts, Elliot 344, 373, 376
Rocks and Gravel' 81, 114
'Rock Me Baby' 363
Rodgers, Jimmie (folk singer) 44, 237, 403, 411
Rodgers, Jimmie (60s pop) 119, 231
Rolling Stones, The 19, 25, 157–9, 171, 180, 194, 196, 203, 220, 239, 255, 267, 369, 405, 410, 412, 425, 434, 448,
   Mick Jagger 130, 180, 194, 216, 220, 227, 235, 267, 269, 341, 369, 426
   (Brian Jones 159, 196, 198, 206, 332,

Keith Richards 206, 220, 227, 302, 313, 347, 353–5, 395
Mick Taylor 345, 348, 356,
Ronnie Wood 319, 341, 347, 349–50, 353–5,361, 363–4, 393,398, 401
Rolling Thunder Revue 11, 29, 273, 280, 299–300, 314–21, 324
'Romance in Durango' 273, 297
Romney, Hugh (Wavy Gravy) 36, 80, 253
Ronson, Mick 315, 317
Ross, Susan 358
Rothchild, Paul 133, 183
Rotolo, Suze 63–5, 68, 79, 80, 82, 117, 121, 124–5, 129, 132–3
Rough And Rowdy Ways 450
Royal Albert Hall, London 98, 130, 177, 210–2, 214, 263, 307
Rubin, Judy 11, 40
Rucker, Darius 295
Rundgren, Todd 77, 256, 305–6
Rush, Tom 169, 283
Russell, Leon 147, 262–4, 353

'Sad Eyed Lady of the Lowlands' 28, 93, 201, 409
Sahm, Doug 265, 269–70, 373, 405
Sainte-Marie Buffy 65, 103, 108, 112–3, 117
'Sam Stone' 111
Sandburg, Carl 132, 140
Santana, Carlos 340, 348–9
'Sara' 299
Savakus, Russ 180, 187
Saved (album) 338–40
Saville, Philip 96–8, 102
Scaduto, Anthony 90–1
Scheff, Jerry 325
Scorsese, Martin 427
Scruggs, Earl 262
Sebastian, John 24, 56, 163, 194
Sedgwick, Edie 141, 199, 200, 202
Seeger, Peggy 32, 38, 45, 67, 96, 106–7
Seeger, Pete
  own career 15, 31, 40, 45–8, 50–6, 62, 69–71, 80, 98, 123–4, 128, 132, 163, 168–9,227, 257
  with Dylan 103–4, 106–7, 111–2, 118, 184–6, 196–7
'See That My Grave Is Kept Clean' 20, 73, 232, 378, 398
Self Portrait (album) 245/6, 259, 262
'Señor' 325
'Series of Dreams' 346, 375, 394
'Seven Days' 319, 398, 406

Sex Pistols 160–1, 312, (Sid Vicious) 28, 327
Shadows in the Night (album) 445
Shannon, Del 123, 388
'She Belongs to Me' 164, 174, 178, 194, 208, 372
Shelton, Robert 32, 40, 60, 64, 66, 68, 85–94, 127, 133, 137, 139, 140, 186, 203
'Shelter from the Storm' 321, 324, 407
Shepard, Sam 315
'She's Your Lover Now' 199
Shot of Love (album) 341, 343
'Sign Language' 319, 439
'Sign on the Cross' 232
'Sign on the Window' 260, 262
Silber, Irwin 140
Simon, Carly 188, 214, 234–5, 311
Simon & Garfunkel 117, 123, 132, 181, 186, 197, 252, 268, 281, 383, (Paul Simon) 14, 66, 117, 180, 182, 212, 217, 260. 281. 331, 337, 394, 412. 444, 447
'Simple Twist of Fate' 293, 299, 324, 348, 368, 395, 424
Sinatra, Frank 146, 250, 266, 275, 344, 405–6, 414, 446–7
Sky, Patrick 282
Slash 389
Sloan, P.F 110, 194
Sloman, Larry (Ratzo) 314–8
Slow Train Coming (album) 333–6
Sly & Robbie 356
Smith, G E 372, 397
Smith, Harry 37–8, 97–8, 356
Smith, Patti 296, 314, 406, 412, 428, 445
Solomon, Maynard 39, 125
'Song to Woody' 52, 54, 61, 63, 69, 73, 99, 143, 274,399
Sonny & Cher 179–80, 194
Sopranos, The (TV series) 419
South, Joe 200–2
'Spanish Harlem Incident' 136, 140
'Spanish Is the Loving Tongue' 277
Spector, Phil 181, 202, 275, 321
Spector, Ronnie 137
Spivey, Victoria 19, 71–2
Spoelstra, Mark 60, 64
Spinners, The 44, 53, 73, 98
Springs, Helena 324–5, 328, 337–8
Springsteen, Bruce 2, 76, 85, 182, 221, 289–90, 342, 356, 363, 365, 366, 369, 371, 372, 382, 391, 403, 405, 412, 417, 434, 443, 449
Staples, Mavis 80, 395
Stanton, Harry Dean 272, 328, 376
'Steel Bars' 392

'Stepchild' 325, 425
Stewart, Dave 358, 359 (a legendary story)
Stewart, John 70, 83, 106, 123, 246, 270, 280, 288
Stewart, Rod 161, 275, 318, 445
Ben & Florence Stone (grandparents) 7–9
Stoner, Rob 325, 327
'Straight A's in Love' 356
Street–Legal (1978) 323, 325–6
'Subterranean Homesick Blues' 106, 138, 163–4, 172, 176, 179, 216, 295, 372
Sullivan, Ed 62, 99, 120, 124, 132, 196, 303
'Sun City' (Artists United Against Apartheid) 358
'Sweetheart like You' 345

'Talkin' Bear Mountain Massacre Blues' 63
'Talkin' John Birch Paranoia Blues' 98, 116. 120
'Talkin' New York' 46, 63, 73
'Talkin' World War III Blues' 116–7, 120, 140, 174
Tampa Red 328
'Tangled Up in Blue' 292–5, 318, 326, 333, 349, 428
Tarantula (novel) 5, 139, 166, 195. 215, 224, 240, 242, 263, 369
Taylor, James 49, 274, 285, 311, 383, 396
Taylor, Elizabeth 17, 357, 359
Taylor, Vince 177
'Tears of Rage' 229, 232
'Tell Me Momma' 205, 209, 211
Tempest (album) 436
'Temporary like Achilles' 202
Terkel, Studs 118–9
Terry, Sonny 23–4, 32, 73
Thal, Terri 69
Tharp, Twyla 428
'That's All Right, Mama' 82
'There But for Fortune' 143–4, 418–9
'Things Have Changed' 418, 423, 427
'This Old Man' 390
'This Wheel's On Fire' 229, 232–3, 400
Thomas, Dylan 35–6, 56
Thompson, Richard 139, 248, 336, 395
'Times They Are A–Changin', The' 123, 128, 130–1, 402
Times They Are A–Changin', The (album) 5, 131, 162
Time Out of Mind (album) 75, 375, 406–12, 418–9, 421–2, 428 432
Tiny Tim 61, 76, 88, 226
'Titanic, The' 437

Together Through Life (album) 432–3
'Tombstone Blues' 171, 187
'Tomorrow Is a Long Time' 78–9, 115
'Tonight I'll Be Staying Here with You' 318
'Too Much of Nothing' 233
'To Ramona' 136, 174, 340, 423
'Tough Mama' 276
Townshend, Pete 136, 231, 332
Traum, Happy 19, 24–5, 38, 50–1, 61, 71, 75–6, 80, 107, 121, 127–8, 194, 227, 234, 264
Traveling Wilburys, The (album) 370–2
Traveling Wilburys Volume 3 (album) 391–2
Triplicate (album) 447
'Troubled and I Don't Know Why' 125
'Trouble in Mind' 336
Trouble in Mind (BBC Arena Special) 338
Trump, President Donald 151, 155, 445, (his dad Fred) 23
'Tryin' to Get to Heaven' 409
Turner, Gil 75, 78, 102, 108–9
Turtles, The 192, 228
'Tweeter and the Monkey Man' 371
Twitty, Conway 32, 145–6
Tyson, Ian & Sylvia 72, 78, 131

'Understand Your Man' 137
Under the Red Sky (album) 388–90
'Universal Soldier' 65, 108, 197
Unplugged (MTV show) 402, 404
'Up to Me' 277, 293
'Uptown' 107
'Usual, The' 364

Van Ronk, Dave 61.64. 68–73, 75–77, 82–4, 138, 188
Van Zandt, Townes 80, 163, 284
'V D Blues' 69
Vee, Bobby 1,31–2, 36, 386
Vincent, Gene 32, 165
'Visions of Johanna' 196–8, 200, 208, 320, 394, 439, 441
Von Schmidt, Eric 32, 68–9, 65, 100–1, 165–6, 245, 265

'Wagon Wheel' 274, 295,363
Wainwright, Loudon, 124, 136, 285
Waits, Tom 126, 141, 190, 286
'Walkin' Down the Line' 82, 162
Walker, Scott 123
'Wallflower' 265
'Walls of Red Wing' 32, 117–8, 132
'Wanted Man' 244, 398

Warhol, Andy 141, 157, 166, 189, 198–9, 225, 381
Warner, David 98
Was (Not Was) 388–9, 391
'Watching the River Flow' 263, 329, 365, 404, 434
Waters, Muddy 137, 157, 178
Waters, Roger 298
'We Are the World' (USA for Africa) 352–3
Weavers, The 50, 70–1, 163
Weberman, Alan J 90, 261–2
'Wedding Song' 76
Weintrab, Jerry 321, 323, 337
Weissberg, Eric 293
'We Shall Overcome' 75, 103–4, 123, 170
Wexler, Jerry 270, 334–5
'Went to See the Gypsy' 258
'What Was It You Wanted' 375, 398
'When He Returns' 336
'When I Paint My Masterpiece' 263
'When the Levee Breaks' 430
'When the Night Comes Falling from the Sky' 356–7
'When the Ship Comes in' 124, 130, 355, 398
'Where Have All the Flowers Gone' 69–71, 106–7, 378'
Where Were You Last Night' 392
White, Josh 44–5, 57, 68, 73, 87, 105, 138
Whiters, Pick 334–5
'Who Do You Love', 83, 147–8'
'Who Killed Davey Moore' 115, 119, 140
'Wicked Messenger' 238, 367
'Wilbury Twist' 392
'Wild Mountain Thyme' 165
Williams, Big Joe 25, 71, 115, 119
Williams, Hank 10, 175
Wilson, Tom 116, 126, 135–6, 141, 163–4, 177, 181, 186, 226

Winchester, Jesse 387
'Winterlude' 261
'With God on Our Side' 1, 115, 118, 124, 180, 313
Witmark Demos, The (2CD) 78
Wonder, Stevie 121, 173
Wonder Boys (film) 417–9
Wood, Ronnie 319–20
'Workingman's Blues, No.2' 430
World Gone Wrong (album) 401
Writings & Drawings 136, 165, 274
Wyatt, Lorre 82, 128

'Ye Playboys And Playgirls' 82, 124
'You Ain't Going Nowhere' 233, 241
'You Angel You' 275
'You Gotta Trust Yourself' 356–7
Young, Izzy 59, 60, 67, 114, 120, 139, 188
Young, Neil 160, 167, 189, 259, 269, 295/6, 310, 312, 345, 355–6, 372, 382, 397/8, 402/3, 410, 425, 429, 449
'You're a Big Girl Now' 292
'You're Gonna Make Me Lonesome When You Go' 292, 294
'You're No Good' 72
'You've Lost That Lovin' Feelin'' 165

Zantzinger, William 126
Zevon, Warren 425
Zimmerman, Abram (father) 6–13. 32, 118, 128, 188, 224, 241
Zimmerman, Anna (grandmother) 6–7
Zimmerman, Beatty (mother) 6–9, 12, 14, 32, 128, 241
Zimmerman, David (brother) 89, 241, 294
Zimmerman, Maurice (uncle) 6–7
Zimmerman, Paul (uncle) 6–7
Zimmerman, Zigman (grandfather) 6–7

ISBN 9780857161659
eISBN 9780857161666

ISBN 9780857161505
eISBN 9780857161512

ISBN 9780857161925
eISBN 9780857160881

ISBN 9780857161888
eISBN 9780857161895

ISBN 9780857160973
eISBN 9780857160980

ISBN 9780857161017
eISBN 9780857161024

ISBN 9780857161345
eISBN 9780857161352